TO ASHES AND DUST

LUNA LAURIER

To Ashes and Dust
Book 2 of the Shadow and Moonlight Series

Story and Art Copyright © 2022 Luna Laurier
Cover Design by Luna Laurier
Editing by Natalie Cammaratta & The Fiction Fix
Illustrations by Huangja

IDENTIFIERS
ISBN 979-8-9859723-8-2 (Ingram Paperback) | ISBN 979-8-3918589-6-6 (Amazon Paperback) ISBN 979-8-9859723-7-5 (Hardcover) | ASIN B0C31YXNGB (ebook)

For business inquiries email lunalaurierbooks@gmail.com

Revised Edition: August 2023

CONTENT WARNING

While these are not all the focus, please be aware that
this series contains scenes of the following

Alcohol,
Anxiety
Assault
Blood
Chronic Illness
Death
Depression
Death Of A Child
Discussion Of Child Loss
Death In Childbirth
Emotional Violence
Fire
Hospitalization
Kidnapping
Murder
Medical Content
Mention Of Self-Harm

Mention of Rape
Misogyny
Needles
Physical Violence
Panic Attacks
Profanity
Pregnancy
Poisoning
PTSD
Reincarnation
Sexual Assault
Sexually Explicit Scenes
Smoking
Suicidal Ideation (Implied)
Terminal Illness
Torture
Violence
War

If you or anyone you know is contemplating suicide, please call the
National Suicide Prevention Lifeline at 1-800-273-TALK (8255). Please
do not struggle in silence. Your friends and family care. I care.

For the most up to date list visit lunalaurier.com

Glossary and Elythian Translations in the back of the book, read with caution to avoid spoilers

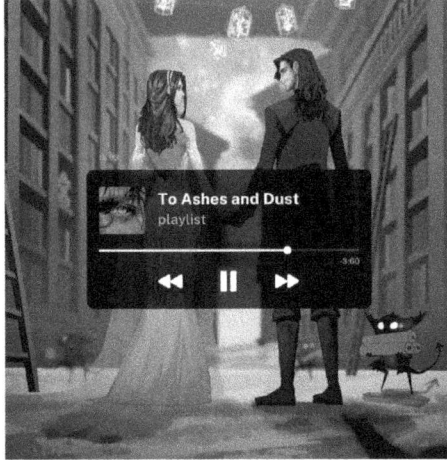

Check out the official OSAM Spotify Playlist

https://tinyurl.com/TAAD-spotify

Want to see a character sheet to see what the characters look like? Or view the pronunciation and up-to-date content warnings?

Chat with other OSAM readers while you read.
Check out the official discord server!
General Chat, Chapter Checkpoint discussions,
end of book discussions, unhinged theories,
quizzes, and more!

https://discord.com/invite/9RvBn2cd3Y

To those fighting unseen battles.
I see you.

PROLOGUE

Death filled the endless wastes of The Shadow Steppes. Thunder and the cries of steel had quieted to an echoing silence as the air shuddered—the realm quaking at the immense toll of the battle—the life and magic snuffed from our world in recent hours.

The soil beneath us had been robbed of life centuries ago when we fought the Titans. No animal had set foot in this land since, and the few trees left standing were stuck in an endless stage of rot.

The very land was cursed.

I hated standing here again, hated fighting my own—ones I had once called allies.

"You have lost. Surrender and return to your domain!" I drew back my bow, aimed at the Goddess before me. Her head was bent low as she cradled her fallen mate, her sobs echoing endlessly across the killing field, melding with the cries of those mourning the dead.

She didn't speak, the agony of their broken bond flitting through the air, as if the very realm mourned her loss.

Arion stomped his large hoof into the dirt beneath me and snorted, his breath strong enough to stir up the dust on the ground. His powerful form rippled with energy, the battle not enough to diminish his spirit. Pride swelled within me, that he was willing to fight on if need be.

He tossed his head before calming, his head lowering. My eyes fell back to the Goddess, and my allies closed in around her. My warriors, though weakened, fell into place, ready to strike if she lashed out. I prayed she would surrender; enough blood had been shed, enough lives lost.

"Surrender!" I repeated.

She hissed, her fangs bared as she clutched her fallen mate, his body, once the very essence of war, now limp in her gray arms—

My arrow protruding from his chest.

"*I will destroy you*," she growled, her body quaking, her voice venom, her promise a curse.

A chill swept over me, and I steadied my bow, Arion's body tensing beneath me.

"And when I've destroyed you." Tears rolled down her cheeks as she lifted her murderous onyx gaze to me, and the sky seemed to darken. "I shall come for everyone you love, everything you hold dear… and you will watch as I make them *suffer*."

I jolted awake, my heart racing, sweat painting my brow as I looked around my chambers.

I was alone.

"Celestia, grant me peace," I whispered, as I laced my trembling fingers together and dropped my head against them.

It had been a long time since I had suffered that nightmare. I wished so badly to forget—

But I couldn't.

I would never be able to forget.

It would follow me forever.

PART 1

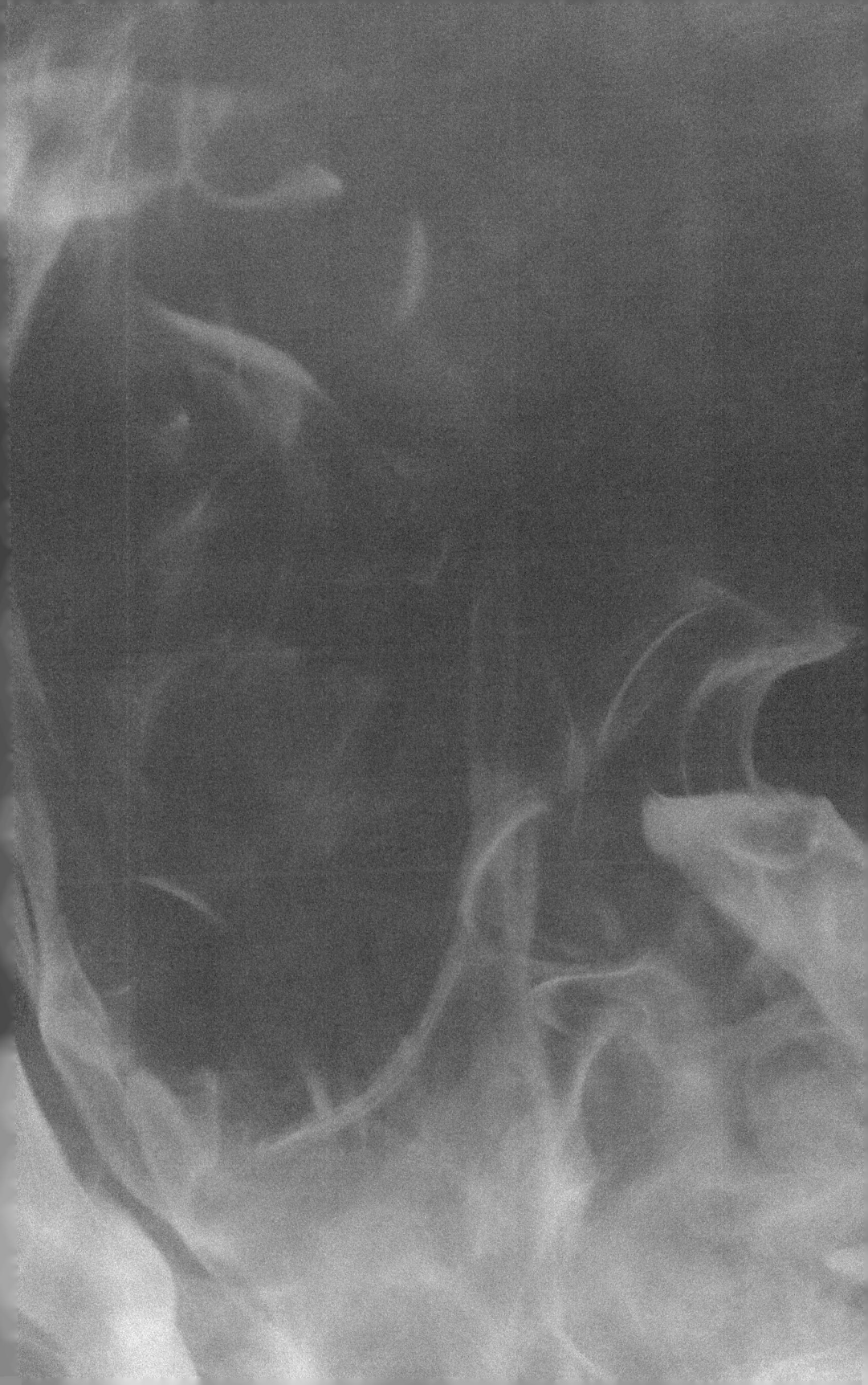

CHAPTER 1

CASSIE

"Watch your back, Cas!"

The mud sloshed beneath my boots as I slid to the side, evading the downstroke of Zephyr's blade. My feet were light and swift as I swung around to face him, and my dagger sliced through the air as I countered. He blocked my strike, sweat glistening on his tawny skin. Barrett and Vincent paced around us, rotating to attack at any given moment. I swiped the damp curls that had come loose from my braid after hours of training from my face.

"A bit close there, Zephyr," Damien growled.

"I wouldn't have hit her," Zephyr responded, glancing away from me. I could've used the opportunity to take him out, but I didn't.

My breaths came in pants as I took a short break. "I'm fine, *mea sol*. If he doesn't swing like he means it, I won't get the full training."

Damien didn't respond, dragging a heavy breath through his teeth as he watched from the sidelines. Zephyr turned back to me, and we resumed training. Damien continued to take note of each move I made, prepared to critique or correct me at the slightest mistake. His long dark hair was half tied back, the rest cascading over his shoulders in soft waves. Color had returned to his skin in the few months since we'd found each other, the olive tone richer, healthier, and his build had filled out, his clothes fitting better. It was a relief to see the change in his overall health. I wondered if it was because he'd begun feeding from me regularly. The thought of it was enough to send my mind spiraling to thoughts of the intimate moments we'd shared over the last few months, the heated drunkenness that came when he fed, and I stumbled as my face and ears grew warm.

Damien's nostrils flared, his amber and ashen eyes flashing as he swallowed. "Mind your surroundings, Cas. It won't always just be one opponent you face."

I cursed internally, wondering if he'd caught on to where my mind had jumped. His movements were tense as he watched us spar, and the way he pressed his knuckles to his lips told me he didn't approve of my training. He had no choice, though; none of us did. It was Selene's order we continue it. I'd be lying if I said I wasn't relieved when she commanded him to continue. It had been a battle to convince him to let me resume my training after...

After Marcus.

The bruises and cuts he'd left had long since healed, but scars remained, both physical and otherwise. I shook the thoughts from my head. There was no time to spare a glance in his direction, but I absorbed his words.

The late January air was icy and bitter in my lungs. Winter was setting in with full force. It was an unusually cold one—Johnstown had been covered in several inches of snow a few weeks earlier. The snow that once covered the training grounds of The Outpost, though, had long since melted from the last few hours of training—leaving the ground saturated and muddy beneath our feet. The hilts of my daggers dug into my leather gloves as I gripped them. Zephyr and Vincent closed in as Barrett stood back, watching for my defenses to weaken. I stepped with them, evading their strikes and meeting them with my own, keeping my thoughts open to pick up on anything I could.

"Watch where you step. Don't throw your weight past your feet." Damien's eyes swept over me in precise assessment as he paced around us. "Use your opponent's weight, not your own." I did my best to listen, focusing on my feet a bit more, maintaining my center of gravity. "Remember to focus on reading your opponent's movements, just like we practiced."

"Come on, Cas. I know you've got more in you than that," Vincent taunted as he jumped in, and my eyes narrowed on him. Unlike Barrett and Zephyr, he didn't wield a weapon, only his hands. It was how he'd always trained, yet I'd never landed a hit. His movements were fluid as the water magic he wielded as he danced around my blades, his hands grappling and hitting my arms and hands as he batted my attacks away with ease. I didn't know what form of fighting it was, what style, but it was almost poetic.

Zephyr leaned in to mutter something to Barrett before barking a warning. "You keep pushing her buttons, you're gonna regret it." I caught a hint of humor in his tone, as if he hoped I'd make Vincent eat his words.

"I'd pay money to see that," Thalia chimed from nearby, where she was supervising the training of the recruits. Her corn silk hair glinted in the winter sunlight, the scar that crossed down her right eye pink against her fair skin from the icy temperatures.

"Pay attention to your own trainees, Thalia," Damien warned without glancing her way.

She didn't respond, but I could imagine the coy grin on her face as she returned to her work.

"I'd like to see her try," Vincent said in challenge, a haughty grin tugging at his lips. There it was, that hint of Barrett's troublemaker personality, hidden beneath Vincent's sweet one. God, he was so much like his cousin.

Make him eat those words.

The dark voice, the one that had lingered since I'd killed Marcus, danced in my thoughts, but I couldn't focus on it as he reached for my arm to block my blow. Irritation flooded me, and I dropped my dagger, slipping through his grip. He fumbled for a split second, shifting away from me as I broke his hold, replicating his own moves as I swatted his hand away. Mud slipped beneath my feet as I shifted forward to close the distance between us, and before I realized what I was doing, I slammed my forehead into his.

We both recoiled immediately, hands rising to our foreheads involuntarily as we cringed from the shattering pain. Vincent groaned, cursing as he paced back a few steps. The others broke into fits of laughter. Damien didn't speak up, but I could've sworn I'd heard a low huff from him as he stifled a laugh.

Vincent hissed as he rubbed his head, shaking it off. "*Shit, Cas!* You've got a hard head."

"You think *I* have a hard head?" I grimaced, pointing at my throbbing forehead. I knew a nasty headache would rear its ugly head later, but the satisfaction was worth it.

Damien remained silent still, but I caught sight of the pride in those stunning eyes. They burned into me, like embers bursting free from ashes—I loved them more than anything. I bit back the smile creeping across my face before returning my attention to the others.

"I think I won that bet," Zephyr muttered to Barrett, barely loud enough for me to hear.

Barrett groaned, reaching into his pocket. He slammed something into Zephyr's outstretched hand: a folded twenty-dollar bill.

Those bastards actually bet on me? Heat flooded my face, and I threw them a dirty look. I guess I should be happy Zephyr had confidence in me, but that was beside the point. For being defenders of the immortal and the human races, they were so childish sometimes.

Damien gave them a warning glare. "I didn't know we were gambling on Cas' training."

Barrett threw his hands up. "What? We couldn't help ourselves!"

I threw up my middle finger at Barrett, who cocked a grin and winked at me. My eyes rolled as I shook my head. He hadn't changed one bit—still loved to pick on me, but oddly enough, I'd grown used to it. In the couple of months since I'd moved in with Damien, I'd become immersed in their group, and they felt like brothers now. While they picked on me and belittled my achievements every chance they got, I knew they would have my back no matter what.

I bent down, swiping my dagger from the ground. I wiped the mud from it on my pants before flipping it in my hand. The weight was perfectly balanced in my palm, as if I'd used it my entire life. I guess if I thought about how many lives I'd lived between Moira, Elena, and Lucia, how many centuries had spanned over those past lives, I *had* used a dagger my entire life.

Even outside of training, I'd spent countless hours getting used to handling a dagger, and I'd ultimately switched to wielding a dual set.

Every day for nearly two months now, I'd practiced twirling and flipping them while I enjoyed my morning tea, while I read, while I sketched—every chance I got.

Damien regularly urged me to take a break, but I couldn't help it. I hoped one day they would be an extension of my arms, wielded with the same level of ease as my own two hands. Sure, it would be a while before I reached that level, but that didn't mean I couldn't try.

When I stepped back into the center of the ring, the others moved back into place around me, and I widened my stance, centering myself. My eyes danced between the three warriors as they paced, watching for the faintest hint of who might make the first strike. I felt so small compared to the three males before me, Barrett being the tallest at over six feet. Before everything happened, I would have never imagined I'd ever, in my life, be able to stand up to them.

Yet here I was.

I could feel their eyes on me as they watched for their moment to strike, and I waited, opening my mind to listen for the first thought, the first sound. They were good, fighting on instinct, for when I opened my thoughts to theirs to listen, all I could hear was a quiet hum.

It was imperative they train me this way—I couldn't read the thoughts of darklings, couldn't use my Nous abilities as a crutch.

My body tensed as I heard the mud squelch under Barrett's boots when he made the first move. I spun around to face him. His arm swung just above my head as I dodged his swing, and I slammed the hilt of my dagger into his gut. He grunted, stumbling back, and I prepped to defend my back for where Zephyr or Vincent would attack next.

A blood curdling scream assaulted my ears, and I whipped around.

Night descended around me, smoke burning my lungs as I gasped for air. The sounds of chaos and the roar of fire filled my ears. My chest heaved as a shroud of unfamiliarity fell, and I took in the strange surroundings. Burning buildings crumbled and screams pierced the night air as people ran in every direction, panic clear on their faces.

My throat went dry as darklings emerged from the shadows in droves. So many darklings... more than I'd ever seen. Their slender, pale bodies crouched low as they stalked their prey, hollow, sunken stomachs and exposed ribs silhouetted in the firelight. Shadowy black mist danced off their skin, slipping from their black hair that hung in tendrils around their faces.

It wasn't the soulless black eyes or the terrible claws that could shred a person to pieces that terrified me. What frightened me the most were those jagged, razor-sharp teeth, skin ripping around them as their jaws spread from ear to ear, snapping and gnawing. Cursed to an eternity of endless hunger and greed, never satisfied, no matter how much blood they spilled, how many souls they devoured.

The fleeing civilians were defenseless against the demons hunting them, unable to fight back. Bile rose in my throat. I watched helplessly as they were slaughtered in the most brutal ways. I wanted to help them, but my body felt oddly weak, as if I'd used up all my energy, my knees quivering beneath my weight.

My braided blonde hair was a mess as it hung over my shoulder, my Elythian leather armor soaked through and stained with a mix of dirt, sweat, and blood—darkling blood. The oily substance stuck to me, the foul stench enough to make my nose wrinkle. How many had I killed?

"Damien!" I searched the burning rubble around me, but there was no sign of him, no sign of the brothers of The Order.

I was alone.

The blood drained from my face when a child's scream cut through the chaos. I twisted around, our eyes meeting as she ran toward me, as fast as her little legs could carry her. She was so small; she couldn't have been older than four or five. Darklings pursued her, not far behind. Gods, they'd tear her apart. Their jaws snapped at her heels, and I ran forward at the sight of them closing in on her.

I reached out, grabbed her hand, and pulled her behind me as I drew my short sword from my side. My feet slid apart as I stabilized myself, and I took my stance as the darklings skidded to a halt, hissing and snapping at me as they maintained a cautious distance.

Her tiny hands gripped my armor as she shook in terror. Her voice was but a whisper of fear as she breathed my name. "Lady Elena, what's gonna happen to us?"

My gaze tracked the darklings as they prowled around us, crouched on all fours, their black claws slicing into the dirt. "It's going to be ok. Do you know where your parents are?"

She didn't answer. The only sounds she uttered were sobs she struggled to hold back. She didn't have to explain; her silence was enough to twist my gut. Her parents must have fallen protecting her, and my heart ached for the horrors she must have witnessed.

15

The air was molten, the smoke so thick that it was difficult to breathe. A cough broke from my throat, and I shielded my face from the immense heat pressing into my skin.

A nearby building collapsed, sending plumes of fire and embers into the air. We shrank away from it, but I jerked my sword in front of me the moment the darklings tried to advance.

I reached my free hand back to grip the child's shoulder, holding her close as we side stepped. "Stay close to me. I'll get you to safety."

It was easier said than done, though. I searched for any means of escape. How would I get her to safety? I didn't even know where safety was. Were there any buildings left standing? How far had they reached? Had the fort fallen to the darklings' attack?

Had Moonhaven, the home I'd known for so many years... fallen? This couldn't be the end. I refused to accept it without a fight.

The hair stood up on the back of my neck as the sound of the darklings' clicks echoed from the darkness behind us. It was faint, but enough to alert me of what was stalking us, and I jerked my gaze over my shoulder. We were surrounded, with no way out. My mind raced, knowing what the outcome would be.

Not her. Not like this.

No matter what, I needed to give this child a chance to escape, to get to safety. She needed to live, no matter the cost. I whipped around, crouching before her, my hands bracing on her small shoulders. "You're going to run. Run as fast as you can. Find Lord Damien. He will protect you."

Her pale eyes widened. "What about you, Lady Elena?"

"I'm going to draw their attention. As soon as I give you the signal, you run. Run like you've never run, *mikros*." I kissed her forehead and stood, turning from her as I gripped the hilt of my sword, eyes following the movements of the darklings prowling around us.

"I can't leave you, Lady Elena," she whimpered.

"I'll be right behind you, as soon as I finish these off." The lie was like ash on my tongue, but she needed hope. I forced a smile as I gestured to her. "Hide, *mikros*. Wait for my signal."

Her hesitation was almost tangible as her tiny, quivering hands gripped my sleeve, but she released me. I tracked her out of the corner of my eye as she stepped back cautiously, hiding amidst the rubble of a cart that hadn't yet caught fire. It became clear the darklings were not interested in her, their abysmal eyes settling on me. They'd never acted this way, had never acted in cooperation with each other. What had changed?

Their foul stench burned my nose as more surrounded me. I cursed under my breath. I was cut off from her.

My gaze drifted over them, counting thirteen, but the number continued to grow as others emerged from the shadows. I knew more lurked, hidden from view by the burning rubble. More would continue to come with each passing second.

It was now or never. I couldn't give them the opportunity to block her escape. A weak smile spread across my face as I mustered as much courage as I could for the child hidden in the rubble. For this little life, full of potential, who had yet to experience everything this world had to offer, it would be worth the sacrifice. If I could just save her, this one little soul; I would be able to find peace in my final moments.

There was no time for hesitation. I took a deep breath, shoving past my fear of death as I lurched towards the nearest darkling. "Now!"

The moment I moved, they leapt to attack me. The pathway opened, and the girl took off, tiny feet pounding into the dirt as she ran down the narrow, fire-lined street. I couldn't hesitate, couldn't back down. It would take just one slip and they would notice her.

I shouted, making as much noise as I could. The action was a double-edged sword; it kept the darklings I fought interested in me, but it also drew the attention of the others in the vicinity who hadn't yet noticed my presence. I'd accepted my fate, had known from the moment I saw how many darklings I faced, I wouldn't make it out of this alive.

If only I hadn't exhausted my magic, I could level this group, could see to the girl's safety myself instead of leaving her to chance. I was exhausted, though, every drop of magic wrung from me in the battles I'd already fought, and I was unable to so much as summon the strength to call out to Damien's mind.

With each darkling that fell to my sword, two more replaced them. Before I knew it, I was surrounded by more than I could handle. My muscles burned, bones ached, and my body cried out for rest. I had to push through. *Not yet.*

Her scream cut through the hot air, and my blood ran cold. I turned in time to see a stray darkling pin her to the ground.

"*No!*" I fought to get past the darklings surrounding me. Pain seared into me as claws raked down my back, shredding my Elythian armor and tearing into my flesh. I twisted around, running my sword through the darkling, but as I did, another struck me.

17

Agony assaulted me and I cried out as the scent of her blood reached my nose. I watched helplessly as the darkling devoured her in the distance. My heart shattered at the sight of her tiny, lifeless frame. Her hand lay outstretched toward me, reaching for the one person she trusted in her final moments, the pale, hollow orbs of her eyes, lifeless, unseeing.

I failed her...

The darklings attacked as my despair consumed me, and I swung wildly. Their black blood splattered me, across my arms, my torso, my face. Many fell, but I couldn't keep up with their increasing numbers. There were too many for me to handle, and my body began to fail, my muscles giving out to exhaustion.

The fires had grown so wide and so high, they stained the moonless sky with orange light. Once proud wooden homes lay in rubble, unrecognizable, and bodies of the slaughtered littered the ground around me.

This was the end... Moonhaven had fallen. The civilians had gathered here for our protection, and we'd failed them.

The attack had happened so fast, there had been no time to prepare. I didn't know if anyone else lived, if The Order had fallen.

If Damien had fallen.

I couldn't feel anything through our bond, as if something were blocking him from my sight, my reach. Agony tore into my soul. I wished I could've seen his beautiful face one last time—kissed him, held him, told him how much I loved him. Goddess, protect him if he was still alive. Keep him safe. Let my sacrifice be the last one suffered this night.

Air burst from my lungs as claws sank into my side, and I ripped myself from the darkling's grasp, sinking my sword into its chest. My knees buckled, but I fought to stay on my feet. The warmth of my blood soaked into my shirt, down my leg, and a pained gasp broke from my lips. The world swam around me, the movements of the darklings blurring. My gaze drifted over the countless darklings surrounding me. There was no help in sight. I was alone.

I would die alone… but I'd be damned if I didn't take out as many as I could when I fell.

Voice hoarse, I roared. *"Come at me, you bastards! I'm right here!"*

They crouched before I could ready myself further, and they attacked. My strength failed as they lunged through the air, my body no longer heeding my commands. They fell on me, claws and teeth sinking into my flesh as I cried out.

"Cassie!"

Damien's voice reached my ears, barely audible over my cries. I couldn't find him through the flurry of darklings ravaging me, and I couldn't breathe for the pain as they tore at me. A blur of voices yelled around me, dancing in the darkness of my consciousness, echoing in my ears. The earth opened, swallowing me whole. I sank into the black depths, sinking farther and farther into the ocean of darkness.

"Calm down, it's us!"

"Get those daggers away from her!"

Air flooded my lungs as I opened my eyes, my back slamming into something hard, gravity pulling me to the earth as light blinded me. The pain and sorrow, still fresh, overwhelmed me. Someone held me tightly, bracing me as they tried to pull my daggers from my hands. I gripped them tighter. They would only get them after I took my last breath.

"No!" I fought against the arms binding me, my body panicking, twitching as it felt like death was gripping me in its clutches. The fresh puncturing pain of the darklings' claws and jagged fangs lingered in my flesh, my body recoiling, air ripping from my lungs as my chest caved in.

Damien's voice was calm in my ears as he held me firmly against him. "Return to me, *mea luna*, please. You're safe. It's not real."

CHAPTER 2

DAMIEN

"You're safe now," I whispered into her ear as I held her tightly against me, her back pressed into my chest. She thrashed and struggled against me with everything she had, but whatever battle she fought, she was losing. Horror filled my brothers' eyes as they watched helplessly out of reach. We'd finally managed to pry her daggers from her hands, but not before she'd injured Zephyr. Fresh blood dripped down his forearm where she'd struck him when he'd first tried to calm her.

"*No! I don't want to die alone!*" she sobbed. Those words pierced my chest like a knife.

She blinked, her eyes wild and terrified, and for a moment, she seemed to realize where she was. I supported her as her body spasmed and twitched, and she felt over herself frantically. She gasped for air, suffocating in whatever vision she'd lost herself in. The terror she felt overwhelmed me, our proximity sending resounding, icy dread down our bond. I lowered her to the ground as her knees gave out.

Cassie sobbed as she twisted in my arms to press her face into my chest, gripping my sleeves tightly, too afraid to let go. My eyes met Zephyr's, then lowered back to her as I embraced her, giving her the time she needed.

She muttered something, so low I almost couldn't hear her. Panicked words escaped her lips with each breath. *"I don't want to die alone... don't want... alone."*

The recovery of her memories had never been so violent before. In the past, they had been more of a merging of thoughts, fitting in as if they had merely been forgotten pieces of a puzzle, falling into completion. However, her human mind struggled with the weight of them. It was unnatural for her mortal body, and it resisted with each new memory. The pleasant ones had been easier for her, but the more painful ones...

It had been difficult to watch, for that was all I could do. I wished I could share the burden she carried, that I could take the pain from her. Unfortunately, I could only be there to catch her when she fell.

Her hazel eyes rose to mine finally, bloodshot and glassy. She looked over her shoulder at the others, and her body tensed when her eyes landed on Zephyr.

She cupped her hands over her mouth as she pushed away from me to stand, and she rushed to him, stopping before she reached him, as if she were afraid to get any closer. "I'm so sorry, Zeph. I—" Her voice broke, and I watched as sorrow rammed into Zephyr, his black spruce and wintergreen scent overwhelmed with the musky scent of fallen rain.

"It's ok, Cas. This is nothing. I've suffered worse." He forced a weak smile, attempting to comfort her. "Are *you* ok?"

Her eyes drifted around us; all our gazes focused on her. Barrett and Vincent were silent, shaken at how she'd fought while trapped in her vision. Thalia and the nearby recruits had ceased their training, now standing in horrified silence.

If I hadn't known she'd been suffering, I would have been overwhelmed with pride at the skill and strength she'd displayed. It had taken every one of my brothers to stop her, to contain her. Her desperate cries had shattered me in those final moments, though, as I held her back. The question lingered on my lips; I wished I could let it go, but I needed to know. "What did you see?"

She turned to me, those beautiful hazel eyes full of agony. "It was Moonhaven again…"

I bit back my own despair, knowing from her reaction what she'd seen. My eyes moved to Zephyr, feeling his own pain at her words. He knew as well as I did why she'd reacted the way she had, why she'd fought so desperately.

She'd been fighting for her life… and had failed.

"I tried to save a little girl—" The moment the words left her lips, her voice cracked. I knew who she spoke of, remembered the child's lifeless body when I'd found her.

Children were, unfortunately, a rare gift for our race, often cherished above all else. We'd been too late to save either of them, to save many lives. When Zephyr and I had found Elena, her body was ravaged almost beyond recognition amidst the countless darklings she'd taken with her into death.

Zephyr didn't speak, his eyes burning into the ground at his feet.

I drew a deep breath. "Training's done for today. You guys can go rest. Zephyr?" I glanced toward him, and he lifted his eyes to me. He nodded in response, understanding my meaning. He'd been hesitant to *really* talk with Cassie, to get to know her more, but he needed to. Elena's loss had been painful to endure for him as well.

For while Elena was my mate, she was *his* sister.

Flames crackled in the fireplace, warmth filling the room, driving out the harsh cold of winter. It had taken a few hours, but Cassie had finally settled and was resting easy in the crook of my arm, legs propped up under her as she watched the fire. Her chest rose and fell in a steady rhythm. It was in these peaceful moments I found the most solace—just hearing her breathe, feeling her skin against mine.

If only it could remain like this.

Her eyes danced around the room before her gaze settled. "Wait. That painting…"

I followed her gaze to the portrait hanging next to the fireplace.

"I completely forgot about it. I saw it when you first brought me here, but... Did you take it elsewhere the last couple of months?"

I nodded. "Yeah, I thought it might be best to put it away in case your parent's saw it."

"When I first saw it, I thought it was some great grandpa of yours or something, but now that I know what I know, I figured it's you, but who's the woman?"

I looked over the delicate skin of her painted face. The artist had been talented, but the portrait paled in comparison to her natural beauty. Her moon-like eyes burned into me as I stared, the rich, black wavy hair framing her face as she leaned against me in the picture. I remembered sitting with her as if it were yesterday.

"It's Lucia. It was painted shortly after The Fall of Kingdoms. You were pregnant then, and after the daughter of Matthias fell, the darklings had gone into hiding for a while. It was a happy time for us, we had a chance to finally enjoy peace."

If only our dreams had become reality. If only we had gotten to experience the joys of raising our family together. She would have been an amazing mother, and I regretted more than anything that she hadn't even been able to hold her own child before she took her final breath.

She rose from the couch, gravitating toward the painting. I saw so much of Lucia in her, saw *all* her past lives in that sweet face. The striking features were more subtle in her human form, hazel eyes instead of the moon-gray ones common for our kind, eyes every immortal inherited from Selene herself. Her warm rosy cheeks took the place of the delicate, pale porcelain skin each of her reincarnations had shared before her.

No matter how much her mortal form tried to mask it, I would have known her regardless—the electric current that sparked between us with each brush of her skin, the gravity of her presence, the voice that drove me crazy with each word that slipped from her lips. She was like a drug—one I'd suffered the worst withdrawals from while awaiting her return.

"When is your next therapy session?" I asked.

She lingered a moment before glancing over her shoulder at me. "Tuesday."

"That's still a few days away. Do you want me to call Salwa in early?"

"I'll be ok. I'm feeling better now. It isn't as fresh anymore." Her eyes didn't meet mine, and I knew she was hiding the brunt of it from me. It hurt to see her hide the pain away. She was far too considerate of others, and I couldn't help but feel that she'd likely been that way her entire life, sheltering her grief alone.

"Have the sessions been helping? I know you only just started a few weeks ago, but I want to make sure it isn't too much."

Her smile warmed me. She and Salwa had developed a relationship that went beyond therapeutic. "Salwa's been so wonderful and kind. I'm glad to have her help. She's good at what she does. She has a special gift; I can't explain it, but it makes it easy to talk to her."

Though she brushed it off, I knew she still suffered from Marcus' torture, the mental manipulations he had put her through. She hadn't been able to bring herself to talk to me fully about it, but I never pressed. I wanted her to come to me when she was ready. "I'm glad to hear that."

Salwa was a therapist for The Order and civilians alike. As a member of House Nous, she used her telepathic abilities to benefit those in her care on a deep level. What set her apart from a normal therapist, though, was that she didn't simply speak with her patients. She entered their minds to help smooth out the ripples of trauma, help heal from the inside out.

It had only been part of the reason I'd introduced her to Salwa, though. After Cassie had lost control and set our bed on fire, I knew we would have to be proactive in how she learns to use her abilities—some of which were wiped out during The Fall of Kingdoms. She risked losing control if another resurfaced before she was ready.

Born of the old blood, centuries ago, not only was she talented in her abilities as a telepathic healer, but she was also a well-versed historian of our race, one of the few who had lived nearly as long as I had. I'd hoped she might be able to help Cassie, not only to heal the scars she harbored, but to ultimately assist when she was ready to learn to use the blood traits wiped out in the war with the darklings.

"Is Zephyr ok? That cut on his arm looked bad. Did he have to get stitches?" Cassie's voice cut across my train of thought.

"Don't worry, Cas. It wasn't as bad as it looked. It'll heal in no time. It'll probably be gone in the morning."

The guilt was apparent in her eyes, and I stood to walk over to her. Her hands grazed her forearms in a back-and-forth motion, a nervous tick she'd developed. I hadn't noticed it when we first met, and I didn't know if she'd always done it, or if it developed after Marcus had captured her. I placed my hands over hers, easing her anxiety as best I could.

She stopped the moment she realized what she was doing and rested her forehead against my chest. "I'm so sorry. I was so lost in the vision of Elena... It's like I lose all sense of reality."

The painful memories tore through me, but I forced it back, leveling my emotions. I wouldn't let her feel the pain I felt. The wound of Elena's death had never fully healed. To have died alone, at the claws of countless darklings, to know how it ended for her, and to have been unable to be there with her... I still remembered the horrible feeling through our bond when she fell, her presence vanishing without a trace. It's a kind of pain I'd never truly recovered from. I could still feel the weight of her body in my arms in those moments after I'd found her.

I wrapped my arms around her, her body so small against mine. "I wish I could spare you the pain of reliving those events."

Though she housed such power, power that could destroy my brothers and me, power that had wiped out armies of darklings, she felt so small, so... fragile. I knew she wasn't, though. She was stronger than anyone I'd met, but that strength had been wavering lately.

Whatever Marcus had done to her left more scars than I could fathom. Something inside her had fractured, and I was lost at how I might help her heal it.

Salwa had found no trace of what happened to her at the metal shop where we fought Marcus. Cassie hadn't been in control of herself when she'd ended him, that much was certain. *Something* had compelled her to act, though, and it was unnerving to not know what that something was.

The sight of her consuming the flames in the metal shop, when she'd burned Marcus in a fire so hot, he'd been reduced to ashes almost instantly, had been terrifying to behold. Such unbridled power had ignited within her, and I feared I may have lost her to whatever darkness clouded her mind, lost her to the fires filling her body.

What concerned me most was that she hadn't been in control of herself, but more of a spectator through her own eyes. Her past lives had compelled her to act before, but she'd expressed the difference of this situation, and Salwa confirmed what she'd said to be true.

That Salwa found nothing out of the ordinary led me to believe Cassie was influenced by an outside source, but who? Marcus? It wouldn't have made sense for him to off himself like that. I knew he wanted to get under our skin, but the look on his face made it clear *that* wasn't in his plans.

"I just wish I could've saved the girl, at least."

I swallowed. "You've always been a powerful warrior, Cas, always quick to sacrifice yourself for others. I never knew what happened, but I'm not surprised you did what you did." Her eyes lifted to mine. She needed to know what had happened that night—why she'd died.

"We got separated in the chaos of the darkling attack that night. It happened before Barrett and Vincent's time, but Zephyr was there. Moonhaven was one of the largest villages we'd built since the darklings first appeared, after our home had been destroyed, our people scattered. It was the first time we had a home for both warriors and civilians." It had become a true home to us, one I missed dearly. "That night, the darklings attacked without warning. We were unprepared and overwhelmed by how many came."

I gazed into those hazel eyes, the agony of the memory sinking into me. "I never should've left your side."

Her eyes fell as she listened, and I couldn't help but run my thumb against her cheek, her skin warm and soft against mine. The faint hum of our bond tingled just beneath the surface, weak, but a presence I couldn't help but cling to. "When they attacked the main gates, Zephyr and I left you to guard the civilians, in case any stray darklings broke through our defenses. I thought you would be safer there."

"The attack on the main gates was a distraction, though, and the darklings found a way through the back walls to attack the civilians in hiding. Before I could pull back to go to you, I was notified a fire had broken out in the village. As the guard was speaking to me... I felt your presence vanish through our bond. I immediately went to search for you, terrified the worst had happened. I tried calling through my thoughts, praying you would reach into my mind like you always did to tell me you were safe…" Breathing became difficult as the memories resurfaced, unbridled and painful.

"I never heard a response, and we found you not long after." I momentarily lost myself in the feel of her skin beneath my fingers, reassuring myself she was here with me, that she'd returned to me once more. "The devastation we found, the destruction they'd left in their wake—I couldn't believe it. They hadn't left a soul alive in that part of Moonhaven, and by the time we got to you, the remaining darklings had fled. They didn't even attempt to attack the rest of the fort."

"I can still hear the horrible clicking sound." Her voice was soft, though her eyes didn't rise to meet mine as she watched it play out in her mind. Sometimes, I hated her ability to see my experiences, feel my pain through touch—hated that she relived it through my eyes.

27

Silence hung in the air, and my fingers ran through her soft chestnut curls, combing them out and letting them fall over her back. If we could just destroy the darkling leader, Melantha, and rid the world of the darklings once and for all, we could enjoy the peace we so desperately deserved. I could give her the life she was meant to have, have her at my side as queen once again. If we were lucky enough, we could possibly even try to raise a family together. Nothing would make me happier than to see her carry our children, mother them the way I knew she could.

It was a distant dream, one I clung to.

Her gaze drifted from me to the window, and her hazel eyes lit up. "Damien, it's snowing."

I turned to see snowflakes fluttering on the breeze outside in the dwindling light as the sun set over the distant mountain ridges. If she needed a distraction, I would happily provide one. "Well, grab your jacket. Let's go enjoy it before it stops."

A sweet smile spread across her face and she headed for the foyer, where she grabbed her coat and threw it over her shoulders. Her happiness filled my lungs, the aroma like wildflowers, her scent of jasmine and her citrus shampoo dancing in the air around her. I could breathe that fragrance in all day, bury myself in it.

Cold air flooded the foyer as she opened the front door, and I could barely keep up with her as she raced into the cold. She didn't hesitate as she hurried down the stairs into the front yard.

"Careful you don't slip now," I warned as I closed the door behind me.

"Oh, I'll be fine! I know I'm a klutz but give me some credit." She stuck her hands out, trying to catch the small crystals of ice as they fluttered around her. Dwindling light faded over the horizon as night stretched out around us. The streetlights lit up as darkness fell, and the snowflakes came to life, catching the glow of the lamps.

Her breath billowed out in misty puffs as she watched the falling snowflakes glow in the light. A soft smile spread across her face as she watched it all. "It's so beautiful."

She was a sight I could watch endlessly. I walked over and pulled her against me, leaning my forehead to hers. Her laughter filled my senses, the most beautiful music to ever grace my ears. "Not as beautiful as you, *mea luna*." *My moon.*

Her cheeks turned a beautiful shade of pink. "You're just saying that, *mea sol*." *My sun.*

My chest swelled as she called me by that special name—one she'd called me for centuries. If only she knew how special that name was for us. If only she knew I didn't call her *my moon* as a simple term of endearment. She was truly the light in my life, the light in the darkness guiding me forward. She'd named me her sun, without whom she could not glow as brightly in the darkness.

And I would bask in her glow until the end of time.

CHAPTER 3
CASSIE

My phone vibrated in my pocket with Kat's text.

> I've gotta get to class, I'll talk to you later!

I tapped away quickly on my phone.

> Before you go, are we doing pizza night Friday?

I toyed with the necklace she'd gotten me for my birthday as I waited for her response. It was a simple locket with a photo of us inside, and I cherished it.

Her text came through, and I sighed.

> I'm so sorry, I'm bogged down with midterms. Anatomy and Physiology is kicking my ass this semester, and Cody is taking me on a weekend trip for a concert to force me to take a break. Can we take a raincheck? I feel so terrible, I would have invited you, but I think it's gonna be that kind of trip, if you know what I mean. 😉

I bit back a smile at her implication. I responded with a short 'sure' before shoving my phone in my pocket. It was foolish of me to think she would have time between her job and school, plus things developing between her and Cody. I was happy for her, but it felt like we were growing apart somehow. We'd only been able to hang out a few times since I'd moved in with Damien. We kept up with each other, visiting when we could. She'd even joined us for Christmas with my parents. It had been... interesting, and I giggled at the memory of Damien and his brothers trying to figure out how to celebrate Christmas to give me some normalcy.

It was getting more difficult, though, as Kat got deeper into med school. Her schedule had been a juggling act of hopping from class to work and back to class again early the following morning. It didn't help that my training had taken up so much of my own time. It had been over a week since I'd seen her in person.

I should've known this would happen. How could I maintain a friendship with her when I now lived in a world she didn't even know existed, a world she could *never* know existed? As a human, she couldn't know anything of the immortals, the Elythians... the darklings.

"'Ow would ye like yer eggs t'day, deary?" Ethel shuffled about in the kitchen, working efficiently as she cooked us breakfast, her salty white hair tied into a ponytail.

31

I eased back in the chair. "I'll just take them scrambled. Thank you, *Mitera*."

"You're not going to ask me, *Mitera*?" Damien said, his tone sheepish as he entered the kitchen. By the coy grin on his face, I knew he was teasing her. It seemed to be his favorite pastime, and I rolled my eyes at the troublemaking grin smeared across his face.

Without sparing him a glance, she waved the spatula in the air. "Lord Damien, there's nae a day that ye 'aven't asked fer yer eggs o'er easy. Ah've offered countless times, an' it's always the same."

He walked over to her, resting his hands on her shoulders. "Maybe I'm going to want something different today."

She turned to him, crossing her arms. "*Fine*. Tell me, Lord Damien. 'Ow wuid ye like yer eggs this mornin'?"

The crooked grin remained on his face as he spoke. "Over easy would be nice."

I choked on my drink as she swung her spatula at him with a huff. He evaded her easily, grunting out a laugh, ducking around the table to dodge her as she went after him again. He slid a sideways grin at me as she returned to the stove, to which I shook my head, unable to fight the smile curving my lips.

The front door slammed open down the hall, and heavy feet hurried towards the kitchen. Barrett burst into the room, followed closely by Vincent, Zephyr, Thalia and James.

"You got any food for us, *Mitera*?" Barrett hurried over to her, leaning over her shoulder to look, popping a kiss on her cheek. I didn't know how this poor woman had put up with them for so long.

She swatted his hand when he reached to grab a bite. "Mind yer manners, Barrett. Sit ye arse down, an' Ah'll fix ye a plate when I can."

Thalia shook her head at him as she settled into a seat next to me. Her cornsilk hair slipped over her shoulder as she leaned in to whisper in my ear. "I'd love to see her clobber him with that spatula."

I huffed a giggle. "You just missed her do that to Damien."

Disappointment flashed across her face as she gaped at Damien as he settled into his chair. Barrett joined us at the table, kicking back in his chair. He popped a stolen piece of bacon into his mouth, winking at me as he leaned back in his seat. Everyone was oddly chipper and awake for being out so late patrolling. I couldn't understand how they functioned on such little sleep. Then again, they were immortal, and there was a lot I still didn't understand about their race.

James walked over to Ethel, pressing a quick kiss to her cheek. "G'mornin', Nan."

"G'mornin' deary. Ah'll 'ave ye some breakfast ready ina bit."

James propped his laptop up on the table, and Damien leaned in. "Have you been able to recover any of the footage from Cole's escape yet?"

Adrenaline spiked in my blood, but I did my best not to react. Cole had evaded capture over the last couple of months, and there had been no signs of him since he broke out of his cell at The Complex. Damien had lost two warriors in the process, and it remained a mystery how he'd gotten free.

"Whoever got inta our system knew wut they were doin'. It took a while tae comb throo' everythin', but ah managed tae get some o' eh footage recovered." James typed and clicked away at his keyboard. "And Damien... there's also evidence o' electrical damage."

Damien's elbows settled onto the table, his fingers knitting together as he rested his chin on them. "So, it was one of our kind who helped him, a Stoicheion user."

My brows furrowed and I looked at Damien. That's what he'd called my flame magic. "Wait a minute, isn't Stoicheion flame magic?"

"Stoicheion users are elementalists," Barrett interjected, running his fingers through his short blonde hair. "Vincent and I come from House Stoicheion. Members of our house are born with one set elemental ability, always at random. I can control Flame Stoicheion while Vincent controls water. There's flame, water, lightning, earth, and air, though air and lightning are rare abilities. I haven't seen a lightning Stoicheion user in decades."

My eyes lowered, thinking about when I'd gained the ability to use the flame magic, how I'd wanted to forget that power—refused to test or use it after what happened to Marcus. Would I only be able to use flame magic? Or, given that I was meant to use every house's blood trait, would I be able to use all the elemental powers?

"So, we've got a lightning Stoicheion user and an Aíma. That's a dangerous combination." Damien's eyes hovered on the tabletop, thinking beyond the words he spoke, his knee bouncing faintly beneath the table.

I'd seen Cole's abilities firsthand, so I understood the truth he spoke. He was the sole living heir to House Aíma, manipulators of blood, thought to have been wiped out during the battle of The Fall of Kingdoms. Cole could bend a person's blood to his will with a simple touch. The things he could do were beyond my imagination. My experience was limited to him altering my blood pressure and heart rate to prevent a heart attack when Marcus had—

33

I drew a deep breath, pushing the images out of my mind.

"All right, 'ere we go," James chimed, spinning his laptop around for us to see the video.

I leaned in, eyes scanning the screen. The video was rough, fragmented and corrupted. Cole sat in the cell, the chains loose, but still binding him, keeping him contained. Though I didn't feel any sympathy for him, it was still difficult to look at. The familiarity of being chained in the same manner had never quite dulled.

"It's ok, *mea luna*," Damien whispered in my ear. He laced his fingers with mine, and I realized I'd been rubbing my wrists again, the faint scars still rough and fading under my fingertips. I breathed deeply and resumed watching.

The lights flickered in Cole's cell, and the door swung open. His guards entered, scanning the room. There was no audio, so we couldn't hear what they were saying. The screen suddenly flickered and shook when what looked like lightning shot into the chamber. The currents of electricity surged around the guards, leaving them lifeless on the ground. A woman entered the room; dark brown hair was her only identifying feature, her back turned to the camera. She hurried over to Cole, knelt before him, and cupped his face in her hands as she spoke.

We all watched the screen intently, waiting for a clearer view of who'd aided Cole's escape. She released Cole and helped him to his feet, his arm tugged over her shoulders to stabilize him. Her head turned in the camer's direction, her face blurred and unrecognizable, before her hand shot out and the camera went black. James reversed the footage back to the last clip before the camera went offline, showing the blurred image of the woman.

Zephyr looked across to Damien. "Is that Amara?"

"It definitely looks like it," Damien said, his dark brows furrowing as he scrutinized the image.

Vincent let loose a breath as he lifted his gaze from the laptop. "She hasn't made another appearance since we busted Marcus' hideout. No one has seen or heard from her."

"I didn't know she had any abilities," Damien said.

"It's possible." Barrett sat back in his chair as Ethel brought over plates for the others. "She's not a warrior of The Order, so we wouldn't know of any ability she might have."

"I'm not surprised she would side with Marcus," Thalia said as Ethel set a plate of food before her. "She was always a pain in the ass." She got to work on her breakfast as Ethel continued to set full plates out for everyone.

34

The food sitting before me suddenly looked unappetizing. It wasn't enough for Cole to have a target on my back. Amara already didn't like me, and I could only imagine how furious she must have been to be knocked out by a human.

I'd known from the first time I met her she didn't care to know me. Her mind had long been poisoned by Marcus, and there was no telling what hatred she harbored for Damien and his group—for me now. I'd hoped I could find some peace after we'd stopped Marcus, but clearly it was wishful thinking.

The afternoon sun shined through the clouds above us. It was almost warm for the first time in weeks, so I shed my jacket and tossed it on a nearby chair on The Outpost training grounds. The forest was dormant around us, countless bare trees stretching out for miles, the yard busy with Thalia's recruits working on their training. We'd come here every day since we started my training, after I'd discovered what I was: a demigoddess, born to fight the enemies of the Goddess of the Moon and Creator of The Immortal Race, Selene.

It was still a strange reality to absorb. Only a few months prior, I'd been like every other human, weak and oblivious to the dangers lurking in the shadows around us, to the monsters who'd happily devour you under the cover of night.

One thing hadn't changed, though. My internal clock was still ticking away, still counting down the days until my heart would give out.

I needed to tell Damien. He deserved to know. Still, no matter how much I wanted to, I couldn't bring myself to do it, couldn't find the right words. I'd made numerous attempts over the last couple of months, but every time I gathered enough courage, something would happen, and it would fall through at the last moment. I was such a damn coward.

Damien tugged at my shoulders, pulling me back to his chest as he laid a tender kiss on my shoulder. "Hold still."

A smile tugged at my lips as his fingers combed through my hair before he started to braid.

"I missed doing this for you," he whispered.

Warmth spread through my chest, and I tried to recall the memories he was reliving. "You used to braid my hair?"

"All the time." He tied the end before letting the braid slip from his fingertips over my shoulder, then leaned in to say. "Though I enjoy messing it up even more."

My cheeks warmed, the warmth shifting to heat, and my heart danced as I imagined just how he would do it.

"We gonna start working on training the little spitfire to control her Stoicheion ability?" Barrett cut in from across the clearing.

All heat left me, and uneasiness sank into the pit of my stomach at the thought. He wasn't wrong; I needed to learn how to master it. It was a dangerous ability, and I was afraid if I didn't know how to properly use it, I might set our house on fire this time, or seriously hurt someone.

Get over it.

"We haven't fully finished her shifting training," Zephyr argued.

"She changed into an owl at your last session," Barrett said.

"Yeah, and then she ate dirt when she tried to fly," Vincent added with a teasing grin.

My lips pressed into a thin line. Just what I needed, a reminder of that blow to my pride. It had hurt, too.

"All I know is she lit shit up when we went after Marcus," Barrett said. "That's some serious power in the hands of someone who doesn't know how to use it." A calm passed over his expression, all joking put aside. "Power like that could do some serious damage. She could hurt someone. Besides, if she can master it, she'll have an advantage against the darklings when shit hits the fan."

I glanced back at Damien. His gaze didn't meet mine, and I could see the conflict in those amber and ashen eyes. It would be no surprise if he was worried after what happened the last time I'd used the ability—when Damien had looked on in horror as I burned Marcus alive.

He deserved what he got.

I winced at the voice in my head. No, that wasn't who I was. I was me. I was in control.

"He has a point," Damien said, and looked back at me. "Do you think you're ready for this?"

"I really should try. I don't want to risk hurting anyone."

Barrett stood and walked over to me. "All right, let's get to it, then!"

36

I forced a smile to ease Damien's concern as I stepped forward. Zephyr, Vincent, and Thalia eased down into chairs to watch from the sidelines. Damien didn't budge, though, and he remained a short distance behind me.

"Like Damien's shadow magic, the different elements used by House Stoicheion can be directly influenced by your emotions," Barrett explained. "Anger and passion can enhance fire. Too much, and it will burn out of control, too little and it won't sustain the spark. You must maintain a balance."

I tilted my head. "Your hotheaded personality suddenly makes a lot more sense."

Barrett cracked a grin, his steel eyes lighting as he stared down his nose at me. "Cool it, spitfire, or I'll teach you how to wield the flame a different way. And you won't like that, I promise."

"I'm really interested to see you try," Damien warned.

I rolled my eyes when Barrett threw his hands up in surrender, a haughty grin spreading across his face. I firmly believed Barrett lived for confrontation—always eager for a fight, likely due to the fire-laced blood flowing through his veins. Given the chance, he'd enjoy watching me dance around his flames to elicit some sort of response with my own. It wouldn't end well for him, though, wouldn't end well for any of us.

He lifted his hand, and small flames came to life at his fingertips. The smile left my face as I watched them dance, growing slowly until they enveloped his hand. My throat went dry as I watched the fire move lithely against his skin.

"Do you use these abilities when you're hunting darklings?" I asked, unable to pull my gaze from his lit hand.

He watched me, gauging my reaction. "Not always. The key to what we do in this era of humanity is discreteness. Still, having this arsenal in our back pocket can be the deciding factor between us putting them down, or them slaughtering us."

There was no greater truth than those words, and after seeing the devastation of Moonhaven's fall firsthand, I knew he was right.

Barrett doused the flames and drew closer. He took my hand, holding it up between us. "Now, think about your emotions. Focus on the tip of this one finger." He tapped my pointer finger. "Picture the heat, the fire. Use those emotions as a spark, and once the flame comes to life, level it out and focus on maintaining it. You'll feel it when it happens."

My eyes flickered back and forth between him and my finger, my heart dipping as the nerves curdled my stomach. "What if I can't control it?"

"Don't hesitate. Fear does not mix well with Stoicheion magic. Ignore your fear. Think of your passionate emotions—love creates a more controlled spark. Think of it like a torch at your fingertip. You can widen or constrict the flow of emotions. You won't understand it fully until you try it out. Don't worry, Vincent can put you out if need be."

Vincent's grin widened as he threw up a hand from the nearby bench. "Got my bucket right here!"

I rolled my eyes at the water user's proverbial 'bucket'. There was no bucket in sight, but I guess he didn't need one when he could manipulate the moisture in the air around us, the snow beneath our feet.

I drew a deep breath, shoving the fear down where I might not feel it. I could do this. Easy. I closed my eyes, remembering when I'd accidentally set our bed on fire. As the fear tried to resurface, I didn't allow myself to dwindle on the cause of that meltdown, on the dream that triggered the magic.

What did I feel right now? Barrett had specifically instructed me to ignore my fears and use love instead. So, I focused on Damien, on my feelings toward him. Surely, that would be enough. Passion. Love. Adoration. The warmth cascaded over my skin in the cold air, focusing on that little heat.

Barrett tapped on the tip of my pointer finger. "Good. Now, focus here."

My finger grew warm, warmer and warmer until it felt hot, my passion and feelings for Damien flowing to one point, sparking to life.

"Open your eyes, Cas." Damien's voice was a whisper behind me, and I obliged hesitantly.

The tiniest of flames danced on my fingertip, so small, so... beautiful. The air left my lungs in a sigh of relief and excitement, and a smile spread across my face. "I did it."

Barrett leaned down to inspect the flame as it flickered. "Excellent, spitfire. I knew you could do it. Now, level out your emotion, and keep the faucet at a trickle for now."

The flame settled, and I moved my hand slowly, tilting my finger back and forth as the flame shifted and danced in the winter breeze. It was beautiful to watch, a living flame at my fingertips. It was... mesmerizing.

You can do better than that.

Sharp pain pierced my skull, stretching out to the back of my eyes as I clenched them shut. Marcus appeared before me, his chest glowing as the flames consumed him, the strange look of appreciation on his face as he thanked me. The fire stretched out from my hand as I burned him until nothing but ash remained. My hand grew hotter, and I opened my eyes to find the flames growing, enveloping my hand, my other hand coming alight as well.

I gasped, chest heaving as I panicked. "No!"

Damien appeared before me, his eyes locking with mine. "Breathe, Cas. Close the faucet."

My eyes flickered between the flames and him. I shrank back for fear of burning him, but he held me steadfast. "It's happening again, Damien. I can't stop—"

"*Breathe, Cas,*" he said firmly. "Focus on cutting off the flow. Focus on me, *mea luna.* You can do this."

My breaths came in short bursts, uneven, uncontrollable. The fire fell further out of my hold, climbing up my arms as my heart stuttered. Damien hissed, recoiling his hands as the fire reached him. Cold water doused me, soaking me from head to toe, shocking me out of my panic.

The fire died out.

Vincent stood frozen just a few feet from me, face drained of all color, hands outstretched from dousing me in his magic. Silence hung in the air. Barrett didn't even have a comment to make. My eyes fell to my quivering hands, my palms red.

"I can't do this anymore…"

CHAPTER 4

CASSIE

The training I desperately needed to complete ended immediately after I lost control. I couldn't handle it. I was too weak—too weak to control this fractured part of me Marcus had created.

I leaned back in my stool to look at my easel, scrutinizing a portrait of Elena I'd been working on for the last week. I'd managed to see my reflection in a recent memory of her prepping for a hunt. She'd always worn her thick blonde hair in a braid, the wave of her hair just as untamable as mine. The words I'd shared with Damien rippled through my memories.

You used to braid my hair?
All the time.

Damien had braided her hair for her. *My* hair. It was still strange to grasp that I'd lived not one but three past lives, and it was just as difficult to accept that I was Damien's mate. I felt it, though, that strange pull to him, as if he completed me. I'd felt it from the moment we first met. The way he acted toward me, though, I knew it paled in comparison to what I would feel if I were an immortal like him.

My eyes fell to the Lupai, a wolf made of shadow and black mist, sitting at my side. Its head rested in my lap, where it had remained for the last hour as I worked on Elena's portrait. I smiled, running my hand through its thick, black fur, the mist of shadow magic dancing around my skin, rising to disperse into the air. It wagged its tail, whimpering as it begged for more pets. I chuckled, showering it with affection, but my smile faded.

My training wasn't moving along fast enough, and my time was running short. I'd been lucky to have not suffered an attack. There'd been times during training the last couple of months where I'd found myself at that unmeasurable limit and had to stop. Thankfully, since I was human, Damien and the others never pressed and would typically let me call it a day.

I knew better, though. I couldn't allow myself to believe my powers awakening had somehow healed the damage in my heart. No, the Goddess Selene made it clear what would happen to me when my human body could no longer sustain my magic. It wouldn't be a heart condition that killed me...

It would be my own power.

Tears of frustration dotted my lashes as I leaned in to grab the charcoal and continued working on the details of her face. I needed more time. I'd only started to grasp three out of countless abilities, and one of them I have no control over.

Melantha.

Just the thought of her name sent chills down my spine, the image of her still fresh in my mind. The memory I'd successfully plucked from Cole's mind haunted my dreams. She was such a proud creature, elegant, poised.

Deadly.

I'd felt the raw power she possessed the first time I encountered her, the first time I'd encountered the darklings in the alley.

My brows knitted, a realization crossing my mind, and the charcoal halted against the paper. I'd met Melantha, had been held in her grasp when I first encountered the darklings. Marcus let slip that she

wanted to convert me into a darkling. Why hadn't she taken me then? I was an easy target, and she had her claws around my throat. I'd been completely defenseless.

So why didn't she?

I hadn't known at the time what I was, what I was capable of. She'd sent Marcus after me, to send me out into the streets so she could take me. Perhaps she realized then that I didn't have access to my magic. Maybe she was waiting for my powers to awaken, for me to master my abilities before she tried to convert me.

Unlike the feral creatures she commanded, she was smart, calculated. She'd somehow turned Damien's brothers against him—both Marcus and Cole. She'd played us like a game of chess.

I set my charcoal down, unable to focus on my drawing. Melantha. Marcus. Cole. Amara. Eris. The Goddess of Strife and Discord. They were all pieces of a puzzle scattered in every direction, so many pieces that didn't add up, didn't fit into place.

Damien and I hadn't had any luck figuring out what role Eris played in all this. She was another goddess for me to worry about, one more powerful and dangerous than I could fathom. Whoever she was, she scared Damien, that much was certain, and Damien didn't scare easily.

Unfortunately, Marcus had only mentioned her name. He hadn't spoken anything more of her involvement, and that knowledge died with him.

I hadn't been able to bring myself to tell Damien about Marcus thanking me in those final seconds before he turned to ash. He'd suffered enough at Marcus and Cole's betrayal. I feared it may make him question everything if he knew. No matter how much I thought about it, though, it didn't make sense, and I didn't think I'd ever be able to erase the memory of his smile.

A knock at the study door pulled me from my thoughts, and I looked up from my easel as Damien entered. "Hey, Salwa's afternoon is clear. She's moving your appointment up and coming over."

He approached the window where I sat and passed his hand over the Lupai. It disappeared into nothing, returning to the shadows, to the Godsrealm. "She's thinking it might be a good opportunity while it's still fresh in your mind."

My eyes drifted from him, my shoulders sagging. "I'm sorry I ruined today's training. I wish I could just figure this out."

"There's nothing to apologize for, *mea luna*." He reached out to brush his hand against my cheek and my control slipped, his pain searing through the touch of his skin.

I was hurting him, and I didn't know how I could make it better. How could I heal the wounds he'd been nursing over countless centuries, having lost me over and over? He was afraid of losing me again with each decision he made, I knew it. He just didn't know it would be sooner rather than later, and there was nothing he could do to stop it.

There's nothing to apologize for. Yes, there was. God, there was so much to apologize for. Perhaps it would have been better if we'd never met that day at The Galleria, or if he'd erased my memory and we'd gone our separate ways. Damien had said the Fates were cruel bitches. What he didn't know was just how right he was in that statement.

It was cruel of them to reunite him with his reincarnated mate just to have her die so quickly. Next to the centuries he'd lived, the possible few years he might get with me would be like days to him, like a candle blown out the moment it was lit.

"How have you been since we last spoke?"

I settled into the couch near Salwa, the leather cushions groaning beneath me. "I've actually been doing better. The dreams aren't as frequent."

Nightmares had plagued my sleep for weeks after I'd killed Marcus. It was always the same dream. I would wake up in that cell, irons binding my wrists, chains hauling my hands up until my weight had my shoulders throbbing.

Then he'd appear. Marcus, the same cruel expression on his face, endlessly chanting the twisted things he'd said when he held me captive, how he would break me, ruin me, leave me for the darklings. He would grab me, and the moment his fingers sank into my flesh, he would burn—burn so brightly. His voice echoed in my mind, *thank you*, as I screamed. And I'd burn with him... until I was a husk of what I formerly was.

44

He'd thanked me. No matter how many times I relived the memory, it made no sense.

Salwa lifted her feet up onto the couch, leaning onto the armrest as she jotted down her notes. She lifted her finger to push her gold, round-framed glasses farther up her nose, her silver eyes lifting to me. I didn't think I would ever adjust to the beauty of those pale eyes against her dark brown skin.

"Still the same dream?"

I nodded.

Her eyes moved over me. "It's good to hear you're sleeping better. You look healthier. You were so thin when I first met you. It looks like you're eating better."

I'd noticed the change as well. My cheeks had filled out, my clothes fit better. I'd even needed to go up a size. The exercise I'd been getting during training had built muscle I'd never had before. Aside from my struggles with sleep and nightmares, I felt healthier than ever.

"It's strange. Before I met Damien, I had such difficulty eating. I thought it was my medication making me nauseous."

She rested her clipboard against her knees. "Depression will do that to you."

Depression. I'd refused to acknowledge it for many years before I met Damien—fearful of more drugs, more tests, more doctors poking and prodding into my head, into my life. It was the last thing I needed or wanted, so I never spoke of it. If I ignored it, I thought it might give up and go away.

Damien had somehow changed everything. He'd become a light, driving out the darkness, showing me how much goodness there could be in life, which was funny given he was a Lord of Darkness.

"Have you told him?" Salwa asked.

I parted my lips, but the words clung to my tongue. I knew what she meant. "No."

"Why don't you tell him?"

"I'm afraid..." I struggled to find the words.

"What are you afraid of? Do you think he'll abandon you?"

No, it wasn't that I was afraid of him leaving me. I was afraid of hurting him when he'd already suffered so much, of him seeing me differently, treating me differently. I didn't want to see that horrible look on his face when he learned he was going to lose me... again.

"I'm scared that..."

She waited, watching me. She'd always been so patient, so kind and understanding. When Damien had introduced us, I'd been hesitant to speak to a stranger about what I'd experienced. It had taken time for me to open up to her, but she'd allowed me that time. Salwa had a gift, though, and I couldn't explain the ways in which she'd already begun to heal me.

"I'm scared of hurting him more than he already has been, of breaking him more when he's already been broken enough." I already knew what she was going to say the moment the words passed through my lips.

Her sable bangs slid free of her ear, and she tucked them back into place, away from her eyes as she looked up from her notebook. "He will hurt regardless. Even more so when he loses you unexpectedly."

The truth of her words, the truth I already knew, hurt as fresh as if it were a new thought.

"I say this not only as your therapist, Cas, but as your advisor, as your friend. At least if he knew, he could focus on enjoying the time you have left together."

"Thank you, Salwa. I know you're right. I'm going to tell him, I just…" My eyes fell. "Need to find the right time."

"There will never be a right time for bad news, but you will be there for him, and he can be there for you. He would want to share your pain, no matter how horrible that may sound."

I smiled, nodding.

She looked back at her notepad. "I want to discuss what happened today during your training with Barrett."

I swallowed.

"Was it like last time?"

I nodded, fidgeting with the hem of my sleeve. "Yeah. At first, things were fine. I had control, managed to create a flame on my fingertip… but then I heard it."

She cocked an eyebrow. "Heard what?"

"The… voice. I felt those urges that leave me terrified with myself. I haven't felt it as strongly as when I lost control fighting Marcus, but the moment I conjured the flames, it was like I was being pushed forward, needing to see how far I could go, even though I didn't want to."

"I remember you mentioning this voice."

She'd tried to search for any clues when we first began our sessions, but no matter what we tried, she never found anything. She set her notebook down on the end table, the couch bowing beneath her as she drew closer to me. Her hands rose, gesturing towards my head. "Do you mind if I look? See if I can find any traces of what it might be, or what may have caused it?"

46

A cold sweat broke out over my skin at the thought of her entering my mind. The painful ways Marcus had forced his way into my mind still haunted me, and I had to remind myself I was safe.

Salwa was safe. Salwa was my friend, my healer.

It had taken a long time for me to feel safe enough to allow her to enter my mind. The traumatic mental manipulation I'd suffered at his hands and the scars it left behind left me terrified of letting anyone into my thoughts.

I took a deep breath and tilted my head forward, closing my eyes.

Her fingers slid over my hair, warmth emanating from her fingertips as they passed over me, like a summer breeze brushing my skin. This was one of the things that made her so effective, so talented at what she did. Her touch was so gentle it put my entire body at ease. My shoulders relaxed, and a sigh of relief eased from my lungs.

Her fingers suddenly twitched, and I flinched, an electric spark shooting through me. Her hands recoiled as she gasped, her eyes wide and confused, brows knitted together as her chest heaved.

"Salwa? Are you ok?" She didn't answer, and I reached out, grabbing her shoulders, speaking louder. "Salwa?"

The door flung open as Damien entered. "Is everything ok?"

Salwa blinked, realizing where she was. "Sorry. I..."

I didn't understand what happened, but I'd felt it, as if my mind had shut her out, slamming a wall between us, but I had done nothing. She seemed to understand what happened, though, and it had her looking worried.

She looked up at Damien, still tense. "I'm ok. I was..." She drew a deep breath, trying to compose herself. "I was forced from her mind."

I sat back, eyes dancing between Damien and her. "But I didn't do anything."

"No, it wasn't you." She directed her attention to Damien again. "There's something else. I was unable to see anything, but I felt it. Whatever it was, it's powerful. Powerful enough to shut *me* out."

"Could it be any of my past lives? Maybe pushing me to be stronger?" I asked.

Salwa pondered the possibility. I'd never seen her as shaken as she did now. She'd always been so calm, collected, in control, not to mention an exceptionally powerful Nous user. Whatever this was, it was something none of us could control.

"It's difficult to tell," she said at last. "It was as if a shield went up when I entered your mind. It doesn't want me to know what it is."

I looked at Damien, his eyes darkening as he pressed his knuckles to his lips. "Something powerful enough to shield against you is a cause for concern. I wonder if it *is* one of her past selves. Lucia was particularly skilled in Nous magic, or it could've been Moira?"

I hadn't made any connections with Moira. It was as if she were locked away. The only memories that resurfaced were from Elena and Lucia. There was so little I knew of Moira. Would she push me to become more powerful for Damien's sake, no matter the cost?

CHAPTER 5

DAMIEN

I leaned against the doorway of our closet. "Maybe you should stay behind tonight. We can plan for your first patrol tomorrow instead."

Cassie was preoccupied with inspecting her new gear, but she shifted her eyes to me. "Do you know how much it kills me to sit here each night, waiting, wondering if you'll return alive? No. You don't. I want to be there at your side for once. I've been preparing for weeks; I'm not putting it off another night."

I remained silent.

She lifted her shirt over her head, back turned to me. The sight of the thin pink scars Marcus had left on her arms and back had left guilt settling in the pit of my stomach. "This is what I've trained for, *mea sol*. I want to be at your side. I want to fight."

I would love nothing more than to have her hunt darklings at my side again. She'd always loved to fight, always felt truly alive on the battlefield. She was born for it, a fighter's spirit woven into the fabric of her being.

"Don't mistake my hesitation. I know you'll be a sight to behold when you fight them." But she was human now, and while she excelled in her training, I still feared for her safety. She didn't have the stamina we immortals had, didn't heal as we did, and the darklings wanted to change her into one of their kind. She was their target. We might as well be serving her up on a platter for them.

Selene's warning remained imprinted in the back of my mind, of the damage Cassie's body was suffering under the strain of the magic awakening in her. How long would she hold out? How long until I lost her again?

No. I refused to accept that. No matter the cost, I would find a way to save her.

I drew closer to her and took hold of her hips, pulling her back against me. I knew she didn't feel the bond between us as deeply as I did—humans didn't bond like immortals. It was difficult for me to ignore, every fiber of my being narrowing in on her very existence. I lowered my nose into her hair, drawing her scent into my lungs. Night-blooming jasmine and the citrus soap she used sent my heart into a frenzy, my body hardening against her. She was everything I could ever want, ever need, specially tailored to bring me to my knees with everything she did.

Her giggle sent an electric shock up my spine as I slid my fingers along the soft skin of her waist around to her stomach. "It's your decision to make, whether you go or stay. I just don't want you to push yourself if you're not feeling your best."

"You keep touching me like that, and neither of us will be going out tonight."

My fingers dug into her hips, the temptation too much for me to resist. Her body bowed against me as I moved my hand, dragging my fingertips against her smooth skin until I took hold of her neck, tilting her head so I could lay a kiss against her throat. The life pumping beneath my palm left my fangs throbbing. "That is quite tempting."

She pulled away from me, crossing her arms and cocking her hip as she looked up at me. "Damien, I'm trying to get ready."

I chuckled, throwing my hands up in surrender as I stepped out of the closet to finish readying myself. "I'll leave you to dress. *Undistracted.*"

Gods, I needed a smoke. She was too damned tempting.

"So how does this work? Patrolling for darklings?" she called from the closet as I checked over my gear, ensuring every knife was secure.

"We'll meet the others at The Complex. We leave from there." I grabbed my rolled brierleaf from the box on the shelf and struck a match, holding the flame to the tip as I drew air through the roll, the embers coming to life.

Cassie's voice echoed from the closet again. "Who's joining us tonight?"

I secured the roll between my lips and pulled my leather holsters from the dresser, crossing them over my chest before individually sliding each of my throwing knives into their slots. "Barrett, Vincent, Zephyr, and Thalia."

"Do they all always accompany you on your patrols? I thought you had different recruits and other warriors. Is this overkill?"

"It's not overkill when we are bringing a new warrior on their first hunt, not to mention my mate. I would rather we be safe." It was better to have warriors as experienced as I was on hand, in case she couldn't handle it, or worse, we encountered a large group. The odds of that seemed to be growing lately.

I took one more hit, then set the smoked roll down in the ashtray to allow the embers to douse as I checked the leathers of the holster strapped to my thigh. Once they were situated, I slid my dagger into place. "But to answer your question; no, we don't always go together. Three teams comprised of two to three warriors go out each night to patrol different sectors. We take shifts. Some nights Zephyr, another warrior, and me, some nights they individually take their own teams, and other warriors take our places some—"She emerged from the closet my thoughts derailing. "times..."

I had to swallow back the overwhelming instinct to peel her out of the black leather armor and bury myself deep inside her until the world shattered around us. She was cloaked in black from head to toe, armor hugging every curve of her body. The hood of the coat hung back, the coat split down the front. Her thick chestnut braid draped over her shoulder, the end resting against the holsters and pouches strapped across her chest. Black leather pants hugged her legs down to her boots, and her twin daggers hung on either side, the leather straps wrapping around and anchoring the sheathed blades to her thighs. The gear suited her better than I imagined it would. The sight of her in the Elythian leather armor was... *fuck.*

Gods dammit, I shouldn't have put that roll out.

"This fabric feels similar to what I felt in my vision of Elena... What's it called? It feels like leather, but it's almost... stretchy? It doesn't feel as hot as leather, either. Will it be warm enough?"

I swallowed at the sight of her ass as she turned in place, my gaze dragging down the length of her legs clad in black leather. It would only take a simple phone call and Zephyr could arrange another set of warriors to fill in for us.

Cassie turned to look back at me, her brows high, and I cleared my throat, trying to focus on the conversation. "Elythian leather. It's unlike any leather you'll find in the Mortalrealm. Created in the Godsrealm, it's designed to be easy to move in, yet durable for fighting, and it helps regulate temperature. Trust me, it doesn't seem like it, but you'll be glad it's breathable when you're fighting. Too many layers and you'll be drenched in sweat, even in the winter air."

Her eyes lit up mischievously as I lifted my gaze from her body.

"How do I look?" she asked playfully, propping a hand on her hip, the golden hilts of her daggers glinting in the dim lamp light.

I licked my lips. "Too good. I'm contemplating stripping you down and not leaving this room for the next twenty-four hours." The flush of her cheeks heated my blood, and by the way her scent flooded the room, I knew my words left her as affected as I was.

"But I know how much you've been wanting to go out with us. I promise not to distract you." She rolled her eyes, and I huffed a laugh. "Come here—let me check over your gear."

As she approached, I lowered to my knee to check the straps of her thigh holsters. She pulled her daggers from their sheaths, checking the placement for reach, before sliding them back into place. Her months of persistence with those daggers had paid off, and, through sheer determination, she'd become well versed in using them. I couldn't be prouder of how far she'd come.

I dragged my fingers up her thigh, feeling her beneath the leather armor, the bond calling out to me. I wished there was nothing between our skin. A soft shudder of her breath had my control slipping again, and I rose, hands gliding over her hips, her waist, reaching the straps bound across her chest. I could feel her eyes on me as I fingered the strap holding her harness in place.

"Are you ready for your first hunt?" I breathed, trying to distract myself.

"Nervous, but ready." Her eyes lowered, and I tucked my finger under her chin to lift her face to meet my gaze.

I brushed a gentle kiss against her brow and wrapped my arm around her waist to pull her against me. "You're a force they'll wish they'd never awoken."

The dark of the moonless night hung over the city like a blanket, the lights of the cityscape pressed against the dome of ink above, as if keeping it from swallowing us whole. Cassie sat on the edge of the rooftop, her feet dangling over the brick edge as we waited for the others to arrive. The Complex stretched downward five stories beneath us, the icy winter air dancing over my exposed skin.

"What's the Godsrealm like? You told me that's where Selene and the other gods live, right?"

Her question forced me to draw a deep breath. "Yeah. Selene dwells in an isolated part of the Godsrealm. It's no fairytale world, and it most definitely isn't the Olympus the Greeks believed it to be. It's a realm not only of gods, but of monsters as well."

Her head tilted as she absorbed the information.

"Any creature of myth in the Mortalrealm is a creature that found its way through a ripple in the veil between our realms when they weren't supposed to. The darklings pale in comparison to the power some monsters of the Godsrealm wield." While I missed our home in the Godsrealm, I didn't miss the endless games the Elythians played in their courts, the senseless wars fought out of sheer boredom or over territory.

"The Elythians seldom fight their own battles, despite their power, instead sending fae and other less powerful races to fight in their stead, never suffering the decisions they made. Our kind were created by Selene for that very purpose when they fought against the Titans. Selene's allies gifting their powers to create each of the houses of power to aid them."

Cassie's gaze drifted out toward the city. "It's still weird to know that gods exist. I don't remember too much of our meeting with Selene, just that she was… power. Pure power."

"And there are those more powerful than her. Far crueler too."

Cassie turned from the cityscape, her hazel eyes settling on me. The icy winter wind whipped loose strands of chestnut hair around her face.

I continued, settling my elbows on my knees. "In their boredom of their own realm, the Elythians slipped through the veil, sought entertainment in the company of the mortals wherever they could. Mortals were easy to manipulate, easy to deceive, and they acted so differently from the Elythians. Their reactions to the orchestrated tragedies and subsequent rescuing only encouraged the Elythians' behavior. Ultimately, it's how they came to be worshipped as gods."

"Cruel sounds like an understatement," she murmured.

"Eris is among the cruelest of their kind." I'd seen the destruction she'd wrought before, and nothing compared to it. "She will turn friend and family against one another and watch as they tear each other down until nothing remains."

"Have you been to the Godsrealm?" she asked.

I nodded, sorrow gnawing deep within my chest, but I pushed it down. I didn't want to linger on what once was our home. "Within the Godsrealm are numerous kingdoms, each ruling over their own territory or domain. Some of the regions are beautiful. The moment you see them, this world dulls in comparison. The very earth is alive with magic."

Curiosity lit up her hazel eyes. I smiled, imagining the endless paintings she might bring to life if she ever got the chance to see the lunassia flowers bloom on the Astral Mountains during the lunar solstice, or the Valleys of the Stryass where mist danced among the steep, wildflower dusted slopes, or... what once was one of her favorite places to visit, the Stellarion Forest, lit by the pale glow of countless, monstrous Dimós trees.

I shoved back the sorrowful memories. "But while there are many beautiful places, there are places of desolation, void of any life or goodness. If it weren't so dangerous, I'd love for you to see the beautiful parts of it, but it isn't a safe place for humans to enter. The few mortals who've happened upon ripples in the veil disappear and become the center of mystery and horror stories you humans enjoy."

I smiled at the continued look of curiosity on her face. "The shadow creatures I summon..."

"You mean the shadow puppies?" A smile laced her tone as she threw a mischievous look my way.

I rolled my eyes. "The *Lupai* come from the Godsrealm." I knew she wasn't serious, and I refused to admit it out loud, but it was

54

adorable, innocent even, for her to call the Lupai 'puppies.' If the name had slipped from anyone else's lips, it would have been an insult to their power. I reached into the dark void lingering within me, calling out, and a dark creature rose from the darkness pooling on the rooftop behind us. It ignored me, immediately rushing to her side before licking her cheek.

Her laughter lit something in me, and I couldn't resist the smile spreading across my face. I rested my head against my fist, watching her as she interacted with the wolf of mist and shadows. The Lupai loved her, and it was no surprise as she'd once been master to the mother of their kind. Though she was different on the outside, they knew.

Lupa, the mother of the Lupai, was a powerful beast and had been a loyal companion of Moira's over the centuries of her life, fighting faithfully by her side. As formidable as any creature of the Godsrealm, she'd been a powerful ally.

Unfortunately, she'd been an equally powerful enemy when Melantha corrupted her.

It had broken Lucia's heart to fight her old comrade when the darkling queen had risen. She'd summoned the mother of the Lupai, corrupted her form, and while Lupa wasn't anywhere near the size she was in the Godsrealm when we'd faced her, she'd nearly been too powerful for Lucia and me to face. Thankfully, we'd managed to bring her down, and she'd returned to the Godsrealm, free from the corruption of Melantha.

I feared what manner of dark creatures Melantha might try to summon this time.

"Are there other shadow beasts like the Lupai?"

I blinked, her question interrupting my musing. "Many creatures reside in the Godsrealm. I prefer the Lupai, and occasionally the Coronis, which are like crows. They're both loyal creatures, smart, and work well together. There are also creatures resembling snakes, other kinds of birds, even some beasts you don't find in this realm, some made of nightmares."

I could already see another question lingering on her tongue, and her curiosity made me smile. I knew it was fueled by the desire to learn more about our world hidden in the shadows, a world just as much hers as it was mine, one she should've experienced if it weren't for the mortal form trapping her soul.

She tilted her head. "Can others of House Skiá summon shadow beasts like you?"

Others of House Skiá... Her question hit deep, but I wouldn't dampen her mood tonight—not before she was to hunt darklings at my side. "Members of House Skiá can summon all manner of creatures from the Godsrealm depending on their skill or level of magic."

"I can't wait to learn how to use it. I want to summon Lupai."

Dread crawled over my skin at the thought.

"Sorry we're late." Vincent's voice came from the doorway behind us, pulling us from our conversation.

I pushed myself up from the edge, banishing the unease in my gut, and the Lupai on Cassie's lap vanished into dust. "About time. I was wondering if you'd snuck off to Stokers. I was about ready to hunt you guys down."

Barrett, Zephyr, and Thalia appeared from the doorway behind him, fully clad in their own black leather armor, various weapons strapped to their chests and hips, hoods down.

"It took us a while to convince Zephyr to leave his new female," Barrett taunted. "Was kinda bummed we didn't get to see her. No matter what, we can't get him to spill any details."

"Female? Zeph, you got a girl?" Cassie jumped to her feet and ran over to him.

When my eyes met Zephyr's, the familiar scent lingering on his skin hit me like a brick, and the possessive light in his pale green eyes made it clear... he'd bonded to the female.

A heavy sigh slipped from my lips. "*Fuck.*"

CHAPTER 6

CASSIE

"I want to meet her!" Zephyr didn't meet my eyes at first, and I realized he was glaring over my shoulder at Damien. My brows furrowed. "Is everything ok?"

"We'll discuss it later." Damien's voice was sharp, but his eyes remained fixated on Zephyr. His words didn't seem wholly directed at me, but to everyone. The air became thick with a strange sort of tension. I shifted on my feet, wary of the energy in the air.

What had I missed?

"Awe, I've been dying to meet this female of his," Barrett teased, throwing his arm over Zephyr's shoulder. Zephyr's body tensed, thick muscles cording beneath the leathers of his gear, and I feared he might turn on Barrett.

Damien growled a low warning, his eyes shifting to Barrett. "You're walking a fine line. Drop it."

Barrett's brows knitted in confusion, but he obliged, releasing Zephyr, his hands in the air as he stepped back.

"I didn't know," Zephyr said lowly, eyes still locked with Damien's, and my confusion grew.

"I'm happy for you, honestly. No hard feelings, I hope," Damien said.

Zephyr didn't respond, and I looked between the two. "What the hell's going on? What are you guys talking about?"

I looked at Thalia, only to get a shrug in response, confusion painting her face as well.

When Zephyr's silence remained, Damien spoke up. "Like I said, we'll discuss it later."

What was there to discuss? What did Damien know?

Watching the hostile energy fill the air between them, I feared they might attack one another at the wrong word. I walked up to Zephyr and placed a hand on his shoulder. "Hey."

His pale green eyes fell on me, and the harshness melted away, a tender smile returning to his sweet face. "Sorry, Cas. It's ok."

My eyes narrowed, but I didn't say anything. I didn't want to press, but the curiosity was enough to drive me insane.

He took a deep breath before he spoke again. "Let's get out there. I know you're ready, and I'm eager to see all that training pay off when you bring down your first darkling. Your daggers sharp and ready?"

I smiled, nodding my head. "Sharpened them before we left the house."

"If she uses that hard head of hers, she won't need those daggers to take them down," Vincent said, tightening his black fingerless gloves. I couldn't help but feel a little prideful I'd head-butted an immortal hard enough for him to remember.

"Twenty bucks says our little spitfire's too chicken to headbutt a darkling." Barrett ruffled the top of my head, and I elbowed him before smoothing my braided hair back into place.

"Stop calling me that," I huffed.

"I'll take that bet!" Zephyr called over me. The tense air melted away, and for once, I was thankful for Barrett's antics. If it meant whatever happened between Damien and Zephyr was put on pause until it could be resolved, I would suffer it. We didn't need any further division after suffering Cole's betrayal.

Damien groaned, his eyes settling on me. "Please don't try to headbutt a darkling on your first night out, Cas."

I crossed my arms, head tilted. "I don't know which is worse; that Barrett and Zephyr are betting over my courage to headbutt a darkling, or that you think I'm dumb enough to try."

Damien cracked that cocky grin I loved so much, the crystalline amber bursting from the ashen gray of his eyes. The way they settled on me sent my heart leaping against my ribs. "I mean, I don't want you to, but I can't say I'm not a little curious to watch you take one down that way. Maybe when you've had more training."

I cocked my head, smirking up at him. "You keep tempting me and I might try it, Damien."

"Taking bets!" Barrett called out as the four of them turned, heading for the door.

The metal door swung closed behind them, their conversations and laughter fading from my ears. Damien's arms came around my waist and pulled me back to him. I could feel the unease he tried to mask rise to the surface. "Please be careful tonight, *mea luna*."

I melted, turning to meet his gaze, seeing the worry filling his eyes. "I will, *mea sol*. I promise."

The city had settled, the alleys filled with a deathly quiet air as I walked alongside Damien. The others spoke in hushed tones, surveying the darkness at every corner. Vincent took a brief glance at his phone and tapped away.

I could just barely make out Zephyr as he whispered to him. "Anna doing ok?"

"Yeah, she's pulling another late night at Johnson's clinic. She needs to cut back on the shifts," Vincent muttered.

I pulled my attention from them, not wanting to eavesdrop on their conversation. Barrett and Thalia walked separately from Vincent and Zephyr, whispering amongst themselves. For once, it sounded as if it might be a pleasant conversation. There had been a lot of back and

TO ASHES AND DUST

forth with them, some nights pleasant, but some nights they were at each
other's throats as they had the first time I'd met her.

I'd managed to smother my nerves up to this point, but now that
I was here with them, feeling the weight of my daggers, knowing what I
would use them for, it was impossible to ignore the adrenaline pumping
through my veins, my pulse pounding in my ears. I couldn't tell if I was
more terrified or excited to finally be on my first hunt. How many
darklings would we find? The darklings' numbers had steadily
increased in recent weeks—warriors encountering groups larger than
they had in centuries. Would tonight be like my last encounter, when
Marcus had sent me out to be hunted? There'd been so many—too many
to count.

Damien took my hand and squeezed it gently. "Breathe, *mea
luna*. I can feel your anxiety from here."

My gaze snapped to him. "What? How?" I said in a hushed
voice.

"You probably can't feel it like I can since you're human, but the
bond between mates is powerful. In close proximity, we can feel if
something is... off," he explained, but his eyes remained vigilant,
scanning for any sign of darklings that might be lurking in the shadows.
"It grew stronger for me when I first tasted your blood."

I'd been unnaturally drawn to him from the moment we met.
Whether it was the bond, or my past selves, or a little of both, I didn't
know. "I've felt something, but it's very faint. Just this… pull."

A smile lit his face. "I wish you were one of our kind, wish you
could feel what I feel. It's indescri—"

"Damien," Zephyr whispered, his body dissolving into black
dust as he shifted into a large panther. He lowered his muzzle to the
ground. His onyx fur caught the faint glow of distant lights, his massive
paws pressing into the concrete beneath him as he crouched. It was still
a shock to see him shift, and I didn't know if I would ever get used to it.

"They're nearby. They passed through here recently," Zephyr
said, looking away to where the trail led. My breath hitched, adrenaline
spiking in my blood.

"Ready your daggers, Cas." Damien squeezed my hand once
before releasing it, and pulled his own dagger free from its sheath.

The others followed suit—Barrett and Thalia with their own
daggers, and Vincent slid his weapon into place over his knuckles,
gripping the handles in his palms. Vincent's weapons were so unlike the
others; he called them trench knives. The brass knuckles extended out

into a blade from his palm, the sharp point etched with runes and magic necessary to finish the darklings off for good. If their vital points weren't pierced, or their bodies burned, they could reawaken.

This is it. This is what I've trained for. The hilts of my daggers were cold against my palms, despite my fingerless leather gloves. I pulled them free from their sheaths, metal hissing against leather, and we waited, listening to the nothingness in the air. Zephyr's low growl startled me.

Then, I felt it.

The temperature plummeted, that familiar chill that came with the presence of the darklings descending on us, as if they leeched the very life from the air around them. I shuddered and looked back over my shoulder to where we'd come from. The streetlamps in the distance flickered before dousing, plunging the area into darkness, and for a moment, I was blinded to my surroundings.

This was their territory.

Silence. The silence was so heavy, like water pressing in on me, suffocating me. Air grew thicker in my lungs as I tried to breathe through the fear. I waited, listening as short breaths escaped Barrett, Vincent, and Thalia's lips, filling my ears with our collective anxiety. In this moment of silent anticipation, I hated the vulnerability of my mortal form. I was at a disadvantage in the dark. Humans weren't built like the immortals; we didn't have the perfected vision, the sense of smell, or the heightened hearing. Immortals were hunters, built to fight under the veil of night.

I was prey.

No, not anymore. I was no longer the defenseless human I was three months ago. I'd undergone the same training every warrior of The Order did.

Click—click—click—click—click. The horrible sound rippled from the darkness, the hairs on the back of my neck standing on end. I thought back to my vision of Elena, remembered how the darklings stalked me before we fought, the feeling of their claws and teeth tearing me apart before I died.

"Remember your training, Cas. Blade in the heart or between the eyes, or they'll get back up," Thalia whispered. "Don't try to be a hero. Ask for help if you need it."

"You've got this," Zephyr said without looking at me.

"Keep your mind open to me, Cas. Don't hesitate to reach out if you need help," Damien's words were a warning of how easily things could get out of hand in the moments to come. There was no telling how many darklings we stood to face. He may be too preoccupied to keep a watchful eye on me. If we faced more than we could handle, it would be difficult for Damien to keep track of where I was or what I was facing.

I would be solely responsible for my own safety.

My eyes adjusted to the darkness shrouding the area, and I saw faint movements from round the corner in the shadows ahead of us. The clicks grew louder as they approached, their black claws scraping against the pavement as they stalked the alleyway. How many were hidden from our view? Did more watch us from the shadows?

My heart hammered against my ribcage as I caught sight of the first darkling peering at us. The darkness licked at its shallow skin, rising like steam from every surface of its hollowed body. Zephyr crouched low as the dark creature crept along the alley, followed by several more.

"They're traveling in larger groups," Thalia whispered to Damien, not pulling her gaze from the approaching creatures.

"Their numbers are growing," Damien responded. "We'll have to pull more warrior candidates from the houses."

The darklings hissed and clicked, lips ripping and curling off their razor-sharp teeth, and the others started towards the walls. Zephyr didn't give them the chance to flank us, as he launched at the nearest one, setting off a chain reaction.

The moment he slammed into it, the other darklings turned on him, their screeches piercing the air. Damien and the others jumped in, intercepting their advance on Zephyr.

When I tried to engage, though, my legs froze, hands trembling as I gripped the hilts of my daggers. *Fuck, not now.*

"Heads up, spitfire! This one's yours!" Barrett yelled as one slipped past him, the creature barreling for me, claws scraping the asphalt as it ran on all fours.

Seconds. I had seconds to get my shit together, or it was going to take me down. It leapt into the air, and I lunged forward, dropping to my knees as I slid against the pavement under it, ducking my head to evade its claws as they reached for me. It crashed into a heap on the asphalt, furious clicks and growls slipping from its teeth as it pushed itself up. I jumped to my feet, spinning to meet it, daggers drawn and ready.

Heart or between the eyes. Heart or between the eyes.

I ran forward as it recovered and lunged at me once more. It reached for me, black claws extended, and I remembered the damage they could do. I shifted to the side, its claw grazing my cheek as I swung my dagger up, the blade slicing its arm. It recoiled the moment metal tasted flesh, and a hiss rose from the wound, as if it were burned.

Damien had told me my daggers, no, all the weapons at The Order's disposal were engraved with runes by Selene—markings that hurt the darklings. It wouldn't kill them, but it hurt enough to leave them recoiling for a moment. A moment was all I needed.

It didn't hesitate long, reaching for me again, and I sank below its grasp, and rammed my dagger into its chest. A scream pealed from its lips, filling my ears, and I winced as the shrill sound clawed into my mind. It disappeared in a cloud of black dust.

I stood there a moment, chest heaving, heart racing. I did it. I'd killed a darkling.

This isn't the time to celebrate!

I turned in time to see more round the corner.

"Fuckin' hell. How many are there?" Vincent barked.

"Can't handle a few extras, Vincent?" Barrett responded. "Bet I can take down more than you!"

"Focus! Play your games when it's just the two of you," Damien yelled.

I ran for them as a darkling charged for Damien as he tore his blade from a darklings' chest. He swung his leg around, slamming his foot into the creature's jaw. It crashed against the far wall, jaw broken and hanging limp at an odd angle. Damien pulled a knife from the leather holster strung across his chest and flung it through the air. The blade sank between the darkling's eyes. It hissed and screamed, body convulsing before it vanished as the others had.

"I hate that sound," I groaned as I stopped at his side, catching my breath.

"You're not the only one. Thankfully, humans can't hear it. They aren't magically aware enough to pick up on it. It's kind of like a sixth sense sort of thing."

I cocked an eyebrow. "They really can't hear it?"

Damien shook his head, switching his dagger back into his right hand. I hadn't even considered it, but that would explain why Kat hadn't heard the scream when I'd seen them kill a darkling months ago.

Zephyr sank his teeth into a darkling's throat, tearing its head free of its body, and I gagged at the sound of bone snapping.

Damien immediately reached to stabilize me. "That's another way to do it, but I didn't think you'd be up for that quite yet."

I swallowed back the nausea, looking around in the darkness. "Was that all of them?"

Everyone stood in silence, listening, but there was no sound, no sign of more darklings. For now.

I turned back to Damien, who was already looking at me. His hand rose, his thumb brushing away a smear of my blood from the cut on my face. He didn't say anything, but the pride in his eyes shined brighter than any light I'd seen. I reached out to his mind.

It's just a scratch. How did I do?

Immaculately, mea luna.

I smiled and swiped the black liquid from my blades on my pants before sliding them back into their sheaths and I sagged against the brick wall. My muscles quivered and twitched, remnants of adrenaline still pumping through my system. My heart raced, but it remained in check, no pain to be felt. I breathed a sigh of relief.

"Shit, spitfire! I thought I was gonna have to pull you out from under that darkling!" Barrett rose a hand in the air, and I huffed a laugh as I met his high five. "But you got some catchin' up to do. I got three darklings; how many you got Vincent?"

"One," Vincent muttered, shaking the black blood from his knuckles.

"Gotta be faster than that," Barrett teased, and I couldn't help the chuckle that slipped from my throat.

Zephyr shook, his black fur swaying with each jerk of his body. I'd never seen a panther in person, but he was huge compared to what I'd imagined. He stalked passed me, his back high enough to reach my waist. I resisted the urge to reach out and find out how soft his fur might feel.

He lifted his head, his form melting into black dust as he shifted back. "I don't smell any others nearby, but they could be hiding in the scent of the ones we just fought, so stay aware."

"We'll keep moving then. Cas, you feel good enough to continue?" Damien looked at me, and the others followed suit.

I shook the quivers from my hand, fresh adrenaline pounding in my ears. It wasn't from fear, though. No, it was anticipation, almost excitement. I wanted to see just what I could do, how many darklings I could take down before the night ended.

"Lead the way, Zeph."

CHAPTER 7

CASSIE

The wood floors creaked under Damien's feet as he carried me on his back into our room. My head hung over his shoulder, body melted as if I'd molded against him. Every part of me was sore, every bone and muscle so tired that I couldn't imagine lifting them. I didn't know what time it was, but I longed for a bath and the warm comfort of our bed.

"You still with me, *mea luna*?"

I groaned, sarcasm painting my words. *"No, I'm dying, Damien."*

He laughed under his breath as he lowered me to my feet.

"I wish I weren't human. This would be so much easier if I was like you." I teetered for a moment, and Damien hesitated to leave my side. "How do you do this every night?"

"We don't need as much sleep as a human does. I could go a couple nights before I start to feel it." He slipped my hooded layer off my shoulders and undid the buckles of my harnesses.

"I gathered that," I groaned in irritation.

He set the harnesses on the floor, the handles of the spare daggers clinking against the wood. The black leather armor was splashed with darkling blood, the smell sticking to my nose. I was a mess, skin sticky with sweat. I dreaded to think how much darkling blood might've soaked into my hair.

What I wouldn't give for a hot shower.

"How many did you take out tonight?" he asked, eyes gliding up to my body as he continued to help me remove my gear.

"Four? No, five."

"Not bad for your first night, and you made it with only a cut on your cheek. If Barrett ever pisses you off enough, you can rub it in his face how he ended his first hunt with a nasty wound that left a scar on his side." He smiled to himself. "You didn't hear that from me."

I huffed a laugh, imagining the look on Barrett's face if he ever found out I knew I'd outdone him on my first hunt. "I'll stick that piece of info in my back pocket for later."

Damien barked a laugh. "He actually wanted to take you out to Stokers to celebrate your first hunt, but I knew you wouldn't have the energy tonight. So, we're going to celebrate tomorrow night."

I raised a brow in question. "Stokers?"

"It's a bar we frequent. Haven't been able to go in a while, but it's owned by two of our own, so it's ok for us to be... ourselves."

"Do we have time to celebrate? Shouldn't we be training or out hunting darklings?" I asked, reaching for the straps anchoring my daggers to my hips.

Damien stopped me, firm hands grasping my own as he met my eyes with an intensity I couldn't look away from. "There will be plenty of time to fight the darklings, Cas. There will come a time when we don't have the luxury to celebrate the little victories. So, while we can, we celebrate. We bask in what little joys we find. We may live to regret it if we don't savor the time we have left."

His words were from experience—painful experience of wars he'd fought in the past, losses he'd suffered. How many of his friends had he laid to rest in this endless war? "Do you think it will be like The Fall of Kingdoms? When we face Melantha?"

His eyes wavered, and I didn't invade the privacy of the memories I knew he was reliving. "I prayed we would never have to fight another war like that, never have to experience that pain again, but

67

the signs are all the same: the darklings growing in numbers, the appearance of Melantha. I fear what the betrayal of our own kind will mean this time. I hate to think about fighting our own on the battlefield, not to mention the humans who may get caught in the crossfire."

The humans who *would* get caught in the crossfire. My parents, Kat...

I took his face in my hands, forcing his gaze to meet mine, and I smiled, if only to comfort him. "I'm here with you, *mea sol*. We defeated her before, and we will do it again. Together."

His smile didn't reach his eyes, and I knew the fear haunting him, knew the one thing that was different from the last war with the darklings.

I was human, and I was weaker for it—an easy target for the darklings to take, to convert to one of their own to turn against them. He would never admit it, never say it, and I appreciated that. I knew my weaknesses, and no matter how hard I tried, no matter how hard I trained, I would never be what they truly needed—an immortal demigoddess fully capable of wielding her powers. I hadn't had any serious issues with my heart lately, which I wasn't sure if I should be relieved about... or worried.

"Can..." My eyes fell. "I know you said a lot of the stories humans share about immortals aren't true."

The question had lingered in the back of my mind for a while now, but I'd been too afraid to ask. Tonight's hunt was a blaring reminder of my limitations as a human, though. It was a stupid question, wishful thinking that there may be some escape from death, but I needed to know. If there was a chance I might not only be able to remain at his side, but to fight on equal ground as him, I would take it.

"Can a human become immortal?"

He drew a breath, and his eyes shifted to my hair, raising his hand to tuck a stray curl behind my ears. "It's..." He released a pained sigh. "It's not possible to become an immortal if you're not born one. It's genetic. The stories of vampires turning humans are just more myth."

A weight sank into the pit of my stomach, but I forced a smile. "It was just a question. It was stupid of me to even ask. I was just curious."

Yeah, stupid. Stupid, wishful thinking.

His eyes lingered on me as I continued to remove my daggers from my hips. His breath stopped, as if he were going to say something, but no words came. I wished he would have said something more, given me some sort of hope that I could enjoy more than a few years at his side.

I looked back at him as I set my daggers down on the dresser, wanting him to say something, anything, but his distant eyes didn't meet mine. He was slipping into whatever dark place haunted the corners of his mind—plagued by my deaths and the hollow, endless pain that always followed. I approached him, taking hold of his face once more, pressing my forehead against his as I captured his gaze.

Come back to me. "I love you, *mea sol.*"

He returned to me, light warming those amber and ashen eyes, and his arms wrapped around my waist. "I love you too, *mea luna.*"

"We will get through this. I believe in you," I said.

"War won or lost... I won't lose you again."

His words sank into my chest, and suddenly I thought I might throw up.

You will, though, and there will be nothing you can do to stop it.

I didn't allow myself the chance to dwell on the thought when my eyes began to burn. "God, I stink."

His smile returned. "I'll get the shower running. You got the rest of your clothes, or are you too sore?"

"I'm sore, Damien, not injured." He almost looked disappointed, and I frowned. "Damien, I'm filthy, sweaty, and disgusting. Let me get clean before you try to get under my clothes."

"Well, get to it then." Oh yeah, he was back, a king of immortals who was impatient for what was his, but it was a relief to hear that tone in his voice. I would give anything to see him happy, to banish the sorrow clinging to him.

I bowed my head, lifting invisible hems of a gown I didn't wear as I curtsied. "As you wish, *Your Grace.*"

His hand shot out to grab me and I ducked out of his grasp, running for the other side of the bed. When I glanced back at him, he didn't approach, watching from the other side of the room with heated eyes. I cracked a cocky grin, sliding my shirt off before letting it fall to the floor, pushing back the urge to groan as my muscles protested the stretch.

He watched me in bated silence, predatory hunger dancing in his eyes as they raked down my body. "I wanted to do that."

"And I want to get clean. I smell like darkling," I grumbled.

A huffed laugh was his only response as he headed for the bathroom. My eyes didn't leave him as he walked, waiting for him to make another move, but he disappeared into the bathroom. I heard the shower turn on moments later.

I couldn't keep the smile from spreading across my face as I removed my boots and pants. "Is there some sort of God's tier brand of laundry detergent we have to use to wash these special other worldly clothes?"

He appeared in the doorway of the bathroom, rolling his eyes at my humor. "Don't worry, *Mitera* will wash them. She's got a talent for getting the smell out of the leathers. Just toss them in the basket."

I approached the bathroom, feeling his heated gaze on my naked skin, but he stepped to the side, holding his hand out in invitation. "It's all yours."

He left me alone in the bathroom to disarm himself. I stepped into the spray, the hot water rolling over my skin, burning away the soreness, and a groan of relief slipped from my throat. The tension in my body eased, and I stood there, basking in the heat as it consumed me.

My head fell forward, and I saw the black swirls of darkling blood mix with the water before it slipped down the drain. I couldn't believe I'd killed five tonight. It seemed like only yesterday I'd been hunted by them, unable to look at them, let alone try to fight them. I was different now, though, stronger. Never again would I be prey.

I lathered soap over my body, the citrus blossom scent a welcome reprieve from the stench of the darklings. It was a relief to have the grit and ick leave my body, let the warmth ease the soreness. Steam filled the room, heat filling my lungs, and I stood there for a moment, embracing the feeling of being clean once again.

Calloused fingers snaked around my hips, the feeling sending chills pebbling across my skin. His lips brushed over the back of my shoulder, and my breath hitched in my throat. Air flooded my lungs in a rush as his hand slid up along my ribs, and his thumb brushed the underside of my breast before gliding over them until he reached my neck. His fingers coiled around my throat as he tilted my head back against him. Shivers skittered over my body as he nipped at the shell of my ear, the sharpness of his fangs causing me to inhale sharply. A low laugh vibrated in his chest as he brushed his lips against my skin, before pressing a single kiss to my neck.

Then he released me.

I glared at him over my shoulder, left hot and craving more of his touch.

A wicked grin tugged at his lips. "I want to get clean."

I rolled my eyes as he threw my own words back at me. "Jerk."

He didn't respond, and we showered in silence as I worked the conditioner into my hair. From the corner of my eye, I watched his tense muscles flex and stretch as he rinsed himself. My hand slid free of my hair, and I reached out to him, only to halt before my fingers could touch his back.

Don't even think about it.

I jerked my hand back and turned my gaze from him, suddenly needing to turn the shower cold as heat flooded me. Despite the need rising, I was exhausted, and though the hot water had soothed much of the tension, I still felt aches in places the heated water couldn't reach.

Sleep. Sleep would be amazing right now.

I quickly rinsed the conditioner from my hair while he soaped his body, and I turned to step out of the shower. He grabbed my hips before I could, pulling me back against his firm chest, his slick skin.

"I didn't say you could leave," he growled in my ear.

If it were possible, I would have become a puddle at his feet.

His hand rose to my neck and tilted my head back against his shoulder as he tasted my skin, tongue gliding up my neck. I struggled to keep myself up, my knees quivering beneath me. He turned me back into the shower, pressing me up against the wall, and I gasped as my breasts met the cold tile.

"Let me help you relax." His heated whisper poured into my ear, his hands massaging my hips. I moaned when his knee lifted between my thighs, and he pulled my hips back, pressing into that sensitive place I wanted him most.

He released my hips and leaned back, just enough to massage up my back, working at every sore muscle. My body sagged against the wall, back arching, and I groaned as he tended to every ache.

"God, you're... good with your hands." I almost couldn't get the words out.

"Mmmm. That isn't all I'm good with," his voice rumbled from his throat as he teased.

If I wasn't enjoying the massage and so exhausted, I might fall over, I would have told him to show me what else he was good with— his hands, what talents he possessed with those fingers, that wicked tongue, his thick arousal pressed against my ass. My mind wandered through every possibility.

He swept my wet hair over my shoulder and his lips grazed the back of my neck, hands still working down my muscles. My back bowed as he trailed his lips down my spine until I was throbbing.

The shower rained down over us, the water's touch mixing with his until my body was twitching, lungs gasping for the oxygen evading me. His hand slid down around to the front of my waist, down my stomach—down and down, farther until his fingers glided over that space between my thighs, begging for his touch. I would have collapsed had it not been for him holding me there against the wall.

Take me. God, take me now.

I hadn't realized I'd slipped my control and reached into his mind until he responded with his own thoughts.

So impatient to order a king around like that.

His hands left that throbbing place between my thighs and he spun me around, plastering my back against the tile as his lips crashed into mine. God, he tasted amazing. I needed to taste more of him, feel all he was. His skin was smooth and slick under my hand as I reached up to touch his chest, his coiled muscles twitching under my fingertips. He groaned into my mouth. I slid my hands down the ridges of his stomach until I found him, thick and hard, but before I could take him into my hands, he grabbed my wrists.

"Not tonight," he groaned against my lips. "Tonight is all about you. Let me ease your tension. Let me help you sleep."

He didn't give me a chance to protest before he dropped to his knees, arms sliding between my thighs, and I nearly yelped as he lifted me, hooking my legs over his shoulders before he dove between them.

I moaned, back arching, head falling back against the tile as his tongue swept up my center. He didn't stop, didn't pause for anything, and my fingers laced in his wet hair as I held on for dear life.

My eyes fell to him, and his gaze lifted to me, glossed over as he stared up at me through his thick, dark lashes. I couldn't breathe, couldn't think straight, couldn't form words. He stopped long enough for me to see a teasing grin form on his lips, his finger tracing lines up and down the underside of my thigh. He watched me, his smile fading into something sinful as he slipped a finger deep inside me without warning.

I cried out his name, tension coiling deep and low, and he groaned before he lowered his mouth to me again, ravaging me until my body gave into the climax.

I laid on his chest, warm blankets draped over us as he held me. My fingers traced the black lines of his tattoo, the symbols bursting from the crescent moon on his pectoral, spiraling in smoky waves down his arm. "Where did you get this tattoo?"

He glanced down at it before letting his head fall back on the pillow. "It's the symbol of my vows to Selene as a warrior and leader of the immortal race."

"It's beautiful," I murmured, tracing over a space within the shadows and text. For some strange reason, it felt as if something were... missing.

"Every warrior of The Order gets one, and the pattern varies depending on their house."

I tilted my head to gaze at him. "Do I get one now that I'm fighting the darklings with you?"

His eyes drifted toward the ceiling, an arm folded behind his head. "I don't know. This is all so new. Everything we've done so far has kind of been learning as we go now that you're human. Why? Do you want one?"

I shrugged. "I kind of do... Do they serve a purpose other than symbolizing a vow?"

"Outside of it being a symbol of our vow, it imbues some of her power into us. It amplifies our magic, but you have to master the magic first. With you, there are so many abilities you've yet to learn. It wouldn't be good for them to be enhanced before you have control of them, and I'd be afraid of it furthering the strain on your body."

What was it like to take vows as a warrior? I traced the black ink down to his elbow. When did he take his vows? Had I been there to see it happen?

"Thank you for the massage."

A smug grin formed on his face, and he licked his lips. "I knew you'd be sore after tonight. You'll still be sore in the morning, but I hope it helped."

I bit back the smile. "Oh, it helped..."

His low laugh filled my ears, and he combed his fingers through my hair before pulling the blanket over my shoulders. "Try to get some rest, *mea luna.*"

I tried to focus on the sound of air filling his lungs, his heartbeat a soothing rhythm in my ear. I should close my eyes and sleep, but I couldn't.

My thoughts drifted to my conversation with Salwa earlier that day, the things I had held onto over these last few months. I hadn't been able to talk to him about the things that happened with Marcus, had wanted to, but...

"Damien?"

"Yeah?" he asked, gaze falling on me. I pushed myself up, and his brows scrunched together. "Everything ok?"

I parted my lips, but the words fell short. How would I even put into words everything that happened in that cell? Damien had told me time and time again that if I was ever ready to talk, he was there for me.

73

"I... I think I'm ready to talk about everything that happened..."

His eyes widened slightly, as if understanding the gravity of my words, and he pushed himself up to sit.

"I just..." I hesitated, chewing the inside of my lip as I struggled to find the words. "I'm sorry. It's late and you're probably tire—"

Damien's hand grabbed onto mine, and my eyes shot back to him. "I'm ok. I told you I would be here when you were ready to talk."

"I just... I don't know where to even begin."

He laced his fingers through mine, lifting them to press his lips to my knuckles, affection sinking deep into my soul. "Then show me, *mea luna*. Share your pain. Let me help carry the weight of it."

I swallowed. Show him? "Are you... are you sure?"

He smiled warmly, his eyes dancing between my own. "We will work through this together, and I will be with you every step of the way."

I drew a deep breath, afraid of just how he'd react. I didn't want him to see what had been done, and yet... I didn't want to be alone anymore.

He lowered my hands, and I scooted closer to him, leaning my forehead against his as I closed my eyes—

And I shared everything.

CHAPTER 8

DAMIEN

Her chest rose and fell in an uneven pattern as she rested in my arms, the salt of her tears still lingering in the air.

The images tore through my memory.

My arm burned, the cut fresh from Marcus' blade, as panic surged through Cassie and his tongue ran over the cut. My view jerked to Cole, who sat nearby, unfazed as he watched.

"Please! Stop this! I've done nothing to you!"

Cassie's voice echoed to the deepest corner of my mind, and Marcus' words overlapped it, the venom in his voice enough to curdle my stomach as his whisper slid into Cassie's ear.

"I can hear your heart pounding, little songbird." His voice blurred, the rest of his words muddled, and the image skipped as Cassie's memory faltered, as if her own mind struggled to relive it.

The memory skipped, and I felt Marcus at her back. The cut on her busted lip burned mine as his finger brushed over it. He jerked her back against his chest as he leaned in to whisper. "Let's see that pretty little mind shatter."

Blinding light pierced my thoughts, fracturing across every inch of my mind as Marcus invaded her thoughts again and again, the pain almost too much to bear.

My blood boiled at the memory, my hands twitching, the dark void in my chest rippling and pressing at the walls containing it. The headache still lingered an hour later after witnessing the things she'd shared with me, the pain still fresh on the surface of my skin, though Marcus had never cut me, never burned me with his cigarettes, never bruised my body with his punches and kicks.

Gods, I couldn't believe all the things Marcus had done to her, each marking he'd carved into her, physically and mentally—how much Cole watched her endure while doing nothing. The void in my chest stirred as rage surged within me, the darkness asking to be unleashed. It begged to find Cole and make him pay for every bit of suffering Cassie had endured under his watch.

For each wound they left, mea luna, I swear, I will give them tenfold.

I wished I'd been the one to end Marcus, to let my shadows tear him apart from the inside out before letting him die in the dirt in the most agonizing way I could imagine. Marcus might be gone, but Cole wasn't. It didn't matter what I had to do to find him. When I did...

My gaze fell to her face, her closed eyes swollen and red. She'd finally opened up to me, though, shared it all with me, revealed every moment of her capture and torment. I hated that she had to endure it, that I hadn't been able to get to her fast enough.

It hadn't been easy, the memories enough to break us both, but I was there to help pick up the pieces, to hold her as she cried. It had taken a lot out of her, and I'd held her for a long while, allowing her the time she needed. At first, I'd feared it might've been too soon, that she hadn't been ready, but I'd seen it in those hazel eyes, seen the relief of no longer bearing those memories alone, understanding that I was there to share her burden.

I inhaled her scent as I eased into the pillow, narrowing in on the sweet sound of her breathing as she slipped deeper into a truly restful sleep.

It was the most wonderful sound.

CHAPTER 9

CASSIE

I felt like death warmed over when I forced my eyes open. Exhaustion lingered in my bones, and my eyes were swollen. I wasn't surprised, what with how much I'd cried the night before. It felt good, though, as if a weight had lifted. Though the chains that had held me in that cell still shackled me, they didn't feel as tight.

The sun leaked in through the curtains, and I realized I'd slept in. For a moment, I didn't know if I could make use of my limbs, let alone the rest of my body, but it didn't matter whether or not I could. Damien's arms held me tightly against him, his rich cedarwood and leather scent filling my lungs with each breath.

"How're you feeling?" he asked lazily as he hugged me close. Nuzzling his face into my neck, he inhaled deeply, and the stubble lining his jaw tickled in all the right ways.

I giggled, shoulders shrugging. "How long have you been awake?"

"Not long. I didn't want to leave you, but I didn't want to wake you," he said under his breath. "You needed the rest."

He kissed my temple and pushed himself up. I groaned as I rolled off my side and up onto my knees. My hair spilled over my shoulders in a mess of loose curls into my face, and my gaze lifted to the window above our bed. It was overcast outside, the sunlight muted behind dense winter clouds.

"Here," he said, approaching my side of the bed, handing me a glass of water and a Tylenol.

"Thank you," I said, and I swallowed them down.

"I'll head downstairs, bring our gear to *Mitera,* and let her know to start making breakfast," he said as he tossed a shirt over his head. He kissed my forehead before grabbing the basket of our Elythian leathers and heading out our bedroom door.

The bed groaned under me as I shifted to the edge. I stood, wincing at the tenderness, feet swollen from all the running and walking we'd done the night before. I slowly made my way to the bathroom.

I quickly used the bathroom and washed up, splashing my face with cold water, and pressing my hands into my puffy eyes—the icy chill of the water soothing. If I was to keep up with late nights spent hunting darklings with The Order, I needed to change my sleep schedule. I pulled one of the drawers out and fished through the mess of things to find my prescription bottles hidden in the back. My doctor had tried switching my medication at my appointment last month. He explained he wanted to try a different approach, and I was now on two different medications. I wished nothing more than to just burn them.

Damien never went into this drawer, as it only held my things, but I'd been careful to make sure he couldn't easily find them. I lifted one of the bottles, inspecting the dwindling supply of tablets. My mother had been getting my refills for me, giving them to me when I went to visit from time to time.

God, I hated this.

I needed to get the courage to tell him, but how would I do that? I'd never told him when we met, never imagined our meeting would lead to all this, and before I knew it, I'd become so entwined in his life that... I couldn't bring myself to. How would I bring it up now? What would he think when he learned I'd kept it from him? I'd managed to mask any hints of my condition from the memories, too afraid to share it all with him, but now... I regretted it.

Nausea pooled in my stomach, and I stopped myself from lingering on the thought further. I took my morning doses before stashing the bottles, then headed for the closet to put some pants on. I paused when I heard the muffled sounds of Damien talking with Ethel below. My stomach growled; Ethel's home-cooked meals sounded like heaven.

As I made my way to the door to head downstairs, my phone rang on my nightstand. I headed over, thinking it might be Kat. My heart sank at the sight of my doctor's name flashing on the screen. My hand hovered over it for a moment, but I grabbed it and answered.

"Hello?"

"Hi, is this Cassie Hites?" a nurse asked.

"Yeah. this is her."

"Hi Cassie. I just wanted to confirm your quarterly exam for next Monday, the twenty-seventh at 11:00 a.m."

My words got lost in my throat. I'd forgotten about my quarterly exam; I'd been so absorbed in my training that I hadn't realized the day was fast approaching. I always dreaded my yearly examinations. They always took so long to complete. From the tedious questions the doctor would ask, to the blood work, to the MRI scans that always left me feeling claustrophobic.

"I'll be there," was all I could say. The nurse thanked me and wished me a good day before hanging up. I braced myself against the nightstand, guilt curdling my stomach at the thought that I'd have to sneak to another appointment without Damien knowing.

"G'mornin' tae ye, Cas," Ethel said as I entered the kitchen. She walked over to lay a kiss on my cheek, her radiant energy helping lift my mood a little. "Ah heard yer first hunt went well."

I gestured to the healing cut on my face. "Would've preferred to avoid this."

"Oh dear. Ah've got some salve 'at'll heal 'at right up. Ah'll get it fer ye after ye've eatin'. Donnae want that tae leave a scar, noo do we?" She returned to the stove, the smell of corned beef and hash reaching my nose. "Ah'll 'ave yer breakfast ready in a moment, dear. 'Ave a seat."

I smiled and joined Damien at the table. He slid over a cup of tea he'd made for me as I eased into a chair. I lifted it to take a sip of the heavenly liquid. "You don't know how special it is that you do this for me every morning, *mea sol.*"

He smiled and leaned in to brush a kiss to my forehead. I noticed Ethel smile briefly over her shoulder at us.

"That I can do it for you again means more to me than you'll ever know."

Damien turned, striking up a conversation with Ethel. I sat in silence, watching as they spoke, their words dancing through the air but not registering in my ears. My thoughts lingered elsewhere, dwelling on darklings and a war my parents and friends would get caught in the middle of, of the phone call I'd received just moments ago, on tests and doctors' visits.

I'd finally shared the burdens of everything that had happened with Marcus, shared everything that happened to me in that cell... but the relief I'd felt after was short-lived. I still felt alone. So alone, despite sitting here with Ethel and Damien. It was as if I were watching them as some intangible being, merely a spectator of their happiness.

For once, I wanted him to know the truth, to know it all. It conflicted with every thought and fear that led me to keep this secret from everyone, but I didn't want to feel alone anymore. I wanted him there at my side to support me. Through everything...

I wanted him to be by my side when I heard how much damage my heart had suffered over the last few months, wanted him there when I might break down and cry.

"*Mea luna?*"

I blinked, awakening to reality, and my lips parted, nearly ready to ask him if I could talk to him, but then I noticed Ethel's curious gaze as she peeked over her shoulder. I forced a smile, trapping the words in my throat and instead saying, "Sorry. Just feeling a little drowsy still. Don't mind me, just zoning out over here."

His eyes danced between mine, and I saw a hint of doubt in them.

"Oh! Lord Damien." Ethel stepped away from the stove, wiping her hands on her apron as she reached to grab a letter from the counter, but I couldn't find relief in her distraction, the guilt clawing at my chest. "Ah forgot tae tell ye. This came fer ye this mornin'."

She handed him the black envelope, and I glimpsed an intricate silver wax seal. His face soured, brows furrowing as he looked at it before tearing it open to read the letter inside.

"It's The Council, isn't it?" Ethel asked.

My eyes danced between them. "The Council?"

Damien didn't answer, reading the letter in silence, eyes flitting over the words on the paper. Whoever The Council was, Damien didn't appear to be fond of them.

His sigh came out in a rush, shoulders sagging as he tossed the letter onto the table. I resisted the urge to pick it up and read it. "They're calling a meeting. It'll happen in a few days."

Ethel sighed. "Ah'm nae surprised wi' the attack 'at happened."

My gaze snapped to Damien, my gut twisting. "Attack?"

His eyes fell before he spoke. "The darklings attacked the home of an immortal family while we were out last night."

The blood drained from my face. "Did they..."

Damien's eyes drifted to me, but he shook his head, the sorrow heavy in his expression. "There were no bodies left for us to lay to rest."

Terror crawled up my spine. The darklings had converted them, growing their ranks even further.

"Human-born darklings aren't as strong as immortal-born darklings. It would only strengthen their ranks," he said. "But this is the first time they've broken into a house. They've never been smart enough to try, and the fact that they're specifically targeting immortal families..."

"'Ow many was it, Lord Damien?" Ethel dared to ask, all the glow and sunshine gone from her face.

"A family of five: a mated pair, and their sons and a daughter. Two of them were to start their training next month. The other was..." Damien's eyes flickered to me briefly before lowering, and I reached out to take his hand, feeling the pain flow through my fingertips. His last, unspoken words lingered in his thoughts.

...a child.

"How did they find them?" I asked.

Damien didn't raise his eyes to me. "I don't know."

Did Cole and Amara sell out their own race to Melantha? Had they started feeding her the locations of immortal families to build their ranks? I couldn't stomach the thought, couldn't bring myself to verbalize it.

"Is that... how the darklings do it? You told me they convert through biting. Is that how they are increasing their numbers, by taking families? I haven't been keeping up with the news to see if there are any new disappearances."

Damien nodded. "They have been, even from the neighboring towns. They have to convert the person before they die. If they die before they change, the conversion fails." He lifted his eyes to me. "That's the only reason you weren't converted when you died as Elena. They'd been so lost to their own hunger; you'd died before you could turn."

The possibility made me dizzy. Thank God it hadn't happened. What would have happened if I'd been converted? Would I have lived on as darkling? Would I have still been reborn? There were so many questions left unanswered.

"Damned monsters," Ethel muttered.

"Who is The Council?" I asked.

"It's comprised of the heads of each house of power. They oversee their houses, and they answer to me, though there are a couple who've become rather entitled over the years. I've been..." He averted his eyes. A feeling of guilt, balmy and cold, crept over my skin from where I touched him. "A bit preoccupied over the last several months, and it's been a while since we've had a meeting."

The heads of each of the immortal houses. What were they like? How many were there? Were they like Damien? It still didn't seem real how there could be an entire society of immortals living in secret amidst the human world, completely unbeknownst to us.

"Are they warriors in The Order?"

He sat back as Ethel brought our breakfast. "The few I can tolerate were once brothers of The Order. Once they took their seat at The Council, they stepped down."

I thanked Ethel as she set my plate before me, and I took a bite, relishing in the salty corned beef hash. "And the ones who aren't?"

"You'll see soon enough."

I halted, head turning before I could take another bite. "What do you mean?"

"You're to join me at the meeting. It's time we made your presence known."

CHAPTER 10

CASSIE

Damien parked his car along a darkened sidewalk. Music pumped through the walls and the neon sign reading 'Stokers' glowed against the brick above the black door. I'd never heard of or seen this place before. It was hidden from the main roads on a small side street, not one you'd typically travel through regularly, and it was most definitely one I'd never been down.

I climbed out of the car at the same time as Damien, the icy wind whipping my hair around me, and I curled into my jacket. "This seems like the perfect place for an immortal bar. Do humans ever come here?"

"Sometimes, a few here and there, but everyone gets kicked out when we arrive," he said with a cocky grin.

I raised a brow, a smile tugging at my lips as I teased him. "Oh? So, you guys are like the VIPs, then?"

"You could say that, or the owners just love us. We never request it." He led me to the door, heavy music spilling out onto the street from within. Avenged Sevenfold's "Brompton Cocktail" blared from the speakers, and Damien waved a hand to the others already settled at the bar.

Black brick walls surrounded us, decorated with assorted morbid oddities and neon signs. My eyes were drawn to shelves full of beautiful, intricate animal skeletons and skulls. The bar's counter extended the stretch of wall in front of us, and behind it stood floor-to-ceiling shelves lined with all sorts of alcohol and liquor. Edgar Allan Poe meets rock seemed to be the running theme.

I noticed Thalia from behind, kicked back on one of the leather couches, sipping some concoction from a glass. She was talking loudly across the room to Vincent, Barrett, and James, who were seated at the bar, nursing their own drinks.

Barrett threw his hand up in the air as he noticed us. "Spitfire!"

I rolled my eyes, slipping my arms out of my sleeves as Damien slid my coat off my shoulders before hanging it on the coat rack. "Can't you just call me Cas like normal people?"

He spun around in the swivel chair and leaned back against the bar, elbows resting on the counter. He cocked his head, his single silver earing swaying with the movement. "I'm not normal people. Besides, where's the fun in that?"

The music's volume lowered. I looked over to see a female turning the dial on the jukebox, and I was relieved I could talk without yelling now.

"Eiko!" Damien greeted, walking over to her as she approached. She leapt, throwing her arms around him. Her short, curly auburn hair bounced just above her shoulders, and her floral dress swayed just below her knees, hugging the swells of her waist and hips. She looked a little out of place in a bar like this—cute and airy.

"It's been too long, Lord Damien!" she said, positively beaming.

"How many times do I have to tell you to just call me Damien?"

"She's too proper to refer to you as anything else. You should know that by now," another female said from the bar. She leaned her elbow on the counter, adjusting her black ball cap which barely hid her onyx pixie-cut hair that blended beautifully against her dark skin. Her eyes, pale silver, drifted to me. Immortal. Damien had explained to me that the pale gray eyes were a trait immortals shared, but Eiko had black ones. Was she human?

84

"Cas, this is Eiko." He gestured to the little female, smiling at his side. "And this is Semele." He held his hand out to the woman behind the bar. "Ladies, this is Cas."

Semele walked around the counter to greet me. Side by side, the females were so unalike, nearly complete opposites. Semele wore all black: a The Used T-shirt, shredded, black, skin-tight jeans, a chain hanging from her hip, and black leather boots. Piercings shined from her ears and lip in the neon glow, and I noticed numerous tattoos peeking from the rolled sleeves of her shirt. Eiko was the complete opposite in her bright floral dress and cute brown leather flats. She glowed with an aura that felt like sunshine and wildflowers.

"Welcome to Stokers, Lady Cas," Semele said, flashing me a pearly smile.

My ears felt hot, and I fumbled my words. "Oh, please! You don't have to call me that. It's just Cas."

"Careful ladies, you'll make her blush," Barrett called from the far end of the bar.

I whipped around, wanting to throw something at him.

"If you want to hit him, I've got a bat behind the counter," Eiko joked in an all too cheerful tone, the innocent smile never leaving her face.

Thalia laughed from her spot on a nearby couch, adding to Eiko's comment. "Eiko and Cas would wipe the floor with you, Barrett."

"Taking bets!" Vincent called out.

I giggled, and Eiko wrapped her arms around my neck. "I'm so excited to finally meet you! Zephyr told me a lot about you."

I tilted my head, brows furrowing. "He did?"

Semele approached behind her. "Sorry, she gets excited to meet new people, and she's been dying to meet Damien's mate since we learned you were found." Eiko released me before wrapping her arms around Semele's waist, Semele tucking her under her arm as she brushed a tender kissed to Eiko's temple.

I smiled. "Damien was telling me about you on the way here. I'm glad I get to meet you guys. Stokers is your place, right?"

Semele nodded. "Yeah. It's a little shithole in the wall, but it's *our* shithole in the wall."

"I love it. It's perfect," I said, eyes drifting over it all again. Immortal lives were woven so tightly with danger, and the glimpse of the happiness they carved out away from the war. It was beautiful. It was something I'd wished I could experience my entire life, but never had the courage to try.

Damien took a seat at the bar as he lit one of his rolls of brierleaf, and Semele took notice, heading around the counter again. "Weak or strong tonight, Damien?"

"We're celebrating tonight," he said, cracking a wicked grin.

She met his wicked grin with one of her own. "Strong it is."

Thalia rose from the couch. "How're you feeling after last night?"

"Still a little sore, but more alive than I felt when Damien carried me in last night."

"You're welcome," Damien said without looking at me, a smug look of male satisfaction on his face, and my cheeks heated, remembering just how he'd eased my soreness.

Thalia's grin turned coy, but she said nothing.

"Still disappointed you didn't head-butt a darkling," Barrett murmured before downing the last of his drink. The rings decorating his fingers glinted in the neon lights as he knocked the glass back onto the counter.

"Barrett! You break another glass and I'll beat you with the bat myself," Semele warned.

"I'll hold him down for you," Thalia offered as she rose from the couch, taking another sip of the amber liquid swirling in her glass.

"Careful now, Thalia. I might take you up on that offer," Barrett said with a smug grin.

I bit back my giggle as Thalia's response fell short on her tongue. I climbed onto the barstool next to Damien. "This is the first time I've been to a bar," I said lowly, surveying the place.

He looked at me incredulously. "First kiss, first time, first date, and first bar? Shit, I'm one lucky male."

I elbowed him, and he grunted a low laugh. "Don't forget to add first kill to your list."

"And damn proud of it," Damien said with a crooked grin.

Out of the corner of my eye, I saw Thalia take a seat next to Barrett, seeming to find her voice after Barrett's remark. They started talking and... she smiled at him. It wasn't a warm and fuzzy smile, but more of a 'fuck around and find out' smile. As she tilted her head onto her knuckles, eyeing him, I realized she was flirting.

I leaned in to whisper to Damien. "This is the second time I've seen Barrett and Thalia talk, and it see almost peaceful."

Damien glanced at them briefly. "Maybe she'll finally bring him down a notch."

"I figured you'd be disappointed if he lost that bit of sparkle," I said, resting my elbows on the countertop as I cocked a smirk.

A low laugh broke from Damien as Semele set his drink on the bartop. "Is that what you call that?" He lifted the glass and glanced at me. "You want one?"

I hesitated, eyes falling on his drink. I wasn't supposed to drink while on my medication. "Um, I think I'll pass for now."

Barrett stood, leapt over the bartop, and slapped his hand on the counter. "This is your party, spitfire! How're you not gonna drink? I'll make you somethin' right now."

"If she doesn't want to, she doesn't have to," Damien said, throwing Barrett a warning glance.

James rested at the bar on the other side of Damien, and I leaned forward to see him better. "I haven't seen much of you lately, James. How've you been?"

"Bin good. Jus' bin tied up diggin' throo any documents I can find tae see if there're any records o' any humans' bein' turned into immortals." He took a sip of his drink as if he didn't just say something that would rattle the very foundation of my reality.

Any words I might've said caught in my throat, and I looked at Damien. "I thought it wasn't possible."

He didn't meet my gaze at first, but his eyes eventually drifted to mine. "I've never heard of it happening, and I haven't found any records, but I wanted to be sure. If you'd be willing to go through with it, I wanted to give you the option. I just... I didn't say anything last night because I didn't want to give you false hope."

I suddenly wished I hadn't asked, the very false hope I'd wished to avoid swelling in my chest. I couldn't let myself give into it. They both made it clear they'd yet to find any proof it was even possible. If Damien had never heard of it happening, then it likely wasn't possible.

"Ah'm visitin' Selene's Temple o'er the next few days tae go throo more documents an' records o' eh immortals. Ah'll keep ye posted."

"Thank you, James," I said, smiling weakly. I didn't want to dwell on the thought any longer. "Where's Zephyr? Is he not here yet?"

Damien glanced around the bar. "I guess not." He looked at Barrett, who was messing around with bottles of different liquors now. "You hear from Zephyr?"

"Probably with his new female."

"You better not waste any of that, Barrett!" Semele called from down the bar, and I giggled. "You'll be replacing every wasted drop, and that stuff doesn't come cheap!"

"Just put it on my tab!"

87

Damien leveled a glare on him. "Your tab is my tab, Barrett. You'll be paying for that out of your own pocket."

Barrett grimaced. "So cold."

I bit back the snicker building in my throat and leaned in, looking at Damien. "I meant to ask; do you know who it is? Zephyr's... female, that is. Is she his mate?"

Damien cleared his throat, his eyes avoiding mine. "Um, listen, about tha—"

"Zephyr! 'Bout damn time," Vincent shouted, and I looked over to see Zephyr entering the bar. My throat went dry at the sight of the beautiful woman walking behind him. She was as elegant as when I first met her a few months prior—shining pale eyes glowing off her golden skin, her posture elegant and poised as Zephyr removed her fine coat.

Calista.

I glanced at Damien, whose eyes were locked with Zephyr, that electric energy I'd felt before sparking back to life. I turned back to the counter, suddenly feeling the world shift under me. "I'll take that drink, Barrett."

A satisfied laugh broke from Barrett's throat as he went to town, mixing a drink for me, and I leveled a look at Damien. "You knew, didn't you?"

Damien didn't answer at first as he turned from Zephyr's gaze. "Yes."

"Why didn't you tell me?"

"I... I didn't know how to."

Barrett set the glass on the bartop, and I took it in my hand, lifting it to my lips to take a drink. I cringed as the liquid burned my throat, but I forced it down, fighting the urge to throw it back up.

Damien cast a glare at Barrett, who threw his hands up, a look of innocence painting his face. "What? She needs to loosen up a little. She's been too uptight lately."

"You should give her a chance, Cas," Damien said, looking back at me as Barrett slipped away before Damien could further reprimand him. "She's truly not a bad person."

"I saw her thoughts, Damien. I saw just how she'd prefer to *service* you, how she wanted to take you to our bed. *Our bed*." I took another drink.

"Cas," he said, and I turned my glare on him, setting my glass on the bartop. Guilt filled those eyes I loved so much. "Give her a chance. She comes from the aristocracy; it's a different world. She's expected to do things, things she doesn't have any say in."

My gaze fell from him, my hand gripping the glass tightly.

Damien let loose a heavy sigh. "I can smell it. Zephyr's bonded to her, and from the looks of it, she's accepted the bond. This isn't something that's going to go away, Cas. The mating bond is permanent once it's been accepted."

I looked back over my shoulder to see them settling onto the couch as Thalia walked over to greet her. Zephyr introduced her to Calista, the two women striking up a conversation almost immediately. I couldn't deny there was something different about the way Calista carried herself—her body not so tense, back not as straight. She seemed more at ease, as if she didn't have to walk on eggshells. Her eyes weren't as cold, now alight with something I couldn't form into words. No longer did she seem like the prideful, high society woman who believed she was better than me.

"Care to join me?" I asked Damien, unable to look at him, my eyes fixated on the nearby trio.

"It'd probably be better if I didn't."

I frowned, brows furrowing as I looked at him. "Why?"

"A newly mated male can sometimes be... territorial. It doesn't help that his new mate serviced me for many years. It's been months since I've fed from her, but he probably smells remnants of her in me." He glanced at them, watching their happy conversation from a far, and I couldn't miss Zephyr watching him from the corner of his eye as Thalia and Calista spoke. "I'd rather not have to fight my brother tonight."

Serviced. That word made my stomach twist. I took a deep breath and lifted the glass to knock back the last gulp, cringing at the horrible taste before setting it back down and swiveling on the chair. I didn't look forward to this.

"I guess I'm on my own then."

CHAPTER II

CASSIE

"Hey, Zeph."

He looked up at me, a smile lighting up those pale green eyes. Calista and Thalia glanced up as well, but Calista's gaze fell before it could meet mine.

"Hey, come join us," Zephyr said, nodding to the couch where Thalia sat.

I hesitated, unsure if I wanted to accept his invitation, if I even wanted to approach Calista. I shoved down the terrible thoughts and took a seat next to Thalia, who was kicked back with a fresh glass of whatever it was she was drinking.

Calista's eyes burned into her lap as she fidgeted with her fingernails. I could feel her fear, her anxiety, her guilt in the air, the sensation skittering over my skin—balmy and icy. Even if I'd lacked the ability to sense it, it would have been obvious. Not that I blamed her; I still remembered the feel of my fingers ensnared in her hair, how she felt under me when I'd pinned her to our couch, my dagger pressed to her throat.

I'd almost given into whatever instinct had overwhelmed me after I saw those images in her mind, almost gave into that very instinct that drove my past lives to nearly take over my body. They'd spoken an ancient language, warning the female of the line she'd crossed. If I'd given in... she wouldn't be sitting here at Zephyr's side.

I'd have slit her throat.

Guilt sank into my stomach, bile rising in the back of my throat. I was still disgusted with myself for reacting that way. Damien had explained it was part of the mating bond; once bonded, immortals were protective over their mate.

It hadn't made me feel any better; it still didn't.

Zephyr tilted his head to her, taking her hand in his in quiet reassurance. She met his gaze before finally summoning enough courage to look at me.

"I owe you an apology," she said, her words shaky and uneven as she struggled to hold my gaze.

I remained silence, and Thalia looked between us, a look of confusion on her face.

"Thalia," Barrett called from the bar, "come here."

She didn't question him, happily accepting the chance to escape what was building into a very awkward confrontation.

"I'm sorry for the way I acted. I never should've done that to you," she managed to say.

I took a deep breath, unsure how to respond, but she didn't give me a chance to. "I never meant to offend you. I wasn't prepared for you to be there, didn't realize what you were to him. When I saw a human with him, it didn't make sense, but I was not there to question. I was there to serve."

Zephyr bristled but held it at bay, his jaw tightening, and I frowned. Had she not been told? My eyes shifted to Zephyr, his eyes locked on Calista, his thumb brushing back and forth across her hand. Such adoration shined in those eyes, as intense a gaze as I'd caught Damien giving me when he thought I wasn't paying attention.

"I should be the one apologizing," I said, and surprise flashed across both their faces. "You're the reason Damien was able to receive what he needed all this time."

Zephyr gripped Calista's hand, his eyes darkening, and I halted. I probably should stay away from that topic, but she needed to understand that I did appreciate her... servicing him all this time in my absence. "I should be thanking you."

Her eyes lowered. "You honor me, mate of my lord."

"*Please*..." I groaned. God, the formalities. "Just call me, Cas. Who withheld the information from you? That I was with him."

Her gaze fell, and I felt her fear, felt this overwhelming dread creep over her. I wouldn't read her thoughts, though. I refused to. The first time had been an accident, and I'd invaded her privacy enough.

Zephyr answered for her. "Her father, Tobias."

My eyes shifted to him. "Why would he do that?"

"He's been trying to get Damien to take her as his mate for the last century. It would only benefit him to have his daughter bear his offspring, to become the new immortal queen."

My blood boiled at his words, that overwhelming instinct I'd felt before swelling in my chest. Damien hadn't mentioned this. Whether he was aware or not, I didn't know. "How—I'm confused. Why would her father have any say?"

"That's how the aristocracy works. Females don't get a say in who they're bound to. They reside with their family until they are mated off, often as bargaining chips to benefit their house." Zephyr's voice descended into a near growl with each word. "Whether they are bonded to the mate or not, whether they love them or hate them, it doesn't matter. Her father would have preferred her live as Damien's broodmare than find her true mate—still wants it."

Dangerous territory. We were stumbling into very dangerous territory. "Zeph," I said, softly.

He took a deep breath. "Sorry."

Broodmare. Damien's broodmare. Those words made me want to vomit. Despite the horrible circumstances of it all, not to mention that she was Zephyr's mate, she would have been able to give him something I never could. A child, children even. I'd always dreamed of one day having a family, and for a long time I'd given into the foolish hope the doctors offered me that I might one day be able to maintain my illness instead of succumbing to it. It was a painful reminder, and jealousy punched deep into my gut.

James and Damien were looking for a way, though. If they could change me, could make me immortal, we could…

I couldn't allow myself to hope, and I dragged myself back to the present, to the issues at hand.

"Can't Damien do anything about it?"

"It's the law," Calista muttered. "Damien is bound to the law just as much as we are. If he were to defy it, it could have severe repercussions. The houses could lash out for not having leeway in other matters, especially if he did it for a friend."

So, his hands were tied. My skin tingled, heat building in my chest. The buzz of the drink I'd downed moments ago was settling in.

I knew nothing about the aristocracy. I needed to find out more about the laws taking away Calista's choice, no, all the females' choices in their world. If I had any say as Damien's mate, this lifestyle would change. It was barbaric for women to not have any say in who they spent their lives with, and I didn't understand why laws like this still existed.

God, I didn't deserve the title of queen. Calista would have made a better one, could have done so much in my place.

"I am truly sorry for what I did to you, Cas," Calista said, pulling me from my thoughts. "I was foolish. My father had told me for so long what I needed to do, and I wanted to please him, wanted to bring honor to our family. For so long, I felt like such a failure to him, and then Lord Damien stopped calling on me, and I feared I had done something to displease him…"

She drew a deep breath. "At one point… I thought I liked him, may have loved him even." A muscle feathered in Zephyr's jaw, but he remained silent at her side. "It only confused me more when I saw you there, and I feared what my father would say or think, and… Gods, I feel so horrible for the things I did—thought. I know now that what I felt before, the feelings weren't genuine, weren't my own."

Her pale eyes snapped to mine when I took her hand. "I forgive you, Calista. I'm sorry you had to go through that," I said, and her pained eyes rose to me.

"I am unworthy of your sympathy, mate of—" She cleared her throat and spoke as if it went against everything she'd ever been taught. "Cas."

I smiled at her correction. "But you are, Calista. I owe it to you."

I lifted my eyes to Zephyr. "Zeph?" His brows rose. "Can you put aside what happened? I know it goes against your… instincts, but can we enjoy tonight without you trying to bite my mate's head off?"

He smiled. "I'll do my best to behave. I promise."

I smiled at Calista. "I'm happy for you guys, really."

Calista beamed, the light returning to her warm, silver eyes, and it was that light that made me wonder if I'd been the first person who'd accepted their union.

"Do immortals get married, like have a wedding? How does that work?"

A low laugh rumbled in Zephyr's throat. "We have a binding ceremony. It's sort of like a wedding, but it's different. It isn't a simple exchanging of vows like mortals do. It's a melding of the souls, a union that goes beyond an exchanging of rings."

It sounded beautiful. "Can I... Would I be invited?" I asked, looking at Zephyr.

He glanced at Calista, but her eyes lowered.

"I don't think we will be able to have a binding ceremony," she muttered.

"Why not?"

Zephyr's eyes darkened. "The law of the aristocracy demands any binding be approved by the head of the female's family."

"So, you can't be bound unless Calista's father approves of it?" I asked.

Zephyr nodded.

"That's bullshit," I said, looking between them.

"It's an outdated law, but it's the law nonetheless, and her father doesn't like me," Zephyr said.

God, I wanted to strangle this Tobias. "Why? You're a warrior and second in command of The Order. Wouldn't that be a *beneficial* binding?"

"It's because I'm lowborn," he said.

I frowned, and I couldn't understand why the term raked against my skin. "Lowborn?"

"Not of the aristocracy," Calista explained. "Impure in the eyes of the high families. He belongs to House Thiríon through ability only, as he was not born of nobility."

Anger rose in my chest. Zephyr was an exceptional person, kind, compassionate, powerful. His birth should have no sway in who he was bound to. "How do we change the law? Women—er females should have a say in who they're bound to."

"The council has to vote on it, but it hasn't been a priority with the possibility of war in the air," Zephyr said.

"I'll talk to Damien. Surely, there's something he can do. The council sent him a letter this morning, requesting a meeting." Perhaps I could do something to help them and all the females caged by this misogynistic law.

"I know. I'll be there," Zephyr said.

I sighed. "Damien's not looking forward to it."

"He never does."

Silence stretched out, filled by music playing from the jukebox and the chatter from the bar. My mind wandered to what was to come; the Council, the aristocracy, war.

War.

There was so much to focus on, so much to do. While I wanted so badly to help Zephyr and Calista, to live my own life, Melantha was out there, building her army. She'd remained hidden since we learned of her existence, and we'd been unable to find the darklings' nest, despite the teams tasked with searching. I'd been exhausted after my first hunt, even with all the training I'd undergone. I couldn't imagine fighting that many darklings at once, not to mention facing their powerful leader.

Damien wanted us to take time to celebrate, to not lose ourselves in the war, but it was difficult, knowing war was creeping up on the horizon. What would become of my home, the people I love, both human and immortal? How could I possibly protect my parents? Kat? I wanted to help them, wanted to change the laws, wanted to protect everyone, but could I?

I took a deep breath. "Well, letting it ruin the night won't change anything." I stood. "You guys want to join us at the bar?"

Calista's brows rose at the informal offer, but she stood to accompany me. "That would be lovely."

Damien watched cautiously as we approached the bar. I gripped his hand in reassurance, kissing his cheek. "Sorry for the way I acted earlier."

"No apologies needed. I should've told you."

Damien's gaze shifted to Zephyr as he approached, his body tensing, and I whispered into his ear. "Zephyr promised he'd relax."

He smiled. "Only for your sake would he manage that."

I frowned, confused, but Barrett threw his arm over Damien's neck before I could ask.

"Round of shots for the brothers!" Barrett said, and Semele brought over the shot glasses. My cheeks already felt flushed, my skin tingling from the buzz of my first drink.

I lifted my hand. "I probably shouldn't—"

"Awe, come on, spitfire! One more!" Barrett said, hopping off of his barstool, and I let loose a breath.

I hadn't been having any issues, hadn't had any signs of an attack... Just tonight. One night of drinking wouldn't hurt.

Semele handed me a shot, different from the ones she gave the others, but I didn't question her as I took the shot glass.

"To our little spitfire." I rolled my eyes as Barrett spoke. "May she rain hell on the darklings and bring a peace like no other."

I didn't speak for a moment, absorbing the words that seemed so unlike Barrett. He stood among our friends, *our family* as they all smiled at me, shot glasses raised.

For me.

I smiled, holding my glass up in response, and we all downed our drinks.

CHAPTER 12

DAMIEN

"She wants to change things," Zephyr said as he sat down next to me, his body still wound tight. He was doing a damn good job of stifling the possessive male instincts I knew were causing his blood to boil.

I leaned back against the bartop as we watched Cassie and the other females talk on the couch. She looked so happy, so at ease, despite everything she'd been through. It was a relief she and Calista had worked things out between them. I dreaded to think how deeply it would have hurt Zephyr if Cassie had refused her. I didn't know what he would have done.

"She's ambitious," I said. "I know she'll do amazing things. I'm just worried."

Zephyr's eyes flickered briefly to me, onyx brows furrowing.

"I fear how they'll react when they meet her. Some of them hate humans." My gaze dropped to the swirling amber liquid in my glass. I'd downed several drinks by now and was only just starting to feel the buzz. The joys of being immortal. Thank the gods Semele was able to import ambrosia liquor from the Godsrealm. She was the only one who'd somehow secured that connection.

"She'll put them in their place, or we'll do it for her," Zephyr said. "Honestly, there're a couple of pompous pricks who need to be brought down a notch anyway."

A smile twitched at the corner of my mouth. "That'd be a sight to see. I don't know what they'd do if a female made them eat their words." My smile faded. "It won't be easy for her to navigate the politics. There's so much for her to learn."

I had absolute faith she could put some of them on their asses. Some of them had never trained, and only the few who served in The Order had ever seen battle. I didn't know which was more of a turn on; the sight of her in her Elythian leathers, or the image of her taking down an immortal male. Gods, my skin tightened at the thought of it, and I had to drag my mind away, or else I'd have to pull Cassie into one of the back rooms.

"Anna!" Cassie's voice echoed through the bar as she jumped up from the couch to greet Vincent's mate as she entered the bar. She hung her long coat on the rack, revealing her scrubs. She must have been working a late shift at Johnson's clinic.

She greeted Vincent as he met her at the door, and I chuckled when he swept her into his arms, kissing her deeply. Her cheeks flushed, and she giggled as he nuzzled her, the glow of the neon light catching on her sepia skin. When he lowered her to her feet and bent to lay a kiss to the swell of her stomach, my heart swelled both with happiness and sorrow.

Vincent's mate had made it safely to her twenty-sixth week of pregnancy and was progressing well. I could only imagine how much it worried Vincent, though. He seemed constantly distracted as of late, checking in on her regularly throughout the day. It must have put a strain on Anna as well, to have her mate out on patrol, in danger. The worry wasn't good for her. I had lightened his patrol schedule as much as I could so he could be with her. If we weren't so tight on warriors, I would have pulled Vincent from the patrol schedule completely so he could stay home with her. I hated putting him at risk.

Zephyr knocked back the last of his drink and set the glass on the counter. "Still can't believe Vincent's gonna be a father."

"He'll make a great one."

I couldn't help but wonder what Emilia would've been like if she'd survived. Would she have followed in our footsteps and joined The Order? Would she have worked as a healer in the medical field? What would she have looked like?

I liked to imagine she would have taken after Lucia: long, wavy black hair, her mother's pale moon eyes, a sweet smile that would have me wrapped around her finger. My mind drifted to what ifs and possibilities, images of what could've been dancing in my thoughts: Lucia tending to Emilia as a newborn, the two of them making a mess in the kitchen as they baked a cake for Emilia's birthday, how proud I'd have been to have the chance to teach her how to wield a dagger, watch her knock her uncles on their asses.

Zephyr's eyes flickered to me, as if noticing the sorrow lingering in the shadows of the happiness I felt for them. "Sorry..."

"No." I cleared my throat, pulling myself from the depths. "It's about time one of our brothers started a family. Gives us something to hope for."

Anna would survive, Vincent would survive, and their babe, whether male or female, would have one hell of a family there to help raise it. My eyes trailed over to where Cas cheerily spoke with Anna on the couch. She leaned in, her hand on Anna's baby bump, waiting, and her eyes lit up when, I assumed, the tiny babe kicked.

While I was still annoyed Barrett had coaxed Cassie to drink when she'd originally turned it down, I couldn't deny how carefree she looked—more so than I'd seen in weeks.

"When are you going to tell her?" I asked Zephyr.

He drew a deep breath. "I'm not sure."

"Maybe during your next training session?"

Zephyr didn't answer, turning back to face the bar.

I turned to him, resting my drink on the counter. "Zephyr, you know better than anyone what's going to happen. You may regret not telling her while you have a chance. She deserves to know, and it wouldn't be right for me to tell her. It should be you."

"I know."

"She may not realize it, but I think she feels it. I can tell she feels closer to you than the others," I said. "She looks up to you."

"What are you two sulking about over here?" Cassie's voice seemed a tad higher than usual. I tilted my head to look back at her. Her cheeks were flushed, and while she seemed aware, I could tell just how drunk she was by the way her legs shifted ever so slightly to maintain her balance, her hazel eyes glossy.

"Talking about how you've had enough to drink," I teased.

"I'm not *that* drunk," she argued, reaching for my glass, but I lifted it out of her reach.

"No, you don't. This is not for you."

She put her hands on her hips, cocking an eyebrow. "Why? Is it too strong for me?" A sarcastic tone painted her tongue.

Gods, the sight of her flushed cheeks, the sound of the attitude in her tone—I wanted to steal her away to the back room, strip her down, and sink between those pretty thighs. The music would be loud enough to drown out the moans I wanted to drag from of her. "Let's just say this stuff is strong enough to put a human down for good."

She scoffed. "What is it, some sort of nectar of the Gods or something?"

"Ambrosia liquor." Eiko leaned over the bar to rest her chin on her hands. "Semele has a contact in the Godsrealm. She's the only bartender who serves it on this side of the veil."

Semele snuck up behind Eiko, her hands wrapping around Eiko's waist as she pulled her back from the counter before nuzzling into her neck. Eiko's sweet laughter filled my ears, and I smiled as she wrestled free of Semele and slipped from behind the counter.

"Is Eiko human?" It was cute how she leaned in to whisper, but I knew she might be afraid of offending her.

"Half," I whispered back.

"I like them, a lot," she said, watching them from afar. "Can we come here more often?"

I nodded. "Anytime you have energy after a patrol or we're off shift for the night, we can come here for a drink."

She smiled, and Semele brought her over a fresh drink.

"Where'd you go, Cas?" Thalia called. Barrett was at her back, an arm wrapped around her waist. I blinked. *Well, shit...*

"Coming!" Cassie grabbed her drink as she thanked Semele and popped a kiss on my cheek.

I glanced at Semele, who winked at me. "Her drinks have been light tonight, but I think she's had enough. That one was a virgin."

I huffed a laugh and looked back at the group congregating around the couches.

Eiko squealed when a song came on the jukebox, the beats vibrating through the counter, and she grabbed Cassie, who grabbed Anna and they all migrated over to the open floor to dance.

Tonight was for celebration. I'd watch and let her enjoy herself, watch her drink and dance with our family. *Our family.* And while I hoped we'd have more chances to enjoy our time together.

I knew few nights like this may remain.

The wood steps creaked under my feet as I carried Cassie up the stairs. Her curls hung over my shoulder, her face pressed against my neck as she lay draped over my back.

She groaned. "Sorry you have to carry me up the stairs again."

I laughed. "I'd carry you up these stairs every night for the rest of my life if I needed to."

She tilted her head, her nose pressing into my neck as I nudged our bedroom door open, heading for the bed to lay her down. She inhaled deeply, and I could hear the smile in her voice as she spoke. "Have I told you lately how wonderful you smell?"

If only she knew how easily her scent could bring me to my knees. "I think you've had a little too much to drink, *mea luna.*"

"Nonsense!" she huffed as we neared the bed. "I bet I could walk a straight line. Go ahead, test me, Mr. Officer."

I chuckled. "The fact that I had to carry you up the stairs says otherwise."

"Oh! Wait." She pushed to be let down, my grip slipping. I readjusted to lower her to the floor, surprised by her sudden burst of energy.

"What's wrong?" I asked, turning to her.

She giggled, pressing her finger to my lips as she shushed me. I bit back the urge to laugh at her drunkenness. Her eyes were glazed over, her cheeks and the tops of her ears red, and she struggled to keep herself steady as she gripped my arms. She'd had way more than I'd expected, but I couldn't stop her fun. I was relieved when Semele had intervened where I couldn't. Barrett, for once, was right. She needed to let loose, take a real break from everything she'd been thrown into.

She pushed herself up on her toes to kiss my nose, her balance wavering, and I steadied her. "You can't put me to bed just yet. I gotta take my pill." She left me before I could respond, swaying into the bathroom. I stood there, blinking, brows furrowing as I processed her words.

Pill?

I stood there for a moment, confused. Was she on birth control? Immortals rarely conceived, and the odds of an immortal and human conceiving were even slimmer. I could tell her she didn't need it, but perhaps there were other reasons she was on it—I wouldn't pry.

I used the moment of her absence to head downstairs to fetch her a glass of water and some painkillers for tomorrow's hangover. I lingered a moment, and when I returned, she was sitting on our bed, wearing—Gods... nothing but a shirt.

My shirt.

She sat watching me as I closed the door, and that sinful grin tugged at her full lips.

Fucking hell.

My gaze raked down the peaks of her breasts, her nipples already pebbling beneath the fabric, down farther to the fullness of her thighs under the hem of the shirt. My body tightened, and I wondered if she wore underwear, or if she were bare.

Her voice was a near purr as she spoke. "I owe you for last night."

"Is that you or the alcohol talking?" I asked, smiling as I walked over to set the glass and medicine on the nightstand.

I lifted my eyes to meet hers as she shifted onto her hands and knees, crawling across the bed toward me. Gods bless the collar of that shirt hanging just low enough for a better view.

My breath caught in my throat, and I turned, standing at the edge of the bed as she pushed herself up onto her knees. The bedframe was high enough that she was almost level with me, those hazel eyes staring into my soul. While I knew she was still drunk, the playful attitude had dissipated, leaving behind something deliciously enticing and wicked in its wake. She was perfect... and mine.

"Does it matter?" she asked. Desire burned in those eyes, a flame so hot it might burn me, dancing under her skin.

And Gods, I'd dance in those flames, let them consume me.

I lifted my fingers to catch her chin, my thumb brushing over her velvety soft lips, dying for a taste. "No."

She reached out, grabbed the front of my pants, and pulled me closer to her. Never had she been so bold, and I had to hold myself back from pushing her back and taking her.

I swallowed as her hands slid under my shirt slowly. I sucked my breath through my teeth at the whisper of her touch against the expanse of my stomach, higher and higher, the opposite direction of where I wanted her hands. My cock twitched in response, already hard against the fly of my pants, begging me to push her on her back, spread her legs, and bury myself inside her until she was crying out my name.

She lifted my shirt over my head, and I moved to help when it went above her reach, tossing it to the side. Her lips pressed against my chest, and I froze, my eyes sliding shut. Her tongue—Gods, her tongue left me teetering on the edge.

"*Cas.*" I exhaled a ragged breath, and a grin tugged at one corner of her lips as her lashes lifted, hazel eyes watching the reactions she brought out in me.

I inhaled deeply, her scent filling my lungs, the jasmine and citrus soap mixed with her sweet arousal. It shot through me, my cock pressing hard against my jeans, begging to feel her touch. I lowered my hands to her hips, her soft, warm skin dipping under my fingertips as I gripped her. Her body tightened in my hands, a rush of air filling her lungs, and I jerked when her warm breath spilled out over my skin.

She rose from the bed, hands slipping back down my sides. I released her hips and ensnared my fingers in her hair, tilting her head back to stare into her eyes. Her chest heaved, and her eyes glossed over. I wrapped my other hand around her waist and pressed my lips to her neck, feeling her pulse race beneath her skin. My fangs lengthened, throbbing and dying for a taste.

She grabbed my arms, and as if on cue, my body calmed, willed to heel at my mate's signal as she guided me around until I was backed up to the bed. She reached up to kiss me, and her tongue slipped passed my lips. I groaned at how good she tasted; the hint of the pineapple from the cocktail she'd been drinking still lingered on her tongue.

Without breaking the kiss, her hands dipped to the front of my pants. She fought to undo the button, groaning in frustration as her trembling fingers couldn't manage. I couldn't help but grunt a laugh against her lips, and I reached down to guide her hands back to my waist. I undid the button and zipper, dropping my jeans to the ground and kicked them off. All that remained between her hands and where I wanted them were these boxers, which I wanted the pleasure of watching her remove.

CHAPTER 13

CASSIE

My heart pounded, my head swimming in a drunken haze. Everything had been a blur until he grabbed hold of my hips and I sobered up fast.

I didn't want to stop. My body was hot, blood molten in my veins. I didn't feel like myself, and yet, I'd never felt so free of fear, of embarrassment—and God, I wanted him, wanted to feel every inch of him.

Damien watched me, eager to devour me the moment I allowed him. I needed it, needed to feel his mouth on mine, on me. I imagined the feel of his hands as they explored my body, the feel of him filling me until I begged for that sweet release.

That could come later, though. Right now was about him, about wringing the same amount of pleasure he'd drawn from me the previous night. His muscles tightened under my palms, as if he sensed just how much my body was reacting at the mere memory.

The moment his pants were off, my hands slid down to feel the thickness of him pressed against his boxers. His eyes watched every move I made with predatory hunger. My lips curved, tongue dancing behind them in anticipation of what he would taste like.

I drug my fingers lazily over his thighs, taking my time to tease and taunt him. His lashes lowered, and his hands clenched at his sides until his veins popped beneath his skin. I leaned in, taking his nipple between my teeth, grazing the sensitive skin just enough to make him hiss, air sliding through his teeth as he inhaled deeply. The sight of his unsheathed fangs sent my heart into a frenzy, and the room spun a little.

He grabbed my hips, nails biting into me, and I couldn't stop the moan that slipped from my lips. His leg shifted, slipping between my thighs, and he ground me against him in torturous sweeps. I shuddered, my lips breaking away from his skin as I moaned again. God, how badly I wanted him, the throbbing growing so unbearable. I almost lost sight of what I was doing. I grabbed his hands, and he stopped.

"You once worshipped me." I lifted my eyes to meet his as he stared down at me. "Let me worship you now."

His lips curved into a wicked smile. "Worshipped by a Goddess? You honor me, *mea luna*."

My fingers slid under the band of his shorts, and I shoved them down, his length springing free as I pushed him down onto the bed. He didn't protest, obeying as he laid back until he was propped on his elbows. I slid my hands up his thighs as I climbed between them.

He sat in silence, watching me, his scent flooding the room. The intoxicating aroma of cedarwood and leather was so strong it sent my heart hammering. I pushed myself to my knees as he rose. His hand wrapped around the back of my neck as he pulled me into a kiss, his tongue penetrating my lips. I couldn't resist as I reached into his mind, the words a tease of his own from the night before.

So impatient.

He laughed against my lips, responding with his own thoughts. *You taste too good to resist.*

I swallowed, pushing him back to keep myself from being distracted. Before he could do anything more, I took the thickness of him in my hand and he groaned, head knocking back into the mattress. "*Fuck.*"

107

Seeing how affected he was, seeing how my touch made him react, I felt so... powerful. His pulse pounded under my palm as I slid my hand up the length of him, my thumb brushing over the velvety tip as his muscles twitched. I licked my lips at the sight of him. How I wanted to climb over him and feel every glorious inch sink into me.

Instead, I dipped down to run my tongue over the tip of him, and the moan that ripped from his throat made me throb.

Not yet.

My tongue danced over him. God, there was no way I could take him fully. I brought my free hand up to bridge the gap, stroking him slowly. I lifted my gaze to find him staring down at me with hooded eyes, predatory gaze locked on me as I licked and teased him.

I continued bringing him to the edge where I would feel his body tense, his hands fisting the sheets at his side before I'd withdraw. It was too soon for him to be finished. I wanted to shatter him the way he'd shattered me.

His head knocked back as he groaned, "I love your mouth on my cock."

His words left me molten. Liquid heat pooled at my core, throbbing need unbearable, but I continued the delicious strokes. Beads of sweat broke out over his body, and I knew I'd tormented him long enough. Our eyes met again, his length twitching, begging for what he didn't verbalize. I quickened my pace, ready to bring him over the edge.

His fingers tangled in my hair, and when I felt him twitch between my lips, he pulled me up off him, my back bowing to meet his gaze. He rose, catching my lips with his. Hunger, more hunger than I'd ever felt burned into me where our skin touched, and that predator I'd seen in his eyes came to life.

He grabbed my thighs, his calloused palms rough against my skin, and lifted me until I was straddling him. He was slick against me, and I moaned as he slid himself against that sensitive place between my thighs in teasing strokes. Those amber and ashen eyes burned into me, watching as I relished in the feel of him, devouring my pleasure.

"Not before you," he groaned against my lips. He lifted my shirt off, tossing it to the side, and he gripped my hair again, craning my head back to expose my throat. I couldn't resist, didn't want to. I'd give him everything, all of me, whatever he asked.

His free hand found its way between us, and I gasped, my body tensing as his finger slid down my center, brushing against that sensitive place, aching for his touch.

"Mmmm, look how wet you are for me," he growled against my throat. He slipped a finger into me as his fangs sank into my throat.

My body buckled, and I moaned his name.

He groaned against my skin, continuing to give and take, give and take, until I couldn't stand it anymore. When he withdrew his finger, I fell against him, breathless, my body quivering. Before I could do anything, he slid two fingers in, and I cried out. He quickened his pace, thrusting his fingers into me, thumb stroking down my center until I couldn't hold on any longer, and I shattered.

He moaned against my neck, tasting my release through my blood, increasing the sensation tenfold as every bit of my orgasm coated his throat. He withdrew his fingers and released my neck, his tongue trailing over the mark. Before I could move, before I could do anything, he grabbed my hips, lifting me just enough to plunge himself inside me in one fluid thrust. I cried out, my world exploding around me. He pumped into me until I could take no more, and I grabbed onto his shoulders, nails sinking into his skin.

"*Fuck, Cas,*" he growled, thrusting into me until I felt him throb inside me, his own release rolling through him. We came together, the remnants of my last orgasm washing over me in a second wave, my body gripping him as he pumped into me.

I collapsed against his chest, dizzy and drunk on him. He wrapped his arms around me, holding me tightly. We sat there for a long while, connected, melted into one another, no end and no beginning. If I could, I'd never leave this place, never let go of him.

He pressed a kiss to my shoulder, heated, panted breaths escaping his lungs as he spoke. "Shower?"

"That sounds amazing." I pushed myself up off him, reaching my feet to the floor, but the world spun, my stomach flipping, and Damien caught me before I fell. I grabbed onto him, my knees shaking under me, saliva flooding my mouth. Adrenaline pumped through my system, and a cold sweat broke out across my brow as I fought the urge to vomit.

"You ok?"

I swallowed. "No, I think I'm going to throw up."

He laughed lowly. "Yeah, that happens when you drink more than you should."

I huffed. "Yeah? Good to kn—" My hand clamped over my mouth, my body dry heaving, and he rushed me to the bathroom before I fell over the toilet and threw everything up.

"Here, let me help you." He pulled my hair from my face as my stomach rolled, and a heave coiled my gut as I threw up again.

"No, please," I groaned. I couldn't believe this was happening, that he was seeing me like this. "I'll be fine."

A chuckle slipped from his throat, but he remained. "It's ok, *mea luna*. It happens. I'm surprised you lasted this long, honestly. The shower should help."

He held my hair away from my face, his presence calming, and I stifled the embarrassment. No slimy feeling of his shame slid over my skin, though, only the warmth of adoration, and he didn't seem to care how much of a mess I was. He'd done this before when I'd entered Cole's mind and puked my guts up afterwards. Warmth blossomed in my chest at the thought of it, strange as it was.

Relief washed over me when the heaves subsided.

He turned the faucet on, filled a glass with water, and kneeled beside me. "Here."

I took it and rinsed the foul taste from my mouth. "Thank you."

"You get it all out?"

I hesitated, then nodded. "I think so."

Before I could stand, he scooped his arms under me, lifted me up, and carried me into the shower. I sighed as hot water rolled over my skin. My head rested against his chest, and I relaxed to the lulling sound of his heart beating in my ear.

I smiled. "How did I get so lucky?"

"Lucky?" he asked, brows raised.

"To find you."

He didn't say anything at first, just lowered us until he sat in the tub, cradling me against him. The water rained down over us as he held me in silence for a moment. I lifted my gaze to him, and the look in his eyes touched something deep in my soul.

"If only I could find the words to express that it's me who's the lucky one—to have finally found you again."

An ache tore into my chest.

"I'd started to accept I might never see you again, sank to whatever means I could find to numb myself just to get through each day and night—drinking when I wasn't hunting, smoking until I couldn't feel my face, *anything* to try to silence the hollow ache in my chest." He pulled my head against him, holding me. "But I found you again, and being able to hold you in my arms again... I wouldn't trade it for anything in any realm."

I smiled, feeling my body relax against him, my eyes fluttering. I didn't know what time it was, but exhaustion was creeping into me.

"I love you, *mea sol*, and to be at your side means more to me than you will ever know," I said, softly, as my eyes slid shut.

CHAPTER 14

CASSIE

The trees stretched toward the sky around me. Fresh snow covered the forest floor, and I couldn't see the city for the countless trees that spanned the thousands of acres surrounding The Outpost.

A large raven landed on a nearby boulder, and his head swiveled in my direction. He stretched out his wings and shook. The iridescent black feathers swayed with each twist of his frame, crumbling into black dust around him as Zephyr shifted back to his normal form.

He crossed his strong, tan arms. "All right, Cas, it's your turn. Take it slow this time. Keep your tail level. Don't worry about banking; just focus on gliding down the slope."

The last time we'd practiced flying, I'd eaten dirt and snow. It had left me fearful and hesitant to try again, but I needed to master flight before we moved on to another form.

I stilled my nerves, closing my eyes, and I focused on leveling out my breathing. I imagined the wings, the talons, the feathers. A strange sensation crawled over my skin, as if the magic were melting down my body.

"Good," Zephyr said.

I opened my eyes. The ground beneath my feet was closer—my body so light, I feared a good gust of wind might throw me into the sky. I turned my head to see spotted, tawny wings as I stretched them out. My talons scraped against the ground ungracefully as I stepped, pivoting in place along the slope of the mountainside. I swiveled my head backward to look at him, and I giggled. "It's so weird that I can do this."

He laughed, and I turned my body to face him. "Yeah, don't force it, though. Owls have a limited radius. Any farther and you risk tearing a tendon."

"Noted." I looked down at my talons as I lifted my feet, bits of dirt and snow clenched tightly in my grip. The ice chilled me to my bones, and I shivered, my entire body twisting and shaking. I'd been working on perfecting this transformation for a couple weeks now, but it still didn't feel natural. Zephyr had stressed that the first form was difficult to master, but future forms would come more easily.

My gaze drifted down the slope of the mountainside, littered with rocks and boulders, but this area was clear of any trees I'd need to avoid. I stretched my wings out, my head tilting as I looked over my stance, ensuring my limbs were listening to my commands.

"Tail," Zephyr reminded me.

I fanned my tail out, eyes forward to the slope before me. It wasn't far to the base of the mountainside. I could do this; twenty, maybe thirty feet. I stretched my wings high, and with a leap and a swift downstroke, I was airborne.

"Straighten out. Level your wings," Zephyr called out, and I resisted the urge to look at him. I might not regain my courage to try again if I crashed into something.

The icy wind slid over my back, through my outstretched wings. My feathers ruffled against the current, and my heart raced. I tried to keep my eyes forward, focusing to keep my body still, but I felt so free. How did shifters not give into temptation to never shift back? To be able to fly anywhere, see anything.

I blinked. I was nearing the bottom, the base of the slope approaching too fast. Shit. I had to land.

"Talons forward!" Zephyr yelled.

This was where I struggled. I shifted my body, stretching my talons before me, wings reaching behind me.

"Shit!" I tilted too far and hit the ground.

"Tuck your wings in!" Zephyr yelled, but I couldn't heed his command. I felt the bite of my bones hitting the ground and curled into myself in hopes my wings wouldn't break.

The trees spun as I stared up at the sky, wings slack at my sides.

The thud of his landing was the only thing that alerted me Zephyr had flown down. He leaned over me, his raven head tilting as his eyes passed over me. "You ok?"

I breathed deeply, calming my racing heart. "Yeah. I don't think I broke anything."

He hopped around to my head, using his black beak to lift me up off my back and onto my feet. My wings sagged on the ground, quivering from the adrenaline pumping through me. God, if I could just get the hang of it, I could only imagine how amazing it would feel to soar high above the city of Johnstown, see the valley from above, fly over the rapids of the Stonycreek River.

"Don't get discouraged. You almost had it that time."

My head swiveled to him, my feathered chest still heaving. "What are you talking about? That was horrible."

He laughed, shifting back to his normal form, then helped me onto his forearm.

I wobbled, grabbing onto him as best I could, but I feared I might tear into his arm with my claws if I clung too tightly. "I feel so out of sync."

He smiled as he walked over to the boulder, where he'd observed me from all afternoon. "It takes time. You'll figure it out. We'll keep at it until it's second nature. You're getting closer."

He lowered me onto the rock, and I sagged as my feet met solid ground again.

"Was it this difficult for you?"

"It was. My magic awoke when I was 17, but by then the fear of falling is instilled in you. The hesitation makes it more difficult to let your instincts guide you." His words of encouragement did offer me some hope. "I was prepared for it, though, having been raised in a family of shifters."

"I need to figure this out soon."

Zephyr offered me a warm smile. "I know you will, Cas."

"Is it possible to do a partial shift?" I asked, walking around the surface of the boulder, feeling out my legs, stretching and folding my wings.

His brows narrowed. "I'm not sure I follow."

"Like." I frowned, trying to find the best way to explain. "If I wanted to fly but didn't want to shift fully, could I form wings?" I lifted my clawed foot, flexing my sharp talons. "Or form talons on my hands for fighting?"

He rubbed his jaw, his face scrunching as he thought. "I can't say. I've never heard of anyone doing it. It's only ever been a complete shift. While the rest of the immortals can only shift into two forms at most, Elena could shift into nearly any creature as a demigoddess, but she never did what you're describing."

I slumped.

"I mean, I can't say it's not possible. Surely, as a demigoddess, if anyone could do it, you could. The magic was originally gifted to us by Artemis, and she could take the form of anything, man or beast." He pondered another moment. "You won't know until you try, right?"

The transformation seemed to only require an image, imagining feathers over my skin, wings instead of arms, talons instead of toes. I wanted to see if it was possible; it could be useful.

"Try gliding down from the boulder. See if you can land on the ground here. I know we started this way before, but let's take a step back and check your form."

I stepped over to the edge and looked down. In my human form, it hadn't felt so high up, but the small form of a tawny owl I was now made the drop feel farther. I stretched out my wings and leapt. My wings beat unevenly as I lowered to the ground, talons outstretched. My feet met the dirt, a bit harsher than I intended, but it wasn't a crash.

"Perfect. You just gotta master the shift of your body from flight to landing. We'll do it like this until you're more confident."

"I just can't seem to get it when I'm outstretched on a descent. It throws my balance off."

"It took me a while to figure it out, too," Zephyr admitted. "Don't worry."

I let out a heavy sigh. "You seem so natural at it."

He shrugged. "Yeah, that happens when you've had nearly eight hundred years to practice."

Eight hundred years. I shouldn't be surprised, not with Damien being nearly a thousand, but I hadn't realized how old Zephyr was, hadn't thought about how old any of them might be. I couldn't even begin to comprehend or fathom what they'd experienced in their long lives.

Black dust enveloped me as I shifted back to normal. "Damien told me you were there when Moonhaven fell."

The light left his pale green eyes, and his lips parted, but he didn't speak.

I immediately wanted to take it back, wished I hadn't asked. "I'm so sorry. If it's difficult to talk about, you don't have to. I just hoped I could get more answers. No other visions have resurfaced since..." My chest sank when I imagined what I'd seen through Elena's eyes in her final moments, and I didn't let myself continue. "I wanted to learn more about my past lives. I figured I might get to know what she was like."

He leaned against the rock, his voice monotone. "No... it's ok."

I walked over to him, and he offered me a smile, but I couldn't help but feel it was forced.

"I assumed you might've known Elena, so I was just curious if you could tell me anything about her." My lips pressed into a thin line, guilt churning in my gut, fearful I was picking at old wounds.

"I... uh... guess you could say that." He inhaled, rubbing the back of his neck. "I... I meant to talk to you about it sooner, I just couldn't figure out how to bring it up."

Something in me stirred, and I couldn't understand it, but I suddenly felt almost dizzy. "Bring what up?"

His throat bobbed, and his eyes didn't meet mine. "Well... Elena was... She was my sister."

Sister...

Sister?

The world stopped, and yet at the same time, it didn't. Gravity pulled me in all directions, and I thought I might pass out. I'd been Zephyr's sister in a past life?

I remembered the look on his face when I'd relived Elena's death, the fall of Moonhaven. Horror and sorrow had marred every feature of his sweet face when I'd awoken.

"I mean... she was my half-sister. We shared a father, different mothers. My mother died, and our father later bound himself to another female..." The words fell from his lips in a flurry, and I'd never seen him so unnerved, so rattled.

"I think I knew," I muttered. "It's difficult to explain... Maybe it was the part of me that's Elena that knew all this time."

Damien had lost his mate that night. Zephyr had lost his sister. Unlike the form I'd taken moments ago, it somehow felt... natural. I assumed the part of me that was Elena tugged on that connection, welcoming the knowledge back into herself through me.

"What was it like being my brother? What was... I like? I've seen visions, heard stories from Damien, but what was I like growing up?"

His face warmed, his lips curving into a smile, and a light of endearment returned to his pale green eyes. "So much like you are now. You were so timid when we first met. When Damien told me of his suspicions, it was hard for me to believe, but as I got to know you more, I saw it. You were so stubborn. Once you set your mind on something, no one could talk you out of it." His eyes went distant, a smile tugging at his lips. "You were always so kind and compassionate, but shit, did you hate being told what to do." He laughed as he relived some fond memory. "Can't tell you how many times I had to talk you out of trouble growing up."

I smiled, imagining Zephyr cleaning up the messes left by Elena—by me.

"It was hard for you to open up to new people, but once they gained your friendship, there was no person more loyal. No matter what, you would be there, have their back."

It sounded so like me, but why wouldn't it?

"I'm sorry. I didn't mean to dig up those memories."

"No, don't be. Like I said, I've been wanting to tell you." His shoulders relaxed, as if a weight had been lifted. "I meant to tell you months ago, but then I met Calista, and I knew things were complicated between you two. I was terrified of how you would react."

"Zeph, you've always been there for me. I would never turn you away." I turned to lean my back against the rock next to him, eyes lifting to the forest around us. A brother. *My brother*. I'd always wanted one growing up, remembered begging my mom for one as a child, but she'd explained it wasn't possible to have a big brother after I was born first. I'd cried so hard that day. A smile crept across my face at the memory. "It's kind of cool to know I have a brother."

He smiled, laying a hand on my shoulder. "Anytime you need anything. Just tell me. Barrett crosses a line? I'll kick his ass for you."

"Oh no, I want that honor for myself," I said, cracking a cocky grin.

He huffed a laugh.

"Can you..."

His brows rose when I hesitated.

116

"Can you tell me stories of Elena when you guys were younger?" I lifted hesitant eyes to him. "I've always felt so... incomplete. When a new memory resurfaces, I can't explain it, but it's like it was a part of me that's been missing."

A warm smile lit his face, and warmth spread through my chest at the sight of it. He nudged me with his shoulder. "I'd be happy to. If it isn't distracting, I'd be happy to share some while we train."

I smiled and pushed myself up to head back to the slope, feeling energized. "Then let's get back to it!"

"Oh, and Cas."

I stopped, glancing over my shoulder at him.

"If you can make that flight down the hill and stick the landing, we'll try the partial shift before we finish for the day."

CHAPTER 15
CASSIE

"How did training go?" Damien asked as he cut into his roast beef later that night.

"Well, I found out I have a brother."

Damien's dark brows rose. "So, he finally told you."

I nodded, warmth spreading through my chest. There had been a change in Zephyr after he'd told me about Elena. He seemed more... at ease. I could only imagine what he'd felt all these months, knowing what he did and having to hold onto that knowledge.

"I'm glad. I've been trying to get him to for months."

Part of me wondered why Damien never told me, but I could understand why he would feel it wasn't his place. I was glad Zephyr was the one to tell me.

"Were you able to stick the landing?" he asked before taking a bite.

"Yeah. It took a while, but I think I've got it figured out. Now I've just gotta figure out how to not crash into trees."

I didn't want to tell him about the partial shifting we'd tried. It hadn't been successful, but I refused to give up. When I figured it out, then I'd show him.

Damien cleared his throat. "So, about the meeting with The Council..."

I gathered a bit of green beans onto my fork. "I guess I've got a lot to learn before then. It's tomorrow, right?"

He nodded. "Not too much. I just want you present at my side to listen in on the discussions. They need to see you, understand what your presence means and how it'll affect the war, that we have a chance to finish them once and for all if we can bring more warriors into The Order. I'm hoping they'll be encouraged to enlist help more proactively."

He took another bite of his food, chewing and swallowing, before continuing. "You're welcome to speak your mind, just... tread cautiously. Some of the newer heads of the houses have not had to answer to a female, and they've become unreasonable and rude in recent centuries. There's too much for me to teach you in a single day. There just isn't enough time."

I reached out to take his hand. "When is there ever?"

"I apologize in advance for what you might hear tomorrow. Most of them are rather reasonable, but there are a couple who don't like humans. We're going to show them that you're more than that. You're a demigoddess, regardless of whether you're immortal or human."

If I wasn't already nervous, I was now. A group of males who may or may not look down on me as a woman, and as a human? I knew nothing about the members of The Council, didn't know who they were or their names, but Calista and Zephyr had shared just how the aristocracy viewed females of the immortal race. We were objects for their benefit. They'd likely view me in the same light, demigoddess or not.

But I'd be damned if I let them look down on me.

I gripped his hand before releasing it to focus on my food. "So, I guess now's as good as any to start learning a bit more about this *council*."

Damien smiled, finished the last of his food, and rose to take his plate to the sink. "We'll start with learning the different houses for now, but we can wait until you've finished eating."

I took my last bite. "Perfect timing then, because I'm done."

He laughed under his breath as he washed his dish. "I wish I was this excited when I learned to rule as you are."

I set my plate on the counter. The tone in his voice, the emotion I felt in the air, sank into me. "You... didn't want to be king?"

He shook his head. "No. I never did." He took my plate to wash it but didn't meet my gaze. "But we don't always get to choose our paths. I know you understand that more than most."

I'd never thought he might not want to be what he was. I could only imagine the pressures of ruling an entire race, being responsible for their safety. How heavy that must weigh on his shoulders, especially given the losses they'd suffered over the centuries. For years, I'd bent to the will of others, allowing them to choose the best course for me, never taking the consideration to give me a choice. He'd been the first to let me choose my own path, and I loved him all the more for it.

He drew a deep breath. "That's for another time, though. Let's find a comfortable place to sit. There's a lot to go over."

I smiled as he took my hand, leading me to the living room.

"Before The Fall of Kingdoms there were nine houses, each in possession of a power bestowed by Selene and her allies."

My heart dipped as I remembered the horrid sight of the battlefield, the anguish Lucia had felt seeing her friends and family dead at her feet.

His eyes lowered, and he nodded. "House Latros, who were powerful healers, were wiped out during The Fall of Kingdoms. House Aíma, who could manipulate blood like Cole, was left with low numbers. The remaining few were killed off in the years following. One of the houses of power fell when the darklings first appeared centuries before."

"Which house fell when the darklings first appeared?" I asked.

The air grew thick with sorrow, his face somber as he answered my question. "House Skiá."

I frowned. That was Damien's house. "But..."

His face turned to me, and his smile didn't reach his eyes. "I am the last of my house. If I fall, The House of Skiá will cease to exist."

I didn't want to think about it, denied myself the opportunity to imagine a world where he didn't exist. "I won't let that happen."

He pressed a kiss to my forehead, my heart skipping at the tender sensation.

"So that means there'll be six house leaders tomorrow?"

"Yes, there will be six heads at the meeting, in addition to me. The heads of each house are referred to as Kyrios, and I want you to understand that, though you do not lead a house, you hold the same level of command I do as king. You are their queen; do not feel you have to put up with anything they say if you don't like it."

The title made my head spin. "No pressure."

"You're going to be fine, *mea luna*."

Was I, though? There was so much to absorb, to memorize. What if I messed something up, or confused one house for another? This meeting could lay the foundation for whatever I was to be as Damien's mate.

He took my hand. "I don't expect you to remember everything."

Of course, he didn't expect that of me, but I would have him go over the information again. I'd stay up late into the night until I felt I could speak with confidence if I needed to.

"There's one other thing I should warn you about before we continue." I tilted my head to look at him as he continued. "Calista's father sits on The Council. He's Kyrios of House Nóus."

My stomach flopped. "Calista told me a little about him."

"He'll be the one to watch out for. He's not particularly fond of me."

"Yeah, and I'm sure he won't be fond of me either, since I got in the way of his plans."

Damien frowned, brows furrowing. "Plans?"

"He's been trying to get you to take Calista as your wife—er… bonded in my absence."

His eyes flitted away from me as he tried to process the information. "That would have never happened. Why would he—"

"He hoped that she'd… give you an heir." My skin tightened at the thought, and the fact I'd never be able to experience that with him.

His fists clenched. "That fucking bastard. Nothing like that ever happened between us. It never would have."

"Well, he's refusing to accept Calista's wishes to be bound to Zephyr because of it."

121

Damien sighed. "I expect this meeting is going to be loads of fun."

"Yer gown is hangin' oan eh bed, love," Ethel said as she passed me in the stairwell the following morning. I hadn't seen Damien yet, and I wondered where he might be.

I frowned. "Gown?"

"Lord Damien brought it back fer ye. A gift from Lady Selene. Ah'll help ye intae it when yer ready."

Selene had gifted me a gown? Why?

"Thank you, *Mitera*."

She left me in the stairwell to see to her tasks, and I continued to our room.

We'd stayed up late last night going over details of the meeting, and I'd forgotten to set an alarm for myself. By the time Ethel had woken me for breakfast, Damien had already left.

So, that was where he'd been all morning. He'd gone to see Selene, probably to discuss things for the meeting. How did Selene play into it all? I knew Damien answered to her, but it seemed she didn't directly impose her will on immortal society, leaving them to govern themselves so long as they provided warriors to serve her.

I opened the door to our bedroom and froze in place as my eyes found the gown. *My* gown. It was more than I could've ever imagined, hanging delicately from the canopy of our bed. As pale and gray as the moon, the chiffon was inlaid with glittering, crystal jasmine flowers, shimmering vines adorning the bodice as they snaked down to the sloping skirts. I'd never worn a gown before, save the one I'd donned the first time I met Selene, but I'd been too shaken to even pay attention to it, let alone enjoy it.

Why would she give me a gown? I didn't think she even liked me. I hadn't seen her again after our first meeting. Perhaps something had changed in the months since we'd met. Maybe my training was enough for her to think me worthy of her attention. I wasn't sure how to feel about that.

The door opened, and I turned to see Damien enter the room, closing the door behind him. "Selene gave it to me for you to wear. You don't have to. If you prefer, you could wear your Elythian leathers."

I looked back at the gown, and I couldn't deny how stunningly beautiful it was. It was difficult to decide what would be best to wear. If I was to present myself at Damien's side as his equal, wouldn't it be better for me to dress the part? "What did I wear in the past?"

"You wore a gown."

I slid my fingers along the delicate chiffon. It seemed almost poetic if I were to stand up to these... males while wearing it, show them that even in a gown, a woman could be just as fierce as they were, just as deadly. I'd make Calista's father eat his words, and I could only imagine how it might enrage him.

I let the chiffon slip from my hand as I looked back at him. "Did Selene say anything about the gown?"

"She asked me to give you this." He held out an envelope, the paper shimmering with the seal of two warhorses over the fold. I opened the envelope and pulled the parchment free. I frowned at the name.

Moira,
For too long, have these Kyrios
gone without the rule of a queen.
Prove to these males that, though
beautiful, you are lethal.

A queen. I wasn't worthy of that title. Lethal? Did she really think that of me? It was strange to think the goddess I'd met a few months ago, one who'd written me off so easily, would send me a letter like this. Why did she call me Moira? I tilted my head to look at Damien. "Selene really wrote this?"

He nodded, uncertainty in his eyes. "What does it say?"

"She wants me to remind The Council of their place."

"*Shit,*" Vincent drawled as he lowered his hood, revealing his dirty blond hair that hung in loose curls just below his ears.

I stifled the giggle threatening to burst from my throat as he gaped at me in the foyer. Sometimes I forgot Vincent was an immortal and likely hundreds of years older than me.

His pale eyes widened. "Damien's gonna keel over when he sees you."

Barrett entered through the front door, his eyes lighting up when he saw me. It was in a way I'd never seen him look at me before. Close behind him were Thalia and Zephyr, clad in the armor warriors wore to hunt darklings with a half cloak hanging from their right shoulder. They all wore their Elythian leathers proudly, the black armor cloaking them in the same darkness they hunted in each night.

They carried different weapons than normal, though. Strapped to one side of their hips were black, ornately decorated short swords. They reminded me of Moira's sword sitting on display in our room. On their opposite thighs hung equally beautiful, yet deadly, black daggers, much like the ones we used to slay darklings. I took them in, armed and deadly, ready to keep peace at the meeting, ready to defend their king and his mate if the need arose, which almost worried me.

"Damn. Our little spitfire cleans up nice. I hardly recognized you without the dirt and grime on your face," Barrett said, taking my hand to twirl me around. The base of my skirts danced around my feet as I spun, and spontaneous laughter spilled from my lips, overriding the urge to roll my eyes.

Zephyr stepped through the door as Barrett released me, and he leaned in to lay a tender kiss to my cheek. Warmth filled my chest. "You look beautiful, Cas."

My heart leapt, and I wondered if it was Elena who felt overjoyed to hear those words from her brother. I wrapped my arms around his neck, hugging him tightly. "Thank you."

Ethel had worked wonders on my hair and makeup, and it honestly felt like I was looking at a different person in the mirror. My hair was pulled away from my face in braids that overlapped over the curls that cascaded down my back, leaving a few delicate strands of hair to sweep over my collarbones.

Thalia winked as she passed by, her cornsilk hair pulled back out of her face in a braid that stretched down her back, leaving the scar stretching down her right eye on full display. I couldn't help but notice that it seemed more visible, as if she'd been covering it with makeup all this time, but no longer did so. "Damien's a lucky male."

I giggled. "You got my back today, Thalia?"

"We've all got your back, Cas," Zephyr said with a striking calm. "Always." The tone in his voice was like a vow, like I'd never even had to ask it. I knew they'd always be there for me... no matter what.

"Selene made this gown for you?" Thalia asked, lifting the skirt to look at the delicate glittering fabric.

I looked down at myself. "Yeah."

I feared the gown might be heavy with all the material and crystals, but it had been crafted by a goddess, and it was nearly light as air. The neckline was an invisible layer of tulle, gemstone vines full of jasmine flowers breaking free on my breasts and shoulders, layers of tulle spilling out and down from my shoulders in long sweeps. I'd feared it might be too revealing, had nearly chickened out and decided not to wear it after all.

"You got a hidin' place for a dagger under all those layers of fabric?" Barrett whispered.

I crossed my arms, wondering how he'd guessed I had one of my daggers strapped to my thigh beneath the layers of chiffon and tulle. "If any Kyrios decide to piss me off, you just might find out."

A taunting grin crossed Barrett's face. "Twenty bucks says you chicken out."

"Probably not a good idea for Cas to off a Kyrios in her first meeting," Vincent said, kicking back in a nearby chair. Laughter poured from each of them as they continued to joke and place bets.

I opened my mouth to argue with Barrett's particular bet, but I didn't get the chance as Damien's voice drifted in from the stairway. "Fates spare me..."

I turned to him, brows raised. He stood at the foot of the stairs, his eyes wide as he took me in.

He wore all black attire I'd never seen him in before; a black coat decorated with intricate silver patterns along the collar and the hems of his sleeves. The coat reached down to his thighs, revealing sleek black pants and tall black boots. My gaze passed over the details of his coat, the material so complexly woven that when it hit the light just right, more patterns could be seen in the fabric.

He was breathtaking, positively beautiful.

"We'll be below when you're ready," Zephyr whispered in my ear as he and the others left Damien and me alone in the foyer.

I met Damien's gaze, his eyes holding a look of astonishment as they swept over me. Knots twisted in my stomach, my eyes falling to my dress as I inspected myself, suddenly self-conscious. "It's too much..."

"No," he said, approaching me.

My hand rose to my cleavage beneath the sheer fabric. "I was afraid it might be too much. It's really revealing, I feel so exposed."

"You're perfect, *mea luna*. The word beautiful is not enough." Damien pressed a kiss to my forehead, the velvet touch sending my heart into a frenzy. "It's like I'm reliving a memory. I knew you'd look stunning, but..."

My heart fluttered, and I couldn't resist asking. "What memory?"

"The first time I saw you in a gown... as Moira."

"Can you tell me more about it?"

His smile faltered for a moment, and I frowned. "Sorry, our relationship had a bit of a rocky start..."

Something twisted in my gut, and ice skittered down my skin.

"It was complicated, and I didn't deserve you, still don't think I deserve you to this day, but, when I saw you for the first time after we'd been apart, the sight of you... it was like the very earth had shuddered, like my reality had shattered and reforged itself with you as the center of my universe."

My chest swelled, and I smiled as he leaned his forehead to mine.

"I wish I could remember it all," I muttered.

"You will. In time."

My smile faded, my stomach dipping because not only did I feel I wouldn't have enough time to remember it all, his presence meant it was almost time. "I'm nervous."

He took my hand and gave it a reassuring squeeze. "You'll be fine. You're just there to observe. None of us expect you to navigate your way through the politics on your first day." He paused a moment, giving me a knowing look. "You've got your dagger on you, don't you?"

I didn't meet his eyes, biting back the smile forming on my lips. "I don't know what you're talking about."

He turned, tucking my arm under his as we headed down the hallway. "Just think carefully about who you use it on. I'd rather not have to clean up a mess today."

I giggled as we reached the door to the basement. We stepped down the stairs to The Propylaea where we would pass into the Godsrealm to Selene's temple and the chamber in which The Council met.

"You think this will go well?" Zephyr asked, looking at him as we entered.

The shadows were already beginning to dance around Damien, snaking out along the ground around us. "We'll see."

CHAPTER 16

CASSIE

The hall was colossal as we stepped through the arched entrance, the ceilings twenty feet high or more, and I nearly tripped over my dress as I took it in. I inhaled the faint scent of jasmine lingering in the air, but there were none of the delicate flowers in sight—in their place stood something magical.

Surrounding the hall, interlaced with the stone columns, stood those incredible glowing white trees I'd seen when I'd first met Selene. The branches were void of any leaves, the smooth bark nearly as white as the moon itself, and the pale glow of the trunks and branches cast a soothing light over the room.

Just how huge was Selene's temple? Were there other chambers like this?

The hall was empty, save for a long wooden table. It wasn't a man-made table, though. It was as if a tree had grown from the soil beneath the temple and formed the table before me, the marble floor cracked at its base where roots stretched out. Twists and knots decorated the pale trunk, coiling and twisting along the floor, the top smooth and flat.

On either side of the living table were eight stone chairs. At the top of each chair, different insignias were inlaid in stone, I assumed one for each house they represented. My eyes fell on the two larger, more ornate stone chairs sitting at the head of the table. They were so beautifully carved, with runes like the ones on Moira's sword, my dagger, and Damien's tattoo. A crescent moon adorned the head of one, and a swirl of black shadow was on the other, which I assumed was the insignia of House Skiá.

Thrones. They were thrones. A dull ache sank into my chest, my heart heavy. How many meetings had he suffered with an empty seat at his side?

We were early, but we weren't the first ones here. Damien hooked my arm in his, guiding me down the steps toward the large table where one of the Kyrios stood. A pair of guards I'd never seen before were speaking together near an arched entrance at the opposite end of the chamber.

Damien lowered himself to whisper in my ear. "You bow to no one here."

I stiffened, gripping his hand, and nodded. I had to remind myself that while this was The Council, and these were the heads of great houses of powerful immortals, I was mate to their lord, to their king. I was their demigoddess. I was their… queen.

God, did that thought leave my stomach in knots.

Those titles were heavy, and I could understand why Damien had never wanted his. Had any of these Kyrios known me in a past life? Would they have expectations of me? Ones I couldn't meet?

I couldn't let my nerves get the best of me, though as the male noticed our presence, turning to look over his shoulder, I willed the turmoil and nerves to calm within me. There was no room for weakness in this world, only strength.

This was only temporary. I just needed to help Damien convince them to volunteer more recruits. If we could just defeat the darklings, find peace… I could rest knowing Damien and the others were safe.

The male's smile lit up his blue-gray eyes when he saw Damien. "Damien Archonis," he said with a cheerful drawl. "It's been far too long, brother."

Damien released my arm to embrace him. "How've you been?"

"As well as I can be. Looks like I'll be rejoining you and The Order soon."

"We'll discuss that in due time." Damien glanced back at me, taking my hand, leading me to his side. "Xander, this is Cas."

His eyes found me, looking more intrigued than anything as he rubbed his hand against his rough, umber beard. A smile lit his bronze face, and he bowed. Blood rushed to my cheeks, but I didn't allow myself to refuse his gesture. This was the way it was, and I needed to adjust. I scanned my brain for all the information Damien had given me the night before, desperate to make a good first impression.

Xander... Xander. "The Kyrios of House Stoicheion," I stated, smiling. He was of the house Barrett and Vincent belonged to, the house of elementalists. Which element could he wield?

He lifted his head and brushed his medium length umber hair back from his face as he straightened. "I'm honored. Word spreads quickly, and the houses whispered of your return. It's a pleasure to meet you, my queen." My heart stuttered and my lips parted, but no response formed on my tongue. *My queen.* The title left me on unsteady legs, but I shoved it back.

He continued. "I could hardly believe the rumors true that you'd returned as a human, but let no one discredit your current form. You carry yourself like the goddess you are."

"You're too kind, Xander. Damien told me about you," I responded with a smile. "The—" Nerves derailed my train of thought, but I forced myself to calm. "Pleasure is mine."

He cocked a brow. "Good things, I hope." He glanced at Damien. "You didn't sell me out, did you?"

Damien fought the grin hinting at his lips. Xander's eyes drifted back to me, a devious grin spreading across his face. "I can tell you many stories of trouble we got into together over our centuries of friendship."

My smile became genuine, my nerves easing. "Now I'm curious."

Damien gave me an assuring squeeze of his hand and smiled sidelong at me. "You start sharing stories, and we'll miss the entire meeting."

Xander waved him off with a laugh before turning to me. "I hear you have a way with the flame."

I fought the sinking feeling in my chest. "It's coming along." It was a lie, but I didn't want to let on that I didn't have control yet. Would they view me as inferior?

Xander's pale eyes shifted as he noticed Barrett and the others lingering on the steps behind us, waiting for the meeting to begin. "I'm glad to see the brothers of The Order have managed to stick together all these centuries. Zephyr looks well. I'm still trying to convince Barrett to take my place as Kyrios so I can retire."

"Barrett?" I blurted, my gaze shooting to Damien.

Xander smiled. "I've been trying to convince him for years, but he keeps turning me down."

"He knows he'd have to step down from The Order if he took the role," Damien said. "You trying to steal my third in command, Xander?"

Barrett as the Kyrios of his own house. I knew he was talented, smart—but the heir to House Stoicheion? I could hardly wrap my head around it. I wondered if Damien feared he might accept. Barrett was a skilled warrior. If he left The Order, I knew it wouldn't be good for us, not with the possibility of war on the horizon.

"I'm not pressing him, Damien. I know how attached you are to him. The offer is there if he ever changes his mind, is all I'm saying." The smile faded from Xander's face, and his tone grew sympathetic as he cleared his throat. "I heard about what happened with Cole. I'm truly sorry."

Damien sighed. "I'm sure Tobias won't hesitate to bring it up today."

My mouth went dry, nerves kicking in. Tobias. Calista's father—the person I dreaded meeting. How would he act when he found me here, the one who'd derailed his plans?

Xander's face went just as sour as Damien's, and I was relieved he seemed to feel the same as we did. "Let him try. I'm just waiting for him to make one wrong move so I can put him in his place."

"He has a right to speak at the table as Kyrios," Damien said. "Regardless of how little we like it."

Xander sighed. "Sometimes, our laws are easily abused by those who aren't as kind as you or me, Damien. He's worked the system to his own benefit for too long."

"And here I thought I was early," a man's voice called from behind Xander, cutting the conversation short.

He was tall with smooth tawny skin, his silky black hair swept back out of his face. "Damien! Xander!" His eyes settled on me as he

131

stepped beside Xander, and for a moment there was a speculative look on his face, his brows furrowing as he gave me a once over but softened almost immediately. Damien's hand squeezed mine, but he showed no other outward reaction aside from that.

He bowed his head low, laying a kiss on my hand. "Cas, I presume."

I forced a smile, uneasy, and I shifted my weight from one side to the other. "And you are?"

"Forgive me, Your Majesty, I've forgotten my manners. I am Hector, Kyrios of House Psukhé."

I didn't know how many times I could handle being called majesty or queen, or whatever else. My skin heated, but I met his gaze with a smile. House Psukhé, the house that controlled objects with their minds. "It's a pleasure to meet you, Hector."

He turned his eyes to Damien, and the change in subject was unsettling, as if he'd just passed over our meeting to get to other more important things. "You didn't, by chance bring, any of that ambrosia liquor today, did you? I feel we're going to need it."

"Did Semele get another shipment?" Xander asked, suddenly onboard at the mention of alcohol.

"These meetings aren't for us to get drunk," Damien said, a crooked grin breaking across his face.

I slid a sideways glance to Damien before looking at Xander, a smile lacing my voice with humor. "Why do I get the feeling those stories you spoke involved a lot of ambrosia liquor?"

The words almost didn't feel like my own, and a strange confidence settled in my chest. I had noticed that with each new memory, the way I spoke had almost shifted, not quite formal, but just... different. Perhaps it was my past lives speaking through me, a *'merging'*, as Damien had described it. I hoped it would help me navigate whatever games the Kyrios might play, help me appear more like the goddesses who had ruled before me.

Xander laughed. "I'll make a deal with you: a story for a story. You tell me how a human rises to fight alongside the Lord of Shadows as his equal, and I'll tell you a story of how much trouble we got into when we broke into a God's personal stash of Godswine and brierleaf."

I slid a glance to Damien from the corner of my eye, biting my lip as I fought the smile spreading across my face. He met my gaze with a proud smirk.

Murmured voices echoed in from the entrance at the other end of the great room, and I lifted my eyes to find a pair of men entering together, so absorbed in their conversation that I wondered if they even noticed us. Briefly, I met one's eyes as he acknowledged our presence, and Damien politely excused us from Xander and Hector to lead me toward the newcomers.

"Good evening, Your Majesty," one said, lowering his head of brown hair to Damien before he lifted his pale eyes to me. "Lady Cas, I presume?"

My eyes passed briefly over his face. His hardened features hinted he was a seasoned warrior—three faint scars lined his left cheek, stretching over his jaw, leaving a path down his beard like claw marks. I wondered how he'd gotten them. Had he been scarred by the darklings?

Damien spoke for me when I struggled to think straight. "Your presumptions would be correct, Alec."

Alec. I thought through everything Damien had taught me the night before. He was the Kyrios of House Thiríon, the shifters, the house Zephyr and Thalia belonged to. "It's nice to meet you, Alec. I'm happy to finally meet the Kyrios of my brother's house."

Alec's brows rose, as if he was surprised I knew who he was. "Zephyr is an exceptional warrior, my queen. I'm proud to call him a member of my house."

So, he knew Zephyr was Elena's brother. I wondered how old Alec was—how old any of the Kyrios were. Had he been around to know me as Elena? As Lucia? The thought made me even more nervous in the ways I might be compared to them. They'd had a lifetime to prepare to rule and govern.

I'd had barely a couple months, and they hadn't been spent preparing to lead.

I glanced from the corner of my eye at the male standing idly by, listening and waiting. His black hair was cut short along his skull, and he was dressed in a coat of rich emerald that draped over his beautifully rich umber skin. His shoulders were squared, and he stood tall and proud, his face sharp yet so gentle, it seemed it had never been marred with hatred. He looked warm, kind, as if he'd nurture a person's very soul.

He lifted his hand. "Your Majesty," he said with an accent similar to Damien's as he dipped his head to me.

My gaze fell from his pale eyes down to the hand he extended, where a single seed lay. Green light shimmered to life in his palm, and a stem sprouted, twisting and growing until a bud formed. I drew a sharp breath as the bud burst into a full bloom of almost translucent petals, splashed with various shades of blues and grays.

I couldn't breathe as I watched the magic come to life before my eyes. He took hold of the bloom, handing it to me. "It is an honor to meet you, mate of my lord."

My eyes remained fixated on the delicate bloom as he placed it in my hand, captivated by the petals. It was like they had been painted with watercolors. I'd never seen a flower like it.

"It's a lunassia," he said with a gentle smile as if he knew the question lingering on my tongue. "They only grow in the Astral Mountains of the Godsrealm. I hope it pleases you, Goddess."

"Thank you. It's beautiful. It's a pleasure to meet you, Aster," I said with a smile, lifting my eyes to him. Damien told me of House Dendron and the power they wielded to manipulate plants. Recently, I'd found out Anna was of House Dendron, that she used it in her garden, but I'd never been able to see it. I'd struggled to grasp how exactly the magic worked. It made sense watching the power unveil itself before my eyes now. It was beautiful.

"I am honored you know of me," he responded.

"It's been too long," Damien said, wrapping his arms around Aster, who embraced him back.

"You've been busy. It is understandable," Aster responded.

"You visited the Godsrealm recently, I hear," Damien said.

I perked up at the statement, and Aster nodded. "I had the pleasure of meeting Persephone; I was able to tour her private gardens."

Persephone? *The* Persephone? My jaw nearly dropped at the casual mention of the goddess. I'd heard of her, though I really didn't know much when it came to Greek mythology.

"I can only imagine how wonderful that was," Damien said. I hadn't been able to see any part of the Godsrealm outside of Selene's temple, and I wondered what Persephone was like. It seemed Aster and Damien viewed her as one of the friendlier goddesses.

"If you're ever interested, perhaps we can plan a trip across the veil."

Eiko had said that word before. "The veil?"

"Yes, it's what separates the Godsrealm from the Mortalrealm," he explained with a warm smile. "I'd love to take you to the Astral Mountains. The hills come to life with these blossoms under the double moons during the lunar solstice."

"Double moons?" I asked, unable to stop myself.

Aster's eyes lit up, his gentle smile growing warmer. "They're beautiful, Your Majesty. The human's moon dwarfs by comparison."

I smiled, but the smile almost slipped from my face as realization dawned on me. I'd likely never get the chance. Damien stressed how dangerous the Godsrealm was for humans. I wondered if the creatures here might smell me the moment I set foot outside Selene's Temple. Would they hunt me down? I knew Selene's Temple resided in the Godsrealm, but I wasn't sure where exactly. I assumed she kept this place protected somehow.

"Alec. Keeping out of trouble, I hope," Damien said, and I took a deep breath, banishing the thoughts.

"You know I can neither confirm nor deny that," Alec said with a light chuckle.

They continued their conversation, catching up on old times. Alec shared the news of his mate's successful delivery of their firstborn. Aster shared more news of his visit to the Godsrealm, but I couldn't focus, my nerves getting the better of me as my gaze drifted.

Four of the six Kyrios had made their appearance. Xander, Hector, Alec, and Aster were all so kind, and obviously longtime friends of Damien's, which was a relief. I wondered when the last two Kyrios would show up. When Tobias would arrive.

Damien already expected him to cause a scene. He'd likely use Cole's betrayal in some twisted way. I quietly prayed Moira, Elena, and Lucia would give me the courage and the knowledge to have his back when that confrontation erupted—give me the confidence to speak in his defense and do what Selene wished of me.

"Gentlemen, I do believe it's time," Xander said from behind us, interrupting the conversation.

Damien nodded and took my hand, smiling as he placed a kiss on it. A commotion from the far entrance echoed into the hall. Damien glanced over my shoulder, and he didn't look too thrilled at the sight of who entered.

I followed his gaze. The moment I saw him, I knew where Calista had gotten her beautiful tan skin and dark golden hair. It was Tobias. He looked so young, possibly in his late twenties, even though I knew he was far older. It was difficult to imagine he was her father, but of course he looked so young; immortals didn't age past their prime, forever frozen in time.

My eyes followed the man walking with Tobias. I'd never seen a person like him. He was beautiful. Long white hair cascaded down over his back. His skin was pale, and his eyes... his eyes were a blend of pale purple and gray, the colors mixing and mingling together.

Damien leaned in to whisper in my ear. "Tobias is easy to spot, but the other male is Kyrios of House Leukós—Lysander."

House Leukós. They controlled some sort of light magic, like how Damien used shadow magic. Damien told me they were a rare bloodline with dwindling numbers. By his tone and expression, I assumed he and Lysander didn't get along, which was ironic, given he was a Lord of Shadows and Lysander was a Lord of Light.

Damien tugged at my arm, guiding me away from them. "Come, *mea luna*. We should find our seats."

My heart leapt into my throat. The meeting was about to start. The moment I'd been dreading all morning had arrived. I glanced back briefly at Tobias one last time, Damien leading me to our seats. For a moment, Tobias' eyes met mine—

And I couldn't hold his hateful glare.

CHAPTER 17

CASSIE

I eased into the stone chair as the Kyrios approached their seats around the live wood table. I couldn't shake the feeling that the floor might open up and swallow me whole.

Damien lowered himself into his seat beside me, leaning back as he laid his arms along the armrests. The weight he bore suddenly became more real seeing him take that throne, and I felt the annoyance radiate off him. I reached out through our thoughts.

I'm here at your side, mea sol.

His eyes softened, but he didn't meet my gaze.

Thank you, mea luna.

I maintained that connection with him, afraid to be alone with my thoughts. He must have felt it, for his voice reached out to me, so soft and gentle, it felt like a brush of his fingertips.

Be mindful of your thoughts. We don't know whose prying mind might slide in.

It was a gentle reminder there was another Nóus user among us now—one who likely didn't mind crossing boundaries. I ignored the urge to glance toward Tobias, to avoid drawing his attention to us, but I could already feel his gaze burning into me.

Xander offered me a smile of confidence as he took his seat nearby, and I smiled in return. The other Kyrios joined him, settling into their seats at the table, what appeared to be their own guards taking places at their sides. For some reason, the weight of the two empty stone chairs at the table was difficult to look at, the pain and sorrow of those losses leaving a hollow pain in my chest. I didn't know how much Lucia had witnessed during The Fall of Kingdoms, but the sorrow had imprinted so deeply into her soul that it affected me over a century later.

Would I regain all my memories of those lives? Would I have enough time to remember everything I shared with Damien? I wanted to dive into my memories as I'd done with Lucia, see if I could learn how they defeated Melantha, see if I could find any clues as to how we might destroy the darklings once and for all. I pulled myself from those thoughts, though. I couldn't dwell on it. I needed to focus now, on this moment, needed to pay attention in case Tobias attempted to read my mind.

Barrett, Vincent, Zephyr, and Thalia took their places at each corner of the table, their faces unreadable, only the masks of guards who'd tolerate no moves against their king… and queen. Thalia and Vincent stood at the far corners of the table, Zephyr at Damien's side as his right hand, and Barrett at mine.

"You've got this, spitfire," Barrett whispered, barely loud enough for me to hear. His watchful eyes remained on the Kyrios seated at the table.

I smiled, straightening, happily accepting the vote of confidence he'd offered.

I understood why Damien dreaded these meetings. The first hour had been spent going over statistics, each Kyrios sharing tedious details of any occurrences in their houses, disputes, resolutions, and anything in-between. They spoke of how many immortal offspring had been born last year, whether the number of successful births were increasing or falling. There was also a brief discussion of improvements in their medical practices which had increased the survival rate of females during labor and delivery. I couldn't help but wonder what would have happened if those practices had existed when I'd given birth to Emilia. Would I still be alive as Lucia, living my life with Damien and Emilia?

Emilia. I had to swallow back the sorrow creeping into my chest. I could only imagine how wonderful it would have been to live that life with Damien, with her.

Damien's hand took mine, and I stiffened. His thumb brushed over my skin tenderly, the touch rippling over me in a calming wave. We were sitting so close, I wondered if he could feel my sorrow through the bond. I blinked, pulling myself from the depths. I lifted my eyes as Thalia and Zephyr took turns reporting information on The Order.

It was almost too much to bear listening to. To hear how many humans had been devoured or converted by the darklings left my stomach in knots. Given the vision I'd seen in Cole's memories of the darklings' nest and the growing army, it barely scratched the surface of the true number. My heart ached for the people searching for missing family members.

Family who would never come home.

Thalia was speaking now, and I watched her intently, trying to absorb every bit of information I could. She held her head high as she spoke, proud and unyielding, powerful, and just as formidable as any of the male warriors standing at this table.

I hadn't acknowledged him, but I'd felt Tobias' stare intermittently throughout the presentation. There was no telling if he would try to use his abilities on me, but I hadn't felt any sign of someone trying to enter my mind.

Damien squeezed my hand gently, and I could feel the annoyance through our touch. He knew Tobias had placed a target on me the moment he'd entered the room. I wondered how Tobias might use me to get at Damien, what his game would be. Regardless of what his plans were, I'd do everything in my power to fight him.

"We know the numbers," Tobias huffed, interrupting Thalia on the tail end of her report. Her eyes widened slightly as she gaped at him. Heat crawled over my skin.

"Have you no manners, Tobias?" Xander glared at him from across the table.

"We've got more important things to discuss," Tobias said.

My spine stiffened, unease settling into the pit of my stomach.

Before anyone could make a remark, Tobias turned to Damien. "What're you doing about the attack on the civilian family? Darklings have never invaded a home like that. They're getting smarter. If we don't do something soon, they'll be dragging families out until none of us are left."

Damien leveled his gaze on Tobias, his face a mask of calm and calculation. "We're searching for the darkling nest. I already sent out instructions to relocate and secure any civilians who haven't already been moved."

"What about the traitors? I'll bet they're the ones who gave their location away," Tobias snapped back.

Barrett tensed at my side, his hand twitching faintly against the hilt of his sword. The traitors... We knew this was going to come up, but I didn't know how to respond to that.

"How many secrets did Marcus and Cole give the darkling queen?" Tobias barked. "How many more traitors hide amidst the ranks of *your Order*?"

Our Order? Vincent, Thalia, Barrett, and Zephyr tensed at the accusation, gripping the hilts of their swords tightly. As if The Order wasn't something that existed to protect us all, immortal and human alike—to protect him. His attempt to sow distrust disgusted me, but I couldn't deny the possibility was a fear I'd harbored. I'd just been too afraid to acknowledge it. How could we tell who was truly an ally? How many more had Marcus coaxed to their side?

"The warriors' vows are not so easily broken," Damien rebutted. "Your queen herself put an end to Marcus for his betrayal of The Order."

I shoved down the horror crawling over my skin at the mention of Marcus' death and held my head high, eyes forward.

"*My queen*," Tobias scoffed under his breath, and a muscle flexed in Damien's jaw, his eyes growing colder.

"It is a valid concern," Aster said in the gentlest way possible. "We'll have to find a way to validate all the serving warriors."

A wave of uncertainty washed over me. How would we even begin to verify that every warrior currently serving hadn't been working for Marcus? The warriors of The Order weren't the only ones who could switch sides. It could be anyone, warrior or civilian.

"What about Cole?" Lysander chimed, tilting his head to us from across the table, his white hair held back by the intricate braids draped across the back of his head. "He needs to be tried for his crimes."

Damien didn't respond. My skin heated, irritation growing within me. They spoke as if it was Damien's fault that Cole betrayed The Order. Damien had been working overtime to combat what was coming for them, had sacrificed so much to fight the darklings. We should be working together to figure out a way to bring them down. This wasn't the time to battle for whatever power they hoped to gain by turning on Damien.

"Personally, I'd prefer he be executed on sight," Lysander said. "But the families of those he's had a hand in killing deserve to see him sentenced to the fullest extent." He settled his chin on his hand. "Death may be too kind."

"I heard he escaped The Order," Alec said, a genuine question, his tone not as tainted as Tobias' and Lysander's had been. "Have you located him?"

Zephyr answered as second in command. "We're working to locate him. We've found some leads and are closing in on him."

I glanced toward him briefly. Was he telling the truth? Had they found leads? Damien hadn't mentioned anything, but I'd been so busy with training. I hadn't been involved in the search.

"You sure are taking your sweet time fixing this, Damien," Tobias drawled, and a realization crossed my mind. Was he challenging Damien? Questioning his ability to lead as king? Could they remove him from his seat? *Oh my God*… had they planned this from the beginning?

Zephyr growled a warning at Damien's side. "That's '*Your Majesty*' to you."

"And what would you do if you were in his place?" Xander said, coming to Damien's defense. "I don't see you joining in the search."

Tobias leveled a glare at the Kyrios of House Stoicheion, but when he opened his mouth to speak, Xander continued. "No, you're too absorbed in your aristocratic parties and frivolous lifestyle to care. I doubt you could bring down a single darkling, let alone the number our king, our queen, and their warriors face every night."

"We need more recruits," Damien said, cutting into their argument. A strange feeling resonated through me, like a string growing taut, as if it were wound so tight it might snap. Was this the bond he'd mentioned? It was different from the way his emotions felt. I didn't understand it, but I could *feel* his patience waning. I offered a reassuring squeeze of his hand.

Their heads all turned to him, silence falling.

Damien continued. "Anyone willing to fight, willing to train, male or female. It doesn't matter if they have use of magic or not. We will need every able-bodied warrior to fight the darklings. Cas saw a vision of the darkling nest. We stand to face hundreds of them. It could be months; it could be days. At this moment, it's unclear when, where, and how many will attack us. We haven't been able to ascertain how powerful the darkling queen is yet, or what manner of beasts she'll summon from the Godsrealm to fight at her side this time."

Dread crawled over my skin. I'd never thought that she could summon creatures from the Godsrealm, but of course she could. Like Damien, she was a descendant of House Skiá.

She could summon shadow beasts.

My blood chilled as I remembered some of the creatures Damien had told me of, how powerful and horrible they were. The vision of the monstrous six-legged wolf Lucia and Damien had encountered flashed in my mind. Would she summon creatures like that? Or worse?

A user's level of magic dictated just how powerful a beast they could summon. How large the creature would be or how many there were. Melantha wasn't bound by the same limits the immortals were. She could tap into the full power the darkness offered. If an immortal crossed that limit, they would lose themselves to the darkness. Whether they'd become a darkling or something worse, I didn't know. Damien had told me she was limitless—more powerful than him.

I shuddered just imagining it.

"More fodder for you to throw to the darklings? Is that really your approach?" Tobias dared to say. "Was it not enough for you to get my sister killed?"

Damien stiffened, and I winced as that taut string I'd felt turned icy. I glanced at him from the corner of my eye to find a muscle ticking in his jaw, and I held back the urge to ask.

"Vivienne was slaughtered on your watch due to your incompetence. I know you won't care if it happens to the rest of my house," Tobias bit out, and I felt my blood pool in my feet. Vivienne was his sister?

I'd noticed it when I'd first met Calista, how much she resembled Vivienne. She was her niece. My eyes slipped to Damien. I could only imagine how badly that statement hurt him, and the aggravation that flared within me was difficult to squelch. Damien had never forgiven himself for Vivienne's death, and this bastard would use his own sister to get under Damien's skin. I took his hand in quiet reassurance without turning my narrowed gaze from Tobias.

Damien drew a deep breath, squeezing my hand in return. He didn't give Tobias the satisfaction of a response as he turned to Alec and the others. "They would be given the same training as any warrior. Anyone who wants to take a stand to defend their families will be given a fighting chance. Whether they use it to fight at our side when the time comes or to defend their family in their own homes, it will be their decision in the end. I will not suffer them to die defenseless under the darklings' claws."

The Kyrios all pondered silently.

"I won't send more of my house to die," Tobias spat.

I shot up so fast, I hadn't the time to think it through. "Why not give them that choice? It should be their decision to make."

Damien's eyes flitted to me, but he maintained that mask of calm confidence. If he showed even a sliver of doubt in my decision to speak up, it would be an easy target for Tobias to attack—to further divide.

Tobias growled, eyes like daggers as he spoke, enunciating each word as if he were scolding a child. "Because it is my decision to make as Kyrios." He seemed infuriated that I'd even spoken.

"Coward," I spat, my skin growing hotter as I stared him down. Barrett tensed at my side, the cool air growing warmer and warmer by the second.

Tobias' nostrils flared as he shot to his feet, his hands slamming on the table as the venomous words spilled from his mouth. "How dare you even speak to me! You tarnish the name of the goddess you claim to be, human filth! You are no queen of mi—"

My body went rigid as the weight of my dagger vanished from my thigh. A loud thud rang out across the hall as Damien sank the blade into the wooden table, black mist and smoke dancing around it as my dagger manifested in his hand.

He stared at Tobias from across the table, his eyes cold and murderous. "Perhaps I should remove that tongue of yours."

CHAPTER 18

CASSIE

My eyes flickered to Damien as I tried to maintain a calm expression on my face despite my heart threatening to burst. I glanced at Tobias, whose wide eyes were locked with Damien's, his guard frozen at his side, hand on his sword. Who did he ultimately serve? Would he draw a weapon against Damien or stand by? Sweat beaded on Tobias' brow, and though he tried to hide his fear, his golden skin paled.

The hilt of my dagger groaned in Damien's grasp as he clenched it tighter. It wasn't a threat. Dear God... he'd really do it.

"I'd be honored to carve his tongue out myself, Lord Damien," Barrett said from my side. His eyes were also locked on Tobias, his hand on the hilt of his sword. The formality of the title sounded strange as it fell from Barrett's lips, but I knew the role he took at this table.

Thalia and Vincent watched us carefully from the far end of the table, waiting for whoever would make the first move. Zephyr remained solid as stone at Damien's side, his eyes as cold and hardened as Damien's.

My pulse pounded in my ears, and I feared my heart might burst.

Tobias combed his fingers through his hair and he straightened his coat. "If I'd known it was humans you craved, I wouldn't have wasted my time sending Calista your way. Perhaps it could've been any human whore willing to spread her legs."

My cheeks heated, and Damien's body tightened next to me. Barrett and Zephyr stood frozen at our sides, their bodies wound tightly, but they didn't move.

The air around me felt hot, my blood boiling at his statement, not just for Damien, but for Calista who'd been given no choice in what was to happen in her life. The thought of another woman touching Damien awoke some strange sensation in my chest, and that overwhelming presence of Moira and all her reincarnations echoed in the back of my mind.

Mine.

I drew a deep breath, trying to squelch the flame threatening to come to life. The last thing we needed was for me to burn the place down. My eyes opened, shifting back to Tobias, who was still watching Damien. Was he testing him? Seeing how far he could push him?

Tobias smiled when Damien didn't respond. "Perhaps I'll just bind her to another. Let you enjoy your human cun—"

Cold air descended around Damien. The shadows beneath us shifted as black mist and shadow enveloped him. He vanished from his throne before I knew what had happened and slammed Tobias back into his seat as he appeared before him. His knuckles paled around the hilt of my dagger as he sank the blade through the back of Tobias' hand, pinning it to the stone.

Tobias barked a gasp, and Damien shoved his hand into Tobias' mouth, pulling his tongue between his lips. Tobias sputtered unintelligible words as Damien yanked my dagger from Tobias' hand, rich red liquid dripping from the blade and gushing from the wound.

The guard at Tobias' side grabbed his hilt, but before he could draw his weapon, Zephyr was there, dagger pressed to his throat. The guard froze, eyes shifting to Zephyr. It was faint, almost unnoticeable, but Zephyr hesitated. His jaw tightened, his throat bobbed, and his dagger quivered as his blade hovered in front of the guard's throat. The guard seemed unfazed, as if he were in control. I stiffened and shot to my feet.

Release him.

The guard's eyes shot to me, wide, and the color draining from his face.

I ground my teeth together, skin burning as I held his gaze. Of course, the guard was a Nous user. Zephyr would be defenseless against his influence. Zephyr's shoulders relaxed, his body easing. I forced my way into the guard's thoughts, temptation clouding my vision as I shoved the warning into his mind.

Unless you want to slit your own throat, you will surrender.

The guard swallowed, releasing the hilt of his sword, and lifted his hands in surrender. Zephyr quickly released the harness securing his sword and disarmed him. I relaxed, settling back into my chair, glancing at Barrett, whose brows furrowed as he looked between Zephyr and me. Would I have done it? Would I have actually made the guard end his own life? I looked at Zephyr, his pale green eyes lit with thanks as they met mine briefly.

If it meant saving him, I would have.

Damien hadn't spared the guard a look, his eyes locked on Tobias. "That's three times you've insulted my mate, your queen. What more would you say? Go on, Tobias. I'm listening."

Tobias remained silent, his eyes wide with terror.

Damien continued when Tobias didn't say anything, his tone full of a cold calm. "Did you know there's a vital artery in a person's tongue, Tobias?"

Tobias' body quaked under Damien as he continued. "Have you ever seen a man bleed out when it's cut?" Damien laid the black and gold blade across Tobias' tongue. "I wonder if you'd die from blood loss, or if you'd choke on your own blood first."

Tobias shrieked, tears welling in his eyes as he begged wordlessly.

I couldn't speak, couldn't pull my eyes away. Barrett placed a hand on my shoulder and I jumped, looking up at him. His eyes were glued to Damien, but he didn't look fearful. No, he looked confident, prideful even. I reached out to his thoughts.

Should we stop him?

No. This needs to be done. Tobias will never stop, and if Damien allows him to get away with insulting you, his queen, as well as insulting him and questioning his role at this table, it will show him Damien is weak. This is how things are done here, Cas. Trust in your mate.

I willed myself to breathe deeply, my head held high as I looked back at Damien. He held Tobias' gaze, dark power rolling off him in waves. Tobias sputtered as pearls of blood formed where my blade met the flesh of his tongue.

Tobias muttered frantic words I could barely make out as apologies or pleas to stop.

None of the Kyrios moved. If anything, Lysander looked to be the only one who looked nervous. The others—Xander, Hector, Aster, and Alec—all stood by their king in his decision.

Damien released Tobias' cut tongue. Tobias' bloodied hand rose to his face, the rich liquid dripping onto his dark purple coat.

"Know that I spare you your sharp tongue as a favor to your daughter who has only ever honored me," he said as he stepped back, wiping the blood from my blade across Tobias' pants. He turned and walked back toward me as he adjusted his coat, and Zephyr released the guard, sheathing his dagger before following. "You are relieved of your title as Kyrios, Tobias, and are no longer welcome in this hall."

"Who would you hope to replace me? I've been in this seat for over a century," Tobias muttered, still trembling.

Damien didn't answer, not bothering to give him a second glance.

As Tobias opened his mouth to speak again, a thought crossed my mind. I took a deep breath, holding my head high. I'd never felt more confident in any decision I'd ever made, and I spoke, cutting off any words he'd planned to say.

"Perhaps Calista should take your place."

CHAPTER 19

DAMIEN

Silence swept across the hall, the Kyrios all snapping their heads toward Cassie the moment the words left her lips. I almost couldn't stop the smile fighting to spread its way across my face as I left Tobias shaking in his chair.

Well played, mea luna.

She didn't waver, her head held as proudly as any of her past lives had done, and I wanted to kiss her. My mate. My queen. *Mine*, and mine alone.

"W-what?" Tobias stuttered, and I resisted the urge to look and see just how red his face must have been. I almost hoped he'd try to take a step toward her, say another word or threat so I could slit his throat once and for all.

She continued, her voice as solid as the stone throne she sat in. "I'll say it again, since you seem to be hard of hearing, Tobias. Perhaps Calista can take your seat at The Council. With all the new free time you'll have, maybe you can join our ranks in The Order, since you seem to know how to bring down the darklings."

"A female has never sat on the council," Lysander said, almost an argument, but he was smart enough to keep his tone in check.

She leveled her gaze on Lysander. "*A female* has ruled at your king's side for centuries, has fought and destroyed more darklings than you could ever hope to." Her eyes drifted to each of the Kyrios as she continued, her chin held high like the goddess she was. "Perhaps it's time I'm not alone at this table."

She drew a deep breath, and I wondered what was swirling in that beautiful mind of hers. "There will be a change to the laws limiting the lifestyles of females within the aristocracy."

My pace slowed as I neared the head of the table, and for a moment I saw her, all of her, each of her past lives sitting on that throne, as if she'd never missed a day in that seat. The pride swelling within me was immeasurable.

Tobias scoffed. "This certainly doesn't seem like the time to be worrying about such thin—"

"What change are you proposing, Your Majesty?" Xander inquired, paying no mind to the male who no longer held any sway at the table. Tobias stiffened, his lips peeling back from his teeth.

"The laws that place a female of the aristocracy under the rule of another who might exploit her," Cassie said, shifting her gaze to Xander.

I lowered myself into the seat beside her, my gaze drifting across the table, gauging the reaction to her statement.

"You would abolish laws put in place to ensure the safety of those who would carry the future of our race, traditions and laws that have existed long before you were born?" Tobias spat.

The fact that he remained at the table irritated me to no end, and I cleared my throat. Something hummed in the air around Cassie as she leveled her gaze on Tobias, something I'd only felt when Cassie had attacked Calista, when her past lives had spoken through her. They seemed to be influencing her, guiding her, the scattered pieces of her soul fitting into place when she needed them most.

"I would change barbaric and misogynistic practices that hinder our people and do nothing to help our efforts."

Our people. Something built in my chest at the words she'd chosen.

"The truth of the matter is, these practices were put in place when our race faced the possibility of extinction," I said. All eyes shifted to me, and guilt curdled my stomach. "I should've never allowed such a law to pass, but fear and grief pushed me to allow those on the council at the time to make poor choices on behalf of our people. It's time these laws changed. I expect you all to be prepared to discuss these changes at the next meeting."

Tobias opened his mouth to speak, but I didn't give him the chance. "Do not make me repeat it a third time, Tobias. You're relieved of your title as Kyrios. Your presence here is no longer needed. I expect your things to be removed from the house provided to you by the end of the week."

I leaned my elbows on the table and rested my chin on my interlaced fingers as I locked eyes on him. Tobias gaped at me and turned to look at Lysander, as if expecting him to speak in his defense, but Lysander wouldn't meet his gaze.

He rose slowly, eyes lowered, hands trembling in fists at his side. Before he disappeared through the doorway, he muttered under his breath, so low I almost didn't hear it.

"You'll regret this..."

I glanced at Cassie, whose eyes remained fixed on the doorway where Tobias had vanished, our bond humming with the flames surging within her, the power reflecting in her expression. Pride wasn't a strong enough word for how I felt about her. She'd handled herself better than I could've ever imagined.

"We shall vote on the new Kyrios of House Nous," I said, and she turned her gaze to me, a subtle light of triumph in those hazel eyes.

I looked at the remaining Kyrios. "You all know Calista. She is a fine female, smart and well versed in our laws. Those in favor she be presented the option to become Kyrios of House Nóus?"

It was Xander whose hand rose first, followed by Aster, Alec, and Hector. Lysander hesitated, but his hand rose.

"Good. It's unanimous. Cas and I will present the terms to her. Should she accept, we will reconvene with her at the next meeting, where we will discuss the changes to the laws."

The meeting ended shortly after Tobias' dismissal. The Kyrios openly accepted the terms to offer any male or female the option to train and fight with The Order. Details of the training were laid out, and the Kyrios were to reconvene to discuss the new laws, hopefully with the new Kyrios of House Nous. I still felt uneasy about Tobias' words as he left, and I resisted the regret blossoming in my chest at the fact that I hadn't cut him down.

The taps of Cassie's shoes echoed off the stone walls as we walked side by side through The Council's chambers. Zephyr and the others had left to return to the mortal realm, leaving Cassie and me to explore Selene's temple before we returned home.

Cassie's fingers glided over the knots and twists woven into the surface of the Stonetree table. "That was an interesting first meeting."

A grin cracked across my face. "I wish I could've taken a picture of Tobias' face when you called him a coward."

She giggled, and I basked in that sweet sound. Gods, just when I thought I had her figured out, she would throw me for a loop. She'd been so reserved when I first found her, yet today, she shared just how sharp that tongue of hers could be.

"I would have it framed and mounted on the wall," I added.

"Right next to his tongue on a plaque. The guy looked terrified." She chuckled as she linked her arm with mine, the skirts of her silver gown dancing across the marble with each step.

Her smile faded, and I hated to see it go. "Was Zephyr telling the truth when he said you guys got a lead on Cole?"

My thoughts halted, and I swallowed. "He was. Not enough to give us his whereabouts, but…" Pain crept into my chest, raking through me like claws. "Thalia picked up his scent at the house where the immortal family was taken. It led to the woods, but then vanished."

The news tore at the wound of his betrayal, and I was relieved Marius and Farah didn't still live to see what their son had become, the terrible things he'd done. My gaze flitted back to Cassie, her expression a mass of conflicting emotions.

"You made a good call," I said, all too eager to change the subject.

Her chestnut brows rose as we neared the arched entrance to the halls.

"When you recommended Calista to take his place. I think it will be a step in the right direction to have a female on The Council. I don't think I could've made a better call, and while now may not be the time to focus on other laws, there may never be a good time. So, we must move to make things better for everyone while we can."

She gave a half smile, eyes going distant as she looked forward. "I want things to change. Calista knows what it's like for females of the aristocracy. If there's anyone who would know how to better things, it's her."

"I agree."

"Zephyr's going to tell her about what happened at the meeting, right?" she asked, and I could feel the anxiety spiraling within her. "I hope she's not upset I brought her into this."

I wished I could take that worry from her. She held far too little confidence in herself. I nodded. "He'll fill her in so she isn't blindsided, and we'll discuss it with her more later tonight."

"I hope she accepts."

"Me too, *mea luna.*"

CHAPTER 20

CASSIE

I struggled to absorb the beauty of Selene's temple as we emerged from The Council's chamber: the intricate stone architecture, vines full of night blooming jasmine climbing the pillars and walls, and those beautiful pale, glowing trees—

They were mesmerizing.

"What are these called?" I asked, reaching out to touch the delicate, glowing bark. It was so smooth under my fingers, velvety and oddly warm.

"Dimós trees," Damien answered. "There are some in this world believed to have existed before the first Elythian. They say the first dimós tree sprouted from a tear shed by Celestia when she cast out her mate for his betrayal."

I tilted my head. "Celestia?"

"The deity the Elythian's worship."

 Gods worshipping gods… "How long have the Elythians existed?"

"I honestly don't know. This pantheon isn't the first, nor is it the only still in existence. There are records of the first race who descended from the stars—the children of Celestia. When they first laid claim to the lands of the Godsrealm, there was a split, and that was when the different pantheons were born."

"Pantheon?" I asked, cocking an eyebrow.

"It's what we call this"—Damien pondered his response—"Generation, I guess you could say. There are different continents within the Godsrealm, all ruled by different pantheons. The Elythians rule Elythia."

The Godsrealm seemed to be more like the Mortalrealm than I'd originally thought. I couldn't imagine it, different pantheons… different gods? Was it not only those worshipped by the greeks that resided in the Godsrealm? Were there other deities that had been worshipped?

"I know you said House Skiá had a history of nearly two thousand years, so has this Pantheon of Elythians been around for a similar length of time?" I ran my hand along the silky bark. My gaze followed the length of the tall trunk to the delicate bare branches stretching out above us, nearly bridging the gap to the dimós trees on the other side of the hallway.

"Longer. Eons, if we were to try to measure the span of time," Damien answered casually.

"Eons?" I said, jerking my gaze to him. "Eons that's—what?" I was horrible at math. How long was an eon?

He chuckled at me. "Hundreds of thousands of years, probably even longer." He took my arm, tucking it into his as he guided me back down the hall.

My brain jumped in so many directions. I couldn't even try to comprehend just what it would be like to live that long. "That's… *insane*."

"You have no idea the insanity of this realm."

"I couldn't imagine living that long." My eyes fell to the marble floor as we continued down the hall, the veins of sparkling silver and gold stretching and branching out in different directions. I wasn't sure if it would be amazing to live that long or terrible.

"It's the reason they tend to lose touch with their... humanity?" His brows furrowed, as if he wasn't sure that was the right word. "Life isn't as significant to them because of their long lifespan. Everything is replaceable in their eyes. Don't get me wrong, there are some gods and goddesses who are kinder, still appreciative of the beings around them, but there are many who would watch life flicker out before them without batting an eye."

I tilted my head to him. "You told me Selene was once very kind."

"She was." His eyes grew distant. "When I was little, she used to play with me in the gardens of our kingdom. Before you were born— er, before Moira was born."

"Kingdom?" I came to a stop. "Did the immortals not always live in the Mortalrealm?"

He realized I'd stopped and turned back to me. "We used to reside in the Godsrealm. Our home was the Kingdom of Lunoscia."

The immortals didn't always live in the human world? I shouldn't be surprised by that, but... why? How had they ended up there? He smiled softly, but it was somber. A deep ache sank into my chest, and I couldn't understand why.

"We did before The Darklings' Descent." His gaze drifted away from me, dulling. "After Matthias fell, we hunted the darklings until they passed into the Mortalrealm. Selene tasked us with eradicating them to prevent the human world from falling into darkness, and here we are today."

"Darklings' Descent?" I asked, head tilting to gaze up at him.

Damien drew a deep breath, as if preparing himself for what he was about to share. "When Matthias became corrupted and the first darklings attacked, destroying our home..."

The sorrow filling his eyes was too much to bear. I wanted to know more, wanted to ask, but I couldn't bring myself to push. I wondered if the vision I'd seen through his eyes of Moira when we'd begun training was from the time Damien spoke of, when the immortals were prosperous, ruling their own kingdom in the Godsrealm. I could only imagine how wonderful that time might've been. I'd looked so happy through his eyes. I wouldn't press, though, couldn't stand to pull him through the difficult memories of the kingdom's fall.

"What's going to happen to the humans in the city when things get worse?" I asked, unable to resist asking the question that had been burning in the back of my mind for months. Recalling the terrible night of Elena's death, I couldn't stomach the thought of suffering that fate again, watching my home, my family, my friends all die. My mind wandered to my parents, to Kat and Cody. How could I protect them from something like that? Would I even be able to help them when the time came if I'd failed as Elena?

Would I live long enough to face Melantha at Damien's side?

"I fear for them." Damien let out a ragged sigh, and his words pulled me from the spiral of doubt. "We can use our influence to try to evacuate as many as we can without revealing the truth of everything, but I fear many will die. The humans living nearby were caught in the crossfire when we fought Melantha during The Fall of Kingdoms, and we were left with a tremendous mess to clean up. There was so much destruction, we had to create a natural disaster to cover it all up."

I halted, my brows furrowing. "You... created a natural disaster?"

He nodded. "The Johnstown flood of 1889. The two thousand humans who died in the flood were really casualties of the war. We had no other option to clean up the mess in a way that would cover up any proof of our existence. Any survivors had their memories altered. We couldn't risk the humans learning of our race."

My heart sank. I hadn't connected the dots, counted the years. I swallowed. Two thousand people... slaughtered, not drowned.

"I need to get my family out of the city."

Damien frowned and his lips parted, as if he might say something, but didn't.

"What?" I dared to ask, hopeful for anything that could be done to keep my family safe.

"We have connections. If you could somehow convince them to leave, I could pull some strings, get your parents jobs elsewhere—somewhere safe. They'd be well cared for."

A thought crossed my mind. "Are there darklings elsewhere?"

He shook his head. "We've only seen darkling activity here in Johnstown. There's been signs in the cities surrounding us, but very minimal, as if they won't go any farther."

"Why, though? What keeps them here?"

He shrugged. "We aren't sure. I think there's a ripple in the veil somewhere, where they slipped through when they fled from the Godsrealm. Perhaps it's the subtle hint of magic lingering around Johnstown, leaking through the ripple in the veil."

"There's magic in the air in Johnstown?"

Damien nodded. "Not enough to affect anything, but it does draw in creatures. Think of it like tossing a raw piece of meat in the woods. Predators would be drawn in by the smell."

If he could relocate my parents, they'd truly be safe from the darklings. There was no way I'd ever be able to convince them to leave, though, not with me here. My mother would never leave me behind.

"Sadly, I don't think I could convince them to leave that house behind for all the money in the world." I sighed. "You mentioned Selene changed. What happened?" I asked, shifting to a different subject.

Damien eyed me warily. "I don't know. No one does. It wasn't long after you were born that she changed, growing so cold and distant with those who once loved and cherished her." He came to a stop as we neared the end of the hall.

"How did we meet?" I asked, and his brows rose, as if he were surprised by the question.

He smiled then, those amber and ashen eyes lighting with... endearment? "I was five when we met."

Five. What did Damien look like as a child? I couldn't fight the smile tugging at my lips as I imagined it. Bouncing black-brown curls, those intense, full eyebrows that amplified every expression that danced across his face. He probably got into the most trouble.

"I'll show you."

I stiffened as he leaned in, pressing his forehead to mine. "Are you sure?"

He smiled, closing his eyes in silent confirmation.

Hesitation stiffened my body, but my lids fell shut, feeling that connection, that bridge between us. I reached out, slipping into his thoughts, warmth washing over me. When I opened my eyes, I was... I was elsewhere, standing in a hall of warm sunshine, the smell of lush forest and stone filling my lungs. Tall, stained-glass windows broke up the walls around me. Depictions of battles and creatures filtered the sunlight shining through the panes. It was similar to the place I'd first seen Moira through Damien's memories, the only vision I'd ever been able to see of Moira. Her memories had remained unreachable, and I couldn't seem to figure out why.

"Damien."

I turned to the gentle call of my name. No, not my name. This was Damien's memory, not my own. It was still strange how my mind melded with his as I gazed through his eyes.

A strange sensation rose in my chest as I found her, sitting at the far end of the room from where I stood in the doorway.

158

Selene.

She was beautiful, with milky white hair splayed around her as she sat before me. The light fell against her back, illuminating her as her moon-like skin refracted the sun's glow. There was something different about her, and I suddenly understood what Damien meant. There was an air of kindness, warmth, love surrounding her, and her soft blush lips curved in a gentle smile.

A tall man clothed in black stood at her side, but I couldn't make out his features, his face almost obscure as he observed us. Perhaps I couldn't see his face because Damien himself couldn't remember or hadn't paid attention to him as a child.

Who was he?

"Goddess!" Damien's tiny voice sang out as I—he bounded for her.

In her arms was a tiny bundle of shimmering cloth, the fabric laced with starlight. She shifted in her cushioned chair, her white silken gown dipping and shifting against the curves of her body, down the swell of her belly, which wasn't as full as it had been the last several months.

"I want you to meet someone," she said warmly, opalescent eyes glowing with adoration.

That strange sensation filled my chest again, growing stronger and stronger, and my pace slowed, little legs coming to a stop as I neared. There was something here, something pulling me, drawing me in as if gravity had shifted.

She lowered the bundle, revealing a tiny babe with pale skin and near white hair curled up in the blanket of starlight. My heart leapt, chest swelling as I gazed down at the infant. The babe's white lashes lifted, revealing pale aquamarine eyes that shimmered as she looked up at me.

"This is Moira," Selene said, the warmth of her gaze filling me as I glanced up at her before settling my eyes back on the babe.

"Moira." I repeated, my voice so small, so... enamored.

"You must protect her, Damien," Selene said, her voice growing softer. "Promise me. She is vital to the future of our kingdom."

My eyes met hers again, and a smile spread across my face. "Always, Goddess."

She smiled, glittering constellations dancing across her porcelain face. "She means everything, Damien, more than you can understand now, little shadow lord, but I know you will understand in time. You must protect her, guide her, remain at her side. Always."

My eyes fell back to Moira, to those beautiful pale eyes beaming up at me.

"I promise to protect you, Moira," I said as I lifted my hand when she reached toward me. Her little fingers wrapped around my finger, and my heart swelled, my entire being drawn in by all she was. "Always."

I pulled back, and Damien's arm came around my waist as I nearly tripped on the hem of my gown.

"Woah there," he chuckled as he braced me against him.

"Sorry," I breathed, trying to find the ground beneath my feet, my hands grabbing onto the lapel of his coat.

"What did you see?" he asked.

"Moira. I saw Moira," I answered, smiling and breathless. "Selene was like a completely different person."

Damien nodded. "Something happened several years after you were born, she turned cold and distant."

"Who was the man in the room?" I asked as he released me.

His brows knitted together. "Man?"

"There was a man in the room, standing next to Selene, but I couldn't make out his face."

"I—" His eyes shifted as he sank into deep thought. "I honestly don't really remember. It was probably just a guard or something."

Perhaps. She was the creator of their race, after all. She would have guards, right? He took my hand, guiding me through the tall archway before us, and my jaw dropped.

The largest, most ancient library I'd ever seen stood before us. Shelves, filled to the brim with all sorts of books and scrolls, stretched up and up. I gasped as my eyes found the starry sky trapped within the high ceiling. Countless floating lanterns danced amidst the starlight, casting a warm glow down on us. The library was mostly quiet, save for the skittering sounds of—my brows furrowed as I caught sight of the tiny creatures shuffling about, carrying books and scrolls in different directions.

"What are they?" I whispered, leaning into Damien.

"They're the librarians," he whispered back, a hint of amusement on his tongue. "Astral sprites created by Selene to care for everything. There are others like them who tend to the rest of the temple."

They were so small, like toddlers, their skin—no, it wasn't skin. Their bodies didn't even seem wholly physical, and yet, they weren't quite like the shadow beasts. They were like pure night, their forms black, shimmering with starlight, with thin tails that swayed ever so slightly as they walked. One of the tiny creature's eyes found me as it passed, the soft white, glowing orbs among the darkness of its body so sweet and innocent, so curious. Its little round head tilted, long pointed ears bouncing as it continued its pace, the scrolls held tightly in its arms.

I tensed. "Oh, watch ou—"

The sprite bumped into another ahead of it, and it fell back onto the marble floor, the scrolls in its tiny claws scattering. The sprite it bumped into turned to look down at it and chittered in a little fit. The sounds it made were like a mouse as it scolded the little librarian before it turned to continue carrying its own books to their destination.

I rushed to the fallen sprite's side, the hem of my gown whispering against the marble floor. I knelt to gather the scrolls as it recovered and scrambled to do the same. I held out the few I'd gathered.

"Here you go," I said, softly.

It lifted its glowing eyes to me, tiny claws reaching out to receive the scroll. It dipped its head shyly before scurrying off after the others.

"That was awfully kind of you."

I started at the familiar voice that reached me from the nearby bookshelf. "Salwa?"

Salwa smiled brightly as she set a stack of books down on a table. "I didn't expect to see you two here."

"I wanted to show Cas the Archivallia," Damien said as he walked up beside me. "Figured we might find you here."

I frowned as I stood, looking at Damien.

"Salwa is the Tabularius," Damien explained.

Tabularius? That only confused me further. Damien must have noticed, for he chuckled at me, and I wondered what my face looked like.

"Don't confuse the poor girl, Lord Damien," Salwa said, her sable brows cocking as she smirked at him.

His shoulders sagged as he sighed, and I chuckled. "Just Damien, Salwa."

Salwa turned her pale eyes to me, her dark skin glowing in the soft light of the floating lantern. "I'm the historian of the immortals. I've documented everything of our race since I inherited the title from my predecessor nearly seven hundred years ago."

Nearly seven hundred years? God, she was nearly as old as Damien. No matter how many times I learned of another immortal who'd lived hundreds of years, it never got any less surprising. I didn't know if I would ever get used to it.

161

"That's amazing. So, all of this..." I turned to look across the vast expanse of the library.

"Is every text to ever exist regarding our race, at least what survived The Darklings' Descent," she said.

I bit my lip. The Darklings' Descent. I resisted the urge to ask more about what happened when the darklings first appeared. Did it have something to do with why I'd yet to see any of Moira's memories? The darklings had first appeared during her lifetime, and the way Damien reacted when he mentioned it, the look of sorrow in his eyes. I could only imagine how bad it must have been to live through.

"I need to report to Selene and discuss some things with her," Damien said. "Salwa, do you mind keeping Cas company? It won't take long."

"Of course," Salwa said, her smile infectious. "She's always welcome. I know how much she loves to read, and she'll offer better conversation than the sprites, that's for sure."

I giggled, trying to imagine Salwa holding a conversation with the tiny creatures.

"I'll leave you ladies to enjoy yourselves then," he said, leaning in to brush a kiss against my temple before heading for the tall archway.

I turned back to Salwa, who held a stack of books against her chest.

"I didn't even know this all existed."

"It's not open to everyone. Only a select few within The Order and The Council are allowed here," she said as she headed toward a nearby table.

I followed behind her, and as I did, the warm glow of a glass display case caught my eye. It was ornate, the glass framed in glittering gold. Within it sat three old, leather-bound books, each unique in their own way, with gold embellishments and engravings.

"So, are you looking for anything in particular?" she asked, and my attention was drawn back to Salwa as she set the stack of books on the table with a loud thud.

"I think Damien just wanted to show me the library while we were here. There's still so much about your world I don't know. I'd love to read up on anything I can."

A soft chuckle slipped from Salwa's lips. "I don't think you'd be able to read every text in this room in the lifespan of a mortal." Her smile faded, realizing the weight of her words to me. "I'm so sorry, Cas."

I forced a weak smile, knowing she hadn't meant anything by it. "It's ok, Salwa, really."

Her eyes drifted away from me as she bit her lip, and I hated the guilt she felt.

It was true, though; my time was limited, and there was so much I needed to do. The darklings had to be destroyed, and I needed to get my parents and Kat to safety. Damien had a means of getting them out of the city, but they wouldn't leave. It was all I could do to reassure them over the last few months that I was doing well on my own. They'd finally settled around Christmas when we'd had them over and hadn't brought up the subject again. No, there was no way they'd leave me behind.

Not unless I wasn't something that would hold them back...

"Salwa."

Her sable brows rose as she looked back at me, momentarily pausing over the text she'd opened.

"Damien told me your kind could erase yourself from the mortal memories."

"Yes..." she said tentatively, brows scrunching in confusion.

"As a Nous user... if I wanted to remove myself from a mortal's memories, how would I do that?"

She paused for a moment, as if contemplating what exactly I planned to do with that knowledge. "It's a complicated process. The fewer memories exist of us, the easier it is. It would be a simple task to remove the memory of our presence from a few hours of interaction. Simple enough that any immortal, even if they don't have the Nous affinity, could do it. If the memories span months, years, it requires more care, only a Nous user could remove those memories. Only a skilled Nous user could remove memories that span years, and they would have to take great care in doing so." Her pale eyes narrowed. "Why do you ask?"

"I..." I inhaled deeply, gathering the courage to do what was necessary. "I need my parents to get out of town before things get terrible."

She remained silent, her eyes slipping from mine.

I swallowed, chest swelling as I fought the emotions rising in me. "I don't have much time left, Salwa. I just want to know they're safe."

"Are you sure?" she asked, looking back at me.

I didn't meet her gaze, grasping for any courage I might find. "Please teach me, Salwa."

"You already have the skill, Cas. You're a very talented Nous user. You have to be careful doing it, you could erase a vital memory if you're not careful or mix things up and leave the person incapacitated permanently, but... you simply have to enter their minds, find all that is you and erase it."

The thought of hurting my parents if I made a mistake left my stomach rolling. "All that is me?"

She nodded. "You're a demigoddess. It would be far easier for you to do it than any of us." Her chest heaved as she prepped to tell me everything. "When you enter their mind, you must find every familiar piece, search for yourself in them. Think of it as if you're looking through a picture book, but each picture is a memory. It may be difficult; you have twenty-one years of memories to remove."

"I just want them safe, and if it means they don't know I exist—" I swallowed and lifted my eyes back to her, forcing a smile. "I'm ok with that."

Salwa smiled softly at me, but it didn't reach her eyes. "Do what you think is right, Cas."

She laid a tender hand on my shoulder, her pale eyes slipping closed as she tilted her head closer to mine. Soft, familiar words of a language I didn't understand slipped from her lips.

It was a prayer. She was praying for me.

I smiled softly, closing my eyes, as I leaned into her, pressing my forehead to hers, absorbing the loving words she spoke. I didn't belong in the world of the mortals anymore, and if it meant my parents and Kat would be safe—

I'd erase every trace of my existence.

CHAPTER 21

DAMIEN

    I stole one final glance at Cassie. The way her eyes lit up and the smile that painted her face as she took in the massive room made it difficult to leave. She was truly at home among books, and I knew, if it were possible, she'd spend hours here, learning all she could. I wanted to show her everything, every book that might interest her. I wanted to teach her about the creatures of the Godsrealm, the ones she'd believed were myths and legends just last year. Perhaps one day, I could take her to see the wyverns of Hesperian's Reach, or the coasts of Thesos at the edge of the Cloist sea where the sand was black as pitch, and the waters were the richest turquoise.

The astral sprites bowed as they passed, starlight dancing over their tiny bodies, and I dipped my head in acknowledgement before slipping through the archway. The echo of my boots danced off the stone hall as I headed for Selene's private chambers. More of the tiny sprites crossed my path, cleaning or tending to the plants and dimós trees. I wasn't sure how many of her astral servants existed at this point, but I was relieved she had the company.

Imprisonment had a way of leaving a person lonely.

"Your aura is warm, warrior."

I lifted my eyes to find Selene admiring the dimós trees down the hall, her silken white hair unbound and cascading to the marble floor. Her voice was soft, gentle, as if it were but a whisper, yet it carried far and clear. The pale light of the dimós trees reflected off her radiant skin as her gaze drifted toward me, her constellation freckles shimmering as they shifted and danced across her face.

I crossed my arm over my chest, dropping to my knee as I bowed my head. "Goddess."

"You may rise." Her opalescent eyes traced my movements, unreadable. "I assume we have much to discuss after The Council meeting."

I rose. "Yes, Goddess."

"Come, walk with me," she said as she glided across the marble floors, long and delicate hands folded neatly together in front of her.

How I wished she were as she once was, the goddess who felt like home, but the sweet goddess was long gone, leaving behind something cold and distant. I hated it, and never stopped wondering just what could've happened to turn her so icy.

"I do believe I heard the footsteps of an angry Kyrios earlier," she said, and there was almost a hint of amusement in her tone.

My pace slowed as I reached her side. I always marveled at just how small she stood next to me. She was of similar height to Cassie, the top of her head barely reaching my shoulder. Still, despite her size, the power she possessed would be enough to end me. "Tobias was dismissed. He's no longer Kyrios of House Nous."

She tilted her head, opalescent eyes shifting to me as a delicate white brow arched, but her pace did not falter. "Dismissed?"

I swallowed. Was she displeased? "He refused to work with us in securing more warriors for the coming battles, tested my rule, and disrespected his queen."

She didn't respond, and my heart hammered in the silence, the weight of her reaction pulling me down. No new Kyrios had been named since The Fall of Kingdoms, and it had been centuries since one was removed from their seat. It was odd to be back to walking on eggshells, avoiding her wrath. There'd been times after Lucia's passing where I'd pushed the limits of Selene's patience, hoping she would lash out and end me, but all that changed when I found Cassie. For the first time in over a century, I no longer craved the peaceful rest of death. No, for the first time in a long time, I wanted to live.

She finally spoke. "I never liked the fool anyway."

Relief washed over me, and we turned down another hall, where the walls opened into massive archways, the endless night sky glistening with countless stars beyond. The second moon of the Godsrealm shined in the near distance, casting its pale blue light on us. This was the view I wanted to share with Cassie, but I wanted to mentally prepare her for the knowledge of just where Selene's temple resided—that we weren't on the soil of our ancestors, but of a moon.

"Who shall take his place?" she asked.

"His daughter, Calista."

Her opal eyes lifted to me briefly, a sense of speculation filling them, but then slipped elsewhere. "His daughter? I did not know he had a daughter."

I nodded, a little leery of the tone in her voice. How could she have not known something like that? Had she become so disconnected? "She's versed in our laws, has a sharp mind, and I know she'll better serve our race than Tobias did." There wasn't a doubt in my mind Cassie had made the right call. Pride swelled in my chest at the thought of her sitting proudly at the head of The Council's table. Calista *would* serve House Nous well.

"Perhaps we should've made the change earlier, then." She paused, her pace unchanged as she added, "How fares, Moira?"

"Despite her mortal form, she's working hard to learn all she can. She's the one who suggested Calista take Tobias' place." I watched her from the corner of my eye, trying to discern what she might be thinking. "She has truly come a long way."

For a second, I wondered if I imagined a smug grin tug at the corner of her lips, for it lasted only a second. "And her training?"

I cleared my throat, praying she would be understanding, given Cassie's mortal form, at how far she'd come in the recent months. "She's currently working on mastering flight with Zephyr. They're to learn more forms once she's mastered that. She's made great progress in learning to harness Nous and wielded it beautifully to communicate with us during her first patrol. She's made great leaps and bounds in sparring, managed to take out five darklings during her first hunt, and we are hoping to resume training on wielding her flame magic soon."

"What is keeping you from resuming it?"

I fell a step behind but quickly returned to her side. "She's... struggled after what happened with Marcus."

"Salwa is healing her, correct?"

The coldness of her words hit me hard, as if it were so easy to heal something so traumatic. It wasn't a cut that could be mended with a bandage. My chest twisted at the memory of the horror that had marred Cassie's face after she'd burned Marcus to ashes. What happened couldn't be erased. It would take time. I nodded, though, knowing she wouldn't understand.

"It is a good thing she put an end to that miserable creature."

I winced at the mention of Marcus, not because of the end he'd met, but because of what his death had done to Cassie, how much she still suffered because of him. I knew, though, that hunting down Marcus and the other deserters had been a matter of great importance to Selene ever since he'd disappeared. We still hadn't been able to figure out how they'd avoided the cost of breaking their vows to Selene. A warrior didn't just betray our goddess without consequences.

"It sounds as if, despite her mortal form, she is somewhat meeting expectations." Her tone almost sounded snide.

"Better than I could've hoped," I said.

Her head turned, chin lifting to meet my gaze. "You sound proud, Damien."

I stiffened at her use of my name. It was rare for her to reference me as such, and I never knew if it was in distaste or praise. "I'll always be proud of my queen, no matter her accomplishments."

She turned from me, and the scent of jasmine filled the hall, but I couldn't see her expression, nor read what emotions she might be feeling... if she still felt them. Her gaze lifted to the nearest dimós tree, where astral sprites tended to the soil at its roots. She bent, her white hair spilling in decadent waves over her shoulders as she reached her hand out to offer something to one of the creatures. "There is another down the hall that could use some extra care."

The little creature nodded, taking what she offered before bowing its head and skittering off. I knew she was fond of these creatures, but I rarely witnessed her interact with them. She spoke so softly to them, and perhaps it was because they were her only form of companionship.

She seemed to be in a good mood today. I wonder if… no, she'd made it clear that she wouldn't help Cassie. But—

Gods damn me. "Is there really nothing we can do for her?"

Silence loomed in the great hallway, and I braced myself for her to lash out in annoyance.

"You know as well as I why I can't, Damien." I couldn't ignore the vulnerability in those words. "I wish I could, but I am bound and forbidden. You know the price of interfering with mortals, regardless of their relation to me."

I remained silent, a heavy sigh escaping before I could mask my disappointment.

"Be thankful the twelve only saw fit to imprison me here." She rose, pale eyes low as she turned to me. I hated what they had done to her, punishing her for another's actions. She inhaled deeply. "For what happened, they could have easily sentenced me to oblivion."

CHAPTER 22

CASSIE

"What did you think of the Archivallia?" Damien asked as we walked down the halls. I couldn't help but bask in the soft glow of the dimós trees as we passed one after another.

"I want to come back when I have time to really look around," I chuckled, the hem of my dress whispering along the marble floor. "When I'm dressed better for reading."

The corner of his lips curved into that crooked grin I loved so much.

He hadn't left me with Salwa for long. We'd barely started to tour the Archivallia when he found us, guided by a lone astral sprite. The creatures were so sweet once they came out of their shell, and they had even danced at my feet in excitement as we strolled the grand library wanting to show me things.

We neared the entrance to The Council's chambers, and before we entered to head home, I noticed a massive set of black wooden doors at the end of the hall I hadn't seen before. Dimós trees were merged into the wall, forming a bridge of glowing branches over the arched doorway. Carved into the doors were two rearing warhorses, riders mounted on their backs.

On one, the rider was clad in leather armor and a hood, similar to the armor warriors of The Order wore when we hunted darklings, a short sword in his outstretched hand. On the other door was a cloaked figure, body cast in shadow. Its face was void of any sign of humanity, like death itself, with a maw of razor-sharp teeth and hollow eyes. Chills skittered over my skin at the sight of its claws tearing into the warhorse's neck as it roared at the warrior on the opposite door.

"What do those doors lead to?" I asked.

Damien paused before we could enter the doorway to return home, dark brows rising as his eyes followed where my gaze led. A somber air descended around him, his sorrow crawling over my skin, icy and hot all at once.

"Moira's Rest." Something twisted in my chest, but his eyes remained fixed on the massive doors and what lay beyond them. "The remains of our fallen brothers and sisters reside there, whether warrior or civilian. It's a place for them to rest when they leave for Elysium, the afterlife."

My eyes drifted over the details of the doors. The carvings were a depiction of their war, of everything they'd lost when the darklings appeared. I turned, taking a step, but hesitated. Would it be right for me to visit their crypt? I feared it would be disrespectful as a mortal.

Damien silently stepped to my side, and I stiffened when he took my hand. "Would you like to visit?"

I couldn't meet his gaze. It wasn't right. I had no right to enter where immortals rested. It wasn't curiosity pushing me toward that tomb, though. My body begged me to take a step forward, to go to whatever rested behind those massive doors. I reluctantly nodded, swallowing as he led me forward, my mind wandering. What would I see on the other side? It was called Moira's Rest. Did Moira's remains reside within this hall? Were Elena and Lucia there?

Was... Emilia there?

My heart raced, thundering in my ears as we grew closer, and Damien gave my hand a gentle squeeze. I smiled, thankful for his reassurance, but it did little to calm the maelstrom raging in my chest. The doors opened on their own, swinging slow and wide, revealing what lay beyond them. I stopped breathing.

The chamber was monstrous, black stone walls forming a massive circle. Blue flames lit sconces high above us, and resting in alcoves on the walls were rows and rows of glass jars, each labeled with delicate inscriptions. I realized they were ashes.

Oh God. I couldn't count how many immortals rested within this hall. The air was heavy, an invisible weight bearing down on me as I stepped inside. I turned to find a small archway leading to what I assumed was another chamber like this one. How many immortals rested in this place?

A pair of immortals appeared from the dark depths, their faces worn and weary. Their eyes found me, and I hesitated, fearful of what they'd think. Did they know I was human? They dipped their heads as they passed, somber smiles barely lighting their weary faces. I dipped my head in response, which I wasn't sure was the right thing to do, but it felt right.

Damien released my hand, his pace slow as he drifted toward the center. How many of these immortals did Damien know? How many of his friends rested here? My eyes followed to where his path led. I froze, heart threatening to burst from my chest at what lay before us.

It was her. No... It was *me*.

In the center of the hall, illuminated by moonlight spilling in from an opening in the ceiling, stood an ornate, gold glass case. Dimós trees curved and wound their way to form a base around the case, tilting it upward. The branches fanned out, supporting numerous burning candles on their twisting limbs, and I couldn't help but feel like they resembled the folded wings of a moth.

Nestled inside, amidst a bed of countless delicate pale flowers, lay Moira, as if she were merely sleeping. Her near-white hair lay in curls around her, her hands folded neatly over her stomach. She wore a white silk gown, the fabric shimmering as it captured the light of the moon. She was as beautiful in death as she was in life.

Damien stopped before her, and I gathered the courage to join. I couldn't believe what I was seeing—that she was really here, that it didn't look like a day had passed since she... since I'd died. I still felt so disconnected from her, my memories locked away. I couldn't deny, though, a strange, almost thread-like connection between us, as if drawing me to her.

My fingers laced with Damien's, and his head tilted, offering me a somber smile. He kissed my forehead, and my gaze drifted back to Moira. My brows furrowed as I noticed two urns woven into the branches on their own pedestals, labeled with delicate inscriptions in a language I couldn't read.

"There rests Elena—" Damien gestured to the one on the left, before turning to the one on the right. "And there rests Lucia."

I couldn't find words, my gaze locked on the sleeping demigoddess. "She... I look like I might wake up at any moment."

"Gods and goddesses do not die like we do. Their bodies do not wither and decay," Damien explained. "Moira's body will rest here until this temple crumples and the world falls to ruin."

"I wonder why I can see Lucia and Elena's memories but not Moira's."

Damien didn't speak.

"Were Elena and Lucia able to remember?"

Damien swallowed. "Moira's memories were always difficult to access. When you returned as Elena, they returned easier, but there were... gaps. When you returned as Lucia, Moira's memories became more difficult. I wondered if maybe the memories of multiple lives were too much for one soul to bear. Maybe, with each rebirth, you grow further from Moira."

I lifted my gaze to him, to the pain etched into his face. He'd shared so many experiences with Moira since they were children. To know I may never remember the times we'd shared, it must be painful for him.

"She's beautiful," I said, if only to break the painful silence.

"You are, and you're just as beautiful in mortal form as you were in any immortal form you've taken."

I smiled, his words touching me, but the smile faded. I lifted my eyes, my gaze drifting across the thousands of remains surrounding us. My heart hammered, and I feared what Damien might think of me for asking, but some deeper part of me needed to know. "Is... Emilia here?"

His amber and ashen eyes drifted to me. His sorrow seeped into my skin where our hands met, the icy-hot chill sinking into my chest. "She is. Would you like to visit her?"

I parted my lips, my eyes burning, and a cold hollow feeling tugged at my chest. I couldn't help but feel foolish. Was it right for me to feel this way? I hadn't physically lost her, and yet... I had. I'd dreamt of her many times since I'd remembered, tried to piece together any possibility of what she might've looked like.

"I feel like it's not my place," I said, voice quivering, and I blinked, furious that I was barely able to hold the tears at bay. Damien should be crying; he'd suffered the loss. Lucia had suffered the loss. Me?

I simply remembered the loss, and yet... it stung so badly, the pain sinking so deep into my chest, I thought I might fall to my knees. All I could think about was how badly I wanted to hold her, to see her face, to watch her grow and thrive. So many things I'd wanted to do, and I'd never gotten the chance.

"It is, *mea luna*. Emilia is just as much yours as she is mine."

I couldn't meet his gaze, guilt and overwhelming sorrow clouding my thoughts.

"Come." He took my hand, guiding me. I followed reluctantly, eyes never leaving the face of my sleeping self, nestled amidst the pale blossoms.

We came to a halt at the back wall. Carved into the black stone was an alcove. Along the interior walls were carved out shelves, which held thick, half-melted candles, lit with delicate blue flames. Wax cooled and hardened as it dripped down the candles and onto the walls, except for one which had fully melted, the wick dying out just as the flame extinguished. I drew a sharp breath when the melted wax snaked back up the wall, reforming the candle, the delicate blue flame springing back to life. It was mesmerizing.

On the arched opening were words written in a language I couldn't understand, and I wondered what this special place was. My eyes fell to the three ornate urns before me, nestled in their own smaller alcoves, more inscriptions labeling each one, more words I couldn't read.

"My mother and father rest here," he said as he approached the wall. He laid his hand against one of the clay urns at the top. His eyes fell then to the single smaller urn beneath them, and a sad smile stretched his lips. He knelt, his hand sliding from the urn and down the black stone, until it rested against the lone clay container of ashes.

Sweet words left his lips in a whisper, his loving gaze drifting over the ashes. "*Mouńn Elispsais, mea stellaros.*"

I hesitated, my heart pounding. I couldn't do this, couldn't face it. I wanted to run. I wasn't ready to see her, not yet… but my feet cemented in place, my body refusing to leave.

She's here... She's so close...

His eyes drifted to me, and he held out his hand. My hand shook as I took it, stepping to his side before lowering to my knees. He lifted my hand to the case. My chest grew heavy, something building in the back of my throat, and I cupped my other hand over my mouth as my palm met the cold clay, a tear rolling down my cheek.

Something in the deepest recesses of my mind pushed past any sense of decency. Perhaps it was Lucia who begged me to do it, a mother so desperate to hold the baby she'd never gotten to see. My other hand

reached out, and I took the small urn, folding it against my chest. I curled into myself, feeling the cold clay against my skin. My breath grew shallow, my chest expanding as I tried to hold it in, tried to fight it, but I couldn't anymore, and I let go. His arm draped over me, pulling me close as I crumpled, sobs threatening to burst from my chest.

Damien held me there for a long time, allowing me to cry into his chest as I held her—the three of us together at last. I held her for so long, not wanting to let go. I didn't know how much time passed, and at some point, we'd ended up resting against the wall of the alcove. My head leaned against Damien's chest, my body lying against his as I rested between his outstretched legs. I took a deep, uneven breath, my eyes puffy.

"What happened?" I dared to ask, my eyes staring into nothing. "She'd sounded so healthy."

Her cry echoed in the depths of my memories. I'd only heard a handful of cries before she'd been rushed out of the room. It was all I had of her, and I'd clung to that little piece ever since the memory had resurfaced.

He drew a deep breath, his voice thick as he spoke. "She started off strong, but a few days after you passed, she... started to struggle. Over the course of a week she withered, growing weaker and weaker with each day."

His fingers glided up and down my back, and I gave into that warm touch. "It's difficult enough for immortal infants to survive delivery with their mothers there to nurse them, to give them those nutrients only they can give. When you passed, it was only a matter of time." He paused, and I lifted my gaze to his. The sorrow was heavy in his eyes. I brushed a kiss against his cheek, and a somber smile tugged at his lips. "It was shortly after The Fall of Kingdoms. We'd suffered so many casualties, and many were still recovering from injuries. The few mothers who'd survived struggled to keep their own infants alive. One had tried to sustain both her child and Emilia, but..."

"Did she pass alone?" It was my own fear, the fear that I'd die alone, with no one at my side. I prayed she hadn't, that even if she didn't know or understand, he'd been there.

He swallowed, his arms wrapping around me in a tight embrace. "She passed in my arms."

Tears threatened to spill again, my chest tight as I imagined him, alone, suffering. "Thank you for bringing me here."

"You're welcome to come here anytime. Anytime you want to visit her, I'll gladly bring you."

"I'd like that."

He brushed a kiss against my temple. The touch pulled me back to the present, and I lifted my head from his chest. I'd completely forgotten we were supposed to meet Calista and Zephyr to discuss everything that had happened. I brushed my hands across my eyes, wiping away the residual tears. I could only imagine how much of a mess I was.

"I completely forgot about tonight. Do we have time for me to shower and clean up before we meet with Zephyr and Calista? I probably look terrible," I said as I pushed myself onto my knees. I pressed a kiss to the small urn, and that pull I'd felt before came back to life, as if Lucia wasn't ready to part ways.

Damien shook his head. "We aren't going tonight."

I looked back at him, brows high. "I don't want to hold things up—"

"You're not holding things up. You've done enough, *mea luna*. Take the time you need. Everyone will understand."

My chest swelled. "Thank you."

It hurt to set that urn back into its alcove, and for a moment, I almost hated that Lucia was trapped within me—forever unable to walk with her child in whatever afterlife awaited them.

I rested my hand against the urn, my body not wanting to leave. I would be back, though, would visit more, while I still could. There was so much to do, but I would do everything in my power to prevent more losses like this, whatever it took.

Words drifted from my lips that weren't my own, and yet they slipped from my lips with unnatural ease. It must have been the language of the Elythians, words spoken by Lucia.

"Revinia aleirene, mea hallos."

Rest peacefully, my love... my heart.

178

CHAPTER 23

CASSIE

"I'm so sorry. I should've spoken with you before volunteering you. It just kind of happened."

Calista sat beside me on the couch at Stokers the following night. Damien and I had taken the entire day off to be with each other. It was time I hadn't realized I needed so badly after visiting Emilia for the first time.

The bar owned by Semele and Eiko was already alive with our group. Damien, Zephyr, Calista, and I sat on the couches, Barrett, Thalia, and Vincent seated at the bar. It was foolish of me to volunteer her to take

Tobias' seat on The Council without speaking with her first, but everything had happened so fast.

She smiled, a soft chuckle leaving her lips. "It's okay, Cas, truly. I was a bit surprised when Zephyr told me of what happened at the meeting. I'm honored you recommended me for it." Guilt crept into those dazzling silver eyes. "I'm so sorry for the things my father said. He's become so bitter over the years. He wasn't always like this."

"I'm not worried about that. Has he reached out to you at all? I didn't think about him taking his anger out on you. He was so furious when he left."

She shook her head. "I haven't seen him. I went to check on him last night, but no one answered, and his house looked empty."

"I'd like to see him try," Zephyr said in a low growl at her side. "I'll finish what Damien started if he even tries to lay a finger on her."

"If he does, you have my blessing to end him," Damien told Zephyr.

For a moment there was a brief flash of hesitation and... fear in Calista's eyes. "He use to be kinder, he wasn't always like this."

"Yeah, when you bent to his will and did everything he asked of you," Zephyr growled. "The moment you started going against him he started treating you like dirt."

Calista swallowed, her eyes falling to the floor briefly, and guilt replaced the bitterness I felt toward Tobias. While I didn't like him, he *was* her father. Even if he didn't care for her feelings, she likely still loved him.

"So, you accept?" I asked, looking at Calista. I tried to hide the hope in my eyes as she turned back to me.

She smiled, nodding as her eyes lit up with her own hope. "Of course! It's the chance we females have needed for centuries. It's won't be easy, but it'll be worth it."

A grin spread across my face as I wrapped my arms around her neck, and she giggled.

"Cas proposed changes to the existing laws revolving around the rights of females in the aristocracy, so all that's left is to lay out how we modify the laws or repeal them entirely. You have my support, and I know the others will likely support the changes you bring to the table. Lysander might offer resistance, but he's only one seat," Damien said, giving her some assurance. "I'm starting the paperwork tomorrow. The Kyrios house will be cleared and ready for you to move in by the end of the week. Whenever you're ready, it's yours."

Calista smiled. "Thank you, Lord Damien."

Damien waved a hand, offering her a friendly grin. "No formalities here. Please, just call me Damien."

She nodded, her eyes flickering as if she were struggling to override the etiquette that had been hardwired into her over an immortal lifetime. "Apologies… Damien. Thank you for your support."

"So…" I started, glancing at Damien, who raised a dark brow. "If you're the head of House Nous, I would assume your title overrides the head of your family's, and you would be the one who determines who you can and cannot take as your bonded. Would that be right, Damien?"

A realization passed across Calista and Zephyr's faces, and a crooked grin curved Damien's lips. I'd seen this look before—right after I'd made the call to replace Tobias with Calista. I couldn't miss the pride in his eyes, or the heat.

"You would be correct in that," he said, hunger painting the tone of his voice. He gripped my thigh, fingers digging into my skin and my skin heated. I bit my lip, smiling as I pulled my gaze.

Calista and Zephyr looked at each other, shock and hope lighting their faces.

"We… We could…" Calista clapped her hands over her mouth.

Zephyr smiled and leaned his forehead against Calista's. "I think it's time we made this official."

My heart swelled at the happiness I felt in the air, the warmth of his adoration drifting over my skin, the scent of… wildflowers filling my lungs. I frowned; wildflowers?

"Drinks on the house to celebrate a female on The Council!" Semele called from the bar, flashing a pearly grin as she grabbed glasses. "And to celebrate this beautiful union!"

"Water for me please, Semele! I'm still recovering from the party the other night," I said with a smile, remembering how drunk I'd gotten.

Barrett laughed from the bar with Thalia, and I cut him a sharp look. I hadn't said anything, but Barrett and Thalia had been talking amongst themselves privately the entire time we'd been here. The last time I'd seen them together, they'd been awfully affectionate.

Vincent didn't seem to be involved in their conversation, as he'd been talking on the phone. The way he smiled when he spoke led me to believe he was talking to Anna. She must've been working at Johnson's tonight. I wondered how much longer she'd work with her pregnancy. Would she go on leave soon?

I leaned in to whisper in Damien's ear. "Barrett and Thalia seem to be getting closer."

Damien's eyes drifted to them. "It would seem so."

181

I pushed myself up and headed for them. They'd left together after the party we'd held the other night, celebrating my first hunt, and I'd been curious about where things were heading for them. I hopped onto the barstool next to Thalia. Her pale eyes drifted to me, lit with her smile.

"You fucking killed it in there yesterday!" she said, shaking my shoulder.

Barrett didn't look my way, but I saw the quirk of a grin creeping across his face as he swirled his drink. "I knew you'd chicken out on putting that dagger to use."

"Oh shut it, you lost the bet. You thought she'd set Tobias on fire," Vincent chimed in from his other side.

I balked at him. "You seriously thought I was going to set someone on fire?"

Barrett elbowed Vincent as he huffed a laugh before saying, "I was hopeful. Those meetings are boring, we need something to liven them up."

"I think Damien livened it up quite a bit," Thalia said, her head dipping as she snickered.

"I swear he pissed his pants," Barrett added, his steel eyes sliding to me, and I bit back the laugh bubbling up in my chest.

"I'm glad you brought up the laws regarding females in the aristocracy," she said, her face softening as she turned to me. "I wish someone had changed them earlier. So many females have suffered because of them."

Her eyes flickered to Barrett, who had gone quiet. She reached out a tentative hand, as if she were going to take hold of his, but she drew it back, hesitation flitting across her face. My heart fluttered at the sign of affection, but then my thoughts narrowed in on her words, on the way Barrett reacted. Did he know someone affected by the laws?

I tilted my head just enough to catch a glimpse of his face, of the muscle feathering in his jaw, his eyes burning into the swirling amber liquid in his glass, and an icy hot sensation crawled over my skin. He drew a deep breath, blinking, as if he were shoving whatever he was feeling down and took a swig of his drink.

It wasn't my place to ask, though I wanted to. Instead, I leaned in to whisper in Thalia's ear, eager to change the subject. "So, are you guys..."

She glanced at me, pale brows raised, and the look of surprise melted into a bashful one, her cheeks flushing. "It's complicated."

"You girls whisperin' about me over here?" Barrett asked, tilting his head to see around her.

"Not every conversation revolves around you, numbskull," Thalia said, but for a moment, something like regret flashed across her eyes, and she almost recoiled.

"Such hostility," Barrett said with a teasing grin. "And here I thought you were getting all sweet on me."

Thalia rose to her feet, hands planted on the counter. "Why is everything a joke to you?"

I stiffened.

Barrett raised his hands in surrender. "Woah! I didn't say it was."

"Then perhaps you could just be honest and talk like you mean it," Thalia snapped back. "I've been trying to get you to open up to me for days now, but you keep avoiding the subject. It's obviously eating at you."

His face hardened, his irritation burning its way over my skin. "I'm not avoiding anything."

"Then why won't you talk about what happened the other night? Why did you shut me out? Why won't you open up more about Cali? You won't talk to Salwa about what happened to her. You can't keep shoving it down. You can't keep doing this to yourself!"

My eyes darted between them. Cali?

"Don't you dare bring my sister into this," he growled, and something like shame darkened his face as he failed to hold her gaze.

Something curdled in my stomach at the mention of a sister I'd never heard of—a sister I hadn't even known existed. I struggled to process it. I'd spent so much time with him. He'd mentioned nothing about her... or any of his family for that matter.

"Are you just going to pretend it never happened? It did, Barrett… and it's not your fault," Thalia said lowly, placing a hand on his shoulder.

He jerked his shoulder from her grasp. "You know nothing."

"There was no way you could've stopped it, you were young," she said, her tone reassuring despite the anger brimming beneath the surface.

Barrett huffed, turning from her.

"Seriously? That's it?" When he didn't respond, she groaned. "Gods, you never change."

A muscle ticked in Barrett's jaw before he shot ot his feet, his stool falling over, and the bar went quiet. "You think I enjoy being like this, Thalia? You think I enjoy fucking everything up? You think I haven't questioned every decision I've ever made wondering if it was the right one or if it cost someone their life?"

Thalia stiffened, and I glanced at Damien and the others, who had silenced their conversations, now very aware of the argument building at the bar.

Barrett didn't seem to care of the audience, continuing. "It goes both ways. You can't push me to talk but refuse to open up about Micah."

Hurt flashed across her face before her brows furrowed, her anger hot over my skin, and she bristled. "Even if I did talk, I doubt it'd be enough. I swear, the way you act, it almost seems like you want to be alone the rest of your life. It's people like you who end up alone in their final moments—" Her words fell short the moment they left her lips. Pain danced in his steel eyes as they widened. She hesitated a moment, the silence hanging between them so potent. Her lips parted as if to say something, her hand lifting, but she retracted, and shoved past him, storming for the door.

I stood, ready to follow her, but Vincent lifted his hand, and I paused. He sighed, rising from his stool before getting off the phone. "I'll go talk to her."

Barrett's gaze followed Thalia as she shoved through the doorway, Vincent hot on her heels. My heart dipped at the regret and anguish in those steel eyes.

His shoulders sagged, and he rested his elbows on the counter. His eyes burned into the bartop as he hung his head. "Sorry you had to see that, Cas."

God, he'd called me by my name. Despite the annoyance I felt when he called me spitfire, it felt oddly weird for him to call me Cas. This was so unlike him. I'd never seen him so worked up like this.

What had happened to his sister?

"What's going on with you two?" I asked, trying to be as gentle as possible as I slid onto the stool beside him. "Every time I think you're gaining ground and getting closer, something happens."

"Noticed that, did you?" He groaned before taking a sip of his drink.

The sarcasm in his tone made me wince. "We all have."

"It's just..." He sighed. "It's hard."

"Why? She likes you Barrett, and it looks like you like her too. I think you guys could be good for each other, if you'd just stop putting your foot in your mouth. Are you trying to push her awa—" I clamped my mouth shut. When had I become so comfortable with Barrett that I felt I could talk to him like this? "Oh my God... I'm so sorry. I shouldn't have said that. I shouldn't be butting in. Forget I said anything." I pushed off the barstool to leave him alone, but he grabbed my arm, stopping me.

"Don't. You're fine, spitfire."

A strange relief washed over me to hear him say the name, and a grin forced the corner of my lips to curve. "You're never going to stop calling me that, are you?"

He shook his head, that cocky grin returning, and I'd never felt more relieved to see him smile.

"So, what's going on with you guys?" I asked, resting my elbows on the bar as I settled back onto the barstool. "If you don't mind me asking, that is."

"It's... complicated."

I fidgeted in my seat. "If you don't want to talk about it... or your sister, I won't push you. I just want you to know I'm here if you need."

"What happened to Cali... I—" His eyes flickered, and a flash of hot anger washed over my skin before icy claws of sorrow replaced the heat.

What happened to Cali... My heart lurched at the unspoken meaning behind those words, and the laws that seemed to somehow play into it.

"We don't have to talk about it, Barrett. If you're not ready, it's ok."

He drew a deep breath and took another drink.

God, I shouldn't pry, but I wanted to help him talk about something, *anything*. I wanted to help him at least work through the issues with Thalia, even if just a little, but I barely understood or knew what was happening between them.

"I heard Thalia... I heard she was bonded before."

"She was." For a brief moment, he almost seemed relieved to change the subject, but it was short-lived. His steel eyes dulled with a sadness I'd never seen before. "He was a friend of mine."

Was. Damien had clarified as much. Thalia *was* bonded, but what happened? She never spoke of him, and Damien had said it wasn't his story to share.

Barrett went on, fidgeting with the empty glass in his hand, the glow of the nearby neon light catching the rings decorating his fingers. "His name was Micah. I met him around the same time I met Thalia when I joined The Order. They were already a thing when I met them. You would've liked him; he was a male you could always count on." A soft laugh slipped from his lips as his eyes grew distant. "Thalia

185

regularly scolded us for getting into trouble together. Constantly told me I was a bad influence."

He took a deep breath, the empty glass ringing as he set it on the bar. "I can't tell you how many times she kept me from getting kicked out of The Order. I didn't always have Damien to get me out of trouble." His eyes shifted to me. "I actually knew you before I knew him."

I remained silent, absorbing everything he told me. He'd known me. I wondered which one, surely not Moira. I didn't think he was as old as Damien. Maybe Elena or Lucia? Had he fought in the Fall of Kingdoms? My mind pooled with so many questions.

It was difficult to resist the urge to reach out to his thoughts, to see Thalia when she was younger, to see the man who she'd been bound to, but it was a boundary I wouldn't cross.

"They had already bound themselves to one another when we met. They weren't *mates* like you and Damien are, but they were happy."

My brows furrowed. "What do you mean?"

"Not everyone in our race is mated to their one true match. It's not rare, just… uncommon. Few are lucky enough to find what you have in their lifetime. Sometimes, they're born too late or die before they find each other; sometimes, an immortal's other half resides in the Godsrealm. Many of our kind are lucky enough to fall in love, but they don't feel that fated *bond* when your soul meets its other half."

I didn't know enough about Thalia to know where she came from, if she was part of the aristocracy. Had he been chosen by her family? Or had she chosen him herself?

"Did she... love him?" The weight in my chest made it difficult to get the words out.

Barrett smiled, warm and pained at the same time. "Yeah, she did. She used to smile so much more. Micah and I were the best of friends, but I couldn't ignore how much I—" His words halted a moment, guilt flickering across his steel eyes. "Was drawn to Thalia. Everything about her was just wonderful, breathtaking. I suspected she might be my mate, but it made me sick with myself, because she'd already chosen who she wanted to be with." He didn't speak for a moment, the weight of his silence crushing. "I don't think she felt it as I did, and the bond never snapped into place. I never told either of them. She'd already chosen him, and she was so happy. It was enough for me to know she was. I wouldn't ruin that for them."

I hesitated but asked, "What happened to him?"

"He was killed on patrol almost forty years ago." His eyes grew distant. "I was with him when it happened."

A weight pulled on my chest. I'd never seen this side of Barrett, had never seen such sadness in his eyes. Semele brought a fresh drink over to him, switching the empty glass with a fresh one before offering him a soft smile and leaving to see to her work.

He thanked her before taking the glass. "I was pinned down by a darkling when three more surrounded him. They took him down and by the time I got free." His voice faded and for a moment I wondered if he'd shared as much as he could bring himself to, but he continued. "He'd taken them out, but not before he'd been bitten. I tried to draw out the venom, to save him. He wouldn't let me, for fear I'd be infected, begged me to end it as he began to change..."

We sat there a moment in silence, and his hand gripped the glass, I feared it might crack in his grasp. Damien had warned me of how dangerous it was to draw out the darklings' venom, and while I felt terrible that Thalia had lost her bonded, I was relieved Barrett hadn't been lost.

"I failed her when I let Micah die that night. The look on her face when she'd opened her door to find me instead of him, the look on her face when I had to tell her what happened—" His skin paled, his hand quivering as he clenched his glass. "It still haunts me to this day. I almost wish I'd been the one to fall and he survived."

Before I could stop myself, I reached out, my hand resting on his forearm and the tremors eased. "You can't think like that, Barrett."

"I've done everything I could to keep her safe since he fell, kept her off patrols, had her train warriors instead. I couldn't imagine losing her." He drew a deep breath. "I feel like I'm betraying him every time I try to get close to her, and I can't help but feel I don't deserve her. Because I let him die, because I showed up at her door that night instead of her bonded... her chosen."

"Barrett..." Sorrow twisted in my chest, seeing the depths of my own regrets reflected back at me in his steel eyes. "You didn't fail her, and you're not betraying Micah. You said so yourself; to find your true other half, it's rare, you shouldn't hold back from something so rare. I'd like to imagine that—" I tried to hold his gaze, and I nearly faltered. "He would want you both to have that kind of happiness."

I knew Damien would eventually find happiness, hated that he'd have to suffer when I passed, but I would return. I would return in the next life, and we'd have that time together, all the time we never had in this life. If I could help them destroy Melantha, maybe we could enjoy the peace we deserved, all of us.

Barrett gave a half smile, his eyes falling to the amber liquid swirling in his glass. If I could, if it wasn't a violation, I'd have loved nothing more than to reach into his thoughts as Salwa did, take every ounce of pain and sorrow consuming him and smooth it all away. I'd take it all, bear every bit of it if only to ease his suffering, all their suffering.

"The thing is, Barrett." His head tilted to me as I continued, his short blond hair catching the neon light. "We don't know how long we have left to live. We could find a way to defeat Melantha, destroy the darklings once and for all, and live long happy lives together, or the darklings could launch their attack before we're ready. We could die tomorrow night on patrol." The world shifted under me as I imagined what I knew awaited me in the near future, fearful of the news I'd receive at my next doctor's visit. "All we can do now is live our lives to the fullest. I know Thalia has feelings for you, more than you probably realize. She might be feeling the same pull you are. She may feel the bond but think you don't. Let her decide for herself. You may regret it if you don't take the chance for you both to find happiness."

He considered my words for a moment before he took a deep breath. "I missed talking to you like this."

I frowned. Had we talked like this before?

"Sorry. Lucia. I used to talk to her—er... you when I needed advice. You were always open to talk if I needed it." He smiled, seeming a bit more optimistic. "Thank you for that."

Warmth filled my chest. "Always. Just don't push her away anymore, Barrett. I want you to be happy."

"Me too, spitfire. Me too." He swallowed back the remnants of his drink and set the glass down before he rose from his stool. "I guess I'd better go talk to her then."

The full moon leaked light in through the curtains at the head of our bed. Damien's level breathing filled my ears as he curled up in my arms in deep slumber. Sleep had evaded me tonight. I didn't know how late it was, and I wouldn't dare move or risk disturbing Damien's rest to check.

I ran my fingers through his dark hair, the silken strands falling over his shoulders as I held him. His arms tightened around my waist, his face pressing into my chest as he made a sweet noise in his sleep, and I smiled. Warmth filled me as I watched him, that strange sensation in the very core of my being pulling me toward him. If I could, I'd lay here for the rest of my life at his side.

The words I'd spoken to Barrett earlier lingered in my mind. Who was I to tell him their time might be limited? God, I was such a hypocrite, and I hated myself for hiding it from everyone. I should tell them. I needed to tell them.

After my doctor's appointment; I'd do it then, when I had a better idea of what state I was in, how my powers were affecting my body. I needed more time. There was so much to do, and I wasn't any closer to figuring out how to destroy Melantha or the darklings.

We had to find Cole, find out what he knew. Maybe he would know what connection Eris had to Marcus. I needed answers, needed to find out what I could do to help Damien, to help all of them. *I* had limited time, but that didn't mean they all did. If only I could find a way to stop Melantha, to destroy the darklings once and for all. Surely there was a way to stop them.

I'd do anything to end Melantha, to ensure the others survived.

To ensure Damien survived, I'd gladly give my life.

CHAPTER 24

CASSIE

Darkness held me in its clutches, imprisoning me in the black depths of an endless abyss. A dark, primal power licked at my skin, coiling around my arms and legs. I searched for something, anything, anyone who might be there for me to reach out to.

Nothing. Pure nothingness surrounded me. Like an ocean, it stretched for miles, farther than I could see. Despite the pitch emptiness around me, despite the fact there was no one to be seen, I could feel it.

A tingling sensation crawled over my skin, the hairs stood up on my arms, and my eyes grew sharp as I searched. I was being watched, though I couldn't see who it was.

"Who's there?" My words didn't so much as echo, the void swallowing my voice as it left my lips. "Show yourself."

Silence.

A grayish hand appeared in the darkness before me and caressed my cheek. I tried to pull back, but my body wouldn't move, muscles unresponsive to my commands.

"Easy child." A woman's voice slithered into my ears, sharp and low. "I don't bite." She laughed under her breath "Much."

"Who are you?"

The hand slid down along my jaw until her finger lifted my chin. "You don't know?"

Her face faded into view. Narrow onyx eyes stared into mine, silver power simmering within them like ripples of water. A smile curved on her dark lips, but it didn't feel friendly. No, this smile was sinister, manipulative. Cruel.

Her smile widened when I didn't answer. "I'm surprised you haven't figured it out yet."

She circled me, a gown a mass of black mist and shadow encircling her. The enchanting fabric barely covered her sultry frame, splitting down the front to expose the swell of her breasts before it met below her navel and stretched down to her feet, where the misty gown danced with movement. I watched her, wary of any sign she might attack me. I didn't know why I bothered; I couldn't move, let alone defend myself.

The power lingering under her gray skin was enough to make me shake. It danced in her veins, stretching out to every edge of her being, so unbridled that with a single snap of her fingers she could end my existence. This wasn't my first time experiencing it. I'd felt this intense power before, when I met Selene.

This was a goddess—an Elythian, one more powerful than Selene. I could feel it, feel every ounce of power that might destroy me if I said the wrong thing. Damien had warned me how the Elythians, the powerful beings of the Godsrealm, had killed for less.

"I guess you wouldn't recognize my voice," she said, her tone casual as she inspected her long, sharp black nails.

A twisted smile stretched across her perfect face, her voice changing as she spoke again. It became my own, laced with a malice that made my skin crawl. "You'll have to forgive me. I mean, you needed a little nudge to do what was necessary, and it was so easy."

My throat tightened. *That voice.* The dark voice spoke into my mind once more, rippling like a memory that burned me with each nightmare that forced me to relive it.

191

He deserved what he got.

"It was you..."

She laughed, arms wrapping around her waist as she reveled in my shock, her inky black hair dancing in weightless silken waves around her.

"You blocked Salwa from entering my mind."

Her laughter faded, eyes darkening, as if she were annoyed by the memory. "I should have fried that brain of hers. So rude to trespass like that, but I didn't. You're welcome."

"Who—who are you?"

The wicked grin returned. "He shouted my name, child. Shouted it so loud I feared you might discover me before I wanted you to. Oh, Marcus was so furious that I kept your secret from him, but it wasn't the right time for him to know."

As if it'd happened yesterday, I remembered it, remembered feeling the bindings on my wrists in the metal shop—Marcus yelling to an empty room, cursing the goddess for withholding information about me.

"Eris..."

She shot toward me, and I sucked in a breath, her face inches from my own, eyes wild with excitement. "I'm so thrilled to finally meet you, Cassie, demigoddess of the immortals." Her voice dropped to a whisper in my mind, laced with venom.

Selene's precious little project.

The way she said Selene's name, like the name tasted sour on her tongue... did she hate her? I opened my mouth to speak, but I clamped my lips shut. Damien had warned me of how dangerous she was, the Goddess of Strife and Discord. She delighted in conflict, in despair.

I had to tread carefully, choose my words with caution. "What do you want?"

She inspected me, lifting her hand so her dagger-sharp nail could graze up and down her long neck as the gears turned in her mind. Would I be able to read her thoughts like I did others, see what plans she had in store?

"I wouldn't try that if I were you," she hissed.

God, she was in my head. She'd know everything I would do before even I did. Marcus knew her, but I wasn't sure how. Was she working with him? With the darklings? I'd been so desperate to find out what had come over me in the metal shop, what had compelled me to lose control. Now that I knew, it only uncovered more questions, more pieces to the puzzle we couldn't put together.

When her eyes met mine, I fought to hold her gaze, my body trembled but I couldn't back down. She seemed amused by that. "Did you know each of your past lives has had a certain affinity for particular abilities?"

I remained silent.

"Moira was especially gifted when it came to shadowmancy and healing. Strange combination, if you ask me." Eris' hand passed through the air, summoning an image of Moira in the darkness, her moon white hair hanging in curls around her face—my face. Pale aquamarine eyes looked through me, unseeing, her chin held high. It was as if I were watching a moment frozen in time, her standing before me though she was long gone.

"Elena—" She moved her hand through the air, an image of Elena coming to life beside Moira, her blonde, braided hair hanging over her shoulder. She wore the black Elythian leather armor of The Order. "Was a talented shifter."

"Lucia had a particular affinity for bending the mind." Lucia appeared before me, so real, her rich black hair lying over her shoulders, pale eyes almost glowing, the eyes they all shared...

The eyes I didn't have.

"You, however." Eris' eyes shifted to me. Moira, Elena, and Lucia images disappeared into inky blackness. "You have a flame dancing within you."

"Flame?" I asked hoarsely.

"They say Hephaestus was the one to give the immortals flame magic, but the tales are lies," she said, as if losing track of her thoughts, her voice dropping into a near whisper. "The ancient souls of Hesperian's Reach were the true bearers of the flame, the true source. Oh how it angered them when Zeus changed the history, snuffing out any record of their contribution. They still harbor hatred to this day, stewing in their caves..."

I couldn't make sense of what she was saying as she continued on, muttering on and on about places and things I'd never heard of, but I latched onto the one thing that stood out to me. "You're saying I'm better suited for using flame magic?"

She cocked her head, her sharp nail gliding up along her neck. "I must say, I admire that fire of yours. I've wanted so badly to test the true limits of it." Her eyes grew wide with excitement. "I wonder if we could burn this very city to ashes."

She leaned in, her breath ice cold as she whispered into my ear. "We could burn the world to ashes if we wanted, bring both realms to their knees. Imagine what we could do together. We would be *unstoppable*."

"Is that why you've been in my head all this time? So, you could push me to do those horrible things? So, you could use me?" I tried to hide the shake in my voice, tried to hold her gaze as she shifted away from me, but I was wavering.

"It was fun, I will admit, feeling those powers you possess, seeing just what you could do with your mortal limitations." Her onyx eyes roamed over me, as if assessing. "It's a shame you're not immortal."

That statement cut into me like a dagger, sinking into a deeper part of me.

She reached out, and my body tensed as she dragged her nail up my arm. I braced myself for her to sink those claws into me, to tear me apart. "You were too soft, too inexperienced to wield them the way they should be. Call it a gentle nudge in the right direction."

"Right direction?" I couldn't stop myself from scoffing. "I've been tormented by those decisions *you* pushed me to make!"

Her eyes flashed to me. "If I recall, you asked for my help, mortal. Begged me to save your mate when Marcus might've ended his life, and I did. You should be thanking me."

My eyes left hers. "I didn't ask you to kill Marcus the way you did."

"Oh hush, you wanted him dead as much as I did."

I stopped breathing. She wanted Marcus dead? Why?

"Because he would have gotten in your way," she said, answering the questions in my head.

My heart stuttered. "What do you mean?"

Her eyes drifted down as she turned away from me. "You are going to face far greater horrors to come. You were such a weak little lamb; you wouldn't be where you are now if I hadn't helped you."

I frowned. What benefit would she have if I mastered my powers? How exactly had she been helping me? "I've been getting along just fine mastering my magic without your help."

She whirled to me. "Oh?"

My breath hitched in my throat as she appeared before me, her lips peeling into a crazed grin. Black mist danced around her as she pressed her nail to my chest. Shattering pain pierced me so fast and hard I gasped, body recoiling.

Those wild eyes watched as I seized. "Haven't you noticed how good you've been doing? How you've been able to train without issue? Why do you think you've had no attacks?"

I grimaced, but I couldn't lift my eyes to her. My chest threatened to cave in, my lungs refusing to fill with air, and I couldn't hold back the scream clawing its way out of my throat. Agony rolled through me, coiling every muscle until tears welled in my eyes.

"I know your little secret. I have kept it at bay to allow you to train uninterrupted, so you might harness that power to use when the time comes."

She pulled her hand back, and the pain rushed from me. I collapsed. My lungs filled, but it wasn't enough, and I gasped, desperate for any air I might find.

"I would think you would be more appreciative of my generosity. Especially when you pushed yourself past your limit and suffered a recoil. I was impressed when you forced the doctor to keep your secret."

Generosity. The Elythians were anything but generous, and they never made deals or offered favors unless it benefited them.

"I would rein in those thoughts, little goddess. I'm the only thing keeping you from meeting that end you so dread."

My blood ran cold. She'd stopped the pain, prevented the heart attacks, but had she stopped the damage? What would happen if she stopped keeping the heart attacks at bay? I'd fought the hope that maybe something had righted itself. I couldn't deny there was a part of me that had wished something good might've happened to me. I was foolish to think it.

"Don't worry, little goddess. Your secret is safe with me."

"Why help me? What do you get out of it?" I bit out.

"Entertainment." She inspected her nails coolly. "It gets boring in the Godsrealm."

Bullshit.

"Watch your thoughts, little goddess. I could kill you now, shatter your mind, and leave you a shell. Or maybe I'll burst that little heart of yours." Her eyes met mine, her gaze ice cold. "Oh, how horrible would it be for the Lord of Shadows to find his mate gone at his side when he wakes?"

The blood drained from my face, my heart stuttering.

She smiled at my silence. "Smart girl." She turned from me. "You focus on building your strength and mastering that magic of yours. You may yet live to see this war through."

And she faded into nothing.

195

CHAPTER 25

CASSIE

I shot awake, gasping for air, and Damien startled from sleep.

He reached out steadying hands to brace me. "It's a dream, *mea luna*. It's not real." He pulled me close, allowing me to fall into him as my body trembled. "It's ok. You're safe. I'm here."

I was safe in our room.

Too many times. Too many times had I awoken Damien like this. He was so used to it now, he immediately knew how to bring me back to reality. It'd been a while since it happened. The dreams of those chains binding my wrists in that cell still lingered in the dark corners of my mind, and there were so many times in the days after I killed Marcus that I'd awoken in terror, throwing my guts up and unable to fall back asleep.

I never wanted to relive those weeks again.

"It was just a dream," Damien whispered, running his fingers through my hair.

I drew a deep, uneven breath before the trembles ebbed, and I looked out the window. The sun hadn't yet risen, but dim morning light had started to paint the sky in faint shades of blue and pink.

"Does it ever get easier?" I whispered, even though I knew it wasn't a dream I'd woken from, that it wasn't the nightmares he'd thought I'd seen. "Do the nightmares ever stop?"

He inhaled. "No... It doesn't. I still have them myself, but I'd be worried if it did get easier. I like to think that the difficulty proves there's still a sliver of good keeping me from that final descent. Taking a life is never easy, no matter how much they deserved it."

I didn't speak then, my mind racing with everything I'd learned.

"You want to go back to slee—"

"No." The word flew from my mouth without thinking. I turned, sliding my feet off the edge of the bed as I braced myself, my skin crawling at the memory of Eris.

"Was it that bad?" he asked, pulling himself to my side.

"Just… too real. I don't want to risk going back into it."

I couldn't tell him about Eris. She'd nearly destroyed Salwa's mind. I didn't want to think what might happen if I told Damien about her. Was she always there, lurking in the depths of my mind, watching? Even now, was she listening in on our conversation?

"You think you can stomach breakfast?" Damien's question pulled me from my contemplation.

I shook my head, stomach churning already at the thought of food. "No food, please."

"Why don't you go take a good hot shower? It should help."

"That sounds like a good idea."

I pushed off the bed, grabbing onto the frame to steady myself. The headache worsened, and I winced.

"I'm going to call off training with Zephyr this afternoon," he said as he stood from the bed, heading to grab his phone.

I turned my head to him. "No."

He glanced back at me, hesitation and worry painting his face.

I needed to do more than sit in the house all day. Training would be a welcome distraction. It might get my mind off Eris and whatever plans she might be orchestrating. "I'll be fine. I just need a shower. I'll be ready by then."

"Are you sure? It's ok, *mea luna*. It's just one day."

I forced a smile. "I'll be fine. I'm tough."

I stood at the base of the mountain at The Outpost, the melting snow squelching under my feet. Zephyr's iridescent black feathers shimmered in the morning sun as he stood on a nearby low branch, observing. I ignored my exhaustion. I didn't know how late it had been before sleep finally claimed me, and I'd barely made it to our daily training on time.

I'd managed to successfully fly in my owl form and land without crashing a few times, which had given me a boost of confidence. My mind had been swirling with questions and possibilities about Eris all morning, and there were times when Zephyr had caught me in a distracted daze, had even teased me when he needed to repeat himself.

Zephyr leapt off the branch, his ebony wings sweeping out as he glided toward me, landing in the nearby grass. Black smoke enveloped him as he shifted back into his immortal form. "You gonna try the partial shift this time?"

I nodded. "Let me know if you see anything," I said as I pulled my black top over my head. The icy winter air chilled my skin. I'd worn a tank top under my training attire in preparation for this. I didn't want to risk tearing my clothes or injuring myself if I managed to form wings, regardless of how small they might be.

Zephyr moved to stand at my back. "All right, ready when you are."

I took a deep breath and closed my eyes. I focused on my shoulder blades, imagining wings stretching out from there instead of my arms. We sat in silence for so long, I was about to give up when a strange tingling sensation crept up my spine. It built, spreading out across the muscles in my shoulders. Zephyr sucked in air.

"Whatever you're doing, keep doing it," he breathed.

I did, focusing and imagining bone, tendon, muscle, feathers... I winced as my muscles protested but pushed through it, feeling a weight settle at my back.

"You're doing it, Cas," Zephyr said, his voice a low whisper of disbelief.

I gasped, air rushing into my lungs in short pants when I realized I'd stopped breathing in my strain. I leaned forward to brace myself against my knees, unable to continue.

"Gods, it's amazing," Zephyr said, and I glanced over my shoulder.

They were huge, fully feathered in a mix of tawny and white like my owl form. I tried to focus on moving muscle and bone, discovering which signals to send to flex and extend them, shifting my shoulder blades in hopes of somehow controlling them. One wing extended while the other folded, and I would have fallen over if it weren't for Zephyr catching me.

"How do you feel?" Zephyr asked as he stepped around to face me, arms extended in an offer of support.

"A bit tired," I admitted.

"The fact you can even do it is amazing," he said as his eyes rose to my wings again.

"No one's done this before?"

He shook his head. "None that I've heard of."

"Now I gotta figure out how to fly with these," I said with a grin. "Imagine how shocked the darklings will be when I attack them from above."

"Just take it slow. I know you're excited, but we have to make sure they'll sustain your weight before you go leaping off a cliff. Your bones aren't porous and light like they are when you're an owl." He glanced at me once more, and the speculation in his pale green eyes left me wondering if I looked as tired as I felt. "Are you ok, Cas?"

A sigh slipped through my lips. Maybe it was that uncanny brotherly instinct tipping him off. "I didn't sleep well last night."

I straightened, looking over my shoulder as I began to figure out how to move my wings, folding them in tightly at my back before extending them out again. They were so light, yet my balance seemed to shift with each movement of them.

"Everything ok?" Zephyr asked. "Still having the dreams?"

"No, it wasn't the dreams. I just..." How could I tell him what had kept me up? I was still scared of what might happen if I mentioned Eris to anyone. "Just a lot on my mind."

"Like what? You can talk to me."

I smiled, warmth filling my chest, and I knew the offer was genuine. "I'm just worried."

I closed my eyes, focusing on shifting back to normal, and slowly but surely, the weight on my back dissipated. My shoulders sagged as I righted myself and grabbed my sweater to pull it back on.

199

"Worried about what?" he asked as I lowered myself to sit on a rock.

"Everything." It wasn't a lie. There'd been so much on my mind since I'd learned about them, about their world and the darklings. It wasn't just Eris plaguing my thoughts, though she now held the most weight.

The inner corners of his onyx brows curved upward as he eased down beside me.

"I'm worried about my parents. I'm worried about Kat and Cody, what's going to happen to the mortals who live in the city, to the immortals who can't defend themselves like the family that was taken. I'm worried I won't be enough to help stop Melantha. The meeting with The Council went well, but..."

He tilted his head.

"I don't think I deserve to stand at Damien's side... I don't deserve the title of queen."

"Cas." He smiled as his head dropped, and I frowned. "I couldn't disagree with you more."

If only he knew what I'd hidden from them. Would he still think the same of me if he knew how I'd lied to them all?

"You care about people, Cas. You sacrifice more than you're willing to admit for others. It was your first meeting; you still barely know anything of ruling a kingdom, and yet..." He turned his gaze back to me. "You stood up against Tobias, in favor of giving the immortals a fighting chance, immortals who you've never even met. You made the decision to replace him with Calista, a female of worth who's well equipped with the knowledge to better serve House Nous. You fight alongside us hunting darklings, risk your life to protect both immortals and mortals alike. You give so much and ask for nothing in return."

I swallowed, fighting to hold his gaze, to not shift away from him.

"Cas." His eyes pierced through me, intense and profoundly genuine. "You are more than qualified to lead our people at Damien's side. I couldn't imagine serving anyone else."

"But... I don't know the first thing about leading a kingdo—"

"That can be learned," he said with such a calm. Any other words I might utter halted on my tongue. "A king or queen can learn to rule, can learn the laws and how to govern, but the care and dedication you show the people through the sacrifices you've made? That's something that can't be taught. It's something you're born with."

I smiled, my gaze falling from his, and while his words warmed me, the guilt sank further into my stomach. I wouldn't be able to meet his expectations, wouldn't be able to meet any of their expectations or needs. We'd be lucky if I lasted long enough to fight the darklings and bring Melantha down for good.

"Thank you, Zeph."

"I mean every bit of it," he said, resting a hand on my head as he leaned in to press his forehead to mine. "I'd never lie to you, Cas."

I forced a smile, chest swelling as I felt the adoration seep through the connection. The guilt lingered, swirling in the pit of my stomach until I couldn't hold his gaze any longer.

I'd never lie to you.

"First thing tomorrow I want to try to glide off a rock with just the wings," I said, eager to change the subject, to escape the guilt leaving me nauseous.

His mouth opened, then closed, and I couldn't ignore the concern in his eyes. "We can try, but promise you'll take it slow. Damien will kill me if I let you hurt yourself."

I chuckled. "I'll be fine, Zephyr. I promise to be careful."

"I'd appreciate that. I prefer my head on my shoulders."

I shook my head, giggling as I stood. "Can we try flight in my owl form a few more times before we finish up?"

"If you're feeling up to it, you can start navigating around trees."

I smiled and turned, jumping up onto the boulder, shifting mid leap into my owl form and landing, wings spread and ready for flight.

"But first you need a break," Zephyr said with a knowing smile.

My wings sagged to my sides as I let loose a heavy sigh. "Fine."

"Bank!" Zephyr coached from the tree before me.

I tilted my tail feathers, heart racing as I drifted around the trunk of the tree and landed on the branch lithely. The wind ruffled my feathers, but each movement I made, each sweep of my wings, left no sound.

"Excellent!"

I'd gotten a second wind after we stopped for a break, and we'd continued our training for an additional hour. I stretched my wings out once more before I folded them in at my side.

The bark of the branch crumbled under Zephyr's talons as he landed beside me. He tilted his head to me, onyx eyes assessing my wings. "I think we should end on that note. We'll glide down and be done for the day."

"Ok," I responded as he leapt off, gliding down to the base ahead of me.

As soon as we were done, I'd be able to focus on Marcus and Eris, revisit every interaction with him, see if I'd missed anything that might hint at his connection to Eris. I wondered if I could dive into my own mind and watch those memories, see if I could pick out anything that might give me any clues. Maybe I could see Lucia's memory of when they'd fought Melantha the first time, too.

Zephyr now stood on the ground below, already shifted. My eyes drifted across the expanse of the slumbering forest, snow blanketing every inch of the forest floor nearly thirty feet below. Confidence surged through me as I stretched my wings out. I'd glided farther distances. For once, there wasn't any doubt in my mind as I pushed off the branch.

The wind caressed my feathers, my body, as I descended. I loved this feeling. It was like freedom. Pure freedom, and I couldn't imagine how I'd lived without experiencing this, how someone could live tethered to the ground, unable to taste the wind, feel the breeze under their wings.

It was strange how quickly these things were becoming second nature, but Damien had explained before how the merging of the memories brought with them the experiences of my past lives. He was right. The lost parts of myself had slowly begun to fall into place as if I'd been incomplete my entire life.

I feared I would never get to experience that feeling of completeness before the end.

My thoughts drifted to darker places, to the end. Had Marcus known his was coming? Had he known I'd kill him? I tilted my wings and shifted to bank around a branch when Marcus' voice shot across my thoughts.

Do you hear it?

My concentration slipped, my balance failing. For a moment, I could see Marcus before me in the salvage shop, and my stomach dipped. His bloodied face lifted to me, as it had in the moments after I'd snapped and punched him. That cruel grin spread across his face.

I was wondering why it got so quiet after I had you in that cell.

I narrowly missed the branch I'd dipped under, my wings and tail tilting and flexing as I attempted to right myself. Marcus' voice flitted across my mind once again.

Thank you.

"Cas!" Zephyr yelled.

My gaze shot forward, and I slammed into a thick tree limb.

Whispers of an unknown language danced across my mind in the darkness—violent, surging, and overlapping. I was in chains, the metal icy against my tender skin. Eris' voice, disguised as my own, slid over me like a snake as I waited for Marcus to awaken me in that cell again.

He'll return. When he does, bite back.

The chains dispersed, and I plummeted through the concrete, crashing onto the couch at The Complex, head throbbing from diving into Cole's mind. Damien cursed as I told him of Marcus' involvement with the darklings.

Dammit, Marcus! What would possess him to side with them?

The memories and voices surged faster, overlapping with one another until I almost couldn't keep up. Marcus yelled in a rage as I slammed into the chair at the salvage shop, Damien bound and unconscious beside me.

Eris, you dumb bitch! You knew all this time I had Selene's daughter? I'm not playing your fucking games anymore! Show yourself!

Damien's words cut across as panic crept over me, my heart pounding like a drum, almost drowning out his voice as it built and built, threatening to explode.

Eris is the Goddess of Strife and Discord. She gets off on sowing chaos and ruining people's lives. She's turned countless families, friends, and Gods against one another, just for a good laugh.

Damien's face melded into shadow, and once more, Marcus was before me backed against the frame of a salvaged car, my vision red as I fought him, every ounce of hatred pouring out of me as I slammed my fist into his face again and again.

What did you do to me?

That terrible grin spread across Marcus' face as the venomous words poured from his lips.

Oh? Do you hear it? I was wondering why it got so quiet after I had you in that cell.

His final words slipped across my mind, his face turning to ash before me.

Thank you.

"Cassie! Wake up!"

I shot up from the darkness, air slamming into my lungs. Hands held me as I opened my eyes. I panted for any air I could get, but my lungs refused to expand, my chest collapsing.

"Easy; slow breaths."

I couldn't see for a moment, the world spinning so fast, whoever was with me was a blur of motion, but I knew that voice, the name I loved to be called.

"Dam—" I gasped, air finally finding its way into my lungs.

"You're ok, Cas," Zephyr said. "You fell."

I looked around. We weren't outside anymore, and I was in a bed, no longer in my owl form.

My mind reeled, the pieces falling into place. Eris and Marcus *were* connected, so much more than we could've ever imagined. Damien had told me how he changed after Vivienne died, how he'd snapped and nothing he did made any sense after that, but of course it wouldn't—

Because it wasn't him who'd done it all. His mind had been poisoned, corrupted.

"Damien!" I managed to get out.

Damien's hand came to rest on my shoulder. "Easy, *mea luna.* Johnson is checking for any broken bones."

"Eris manipulated Marcus!"

He steadied me, dark brows knitting together. "Slow down. What are you talking about?"

I couldn't get the words out fast enough, my voice unsteady as air forced its way into my lungs in uneven bursts. "At the salvage shop, he said something to me, asked if I could hear it, then he said how quiet it had been since he had me in the cell." My vision began to settle, and I winced as Johnson's fingers pressed into my rib cage.

"She may have broken a rib or two," Johnson said calmly over the chaos painting my voice.

Damien's eyes burned into mine. "Hear what? What are you talking about, Cas?"

"You told me Eris had turned friends and families against each other before! I never told you; Marcus thanked me when I killed him. I couldn't understand why he'd do that. It was because he didn't have control over himself! It was Eris!"

The pieces began to click into place in Damien's mind, realization dancing across his face.

"It wasn't him who did all those things! She corrupted him. The voice I've been hearing, it was Eris!"

Foolish girl. You just couldn't keep your mouth shut.

Pain assaulted me, claws sinking into my mind, and something coiled around the frail organ in my chest. My body buckled, back straightening, as I cried out.

Damien's olive skin paled. "Cas, what's wrong?"

"It's Eris!" I cried out, and Johnson stumbled back as I lurched.

Shut up, girl.

"She's the voice! She's the one who made me lose contro—"

SILENCE!

I gasped, my heart hammering, my skin burning and melting from within as Eris' claws threatened to split my mind in two. I fought back as she tried to stop me from speaking further, invisible hands snaking around my throat.

"Take me to Selene! Now, Damien! Plea—"

CHAPTER 26

DAMIEN

Cassie cried out, and her pupils expanded, eyes hazing over as she clutched her throat. My heart sank. She couldn't breathe. Gods, she was suffocating. Eris was killing her.

Take me to Selene!

Her voice echoed one final plea through my mind, and I snapped from my terror, shoving Zephyr and Johnson away before wrapping my arms around her. Icy air and darkness descended around us, the medical room of The Complex melting into shadows. I didn't have enough time to think, couldn't focus on anything but Cassie in my arms as Eris assaulted her.

We slammed into the stone floor of Selene's temple so violently my knees screamed at the contact, my body recoiling from the cost the magic demanded to pass through the veil. Cassie nearly spilled from my arms onto the floor before me as she gasped for air, body convulsing, fighting something I couldn't see. I held her, eyes darting around the room for Selene.

"Selene!" I yelled, bracing myself as the room spun.

She stood on the dais at the head of the hall. She wasn't alone, but I couldn't care enough to see who it was as my eyes fell back on Cassie. Short bursts of panicked air slipped from her lips, and her back arched violently.

"Fight her, Cassie!"

"What's happened, Damien?" Selene asked as she appeared beside us, her white silken gown and hair pooling around her as she fell to her knees.

"It's Eris!" I took Cassie's hand, her other one clutched at her chest.

Selene's eyes went wild, and a fury I'd never felt rose off her. "Eris?"

The scent of her anger, like smoldering oak and jasmine, filled my lungs, but another scent faintly lingered beneath it, one sour and acrid. Fear?

"She's killing her!"

Someone knelt beside me, and a strange hand shot out for Cassie. Something stirred in the dark void in my chest. My body reacted, grabbing his tanned arm, and my fangs unsheathed, instinct taking over to protect my mate no matter the cost.

"It's ok, Damien. I mean her no harm." His deep voice, powerful and deadly, yet calm and soothing, eased the instincts that had momentarily raged out of control. Still, I hesitated, dread crawling over my skin as the memories threatened to resurface.

"Erebus..."

My eyes met his, and the God of Darkness offered a smile of reassurance. Instinct nearly consumed me at the thought of his hands on her. My body resisted as I forced my grip to loosen, if only to give him the chance to save her.

An agonizing scream tore from Cassie's throat, and my gaze darted to her. Erebus lowered his hand to her chest, darkness seeping out where they were connected, and his palm sank into the dark void that formed in her chest. Her body shot up, back arching. My heart sank.

Black mist and inky darkness spilled out of that dark place Erebus had reached into, slipping over the marble floor.

Her body seized.

"Easy, Cas," I pleaded, plastering my hands on her shoulders. Her body jerked, instinct for survival taking over, and I fought to hold her in place. Her eyes were unseeing, as if she wasn't here, instead deep within her writhing body, fighting to live. Gods, she was dying. It pained me to no end that I couldn't help her, that the only thing I could do was watch. Suddenly, I wasn't holding Cassie, I was holding Lucia as the life slipped from her body, holding Elena after the darklings had ravaged her, watching Moira speak her last words as she...

I'm so sorry...

"Damien!" Erebus demanded through gritted teeth, pulling me back to the present.

I blinked back the burn in my eyes, shoring up my grip on Cassie, holding her in place. I lowered to her ear, praying I could help her in some way, to keep her tethered here. "Stay with me, Cas! Stay with me!"

Fates please. Not like this... Not again.

Darkness continued to pour out of her, spilling onto the marble floor around us as Erebus reached deeper into the void he'd found. Seconds felt like hours as he fought with whatever struggled to cling to her. I jerked my gaze to Cassie's chest as his weight shifted and he pulled back. With his hand came something so dark, so evil, it sent my hairs on end.

The pale white light from the ageless dimós trees dimmed, as if they might die out entirely. Dark wind sliced through the air, and the blue flames of the sconces surrounding us flickered as the shadows spread. The winds whipped around us, ripping the delicate petals of the night-blooming jasmine from their buds. Something within me stirred, that dark void deep within me, enticed by something. I'd felt it before, though it had been hundreds of years. I'd never been able to forget this feeling, this pull. I bit down, keeping myself in place, forcing that void within me to still.

Selene's war horses came to life at her altar, their heads whipping around, hot air spilling from their flared nostrils in puffs as they snorted, hooves smashing into the marble floors as they reared and pawed.

"Gods." The word left my lips on barely a breath as Erebus pulled it from Cassie.

Not *it*.... *her*.

"Eris." Selene's voice was laced with more fury than I'd ever heard mar that angelic tone. Her lips peeled back from her teeth, her canines sharp and bared at the mass of black mist.

Erebus rose, his hands clasped around something within the shadows as he held it above Cassie. The black mist dispersed, melting and fading as it drifted down her body, revealing the Goddess whose rage had become so palpable. I almost couldn't breathe for how it tainted the air around us. Her onyx hair flowed around her, the darkness still faintly licking her gray skin as her onyx eyes narrowed on Erebus.

A wicked grin spread across her face. The fact that Erebus' fingers were wrapped around her throat seemed to be of no consequence to her, but why would it? Selene, having been weakened in her imprisonment, couldn't stand up to her, and Eris' power rivalled his. Erebus turned, carrying her away from us.

I couldn't focus on the Goddess as she glowered down at Erebus, my eyes immediately falling to Cassie as she lay on the floor, unconscious.

My heart sputtered. Her skin was pale, cold to the touch. Her lips, once blush and bright, had turned a pale shade of grayish purple. My eyes drifted over her body; she was so still and for a moment I couldn't see even the faintest movement of breath. *Please Fates, no...*

"Cas?"

I pressed my ear to her chest. It was quiet, weak, but I was able to hear her heart beating. I reached up to lay a hand just above her parted lips. The softest of breaths caressed my skin, but I didn't know how far gone she might be, or how much damage Eris had been able to do before she was pulled from Cassie's mind.

"She's breathing." I cupped her cheek, leaning over to rest my forehead to hers. I'd give anything to see those eyes open. "Cas? Stay with me, please."

Gods, I felt so damned useless! Physical wounds I could help with. If she were bleeding, I could staunch it, could stitch it closed, but this? There was nothing I could do but watch helplessly at her side, praying the fates might smile down on her and give her another chance.

Selene didn't speak, and I lifted my gaze, ready to beg her, whatever it took. I froze. I couldn't believe what I saw. Worry filled the Goddess's eyes as she stared down at Cassie, a mother's worry. It had been centuries since I'd seen such emotion in those opalescent eyes, and I'd feared she'd forgotten, that she'd become numb, like many of the Elythians had.

Words escaped me as Selene extended her hand to Cassie's forehead, her eyes closing. A warm glow came to life in her palm, and I wondered if she could sense what Eris had done to her, if she could repair whatever damage had been wreaked.

"When did Eris get her hands on Moira's mind?"

"I-I don't know. She had a training accident and was knocked out. When she came to, she started telling me that Eris manipulated Marcus, that Eris was the reason she's been struggling with her magic, but this is the first she's told me about it."

Selene opened her eyes as she continued to push that light into Cassie, and I watched in silence, praying to gods I hadn't believed in for centuries.

"Eris has been holding her captive," Selene said softly, eyes intense as she focused.

My stomach twisted, my mind flying through every occurrence that might've hinted at Eris' involvement. How long had Cassie known and been unable to tell me? How long had she suffered under Eris' watchful eye while I was oblivious?

"What do you think you're doing, Eris?" Erebus asked from behind us, and I glanced over my shoulder.

A grin spread across the Goddess' face, and I restrained the urge to snap her neck. "I was merely helping the little goddess."

"It didn't look like that to me," Erebus said casually, a dark brow cocked.

I pulled my gaze from Erebus and Eris to look back at Cassie. Air slammed into my lungs in relief as the color slowly returned to her skin. She groaned, her face scrunching.

"Cas?" I lifted my hand to brush my fingers along her cheek. She already felt warmer.

Her eyes fluttered opened, those hazel eyes I loved so much lifting to me, and my shoulders sagged. She tensed and tried to sit up, her hand cupping her side as she grimaced. My hands shot out to help her.

Selene turned to glare over her shoulder at Eris, who remained in Erebus' clutches. "*You.*"

Eris' eyes shifted to Selene, the grin never leaving her face. "Hello, Selene. It's been far too long. You didn't think I'd just live out the rest of eternity in my domain, did you?"

Cassie stiffened when her eyes found Eris, and she grabbed onto me. Terror welled in her eyes, and it was as if the memory of all that had happened had slammed into her. I laid a hand over hers as it clung

211

to me, and I turned my gaze on Eris, body tensing. She was far too cheerful for someone who'd been caught red-handed breaking the laws of the Godsrealm. It was expressly forbidden to interfere with mortals, and while Cassie had the soul and powers of a goddess, she was technically mortal.

Selene rose, her hair fluttering around her. Whatever power remained within her threatened to burst free. "How dare you interfere with my daughter."

"Oh? You suddenly care?" Eris' onyx eyes glided over Selene, sizing the Goddess up. "Last I heard, you were willing to let her succumb to whatever fate would befall her when her powers fully awoke."

"Are you the one who interfered with Moira's reincarnation?" Selene demanded.

Eris' gaze shifted away, false innocence flitting across her face. "Moira's reincarnation? I don't know what you're talking about."

I whipped around, pushing Cassie behind me. I'd slice the bitch's throat for what she'd done, the suffering she'd caused Cassie. If she'd been the reason for her reincarnating as a mortal... I stretched my arm out, tapping into the shadows as I summoned my dagger. The weight fell into my grasp and the black mist melted away, revealing black Elythian steel that begged to be wielded. I locked eyes on Eris, whose gaze had shifted to Cassie and me. Would Erebus be able to contain her? I didn't know how powerful she'd become over the centuries, but I'd be damned if I let her lay another finger on Cassie.

"You know the laws, Eris," Erebus said.

Eris looked back to Erebus and her eyes narrowed, but that smile still lingered. "Are you going to scold me, Father? Tell me how bad I've been? You're no upstanding saint yourself. He still suffers after what you did to him, you know." Erebus' eyes briefly flickered to me, but I avoided his gaze. Eris looked back to us, to Cassie. "If anything, you should be thanking me."

I froze as Cassie gripped my shirt and yelled at Eris. "I'd never thank you!"

Eris' eyes flared, her smile growing crazed. "You made a grave mistake in revealing my presence, girl. You will live to regret this."

"And you will regret the moment you chose to tamper with my daughter," Selene yelled, her opalescent eyes nearly glowing with rage.

"So, the moon goddess *does* have bite." The taunt was obvious. Eris wanted her to attack, wanted the fight. "And here I thought you'd mellowed out after all these years."

212

Eris' eyes roamed over Selene. "I can feel it you know... You aren't what you used to be." Her expression shifted then, into something cold and calm, the rage reflecting in her onyx eyes unsettling. "I promised you, didn't I?"

Selene hesitated, her body stiffening, and the grin returned to Eris' face at the sight of it.

Gods, this was spiraling out of control. We couldn't linger here any longer. I needed to get Cassie out of here. Elythians rarely fought each other personally, but when they did, the display of power was enough to level cities, kingdoms, even. I'd been told the tales as a child, saw the ruins of cities that had fallen with my own eyes. I shuddered to think of the destruction if Selene and Eris fought. If Erebus joined in, Selene's moon could be reduced to dust.

We were fucking powerless, and I wouldn't be able to protect Cassie, not with my magic drained after jumping across realms. The darkness within me stirred again, offering the depthless power it could give. If I tapped into it, I might...

I glanced back at Cassie, taking in that beautiful face, her hair— inhaled her scent of jasmine and citrus. If it meant she lived, I'd open myself to that darkness, use it to fight Eris, to protect Cassie—

And pray I didn't fall as Matthias did.

"Don't worry, little Lord of Shadows," Eris said. "I will not be fighting your lady and master today." My gaze snapped to her, and a low growl ripped from my throat at the invasion of my thoughts. "I have more important things to do, so I will be taking my leave."

"You don't get to make that decision," Erebus said, his jaw tightening. His own darkness swelled at his feet, the dark tendrils reaching for her.

"Try and stop me, Father," she said with a smile, all light in the space flickering.

Erebus growled as Eris' own dark magic slid off her body like snakes, coiling around his arms. His hand recoiled as it bit into him. "Dammit, Eris!"

Eris' manic laughter filled the room as the black mist built and built, consuming her, the wind lashing around us. My heart lurched, Cassie's fingers digging into my arm as she clung to me. I turned, wrapping my arms around her, shielding her as best I could. Selene slid before us, extending her arms outward, and a shield of light streaked around us as Eris unleashed a blast of power.

She vanished.

CHAPTER 27

CASSIE

An eerie silence filled the room, the light of the pale glowing trees flickering, and I couldn't stop the shaking overtaking my body as I gripped onto Damien's shirt. "Is she gone?"

Selene rose, scanning the massive room. Moments passed without a response from Damien as we surveyed the chamber. Selene's warhorse statues pawed on the dais, snorting but settling. Jasmine petals drifted to the stone floors as the harsh winds finally died down, and the sconces returned to life, flames illuminating the temple hall in a pale blue light.

Damien turned to me when there appeared to be no sign of Eris, his hands shaking as he held me. "Are you ok?"

I didn't know how to answer. I felt so weak, so tired, I couldn't even bring myself to stand. "I-I think so..."

"You're lucky to be alive, little goddess."

My gaze jerked to the source of the deep voice echoing off the stone walls, dripping with such power I almost forgot how to speak. His sea foam eyes passed over me, tan skin as unblemished and smooth as Selene's. He swept back his onyx curls before kneeling beside us, and the power contained in his massive body washed over me.

Damien tensed when the man grew closer, as if he were preparing to do whatever it took to protect me. Was he bad? What was he doing here? What were *we* doing here? How did we get here? My mind raced, memory clouded and unclear beyond the medical room at The Complex.

"When did you first notice Eris' presence?" the man asked.

I snapped back to the present. How did he know about that? "I..." I glanced at Damien, who nodded that it was safe to speak to him. "I didn't know it was her until just a few days ago... but I've felt her since I was held captive by Marcus."

Damien's gaze snapped to me, a horrified look on his face. "That long?"

I swallowed and nodded, my eyes faltering. "I'm sorry, I couldn't tell you. I was afraid of what she'd do."

"What did you mean, Eris manipulated Marcus?" Selene asked, turning to look at me.

Damien's eyes remained fixated on me, just as eager for an answer.

"I... I think she corrupted him. Damien told me something changed in him after he lost his mate. I saw him in Damien's memories. He'd been a completely different person from the Marcus I knew." *Knew.* The thought felt like poison in my mind. I knew him all right, more than I cared to acknowledge. I knew every twisted thing he had the potential to do to a person. Or... had I? It wasn't the true him I'd known, but the twisted corruption Eris had woven into his mind over the last century. He'd been held captive, just as I had.

Selene considered my words for a moment, her pale eyes lowering to the marble floors.

"It definitely sounds like something she would do," the man said, turning his face to me. My brows furrowed as I met his gaze. "Apologies. My name is Erebus. I am an ally of Selene's."

He gave a soft bow of his head, and his smile lit up those rich, sea foam eyes.

"Erebus is the God of Darkness," Damien explained, eyes fixed on the man. "He's the one who offered shadow magic to Selene when she created our race." I couldn't help but notice a hint of hostility in Damien's voice. Did he consider Erebus an enemy? I vaguely remember Eris calling him Father after I woke, but where had he come from? Was he here when we arrived?

Erebus didn't seem phased by Damien's tone, his eyes so piercing, I had to look away.

"Forgive me for staring. I'm intrigued by you, little goddess." I could almost feel his eyes roaming over me, and I stiffened. "You are unlike other demigods, for you have the combined gifts of many of our kind. One might say you could be the future of the Elythian race. Any god would be an unstoppable force with you at their side."

Damien's lips peeled back, revealing his fangs, and... God, his eyes. They'd become crystalline, the amber in the center of the ashen silver burning like embers. His pupils contracted and expanded at the slightest movements. I gripped Damien's sleeve, and his hand raised to cover mine in acknowledgement.

"Do not fret, Lord of Shadows. I do not intend to steal your mate," Erebus said, a coy grin spreading across his face as he rose. "I do not force my servants to stand at my side." His eyes settled on me again, that smile remaining, and the hair on the back of my neck stood on end. "They come willingly."

Selene paced, her gown shifting and gliding over her body with each movement, the light of the blue flames reflecting off the shimmering fabric. "Did you learn anything else from Eris?"

I opened my mouth, but the words wouldn't come, and I had to think through everything. "She... visited me in a dream last night."

Damien's eyes fell from Erebus, frowning as he turned to meet my gaze. "The dream you didn't want to go back into..."

I nodded, painfully aware of how much I hated that I hadn't been able to talk to him about it. "I didn't get much out of her; she was closely guarded. She was helping stabilize my body while I learned my abilities."

"She was helping you?" Damien asked in disbelief.

"Yeah. I don't understand why she'd want to help me, though," I muttered, eyes falling to the marble floor, littered with jasmine blossoms. A thought crossed my mind, and I looked back at him. "She did let something slip."

Selene's white brows rose, her head tilting as she waited for me to continue.

"She wanted Marcus dead. I don't know why."

Damien's eyes lowered as he considered the possibilities. "Maybe he knew something."

"I don't know…" Any knowledge Marcus might've had on Eris died with him. There was no getting that information now.

"She claimed she was manipulating me when I killed Marcus to make me stronger for the battles to come. Was she talking about the war with the darklings?" I asked, glancing at Selene.

Damien pressed his knuckles to his lips as he sank deep into thought. "She's never sided with us. Why would she care about our battle with the darklings now? And why do it after she had Marcus work with Melantha? Is she playing both sides?"

"Does she have any ties to the darklings?" I asked.

Damien shook his head. "There's never been any signs, outside of Marcus. She's never involved herself in our affairs, and the only time she's ever been seen in the Mortalrealm was to cause trouble for mortals, which was a typical sport for her. I hadn't heard of her actively interfering in the affairs of another god or goddess recently. She's remained secluded in her kingdom for centuries."

Selene's eyes flickered as Damien spoke, but she remained silent for a long while before she glanced at me, her face unreadable. "Are you all right, Moira?"

The words clicked in my head, and I straightened, realizing she was talking to me. "I-I think I'm ok. I just feel a little weak, sore from the training accident…"

It almost seemed as if her shoulders relaxed, but only for a moment before she squared them, her head held high. "Good. Damien, you may take her. Report to me if you learn anything new of Eris' involvement."

Damien bowed his head. "Of course, Goddess."

The Propylaea was cold and dark when we returned, which was strange. Normally, blue flames came to life the moment we entered. Thankfully, just enough light shined down the stairwell, just enough for me to see. I couldn't ignore the exhaustion filling Damien's eyes.

"Are you ok?" I asked, stopping him.

"Just a little worn. It takes a lot for me to pass to the Godsrealm without assistance from the Propylaea. It acts as a bridge between our worlds, but there was no time. I had to get you to Selene."

"Is it dangerous to do that?" I asked, realizing the weight of what he'd done.

He smiled weakly. "I'll be fine, *mea luna*."

Why did I not believe that?

He led me toward the stairway, but I didn't move, and he looked back when my fingers slipped from his grasp. I froze—listening, feeling, realizing. There was a resounding, peaceful silence in my mind. The doubt and dread that had clouded my every thought had faded. I stood there in a moment in disbelief, letting it all sink in. I was finally alone. The darkness that had lingered at my back every moment since Marcus held me in that chamber...

It was gone. I was finally alone with my own thoughts.

"Cas?" Damien asked, worry painting that beautiful face.

"I'm ok. I just feel... so light," I breathed, my gaze falling to my hands. Was all the hate and fear nothing but Eris' presence? Was that how badly she affected me? God, I could only imagine what Marcus must've gone through, what her presence had done to him for so many years.

Damien stepped closer, his hand lifting to brush through my hair. I smiled up at him, and a calm rush of relief washed over his face, his smile warming me. "How do your ribs feel? Johnson said you might've broken a few."

"They're a bit tender," I admitted.

"Do you mind if we go back to The Complex? I'd feel much better if Johnson checked you out fully," he asked.

While I wasn't thrilled at the thought, it was probably for the best. "Yeah, that's a good idea. I don't want you exhausting yourself with worry," I said, smirking up at him.

Damien cocked a grin, pulling his phone from his pocket, and pressed a button before holding it to his ear. "Hey Zephyr, are you— easy, brother. She's ok, don't worry... Yeah, Selene and Erebus were able to stop Eris. She's safe now."

I could hear Zephyr's frantic voice over the phone and guilt immediately sank into the pit of my stomach. He'd been with us when Eris attacked me. He'd probably feared the worst.

"I'm bringing her down to see Johnson... Yeah, she's ok. I'll tell you more about it when we get there... See you shortly." Damien hung up and slid the phone into his pocket before extending his hand to me.

"I feel so horrible. Zephyr must've been freaking out," I said, taking Damien's hand. He pulled me in close, the temperature dropping as black mist rose and danced at our feet.

"Are you sure you can take us there?" I asked, worried about how much he'd exhausted himself already.

He smiled warmly. "I'll be fine. I'll rest easy when I know you're ok."

I gripped onto him as the darkness enveloped us. The floor vanished from beneath our feet for a moment before we settled onto tile, and the shadows dispersed, revealing Johnson's office.

Zephyr rushed over to me. "Cas!"

"I'm ok, Zephyr. I promise."

He gripped my arms, agony etched into his face as he looked me over, and his head fell forward in relief. "Gods, I was afraid Selene would be too late."

I stepped closer, wrapping my arms around him to offer him any comfort and reassurance I could. "I'm safe, Zephyr. I'm here."

"Thank the Fates." he breathed, holding me tightly.

"Cas." I glanced back to find Johnson beckoning from the nearby medical table.

"Coming, Johnson," I said, and Zephyr released me before he and Damien stepped to the side so Damien could fill him in.

I groaned as I climbed onto the bed, my sides protesting each movement. The adrenaline was finally slipping away, and I was slowly becoming very aware of how much damage I'd sustained from the fall. "How far did I fall?"

"Zephyr said you fell almost twenty feet." Johnson felt around my ribs, and I winced when he poked my right side. "Thankfully, it seems you were mid shift when you hit the ground, so there wasn't as much force."

It had all happened so fast.

"I think you just suffered some bruising. Do you remember anything?" he asked as he jotted down some notes in a folder. It was strange how refreshing it was to see such a thin file instead of the packet full of countless files my doctor had.

"Not really. The last thing I remember was a branch."

"You seem to be getting around ok. Anything else hurting?"

I shook my head. "Just my ribs."

He pulled a small flashlight from his pocket and clicked it on. "You may have a concussion, so I'm going to run a few additional tests to make sure everything else is good. I want you to look into the light, ok?"

I nodded, bracing my knees as I straightened. "Ok."

CHAPTER 28

DAMIEN

"Damien, you don't look too good," Zephyr said as we allowed Johnson the room to properly examine Cassie.

Gods damn this male and his attention to detail. It didn't matter whether I was okay or not, not when Cassie had come so close to...

I didn't let myself finish that thought.

"I'll be fine," I responded, leaning against the far wall, eyes locked on Johnson. My senses were heightening, my body dredging up every instinct to hunt, to feed, to replenish the energy I'd expelled moving us between realms. I knew I'd pay for it, but there'd been no time. If I'd have taken her to the Propylaea first, it would have been too late.

What did Eris want in all this? Had she really had a hand in the interruption of Moira's reincarnation? Was she the reason Cassie had been born a human instead of an immortal? How would she benefit from this? Was it purely out of boredom? What the fuck was she scheming? Why?

Johnson moved his small flashlight across Cassie's face. Her hazel eyes quickly dilated in reaction to the light. Relief washed over me that she didn't have a concussion, but I feared what hidden injuries might linger beneath the surface.

Zephyr's black brows narrowed, and I resisted the urge to silence him. "You crossed the veil on your own, Damien. I don't even understand how you're standing right now."

"Well, I am."

"Gods dammit, Damien, you didn't stop to think about what could've happened to *you*?" Zephyr said, turning to me.

"It wouldn't have mattered what happened to me if she'd died," I stiffened, my voice louder than it should have been, and I groaned when he met my stare. "Sorry."

Zephyr sighed, pinching the bridge of his nose between his thumb and forefinger, but thankfully, he didn't press further. "What happened? Cas was saying something about Eris before shit hit the fan."

I swallowed, still getting past the fact that Eris had nearly killed her. "Eris has been occupying Cassie's mind since Marcus had her. She's the reason Cas has been struggling with everything, and it looks like Eris was the reason for..." Fuck. I still couldn't believe it. "Cas thinks Marcus was corrupted by Eris this entire time."

The color drained from Zephyr's face. "Gods..."

It would explain everything—Marcus' irrational behavior, why he blamed me for Vivienne's death. Guilt sank into the pit of my stomach as sorrow washed over me. How badly had he suffered all this time, alone? Over two hundred years trapped in that misery, and Eris had tried to do the same to Cassie.

Zephyr hesitated, but asked, "Do you think he was aware of it all?"

Gods, I prayed he wasn't. I could only imagine the horrors he'd suffered if he'd been fully aware of his actions but unable to do anything about it. We still didn't know the extent of the things he'd done, if he'd had a hand in the disappearances, how long he'd worked side by side with his mate's murderers. Had Eris done it intentionally? Was this just another one of her games, like she used to play on mortals? I guess I shouldn't be surprised. The goddess rarely seemed rational.

"He... thanked Cas when she killed him. She only just told me after Eris attacked her." I hated that she'd kept that information to herself, but she'd likely felt guilty, probably tried to save me from that painful knowledge.

"*Fuck,*" Zephyr breathed, running his hand over his face.

Would Eris return? Would she target Cassie again?

"You don't think..." I feared I knew what Zephyr was going to ask next. "You don't think Cole might also be..."

I couldn't let myself give into the hope that Cole hadn't betrayed us of his own volition, that he hadn't truly helped Marcus. I pushed off the wall, leaving him without a response. We still weren't entirely sure how long Cole had been working with Marcus. Whether or not the possibility of corruption, the Cole we'd interrogated didn't feel like the Cole I knew. The Cole I'd seen in Cassie's memories hadn't either. Or… did I ever truly know him at all?

"How is she looking?" I asked as I approached Johnson.

"I don't think she broke anything, thankfully. No signs of a concussion." Johnson glanced back at Cassie. "You're lucky, I'll give you that."

She forced a weak smile, but her eyes slid away from him. I wondered just how badly she was affected by all this, could only imagine what was really going on in her head. Her frantic heartbeat reached my ears, and I had to shut it out. *Fuck.* I couldn't fight the heightened senses, the instincts pushing to the surface, and that meant one thing: I'd crossed into dangerous territory. Zephyr was right, I couldn't deny it. I wasn't good, and it was a struggle to remain firm on my own two feet.

Johnson returned to his desk and set his folder aside. Cassie glanced at me, her delicate eyebrows scrunching. I suddenly became very aware of her, of her breathing, her scent, the pumping of her blood. My fangs throbbed, slipping free, and I clamped my mouth shut. No, not now. She'd been injured, could still harbor wounds we weren't aware of. The last thing she needed was for me to feed from her.

She slid off the bed, head tilting as her eyes danced across my face. "*Mea sol?*"

I forced a closed lipped smile. "You ready to go home?"

She nodded, and I could see the hesitation in her eyes. I took her hand before turning for the nearest dark corner.

"Damien," Zephyr started.

I glanced back at him, and the look he gave me irritated me to no end. "I'm fine, Zephyr."

His eyes wavered before drifting to Cassie. "Just try to get some rest, Cas. We'll skip training tomorrow and Thalia will work with you on Sunday and Monday."

"Actually, I'm going to visit my mom on Monday. I completely forgot to tell you."

She hadn't told me she was going to see her mom, but I was relieved she would be visiting her family. She'd been so busy with training, she'd had little time to visit with her parents. I didn't want her to miss out on them or her old life simply because of us.

"That works for me," Zephyr responded with a shrug.

"I'll see you on patrol tomorrow night," she added.

I stiffened. "Cas, I don't know if that's a good idea."

"I actually feel really good, for the first time in a while. Honest, *mea sol*." Her smile warmed my heart, and I pressed a kiss to her forehead before I drew from the dark void inside me. The shadows shifted from the corner toward us. They twitched and nearly receded back, but I pulled harder, and they gave in, rising around us.

CHAPTER 29

CASSIE

Cold air whirled around us, my curls dancing over my shoulders. Then, the dark mist dispersed, revealing our dimly lit room. Damien's body sagged as the shadows receded, and I grasped his arm, helping to stabilize him.

"Damien?"

He braced himself against the dresser, and when he turned his face to me, I saw them, just beneath his parted lips. The low light of the lamp reflected off the glimpse of his exposed fangs. My breath hitched, heart skipping a beat at the sight of them. He needed to feed. I'd noticed that he'd seemed off at The Complex, and the way Zephyr acted before we left had me suspicious.

Taking me to Selene's realm without the Propylaea must have taken a heavier toll than I imagined. His olive skin had paled a bit, pupils expanding and contracting in the low light with each movement, the crystalline veins almost glowing in his irises.

"What do you need, *mea sol*?"

Confliction flitted across his eyes, and for a moment I feared he might try to bury it. "I'll be fine. I just need rest."

"Don't lie to me," I said firmly, cupping his cheek.

His eyes softened, but the worry remained. "I need to know you're really ok, that you're not just saying you are."

I stifled the fear of what would happen to me now that Eris wasn't here to keep my condition in check. I could be honest about one thing, though. Without her presence, I felt free, unburdened. "I'm ok, I swear. Honestly, I feel better than I've felt in months." I lifted my eyes to him. "Now *you* be honest with me."

His eyes raked over me, and I could see it, that predator lingering just beneath the surface.

"You need to feed, don't you?" He swallowed, eyes averting from mine. I tugged at his chin, forcing his gaze back to me. "Tell me what you need, *mea sol*. Let me help you."

"You. I need to feel you, to taste you." He lowered his face to mine as his finger slid along my neck to my chin. "Yes, I need to feed, but I need..."

The conflict surged across his face, and guilt slammed into me. It was because of me he fought his needs, because I'd been attacked.

"I'm yours," I whispered back when he couldn't bring himself to say another word, our breaths mingling.

His hands slid down to my hips, and I gasped as he gripped me. "Gods, I love hearing you say that," he rasped against my lips before capturing my mouth with his.

The exquisite taste of him never dulled, every kiss just as glorious as the first. He pressed me back against the dresser, his leg sliding between my thighs. I drew a sharp breath, my back arching, heart leaping as his tongue slipped passed my lips. The invasion was divine, and I met his hunger with my own until he withdrew, pulling my lower lip between his teeth. His fang grazed the sensitive skin, nearly piercing it.

"Sorry," he breathed, face scrunching as he momentarily fought with himself.

I lifted my hand to his face. "Damien."

His eyes shot open, meeting mine.

"Don't hold back, *mea sol*. Take what you need." His muscles tensing beneath my touch as I slid my hand up his chest until I reached his shoulders. His features softened, and his lips brushed against my cheek in the most tender of kisses. My heart thrummed, air flooding my lungs as I inhaled deeply. His kisses trailed along my jaw, moving lower until he found my throat. His tongue glided along my neck, and I moaned, head tilting back.

"Gods, I love that sound," he groaned against my skin, and my blood turned molten in my veins. "*There are so many fucking ways I want to take you.*"

His words sent shivers rippling across my body, liquid pooling between my thighs as his fangs dragged along my throat, teasing at the pleasure I knew awaited me. His hand snaked up my back and his fingers ensnared in my hair, tilting my head. The embers in those ash eyes nearly glowed as they reflected the dim light, his gaze piercing through me. God, did it make me melt.

"And I wouldn't just take from your throat," he breathed, his control crumbling but holding. My chest heaved, body melting. "Do you want to know how I'd take you, *mea luna*?"

I swallowed as his eyes held me captive, that predatory instinct he harbored rising to the surface. The words slipped from my lips in a near whisper. "How?"

His fingers glided along my skin to my breast, and my breath hitched. "I'd take from here…" They continued down to my hip. "Here…" His hand descended farther, and I inhaled sharply, heated anticipation coiling deep and low when his hand slid to the inside of my thigh. "Here…" His breathing turned ragged. He cupped me through my jeans, and my body jerked in response. "And *Gods*, will I enjoy devouring you here."

A moan spilled from my lips as he slid his thumb against that throbbing concentration of nerves between my thighs, the feeling muffled by too many layers of clothing between us.

He tilted his head, his eyes burning into me, and my world threatened to catch fire. "Would you like that?"

I couldn't think straight, my knees quivering. With each passing second, I grew more and more desperate to peel him out of those clothes, to touch every glorious inch of him, but as I reached for the waist of his pants, hands as soft as a brush of wind wrapped around my wrists, pulling my hands back against the dresser. My gaze dropped, his hand still in place between my legs, his other entangled in my hair.

Shadow magic.

The phantom hands, made of dark mist and shadow, gripped my wrists, their thumbs brushing against my skin in tender strokes as he held me in place. A low sound rippled from his throat, and I met his gaze, my body coming alive. A wicked grin curved one side of his mouth, revealing a fang, and I nearly forgot how to breathe.

"Don't get ahead of yourself now. You didn't answer my question." He lowered himself to my ear, his breath causing me to shiver. When I didn't answer, his hand grasped my hip, and he pulled me forward, grinding me against his leg as my body buckled. "Would you like that, *mea luna*?"

"*Yes*," I gasped, hot air spilling from my lungs in a breathy moan.

I lifted my eyes to him. He was different. Something inside of him had been set loose, but I wasn't afraid, because I knew, in the deepest parts of my soul, that he'd never hurt me. He kissed me deeply, the shadowy hands releasing me as he furiously worked to remove my sweater, nearly tearing it apart before I helped him pull it over my head. He threw it aside before his hand found my breast and my head fell back as he pulled my bra down impatiently, the straps trapping my arms at my sides as his lips found their way to my chest.

He struck, fangs sinking into the tender flesh of my breast, and I gasped as the faint sting melted into something wickedly delicious. His moan spilled out over my skin as he drank, tasting every ounce of pleasure flooding me. It didn't last long enough, and he broke the connection a few short moments later. My body sagged against his, my skin tingling, electric currents dancing across every inch of my body. His arm wrapped around my waist as he absorbed my weight. I lifted my eyes, my chest heaving as I tried to regain control over my body.

His eyes fell to my breast, a sinful, crooked grin tugging at his lips. His tongue passed lazily over one of his fangs, and my heart leapt at the sight. "I like the sight of my mark on you."

I followed his gaze to the two small punctures on my breast, encircled by red and purple skin. My body quivered, air escaping my grasp as the rippling sensation continued to radiate through my body. He was wicked, unleashed, and I wanted him, wanted him to do all the things he promised and more. His hand slipped around my back to unclasp my bra before pulling it down my arms and tossing it aside. I braced myself against the dresser, knees shaking under my weight as the effects of the feeding left me high. He licked his lips, and his eyes met mine once more, fire burning in them. Did he know how badly I wanted him?

As if to answer the question lingering on my lips, he hooked his hands under my thighs and lifted me. I wrapped my arms over his broad shoulders, capturing his lips with mine, and he groaned against my mouth. The coppery taste of my blood lingered on his tongue, and it sent my heart into a frenzy as he carried me toward the bed.

The mattress dipped as he lowered me down, and he released me to pull his shirt over his head. His pants hung low on his hips, the swell of his arousal pressed firmly against the zipper. I wanted to touch him, to feel every part of him under my fingertips.

I rose onto my elbows to gaze at him. My eyes fell over his chest, his muscles taut, veins popping across his hands and forearms. I pushed myself up to reach out, running my fingers along the grooves of his stomach, over his pectorals. His heart raced beneath my palm, matching mine with each beat. His eyes tracked my movements, but when I met his gaze, I thought he might devour me at any moment—

And, God, did I want it.

My lips curved into a grin as I watched the way my touch made him react, every twitch of his muscles, every shudder. He was stunningly beautiful, as if he were sculpted by the finest artist, and he was mine. Something bloomed in my chest at the thought, and he shuddered at that very moment.

My hands slid down to unclasp the button of his pants, and I lowered the zipper at a painfully slow pace, holding his gaze. His burning eyes remained fixed on me, his chest expanding and contracting in fluid motions as he restrained himself. I took hold of the waist of his pants, pulling them down along with his boxers. I swallowed at the sight of him, thick and free, begging to be touched.

His scent filled the room, flooding my lungs with that musky aroma of cedarwood and leather I loved so much. He kicked his pants off and pushed me back onto my elbows. His hand planted firmly on either side of me, he leaned down until his face was inches from my own. His lips curved into a crooked grin. "I like that look in your eyes."

His weight shifted, his face lingering inches from my own as he watched me. He clasped his hand over my breast and brushed his thumb over the sensitive peak, drawing a shudder from me. "But I love the way you look when I make you come even more."

He released my breast to slide his hand down, finger grazing my sternum, and I shivered. Lower and lower, he traced over my stomach until his finger hooked into the top of my jeans. He pulled my hips forward, and his lips were on mine, devouring me as I drowned in the taste of him. Coppery and sweet, salty and sinful. His tongue danced over mine, and I slid my tongue against one of his fangs.

His body jerked, a groan spilling from his throat, and I wondered if he felt that, wondered just how sensitive his fangs might be. He undid the button of my jeans and broke the kiss to nuzzle against my neck as he pulled them off me. He grabbed my hips and pulled me to the edge of the bed, his knee pressed into the bed beside me, his hard length hot against my thigh.

"You keep doing things like that with your tongue, and I won't be able to resist sinking myself so deep inside you we both forget our names," he growled against my lips.

Desire spun inside me, writhing and coiling, begging for more. I parted my lips to make a smart remark, but the words fell short on my tongue—a moan slipping from my throat as his finger slid up my center through my underwear.

"What was that?" he asked, that wicked grin returning as his eyes roamed my face.

Before I could respond, he did it again, and he dipped down to take my breast between his lips, his finger stroking torturously against that throbbing bundle of nerves. His name burst from my lips, and my head fell back as he teased the sensitive peaks of my breast with his tongue and teeth.

He lifted his face to me as he continued the wicked rhythm between my legs, relishing in the expressions he elicited. It was all I could do not to come undone when he slipped two fingers past my underwear, plunging them deep inside me. My back arched, hands grabbing onto his arms as my body bucked. His other hand grasped the back of my neck as he held my gaze.

I pushed myself against him, kissing him deeply, tension winding and building as I grew closer to that edge. My lips parted against his as I moaned once more, his thrusts deep, momentum building and building.

"Fuck, you're beautiful," he said against my lips as he withdrew his fingers, leaving me teetering on that precarious edge. He lifted those two fingers and drew them between his lips. I inhaled deeply as a low rumble ripped from his throat at the taste of me on his tongue.

Something snaked up my legs, and my eyes fell. Shadows. They rose, brushing over my calves and thighs until they reached my hips. Like hands, they glided up my stomach.

"Another of your talents?" I breathed, smiling at him, and I shuddered as that shadowy hand grasped my breast.

His heated gaze met mine. "I have many."

Need shot through me as he sank to his knees before me, pulling my underwear off and throwing them to the side before spreading my thighs apart. He dipped his head to drag his tongue up my center. My back bowed as I gasped his name, and the shadowed hands braced me, one wrapping around the back of my neck, supporting me. My gaze fell to him, ready to beg for that release laying just out of my reach, the tension too much for me to bear any longer.

His arm slipped under my thigh, my legs resting on his shoulders as his arm wound around my lower back, keeping me upright. His eyes lifted to me, glazed with hunger as he whispered. "Spread for me."

I couldn't think straight, my legs tense and twitching. When I didn't move, the shadows snaked up my legs, misty hands grabbing my thighs and spreading them apart. His head dipped low, tongue passing up my center. My body buckled, head falling back, and I cried out as the rippling effects of the feeding sent a wave of ecstasy rolling through me.

"Gods, you taste heavenly, *mea luna*," he whispered against my throbbing flesh.

"Not as good as you feel," I breathed as I gazed drunkenly down at him.

He groaned against the sensitive place he worshipped, those intense eyes locked onto mine, and with the next flick of his tongue, he thrust two fingers into me once more. My body spasmed as a wave of pleasure surged through me, overwhelming and glorious. He continued in slow, deep thrusts, pleasure building and building as he licked and teased me, pulling me back to the edge of the abyss. Just as the tension coiled tighter and tighter, just as I thought I was about to find that release I was so desperate for, he sank his fangs into the inside of my thigh.

I cried out his name, body spasming as the orgasm shot through me. The shadows quivered against my skin, their grip slipping. Every muscle locked up and released as he drew from me. My toes curled, and he moaned against my skin as he drank deeply, drawing me into him. He didn't stop, continuing to drink, dragging out the wave of pleasure until my body writhed against him.

He lifted his face from my thigh. Remnants of my blood lingered on his lips, and he licked the rich liquid lazily, basking in the flavor. He leaned into me and, God, he was beautiful, those embers in his ashen eyes burning intensely.

"I'm not done with you yet."

My thoughts were so scattered, my orgasm still rippling through me so much so that I couldn't form words as he flipped me onto my hands and knees. I hadn't realized it, but the shadows had vanished. The bed dipped as he leaned into it, his knee pressing into the mattress behind me as his hands found their way to my hips. His chest slid along my back, his body slick with sweat.

"I like the look of you laid bare before me." His words were warm against my ear, his arm snaking around my ribs until he took hold of my breast. My body buckled, and I moaned his name, my head falling forward against the bed. His length pressed against my ass, throbbing as badly as I was. I wanted him inside me, needed it so desperately, I thought I might lose my mind. I turned my head to glimpse him as he pulled my hair over my shoulder, pressing sweet kisses up my spine, torturously slow until he reached my neck. My body quivered and twitched with each brush of our skin, electric charges flitting over every inch of my body from the feeding, every sensation heightened.

"Why—" I gasped at the brush of his lips. "Do I get so sensitive every time?"

"Feeding has an... aphrodisiac effect," Damien whispered, his breath hot as it spilled against my skin in heavy waves.

"That's an interesting effe—" I moaned as his hand found its way around to the front of me, his finger grazing down my center.

He chuckled against my neck. "I love how wet you are for me."

God, did this man know how to make me melt with his words.

He rose from my back, my chest heaving against the blankets. His finger trailed down my spine until he grasped my hip with one hand. I gasped as the head of him slid against my entrance. He glided his hard length in lazy strokes along my center, and then he sank into me so deep, I cried out his name.

"*Fuck.*" He pulled me up against him as he buried his face into my neck, biting down once again. He surged inside me, stroking me in ways I didn't think possible, my body tightening around him. He drank deeply now, as if he were truly feeding, as if every other sip of my blood before this had just been a taste. My body came alive, that electric sensation overlapping with his deep thrusts. My head fell back against his shoulder, every inch of my body hypersensitive, every brush of our skin sending chills dancing over me, and I thought I might shatter.

He didn't stop, though, tasting every sensation, every feeling surging through me as he drove himself into me again and again and again. My muscles tightened and loosened all at once, my back bowing against him until it crested, and his name burst from my lips on a moan as another orgasm rolled in uncontrollable waves through me. He held me in place as he drank my orgasm down, riding the wave with me. I felt him spasm deep within me, felt his body go absolutely tense against my back as he came.

"*Cas*," he moaned against my skin.

I melted against his chest as he took a few more deep pulls, and I sighed as I felt myself flow into him. He eased, releasing my neck before passing his tongue over the puncture wounds, my skin tingling as the wounds sealed.

His arms trembled as he lowered me to the bed. I melted into the blankets, shifting to my side as I tried to remember how to breathe. He settled down beside me, looking just as affected as I was. My breath came in short pants, my body twitching and shivering as his hand passed over my arm, my hip, my thigh.

His eyes had returned to normal, the predator slipping back beneath the surface. I reached up, running my fingers through the stray waves of his dark hair and tucking them behind his ear.

"Sorry, I—" He panted, his broad chest heaving. "I kind of lost control there."

"No apologies, *mea sol*. I loved every minute of it." I gave a drunken giggle. "The shadows were a nice touch."

"They couldn't resist the temptation," he whispered back, pressing his forehead to mine. We just laid there for a moment, basking in each other's presence. I inhaled his scent, felt his warmth as he held me in his arms.

I opened my eyes, gazing at the other half of my soul staring back at me. "I have to ask."

He tilted his head, curiosity lighting up those beautiful eyes. "Ask away."

I bit back the grin forming on my face. "Can you feel things with your fangs? I couldn't help but notice a certain… reaction earlier."

He chuckled softly. "Our fangs are sensitive, yes."

I cocked an eyebrow. "*How* sensitive?"

That wicked grin returned, and for a moment, I couldn't believe it, but I could feel him hardening against my thigh as he lifted himself onto his elbow to lean over me. "You could say it's—" His tongue slid over the shell of my ear, his breath tickling my skin. *"This sensitive."*

I shivered, and his hand slid under my neck, fingers tangling in my brown curls as he lifted my head.

"Or maybe…" He lowered further, his dark hair spilling over me. Chills broke out over me as he nuzzled against my neck, the stubble

233

along his jaw scratched deliciously against my skin. My breath hitched as that throbbing heat returned.

His voice descended into a near rasp. *"This sensitive."*

"Mea sol," I breathed, chuckling softly to try to hide how affected I was. I couldn't understand how I could want him again so soon.

He lifted himself, his gaze sweeping over me once more. That hunger returned to those amber and ashen eyes of his. His hands dragged over my waist, further, until he reached the back of my knee and hooked it over his hip.

I moaned as he slid inside me once more.

CHAPTER 30

CASSIE

"How're you holdin' up, spitfire?" Barrett whispered as we turned onto a dark street. "I heard what happened last night with Eris. I couldn't believe it when Zephyr told me."

"I'm actually feeling good," I said, shaking most of the darkling blood from my dagger before swiping the last remnants of the black liquid on my pants.

My eyes had long adjusted to the darkness, yet it was still so dark that I could just barely make out his face hidden in the shadow of his black hood. The night had been quieter than the last few hunts I'd been on, which was a relief. Damien had been hesitant for me to hunt tonight. It probably would've been smarter for me to skip, but I was so antsy that I couldn't stay behind while Damien went to patrol with the others.

I was well rested, had spent most of the day sleeping, and I wondered if it was due to Damien's feeding the night before. I didn't know how late we'd stayed up, or how many times we'd made love. A smile tugged at my lips as my mind wandered to the healing bite marks on my breast and the inside of my thigh. My heart fluttered at the memory—how he spoke, how he touched me. God, he was amazing, wickedly amazing.

Despite that reprieve from reality, I was afraid to be alone with my thoughts. While I relished in the peace left in Eris' absence, the weight of her absence was heavy in my chest. In a few days, I'd find out how my body had fared over the last few months of training. How much damage had I unknowingly caused? No, if I remained behind, alone, it would be too much to bear.

"I actually wanted to ask if we could retry the flame Stoicheion lessons again," I said, lowering my hood.

His head jerked to me, and he tugged his hood down as well, revealing his short blond hair. "You sure?"

I nodded. "I can't explain it, but I feel... amazing, actually. Maybe it was Eris who was making it so difficult."

We rounded the corner, and I could faintly hear Damien and Zephyr talking ahead of us, but I couldn't quite make out what they were saying. "I don't feel as affected by Marcus' death anymore." I hesitated, the weight of what I'd just said heavier than I expected. "Knowing what I know now, I can't help but feel like it makes me a terrible person."

Barrett let out a heavy breath. "Marcus did a lot of terrible things. Zephyr told me about Eris' corruption. I can imagine that might make it more difficult for you to accept what you did."

"It does in a strange way." I turned my head to him, sliding my daggers into their sheaths. "I wonder if I've been struggling with it for so long because of Eris, like she's been trying to corrupt me all this time, the way she did him."

"It's never easy to take a life, but you did what you had to do. Don't think you're a terrible person for finding the peace to move past it," Barrett said.

"Wow," I chuckled. "That almost sounded mature of you."

He cracked a crooked grin. "It's been known to happen. If you want to start training again, we can start immediately. We can do it in the afternoons after your training with Zephyr if you're feeling up to it. Vincent can even join us. We can try water Stoicheion as well."

"Sounds like a plan." A realization dawned on me. "Barrett."

He glanced back at me, brows raised.

"What if..." God, I was afraid to think it, but a part of me hoped. "What if Marcus wasn't the only one corrupted? What if Cole was corrupted, too?"

His steel eyes fell to the pavement, and the look of sorrow and shock on Barrett's face was enough to tear my heart in two.

"You really think it's possible?" he asked, and I almost regretted mentioning it. There was a hint of hope in his voice, but... what if I was wrong?

"I don't know. He was different when I saw him while I was being held. It's difficult to let go of everything, but..." My eyes drifted along the buildings around us to the moon hidden just behind the clouds. "What if he didn't have a choice in it all?" My voice trailed off as I came to a stop, eyes narrowing as I caught a glimpse of a figure on the rooftop.

"Cas?" Barrett said from my side, confusion lacing his tone.

I blinked, and the figure disappeared, the roof left bare. Had I imagined it? I didn't sense any darklings nearby. My lips parted to call Damien but tensed, gripping the hilts of my daggers as Zephyr shifted into his panther form without warning, his conversation with Damien ending abruptly. I reached out to Damien's thoughts.

Darklings?

Damien took a hesitant step back, pulling his dagger free from its sheath. His head turned to scan the darkness around us.

I don't know. It's... different.

What did that mean? If not a darkling, what else could it be? What else was there?

Is it Melantha? I think I saw some—

The temperature plummeted around us at such an alarming rate, I couldn't even prepare myself. I shivered, breath spilling from my lips in white, misty puffs. It was more intense, so much more powerful than the sensations darklings gave off when they approached.

Then, I felt it.

It was a strange prickling on my skin, my entire body screaming to run, to get away. Damien turned, his eyes meeting mine, horrified.

His name left my lips in a shaken whisper. "Damien?"

A screech rang out over the air, and my hands shot to my ears. The scream was so shrill it pierced into my mind. I gasped, hitting my knees, and I cracked an eye open to see Damien, Zephyr, and Barrett in similar positions.

Then, silence.

"What the fuck was that?" Barrett barked, releasing his ears, his eyes darting around the darkness.

Metal hissed against leather as Barrett and I drew our blades, and Zephyr shifted back into his immortal form, drawing his own weapon. We whipped around, backing into a tight circle. My senses heightened, heart hammering in my chest as I searched for something I couldn't see. Something watched us, but I couldn't understand what it was. It felt... cold. Ice crawled over my skin, the hair on the back of my neck standing on end.

Can you feel it, too?

Yeah, but what is it?

The same horrible clicking sound the darklings made echoed in the darkness. The way it bounced off the brick made it difficult to pinpoint where it was coming from. One thing I was certain of, though; this feeling, this sensation, it wasn't from darklings. This presence was so much stronger, so much more terrifying.

Damien whispered, "Zephyr, if this gets bad, we fall back, and you get Cas out of here, no matter what."

"I stay with you," I said sharply before Zephyr could respond.

"Cas, I don't know what this is."

"We'll take it down together or we'll fall together." My voice was unwavering. I felt Damien at my back, his presence an unexplainable reassurance.

I love you.

His voice echoed in my mind, and I took a deep breath, gripping my daggers.

I love you too, mea sol. Always. If we fall... I swallowed. *We'll find each other again, just as we always have.*

Another screech spilled out into the alley, and I gasped as invisible claws sank into my mind. I ground my teeth, pushing through the agony as I opened my eyes, gripping my daggers tightly, prepared to fight off whatever stalked us.

"Above us!" Zephyr yelled.

I jerked my gaze up, and my blood ran cold at what stared back.

CHAPTER 31

CASSIE

Brick crumbled under the massive black claws of the beast clinging to the edge of the roof. Dust and bits of brick tumbled to the concrete below, the clattering drowning everything else out as my adrenaline spiked. It growled as it stared down at us, and my heart hammered in my chest, hands shaking. This was unlike any darkling I'd ever seen, more beast than human.

Its very being was shadow and darkness. I could just barely make it out under the cover of night. Black liquid dripped from its maw of razor-sharp teeth. Its massive, oblong head jerked in our direction, thick neck twisting as it cocked its head to the side as if it were watching us. Only... it wasn't *looking* at us.

Its head tilted back and forth in short twitches, its neck rippling with each movement, the darkness rising like steam all the way to its arched back, where broken spikes jutted down its spine. It clung to the brick as it crept down off the roof and onto the wall in slow, calculated steps, as if stalking prey. That horrible clicking sound echoed from between its razor-sharp teeth. Was it calling to other darklings?

"Damien," Zephyr whispered.

The beast perked, its body freezing as if it heard them.

"I've never seen anything like this," Damien responded.

It lunged from the wall, dagger-like talons stretched out as it soared through the air at us, that horrifying scream piercing the air. My feet wouldn't listen for a moment, my body freezing as the beast's jaws opened wide.

Damien pulled me to the side as the others dodged in the opposite direction out of the creature's way.

The beast slammed into the concrete, sparks lighting where its claws scraped asphalt as it slid to a stop. It crouched low, head turning in various directions as it hissed. God, it was massive, reaching easily seven to eight feet. I froze as it seemed to search.

It couldn't see us. I opened my mouth to speak, but immediately clamped it shut.

Damien! It can't see!

Damien's eyes snapped to me before looking back at the creature. Its head turned slowly, scanning the area. He glanced at Barrett and Zephyr frozen against the brick wall opposite the alley from us. He pressed a finger to his lips, and they nodded.

My heart hammered, adrenaline pulsing through my body as I watched it. The creature quieted, the air falling dead silent, and its head jerked in my direction. I froze, my blood running cold. How strong was its hearing? Could it pick up something as quiet as breathing? A heartbeat?

The gravel ground into the bottom of my boot as I stepped back, and the creature locked onto me before lunging. I shoved Damien out of the way and dropped beneath the creature as it crashed into the brick wall, ramming my dagger up into its chest.

The blade met nothing. Its body wasn't physical.

"Fuck," I breathed, head pressed against the brick as my eyes lifted, pinned beneath the creature, trapped. The creature's head tilted down to face me—

And I met death's gaze.

Something grabbed hold of my feet, and I was dragged between the creatures' legs and out from under it. Its head slammed into the pavement where I was a split second before. Damien and Barrett grabbed my arms, hoisting me to my feet. Before I could think, we were running. Darkness swirled around us, the Lupai rising from the depths, and they surged past us to attack the creature. Their glowing blue eyes turned red, their jaws widening and splitting as they bared their teeth.

"How the fuck are we gonna take that thing down?" Barrett barked as we rounded the corner.

I glanced over my shoulder, the creature's shriek ringing out behind us. The Lupais' growls and whimpers filled the alley in response as they fought the creature.

"I don't know," Damien said.

"Its body isn't physical," I panted, my boots slamming into the asphalt as I quickened my pace to keep up with them.

"Like the Lupai?" Damien asked.

"Almost, but I couldn't even touch it. My dagger went into it, but there was just... nothing. Do you think Melantha summoned it, like how you summon the Lupai?" I said through short breaths.

"More than likely," Damien answered.

Melantha had the same abilities as the members of House Skiá, and Damien had told me the types of creatures a user could summon were dictated by the power of their magic.

We came to a halt around another corner, Zephyr tight on our heels, and I collapsed against the brick, panting. I winced as a sharp pain shot into my ribs. *Fuck. Not now.*

"You ok?" Damien asked between breaths.

"Yeah." I swallowed back the pain, forcing a smile. "Just winded."

God, I hadn't realized how much Eris had been helping in keeping the pain at bay. Would it have been like this always? If I couldn't stand up against a creature like this, how would I ever be able to face Melantha?

Zephyr glanced back around the corner, checking to see if the creature followed us before asking, "Well, if physical attacks won't work, how are we going to take it out? I don't know if the Lupai will be able to take that thing on their own."

"We may have to use your flame to fight it," Damien said.

"Flame Stoicheion is effective against darklings. Maybe it could work." Barrett ran his hand through his hair, his jaw working furiously

241

as he thought. "Shit, this is gonna make it difficult to keep from drawing human attention."

The sounds of the distant fight quieted, and I froze as Barrett and Damien continued to discuss ways to take this monster down. "Guys—shh—listen."

Silence. I clamped my hand over my mouth as I tried to calm my heavy breaths.

Damien scanned the area as we listened for a hint of what happened, but there was no response, no sound, no sign the Lupai might return to us.

Zephyr inched to the corner, shifting his weight to check the alley. The creature slammed into him, pinning him face down on the ground. Barrett didn't hesitate, slamming a blast of fire into the creature. A painful screech peeled from its lips, and I grimaced as the horrible sound pierced my mind again. It flailed off Zephyr, retreating to a nearby wall and climbing it with ease.

The creature whirled, head snapping in our direction, and bits of brick crumbled and clattered to the street beneath it as its sightless gaze locked on us from the wall. Its jaws peeled open as it shrieked at us, furious at the damage the flames had done to it.

Flames flickered atop Barrett's fingertips as he prepped to hit it again. "Ok, fire works on it!"

The creature lunged the moment Barrett spoke, the flames extinguishing as he narrowly avoided being impaled by its claws. God, those claws were terrible, so long it was like it wielded daggers. It would be so easy for it to run one of us through. The alley spun as I remembered how it felt through Elena's memory to be gutted by the darklings' claws. This would be so much worse.

"This thing's smart!" Barrett grimaced, clutching his side.

Zephyr shifted into his panther form, crouching low and growling, dragging his claws against the pavement to draw the creature's attention. It worked. The creature turned on Zephyr as Barrett recovered. He grasped the shredded side of his leathers where the creature had grazed him, blood soaking into his armor. I looked back and forth between Barrett and the creature.

Flame. *I* could use flame Stoicheion too.

I hadn't dared try since our last attempt when it had fallen out of control. Could I do it? Would I lose control again? Vincent wasn't here to assist if things went south. I looked to Damien, who met my eyes, and his brows furrowed before I reached into his mind.

I'm going to help Barrett.

He swallowed, but nodded.

She doesn't hold power over you any longer, Cas. You're free now. You can do this.

Damien summoned more of the Lupai to assist Zephyr, the wolves rising from the shadows to surround the creature. The demon blindly spun, the shadow wolves snapping their jaws and barking from all directions. One of them leapt onto the creature's hunched back, biting down onto its neck. The creature stretched its long arm up and knocked the Lupai wolf into a wall. I flinched at the whimper that tore from the Lupai's throat as it slumped to the ground and disappeared. I reached out to Barrett's mind.

Barrett, we're going to tag team it.

Barrett's gaze snapped to me.

You sure, spitfire?

Yeah. I'll go first. When it turns on me, get its bac—

The creature sank its jaws into the back of one of the Lupai. My chest twisted at the cry that ripped from the shadow wolf's mouth as the creature thrashed it in the air before slamming it to the ground. The monster stepped up onto the shadow wolf as it began to fade into nothing, the creature's massive head turning as it listened intently.

I ducked away from Barrett and spun on my heels as I summoned the courage to call forth the flames. They came to life on my hands, warmth dancing over my skin. Before I could risk losing control, I shot my hand out, hurling every bit of that heat at the creature.

Its head snapped to me and it darted to the side, the flames sliding over its back, barely grazing it. It leapt onto the wall, running along the brick. Barrett shot to his feet, sending a wave of fire at the creature's back. The flames slammed into it, and the creature crashed onto the ground. It slid to a stop, writhing, but it wasn't enough. The fire died quickly, and the creature rose, thrashing its head as it screeched. It recovered faster this time, lunging at me before I could react.

"Cassie!" Damien yelled as they ran for me.

There wasn't enough time. It slammed into me, my back meeting the pavement, the side of my dagger grinding into my palms as I held it between the creature's jaws. My dagger wasn't long enough, my hands just barely outside of its jaws. If it moved, it could bite down on me. Would I turn into a darkling? Would it tear my arm off?

The creature barreled down, trying to force its way down to me. My muscles quivered, threatening to give out as it inched closer. Its jaw was physical, the only part of it, it seemed, that was not made up of shadow and mist.

"I can't burn it with Cas under it! The creature might hurt her!" Barrett yelled. I couldn't focus enough to pay attention to what the others were doing. I could burn it—was in the perfect position.

A Lupai leapt onto the creature's back, but it ignored the shadow wolf, slamming its claws into the pavement in such a fury, I struggled to shift out of their path. I breathed deeply, letting the fire come to life beneath my skin, the flame sparking in my palms.

A scream echoed out over the streets, and both the creature and I froze. Its oblong head jerked upward and it sniffed the air. The black mist peeled off his teeth as it growled, and before Damien and the others could do anything, the creature leapt off me, taking off into the darkness.

I lay there a moment in shock, fire doused, chest heaving.

Damien appeared at my side, grabbing hold of my arm and pulling me to my feet. "Gods, are you ok, Cas?"

I couldn't answer, terror washing over me, but it wasn't from being face to face with that creature again.

"Was that a human scream I just heard?" Barrett asked, eyes following where the creature had run off.

Damien looked me over, but I didn't meet his eyes, my gaze locked down the stretch of the dark street. My heart hammered.

The scream wasn't far.

Zephyr shifted back to his normal form "Shit, if that creature gets a hold of her—"

The same scream pealed out in the night air, followed closely by a plea for help. My throat tightened, my heart nearly stopping.

It was Kat's voice.

CHAPTER 32

CASSIE

"Cas!"

Damien's voice echoed off the walls, but I ignored him, my body moving on its own. Instinct overrode rational thought as I ducked into an alley—searching, listening for any possible sounds of darklings, of the creature, of Kat. I don't think I'd ever run as fast as I did, Damien and the others not far behind me. There had been no other scream, no other sound.

Please, God no.

Not Kat. I couldn't lose her, couldn't imagine anything happening to her. When had we last spoken, like actually spoken? When had I last seen her face? When had I last told her how much I loved her?

"Cas!" Damien's voice reached me, closer now, but I didn't stop.

I rounded a corner to find her on the ground. The creature stood over her, snarling at the darklings who prowled nearby. My heart sank as I grew closer. Her eyes were closed, and blood coated the side of her head. The demon we'd just fought lowered its head to her, its powerful jaws spreading as it inched toward her face.

Oh my God, it was going to eat her!

"No!" I shot out my hand, and the moment the creature's head snapped in my direction, flames erupted from my fingertips. The flames shot through the air, avoiding Kat and slamming into the creature. It smashed into the nearby wall, its screech piercing the night air as I incinerated it.

Barrett and Zephyr flew past me, attacking the few darklings lingering nearby.

Damien stopped at my side, eyes wide as he watched. I didn't let up, pouring everything I had into the fire, all sense leaving me as I imagined the worst.

The creature's head shot up, its screech never-ending, and finally, its body dispersed into nothing. My hands fell, the fire dying out as Barrett and Zephyr made quick work of the darklings. My knees shook, heart slamming against my ribs so harshly, I winced, clutching my chest.

Damien braced me. "Cas? What's wrong?"

I didn't respond, his words distant in my ear. Was she? Please no, not her. I tore from Damien's grasp, running for her. "Kat!"

I fell to my knees at her side, chest heaving as I looked her over. She was a mess, blood seeping from a wound in her coppery hair, clothes torn and filthy. I searched her frantically as Barrett, Zephyr, and Damien approached. She was breathing, her chest moving softly beneath her shirt, but had she been bitten?

"Kat!"

Zephyr hesitated beside me. "Was she—"

"I don't know!" I shouted. He didn't move, didn't get any closer.

I moved her shirt, checked her neck, her arms, her legs. My vision blurred, tears rolling down my cheeks as I tried to find some proof that I hadn't just lost her to the darklings, that she wasn't going to turn into one of them.

"Cas," Damien said calmly, easing down to his knees. "It doesn't look like she was bitten."

My hands shook as I checked her head.

"We need to get her to a hospital," Zephyr said, his tone calm.

"Please, Damien," I sobbed, lifting my gaze to him, unable to say anything more.

Damien nodded to Barrett and Zephyr before he scooped Kat into his arms.

The monitor's beep filled the dark hospital room. Kat rested peacefully beneath the blankets, IVs hooked up to her arm. The nurses had cleaned her up, dirt and blood no longer tarnishing her beautiful face. Damien stood at my side, tracing comforting circles against my back as he quietly spoke with the other patrols on the phone.

We'd changed out of our Elythian leathers into normal clothes before arriving. I'd been so frantic, he had to stop me before I rushed into the ER to call for help, wrapped head to toe in black leather and weapons, covered in the black, oily blood from the darklings I'd slain.

"Let me know if any more of those things make an appearance," Damien said, and hung up before sliding his phone into his pocket.

I sighed, head falling forward as I held Kat's limp hand. This wasn't where she belonged. She deserved better than this. She deserved it all—a life, happiness, safety, everything. It wasn't just sadness that filled me, but anger. Anger at Matthias for starting all this. Anger at Melantha for creating more misery. If it wasn't for her, none of this would be happening.

"She's going to be ok," Damien said softly.

"I almost lost her," I said, barely loud enough to hear.

"I know. I'm so sorry she got caught up in this."

"I want you to see what you can do to get something set up for Kat and my parents away from here," I said, unable to look at him.

Damien went rigid at my side. "I thought you said you wouldn't be able to convince them to leave."

"I'll make them."

His warm eyes flitted over my face, dark brows narrowing.

My eyes drifted to Kat. "If they don't know I exist, there'll be nothing to keep them here."

"You can't do that. You'll—"

"Salwa explained how to do it," I said, my voice flat, a hollow numbness filling my chest.

He hesitated, but I couldn't pull myself away from Kat to try to figure out what he was thinking. "Are you sure about this, Cas? You can't reverse something like that…"

"I know. I know that once it's done, it's… done." I swallowed, feeling the warmth of Kat's hand against my skin, proof that she was truly alive. "But I'd rather them be safe and happy than know who I am."

"Sometimes…" He took my hand as he lowered himself to my level and cupped my cheek with his other hand as he forced my gaze to him. "Sometimes, I fear you're too strong, *mea luna*, that you're willing to sacrifice too much for others. I don't want you to suffer any more than you already have, and to see someone you love and them not see you, not know you… It's more painful than words can describe."

His words stung, and I knew he knew the truth better than I could. He knew from experience when I hadn't known who he was, when I'd had no memory of him. I could only imagine how deeply it must have hurt.

I met his gaze, steeling my nerves. "I'll suffer more if I lose them to this."

His eyes wavered, and he squeezed my hand gently before lifting it to press a kiss to my knuckles. "If this is what you think is best, I'll be there for you every step of the way. I'll make arrangements for them elsewhere. You can plant false memories to help them transition better once we get them out of the city. Just don't do anything until I have plans in order."

I nodded. "Please do it as soon as possible. I'm sorry to ask this of you. I know it's a lot."

He didn't respond, and the sorrow that seeped into my skin through his touch was enough to make my eyes burn, tears threatening to fall again. "You could never ask too much of me, *mea luna*."

"I'm going to stay with her until she wakes up," I muttered as I looked back to Kat, to the bruise marring her jaw, the scrape on her brow.

"I'll give you some time alone. Call me when you're ready." He pressed a kiss to my forehead.

He hesitated, then pulled himself away, the metal door clicking shut as he left, and I sat there in silence. The lights in the room were off, the orange glow of the streetlights leaking through the closed blinds, the light in the hall creeping in from beneath the closed door. I didn't know how late it was, but I could hear the doctors and nurses going about their nightly routine in the hallway. It was all too familiar…

I hated it.

It should have been me there, laying in that bed, not her. She didn't deserve this.

It was a relief she hadn't suffered any serious injuries. The doctors had assured me there was no sign of brain damage. She'd suffered a concussion, though, and she'd been unresponsive since we brought her here. My eyes roamed over her again, noting the subtle rise and fall of her chest beneath the blankets.

I needed to let Cody know she was here, that she was ok, but I didn't know how long it would be before she woke up. As I reached for my phone, I realized I didn't have his number, and Kat's phone hadn't been on her. It was probably lost in the alley; I hadn't even taken the time to try to look for any of her belongings. I'd been so panicked.

Thankfully, it was easy to convince the doctors she'd been mugged. The police were called, a false report given. It was strange, but I didn't feel guilty lying to the officers. I felt plenty of guilt, but not because I'd fabricated this false story. No, the guilt was because Kat had been caught in the middle of this war, because I hadn't been able to protect her.

I wondered what she would remember when she woke up, what exactly she'd seen. Would I have to erase parts of her memory? I hated the thought of invading her mind, hated the thought of doing it again when I erased myself from her memories, but she couldn't know, and I wouldn't let anyone else touch her.

It was a relief that Damien had connections to get Kat and my parents safe and as far away as possible. I began to wonder just how much influence their kind had in our city, in our world. They'd been around since before the founding of our country; I could only imagine just how much sway they might hold.

Kat's faint groan pulled me from my thoughts, and I jumped to my feet.

Please God, don't remember what happened.

Her coppery lashes fluttered, brows scrunching as she woke. Confusion marred her beautiful face, and her hand rose to her face. She stopped when her IV and the probe clamped to her fingertip tugged at her arm.

"Hey, Kat," I breathed, offering her a weak smile.

Her tired eyes found me before drifting across the room, and she frowned as if she were trying to make sense of what happened and where she was.

"You're ok. You're in the hospital," I explained.

She groaned, trying to push herself up.

"You have a concussion, Kat." I reached out to her shoulder, urging her to stay laying down. "Try not to move too much. Just try to relax."

She slouched back into the pillow.

"Do you remember anything?" I asked, dreading her answer.

She blinked, eyes shifting around. Her voice was hoarse, cracked as she answered. "I... I don't know..."

"Do you remember what you were doing? Anything at all?"

She parted her lips, but it took a moment for the words to form on her tongue. "I was... I remember I went to get a pizza."

Relief washed over me before guilt hit me low in the gut. I shouldn't be relieved that she'd experienced something so traumatic that she may not remember. How long would that amnesia last, though? Would the memories resurface?

"Do you remember anything else?"

She shook her head, her face haggard as she blinked, fighting to keep her eyes open. "Is there a glass of water I can have?"

"Yeah, let me get it for you." I rose, hurrying to the other side of the bed to retrieve the plastic cup of water on the rolling tray. "Here, let me help you."

I reached behind her shoulders, helping her sit up just enough to take a sip. She sighed as she drank the cool liquid down before laying back down on the pillow.

"Thanks." She inhaled deeply, body easing into the pillow. "What happened?"

Guilt curdled in the pit of my stomach. "You were mugged."

Her eyes flew to me before they drifted back down, and for a moment, she remained silent. Frustration painted her eyes as she struggled to remember, but she didn't say anything more.

"Does Cody know? Have you called him?" she asked.

"I was going to, but I realized I don't have his number. Your phone wasn't on you, so I wasn't sure how to get a hold of him."

She looked at the clock on the wall. "It's so late. How long have I been out? Oh my god, did he—"

The realizations and possibilities started to darken her eyes, and my stomach twisted. "You're safe, Kat. You've been out for a few hours. One of Damien's friends was heading downtown when they heard you scream. The guy ran off when he got to you. The mugger didn't touch you. I promise. Damien's friend called us, and we helped him get you to the ER."

She remained silent, but thankfully, there was a small amount of relief in her expression as her head eased back into the pillow. I settled back into my chair. I hated seeing her like this, hated how freaked out she looked. "There's nothing else wrong, just the concussion. The doctors wanted to keep you here for observation. They'll probably release you once they see you're awake."

She drew a deep breath. "I can't believe this happened."

Her gaze drifted around the room to the monitors, then down to her arm where the IV was attached. She sighed, a somber darkness flickering in her green eyes. "Thank you for sitting here with me."

I gave her an incredulous look. "Of course I'd be here."

She smiled weakly at me, and I was confused by the guilt in those fern-green eyes. "I'm such a horrible friend..."

My brows knitted. "Why would you say that? You're not a horrible friend. What would even make you thin—"

"You've had to suffer things like this alone for so many years." Her eyes lifted to mine, but she couldn't hold my gaze.

I froze, straightening in my chair as I tried to understand, and I couldn't stop the nervous laugh. "What are you... what are you talking about, Kat?"

"I know," she muttered, her hands clutching the blankets.

I had to force myself to breathe, and an icy chill crawled over my skin. The room spun as I sat in silence, absorbing her words. My stomach flipped so hard, I thought I might vomit.

"I've known for a while." Her throat bobbed. "You didn't tell me, so I didn't pry. I hoped you might open up one day, figured you probably had some stupid reason for not telling me. You always get these crazy ideas in your head," she said, smiling weakly. "Probably thinking you were protecting me or something stupid like that."

I couldn't think of what to say, couldn't look her in the eyes, and the only words I could form spilled from my mouth in a quivering voice. "I'm sorry."

She knew. *God, she knew.* All this time. I was such an idiot. Of course she knew. How could I be stupid enough to think I could hide something like that from her, from my best friend? She knew me better than anyone.

"Don't be sorry, Cas." She hesitated, but continued. "Your mom called me when they rushed you to the ER, when you had that heart attack last year. She was so afraid we'd lose you that day. I've never been so scared in my entire life, but you came back, and I hoped you might tell me. You didn't, though, and I was afraid you were holding it all in, dealing with it on your own."

She bit her lip. "I can only imagine what you've endured all this time. I just hate that you've had to do it alone." Her eyes fell to her hands in her lap. "I wanted to talk to you about it, wanted to let you know you weren't alone, that I was here for you, but I was so afraid you'd be upset with me. I didn't know how to approach you."

I didn't know what I should be feeling, saying, or thinking. All I could do was clench my fists as I braced myself against my legs, head hanging as tears dotted my eyes, sobs building in my chest. "I'm so sorry."

Kat tensed. "Cas."

"I'm so sorry," I repeated, the tears rolling down my cheeks as everything I'd been hiding all these years broke free. She'd known all this time, known what I was hiding, known all the lies and twisted truths.

She pushed herself to the edge of the bed and wrapped her arms around me. "Don't apologize, Cas. I'm here. I know we've been distant these last few months, and I feel like the biggest piece of shit for not knowing how to handle talking to you about everything that happened when you were kidnapped. I hate that I got so absorbed in school and work that I left you to deal with everything alone. I don't want you to suffer alone. I want to be there with you, I want to face it all with you."

I cried into her shoulder, wrapping my arms around her. An overwhelming rush of relief washed over me. She knew. I didn't have to lie to her or hide it from her anymore.

We sat like that for a while, crying with each other, and she cupped my face, thumbs brushing the tears from my eyes. She embraced me once more, holding me, allowing me the time I needed.

I wasn't alone. I wasn't alone.

Damien.

God, the fact that she knew and Damien didn't only left me feeling sick to my stomach.

"I need to tell Damien," I admitted with a shaky voice into her shoulder.

"You haven't told him?" she asked, pulling away to look at me.

"I feel horrible about it. I never imagined it would get this far, that we'd ever get to where we are now, but now, I don't know how to tell him. I've tried multiple times, but every time I do, something comes up and I lose my nerve."

She pressed her forehead to mine, taking my hands. "Cas, I've seen how he looks at you. I'm sure he won't hold it against you."

"I know, I just…"

Her eyes roamed over my face, sorrowful. She knew. She knew I had limited time.

"I wish it wasn't something I had to tell, that we could just live our lives."

Tears welled in her eyes. "I wish you didn't have to, either."

My eyes dipped low. Her voice was thick and quivering as she held back the tears. "Just know I'm here for you. You're not alone, not anymore. No matter how bad it gets in the end."

I couldn't answer, could only cry as I embraced her; and while I felt horrible that I still hadn't told Damien, I felt such profound relief to know I was no longer alone, even if only for a short time.

CHAPTER 33

CASSIE

Damien and I walked through the training yard of The Outpost the following afternoon, the snow crunching beneath our boots. My mind had been occupied by my night spent with Kat in the hospital. Thankfully, the doctors had released her in the hours before the sun had risen, and Damien and I were able to get her home and settled. It was such a relief that she hadn't suffered more than a concussion. She'd have to take it easy for a few weeks, but she was alive. She hadn't been bitten.

Sadly, the sun had been rising when we'd made it home, so I'd only managed to take a nap.

Kat had known all this time.

I'd been nauseous since I learned, but despite the guilt, there was relief at the same time… I could talk to her about it, open up. There was no need to hide things from her anymore. She was there for me, would be there when I needed her most. I wished I'd told her sooner, and I hated that I couldn't find the way to tell Damien.

Would it feel like this when I finally got the courage to tell him? Or would he be angry that I'd kept this from him? I'd tell him Monday, no matter what came up, no matter what threatened to interrupt us. I'd tell him the truth.

Monday, I would know if any new scar tissue had built up in my heart, whether things had remained stable… or worsened. Eris claimed she'd been helping me; maybe she'd somehow reversed some of the damage.

Regardless, after my appointment, I'd tell him. I'd tell him everything there was to tell, from the very beginning, so that we might face it head on together, no matter what end awaited me.

I wanted him at my side when I took my last breath.

The Outpost seemed livelier than usual, the yard full of warriors training with recruits, a mix of both men and women. Everyone had stepped up to help Thalia with training, which was a relief. I couldn't ignore the curious eyes of the new recruits following me as we approached the building, some pairs pausing their training to watch.

I knew why they were watching me—I was with Damien. Did they know I was Moira's reincarnation? Perhaps I should acknowledge them. I was mate to their lord, their… I still couldn't acknowledge what it meant to be the mate of the King of the Immortals. I didn't feel worthy of a title such as queen, and there hadn't been any formal ceremony to name me as such. Was that something that happened? Did I just assume the title every time I was reincarnated?

Inhaling deeply, I offered them a soft smile and a nod as we passed. Some smiled back, dipping their head to us, some remained frozen in a curious state, silver eyes transfixed on me. While it was unsettling being the center of attention, it was a relief to see new faces, the first of hopefully many sent by the Kyrios to aid us.

"Lady Cas! Lord Damien!" The familiar voice caught me off guard, and I looked over to find Alec and Xander approaching us. My brows rose, surprised to see the Kyrioses of House Thiríon and House Stoicheion here. They were once warriors of The Order, and their experience would be a tremendous help, but would they fight as well?

"It's nice to see you both again," I greeted as they approached.

"Alec, I swear I'm going to knock your feet out from under you, if you call me that again. We're not in a meeting," Damien huffed, but I couldn't miss the smirk threatening to curve the corners of his lips.

Alec simply laughed in response, and I bit back my smile, elbowing Damien. Damien gave me a wink.

"Looks like you guys are fitting in well," Damien said, crossing his arms over his chest.

"Honestly, I kind of missed this, but damn, am I out of shape," Alec said, sweeping his brown curls from his face, the scars on his jaw a faint pink against his skin. "I'm probably too rusty to take on the Lord of Shadows. Care to go for a round, Damien?"

"I may just take you up on that offer." Damien's eyes shifted behind them. "I see we have some new faces."

"It's not nearly enough, but we managed to bring some new recruits today," Xander said, a sheen of sweat painting his umber skin. How long had they been out here training?

I'd learned more of how The Order operated in the recent weeks. Training was treated as a full-time job for the warriors, done in shifts around their patrol schedule. They were paid a full wage that provided them with more than a comfortable life, medical benefits, paternity and maternity leave when they were expecting, and so much more. When Damien had told me of all The Order offered those who served, I'd felt such pride. Countless benefits were available to everyone who served in whatever capacity they could, and when a warrior fell, their mate never had to work another day in their life. They were given council and aid, allowed the time and space to grieve in their own way. It showed how much Damien cared for his warriors and anyone who aided in protecting the immortal race.

Tobias was a fool to think otherwise, and I was more than relieved to see him no longer serving on The Council. I wondered where he'd ended up, if he'd given Calista any trouble during the transition.

"How many have you brought?" Damien asked.

"Fifteen between both our houses today, but we're expecting at least ten to twenty more tomorrow," Alec said. "The other Kyrios are still working. Calista's been settling into her new position nicely. She performed beautifully at yesterday's meeting."

I smiled, happy to hear how well Calista was being received.

My eyes drifted across the busy training yard, running the numbers through my head. Adding the new recruits to the current warriors and recruits, that made nearly sixty warriors. Less than forty of them were fully trained, and while the new recruits could work at a faster pace than I could, they'd need weeks, maybe months, to be able to defend themselves, let alone stand up against a horde of darklings. What if we encountered more creatures like we'd faced last night? We needed to share with everyone their weakness to flames. There were so few warriors to start with; we couldn't risk losing anymore.

I remembered the numbers presented at The Council's meeting. The immortal race was dwindling, the census barely breaking a thousand. Only a thousand... It was difficult to believe how an entire race that had existed for millennia was on the verge of... extinction.

My heart sank, and I quickly pulled my thoughts elsewhere, not wanting to imagine it.

That number included children, pregnant females, as well as immortals who didn't harbor the talents or abilities for fighting darklings. Would we be able to gather enough to fight Melantha? Train them enough to stand a chance? We didn't have enough time. We had to make every minute count.

"Can I help with training them in my spare time?" I asked, glancing up at Damien.

Xander and Alec's brows rose, and they glanced between one another. "We'd be honored," Xander said to Damien. "It would most definitely boost morale to have Moira's reincarnation training with the recruits."

Damien smiled down at me. "I've no issues with it, just so long as you don't push yourself too much."

I smiled up at him before looking back out across the training yard. This was where I wanted to be, helping anyone I could while I could.

Here, I could make a difference.

"Well, while we'd love to stay and chat, Cas has training with Barrett and Thalia," Damien said.

"They arrived earlier this morning. I think they're inside," Xander said as he and Alec dipped their heads before returning to their recruits.

Damien held the door open for me, and I stepped into the warmer air of the training facility. I rubbed my chilled hands together and slipped my jacket off, hanging it on the hook. There was no sign of Barrett or Thalia in the main lounge. There was no one, not even recruits, and it was oddly quiet.

"They're probably downstairs in the sparring room, warming up. Go ahead and head down. I'll grab us some water," Damien said, surveying the room before he started for the kitchenette at the far end.

I nodded and headed for the door to the stairwell. Flame magic. I couldn't stifle the excitement swelling in me, couldn't wait to learn how to use it properly. Our first attempt to train had been a disaster, but this lesson would be different. I knew it. I hadn't lost control when I'd used it last night, and I was eager to learn just what I could do without Eris' interference. I pulled my hair tie from my wrist and braided my hair as I descended into the basement level.

There was so much I needed to learn, and I wondered if I could learn every element House Stoicheion had at their disposal—flame, water, lighting, earth, air. I was intrigued by how they were all used. I wanted to learn how Aster used his magic to command plant life. How did they fight with it? My excitement waned as I reached the foot of the stairwell, the list of all the different houses of power building in my mind. Did we have enough time before the darklings attacked?

Did... I have enough time?

I smothered the dread rising in my gut as I opened the door to the sparring room. "Barrett? Thal—"

I froze in the doorway when my eyes found them.

Thalia was pressed against a wall, Barrett's hands roaming up her shirt, her pants undone and low on her hips where his other hand had vanished. His face was buried in her neck. Her pale skin was flushed, chest heaving.

Their gazes met mine, Barrett's blazing with that intense flame raging inside him, and Thalia's face held that same heated drunkenness I knew came with feeding. My face burned, and my feet cemented to the floor for a moment before I pulled myself away, my eyes flying in any direction but toward them.

"I'm so sorry!" I ducked back out into the hallway, slamming the door behind me. My back met the wall as I clasped my hands over my face. What would I have walked into if I'd arrived ten or fifteen minutes later? My mind wandered, unbound and wild and—Oh my God, no. *Stop thinking!*

"Cas?" Damien's voice alerted me of his approach, pulling me from the thoughts which left me even more embarrassed, even though he couldn't read them. I had never been more thankful that he wasn't a Nous user.

My face was likely beet red, and when his eyes met mine, his confusion melted into something sinfully humorous. God, could I be more obvious?

He grew closer, leaning in to whisper, "Did you walk in on something, *mea luna*?"

"No!" I blurted.

He lowered his face to my neck as he inhaled deeply, and that smile turned wicked. "Your scent tells me otherwise."

259

I swallowed, averting my gaze from him, wishing the floor would swallow me whole. His warm gray eyes shifted to the door, and he reached for the knob.

My hand shot out, stopping him. "We can't go in there!"

"Oh?" he said, a mischievous grin tugging at the corner of his lips. "Why not?"

The doorknob clicked seconds later, and the door opened, revealing Barrett and Thalia, looking a bit more put together than they had moments before, although Thalia was still fixing her disheveled braid.

Thalia gave me an apologetic grin. "Sorry about that, Cas."

"Didn't realize it was already that time," Barrett added, and it annoyed me how put together he looked, as if I hadn't just walked in on them—the heat spread from my face to my ears and the back of my neck as my mind relived what I'd seen.

I waved my hands in a flurry. "No! You're fine!"

A shit-eating grin spread across Barrett's face. "Awe, spitfire's embarrassed,"

Damien bit his lip as he became preoccupied by the detail of the barren walls around us.

"Barrett, leave the poor girl alone," Thalia said as she passed him to head for the stairway.

"Maybe next time, you two could join us," Barrett added with a wink as he passed me to follow her.

"Barrett!" I balked, searching for anything I could throw at him.

Thalia chuckled as she ascended the stairs. Damien bit back the urge to laugh, but I heard the low huff that escaped him.

"Damien!"

He gave me an incredulous look. "What?"

I slumped and followed after them.

"It's nothing to be ashamed of if it got you feelin' a certain way, spitfire," Barrett teased.

"*Oh my God.*" I groaned. "I'm going to set you on fire, Barrett."

Barrett let out a bark of laughter. "I look forward to it."

Damien rested against a nearby maple tree as he observed us from a distance. He'd insisted on being here instead of helping Alec and

Xander train recruits. After how our last attempt to train with flame magic had gone, I didn't blame him.

I stood in the center of the clearing, transfixed on my hand. Small flames danced in my palm, the wind causing them to shift and ripple. They were mesmerizing.

"Now that we know you've got the basics down, there are techniques for using flame Stoicheion, and you'll notice when you start to learn the other Stoicheion that there are similarities. You can shoot the fire as a projectile." Barrett allowed the flames to climb up his arm, his skin nearly glowing wherever the fire crept. He turned, shooting his hand out as fire erupted from his palm, sending a blast into a nearby target.

"Or you can use it as an extension of yourself." He spun around, the flames extending out from his arms like a whip as he swept them through the air. They stretched out to slam into another target, pulverizing it, the remnants dousing in the snow as they crumbled.

"I'd have Vincent show you the similarities between flame and water, but Vincent's not gonna be able to make it today. Something came up last minute with Anna. He'll be here Tuesday, so you can try then."

My stomach dipped. "Is Anna okay? Is the baby okay?"

"She's fine. It's more of a precautionary visit with Johnson. I spoke with Anna a couple hours ago. Her blood pressure was a little high and Vincent freaked and wanted her checked out," Barrett said, and my shoulders sagged.

Anna had told me how protective Vincent had gotten over her. It was sweet to think about someone who was a trained killer doting over his mate. I wished I could've experienced that with Damien, wished I could've experienced the joys of pregnancy and bringing a child into the world with him. I knew there was never any chance of it, but I'd always wanted to start a family, be a mother.

Barrett's voice pulled me back. "You ready, spitfire?"

I nodded, eyes falling to my hands as the flames swayed at my fingertips. There was no time to dwell on the things I couldn't do. I needed to focus on what I could. He'd taught me before to imagine a faucet, but last night I'd let instinct take over. Now that I wasn't in danger, the ability sat just out of my reach.

I imagined it as a ball I could throw. My gaze drifted to the target he'd hit, the hole left in the middle of it still smoldering. I turned, solidifying my stance as I focused on the target beside it. I grasped my hand around the flame, imagining the ball, and I launched it forward.

The flame hit one of the target's legs, and it fell over with a thud, steam shooting up from the snow-covered ground. My shoulders slumped. Well, that was a graceful failure.

261

"It's ok, spitfire. Don't get too down on yourself." A teasing grin spread across Barrett's face. "Try not to think of it as a baseball."

He walked up behind me and took my hand. I stiffened, the flames still alive as they moved over my skin, and I nearly recoiled from his grasp for fear of burning him, but he didn't pull back, and I realized the flames didn't harm him.

"You can touch them?" I asked, eyes darting to his face beside me.

"I can walk through any fire and not burn if I'm aware and maintain control. You can do the same," Barrett said coolly. I remembered when I'd been engulfed in the flames at the metal shop. I wondered just what else the Stoicheion could do with the elements they wielded.

"Now, I want you to hold your hand out, and, just like you did last night, shoot the flames from your palm in a blast, more like a gun. Just like how I showed you."

My gaze fell forward to the target now on its side, Barrett's hand a calm brace on my wrist as he helped me aim. I inhaled deeply, imagining the barrel, the flames building, waiting to be unleashed.

"Set it loose," Barrett whispered.

I imagined pulling an invisible trigger, releasing it, and the fire erupted from my palm, slamming into the center of the target. Barrett released me, and I stood there, staring at the smoldering hole I'd just created.

My gaze snapped to Damien, giddiness rising in my chest as I smiled in triumph at him. "I did it!"

"I knew you could." A warm smile lit his face. "You don't give yourself enough credit."

"I'll say! You should've seen how she incinerated that creature last night, Thalia," Barrett added, his eyes jumping to her.

"I wish I'd been there to see it. Speaking of..." She glanced between Barrett and Damien. "Did we figure out what that thing was?"

Damien shook his head. "James is at the Archivallia with Salwa researching it as we speak. I'll be joining them this evening to help."

My brows rose. He hadn't told me James and Salwa were there. I'd wanted to visit the vast library again. I desperately wanted to see what types of books were contained on those shelves and see the little librarians again, and I was curious about the glass case with those three thick leather-bound books.

"Can I come?" I asked, a bit too eagerly.

He blinked, somehow surprised that I wanted to go. "You barely got a nap in this morning after we got back from the hospital. I figured you'd be exhausted after training."

"I want to help look, and I want to see the astral sprites again."

He chuckled. "I won't tell you no, Cas. You can do whatever you like."

"Let's get back to work, then. Barrett?" I said, spinning to face Barrett, eager to continue the lesson.

"Such a demanding queen," Barrett huffed, stepping back a safe distance from me.

My eyes narrowed on him, and he laughed. I oddly preferred him calling me spitfire to calling me queen.

"There is another common technique," Barrett started, and he slid his feet apart. "You can use the flames as a shield against various objects."

As if already prepared to assist in the demonstration, Thalia ducked low to scoop up some branches and other forest debris from the snow. Barrett glanced her way as she chucked the mass of things at him and he swept his arm across the air, a wall of flames spreading wide. The branches and damp leaves disintegrated into ash the moment they met the wall of flames. Amidst the branches and leaves, a lone pebble shot through the flames, and it clunked against Barrett's head. The wall of fire vanished, and Barrett threw Thalia a look.

"Whoopsie," Thalia said, eyes dropping to the ground, pacing in a circle as if she were looking to see where it could've possibly come from. "How'd that get in there?" She slid me a quick wink, and I giggled.

Damien huffed a short laugh under his breath, but by the time I glanced back at him, he'd already composed himself. I gave him a knowing smile, and the mischievous one that formed on his face left my heart fluttering.

Barrett ducked to pick up the pebble, leveling a glare at Thalia. "Well, as Thalia so kindly demonstrated, it will not protect against certain objects, but if it's burnable, the wall will protect you."

He wound his arm back before he chucked the pebble at Thalia. I gasped as she leapt, twisting in the air as black mist swirled around her, and dappled white wings fanned out from the shadowy mist, the darkness dispersing to reveal a white falcon.

I stopped breathing, enthralled at the form I'd never seen before, as she darted for Barrett. He stepped back as she careened for him. Black mist swallowed her once more, the smoke building bigger and bigger until a large gray wolf emerged from the shadows, teeth barred as she plowed into him, pinning him to the ground.

Barrett grunted as he hit the snow. Thalia's paws pressed into his chest as her lips peeled back, exposing teeth that could tear him apart, a low growl slipping from her throat. Barrett smirked up at her, unfazed by the deadly creature on his chest.

"If you wanted on top, all you had to do was ask," Barrett said as he met Thalia's deadly gaze with a wicked grin. Her weight shifted as the words left his lips, as if she were thrown off by them. I tried not to revisit the sight of them in the training hall—Barrett pressed against Thalia as he—

God. I shook the thought, turning from the couple, and the coy grin on Damien's face as my gaze found his made it clear he knew exactly where my mind had gone.

His lips parted, and I shot out a hand. "Don't. You. Dare."

He bit his lip, amber and ashen eyes raking down my body, and I wished his nose wasn't so strong. Oh my God. A realization dawned on me, one I almost wished I hadn't thought of. Did that mean Barrett and Thalia could tell when... I wanted to leave, to just disappear as I figured out how obvious any hint of arousal could be to any of them.

Damien laughed and pushed off the tree. "Let him up, Thalia. I'd prefer you not tear the face off my third in command."

I looked over my shoulder to see the black mist slipping off Thalia as she shifted, her pale cornsilk braid falling over her shoulder as she pushed herself up off Barrett's chest. She extended her hand out to pull him up, and he took it, a haughty grin smeared across his face.

I beamed at Thalia as she turned to me, in awe of both of her beast forms. "That was amazing!"

Her brows rose, silver eyes widening slightly. "It's a tactical use of the two forms we Thiríons possess."

"So, there's only two?" I asked as I walked toward her.

Thalia nodded. "A flight form and a ground form. Not all immortals can use both. Those with weaker magic are only able to form one of the two their entire life. You could shift into any animal you desired in your past lives. Zephyr tells me you're working on a tawny owl."

I nodded. I wasn't sure if I'd be able to shift into whatever I chose as I'd done in my past lives. It would be cool, though. "I haven't tried any other forms yet, but I think we are getting close to actual flight lessons, instead of just gliding down from high places. Is your form a hawk? I've never seen anything like it."

She chuckled. "It's a Gyrfalcon."

"It's beautiful!"

I couldn't believe the surprise that flitted across her face at the compliment, the faint blush that painted her cheeks.

Barrett's arms came around her waist, pulling her against him. "Careful, spitfire. She doesn't take compliments well."

She bit her lip, elbowing him in the gut, and he grunted a laugh.

"There's one other thing I wanted to talk to you about before we continue," Barrett said, the humor leaving him. He released Thalia and stepped to her side as he lowered his gaze on me, and the concern that lit his steel eyes left me uneasy. "Damien told me about how you used it."

It? My brows furrowed. What was he talking about?

"This particular technique is typically used as a last resort, when there are no other options or chance of escape, when a Stoicheion concentrates the flames to a dangerous level in their body before releasing it."

I knew what he spoke of, remembered the feel of the heat under my skin as the fire flooding the metal shop entered my body. I'd absorbed every bit of the flame and poured it into Marcus. I remembered the horror in Damien's voice as he called to me from where he'd been trapped.

"Damien was right to be scared for you when you used it," Barrett continued, and the unwavering sternness in his voice left me even more anxious.

"Why?"

"You somehow diverted that power into someone else, concentrating the flames into your target, but it's not typically how that ability is used. Usually it is explosive, like a bomb going off, destroying everything in its path."

My heart dipped, a sinking feeling settling into my stomach.

"You must avoid using it again. Promise me you won't, Cas." His blond brows knitted together, the concern in his voice growing deeper. "Because the person who uses *telos pyrai* is typically destroyed by the flame as well."

CHAPTER 34

CASSIE

Telos pyrai.

Barrett had explained it meant flame's end.

God, had I nearly killed myself that night? Was it only because of Eris I'd survived? Questions swirled in my mind as Damien and I walked through the sparring yard at the Outpost an hour later, the lesson with Barrett done for the day. There hadn't been as much training needed as I thought there'd be. The flames had answered my call with ease, but I'd suspected they might after what Eris had told me. We were to begin combat training using the Stoicheion magic on Tuesday with Vincent, to see if I could wield water Stoicheion as well.

While I'd always been able to use every type of magic the houses of power possessed, each of my past lives had excelled in a specific magic above the rest. Lucia had been talented at bending the mind using Nous. Elena had been an avid shifter, which made sense as she was Zephyr's sister, and he's a Thiríon. Moira... What had she said about Moira? What did Moira specialize in?

My mind always grew hazy when I thought of her, and it still concerned me that I couldn't tap into any of her memories, that none had resurfaced. The only images I'd seen were through Damien's memories.

I did remember one thing, though. Eris had told me my talents, for whatever reason, lay in the flame. I'd felt it when I'd tapped into the ability in the metal shop—it came so easily. Still, I didn't know how much of my control over the flames had been due to Eris' influence.

"Are you her reincarnation?"

I stiffened, halting at the little voice, full of such adoration, a tiny hand taking hold of mine.

Damien came to a stop a few steps ahead of me. "Cas?"

His words didn't register as I turned my gaze to find a little girl at my side. She was so young, not more than six years old. Her wavy black hair was pulled back into pigtails, her pale eyes beaming up at me, her smile wide and infectious. I blinked down at her, my heart fluttering, warmth seeping into my skin where she held onto me. She reminded me of myself at that age, her little round cheeks, tiny button nose...

"Aurelia!"

I lifted my gaze to find a woman hurrying over to us. She pulled the girl back, kneeling beside her. "I'm so sorry, Your Majesties. She doesn't understand she's being rude in asking."

I smiled. "Oh, please, no. Don't apologize. It's ok."

Damien knelt beside me at the girl's level, and the warmth of his expression stirred something in my chest. I liked to imagine it was the way he would have looked at Emilia. "Are you helping your mother train?"

A bright smile spread across Aurelia's face. "I am! Papa's resting at the temple, and Momma couldn't find anyone to watch me, so she brought me with her."

The smiles left our faces. Her father rested at the temple. Moira's Rest. My gaze shifted to her mother, who held a somber smile as she brushed her fingers against her daughter's cheek.

268

"My mate was Alex," the woman said somberly, a weak smile on her face. As she gazed down at her daughter, I knew the smile was for her, strength she mustered for her daughter. "He fell on patrol last year."

Damien placed his hand against his chest, dipping his head. "*Aleirene touen enlisno en solos.*" I didn't understand the words, but it hurt to hear them. He rose, meeting the mother's gaze. "Alex was a strong warrior. I remember him well."

Her smile threatened to fade, her glassy eyes flickering as she blinked back tears. "Thank you, Lord Damien. He always spoke highly of you. I'm honored he was able to fight at your side. When I heard you were opening training to anyone, I knew I had to come. I hope it's ok I brought her. I don't have any family, and I couldn't find a sitter. She's really well behaved, she stays out of the wa—"

"She's always welcome," I said, and Damien's gaze flitted to me, a soft smile curving his lips.

"Startin' them early, I see!" Barrett said as he approached and knelt before the little girl. "Give her a few weeks, and I think she'll be sweeping my feet out from under me."

Aurelia snickered.

"Forgive me, I haven't introduced myself. I'm Lydia," the woman said warmly, tucking her blonde hair behind her ear.

"Cas," I responded, but I immediately realized it may not have been necessary. She knew who I was, and the smile she gave only made it more obvious how pointless the introduction was.

"Your father was an outstanding Dendron," Damien said, his gaze warm as he looked at Aurelia. "I'll bet you take after him."

"Sadly, we don't know what abilities she'll have," Lydia said.

I tilted my head to Lydia, brows furrowing.

"My mate and I adopted her two years ago. Her family was killed by darklings, and there was no information on her background, who they were, anything," Lydia said, the inner corners of her brows curving upward as she ran her fingers through Aurelia's black hair.

My eyes fell to Aurelia, the smile unwavering on her face, as if she was unfazed to know she was adopted. My heart swelled at the sight of that smile. "That just means the sky's the limit. You could be anything, Aurelia."

Aurelia nodded with a smile and spoke again, her tiny voice filling my chest with warmth. "Papa used to take me into the woods and teach me all about the plants. He thought I might be a dendron, but they didn't speak to me the way others do."

Damien and I frowned, glancing at each other.

"She says that sometimes, and I still don't understand what she's talking about," Lydia said, smiling awkwardly. "Children say the strangest things."

"Maybe one day, you'll grow into those same abilities," Damien said.

"Maybe I'll take after Momma," Aurelia said, smiling as she beamed up at me. Lydia's smile widened as she glowed with pride.

"Whichever path you follow, I sense his strength in you, *mikros*," Barrett said. "He'd be proud to see you helping your mother train."

Mikros. I'd called the little girl in Moonhaven that. Watching them interact with the child reflected what I already knew. Children were cherished above all else by the immortal race. They were rare, and when they made it safely into the world, they were treated like the treasures they were.

Aurelia smiled bashfully at Barrett's words as she leaned into her mother, holding her hand. Lydia watched silently, absolute adoration lighting her eyes.

"You want a snack, Aurelia?" Thalia offered, glancing up at Lydia for permission. Aurelia looked up at her mother, who smiled and nodded in return. The young girl turned back to Thalia and nodded.

"There are drinks and snacks inside, whatever you want. Afterward, we can come back, and I'll show you some basics of fighting," Barrett said, holding his hands out. Aurelia's eyes lit up and she hurried toward him. He lifted her up, throwing her up onto his shoulders with ease, her laughter filling the training yard. The eyes of many trainees found us, and warm smiles spread.

My gaze drifted across the faces around us, some still watching us, some not. Seeing both familiar and new, their happiness shining in their expressions, despite everything they stood to face, sparked something within me.

This was what we were fighting to protect. This was worth defending, worth any price. This was where I belonged. My entire life, I'd always felt like an outsider, like a burden. Here, I had a purpose, a place. Here... I felt like I belonged.

Barrett and Thalia took the child into the building, chatting and joking as they went. My heart fluttered when Damien's fingers laced with mine, and I turned to meet his warm gaze.

"Have the energy to head to the Archivallia?" he asked. "After a shower and some food, of course."

I giggled, the smell of smoke, ash, and sweat prevalent on my skin. "A shower and food would be nice, and I'd love to join you."

Tiny astral sprites skittered past my legs, arms full of scrolls and books as they rushed to return them to their home or bring them to whomever requested them. Damien snickered, and I turned my gaze to him.

"What's so funny?"

His eyes drifted over me, a crooked grin tugging at the corner of his lips. "You're just cute when you're around books. You get this look in your eyes," he said.

I cocked an eyebrow, now curious about what he meant. Did I have a funny look on my face? I suddenly became very concerned, my cheeks and ears growing warm.

"Have you heard anything about the arrangements for my parents?" I asked. It felt random, but I'd been eager to know if he'd gotten any word. Monday would be the perfect time to try to... I inhaled deeply, dreading what I knew I needed to do.

He released an uneasy breath. "I have. I landed jobs for them. The company offers a few options for housing, so they won't need to look. Everything is pretty much ready for you, but..."

His voice trailed off. I tilted my head to look at him as he came to a stop. "I just want you to be sure of this, *mea luna*."

My gaze slipped from his, a weak smile tugging at my lips. "I don't really have an option. I need to know they'll be safe from the darklings. I can't focus knowing they're in danger."

"Good evening," Salwa greeted from a nearby table. I hadn't even noticed her and James, too absorbed in our conversation to pay attention.

"Hey Salwa," I said with a warm smile, pushing back the dread, knowing that in just two days' time my parents wouldn't know I existed.

James' coppery brows rose, and he pulled his gaze from the book he'd been preoccupied with. "Oh, hey, Cas. Didnae see ye come in."

"How's it coming?" Damien asked as he stopped at the table's edge, eyes scanning the mess of books they were working through. There were countless stacks of tomes and scrolls, the papers worn and aged.

"No luck on the creature you described," Salwa answered. "We've been searching through any bestiary the sprites can find. I don't know how many we have, and I know we don't have information on every beast across the twelve kingdoms, so there's a chance it might not be here." A couple of sprites approached, stretching onto their little hocks to place a few more books on the table. "I've got every sprite searching for any text that might have any information. This is what they've found so far."

Twelve kingdoms? I parted my lips to ask, but a tiny hand grasped my finger and tugged at my side. I dropped my gaze to the tiny astral sprite, trying to get my attention. Starlight danced across its black form, its glowing, white, orb-like eyes shining up at me. It was so small, barely reaching halfway up my thigh.

I turned, kneeling to its level. "Can I help you?"

It reached for the thick book tucked against its side, and my brows rose as it held it out to me. The book was almost as big as its torso; I couldn't understand how these creatures could carry them around.

"For me?" I asked, curious as to what exactly it was giving me. Did the little librarian know we were here to help Salwa and James?

The sprite nodded, eyes beaming, and for a moment, it looked as if the constellations and starlight that danced across its face formed a smile. I took the thick book, the weight catching me off guard. Goodness, the librarians made them look light. It probably weighed at least fifteen pounds.

"Thank you," I said with a smile.

The creature bowed its head before skittering off.

Salwa chuckled. "They've been in an uproar since you first came."

I tilted my head. "Why?"

"They know who you are," Damien answered with a knowing smile.

I frowned. I'd never been here before the meeting with The Council. How could they know me?

"As Elena and Lucia, you were always in here with the librarians in your spare time. You've always loved reading, and you'd visit the librarians when you could," Damien said, pulling out a seat before offering it to me. "You talked with them. I don't know how you did, but you somehow could. You understood them. They've always been very fond of you."

I remembered how stunned one of the sprites had been when I'd first come to this place, how it had frozen when it first saw me. Movement caught my eye from a nearby bookcase, and I looked up to find a few peering at me from around it. I smiled, giving them a light wave, and they tensed, as if they'd been caught. Another sprite chittered at them, squeaking what seemed to be some sort of remark to get back to work since little sprites scattered, running off to their tasks. I giggled. I loved the little creatures, and I found myself wanting to spend more time here.

Damien smiled as he watched them run off before he glanced at Salwa. "Any books you haven't started? I'll get to work."

I set the thick tome I'd been given on the table and eased into the cushioned chair. As if on cue, a floating lantern lowered until it hovered just above me, illuminating the pages.

"Here," Salwa said, handing Damien a thick, leather-bound book. It looked ancient, the leather worn, the pages no longer a crisp white, almost tanned.

He settled into the seat next to me. I opened the book the sprite had given me, disappointed to find the writing all in the same unreadable text I'd seen in Moira's Rest.

"What's wrong?" Damien asked, lifting his face, then he saw the writing. "Shit, I'm sorry. I didn't think about that. The books are all written in Elythian."

Every book? So much for reading. "At least there are illustrations. I can at least see if I find something that looks like it and let you read whatever it says."

Maybe I'd be lucky enough to find more books with illustrations. I'd have to ask the librarians, and I could have Damien translate it for me or maybe even Salwa, if she wasn't busy.

The table grew quiet as we resumed flipping through pages and pages of ancient text depicting all sorts of creatures. Hours passed, more books appearing on the table as the sprites found them. I became mesmerized by some of the illustrations. Some I recognized from fairytales, but there were many I'd never seen or heard of before.

There were mermaids—or I guess they were sirens, since they had the most terrifying teeth, webbed fingers, and tails with multiple, massive fins. The illustrations, though, made it appear like they took two forms: the first was terrifying, but the second was the most enchanting thing I'd ever seen. I learned, however, that they weren't the scariest creatures as I came across a picture of something far more terrifying. Its fur-covered body was long and spindly, arms dangling low as it hunched over, long claws dragging across the ground, its legs shaped like the hind legs of a dog, but longer. The creature's head looked like the skull of an animal. A horse? Maybe a deer? Its antlers were monstrous, razor-sharp teeth coated in what I assumed was blood. The illustration was so detailed, the hollow black of its eye holes practically stared through me. If I never encountered a creature like this in my life, it would be too soon. I rested my chin on my hand as I turned the page, my eyes growing heavy.

My heart stuttered.

I'd never forget that sightless gaze as it stared down at me before it nearly tore my head off my shoulders. If Damien and Barrett hadn't pulled me from beneath it, it would have. My eyes drifted over what little writing there was, and I frowned. The bottom half of the page was torn, the lower section of the creature missing. Whatever information might've been written there was gone, taking with it the knowledge we so desperately sought.

"Damien," I said, sliding the book to him.

"Ye find sommat, Cas?" James asked, and I nodded.

Damien's brows rose, his eyes falling to the illustration. He frowned when he saw half the page missing. "Salwa, do you know this book?"

Salwa lifted her eyes and walked around to us. "That's strange. Why is the page ripped?" She took the book, holding the place with her finger as she closed it to look at the cover.

James frowned as he stood, walking over to us as Salwa gave him room to see the page.

"It's old, likely one of the few that survived The Darkling's Descent. I can't even read the title. This is probably the first time it's been off the shelf in ages." She opened the book again. "That's strange; this is the only page that's torn."

Unease settled into her pale eyes as they lifted to us. What would that mean? Had someone torn the page out intentionally? And if so, who?

I looked to Damien. "You said not many immortals were allowed here, didn't you?"

Damien nodded. "Very few."

James looked at me, running his fingers through his coppery hair. "I donnae who cuid hev done 'is. Eh sprites ur very protective o' these books. They freaked oot oan me eh other day when ah dropped one by mistake. Ah felt terrible."

Could one of our own have slipped into the Archivallia and taken the page? Did they do it to hide information on the creatures from us? There was still a part of me that had become almost hopeful that Cole hadn't done everything on his own, that he'd been corrupted, like Marcus. I hated to ask, had worried just how divided we could become if we started questioning the few allies we had, but Tobias was right to be concerned.

"Could someone have broken in?" I asked.

Damien pondered. "It shouldn't be possible. The only way to get here is through the Propylaeas in each of the Kyrios houses."

James spoke up, saying what I couldn't. "Do ye think it cuid be someone workin' wi' Cole an' Amara? Another deserter we donnae kno' aboot within Eh Order?"

"If we have any other immortals who've deserted but are working within The Order..." Damien drew a deep breath, his expression growing graver. "They could gain access, slip through to this side of the veil, and steal a page, but it would still be difficult. The astral sprites don't sleep; they're always working."

I tilted my head, frowning. "It doesn't make sense, though. Why tear out just one page? Why not just take the book?"

"Eh librarian's wuid kno' eh moment a book left eh Archivallia," James explained. "They kno' if a book or scroll's removed from 'is chamber. A page might go undetected tho'."

"Sadly, there aren't exactly cameras here, so there's no way to know who's come and gone," Salwa said, her gaze falling back to the illustration. It was clear she felt the weight of what Damien had said. Another possible betrayal, but who? How could I remember each of the warriors I'd seen training at The Outpost earlier that day and not wonder now whether any of them had done this, if any of them might be working with Melantha and the darklings? Another part of me thought back to what Marcus had said. Did the immortals who'd worked alongside them truly believe that siding with the darklings would bring about some sort of revolution—a means to separate themselves from Selene? It was too much to think about on such little sleep, and a headache already lingered in the back of my head.

My eyes flickered between Salwa and the book she held, wondering what little information remained on the page. "Does it say what the creature's called?"

"The Varyoskia," she answered. "Also known as a Varyos."

"Does that mean something?" I asked, glancing between her and Damien.

Damien drew a deep breath, as if he already knew what the name meant as Salwa's pale eyes lifted to me. They wavered, as if she herself were unnerved by the creature. "The shadows that hunt."

"Shadows? As in plural? There's more than one of those things?" I asked, heart sinking.

Salwa looked back to the few words on the torn page. "There isn't enough here to give us much knowledge, what kingdom they reside in, what other abilities they might have, if any." She looked at Damien. "James told me it's weak against the flame Stoicheion. That's a start."

"But if there's more of these things..." Damien started.

Something crawled across my skin, my stomach twisting into knots. More of them? It had taken four of us to take down one, and it was only because Barrett and I could use flame magic.

"What if any of the patrols encounter another one and there isn't a flame user with them?" The worst thoughts came to mind. There were warriors on patrol tonight, males and females who could be torn apart by more of those things. Weapons couldn't touch them, not even the blades imbued with Selene's magic.

"James, get in touch with Barrett or Zephyr. Make sure a flame Stoicheion user is put on every team," Damien said urgently. James nodded, rising to his feet, hurrying for the entrance.

"Damien, do you think she could summon more than one of those things at once?" I dared to ask, afraid I already knew the answer.

His eyes met mine, and he didn't need to respond. The fear and unease there spoke volumes. "I'll speak with Selene, see if she has any knowledge of these creatures and if there are any enchantments that could be imbued into our weapons to take them down."

CHAPTER 35

DAMIEN

I rounded the corner of a bookshelf, the astral sprites chittering at my sides in what I hoped was appreciation for helping them put all the books away. I'd sent Salwa home before cleaning up. She'd pulled enough hours, and I imagined she could use the rest.

"Ready to head home, *mea*..." The words fell short on my lips as I caught sight of her, my heart swelling.

Her head rested on her crossed arms over the thick book, full of illustrations she'd been looking through when I'd left her to put the other tomes up. The gentle lull of air filling her lungs reached my ears in rhythmic waves. I stepped quietly to her side, leaning over to see her face. Her thick chestnut lashes lay low against her cheek.

I was surprised she'd lasted this long, given how little sleep she'd gotten this morning after everything that had happened.

The sight of her stirred something deep within me, my chest swelling. I smiled, looking at the group of sprites gathering around the base of her chair, curiosity lighting their already bright eyes. I pressed my finger to my lips as I looked at them. "Can you help me?" I whispered.

They nodded, taking hold of the chair as I reached across her shoulders, easing her up and against my arm. The sprites pulled the chair back carefully, and I scooped her up. Her warmth seeped into my skin, spreading to every inch of my body as I held her close to my chest. A soft groan slipped from her throat, and she curled up against me, drifting back into the sleep she needed.

"So beautiful," I whispered, as I laid a tender kiss to her brow. I constantly had to remind myself she was mortal, that she needed rest far more often than any of us did, but she made it difficult sometimes. She was persistent, hardheaded, and I knew she hated her physical limitations as a mortal. I hated it for her, but there were no words to express the depths of pride I felt watching her defy all the odds. My mate. Mine.

"Thank you," I whispered to the sprites, and they quietly chittered their responses, which sadly, I couldn't understand. I realized the Archivallia had grown quiet, and I lifted my eyes to find each and every one of them staring up, attention locked on us. They truly admired her, and I understood why they did. I dipped my head to them before I turned, carrying her out of the Archivallia and down the hall to return home.

Home. That word held a deeper meaning now as I slipped through the depths of the darkness, willing the blue flames to life in the Propylaea. This was no longer a house, but a home. My eyes fell to Cas, still resting peacefully in my arms.

She was home.

I ascended the stairs, silence reaching every corner of the house. It was late, Ethel's glowing presence gone for the night. I quietly stepped down the hall and up the stairs to our room, Cas tucked tightly against my chest.

I hadn't heard back from James yet, and I prayed the warriors on patrol were okay, that they hadn't encountered another Varyos. Gods, that creature was terrible. I remembered the terror ignited in my stomach when I'd first sensed it, as if death were watching us.

Our bedroom door groaned as I nudged it open. I inhaled deeply, Cassie's scent of jasmine and citrus mingling with my own. I liked it that way, and I never wanted it to fade. The bed dipped as I eased her down onto the mattress. I made quick and gentle work of removing her shoes and socks, setting them down on the floor. My gaze drifted back to her, to her chestnut hair splayed around her, her hand resting against her chest.

I carefully undid her jeans, and pulled them off her slowly, my eyes remaining fixed on her face for any hint I might wake her. Once the jeans slipped from her feet, she shifted onto her side. I tensed, but she settled back into a deep sleep, her hands curling up against her face. I smiled, pulling the blankets over her before placing a soft kiss to her brow. She curled inward, a faint smile tugging at her lips. Peace settled over me, and I could've sat there, watching her rest for hours.

My phone vibrated in my pocket, and I checked to find a text from James. Perfect timing too, as I wanted to know how things were faring on the patrols.

My eyes fell once more on Cassie, ensuring she was settled and warm under the blankets before rising to head for the door. It must have been important for James to have come at this hour instead of calling. I prayed it wasn't bad news, that there hadn't been any odd occurrences during one of the patrols.

No, if there had been a serious attack, he would have called right away.

The moon shone dimly behind the cover of winter clouds, and pale snowflakes drifted across the headlights in our driveway. James leaned against the hood of his car, smoking a cigarette as I descended the stairs of the front porch, pulling my coat on. He wasn't alone, and he pushed off when he saw me, carrying a file of papers. The person who'd been speaking with him followed.

"Lord Damien," the male said, dipping his head, and it was the first time I'd seen him in a while. His half-immortal black eyes peered from beneath the mess of shaggy black curls on his head.

"Cody," I acknowledged. I had a sneaking suspicion I knew what this visit was about. "It's good to see you again. It's been too long. I hope you've been well."

He tucked his hands into his coat pockets, and I knew he felt uncomfortable. I felt bad enough that he'd been busy with a task I'd given him, one I knew he didn't want to do.

"How's Kat doing?" I asked.

"She's well." He gave a nervous laugh. "She's been in bed all day, complained when she thought she might have to miss school and work on Monday. I swear, she's a workaholic. I don't know how she keeps up with it all."

It was a relief to hear she'd settled in at home after everything that happened. I'd found Cas texting her intermittently throughout the day, checking in on her. I knew she was worried. "I'm glad to hear that."

James held out a manilla folder. "Thought Ah'd gi' ye these. Let ye decide whit tae do wi' them."

I took it the folder. "So, this visit isn't about the patrols? There's been no appearances of the Varyos?"

James shook his head and the tension in my shoulders eased at that bit of good news as I opened the folder to find numerous photographs and documents on Kat. Nestled behind the photographs were countless documents, every detail that could possibly be found: who her parents were, which schools she'd attended, her job, everything. I glanced at Cody, whose eyes drifted from me, and I noted how he chewed his lip.

"Barrett told meh aboot whit happened—'at she wis attacked last night. Wisn't sure if ye wanted us tae continue keepin' tabs oan 'er," James explained before glancing at Cody.

A heavy sigh slipped from my lips. I'd instructed James to dig into Kat's background ever since we'd found Cassie, just to be safe. Never knew when a human might be a darkling, and I wanted to be sure Kat wasn't. I could barely believe it when James had informed me that she was seeing an immortal. She didn't know it, was still unaware of what Cody was, but it wasn't unusual for immortals to have relationships with mortals. I couldn't help but wonder if it were the Gods-damned Fates at work again. If I hadn't bumped into Cassie at the Galleria, I likely would have met her through Cody when he brought Kat into our world, if their relationship ever became serious. I wouldn't have been able to stay away even if I'd wanted to, even if I'd erased her memories, the threads of fate carefully entangling and webbing their way into our lives, forcing us to find one another.

"Thank you for calling me last night, Lord Damien," Cody said, an all too familiar fear creeping across his eyes.

I'd spoken with Cody after leaving Cassie and Kat at the hospital. He'd been distraught over the phone, and it had taken a lot to calm him down. I hated making the call, but he had to be made aware. He needed to know she was safe.

Guilt twisted my gut; not just because I'd given him this task, but because I'd kept it from Cassie all this time. She had enough to deal with, and I didn't want to put any more on her shoulders, didn't want to fill her head with doubt. I'd rather she be angry with me than be in danger. "I'm sorry I had to ask you to keep tabs on her, Cody. I truly am."

His onyx eyes shifted back to me. Cody wasn't a warrior, wasn't even a fighter, never had been. He was among the civilians who attended the college we checked in on from time to time. He was only in his early twenties, a few years past the settling, when an immortal reaches their prime and stops aging, when the need to feed springs to life.

Cody gave a half smile. "To be honest, I wasn't thrilled about it, but I understand why. I heard the darklings have been targeting Moira's reincarnation. I just... when you told me the possibility, I couldn't imagine her being one of them, didn't want to think it could be true."

I nodded, flipping through the documents. I could only imagine how uncomfortable he must've felt, reporting on the one who held his affection. "You swear you haven't seen anything odd?"

"I haven't," Cody assured. "Her schedule is so full. I don't know how she keeps up with it. She works a lot. College during the day, work in the afternoon, then she's usually stuck in her room late into the night studying and completing assignments."

I closed the file and tucked it under my arm. "Thank you, Cody. Truly."

He dipped his head. "Of course, Lord Damien. I'm honored to help in any way I can. I'm relieved she isn't a darkling."

"You can stop reporting on her. When I saw the darklings attack her—" His body stiffened, and I reconsidered my words. "I think it's safe to say she isn't one."

The silence stretched on for a moment, and he parted his lips as if to ask something, but stopped himself.

I raised a brow. "Speak your mind, Cody. What is it?"

"I... I'm hoping to tell her—maybe in the next few months what I am—what we are. When things start to get... bad, will I be able to get her to safety somewhere?" Kat was mortal, and while there were relationships between mortals and immortals, they always walked a fine line before things fell into place. How things ended always hinged on how the mortal reacted when they learned of their lover's identity. Rejections did happen, and the mess left in its wake had to be cleaned up quickly, the mortal's memories erased. It wasn't pretty, and I hated when it happened, hated it for the immortal who had to carry that sorrow with them.

Even more, I feared how it might affect Cassie if it didn't go well.

"Cas and I are working on securing a safe place for Kat. I'll let you know when we figure it out," I assured him.

He smiled. "I can't thank you enough, Lord Damien."

"No. Thank *you*, for helping me ensure our queen's safety."

282

CHAPTER 36

CASSIE

Ghastly shrieks pierced my ears as my feet slammed into grass and dirt. The field erupted in chaos around me as countless darklings clashed with immortal warriors, claws and teeth meeting steel and flesh. Fire erupted in the distance as Stoicheion users on the frontlines collectively mowed down another wave of darklings threatening to descend on us, and I cringed as a flame sputtered before going out entirely. One of them had fallen.

Shrill cries of the Coronis drew my gaze skyward as the mass of shadowy birds flew overhead. Fear curdled my stomach. They weren't here to aid us...

They served her.

The Coronis descended on us in a wave of feathers and shadowy death. I shot my hand into the air, ready to defend those they'd attack. White light shot up before I could act, fanning out in a shield of mist, deflecting the dark creatures, deflecting their descent and they scattered. I dropped my hand, relieved to see House Leukós still stood.

A snarl snapped my attention to the darkling charging toward me, and I whipped around, plunging my sword deep into its chest before pulling the blade free with a grunt. Icy black blood splattered my face before the creature crumbled to dust. I swallowed back the bile rising in my throat as the putrid smell filled my lungs. I lifted my hand to wipe the blood from my face, but it clung to me, oily and slick.

Heavy paws and a snarl alerted me, and I turned in time to see a massive snow leopard charging toward me. I dropped to my knees as it launched over me and crashed into a pair of darklings overwhelming another immortal warrior. Its massive jaws crunched down on the throat of one and ripped its head clean off as the other warrior finished the other darkling off.

Sweat stung my eyes, my black braid flipping over my shoulder as my gaze darted around in search of Damien. Where had he ended up? Was he on the frontlines? He'd been lost to me in the chaos of hundreds, possibly thousands, of warriors and darklings, but I still felt him, still felt that lingering thread connecting us. He was alive, but I needed to find him; we needed to do this together. I reached down the bond, casting my thoughts out to his but I was met with a wall, as if something were blocking our connection. I frowned. Was I that tired? No, I'd barely used my magic; I should still be able to reach him. Maybe my body was too tired, too fatigued from bearing the weight of fighting and what I carried within me.

My chest heaved, magic begging to be unleashed, but I couldn't. I needed to reserve it. The daughter of Matthias hadn't appeared yet, and I needed to be ready when she did. A mangled screech rang out behind me, and I spun around, swinging my sword in a wide arc at the charging darkling. Elythian steel met flesh and bone, and the darkling's head tumbled to the bloodied grass, more oily liquid splattering across my leather armor as it crumbled into dust.

I panted, bracing myself against my knee. Air evaded me, my lungs unable to fill fully. Gods, I just needed a moment, a breath. I dropped to a knee, my head dipping, and my hand came to my stomach, to the life growing inside me.

Emilia. This was for her. We'd destroy them once and for all this time, for her and all the young—for the future of our race.

Exhaustion crept into my limbs, my joints. I bit it back, pushing myself back onto unsteady feet. I had to endure, had to push forward.

"Lucia!" Barrett's voice shot out over the noise, his hand grabbing hold of my shoulder.

Relief washed over me at the sight of his face. He was okay—he was still alive. His face was unmarked, save a single scratch, and I couldn't see any other visible wounds. Gods, he smelled heavily of burnt flesh and ash, and I wasn't sure where he'd been fighting all this time, whether he'd been to the frontlines or not.

Concern and terror painted his face as his eyes danced over me, falling to the hand resting against my swollen stomach. The words flew from his mouth in a flurry, edged with fear. "Are you hurt?"

My brows rose, and I looked down at myself. "Oh no, I'm fine. Just winded."

"Are you sure? I can take you to a healer."

I smiled, despite the bloodshed surrounding us. You'd think he was my mate for how he doted over me, but it was fear for a friend that laced his voice, fear for his brother's mate and child, for his queen.

"I'm fine. Have you seen Damien?"

His jaw tightened, and he clamped his mouth shut, his throat working on a swallow.

I leveled my eyes on him. "Tell me, or I won't ask nicely the next time, Barrett. *Where is he*?"

He let out a ragged sigh of defeat, his eyes dancing anywhere but to mine. "He went to the frontlines. They became overwhelmed when our forces were split to stop the darklings attacking the city and—"

A cry from behind us cut his words short, and I pushed past him as two darklings pinned a warrior on his back, claws ripping at leather and flesh.

"No!" I slammed into them, and we crashed onto the ground before I rolled away and onto my knees, rising to my feet to face them. Barrett came up behind one, using my distraction to plunge his sword into the back of a darkling's head, while I dropped low, sweeping my foot out to knock the other darkling's legs out from under it. It fell onto its back, and I sank my sword into its chest.

The warrior lay on the ground, bloodied. Short, panicked gasps broke free of his lips as he lifted his head to look down on himself. I hurried to his side, his pale, wide eyes finding me.

"Were you bitten?" I asked. "Can you get up?"

285

The warrior let out a painful grunt as he attempted and failed to push himself up, clutching his stomach. I caught sight of the jagged wound, the torn leather armor that revealed... My stomach dipped. They'd nearly gutted him.

"*Were you bitten*?" I demanded, pulling my eyes from the wound.

The warrior shook his head. "They nearly got me, though."

My gaze snapped to Barrett. "Get him to the healers."

Barrett hesitated. "You should take him. I'll stay here and fight."

"He can't stand, let alone walk. Does it look like I can carry him, Barrett?" I barked back. "Get him to the healers and then find me again. That's an order!"

Barrett heaved a disgruntled breath, running his fingers through his bloody blond hair, and he growled his displeasure before pleading, "Come with me."

"I can't. I have to be ready if the daughter of Matthias appears." Fire erupted in the distance once more and I lifted my gaze to the frontlines. I didn't know how much magic the Stoicheion users might have left. They couldn't keep this up. There were too many darklings, our forces stretched too thin between here and the city. The battle had dragged on for far too long now. The darklings were wearing us down, and many of the fallen immortals only replenished the darkling's ranks.

Barrett crouched and pulled the injured warrior's arm over his shoulder before hoisting him to his feet. The warrior let out a wet gasp, clutching his shredded stomach, his face contorting with pain. Barrett's steel eyes met mine, fierce yet fearful. "Be careful, spitfire."

"You too, hothead," I breathed with a smile, and he turned to make his way through the chaos to the healers at the back of the battlefield.

A darkling slipped through the crowd between us, its dark gaze shifting to me before its head whipped back to Barrett. Shit, the fresh scent of the injured warrior's blood must have drawn its attention. My heart lurched as it lunged for their backs. They were too far; I couldn't get to them in time to intercept its attack.

I shot my hand out, my sword falling to the ground as my thoughts curled and wound around the creature. Roots shot from the ground, snaking up the darkling's body, anchoring it in place. The darkling twisted, fighting against the tethers, clawed hands snatching through the air at Barrett and the wounded warrior. My other hand shot forward as I closed my fingers, twisting my wrist in a circle. The roots twisted and tightened, biting into the creature's flesh. The darkling shrieked as Barrett looked over his shoulder with wide eyes. I gritted my teeth, jerking my hand back, tension coiling as the roots plunged into the darkling's chest, ensnaring its heart and crushing it.

The darkling collapsed into dust.

My shoulders sagged, arms falling to my sides as I panted. "Go!" I yelled, and Barrett dipped his head before hurrying to the healers. I prayed he made it there safely, that he would return to me unharmed. I prayed Zephyr and Vincent were okay, wherever they were.

I turned from where Barrett had vanished, my eyes set on the worst of the battle: the frontlines. Damien was there. He was fighting, and I didn't know how he fared. Was he hurt? My thoughts stretched out once more, desperate to reach him, to hear his voice, but it hit that wall again, as if something were holding me at bay. I needed to get to him; we needed to be together, to watch each other's backs.

The ground was slick with blood as I stepped forward, ducking to grab my sword. There were few bodies on the ground, the lucky few who'd died before they'd changed. Gods, how many had we lost? How many of our own had been turned since the battle began? My gaze lifted from the dead bodies, and I leapt into a run toward the frontlines when a wave of power shot over the field from behind me, sending countless darklings and warriors to the ground. I slammed into bloodied grass and mud, cries and screeches replaced with near silence.

Ringing filled my ears, and I grimaced as I pushed myself to my knees. An unnatural presence crawled over my skin. My eyes drifted forward, to where I knew Damien was. The frontlines hadn't been hit by the blast, didn't seem to realize it had even happened.

"The healers!" cried a panicked voice from nearby. My gaze snapped behind me, to where the healers of House Latros had resided for the last few hours, to where Barrett had disappeared into the crowd of death. Black mist enveloped it all.

My heart sank. No. No. Where was he? My eyes searched, but I didn't see him. In the distance, undulating tendrils of darkness stretched out where tents and healers once worked. I couldn't see anything through the black mass consuming everything, through the swirling darkness, marking the arrival of what I'd dreaded.

The daughter of Matthias had made her entrance. The frontlines were a distraction. She'd somehow flanked us, slamming into our under-guarded rear where the injured were being tended to. How had she slipped past us unnoticed? Where was the rear guard? Had she wiped them out?

"Gods…" I breathed as I pushed myself to my feet in a daze of disbelief. The world spun as the smoke and dust cleared. Nothing remained. She'd destroyed them, in an instant, every last healer, every recovering warrior.

They were all gone. House Latros… Gods, no, it couldn't be gone.

I gripped my sword, my heart thrumming as the darkness at the core of my being writhed and tugged me toward her. It was too tempting and terrifying all the same, the dark void offering me power that would turn me against those I fought to protect. Terror crawled over my skin, and I forced it down as the very creature I dreaded facing rose from the darkness, tendrils of darkness shooting out from her lower back, knocking every warrior who charged her back.

Her dark gaze drifted across the field, her long black claw dragging across her lips idly as she searched. For what? What was she searching for? Those hollow black eyes locked with mine. She'd been looking for me.

My magic pulsed, begging to be used. I took a step forward, holding her gaze as a cruel smile spread across her face, revealing those terrible serrated teeth behind her dark lips. The deaths she'd caused didn't seem to faze her, and my blood boiled in response. I would end her, once and for all. I had to. There was no other option. Only one of us would be leaving this killing field alive. For Emilia, for Damien, for our race; I would destroy her.

I stepped forward, primed to unleash myself on her, but time slowed, my vision skipping and cracking. My feet slipped through the ground into nothing, plummeting into a pitch darkness that swallowed me whole.

No!

I slammed into something solid, and I gasped, eyes shooting open. Warm, strong arms wrapped around me, pulling me back against a firm, powerful chest.

"Easy, *mea luna*. I've got you." Damien's calm, tender voice slipped into my ear as gentle as a caress, and I blinked as I tried to catch my breath.

The scent of burning flesh and blood was quickly replaced by the smell of cedarwood and leather, of the fire burning in our fireplace, of home. The familiarity of it, of his touch grounded me. My heart thrummed, my hands twitching and clammy where I'd just been gripping my sword. My shoulders sagged as my head fell into the crook of his shoulder.

"How'd it go? Were you able to find anything this time?" he asked, reaching for the glass of water sitting on the nearby table. When he offered it to me, I downed the liquid, desperate for its soothing rush. It slammed into my parched throat so hard, I nearly choked.

I coughed, and Damien eased the empty glass from my grasp.

"Nothing. Something keeps interrupting it, like I'm hitting a wall," I said through shallow pants, frustration lacing my words.

I'd been at this for the last hour or two, diving into that memory of Lucia's when she'd fought with Melantha, searching for any clues as to how I'd defeated her. Every time I got to that point, right as I was about to attack her, I'd slip from the memory as if it were wet paper in my hands, disintegrating before me, or the world would shudder, and I'd wake up on the other side of the battle. It didn't make sense.

"Why can't I remember?" I muttered, brows furrowing as I rested my elbows against my knees.

"You never spoke of what happened after Melantha fell. Whatever you did, it seemed to haunt you. I didn't think it would ever be something I needed to know, and I couldn't bring myself to ask."

I leaned into him, my gaze lifting to the painting of us hanging on the wall—of a time when I was Lucia, and we were excitedly awaiting the arrival of Emilia. It was strange how it was all falling into place, as if the lives I'd lived simply felt like a far-off time. It hadn't been someone else's time, but my own.

"Maybe you suppressed the memory," Damien suggested, fidgeting with a stray lock of my hair. "It's quite common."

It was possible, but what could've happened that would be so horrible that I couldn't, or... *wouldn't* remember?

"Something else happened. I kept trying to reach out to you through our thoughts, but it was as if something was blocking our connection."

Damien's brows furrowed. "You never mentioned that."

What could've caused it? Could Melantha have somehow interfered? Was that even possible? Something else resurfaced from the memories I'd relived several times this evening, and I paused.

My gaze turned to the plant nestled in the corner by the bay window. "I wonder..."

I pushed up to my feet, and Damien watched me curiously as I approached it. "What are you doing?"

"I used the abilities of House Dendron in the memory. I don't know how to explain it, but I think I remember how to use it."

Damien rose, his brows pinched as he followed me.

I bit my lip as I stopped before the plant. It was a fern, its long stems full of leaves stretching up toward the ceiling. I pulled from the memory, letting my will slip over my fingers as I reached my hands over the fern. My eyes slid closed as I focused, and my thoughts took the form of roots, of the tendrils of life that flowed through them, tunneling my will into countless stems stretching out of the pot like a firework. My hands became an extension of that life, the warmth seeping into my skin, pulsing through my veins. I stretched my fingers out, like leaves fanning out for more sun.

Damien stiffened at my side, a short breath hissing through his teeth, and I opened my eyes to find the fern's stems lifting, the leaves stretching out the way my fingers did. I gasped, my hands recoiling, and it slowly eased back into its upright position. A smile formed on my lips. I'd done it.

"Have I told you lately how much you amaze me?" Damien's strong, warm arms came around me as he pulled me back against his chest.

I smiled to the side at him. "I do try."

He gave a light chuckle, the sound causing my heart to flutter. "You should probably stop for the day. You're starting to look a bit pale."

My eyes fell from his, the truth bringing a rush of annoyance. "You're right."

I wanted to continue, but I could feel that unseen limit drawing closer, where my body couldn't keep up with the power's toll. It was dangerous territory. I'd suffered from a recoil the first time we'd practiced my Nous ability. I'd pushed far beyond my limits, and it hadn't ended well.

"I've got some paperwork I need to complete. If you'd like, you're welcome to grab a book and keep me company," Damien offered, and the corner of his lip tipped up into a crooked grin as his finger drifted across my lower stomach. "It might encourage me to work faster."

Heat rose in my chest, but I cocked my head to look at him over my shoulder, lifting a brow. "Would my company be an encouragement? Or a distraction?"

He licked his lips. "That's yet to be determined."

Part of me was curious. I'd never really been in his study; not for any reason, it had just never happened. We had been preoccupied elsewhere, and Damien rarely spent time in there to begin with.

"I guess I can grace you with my presence, *my king*," I said in a teasing tone, pulling free of his arms.

Damien grabbed my hand, pulling me against his chest with such force that I nearly gasped. His forehead pressed to mine, eyes molten. "Ok, *that, mea luna*, is *very* distracting."

I bit my lip, and for a moment, I was conflicted as to whether I should be as distracting as I was tempted to be, or if I should pull away and make him that much hungrier for me.

"I promise not to tempt you," I said with a coy grin.

He gave me a knowing look, as if contemplating whether I truly meant it. I pushed myself up to kiss his cheek before slipping from his grip. His eyes followed me, and I bit back a giggle as I headed for my study to grab a book.

I was curious to see his office. What did he do? What kind of paperwork did the King of Immortals need to complete? My fingers drifted across the spines of my books, unable to decide on one. I settled on a book I'd bought recently but hadn't been able to read yet, tucking it against my chest.

The wood floors creaked under my feet as I stepped out of the room, heading upstairs and down the hall in the opposite direction of our bedroom. The door to his study was left ajar for me, and I quietly opened it, peering inside. Damien stood behind a large, ornate wooden desk, already sorting through paperwork. I bit my lip, smiling at the intense concentration already forming on his face.

My eyes explored the rich wooden space, the walls lined with shelves of dark walnut. There weren't nearly as many books on the shelves as I had in my study, but where books were missing sat all sorts of knickknacks and items that piqued my curiosity. Some of the objects had to be from the Godsrealm—a few large clusters of crystals, including one that emitted a soft glow, as well as a few small skeletal displays of creatures I'd never seen before.

Damien pulled his attention from his work and extended his hand toward an emerald chaise at the other end of the room. It rested near a fireplace as grand as the one downstairs, decorated with finely carved, walnut-stained wood. A cozy fire was already lit, warmth emanating throughout the space. I set my book on the chaise, taking every detail in before I turned my gaze on Damien, who'd resumed his work. I drifted toward the desk. God, there was so much paperwork.

"Do you mind handing me that pile over there?" he asked as he tapped the edge of a stack of papers to line them up. I glanced to a loose pile of documents and paperwork sitting at the far front corner, a manila folder resting on top.

"These?" I asked, laying a hand on it, and he nodded absentmindedly. I carefully scooped up the pile, the stack heavy as I rounded to where he stood.

"You're rather messy for a king," I teased, and he cocked an eyebrow at me.

"Apologies, my queen. I shall do better," he responded with a wry grin, and my damn heart fluttered hearing the title on his tongue.

I laid the stack before him, but it shifted, the manila folder and papers sliding across the desk. He stiffened as photographs slipped from the folder.

"Shit! I'm so sorr—" My gaze snagged on the photos as they spilled over, my brows furrowing. They were pictures of Kat. Not selfies or snapshots with friends, but ones taken without her knowledge. I reached across the table and grabbed the folder before Damien could stop me.

"Cas..." Damien started, but I opened it, my breath catching in my throat.

It was filled with photographs of Kat—of her on campus, entering work, even eating out with Cody. My stomach twisted, and I flipped through to the contents. There weren't just photos, but documents on her parents, the schools she'd attended, everything.

"What's this?" I demanded, dropping the folder on the desk, my attention snapping back to him.

Guilt flickered across his features. "I can explain—"

"You need to start doing that right now, Damien. Why are you spying on Kat?" Oh God. Had he spied on me at some point? Had he dug up files like this on me? Did he—

"It was necessary—"

"*Why though?*" I bit out, nearly cutting him off.

His gaze flickered from me, and he drew his hand across the back of his neck as he carefully chose his words. "I needed to make sure she wasn't a darkling."

I stilled. "A darkling? You seriously thought she was a darkling?"

His lips parted, and he hesitated. "I couldn't know for sure until we looked into her background, kept tabs on her whereabouts. I wanted to make sure you were safe."

"Did you spy on me like this?" I asked, heart racing.

He looked at me as if shocked I'd even considered it. "Of course not, *mea luna*. I knew what you were the moment I met you."

293

His statement came with a small measure of relief, but it didn't erase his actions.

"Who?" I breathed, trying my best to remain calm, even as I struggled.

"Who what?"

"Who else was a part of this? Who else knew?" I ground out, my irritation growing.

"James and... Cody," he admitted.

"What the hell, Dami—wait..." The name clicked through me, halting any thoughts or words I had. "Cody?"

Damien nodded, and my brows furrowed. An icy feeling crept through my chest, and it stung to know he'd kept this from me. "Kat's... boyfriend, Cody?" I confirmed.

"Cody's an immortal. Half, to be precise."

"Cody's an immortal? Since when—I mean, of course his entire life, but—God, Damien, I—" My mind flew into a flurry, my skin hot. "Was he actually with her? Or was it just so he could spy on her this entire time?"

"His affection for her is genuine, Cas. I promise you, and I felt terrible asking him to keep tabs on her. After she was attacked, I figured it was safe to assume she's not a darkling—"

"So, it took her being attacked for her to clear her name? It took her nearly dying for you to figure that out?" I scoffed.

He winced. "There was no other way to confirm she was mortal, Cas. I couldn't exactly walk up to her and ask her if she was a darkling."

"Why didn't you tell me?" All heat left me the moment the words left my lips, guilt sinking into the pit of my stomach. God, I was such a fucking hypocrite. What right did I have to be upset with him for keeping this from me? He'd done it for my safety.

I'd kept something far worse from him, and for what?

Damien tried to reason with me, tried to explain further, but I couldn't meet his eyes, all fight leaving me as I stepped back, hugging myself. "I wanted to, but I couldn't do that to you. You've had enough to deal with these last few months. I didn't want to put that concern on your shoulders, didn't want you fearing whether you could trust your own friend. I hated keeping this from you. I was going to tell you once I knew without a doubt that she wasn't, I just haven't had the chance."

He was right, and I couldn't deny it. If I'd have known there was any chance Kat might be a darkling, it would've torn me apart. I clamped my mouth shut, nausea building in my stomach. I had no right to be upset with him for this.

"I truly am sorry."

I couldn't speak, my mind a whirlwind of guilt and confliction, of everything I wanted to tell him but was too afraid to.

"I'm sorry I got mad," I muttered, and Damien's brows furrowed.

He lifted my chin to meet his gaze. "You have every right to be, Cas. I deserve it."

"No, you're right. You told me yourself; you can never know who's a darkling and who's not."

His gaze fell, and he drew a deep breath, lifting the folder and collecting the few photographs that lay across his desk. "I spoke with Cody and James last night after we got back from the Archivallia. They're no longer keeping tabs on her. Cody told me he plans to tell her what he is in a few months."

My gaze shot to him. "What?"

"It's... not guaranteed everything will work out. If their relationship continues, though, he'll reveal what he is, reveal many of the things I've shared with you, about the immortals, about our world," he said as he approached the fireplace.

The guilt and hurt were replaced with something else—hope. Kat might be welcomed into our world. I wouldn't have to erase her memories of me. She would know what Cody was, what they all were. God, I could talk to her about, well, anything, everything. There'd been so much I'd wanted to talk to her about, to tell her.

"There will be protocols he'll have to follow," Damien warned, and I glanced back at him as he came to a stop before the fireplace.

"Like what?" I asked, unease settling over my skin.

"Well, it could go one of two ways. If he tells her and she's accepting of the information, she'll be allowed to take a vow of silence every mortal takes when joining our society. If she doesn't take the information well..."

My stomach dipped as his words trailed off, and he tossed the folder into the flames, the paper and pictures curling into themselves as the embers crawled across them. "What happens then?"

"Her memories will have to be erased."

CHAPTER 37

CASSIE

The cold chill of the doctor's office seeped through my thin gown as I lay in the MRI machine. Why did doctors keep their offices so damn cold? The machine hummed as it scanned my heart, the tunnel hovering less than a foot above me, the sounds of the machine nearly loud enough to drown out my own thoughts. My eyes flitted around, my heart racing, breath shaky. The white walls felt closer than they had a few seconds ago, as if they were closing in.

Sit still. Breathe. I inhaled deeply. *Five. Four. Three. Two. One.* I exhaled. I don't know why I bothered with the breathing exercise. It did little to calm my panic. I closed my eyes, imagining I was elsewhere, anywhere.

"We're halfway there, Cassie. Twenty more minutes. Just relax. Try to keep still," the MRI tech said through the speaker.

I swallowed and inhaled, counting again. *Just twenty more minutes. Twenty more minutes.* My thoughts drifted to the time when Damien and I sat on the bank of the creek at Stackhouse park, when I'd sketched him, before I knew of their world, of the horrors lingering in the shadows. I focused on the way his eyes had glowed in the rays of the sun, how the amber exploded amidst the ashen silver of his eyes, the feel of the charcoal in my hands as I sketched out the details of his sharp jawline. Details, focus on details, anything else but this damned tunnel.

The remaining twenty minutes felt like hours, and when the bed creaked, rolling out of the machine, I couldn't sit up fast enough. The nurse opened the door, gesturing for me to follow. I did, eager to get out of this room. My eyes burned into the nurse's back, avoiding the knowing gaze of the staff. It didn't help that half of them had been here the entirety of my treatment and knew what I was facing. It was refreshing when I'd see new faces who didn't know my situation over the years, but it never took long for them to learn and the pity to sink into their not-so-subtle glances.

"He'll be with you shortly," she said as she led me into the room, setting my thick medical chart on the counter. I wanted to burn it where it sat. I could. It wouldn't take but a second, a thought, and I knew the chart would go up in flames.

I sighed, settling onto the bed, my feet dangling over the edge. The nerves set in then. I dreaded this waiting game, dreaded the news, dreaded what I knew was going to happen when I visited my parents afterward.

Anywhere but here. My thoughts drifted again. Damien thought I was with my parents right now. The lie left gravelly guilt in my gut, which had only been amplified when I'd exploded on him yesterday for doing what I'd done from the start. I needed to tell him, but today was going to be hard enough without breaking that news to him.

I wanted to. I wanted so desperately to tell him everything, but I couldn't now, not when I knew that within the next few hours my—

My parents wouldn't know I existed.

It needed to happen, though. I had to ensure my parents were safe first. After this, I could tell him everything.

"Here are the details of where they're going so you can work it in to help the transition. My contact will be reaching out to them tomorrow to start the process," Damien said, slipping me a piece of paper. *"We'll switch out their*

phones with new ones so no one can contact them. James will email resignations to both of their jobs.

"Thank you," I said, taking the paper and unfolding it, scanning over the few details I'd need to make this transition easy.

"The company's in Washington. The job comes with housing, excellent pay, and lots of benefits. I'll be able to keep tabs on them as well, so you'll know they're safe. They'll have everything they'll need, and they'll be able to retire at an early age."

I lifted my eyes to him, disbelief rushing through me. "Damien, this—"

"Is the least I can do for the sacrifices you've made for our kingdom..., for me," he said, and I pressed the paper to my chest, tears welling in my eyes. He pulled me into a tight embrace. "I'm only sorry this is all I can do, and I'm sorry I kept everything about Kat hidden from you."

I forced a smile, despite the dread filling my chest.

Damien's forehead eased to mine, warmth filling me as he offered me what comfort he could. "I'll be here every step of the way, mea luna. Reach out to me when you're ready."

The metal door clicked open, pulling me from the memory of this morning, and I stiffened as Dr. Robertson entered. His brows rose as he tilted his head forward to gaze at me over his reading glasses. "Wow, Cas. You look like a completely different person since I last saw you."

I forced an awkward smile. "I've been eating better."

He opened my file, reviewing the notes from the nurse. "I see that. Your weight's perfect." He lifted his chin, glancing at me before continuing to read the notes. "Have you been exercising?"

I nodded. "I started jogging again and I've been learning self-defense."

"Your blood pressure is the best I've seen in years," he said, glancing back at the file.

Something swelled in my chest. He sounded the most hopeful I'd ever heard. Had they already finished reading the MRI?

"How did the MRI look?" I dared to ask.

"They're still reading it, but it should be ready before you leave." He approached me, removing his stethoscope from around his neck. "How have you been feeling since your last visit? Any issues?"

I sat back as he pressed the stethoscope to my chest. "Good. Nothing out of the ordinary, some chest pain here and there."

He listened to my heart, changing position a few times before moving to my back. I sat in silence, waiting for him to speak. "Breathe for me."

I inhaled deeply, holding it for a second before slowly exhaling.

"How has your implant been? Is it still in place? Has it caused any issues?"

I scratched my arm at the reminder of the birth control they'd placed there several months ago. It would've been too risky for me to get pregnant with the complications and the medication I was on. I'd been against it at the time, not seeing the point, as I wasn't sexually active. Now that I was with Damien, though, I was glad to have it. "It's still in place. I haven't had any issues."

"Did your period ever start back up?"

I shook my head. My periods had been irregular for years, and then at some point over the last two, they had stopped entirely. The doctors had ruled it as a side effect of my medications and treatments. It didn't matter either way.

He placed the stethoscope back around his neck. "We're gonna run some blood tests and run an EKG while we wait for them to finish reading the MRI."

I nodded, and a knock sounded at the door.

"Ah, perfect timing. Come in, Jenn," he said.

The nurse opened the door. "I'm going to draw some blood, Cas. Is that ok?"

I smiled weakly at the nurse, who'd been here for as long as I could remember. "Yeah."

Dr. Robertson turned back to me. "I'll be back as soon as the MRI's done."

"Okay," I said, and he slipped out of the room.

Jenn headed for the counter and pulled various things from the drawers. The gloves snapped and squeaked as she pulled them on, the sound echoing off the walls as she rolled the tray over to the bedside, pausing to grab the rubber tourniquet.

"All right, Cas. Extend your right arm for me, hun," she said tenderly, her dark hair slipping free from behind her ear as she leaned forward.

I stretched my arm out, straightening my elbow. She turned from the rolling tray to face me. I couldn't miss the brief hesitation as her eyes found the long scar spanning the length of my forearm, one of the few scars remaining from when Marcus had kept me imprisoned. She didn't say anything as she wrapped the strip of stretchy material around my bicep, tying it tight.

She quickly prepped my skin, rubbing it down with alcohol before reaching back to grab the needle and syringe. Her thumb pressed into the crease of my elbow as she lifted her eyes to mine, a reassuring smile on her face. "Ready?"

I nodded, taking a deep breath. I turned my gaze from the needle as she lowered it to the crease of my elbow. My body tensed as the needle pierced my skin, and I closed my eyes, my mind drifting elsewhere again, anywhere but here.

My thoughts wandered to times when Damien and I had spent hours curled up together on the couch, when we'd hosted 'Shitty Movie Sundays'. Barrett choosing the absolute worst movies to watch. The living room would be filled with jokes and comments that left me laughing until my sides hurt.

Those memories helped pass the time it took Jenn to do what she needed until the technician had finished the EKG. I sat in the room, alone again, waiting for Dr. Robertson to return. Anxiety swelled as I wondered how much time had passed. Would it be good news? Bad news? My thoughts wandered and the anxiety grew, clouding my thoughts in a shroud of fear.

No. Not now.

My thoughts drifted to what I feared, to what had happened before, to what I knew would inevitably happen again.

I nudged my front door open, my mom following close behind as I stepped into my apartment, our arms weighed down with every grocery bag that had been in the car as we joked about how we refused to make a second trip for more. I set them on the counter. "Told you we could do it!"

My mom laughed as she set her own down on the kitchen table, and she began unloading the groceries.

"I'm gonna run these few up to my room. I'll be back to help you," I said, skirting past her.

"All right," she said, and I grabbed the bags of toiletries as I headed down the hall. I had plans to meet Kat for a pizza date in a few hours, our weekly ritual we'd managed every Friday night without interruption for years. As I reached the top of the stairs, I stopped, brows furrowing as a tightness spread through my chest. I blinked as it receded, almost as quickly as it had appeared. I shook it off and turned for the bathroom.

When my shampoo, conditioner, soap, and other goodies were all restocked, I started toward my room to drop off the last of my things. I halted. The room spun and shifted, and I stumbled, bracing myself against the counter. A cold sweat broke out across my skin, and I took a step forward, suddenly feeling as if I couldn't get enough oxygen into my lungs.

"Mo—" Pain shot through my chest, knocking the wind from me.

300

Oh God. I opened my mouth to call for help, but the pain shot through me again, down my back, and the room spun until I couldn't see straight. I needed to get to Mom, I needed...

"Cas?" My mother's voice reached up to me from downstairs.

"Hel—" Pain, sharper than before, tore through me, the wind rushing from my lungs, as my knees gave out from under me, the world going dark as I hit the tile.

A wave of electricity shot through the nothingness, sending piercing white light across my vision, and a blur of voices trickled in through the darkness.

"Resuming CPR!"

Weight pressed on my chest in a rapid rhythm, and then my lungs expanded, but I didn't breathe.

"Clear!" The voice was breathless, and the next words were laced with what sounded like irritation or urgency, I couldn't tell. "Get them out of here!"

The shock surged through me again, excruciating and blinding. Then I heard a familiar voice, a woman, her voice filled with tears and terror.

"Cassie!"

A knock sounded at the door, and I jumped as Dr. Robertson entered, carrying a large envelope in his hands. The MRI. I clenched the end of the bed, my stomach dipping. He pulled the results from the envelope and stuck it up on the light panel before flipping the switch. God, I wish it didn't look like a black and white blob.

"So, I have some good news," he said, resting the envelope on the counter as his gaze shifted back and forth between his notes and the glowing picture.

My heart leapt, tension slipping from my shoulders. "You do?"

"There is a bit more scar tissue, which we expected, but not much. Whatever you're doing seems to have slowed the development."

A weight left my shoulders as the news sank in. I was good for now; I still had more time. Was it because of Eris' interference? It was strange to think Eris had truly been helping me. I also wondered if Damien's feeding was somehow helping. Dr. Robertson had said my blood pressure was better than it'd been in years. It was ironic to think Damien believed he was hurting me by feeding, when in fact it seemed he was doing quite the opposite.

"We're gonna keep you on the same medications. You keep doing what you're doing. Keep up the exercise, and let me know if anything happens," he said, pulling the MRI down from the panel.

"Thank you, Dr. Robertson."

He smiled, and it was as if that same weight I'd felt slip from my shoulders, seemed to have lifted for him as well. "I'm just happy to be able to give you some good news for once."

CHAPTER 38

CASSIE

A few cars passed as I walked along the sidewalk. The bus stop wasn't a terrible distance from my parents' house, and I needed some time to build up my courage for what I was to face in a few hours. I tucked my hands into my coat pockets, the winter breeze whipping my curls around my face.

My phone vibrated in my pocket, and I pulled it free to see a text from Kat. I tried not to linger on what I'd learned the day before, how Damien had been watching her, invading her privacy under the suspicion she might be a darkling.

How'd the doctor's visit go? Are you out yet?

I typed my response, my heart racing out of habit. It was still a lot to adjust to, to know she knew everything.

I'm out. It went better than expected. I'm the epitome of perfect health.

I typed more.

The scar tissue looks like it slowed, so I guess I'll live to see another day.

My phone vibrated again, her text appearing on the screen, and I smiled.

You and me both. Cody's been stuck up my butt the last two days, doting on me. You'd think I was dying.

I chuckled under my breath. Cody. I still couldn't wrap my head around the fact he was half immortal. The possibility had never crossed my mind, but a part of me almost hoped she'd learn the truth. I'd be able to talk to her about everything. There'd finally be no secrets between us.

I tapped away at the screen.

That's so adorable, it's sickening.

I quickly texted back once more as I rounded the corner and headed up the hill along Coal Street. I needed to clear my head, calm my pounding heart, flush out the nerves that left nausea roiling in my gut. I sighed, knowing that no matter what I did, it wouldn't go away.

I just got to my parents' place. I'll text you later.

She responded quickly.

Have fun! Cody's bringing me lunch. I swear, this man is always concerned about whether I'm eating or not.

I smiled, relieved she wasn't home alone.

Both my parents' cars were parked along the sidewalk, my dad having taken the day off to visit. I drew a deep breath, my gaze drifting over the details of their home, and I pushed my phone back into my pocket as I headed for the porch steps. I silently prayed theirs would be the only memories I'd have to erase in the end.

"Cas!" My mom rose from the couch the moment I stepped through the front door, her dirty blonde hair slipping over her shoulder before she tucked it behind her ear. She'd cut it since I'd seen her nearly a month ago around Christmas. It used to reach down to her shoulder blades, but now it brushed the top of her shoulders.

"Hey, Mom," I said as she hugged me. I wrapped my arms around her, holding her tightly, feeling every part of that embrace, committing it to memory. Her scent filled my lungs, indescribable yet nostalgic. It was the scent of my childhood, of moments I'd cherish forever. "I love your haircut."

She smiled, running her fingers through it. "Thank you. I just got it done Friday."

"Where's Dad?"

"He's in the basement working on some project before we go out for dinner," she said, as I slipped off my coat and hung it on the rack. "You thirsty? I could make some hot cocoa."

I smiled, my eyes drifting over the details of her face, every fine line and wrinkle, the crow's feet stemming from her eyes when she smiled. "Hot cocoa would be really nice right now."

She turned and headed for the kitchen, and I followed, rubbing my hands together to warm them. My feet slowed as my gaze found the countless pictures decorating shelves, the memories that would soon be wiped away. The first time Dad took me fishing, and I'd caught my first fish. I'd never seen him smile as big as he did in that picture, my four-year-old self proudly displaying the tiny fish on my hook beside him. Another picture captured my first art competition, another my first time riding a bike, my private high school graduation they'd done, so I didn't feel left out when Kat graduated. So many smiles.

"How did the doctor's visit go?" she asked, and my gaze shot forward, stepping through the hallway and into the kitchen.

"Oh, it, um… it went good, actually. Dr. Robertson said there's very little new scar tissue."

She glanced over her shoulder, her eyes lighting up as she opened the cabinet and pulled a kettle out. "Really?"

I nodded, admiring the hazel eyes she'd given me—the only feature I'd received from her. Would the sight of those hazel eyes in the mirror haunt me for the rest of my life? Or would they be a tender reminder of her, that she'd always be with me? "He said my blood pressure's the best it's been in a long time. Even said my weight is where they want it."

She filled the kettle with water before moving it to the stove as she turned the knob. The fire came to life after a few clicks of the starter. "You look really good. Did he say anything more? Are they changing your medications? Did he mention any new treatment options? I should've gone with you."

"It's ok, Mom. You were held up this morning. I'm good with doing this on my own." I reached into the cabinet to fetch the hot cocoa mix for her, right where it had always been. "He's keeping me on the same regimen. No point in changing things if they seem to be working."

She nodded. "How's Damien? Are you guys doing well?" She glanced back with a knowing smile.

My heart skipped, and a warm smile curved my lips. "He's great. We're doing really well."

"What does he do for a living again? I can't remember if you told me." She pulled two mugs out of the cupboard.

I pressed my lips into a thin line, trying to think of what I would tell her. "He's um... runs a company in another city."

Her brows rose. "He's so young."

I tried not to laugh at the statement. If only she knew he was nearly a thousand years old. "Family business."

"Ah," she said, as if that suddenly made more sense.

I cleared my throat. "Did they rent out the apartment next door again?"

She shook her head. "No, they've been talking about remodeling after the damages. They got most of it cleaned up, but there's going to be quite a bit of repair work needed."

I didn't say anything. I hadn't set foot in that apartment since I'd left, and I never would.

She poured the hot cocoa mix and a few scoops of mini marshmallows into the mugs as I settled into a chair at the small, round table.

She glanced back at me. "How've your classes been? Settling into the new semester?"

Guilt crept in, and I forced a smile. "They're going well. Boring as usual."

There was no point in stressing them out about me stopping. It had been a difficult enough transition with me moving out. So I'd lied, kept up the façade that I'd continued attending classes. It wasn't like they went to campus or received emails; that was something I'd always managed.

"That's good." She turned to rest against the counter while she waited for the water to boil. "How's Kat been? Still dating that boy?"

I loved her questions, loved hearing her talk. It wouldn't matter in the end if I gave her answers or not, but I would answer them all the same, anything she wanted to know. I didn't care if it made my job more difficult. I'd cherish what little time we had left...

So, I answered.

The afternoon sun warmed my skin as we sat on Devil's Rock. The wide expanse of the Johnstown stretched out below us in a web of buildings and streets converging in the valley, the Conemaugh River winding through the center. The last hour had been spent reminiscing on fond memories and funny times we'd shared. It had been the most wonderful afternoon, more than I could've hoped for.

The sight of the sinking sun, though, twisted something in my chest. I turned my eyes to my mom and dad, who sat together on the quilt, heads leaned against one another as they watched the horizon. They loved each other so much, and the sight of them together warmed my heart.

"I'm glad we came here," I breathed, wrapping my arms around myself, the cold winter breeze snaking through my hair.

"It's been a long time since we came here last. I think you were…" Dad paused, glancing at Mom. "She would have been what? Twelve? Thirteen?"

"I think so," Mom sighed. "We should do this more often. I've missed you around the house."

My smile became painful. I shifted, scooting closer until I was between them. Their eyes followed me as I kneeled between their legs and wrapped my arms around their necks, pulling them into a tight hug. "I love you guys so much."

They hesitated, their confusion seeping into my skin in tingling waves, but their arms came around me. I bit back the urge to cry, fought the tears that threatened to well in my eyes.

"We love you too, Cas," Dad said warily. "Everything okay?"

"Sorry," I said, remaining still. "So much has happened. I've just missed you guys so much."

My dad pressed a kiss to my head, his hand gently brushing my back as I leaned my head against his shoulder. "I'm sure it's been a lot to adjust to."

Silence hung in the air, and dread flooded my chest, sinking low into my gut. It couldn't be time already… not yet. I wasn't ready.

I needed more time. Just a little more time…

I wanted to say so much, wanted to thank them, to tell them to take care of each other, to always give each other warm hugs, to always smile the way they did.

"I love you so much," I breathed one last time, reaching out through my thoughts, finding the walls of their minds. "Thank you for everything."

"Cas—" Mom started.

Sleep.

It was barely a second before their weight settled against me, and my heart stuttered. I eased them down onto the blanket, their faces peaceful. I reached out to brush the dirty blonde strands of hair from my mom's soft face. My eyes drifted to my father, to the wiry short chestnut hair, the wrinkles around his mouth etched from how wide he always smiled, the frown lines that had set into his forehead from all the years of scolding me when I'd break the rules as a child.

I bent down to press a kiss to his forehead, and the tears broke free, rolling down my cheeks before dripping onto his.

No, I couldn't do this now. I needed to get to work, needed to get them to their car. I should call Damien. Air flooded my lungs, and I closed my eyes as I stretched out my thoughts, finding that tether that tied Damien and me together.

Mea sol…

His voice brushed my thoughts, the caress as gentle as his fingertips against my face.

Is it time?

My throat thickened, my chest filling with something so hard and painful that I whimpered, but I clasped my hand over my mouth.

I…

I couldn't bring myself to say yes, to verbalize what I was about to do, the line I was about to cross. It was for the best, though. It would ensure they survived. The scent of cedarwood and leather drifted on the breeze, and I lifted my gaze to find him stepping from the tree line, followed closely by Zephyr and Barrett.

"Damien," I breathed, my vision blurring. I swiped my hands across my eyes.

He kneeled beside me. "I'm here, *mea luna.*"

Barrett and Zephyr came to a stop behind him, their eyes passing over my parents. My parents never met them, and I wished so badly they had, wished they could've seen how happy I'd been the last few months. My mom would've liked Zephyr, and, once she got to know Barrett, would've possibly even considered him adorable for his childish antics. It would never happen now.

"Their car's parked not far from here. It'll seem like they went on a date and fell asleep watching the sunset," I said, more to myself than them.

Damien didn't say anything, tenderly tucking a loose curl behind my ear. "We'll keep watch while you work."

"Thank you," I said as my gaze fell to my father. I placed my hand over his eyes before pressing my forehead to his, feeling that connection, that bridge between our minds. I began my search for all that was me residing within the recesses of his mind, of his memories. I followed the familiar pull of myself lingering within him, following that guiding light until I found each memory that resided in the depths of his consciousness... and I wiped it all clean.

"Can you take me to my parents' house?" I asked as we settled my parents into their car. Damien tilted his head to me, dark brows rising.

The sun had long since set, the crisp night air filling my lungs. It had taken a few hours to fully comb through every memory, to plant the false ones and information. Exhaustion had settled into my bones. It had taken a lot out of me, and I was so desperate for rest. We weren't done, though. James had been tasked with hacking into and removing any information of me linked to them. We didn't have any living relatives to remember me, and my parents only had a few friends, mostly work friends; none close enough to call or come check on them, though.

It would be as if they'd never had a daughter.

It was colder now, the night temperature dipping, but the effects of the sleep I'd placed on them would wear off soon. They'd awaken with no memory of what had happened.

"I can stay here and keep an eye on them," Zephyr offered.

"Thank you," I said, unable to force a smile as I watched my mom's chest rise and fall.

"Come," Damien said, offering me his hand.

I took it, no words left on my tongue as he led me into the shadows of the forest. I lost myself in the feel of the darkness sweeping over my skin as it enveloped us. Seconds later, we emerged into the darkened stairway of my parents' house.

"Can you give me a moment?" I asked, the words barely breeching my lips, as if they didn't want to be spoken.

He hesitated, but nodded, giving my hand a gentle squeeze. "I'll be outside. Take all the time you need."

I lingered in the living room as he stepped through the kitchen and out the backdoor. My feet were cemented there for a moment, my eyes moving over every detail. Memories of my childhood resurfaced, my thoughts drifting to pillow fights on the old couch in front of me, the couch where I'd watched countless football games with my dad until he was on his feet, shouting at players who couldn't hear him. I thought about the time I'd spilled red acrylic paint all over the wood floors, red still visible to this day in the joints in certain places. Those memories only existed within me now.

There was too much here to tie me to them, too many pictures, too many keepsakes. I walked over to the shelves, to the countless portraits, the art projects.

This couldn't be here when they got back…

I neared the bookshelf nestled in the corner and stretched onto my toes to reach for a picture on the top shelf. I eased back down, the small frame cold in my hands. It was a picture of the three of us. I was six or seven years old, sitting on my dad's shoulders, my mom grinning widely up at me as I ate an ice cream cone. I smiled as I took it in. My tiny face was a mess of chocolate, and I remembered how my mom had told me that after it was taken, the ice cream had dripped onto my dad's head. It was a time when things were simpler, happier, a time before I'd been diagnosed.

I pressed the portrait to my chest, tears welling in my eyes. They would be safe. They would be protected. They would be far from this mess.

They would be free of the burden of my death.

I drew an uneven breath, lifting my eyes, and I wiped the tears away as I glanced down the hall. Through the kitchen window, I could see Damien in the backyard. I wouldn't make him wait any longer. I needed to do this before my parents woke and returned.

One final loose end.

I lifted my hand, my eyes falling to the tiny flames that sparked to life at my fingertips. The fire danced and swayed as I placed my hand against the bookshelf, the warmth seeping out of my body and into the wood. It smoldered and blackened before catching fire. I started toward the couch and my fingers grazed the threads, the fire creeping slowly across the armrest.

I clutched the tiny picture frame tighter to my chest, my hand quivering as I turned, the flames growing along my palm as I dragged it along the surface of everything I passed. It would be quick. There'd be no trace of me, nothing left to tie them to this place.

No turning back.

It didn't take long for the fire to spread as I stepped through the hallway and into the kitchen. I glanced back over my shoulder, the flames already crawling across the living room, the glow lighting every inch of the space.

Cas?

Damien's panicked voice shot through my thoughts, and I hadn't realized I'd reached out to his mind. Maybe it was a part of me that didn't want to be alone that caused me to slip, that led me to reach out to him. I continued through the kitchen, and I heard Damien's heavy footsteps on the porch as I stepped through the back door to find him wide-eyed before me.

"What're you doing?" he rasped.

"Destroying the last of it," I said numbly. "There's too much of me here."

He looked past me, through the doorway to the quickly spreading flames. "But—"

"It's better this way." My eyes drifted back to the flames spreading through the kitchen. I placed my hand to the wall, the flames coming to life beneath my palm. The fire stretched in every direction as I unleashed the destructive power. Nothing would remain; nothing would be salvageable. It would be a fresh clean slate for them—a new life, one untethered to the sorrowful filled memories lingering within these walls.

The fire gradually consumed the house as Damien and I stepped back off the back porch. He watched the fire grow with uncertainty, but there was no stopping it now. A commotion broke out in the streets as the neighbors emerged from their homes.

"We should go before someone sees us," Damien said, squeezing my hand.

I clutched the lone picture to my chest, the only thing that remained. I turned my head to him, nodding. "Ok."

We turned, walking to the farthest corner of the backyard. I glanced over my shoulder as he held onto my hand, guiding me into the shadows. Wood crackled and splintered as the fire rose and climbed to the sky, embers dancing through the air. A loud crack rang out, and the roof caved in on itself. The flames were intense, the magic powerful, and it would likely be a pile of ash within a few hours.

Faint sirens stretched out across the sounds of the city just as the shadows swept over us, dousing my sight in inky blackness. I found myself in our room, the smell of ash and smoke faintly lingering on my clothes. I stood there, an odd coldness stretching through my chest. My knees gave out, and I collapsed to the floor.

There was no going back. They were gone. I'd never see them again. Tears flooded my eyes as Damien lowered himself before me, his hands resting on my shoulders.

"It's done," I whimpered.

"It is, *mea luna*."

My chest tightened. "Tell me I did the right thing, Damien."

His throat bobbed, and his lips parted as my vision rippled, tears spilling down my cheeks.

"Tell me they'll be safe. Tell me—" My voice broke, sobs breaking from my throat as I cried, the tiny frame held tightly against my chest. He pulled me into him as I sobbed, and his voice was so tender, so soft, so strong and warm.

"It was the right thing. They'll be safer this way."

CHAPTER 39

DAMIEN

Six days. It had been six days since Cassie erased every trace of her existence from her parents' memories. Yet, here she was, training with recruits at The Outpost, as if nothing had happened.

To say I was worried was an understatement. She'd cried for the longest time when we'd returned home that night, and it tore me to pieces to see her like that. She'd had the courage to do for them what I couldn't do for her when I'd found her again, the courage to give her parents the chance of safety, of happiness, despite the fact that they'd never know who she was.

I feared she might be handling this too well. That, or she was internalizing it, not sharing the full weight she was bearing. The only relief was that she hadn't skipped her weekly therapy session with Salwa, but I was never present for those. I wouldn't intrude on her unless she wanted me there.

Cassie widened her stance, three recruits surrounding her as they sparred—Zach, Sasha, and Liam. They were in their third month of training and, if they continued at the pace they were, they'd take their vows before Selene as warriors of The Order in a month. Cassie's grip tightened on her baton as Zach lurched forward, swinging it down on her. She stepped to the side, absorbing the blow with her baton before guiding his weight past her. He stumbled forward, crashing into the dirt.

Zach had always been a little impatient, quick to move when it wasn't the right time. His attack sparked a chain reaction as Sasha and Liam, in unison, went for Cassie. She moved lithely as the two came at her from the front and back, blocking Liam's strike before stepping to the side. Sasha's baton missed Cassie, smacking Liam square in the face. He recoiled, his hand flying to his face, baton falling to the ground.

"Oh, Gods! I'm so sorry, Liam!" Sasha said.

Zach burst out laughing as he sat on the dirt where he'd fallen.

"I wouldn't laugh," Cassie told him. "You made the biggest mistake here." Zach's laughter stopped, embarrassment clear on his face. "You would've been the first to get taken out."

Cassie turned back to Sasha, who was checking Liam's red nose. "While you're trying to strike your enemy, you've got to be aware of your allies," Cassie said with a knowing grin. I fought the smile tugging at my lips, recalling a time when I'd shared that very same bit of knowledge with her. "Taking out a darkling is wonderful and all, but you'd have split Liam's face in two if that were a real dagger."

Pride swelled in my chest at the sight of her. My queen, my strength.

While she hadn't recovered her memories fully, the experiences she'd gained across her lives were resurfacing, propelling her training forward. She was mortal, but she never used it as an excuse, always pushing forward.

Sasha apologized profusely as she dipped her head. Cassie smiled, encouraging her to keep working at it. She dismissed them, training ending for the day. The three of them bowed their heads to her before heading for the Outpost's lounge, picking on one another.

Cassie lingered, the other recruits barely aware of her as they finished the last of their own training, and for a moment, I saw it; the weariness. Her eyes drifted downward, as if the moment without a distraction had allowed whatever she held in to resurface. My heart twisted.

Despite the snow and unrelenting cold, a sheen of sweat glistened on her brow, which she swiped away with the back of her arm. She'd thrown herself into training, hunting darklings, anything to keep herself busy. Today, she'd been training for hours, switching between recruits, helping wherever she could. If she hadn't been stopping for periodic breaks, I would've stepped in and forced her to stop.

It would've been hypocritical for me to do so. How many times had I lost myself in whatever distraction I could find to drown out the thoughts, the pain? I'd found myself in that very place she was struggling to climb out of now, and I somehow felt useless, unsure of how to pull her out.

I shifted my gaze to the recruits I'd been working with. "That'll be good for the day. Rexy, Angie, make sure you check in with Barrett before you leave, and I'll see you tomorrow."

The females nodded and headed toward the building to put their equipment up.

"Lady Cas!" Aurelia's tiny voice drew my attention back to Cassie as the child crashed into her legs. She nearly knocked her over, and Cassie broke out in laughter as Aurelia's mother, Lydia, chastised the child.

"Gonna have to watch your back, Cas. Aurelia's the next top warrior of The Order," Barrett said as he and Thalia approached, their recruits also done for the day.

I made my way toward them, the soggy ground squelching under my boots. Cassie smiled when she saw me, and the sight of her with Aurelia filled my chest with warmth.

Gods, I wanted a family with her.

"I heard Barrett taught you to punch," I said as I knelt to Aurelia's level. "Let me see that right hook."

Her bright eyes shifted to me, and she released Cassie's leg with a determined look as she balled her tiny fists. I held my hand up, nodding for her to hit. She swung her arm forward. It was the gentlest blow I'd ever felt, but I pulled my hand back, feigning a recoil and fell back with a grunt.

Aurelia's eyes went wide, and I pushed myself up, shaking my hand with a forced grimace. "That's quite the hook you've got there."

Cassie cupped her hand over her mouth, biting back a laugh, and I slid a grin her way.

316

"Are you okay?" Aurelia asked, brows curving upward as she hurried to help me up. My heart swelled at the care and concern in her pale eyes.

"I don't know, I may have to go put this hand on ice." I flexed the hand in question.

"I told you, Aurelia. You've gotta be careful. You're too strong for your own good," Barrett teased, ruffling her black hair. Her giggles spilled out as her nose wrinkled, and she pushed Barrett's hand off her head.

"Come on, Aurelia. Training's done for the day," Lydia said, her loving gaze shining down on the sweet child.

"Awe, but I wanted to see Barrett shoot fireballs!" Aurelia whined.

"Tomorrow, *Mikros*," Barrett said, patting her head once more. "Be a good girl and listen to your mom."

Her tiny shoulders slumped, her lower lip jutting out as she pouted. "Alright."

Lydia hoisted Aurelia into her arms. "We'll see you all tomorrow. Come on, let's go make some hot cocoa."

Aurelia's cheers quickly replaced her previous disappointment at the promise of hot cocoa. I shifted my gaze to Cassie, who'd stepped away to return her baton to its stand.

"How's she been?" Thalia asked in a hushed tone as I pushed myself to my feet.

I sighed. "Too well."

Barrett ran his fingers through his short blond hair, his concern thick in the air. "I still can't believe she burned the house down."

I couldn't either, but she'd been right. Too much of her remained in that place. There would've been no way to remove her from the portraits decorating the home, to ensure there were no photos or documents tucked away somewhere. It was too great a risk.

I let slip a heavy sigh. "She didn't really have a choice."

I slowly opened our bedroom door later that evening. Cassie sat on our bed; the small picture frame she'd taken from her parents' lay in her hands as she gazed down at it. She stiffened when she realized I'd entered, her hands frantically brushing aside the few tears lingering in her eyes.

"Hey," I said.

She set the picture down on her nightstand, her hand lingering a moment on the frame before withdrawing. "Hey."

I hesitated in the doorway, unsure of what to say, unsure of how I might be able to help her. Nothing would help ease the pain, nothing would soothe the sorrow she felt.

"Thank you."

My attention snapped to her, confused. "I—" I'd done nothing. What was she thanking me for? "I'm sorry, I'm... not sure what I did."

"For giving me time." She drew a deep breath. "I just… needed to process everything."

My heart twisted; I understood that more than I could put into words. I approached her, lifting my hand to brush a stray curl from her face. "How're you holding up?"

"I'm—" Her gaze left mine, and I wondered what she was thinking. Would she put up a front? Tell me some bullshit that she was okay? Her lips pressed into a grim line, hesitation clear on her face. "I've been better."

Relief washed over me when she didn't try to hide it, but it wasn't enough. She still held something back.

Don't hide it away. Please, just open up to me.

"It hurts." Her voice was thick. "I miss them so much already."

I eased onto the bed beside her, brushing my hand along her back. Her gaze fell to her lap. The silence stretched on, but I didn't speak.

"I don't regret it, though," she finally managed to say.

"You made the right choice. They'll be safe, *mea luna.*"

"I know," she whispered, and her weight shifted as she leaned into me. "I just… need time to adjust."

"Take your time, as much as you need."

PART 2

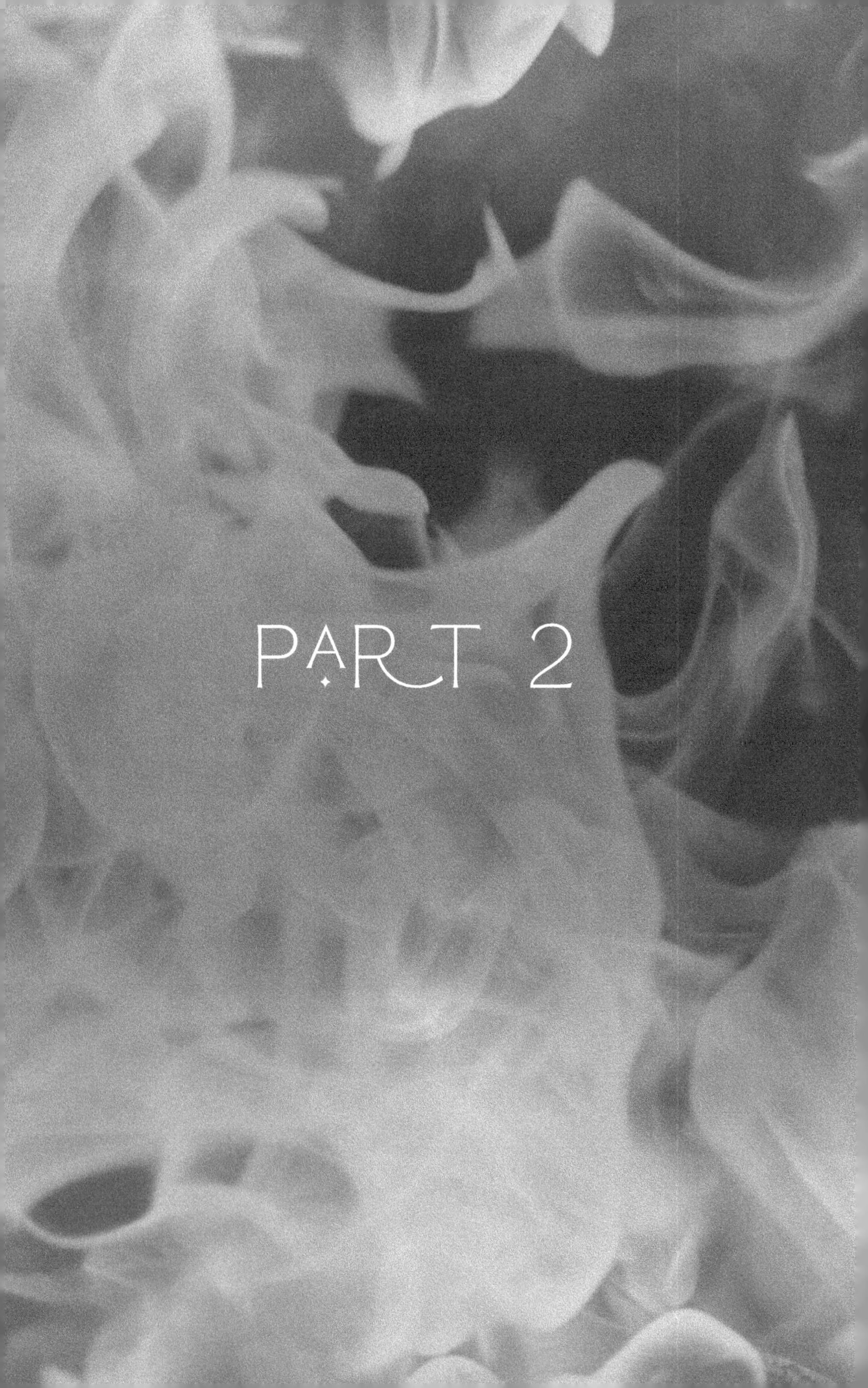

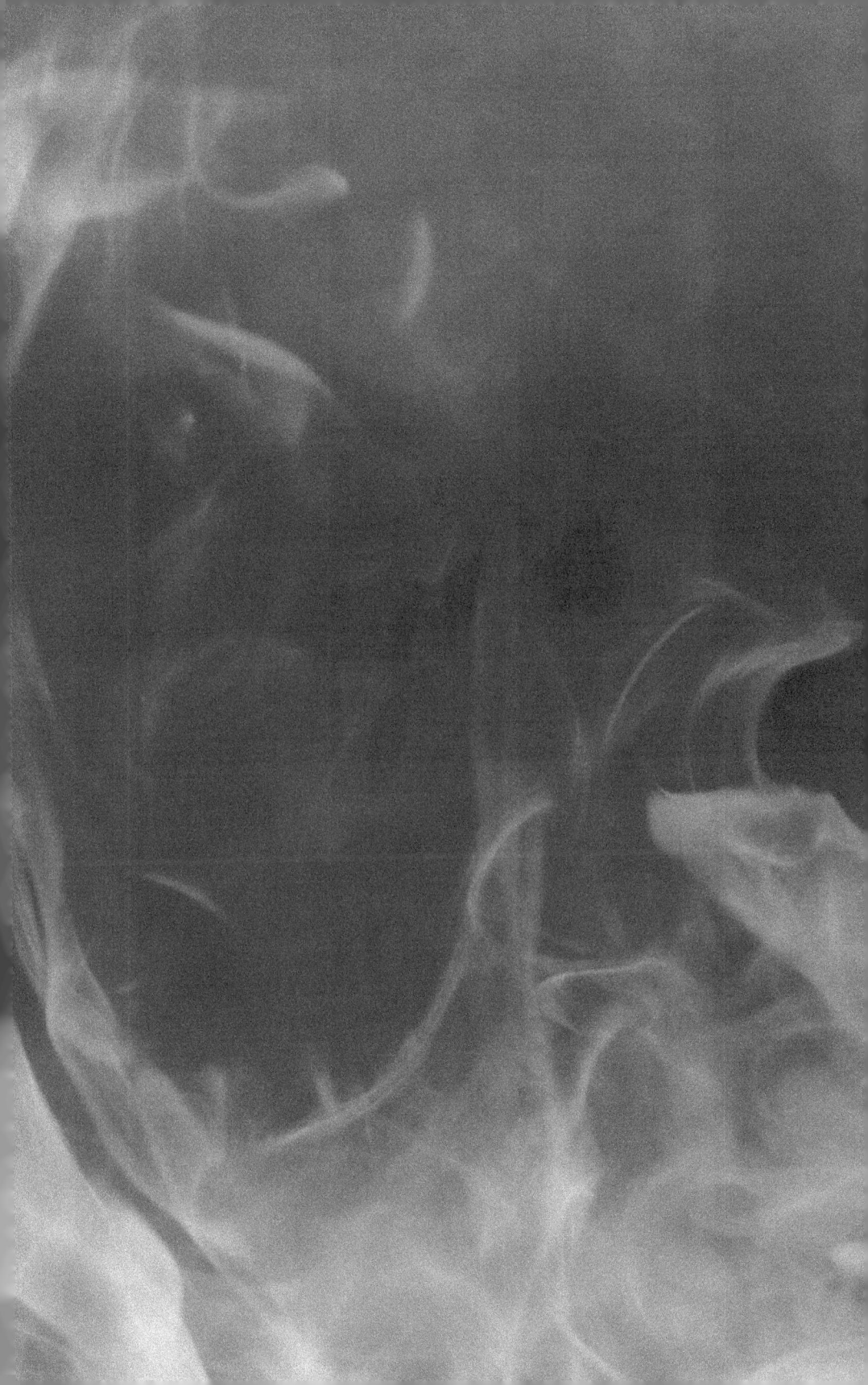

CHAPTER 40

CASSIE

White puffs of mist slipped from my lips as I breathed in the icy night air. My eyes drifted over the dark expanse of the alleys below as I crouched atop the roof of a building, my Elythian leather armor groaning as it stretched and shifted against my skin. Thalia and Barrett searched below us. Barrett remained alert, watching their surroundings as Thalia shifted to her wolf form. Damien stood at my side, eyes scanning the area behind me. It was inching toward midnight, the night unusually calm, and we hadn't encountered a single darkling.

I didn't like it.

It had been two weeks since I'd erased my parents' memories, and while I missed them deeply, the pain had lessened. I knew it would never leave me. It would remain a dull ache for the rest of my life, but it was worth it to know they were safe.

Damien kept tabs on them, that much I knew, but I hadn't had the courage to ask him for any updates, fearful talking about them would only pick at a wound that had just begun to mend. They were settled in a local hotel until their house in Washington was ready, and it would only be a matter of time before they were gone for good. The idea hurt to think about.

I drew a deep breath, stretching my thoughts out to the group patrolling the south sector.

Any updates, Aiden?

Damien lowered to his knee at my side, his eyes locked on the massive gray wolf below us, her nose to the ground as she searched for any scents to follow. It had been hours since we'd started our patrol, but Thalia had been unable to find any fresh signs or scents to track, and it left us all uneasy.

Nothing here. Not even a trail to follow.

Nothing? I chewed my lip, resting my elbow on my knee as I leaned toward the edge of the roof, lifting my gaze to the rooftops before us. Aiden's usual irritation slipped through the connection, bristly and hot. I spoke through the connection again.

Have Leo reach out to me if you find anything. Be alert.

Understood.

I reached out to the group patrolling the north sector. Over the last few weeks, we'd begun to see just how far I could communicate mentally, the distance growing with effort.

How're you guys faring, Logan? Encounter any darklings?

He responded a second later.

Nothing, Lady Cas. Owen's shifted right now, but he hasn't been able to pick up any fresh trails.

I found myself chewing my nail in frustration. What was happening? Had Melantha pulled the darklings back? Where had they all gone?

Okay, keep us updated. Call us if you find anything.

Understood.

I let out a heavy sigh, and Damien's gaze shifted to me. "Nothing?"

I shook my head. "Neither of the groups have had any luck. Something's wrong, Damien. What does this mean? What could they be up to?"

"I don't know." His voice wavered, uncertainty clouding his eyes as he ran his fingers along the coarse stubble on his jaw.

My eyes dropped to Thalia, who seemed to have given up, for she'd shifted back to her normal form. I reached out to her, Barrett, and Damien.

The other teams haven't seen any darklings either.

Thalia's voice drifted through my mind.

The only scents I'm picking up are old. There've been no darklings here for a few days at least.

I pondered for a moment, trying to make sense of it all, but no matter what, I couldn't come to any conclusions.

I guess we should…

The words faded in my mind, the connection halting as I peered through the distance to the rooftop a couple buildings over.

Damien's face turned to me. "Cas?"

My eyes narrowed on the small dark lump on the ridge of the roof, and for a moment I thought I saw it move. From the corner of my eye, I caught sight of Thalia and Barrett in the alley below us, faces raised to us in confusion.

"Damien, I think we're being watched," I whispered, eyes fixated on the shadow.

Damien's head tilted before his gaze followed mine. "What are you—"

The dark figure rose, and Damien and I tensed. It was a person. How long had they been watching us? My hand went to my dagger, and I wondered why I didn't sense darklings, didn't feel that cold presence pressing against my skin. It was in that moment I realized—this wasn't a darkling.

"I think I saw whatever it is before," I breathed, my heart rising in my throat as familiar dread crawled over my skin.

Damien's eyes snapped to me. "When?"

"Right before the Varyos attacked us. I thought I was seeing things because it was out of the corner of my eye. It was gone when I looked, but I swear, I think it was that."

The figure moved then, turning to run along the rooftop.

"What's going on?" Barrett called as Damien and I took off down the stretch of rooftop.

Thalia shifted into her flight form, dappled white wings spreading from black mist as she took to the sky. Barrett trailed on foot through the alley alongside us. I reached out to their thoughts.

Someone's been watching us.

Thalia banked, lowering to fly alongside us as we reached the end of the roof and leapt to the next. I glanced briefly in her direction before pointing to the fleeing figure. Her head tilted toward where I'd pointed, and she took off ahead.

"Don't let go," Damien said, grabbing my hand as he turned, leaping off the roof. I gasped as he took me with him. Shadows spread across the pavement below, and Barrett jumped into the black depths along with us.

We passed through the darkness, feet meeting the shingles of another roof not far from the fleeing figure. The person stopped, head whipping to us. The hood barely hid the black mess of curls and black eyes, his tawny skin covered in a sheen of sweat.

"Cole," Damien growled.

Cole smirked before he took off, faster than before, and we followed. A shrill cry rang out from Thalia as she swooped into him, slamming her wing across his face. He twisted, rolling off the roof and onto the dark road below. We hurried to the edge to find him jumping to his feet, taking off once again into the streets.

Damien lifted me into his arms, and I held on as he and Barrett leapt down to the asphalt below. He set me down, and our eyes searched for any sign of Cole.

"Where the hell did he go?" Barrett barked, stepping ahead of us.

Thalia's shrill cry alerted us ahead, and we took off, following the direction of the sound. I reached out to Thalia, bridging the connection between the four of us.

Do you see him?

He's on Vine Street, headed east.

We'd grown closer to the edges of the city, to the neighborhoods surrounding it. Where was he going? Where had he been hiding all this time? I caught sight of him running up the sloped street toward the forests.

"Is he leading us somewhere?" I rasped as we ran, my lungs burning from the icy air. I feared I was holding them back; I couldn't run as fast as they could, and Cole was slowly gaining distance.

He halted at the edge of the forest, and we came to a stop at a safe distance. My chest heaved as I tried to catch my breath. I winced as a tinge of pain slipped through my ribs with each inhale. I'd run too hard. I focused on calming my heart rate, on controlling my breathing. *Shit. Not now.* We couldn't afford the delay. I couldn't slow us down, couldn't let him get away.

We'd only just finally found him... or he'd found us.

A gravelly unease settled into the pit of my stomach. I pulled my daggers from their sheaths, the metal whispering against leather as I prepared for whatever he might have up his sleeve. Barrett and Damien did the same, eyes locked on him.

"Long time no see," Cole said casually, tugging his hood down.

"Is that really you talking Cole? Or someone else?" I barked.

His black eyes jerked to me, and a cruel grin spread across his face. "Hello to you, too, Cas. Miss me?" His expression shifted to one of inflated pity. "Damien keeping you company in my absence?"

I bit back the words bubbling up my throat, irritation causing my skin to heat. This wasn't him. This wasn't truly Cole.

Or was it?

That icy feeling crept over my skin, and my heart stuttered, but it was faint, the temperature not as cold. Thalia flew low, perching on the edge of a roof, her falcon eyes searching our surroundings.

"Darklings," Barrett breathed as his gaze swept back and forth around us, turning to guard our backs. "But where are they?"

Thalia leapt off the roof, dark mist enveloping her as she landed on her feet beside me, pulling her dagger free from her chest holster.

"They can't be far," she said, back to mine as she scoured the city behind us.

A darkling's shriek pierced the night sky, and our heads snapped in its direction.

I looked back to find Cole's eyes locked on us, and his grin made my skin crawl. "You really need to improve your tracking."

My heart sank. "What're you talking about?"

A scream reached my ears, and conflict roiled through me as Cole took a few steps back, arms outstretched. "What will you do?" he asked, a coy grin on his face. "Will you go after me? Or go to their rescue?"

Damien growled, his fangs unsheathing as he locked gazes with Cole. "Fucking bastard."

Cole glowered at him. "Oh, so feisty, Damien—oh, sorry." He took a dramatic, low bow. "Your Majesty."

Another cry rang out, and I looked to Damien. He drew a deep breath before his eyes passed over me to the direction of the darkling attack.

"*Fuck*," he breathed and nodded to Barrett. His murderous gaze locked back on Cole. "I'll find you again."

Cole tilted his chin up, his black eyes meeting Damien's. "I look forward to it, Lord of Shadows."

CHAPTER 41

CASSIE

My feet barely met asphalt as we ran, the road stretching on before us. Thalia's large paws slammed into the pavement as she ran alongside me.

Her head tilted in my direction before glancing to her back. "Get on!"

She slid to a stop before me, and I looked across her back, unsure. Damien and Barrett stopped, brows raised.

"Go ahead! We'll catch up!" I shouted, and they nodded before taking off again.

She was huge, her back reaching past my waist, thick muscle hidden by her dusty gray fur. Could she really carry me? I looked ahead at Damien and Barrett. There was no time for uncertainty. I reached out, grabbing hold of her fur, and threw my leg over her back. She absorbed my weight, her body barely reacting to me.

"Hold on!"

She took off, and I held on for dear life, her body rolling and shifting beneath me. Oh God, I was going to fall off. This was a horrible idea. My legs tightened against her sides, my heart thrumming, the asphalt a blur beneath us. I didn't fall, though, and it was only a matter of seconds before we caught up with Damien and Barrett.

We cut through back streets to the edge of the forest, then up the lone road that snaked into the trees. The screams had stopped some time ago, and I feared the worst.

The cold presence against my skin receded, replaced with an even icier dread. Had the darklings left? Were we too late? I passed a nervous glance to Damien, who couldn't meet my gaze. We reached a curve in the road, an unfamiliar house coming into view from behind the tree line, and my heart lurched as we came to a stop in the gravel driveway. Thalia lowered herself to let me down.

The house was dark, the shroud of silence deafening. Where there were once windows was nothing but shattered glass, the front door now a gaping splintered hole. Thalia stood between Barrett and me, her ears folding low as she dipped her head down, a painful whimper slipping from her throat.

"I know, *Kelisa*... I smell it too," Barrett muttered, running a hand through her fur.

I tilted my head at the name, but I couldn't linger on it as his words caused my stomach to churn. I swallowed. "What exactly do you smell?"

Barrett's brows furrowed, sorrow sweeping across his face. "Blood."

"Call the other teams," Damien said grimly as he glanced at me before stepping toward the porch, pulling his dagger from its sheath.

I swallowed as I stretched my thoughts out to the different teams, beckoning them here immediately. My heart pounded, my pulse drowning everything out as I inched toward the house. Icy horror shot down my spine at what I saw.

Flames came to life in Barrett's hand, illuminating the traces of blood that formed a broken trail leading into the forest. I followed his lead, lifting my hand, focusing on the warmth in my skin, and my flames lit. We reached the steps, my eyes following the blood until I found what looked like lines etched into the wood porch, and bile rose in my throat at the sight of a lone bloodied fingernail. Oh God... they'd been dragged from their home.

329

Damien reached the door before I could, looking inside. His hands balled into fists as he shifted back, his eyes closed. Thalia remained in her wolf form as she and Barrett came up behind me. She lowered her muzzle, sniffing briefly before she peered through the doorway.

I carefully stepped around the smears of blood and went to pass Damien, to see for myself what was left in the house, but his hand came up, stopping me.

"You don't need to see this, Cas."

My heart lurched, but I steeled my nerves. "I do."

There was no denying that at some point, I was going to see worse. I'd seen the horrors left in the wake of the darklings through not only Lucia and Elena's memories, but his as well. Damien's chest expanded as he drew a deep breath and turned to step into the house.

Barrett passed through the shredded doorway ahead of me, the flames in his hand illuminating the room, and Thalia followed close behind me. No amount of preparation could've readied me for what I saw.

God... there was so much blood, too much blood, splattered across walls and wood floors. Thalia crept through the room, head low as she prowled, searching, whether for hidden darklings or survivors, I didn't know. I couldn't imagine how there could be any survivors. Furniture was flipped over, shredded, splattered in what appeared to be a mix of red and black blood.

Thalia stopped, perking her head up toward us. Barrett walked over to her to see what she'd found.

"They didn't go down without a fight, that's for sure. Took one out," Barrett said as he crouched low, swiping the oily black liquid from the floor before lifting his gaze to look around.

They'd taken out a darkling? "Were they immortals?"

Damien nodded as he cautiously stepped through the room, stopping to survey every detail of destruction. They'd managed to take out a darkling; could one of them have been a warrior? A recruit? Did we know them?

Barrett and Thalia split off through the house; Barrett took the stairs to the second floor, while Thalia entered the far hallway to search the rest of the lower level. My heart pounded, my pulse roaring in my ears as I braced myself for the possibility of a darkling launching at us from the darkness.

"Do you know who lived here?" I asked, careful of where I stepped.

330

Guilt flickered across his face. "I don't."

"Damien!" Thalia called from the hall, the sound followed by the thunder of Barrett's steps rushing back down the stairs.

Damien and I hurried toward her. Thalia had shifted back to her normal form, her ear pressed to the door.

"We're here to help you. Can you open the door?" Thalia said, working the knob, but it didn't budge.

My heart lurched into my throat. Had someone survived? Barrett, Damien, and I came to a stop in the hallway. At first, I didn't hear anything, but then it reached my ears; the faintest sound of a painful sob, short and weak.

Barrett stepped up to the door, his voice heavy. "We're with The Order. We're here to help. Can you unlock the door?"

A weak voice drifted on the quiet sobs. "Please..."

Damien and Barrett's eyes shifted to each other, and their expression didn't settle well in my gut.

"We're coming in. Stand back," Thalia called, her ear still pressed to the door, but no response came. Thalia stepped back, grabbing Barrett's hand to steady herself. She lifted her leg and slammed her foot against the door. It didn't budge. She kicked again, slamming her weight into it, and it burst free. She pulled her dagger from its sheath, and Damien readied his as Barrett held his hand forward, flame lighting the stairwell. They moved in calculated unison, filing down the stairs, ready for anything that might lunge at them from the darkness. I followed, finding a trail of smeared blood down the stairway.

"Gods," Barrett let out on a breath as he reached the foot of the stairway, holding the flames high. Damien and Thalia sheathed their daggers as they approached whatever Barrett saw. I cautiously stepped down. Short gasps of pain reached my ears, and I stopped at Barrett's side.

I swallowed. A woman sat slouched, her back against the wall. Her clothes were torn, covered in so much blood that I couldn't tell where exactly she was wounded.

Claw marks raked up her exposed arms, her chest heaving unevenly with each painful gasp. Damien approached cautiously and knelt beside her.

"We're here," he whispered tenderly. "You're not alone."

Her blonde lashes lifted, just barely, just enough for her to tilt her head to see who spoke. "Lord... Damien." she muttered, what I could only describe as pure relief washing over her face. Then she coughed, grimacing as her body tightened, and a whimper of pain left her throat.

"Yes, it's me. How many lived here?" he asked, his voice thick.

She drew a deep, uneven breath, and tears welled in her eyes as she spoke, her voice thick. "Four..." She coughed again, and I tensed as blood dripped from her lips. I hurried over, eager to help in any way I could. We needed to get her help, get her somewhere safe.

Damien grabbed me, stopping me before I could touch her. "Don't. Stay back."

I jerked my gaze to him. "But—"

"It's too late for her," he said, his eyes locked on the woman.

I turned to look at her as she rested her head back against the wall. Her eyes found me, and realization lit them as she took in my face. A faint smile tugged at her bloodied lips.

"It's true," she said on a weak breath, her chest expanding with each word. "You... returned... to us."

"I'm here."

Her lips parted to speak again, but she tensed, her face scrunching as she clutched her stomach, a broken sound ripping from her lips. Damien pushed me back, but she eased, her head falling back against the wall again.

"What's your name?" Thalia asked from her other side.

She sat there a moment, her breathing becoming more difficult. "Lee... Dreevas."

Damien's eyes wavered.

"Please..." she whimpered, her unsheathed fangs revealed by the parting of her lips.

I frowned. Please? What was she asking for? Barrett's hesitant footsteps approached from behind until he came to a stop beside us.

She coughed again, a broken sob breaking from her throat as she looked to Damien. "Please..."

Throat bobbing, Damien's gaze passed over her, over the wounds she'd suffered. His eyes found mine, and the agony in them sank deep into my chest. He looked at Barrett. "Get Cas home."

I stiffened. "What? Why?"

"*Please*," Lee rasped again.

My eyes snapped to her and my heart faltered. Darkness swirled in the whites of her eyes, black veins creeping around them. Her complexion had paled since we'd arrived, turning a sickly gray, and the veins beneath her skin had become visible, impossibly dark and branching down her throat, across her arms. The blood trickling from the cut above her eye was a swirl of red and black. It wasn't too late for her because of her wounds. She'd been bitten; she was changing.

"Take her, Barrett, now," Damien muttered once more.

Barrett hesitated. "Damien, you don't have to do this again. I can take care of her."

My head snapped in Barrett's direction. Again?

"Now, Barrett," Damien ordered before turning his gaze back to Lee. She tensed, that same painful sound breaking free of her before she eased once more against the wall.

Barrett parted his lips but didn't speak, and his hand clasped my shoulder. "Cas," he said lowly, but I pulled free from his grasp.

"Damien, no." What was he going to do? Was he going to kill her?

"I don't want you to see this." Damien said, pulling his dagger from its sheath, his gaze remaining fixed on the dying immortal. "Please, *mea luna*."

I swallowed, looking back to Lee, the darkness nearly enveloping the whites of her eyes now, the pale orbs threatening to be devoured next by the darkness taking root. She offered me a weak smile, her arm falling slack in her lap, exposing the jagged wound crossing her belly. The blood drained from my face. They'd torn her apart.

"Come on, Cas. There's not much time," Barrett warned, and I rose tentatively. He tugged my arm, leading me away from them as Damien shifted into a crouch, lifting his dagger.

"It'll be over soon," Damien whispered to her.

"Don't watch," Barrett warned as we reached the foot of the stairs. I tried not to, but my gaze remained fixated on Damien as his hand came to rest on the female's shoulder.

"Thalia, brace her." Damien's voice dipped almost to a whisper.

My foot reached the first step.

"I'm sorry," Damien whispered again. "I'm so sorry."

Lee's body tensed and she grimaced, a strange sound slipping from her lips, one that didn't sound wholly human as Thalia braced her, and then she settled back against the wall. My foot reached the second step, and I forced my gaze forward, my heart pounding.

"*Aleirene tauen enlisno en solos,*" Damien's prayer barely reached my ears.

Third step... Fourth step... Fifth step...

She began to cry then, her voice changing, hoarse and shaky. "Thank you... Lord Damien..."

Something pressed into the back of my throat as we reached the sixth step, then the seventh, my pulse pounding in my ears as Barrett's hand pressed to my back, urging me forward. My foot reached the eighth step, my stomach dipping as I tried to focus on the air filling my lungs, on anything but what I knew Damien was about to do. The wall blocked our view now.

Then I heard it; a wet gasp and gurgle. Something knocked and shook against the wall, scuffing against the concrete floor. I covered my ears as Damien and Thalia's struggled grunts reached us.

Then, there was nothing.

CHAPTER 42

DAMIEN

My blade met no resistance as I sank it deep into her chest. Her body jerked, spasming against mine and Thalia's hold as the conversion began to take root. *Fuck.* We'd waited too long; she was further gone than I thought.

She fought against us, blood splattering from her wounds as she flailed, warmth dotting my face. Thalia gritted her teeth as she braced her elbow against Lee's throat, avoiding the snaps of her fangs as she lashed out, and I absorbed the bite of her nails as she dug them into my arms. It wasn't her fighting, though. It wasn't Lee who stared back at me through those depthless black eyes.

"I'm sorry," I muttered as I forced her back against the wall, her shoes scuffing against the concrete before her body finally began to settle.

Her movements slowed, nails unable to dig as deep as they had before, muscles twitching as nerves shorted out. I maintained eye contact, wholly present at her side until, she crossed into the afterlife. She wasn't alone; I wouldn't let her feel alone in her final moments. She'd suffered enough. The shadows receded from her unseeing eyes, the silver revealed once more.

Her hand slid from my arm, falling limp into her lap, and Thalia swallowed as she hesitantly released Lee. My hand remained, though, planted firmly on her shoulder, where I'd reached out to offer her any comfort I could.

I sat there a moment, unable to move, her bloodied face engraving itself into my mind, and suddenly, it wasn't her face I was looking at. Countless faces flashed before my eyes, all pale, all covered in blood, all dead by my hand before they could turn. My breath grew shallow as the weight of their unseeing gazes burrowed into me, their hands grabbing hold of my arms as they fought against me.

"Damien." I jerked as Thalia's voice cut across it all, dragging me back. "Damien, she's gone," she whispered, her hand resting tenderly on my shoulder.

I blinked, swallowing as I eased the dagger from Lee's chest. She hadn't turned to dust; we'd managed to end her before she fully changed. It was a small blessing. At least she could rest alongside her kin in Moira's Rest. If she had any living family, they could mourn her properly. She deserved that much.

Gods, when would this end? I slid my hand under her blood-matted, golden hair to the back of her neck, dropping my head as I silently prayed for her soul to find its way, that despite the horrible way she'd passed, she could find peace at last.

Thalia shifted to the side as I eased Lee to the floor, and I lifted my hand, closing her eyes. My gaze wandered over her wounds, my skin crawling as I remembered the same wounds marring Elena's body when we'd found her.

No one deserved to die like this.

"You can't keep doing this to yourself," Thalia whispered.

"I'd never ask that of any of you."

"It's not something you need to ask of us. Barrett would've done it. I would've done it."

"Barrett carries enough with him." I knew how badly Micah's death haunted him. I'd never ask him to do this. Never. I lifted my eyes to Thalia. "And if I can help it, you'll never carry that burden... *ever*."

"Damien?" Aiden's voice echoed from upstairs, and I looked over my shoulder as the young warrior peered in from the stairwell. The moment he found us his eyes widened. "*Shit*."

I wiped the blood from my dagger and rose to my feet as I slid it back into its sheath at my hip. "Her name was Lee Dreevas. Contact James to find out if she has any living relatives. I also need to know who else lived here. She said there were a total of four."

Aiden nodded, his jaw tight as he pulled his phone from his pocket.

"As of right now, she's the only one who didn't get taken. Did you see any darklings on your way here?" I asked, heading for the stairs.

Aiden shook his head. "None."

How did Cole play into this? Had he been a distraction? Had he set the darklings on this family? Gods, I wanted to believe he'd been corrupted, that none of this had been his doing, but it was getting more and more difficult each day to separate him from everything.

"Thalia," I called, glancing back at her. Her brows lifted, and she rose from Lee's side. "We need to get her body down to the morgue and get her cleaned up before whatever family she may have sees her. Can you arrange that?"

She nodded. "I can do that."

The rest of the house needed to be searched to make sure there weren't any others who might've died before they completed the conversion. I knew none remained alive—if they had, we would've already been attacked. The warriors who'd answered Cassie's summons didn't speak as I found them in the living room, already hard at work looking over the scene—their sorrow a heavy scent in the air, like freshly fallen rain.

What had changed with the darklings? This house was so far from the city. Darklings didn't roam where immortals and humans were scarce; they had no reason to, not when there were easier targets roaming the streets. My greatest concern was that darklings never entered homes unless they were led to them. This was the second house darklings had broken into, had attacked immortals unprovoked. Were their senses strengthening? Were they getting smarter? Gods help us if they were.

"Logan, Maria." The two warriors lifted their eyes to me, pulling away from what they'd been inspecting. "I want you both to check upstairs, make sure there aren't any others who might've died before the transition. I don't want any left behind when we torch this place."

They both nodded, heading for the stairs, the wood creaking with each step. The only sound of Thalia's approach was her heavy sigh. I turned to see her carrying Lee's body.

"Johnsons got a car on its way to transport her," she informed me, and I nodded.

"Thank you, Thalia." I stepped to the side, allowing her room. The warriors lowered their heads as she passed them, offering their respects.

"Aiden," I said, and the Flame Stoicheion user turned his gaze to me, black brows rising. "I'll need you to take care of the house once it's cleared."

CHAPTER 43

CASSIE

I sat on our couch curled under a blanket, the fire crackling in the fireplace before me. It had been an hour since Barrett brought me home, leaving Damien and Thalia to meet with the other patrols to clean up the mess left behind by the darklings.

Time passed too slowly, the hands of the clock teasing me with each painfully slow tick. I wondered how Damien was doing. Barrett had left to help; I could only imagine the cleanup they'd have to do. I hadn't heard from them, and the worst possibilities churned in my mind. Lee's face remained etched in my thoughts, blood coating her body, her face, the marks left by the darklings' claws and teeth. I could only imagine the horrors she'd witnessed. Had she watched her loved ones die? Had she watched them change?

I drew a deep breath, lifting my teacup to sip the warm caramel liquid. I'd bathed and changed out of my leathers, but I couldn't wash away the image of Lee in my mind, the pained look on Damien's face as he prepared to end her life.

It had to be done. She would've changed, and I knew it was a mercy to do it before she did, but what Barrett said clung to me.

Again.

How many times had Damien done this? I never knew, had never considered the possibility, and I hated that he carried that burden.

Wood groaned down the hall, and I shot to my feet, setting the teacup on the end table as I rounded the couch. I peered into the hallway to find Damien, his back pressed against the wall, eyes downcast.

My heart twisted at the sight of him. Splattered blood painted his face and armor, sweat glistening on his brow. He remained where he stood, staring into nothing. He slid down the wall until he sat on the floor, his arms resting loosely on his knees.

I approached him slowly, my voice soft. "Damien?"

He didn't look at me, seemingly lost in his own thoughts. I lowered myself to my knees before him, lifting my hand to touch his cheek. That touch seemed to awaken him from wherever his mind had wandered, his amber and ashen eyes finding me. He looked... exhausted, worn... defeated.

"*Mea sol,*" I breathed. "Stay here. I'll be right back."

I pushed myself to my feet and hurried to the kitchen, where I grabbed a large bowl, filled it with warm water, and grabbed a rag. He hadn't moved from where I'd left him, his eyes burning into the wood floor. I set the bowl down, settling back down on my knees between his legs. He remained still, his eyes low as I dipped the rag into the warm water and lifted it to his face.

His hand shot up, grabbing my wrist. Confusion marred his face, but I offered him a smile. "*Mea sol.* Your face; let me clean it."

He blinked and released me to touch his face. The crusted blood broke onto his fingertips as he pulled his hand away to look at it. Had he not realized?

I lifted the damp rag to wipe it away. "It's ok."

"I'd... hoped you'd be asleep," he muttered. "I didn't want you to see me like this."

"I wouldn't have been able to sleep with you out there, not with what you had to face." I dipped the rag into the water once more and wrung it out before returning to his face.

"You've... had to do that before," I said—not a question, but an acknowledgement, an invitation. "You don't have to talk about it if you don't want to, but I'm here. You can tell me, *mea sol*. Let me share that burden."

He remained silent for a moment, eyes drifting away from me. I didn't press, and I finished wiping away the last speck of dried blood and lowered the rag into the bowl. I cupped his face, pressing my forehead to his.

"Come, *mea sol*. Let's get you washed up," I whispered, rising to my feet. I took his hand, giving him no option but to follow.

He didn't fight me and let me guide him up the stairs. His hand gently squeezed mine, and my heart swelled, relief washing over me at the first real reaction I'd gotten.

I left him in the doorway to our bathroom, as I turned the shower on. He began unfastening the leathers strapping his knives to his chest, setting them on the vanity before removing the holster of his dagger from his hip.

I nodded to the shower once he'd stripped naked. "I'll be right behind you."

He stepped in, the hot water rolling over his body. His face remained vacant, tired. If only I could take some of that pain from him, I would do it in a heartbeat. I quickly removed my clothes before stepping into the shower behind him.

I lathered soap into the sponge and ran it over his chest, his shoulders. The suds slipped down his skin and pooled beneath him. Thankfully, there wasn't much blood anywhere else. I set the sponge aside and reached for him, my arms stretching around his waist as I leaned into him.

His arms came around me, my heart fluttering.

"Forty-seven," he muttered.

I lifted my eyes to his face. "What?"

"I've had to... end forty-seven immortals before they converted."

A chill swept over me. God, he'd had to take forty-seven lives, lives of immortals who'd done nothing wrong. I pushed myself to my toes, pressing a kiss to his cheek. He tilted his head and pressed his forehead to mine. His sorrow seeped into my skin, icy and hot. It hurt so much, and I could only imagine how badly it hurt him.

"I'm so sorry," I whispered.

"Cole's parents were among them," he admitted.

I tensed and swallowed, remembering how Cole had shared the loss of his parents, how Damien had taken him in, raising him in their stead. I didn't know how to respond. Did Cole know?

"Farah had been bitten. Marius tried to draw out the venom, but—" He didn't speak for a moment, his throat bobbing as he tried to form words. "I was too late. It wasn't until he'd been infected and on the verge of the conversion that I'd found them."

Guilt replaced his sorrow.

"It's never easy killing someone. I've done it too many times, fought too many wars. I don't regret killing those I did in war; it was to defend those I loved." His eyes fell from me. "But to see someone who'd never chosen to fight, who'd never done anything wrong in their life, suffer such gruesome injuries, experience what no one should ever have to, and then only be able to ease their suffering by ending it quickly... none of them deserved that. They had a future, a family waiting for them, lovers who would never get to kiss them again, hold them..." Silence hung in the air for a moment before he spoke again. "I couldn't protect them."

I held him, stroking his back tenderly.

He spoke through gritted teeth, his frustration pouring through our connection. "I'm their king. I should be able to defend my people, protect them, but I couldn't."

My heart squeezed.

"I failed them," he breathed.

I failed her. I'd thought those very words as I watched the little girl die when Moonhaven fell. I didn't even know her name, but I felt that weight, that same pain.

I lifted my eyes to him, cupping his face. "You didn't fail them, *mea sol*, and we *will* put a stop to it. We *will* destroy Melantha."

His eyes found me once more, and I could see the exhausting centuries within them. I knew that no matter what, no matter what it cost, I would ensure what I said would be true.

"We will make her pay for every death we've suffered."

342

CHAPTER 44

CASSIE

Rest seemed to have dulled the sharp pain left in the wake of Lee's death. That, or Damien had perfected the art of masking over his centuries of life, of burying that grief so deep, it couldn't reach the surface. I knew all too well how to mask the pain, the sadness, and it only hurt more to know it was what he was likely doing.

"How about I cook breakfast this time, *Mitera*," Damien said, walking up behind Ethel as she worked away at the stove.

"If ah dae that, then ah'd be oot o' work, Lord Damien. Where dae ye expect me tae find work at seventy-four?"

"Nonsense. It's my treat. You make us breakfast every morning. It's time someone made you breakfast for once." Damien slipped in, taking the spatula from her, and the little old woman huffed at him, reaching for the spatula as he held it just out of her reach. He chuckled, and it was the most wonderful sound.

I smiled as I watched them from the nearby table, my heart swelling as I rested my chin on my hand, looking up from the book I'd been reading. Ethel finally gave up and took a seat at the table. The look of irritation melted into one of adoration as she watched him cook. I slid my bookmark into place and rose from my seat.

"No' ye too," she groaned.

"I can't sit back and watch Damien cook for you by himself. I want to help too." I grinned at her as I walked over to him. "You do so much for us."

"I promise, I'm perfectly capable of making pancakes by myself," Damien said over his shoulder as I came to a stop at the counter.

I snickered. "You'll have to show me your flipping skills then, Lord of Pancakes."

A low laugh slipped from his throat as he spread butter over the pan.

The front door opened as if on cue, and a thunder of feet echoed down the hall. The brothers of The Order loved interrupting quiet mornings, but these chaotic moments were ones I cherished the most. Barrett was the first to appear, his blond brows scrunching in confusion as he caught sight of Damien at the stove instead of Ethel.

"Good morning," I chirped with a smile as Vincent, Zephyr, and Thalia entered close behind him. Barrett approached Damien without saying a word, and I frowned.

"I was gonna greet *Mitera* with a kiss for cooking breakfast, but I guess you'll do," he said, and laid one on Damien's cheek. Damien elbowed him in the gut and Barrett grunted.

The others burst into laughter as Barrett recoiled with a throaty laugh, tossing me a wink. I rolled my eyes at him before turning back to the counter, grabbing the mixing bowl of batter.

"You got the morning off, *Mitera*?" Thalia asked, leaning in to place a tender kiss to Ethel's cheek. Ethel smiled warmly as she cupped Thalia's face and returned the gesture.

"Damien decided he wanted tae cook breakfast today," she responded with a woeful tone. "Ah think mah days 'ere might be numbered."

I giggled at her dramatic display as Damien ladled batter into the pan, the sweet, buttery scent filling the air.

"Ah hear thir's a bindin' ceremony tae be planned," she said, turning to smile at Zephyr as he eased into an empty chair.

344

Zephyr smiled, almost bashfully. "Yeah, in a month. We're already laying out the details."

I perked up, excitement blossoming in my chest. "A month? Really?"

Zephyr nodded, his gaze warming as he looked to me. "Calista actually wanted me to ask you if you'd do her the honor of being her attending maiden."

Attending maiden? Was that like a bridesmaid? "I don't know what that is, but I'd be honored!"

His eyes lit up, and I caught a glimpse of Damien briefly smiling toward me before returning his attention to the frying pan, where the creamy surface of his first pancake was beginning to bubble and set.

"Perhaps it willny be long after 'at Vincent and Anna's babe will hev a playmate," Ethel said, sliding Zephyr a knowing smile.

God, I'd love to see that. Would that make me an aunt? My chest swelled at the thought. What would they look like? I knew any child of Zephyr and Calista's would be beautiful.

"Whatcha readin', spitfire?" I stiffened as Barrett picked up the book I'd been reading. Oh God, no. Don't—

He flipped through the pages, stopping somewhere in the middle, and my cheeks heated, praying he didn't happen to flip to any of the *scenes*. I rushed over to take the book from him. Before I could reach him, he lifted his eyes to me, a teasing grin on his face. "*Spitfire.*"

I snatched the book from him.

"*Scandalous*," Barrett added, and I searched for anything I could throw at him. Thalia snickered, leaning into his shoulder, and I narrowed my eyes on Barrett.

"You're lucky Thalia's there, or I'd throw something at you."

"Oh, I'll move if you want to hit him," Thalia offered, and I couldn't fight the laughter that broke from my throat.

Damien stepped back from the stove, interrupting the conversation. "Okay, *mea luna*. Let me show you just how good I am at flipping pancakes."

My brows rose as I turned to face him, and he glanced to make sure I was watching.

"Twenty bucks says he drops the pancake," Barrett muttered to Vincent.

"I'll take that bet." Vincent settled his elbows on the table.

Damien bit his lip as he lifted the pan once, twice, then jerked it up in a swift, calculated motion. The pancake flipped into the air before he shifted to catch it smoothly in the pan. Ethel and I clapped our hands, a grin spreading across my face as he returned the pan to the stove,

giving me a quick wink before he got back to work cooking. The others chuckled as Barrett muttered under his breath.

"Hey Barrett," Damien said.

Barrett lifted his face to look to Damien. "Yeah?"

"I believe you owe Vincent twenty bucks."

I tugged down my hood as we stepped into the lower hall of The Complex later that night, warmth greeting us with open arms.

"Man, I don't know about you, but I'd fight a badger over a fuckin' cardboard box for one of Semele's drinks right now," Barrett groaned from behind me as we headed for the stairway to the third-floor lounge.

"That seems random even for you, Barrett," I said, chuckling as I glanced back his way.

"His existence is random," Vincent said.

"Agreed," Zephyr added, and I giggled.

"Just admit it, you guys love me." I rolled my eyes as Barrett stretched, nearly brushing the ceiling with his hands as he groaned. "Just two more hours and I'll be enjoying that drink. Thalia's meeting me at Stokers. You guys wanna join us?"

"If Cas isn't too tired, we can join you," Damien said. "I don't have any plans. You want to go?"

"I'll never turn down a trip to Stokers. I love visiting Eiko and Semele," I said. "Speaking of random." Barrett perked up beside me. "I—uh, was searching through Lucia's memories the other day."

He cocked a brow, tilting his head down to look down at me.

"It was a memory from The Fall of Kingdoms. I ran into you on the killing field..." The memory still hung in the back of my mind, the horror of it all, the sadness that had remained after the battle was won.

His curiosity doused, his eyes drifting to the floor in front of him.

"How long have you called me spitfire?" I asked, and his brows rose. He seemed genuinely surprised that was what I'd brought it all up for.

"A long time. I was a mess when I joined The Order." His eyes darkened briefly, as if the memory haunted him. It faded away just as

347

quickly, light returning to those steel eyes as he looked back down at me. "You used to scold me when I'd get into trouble, and I always joked about how your words were enough to burn even me. The name spitfire kind of just stuck."

"I called you hothead." It wasn't necessarily a statement but more reminiscence, and a smile tugged at my lips.

A crooked grin curved one side of his mouth as he lingered on the thought. "I deserved that. I wasn't always the cool, collected, calculated fighter I am today."

"That's a bullshit statement. You've never been any of that," Vincent chimed in.

"No one asked you," Barrett bit back, swiping at Vincent, who ducked out of the way. I giggled as we made it up the stairs—Damien, Zephyr, and Vincent taking the lead as Barrett and I trailed behind.

"I had a feeling when we first met," he started, and I lifted my eyes to him, one brow lifted. "I didn't wanna believe it. Zephyr and I had given up hope you'd return, but I felt it when we first met you. I was…" He pursed his lips, running his hand over the back of his neck. "I was in denial when Damien started talking to you. There was no way I could see you returning as a human. I tried to scare you off, thinking you just resembled her. I feared how deeply betrayed you'd feel if you returned to find your mate with another female."

I couldn't think of how I might respond to that.

"When Damien confirmed it the night you got attacked, I felt like such a piece of shit for the way I'd treated you." My mind wandered to the first real interaction we'd had on the stairway in front of the library, how he'd teased and taunted me. I couldn't deny I'd been intimidated by him, but before I could say anything, he continued. "I snapped when Damien brought you to The Complex. You were terrified, hurt, and instead of trying to comfort you, I'd threatened to wipe your mind."

His guilt skittered over my skin, and I reached up to place my hand on his arm.

"Barrett, I don't hold any of that against you. I didn't then, and I don't now."

"I'd feel better if you kicked my ass or had Damien do it," he admitted.

"How about this; I'll take you one on one in the training ring tomorrow and kick your ass to make up for it. How does that sound?" I offered.

A cocky grin slid across his face. "Deal. Just know I won't make it easy on you. I've got a reputation to keep up."

"Then I guess you're going to get a real hard kick to the ego."

As we made our way down the hall, we passed a few of the resident immortals. The trio of recruits—Zach, Sasha, and Liam—whom I'd helped train a few times waved as they passed us on their way to Stokers, talking about how they were to meet up with other recruits and warriors. It wasn't long after that we'd encountered a mother with a fussy infant who didn't want to go down for the night. Recently, more immortals had moved into the vacant rooms at The Complex, seeking refuge and protection from the darklings. I wasn't sure how many lived here overall, but I knew at least fifteen recruits had taken up residence while they completed their training.

"We're gonna head to the kitchen, see if we can find something to eat," Vincent said.

Damien lingered in the entry to the lounge, speaking with Vincent, Barrett, and Zephyr briefly before they headed off, their conversation echoing down the hall. Something about Aurelia having a major meltdown, begging Barrett not to go when he had to leave The Outpost that day—how he'd felt bad, he'd had to leave early to get ready for tonight's patrol and wanted to make it up to her. I couldn't help but smile at how close they'd gotten. Barrett and Thalia spoiled her. I couldn't deny that I may or may not have had a hand in my own spoiling of the little girl.

The cushioned chair near the window called to me, and I eagerly took a seat, resting my feet. The lounge was empty at this time of night—no sign of anyone, save the few immortals we'd encountered in the halls. Warmth from the fireplace filled the large room. I'd enjoy it while I could since we'd be back out on patrol within the next half hour, our shift not over for another two hours after that.

I stared out the window to the city in the distance, the twinkling lights illuminating the night sky.

A heavy sigh was all that alerted me to Damien's approach, and I shifted my gaze to him as he eased into the chair before me. He groaned in relief as he settled into the cushion of his chair, eyes drifting toward the window to the view I'd been enjoying. He didn't seem to enjoy it quite so much.

"I can't believe we didn't find any darklings," I muttered, falling back into the chair, my arms falling limp on the armrests.

He didn't say anything, but the hard set of his brows made it clear how heavily it weighed on him.

"What do you think Melantha's up to?" I asked. "Do you think the darklings' disappearance could mean something?"

His eyes drifted from the window, but they didn't meet mine as he pondered my question. "I don't know, and I don't like it. Between the darklings and the Varyoskia, I don't know what she's been up to, but I fear she may be building her horde with creatures far worse."

Was this the quiet before the storm? Was Melantha's absence a sign of approaching war?

"I wish we had more time," I said, pushing myself forward to rest my elbows on my knees.

Damien's eyes lifted to mine, and he reached out to take my hand. "I won't let this war destroy us, *mea luna.* We'll get through this. We'll make it to the other side, and we'll have a lifetime to spend together."

But we wouldn't...

My heart twisted, guilt settling into the pit of my stomach, and I parted my lips.

He took in a breath, as if preparing to say something, but he hesitated and I stopped, brows rising. "Cas, I..." His eyes danced over my face, whatever words he wanted to say lingering on his lips. His shoulders sagged. "It's nothing. Never mind."

"*Mea sol.*" I gripped his hand. His pale eyes met mine. "You're the one who's shown me we shouldn't leave things unsaid. You're the one who's shown me how much we could live to regret it."

He smiled. "I know we haven't found a way to turn a human immortal, and I know that... it won't be as much time as I would like with you."

My chest tightened, my heart dipping.

He took my other hand, his eyes falling to it as his thumb stroked my skin tenderly. "Regardless of that, I intend to spend every moment I have with you to the fullest."

His lips pressed into a thin line as he fidgeted. "I—You can tell me no, but after last night, I don't want to live to regret it. Regardless of whatever time we have together in this life, regardless of if we fall to the darklings or defeat them and you live fifty or sixty years past that..."

My eyes burned. It would never be that long.

"If you'd accept, I'd love nothing more than to be bound to you."

My breath rushed from my lungs, the world shifting under me. "B-bound?"

Though I could feel the hope, the love rising off him, I didn't miss the pain in his eyes. He'd be here at my side, for however short my life would be, regardless of the pain he'd endure again. He'd be at my side when I passed on.

We could die at any time, but he wanted to be bonded, wanted to live what life we had left together as one.

"Damien, I—" His gaze lifted to me, hope lighting those beautiful amber and ashen eyes. I needed to tell him the truth. "There's something I've been wanting to tell you..."

His brows furrowed, and I swallowed. I wanted to cry, to scream. This was so unfair. Neither of us deserved this, not after everything we've sacrificed over the centuries.

"I've wanted to tell you for a long time, but I—" Was this really where I was going to tell him? I glanced around the empty room nervously before turning my gaze back to him. No, I couldn't back down this time. He needed to know.

"I didn't mean to keep this from you. When we first met, I had no idea it would lead to any of this. I've tried too many times to tell you, but—" I froze as the temperature plummeted, my breath leaving my lips in a pale mist. Damien's eyes shifted to the rest of the room, the lights flickering around us. I turned to see the fire sputter, shrinking before dousing entirely.

My heart sank as I turned to look toward the window, ice crawling along the glass in fractural patterns. "Damien?"

He rose from his chair, horror fanning across his face. The doors to the lounge burst open and Damien and I whipped around to find Vincent, Barrett, and Zephyr, their eyes wide as the lights went out.

"Darklings!"

351

CHAPTER 45

CASSIE

A darkling burst through the window, and Damien grabbed me as countless shards of glass rained over us. Damien released me to slam his fist into the creature's face, and it flew into the nearby sofa.

"Get out of here!" Damien yelled, and I lurched to my feet, running to where Barrett and the others flagged us down in the shadows, faintly illuminated by the stray light of the streetlamps. As we rushed through the doorway, Damien and Vincent slammed the doors closed behind us, but not before I caught a glimpse of darklings pouring in through the broken window.

The hall was cast in inky darkness. I could barely see as I grappled for the wall to brace myself while I allowed my eyes to adjust.

"Where the hell did they come from?" Zephyr barked, and something thumped against the double doors. The faint sound of clicks came from the other side, and dread spread through my chest.

Damien's eyes flitted back and forth. "I don't kno—" A scream echoed down the hall. Zephyr shifted into his panther form, taking lead as we hurtled down the hall.

Barrett drew his dagger behind me. "Fuck! We need to get everyone out of here!"

"Johnson's down in the med bay. He'll be trapped!" Vincent said, glancing over his shoulder, and terror stretched over me as I drew my daggers. The dark hall stretched before us with no way of getting out, save the two stairwells at either end. The immortals living here would be trapped. They'd be easy prey. Had the darklings surrounded The Complex? Where had they come from so suddenly?

"I can get people out, but…" I glanced at Damien as his gaze snapped to me, his own words falling short. He could use his shadow magic to get everyone out, but where would he even begin?

A recruit crashed through a nearby door, bracing the jaws of a darkling. He slammed into the opposite wall and onto the floor, the darkling snapping the air inches from his face. Zephyr slammed into it, biting down on its throat as he tore its head off.

Vincent hurried to the recruit's side as Damien peered into the room. Barrett and I scanned the hall behind us.

"*Fuck*," Damien breathed, and he looked at Vincent. "Get him up, *now*."

Terror sank into my bones as the echoes of clicks slipped from the shattered window in the room—the darklings communicating with each other. More were coming. God, how many were there? Vincent helped the recruit to his feet, the male's face drained of color.

"Move, *now*!" Barrett ordered, nudging the stunned recruit. He blinked and turned to follow Zephyr.

"Damien, how are we going to get everyone out?" I asked as we ran.

"We'll move through the shadows, get them to Haver's office in town. I'm limited, though. I can only move so many people at a time. Three is pushing it. I might be able to move four, but everyone's spread ou—"

As we passed an open door, three darklings spilled out of it, crashing into Damien and me. I hit the floor, the darkling pinning me with its icy claws. I grimaced as its terrible smile widened from ear to ear as it tried to bite me.

"Shit!" Barrett barked from behind me, and Vincent and Zephyr joined him as they leapt in, knocking back the few darklings that followed through the open doorway.

I kicked one of the creatures off me, pushing to my feet. It rose, its attention drawn from me to Damien. I plunged my dagger into its back and through to its chest, and the creature shrieked before collapsing into dust.

Damien ripped his dagger from the darkling in front of him. A third darkling crouched low, head tilting as its bottomless black eyes moved over me. I stared the creature down, chest heaving as I readied for it to attack. It bared its jagged teeth at me before Damien's dagger burst through its head, the blade emerging between the creature's eyes, and it disintegrated.

"Damien, get everyone out of here." I panted, and his wide eyes met mine. "We'll distract them."

"No," he said. "I'm not leaving yo—"

"You've already got one." My gaze shifted to the terrified male who stood behind Damien. I didn't blame him. He'd been among the new recruits who'd joined just a couple of weeks ago. He wasn't ready to face this.

I took Damien's hand as I locked my gaze with his. "You'll have a better chance of saving more if I stay behind. I can defend myself, they can't. Get them out of here, and then find me."

Damien's chest heaved as he stared down at me, conflict streaking across his face as he fought between his duty to protect his people and his mate.

"I'll be ok, *mea sol*."

He tilted his head to press a kiss to my forehead. "I just need ten minutes." His eyes fell on me for a moment before he looked back to his brothers, an unspoken request lingering on his parted lips.

"We'll protect her with our lives," Zephyr said as he shifted back into his immortal form. "Get Johnson and the others out."

"We'll buy you all the time you need," Barrett added.

Damien's eyes fell back to me, his hands gripping my arms. "Keep your thoughts open, Cas. I'll come get you as soon as everyone's out."

I nodded, pressing a kiss to his lips. Screams poured out from somewhere in the building, and I released him. "Go!"

Damien took a step back, hesitating, but he grabbed the arm of the recruit and slipped into the shadows, disappearing. Terror crawled over my skin as I watched him vanish.

I clasped my hand over my mouth, shaking. He would be ok. *We* would be ok.

Ghastly shrieks rang out down the hall behind us, echoing off the walls. We whipped around, and my heart plummeted as a mass of darklings rushed for us.

"Get to the stairwell!" Barrett yelled, pushing me forward as we ran for the door at the far end of the hall.

"Where the fuck are they all coming from?" Zephyr shouted.

"I don't know! It was so sudden! They just appeared out of nowhere!" Vincent said as we burst into the stairwell.

I hit the railing, looking down the shaft to the base level. Should we go down, try to get them out of the building? The blood drained from my face as more darklings stalked into the base of the stairwell, searching. Vincent and Zephyr took one look over the edge and pushed me upward.

We rounded the stairs, air catching in my lungs as the air grew impossibly cold. I'd never felt such a strong presence from darklings, and it terrified me to think just how many hunted us. It had only been a few seconds since we'd separated from Damien, but it felt longer.

Shrieks spilled into the stairwell below as the darklings burst through the door where we'd just come from, fanning out as they searched for us.

"Go!" Zephyr shouted behind me. I followed close behind Barrett up the winding staircase, Vincent tight on Zephyr's heel.

Darklings appeared in the open doorway of the fourth floor, their claws stretched out for me and my heart stopped. Zephyr shoved me out of the way as a mass of darklings crashed into him, knocking him into the railing. My palms and knees met unforgiving concrete, and I grimaced.

I whipped around to find the mass of darklings, but I couldn't see—"Zephyr!"

I climbed to my feet, knees throbbing as more darklings spilled from the doorway. I couldn't move, the world going quiet. Barrett shoved past me as a darkling lurched for us, slamming his palm into its chest, flames erupting as the darkling shrieked and dissolved into dust.

Vincent launched into the horde of darklings attacking Zephyr, and I lost sight of him too. *No!*

I ran for them, but Barrett threw up an arm, holding me back. Panic flashed across his face as we watched the mass of writhing bodies, claws, and fangs, darkness rising off them like steam. I clasped my hands over my mouth, horror sinking into my bones.

Water erupted from the mass of darklings in thick tendrils, whipping in all directions. They were knocked back down the stairs and over the railing, their shrieks echoing off the walls as they plummeted.

Barrett released me as two darklings launched for us, intercepting one. I knocked the other's outstretched arm away from me, slamming my dagger into its chest. I stumbled back, nearly falling as another took its place. I dropped beneath the grasp of its claws, slicing the dagger up into its chin and through its skull. The creatures crumbled into dust, but more flew at us, so many more, the darkness below churning like a maelstrom. Barrett pushed me back, and I fell onto the steps as two more darklings crashed into him.

Vincent burst from the horde, Zephyr clutched in his arms as he dragged him into the hall of the fifth floor. My eyes roamed over Zephyr, his eyes closed, body slumped in Vincent's arms. *Oh God, please no.* Vincent's eyes snapped to Barrett and me as I pushed myself to my feet. We couldn't get separated; I needed to get to them. The stairway was too narrow for me use my flame magic. I wasn't skilled enough to not risk burning Barrett and the others in the process, not to mention setting the building on fire.

I primed my daggers to sink them into the darklings' heads as they pinned Barrett down, but both the darklings went up in flames before I could do so. I ducked to grab Barrett's arm as they dissolved into ash above him, using every bit of strength I had to pull him up. "Come on, Barrett!"

He grimaced but pushed himself to his feet, his gaze snapping to Vincent and Zephyr.

"Get out of here!" Vincent yelled, easing Zephyr down before rushing to the door to shut it as darklings climbed the stairs below us.

Barrett pushed me up the stairs, but my eyes shot back to Vincent. "But Zephyr!"

"I've got him! Go!" Vincent yelled before barricading themselves in the top floor hallway.

"Go, Cas, now!" Barrett yelled, pushing me up the stairs. The ghastly howls and shrieks echoed up the expanse of the stairwell. I pulled my gaze from where Vincent and Zephyr had disappeared, rushing up as I reached out to Damien's thoughts.

Damien?

My feet grew heavier with each stair, and when I didn't receive a response, an icy dread crawled over my skin.

Damien!

His voice cut across my thoughts.

Cas? Are you ok? Are you hurt?

I crashed through the door to the roof, the winter night winds whipping through my hair.

Vincent and Zephyr are on the fourth floor! I think Zephyr's hurt! Get to them, please!

Barrett stumbled out behind me, pushing me forward as the shrieks grew louder, countless darklings swarming the stairwell below. I couldn't see how close they'd gotten, the darkness cloaking their ascension.

I searched for anything to possibly barricade them in as Barrett slammed the door shut, but there was nothing. It wouldn't hold up against them, not this many. I searched the rooftop for any other means of escape, of drawing them out of the building until the others could get out. My heart stuttered, my mind trying to grasp what bits of Zephyr I'd seen. He'd looked unconscious. Vincent had to pull him out; had he been injured? Had he been...

I didn't let myself finish that thought as my body trembled.

Something crashed into the metal door, and my attention snapped to it as Barrett came to a stop at my side, his breath ragged. The gravel of the rooftop ground under our boots as we stepped back.

My hands quivered as I gripped my daggers, the sound of their clicks and shrieks muffled by the door between us as they pounded against it. Damien still hadn't responded, and my mind swam with every terrible possibility as the door blew off its hinges. Broken and crushed darklings fell out onto the rooftop, more climbing over them as their soulless black eyes searched for us, their broken bodies snapping and twisting as they healed. I stretched my thoughts out farther, latching onto that tether connecting me to Damien.

Damien!

Silence was my only response.

CHAPTER 46

DAMIEN

I held tightly onto the arm of the recruit, his terror thick and sour in the air like lemons and vinegar. I hadn't yet met him, hadn't worked with him at The Outpost, so I didn't even know his name. Thalia had overseen recruits, and the guilt tore at me—that I'd been too absorbed in my own grief over the years to know. The shadows dissolved around us, revealing the med bay. Johnson whipped around to face me, pale as he braced the double doors. Another male, Logan, was already at work barricading the door, but how much longer would it hold?

"Lord Damien!" I jerked at the voice of a female. There were others here, thank the Gods.

"Were there others in the rest of the building?" I asked, calculating how many trips it would take to get them all out.

"Kyla was in her room last I saw, and Dawson and Lyra had stayed in for the night," one of the males said. "But I don't know if they were found or not."

I knew this couldn't be all of them. More had to have survived. Gods dammit, there was no time to dwell on it. I had to get them out, then check the rest of the levels for those who might've successfully hidden.

I turned to the far corner of the medical room. A group of females were huddled together, holding onto terrified young as they whispered soft words of assurance.

"Johnson, I'm going to move everyone to your clinic. Get ready to go. Grab anything you need," I said, and Johnson nodded, rushing to grab a few things.

I turned to the recruit who'd come with me. "What's your name?"

"Caleb," he answered, trying to force a mask of courage.

I planted a hand on his shoulder, offering him any strength I could. "I need you to stay here. Help Logan keep that door closed while I move the females and young out of here. Can you do that?"

His chest heaved and fear flickered across his face, but he nodded.

"I'll get you out of here, I promise. I won't leave any of you behind."

He nodded once more, turning to help barricade the door.

I turned toward the females huddled in the corner. "I can only move three or four of you at a time."

The females rose and hurried over to me. One of them dropped her gaze to the terrified young, offering them a warm smile. "It's going to be okay. Lord Damien is here. He and Lady Cas are the strength of our race. He'll protect us."

I met the fearful gaze of the toddler clinging to her hand as he sucked his thumb, his teddy bear tucked tightly under his arm.

"Come on. It'll be better if you hold them. I'll take one of you with two of the young," I said, stepping to the darkened wall, tapping into the dark void writhing inside me in response to the mass of darklings, to the corruption flowing within their veins just past the door.

The shadows came to life, and the children tensed, a fearful cry slipping through the toddler's lips as the black mist danced and coiled.

I offered them a reassuring smile. "It's okay. It's safe, I promise."

The female dipped to lift the little boy into her arms and grabbed another child. I motioned her to me, and as she drew closer, I wrapped my arm around her waist.

"I've got you. Close your eyes," I warned, quickly guiding them into the darkness.

The children shoved their faces into her shoulders as she held them, crying out as we slipped into the void. The darkness quickly receded as we reached Johnson's clinic. Anna was there, standing bedside as we emerged. She whipped around to me in surprise.

"Damien?" she gasped, running over.

"Take them, make sure they're okay. I'm bringing more. The Complex is under attack—"

"Vincent?" she said, horror streaking across her face as her sepia skin paled.

"He's with Cas. I'll get him out, Anna."

I turned from her, unable to waste any more time, hating that I couldn't reassure her further. I slipped back through the darkness, finding the remaining group staring wide eyed at the double doors as claws raked the metal.

"Come on!" I called, and the other female grabbed one of the remaining children, rushing to me. I grabbed another child from one of the females, clutching the sobbing toddler to my side as I guided us through the darkness. Pain shot across my skull as we emerged, the caged void in my chest nearly fracturing. *Shit*. That was my limit. I couldn't move more than four, and it was dangerous to do even that.

It took too long to move the remaining few. I needed to get back to Cassie. I hadn't heard from her, and my mind drifted to the worst possibilities. Anna took the child from me before I turned to slip back through the darkness.

Cries pealed out as I emerged. A darkling plowed into me, and my back hit concrete as it pinned me. I braced my arm against its throat, its torn smile stretching impossibly wide as it snapped its razor-sharp teeth at me.

Johnson and Caleb braced the door against the others. Only one had gotten through, it seemed. I yanked my dagger from its sheath, sinking it deep into the creature's chest, shielding my eyes as dust fell over me.

I blinked, rising to my feet as I met Johnson's terror-filled eyes. How would I get them out of here without the darklings taking us down, without them slipping into the darkness with us, to those taking shelter on the other side? I could summon the Lupai, have them handle the darklings while we escape, but it took tremendous power to tap into the void and sustain the forms of the *Skoteino Teras*, the shadow beasts, their forms tethered to this realm only by my magic.

We'd have seconds.

I swallowed, calling out to the Lupai, the pack of shadow wolves rising from the void beneath my feet.

"They'll hold them off. Get to me now!" I yelled. Johnson and Caleb's eyes flitted to each other as the Lupai charged for the door.

"Now!" I urged.

Johnson and Caleb pushed off the double doors in unison, the metal blowing wide open as countless darklings spilled in. The Lupai leapt into the swarm, and the sound of growls and snapping jaws meeting shrieks and howls filled the room. Caleb and Johnson ran for me, the creatures overwhelming the twelve Lupai almost immediately. Their whimpers and cries filled the room, tearing something apart inside me as I grabbed Johnson and Caleb's outstretched hands, pulling them into the darkness with me.

We crashed onto the other side, people screaming as the darkness receded, but not before a darkling slipped through behind us. I jumped to my feet, slamming my fist into the creature's face, sending it crashing into the nearby empty bed. It flailed, struggling to right itself as I pulled my dagger free from its holster.

It hissed and shrieked as it twisted onto its hands and claws, launching at me in a fluid motion. I ducked beneath its outstretched claws, grabbing its throat, ramming my dagger up into its chest. It shrieked, disintegrating into dust, and I dropped my hand to my side as I panted.

I looked back to the survivors, meeting their terror-filled gazes.

"I'll be back," I promised Anna, the fear I felt for my own mate reflected in her pale eyes.

I slipped back into the shadows, appearing in the hall of the first floor. "Is anyone here?" I called, hurrying from door to door, listening for any sign of darklings or survivors, but I was only greeted with silence. I passed through the shadows to the second floor, finding nothing but a few dead bodies. I resisted the urge to grab them, to bring them so their families could mourn, but there wasn't time. There may still be others who'd survived.

Shrieks rang out from the stairwell at the far end of the hall, but nothing emerged from the door. My heart lurched. Were they going after Cassie?

I whipped around as a door creaked open, revealing a female carrying an infant, the one we'd encountered when we'd arrived earlier that night. A young girl was glued to her side, trembling hands clutching onto her. Relief washed over me as her eyes lit with hope. She wasn't alone, a pair of recruits right behind her. I knew them; they'd been in the training program for months and were close to taking their vows. I'd trained with them numerous times.

"Grayson, Cora, thank the Gods you're okay. I'm getting you out of here, but I can only take four of you each pass. Someone will have to stay behind and wait."

"Take them," Grayson said without hesitation.

Cora shot a look of concern toward him. "No."

"Do it, Lord Damien. I'll be fine," Grayson said, pushing them toward me as he looked back down the hall.

I grabbed their hands, nodding to Grayson, before I turned to slip into the darkness.

Damien!

I froze as Cassie's voice shot across my thoughts. I responded to her immediately, both relieved to hear her voice and terrified at the fear in her tone.

Cas? Are you ok? Are you hurt?

She didn't respond, and I tried again.

Cassie?

Nothing.

The females stared at me, confused and terrified as I tried to reach out to Cassie once more. She didn't respond, and I swallowed, reaching out to the darkness. The doorway opened, and I pulled the females in. "Don't let go."

We emerged on the other side, pain searing across my temple, and I released them both to dive back in. Grayson was still there, relieved to see me. I grabbed his outstretched hand, pulling him through.

"Help Anna any way you can," I said, sparing a quick glance to Cora and Grayson. They both nodded before I slipped back through the shadows.

I didn't think, couldn't allow myself to, as the worst thoughts invaded my mind. I was no longer running down the hall of The Complex; I was running through Moonhaven, running toward the last place I'd seen my mate before I'd lost the connection.

It was still there, though. The mating bond still remained. I could still feel her, faint, distant; I just couldn't pinpoint it, though. Had they gotten out? I couldn't see anything but the walls surrounding me. I slipped through the shadows, the night's winter air whipping past me as I emerged just outside the building.

I searched for any sign of Cassie, any sign of my brothers. There were no darklings out here, not a single one. My heart plummeted as I caught sight of Vincent, hovering over Zephyr on the ground, his hand pressed to his abdomen. I ran to their side to find Zephyr unconscious, his golden skin a sickly pale, a sheen of sweat beading his brow. Vincent's chest and hands were covered in blood oozing from the wound in Zephyr's gut. Vincent lifted his gaze as I dropped to my knees, eyes wide. Zephyr didn't move, and my heart sank.

"What happened?" I demanded, leaning over to press an ear to Zephyr's chest. His heart was still beating, but it was slow, his chest rising and falling at an equally slow rate.

"We got hit by a bunch of them. He knocked Cas out of the way but got overrun."

Icy dread shot down my spine. "Did he—"

Vincent shook his head, his voice shaking. "Somehow didn't get bit, but *fuck*. They gutted him, Damien."

"We need to get him to Johnson's clinic. Anna's already there." I hooked my arm under Zephyr to lift him. "Keep pressure on it!"

Vincent helped lift him, kept the cloth pressed to the wound, but the second he was upright, blood seeped farther into it, dripping down to the ground.

"*Fuck*," I breathed, straining under his weight as I called forth the shadows once more. We stumbled toward the doorway, Zephyr growing heavier with each step, his body wholly limp between us.

"Vincent!" Anna cried as we emerged on the other side, but she immediately halted at the sight of Zephyr.

"Johnson!" I called, and the doctor immediately rushed over with two more nurses.

"Get him on a bed!" Johnson ordered, and Vincent and I grunted, shifting his weight toward the closest one, the nurses helping lift him up as we laid him down as carefully as we could.

Johnson took over, shouting orders to nurses, the room descending into chaos. Vincent and I stumbled back, chests heaving as we struggled to catch our breaths. Anna ran to Vincent, wrapping her arms around him. Her relief washed over me as Vincent embraced her, murmuring soft words of love to her.

I wanted to linger, wanted to make sure my brother was okay, but I looked to the dark void connecting us to The Complex. Cassie was still out there somewhere; Barrett was still out there. I turned, heading back toward the shadows, Vincent telling Anna he would be back. I glanced over my shoulder to see her clutching his sleeve tightly, shaking her head as she begged him not to go.

"Cassie and Barrett are still out there," he said, and she stilled.

Anna's wide eyes found me, and I couldn't hold her gaze. Guilt sank into the pit of my stomach as I asked her to risk the life of her mate for the sake of mine. I stepped toward the darkness as Vincent gave her a quick kiss and hurried to my side.

"What happened?" I asked as he reached me. "Where's Cassie and Barrett?"

"We got separated on the fifth floor. Got hit by a horde of them. They could be anywhere by now."

My heart stammered.

Where was my mate?

363

CHAPTER 47

CASSIE

Zephyr hadn't looked good when Vincent pulled him out. Had he been...

No, I couldn't allow myself to think that, but the fear had taken root, my breaths coming in short bursts. Darklings poured out of the rooftop doorway like a swarm of roaches, and I stumbled back, fighting to steady my pounding heart.

Barrett widened his stance beside me as they charged for us.

"Light these fuckers up, Cas!" Barrett shouted, flames coming to life in his hand.

I calmed my racing heart, sinking into the warmth of my own skin, sparking that heat until it ignited in my hands. I fanned out the flame in a wide arc in unison with Barrett, sweeping across the wave of darklings.

They descended into dust, but more emerged through the mist of ashes. I ripped one of my daggers from my thigh, swinging it through the air at one of the creatures' chests as I ducked beneath its grasp. The darkling howled as it crashed to the rooftop behind me. I whipped around as it twisted onto his claws and feet, snapping its torn jaws at me. Barrett's back met mine as he held off other darklings that came for me. The only sounds were his grunts and the hisses of the darklings falling to his blade.

They surrounded us, forming a massive arch as they drove us to the edge of the rooftop. I shot flames out as two darted for me from the mass. Through the thinning horde, I caught sight of more climbing onto the roof from the far wall. God, how many were there?

Barrett and I pivoted, backing against one another as we faced off against the onslaught. I panted, my heart pounding. How much longer could I hold them back? The climb up the stairs had left my legs shaking and my lungs struggling to pull in the bitter winter air.

"So, I hear you've been doing good in your flight training," Barrett said before he slammed his dagger into another darkling.

"I don't think this is the time for chitchat," I ground out, slamming a fistful of fire into another darkling's face, the creature lighting up in flames the second my hand connected with it.

"Nonsense," he grunted as he took out another darkling. "It's always a good time for chitchat. If you can't talk while fighting, you're—" He slammed another darkling onto the roof. "Not in good shape!"

Another darkling turned to dust on my blade, and I stumbled back, chest heaving. I couldn't keep this up—that invisible limit was approaching. I tried to reach out to Damien again. We'd run out of time. We needed to get out of here.

Damien! Did you get Johnson out? Is everyone out of the building?

There was no response at first, and I faltered as another darkling lurched for me. I lifted my hand, shooting a blast of fire into it. It shrieked, falling onto the ground. Why wasn't I able to reach him? My thoughts flitted to Lucia's memory, to when I hadn't been able to contact him. Were the darklings somehow interfering? Was he hurt?

Cas? Thank the Gods. Yes, everyone is out. Where are you?

Relief washed over me at the sound of his voice.

"Get back, Cas!" Barrett shouted, pulling me to the edge as flames erupted from his palm in a wide arc, more powerful than before, engulfing a mass of the darklings in a wall of fire.

We're on the—

A darkling slipped beneath the arc of flames, crashing into me, breaking my concentration, and my heart lurched as my feet left solid ground. I careened over the edge of the rooftop, the icy wind surging around me. Barrett whipped around, grabbing hold of my outstretched hand. His chest met the edge of the rooftop and I slammed into the brick wall, the air rushing out of me. I gasped, air flooding my lungs with unrelenting force as the darkling and my daggers both fell.

"I've got you!" Barrett said, holding my wrist. I lifted my eyes to him as I dangled, gasping for air. I reached my other hand up, grabbing onto him, holding on for dear life. My gaze threatened to fall to the descent. "Don't look down, Cas. Look at me."

My gaze locked on him, adrenaline clouding my thoughts.

"I've got you," Barrett gritted out, his steel eyes meeting mine. "Did Damien get everyone out?"

"Yeah! Pull me up!" I gasped, my sweaty hand threatening to slip from his grip. His other hand shot out, grasping onto my hand.

"I'm sorry for always picking on you," he ground out, grimacing.

"What?"

"You're really good to Damien, you know that? He's happier than I've seen him in a long time thanks to you." His arms quivered as he held me. The darklings' clicks and snarls reached my ears as they recovered from the flames Barrett had just unleashed.

"This is a horrible time to be sentimental, Barrett." My boots slipped against the brick as I tried to pull myself up. My arms shook under my weight, my strength waning.

"Dammit, Barrett pull me u—" I stopped breathing as my eyes locked on his arm. Blood rolled down his leather armor, reaching his hand where he held me, the red blood swirling with... darkness. My eyes darted to his as he swallowed, forcing a weak smile. *Oh God, no.* When had he been bitten? Had it happened on the roof when I'd had my back turned? In the stairwell? Panic shot through me and I pulled harder, trying to climb.

"Barrett!" I jerked against him. "Pull me up!"

Barrett didn't respond at first, and my heart dropped.

"It's too late for me," he said.

"No! I can draw it out! We can draw it out! Damien said it's dangerous, but not impossible!" My boots skidded against the brick as I struggled to climb, desperate to get to him.

366

Barrett tried to reason with me as he glanced over his shoulder. "They're recovering… and there's too many."

"We'll take them out together!" I fought to pull myself up.

"I'm sorry, Cas." A look of pure endearment spread across his face, lighting those steel eyes.

My vision blurred. *"Don't you fucking talk like that, Barrett! Please!"*

"Shift for me. Show me that pretty owl I've heard so much about," he said with a sweet smile.

My heart lurched, tears blurring my vision. No, not like this. I needed him here; we all needed him here. "No, no, no, no, no, no, no!"

"Tell Thalia I love her. Tell her I'm sorry." Tears rolled down his cheeks and fell onto mine.

I sobbed, fighting. "Barrett, pull me u—"

He released my hand, my fingers slipping through his, and I stopped breathing as that warm smile remained on his face.

"Fly, spitfire."

Time slowed; my eyes locked on his. No! Not like this! I stretched my hands out to him as air rushed past me. I wanted to shift, needed to fly, needed to reach out to him, grab his hand. Barrett's warm smile remained on his face, his skin beginning to glow as the black veins crept across his skin. The veins turned molten, his skin glowing brighter and brighter. The claws of the darklings came into view at his back.

"No!"

Pain erupted at my back, feathers flying loose around me as wings shot out in painful urgency. I wouldn't leave him, wouldn't let him go. Darklings came into view as they launched onto him, and he slammed his hand into the brick wall, his body erupting into a blinding light, flames engulfing him and the darklings at his back as the fire exploded, shooting down the stretch of the building, destroying every darkling that remained.

The blast knocked me back, my wings swinging wildly and uncoordinated. I couldn't brace against it, couldn't right myself, and I slammed into the chain-link fence at the far end of The Complex's yard.

Ringing filled my ears, drowning everything out as I blinked. My eyes wouldn't focus, my vision a blur of bright light and darkness. I couldn't move at first, my body unresponsive to my commands, numb and floating. I needed to get to him. I had to get up. I needed to…

Black dots danced across my eyes as I grimaced. The chain-link fence was bent and caved in around me, and my—

I gasped as I tried to move, pain shooting up my spine. I twisted my head around to find my wings shredded and broken at my back, hooked into the chain links. My gaze shot forward, eyes darting around for Barrett, but what lay before me left me without air.

The building was engulfed in a flame so hot I could feel the heat from where I sat. I cried out as I ripped myself from the chain-link and collapsed onto my hands and knees. White hot pain lanced across my shoulder, and I winced as I nearly caved beneath my weight. The ringing persisted, my balance shifting and swaying with each movement, and I vomited onto the concrete, agony rippling out to every inch of my body. I looked over my shoulder, my wings tattered and broken, hanging limply at my back.

My eyes shot back to the building as a hollow blur of words reached me from the distance.

"Ca—ie!"

I searched the flames already spiraling out of control, the magic burning the building quickly. Hands grabbed me.

He can't be...

"What happened?" Damien's voice finally cut through the ringing, the sound replaced by the blazing fire and the screams of darklings filling the night sky as they burned.

"He can't be..." I muttered.

Vincent skidded to a halt, horror painting his face as he caught sight of my wings, of whatever else they could see that I couldn't. Damien's hands hovered at my back.

"Where's Barrett?" Damien asked, his voice laced with panic. Something fractured inside me, tears rolling down my cheeks as I sobbed. The color drained from Damien's face, and his eyes followed my gaze to the burning building.

He couldn't be gone. He couldn't. I pushed myself up, pulling from Damien's stunned grasp. He told me so himself. *Telos Pyrai* wasn't a guaranteed death. He could survive that. He had to.

"No," I cried, tears rolling down my cheeks, burning in wounds I couldn't pinpoint. "No, no!"

I stumbled forward, the concrete searing my wings as they dragged behind me. I didn't have the strength to lift them, couldn't afford to waste time. Damien called for me, but I couldn't listen, couldn't give up on him. Not yet. This wasn't the end. He had so much life ahead of him. I didn't. It should've been me. He had his brothers, Thalia.

"Barrett!" I cried out as I approached the flames. The heat enveloped me, the wind whipping through my hair. I stumbled to the side, nearly falling as the world spun, my mouth flooding with saliva. I could squelch the flames. We could find him. We could draw the darkness out of him. We could save him.

I stretched out my hands, the heat under my skin calling out to the raging inferno just out of my reach. I called it to me, bending it to my will.

"Cassie! Stop!" Damien called from behind me.

I pulled at the flames, willing them to slow, willing them to calm. They raged against me, the power too much to be tamed. I gritted my teeth, fighting against it, commanding it to bend to my will. If I could put the fire out, we could find him. My weight shifted, my legs unsteady beneath me, sweat drenching my brows, and a chill fell over me despite the immense heat.

Not yet! I pushed through the pain, through the nausea swirling within me, through my body's warnings. The flames started to calm; he would be alive. *He would be alive.* Arms came around my waist, threatening to pull me from the flames, and I howled, fighting to stay here. I couldn't leave him.

Fly, spitfire.

Tears flooded my eyes as I strained, my heart pounding. Damien said something, but I couldn't hear him, couldn't process the words as I focused on the only thing that tethered me to Barrett—his flames.

He would be ok. He would be—

370

CHAPTER 48

DAMIEN

The immortals taking shelter in Johnson's clinic stood around us, murmuring amongst themselves. Vincent stood frozen at my side, his fear and concern thick in the air as I tried to reach out to Cassie again. What had happened? Why were we having issues communicating?

Cassie? Cassie!

"Are they ok?" Vincent asked as I started for the shadows.

"I don't know. She asked me if everyone was out." My heart hammered, dread crawling across my skin as we slipped into the shadows. She'd sounded terrified, desperate. "But she isn't responding."

Gods, please let them be ok.

The darkness receded, revealing the abandoned parking lot, the stretch of Short Street and its loading docks. Vincent and I skidded to a halt, eyes searching the grounds for any signs of the darklings, of Cassie and Barrett. Were they still inside The Complex?

Raw power hit me first, sending the hairs on my neck on end, and just as I turned toward the source, fire erupted, a shockwave slamming into Vincent and me, knocking us onto the concrete.

"Fuck," I grimaced, pushing myself to my knees as an intense ringing flooded my ears. What the hell... I froze at the sight of The Complex, the flames surging and writhing as they engulfed it. My eyes swept across the small lot for Cassie and Barrett as I jumped to my feet. Those flames... the raw blast of power I'd felt before they appeared... I hadn't felt that terrible power since The Fall of Kingdoms, since the Stoicheion users at the frontlines had erupted in one final attempt to bring down the waves of darklings overwhelming us. They couldn't have used...

Please, no...

"Gods," Vincent breathed, the color draining from his face.

A wet gasp reached my ears, and I whipped around. The chain-link fence was caved in, feathers cascading like snow around a body. It wasn't until she lifted her head, chestnut hair falling around her face, that relief and terror washed over me. "Cassie!"

I shot to my feet and rushed toward her. She tore herself from the fence, a painful sob ripping from her lips as she fell onto her hands and knees and threw up. Air rushed from my lungs at the sight of the mangled wings at her back, the tawny feathers coated in blood. They were massive, hanging at her sides, limp and broken. I couldn't process where they'd come from, but I couldn't linger on them as my eyes roamed over her body. Her Elythian leathers were torn and ripped, cuts and scrapes marring her exposed skin.

My knees hit the pavement as she lifted her head, her wide eyes focused on the building engulfed in the flames. "What happened?"

Vincent's heavy footfalls halted behind me as he froze in place.

I reached out to touch her but hesitated, afraid of where she was hurt. Her left shoulder twitched and quivered under her weight, the exposed skin already black and blue. She muttered something under her breath, not even seeming to know I was there. I scanned the small lot again, refusing to accept who could've been responsible for the unnatural fire raging out of control.

"Where's Barrett?" I asked, praying to Gods I'd long lost faith in.

Tears welled in her eyes as she stared past me at the flames, and a coldness swept over me. No. Gods, no, it couldn't be true...

"No," she cried, the agony in her hoarse voice shattering me as she cried it again and again, pushing herself to her feet.

I couldn't think straight, couldn't breathe. He couldn't be... Gods. I clung to the last words we'd exchanged, the irritating comments he'd made that morning over breakfast. My brother... He couldn't be...

Cassie stumbled away from me, and I pulled myself from the agony to push myself to my feet. Vincent lingered back in his own shock and pain, disbelief painting his face.

"Barrett!" she cried out, stumbling toward the inferno, her left arm hanging limp at her side, the bloodied wings dragging along the concrete behind her. I flinched at the sound of his name, the pain sinking its claws deep into my chest, but I didn't let it stop me as I ran for her. Her hand stretched out to the flames. What was she trying to do? What was she thinking?

"Cassie! Stop!" I shouted, trying to get through to her.

She'd lost herself, growing dangerously close to the fire. Heat pressed against my skin as I neared her, her curls whipping around her as the fire reached for her in a tendril of destruction, licking at her outstretched hand. I hissed as stray embers burned my skin. I had to get her away from here, get her back. We couldn't linger any longer than we had.

The fire was too powerful, too all-consuming at this point, and I knew it would reduce the very bricks to ash by the time it was sated. She couldn't stop this; it would be too much for her body to handle. I wrapped my arms around her waist, careful of her wings. The heat of her skin seared me, and I cursed at the pain of it.

Barrett was... gone. She couldn't change that. I couldn't change that. Agony tore through me as I tried to force my mind to accept it—but while he was gone, she was still here. She'd survived; he'd protected her, and I wouldn't allow her to waste his sacrifice in her grief.

A shattering cry pealed from Cassie's lips as she fought against me, trying to maintain contact with the inferno raging out of control. The surface of my skin burned, the heat of the fire overwhelming, and sirens sounded in the distance.

"He's gone, Cas. He's gone," I muttered, my voice breaking as my vision blurred.

Her body jerked suddenly, the bond between us shuddering, and my heart lurched, the air punching out of my lungs. Something was wrong. She gasped, body surging, and I froze as the wings began to crumble, the feathers breaking down into dust. It wasn't the same as a shift; there was no black mist. This was a cutoff of magic, the form no longer able to sustain itself.

"Cassie?"

Her hands recoiled, grabbing hold of her chest, gasping for air as she tried to speak. Her knees gave out, and I caught her, supporting her as I dragged her away from the flames.

"Vincent!" I shouted, and he shook from his daze, running to my side. His skin was pale, his eyes red, but he focused on Cassie.

"What happened?" he asked, looking down at her as I lowered her to the ground. She curled into herself, trying to pull from me.

"I don't know. Something's wrong," I said, looking over her. I couldn't see any wounds on her chest, any sign of what could be hurting her. Was it another recoil?

"Hear—" Cassie's words cut short as she panted, her face twisting, the color draining from her skin.

"We need to get her to Johnson." I flinched as a cry broke from her. "I'm sorry, *mea luna*. This is going to hurt."

I slid my arms under her, hating that I had to move her, but I was desperate to get her to the clinic. She cried out as I lifted her, her bruised shoulder pressing against my chest, but it couldn't be avoided. "Just hold on."

Shadows stretched out from the darkness of the nearby building, and I hurried through to Johnson's office, Vincent close behind me. I couldn't allow my mind to wander as panic crept in, threatening to swallow me whole.

"Anna!" Vincent called as I searched for Johnson. Zephyr was no longer in the bed we'd placed him on, and the room spun as my eyes settled on the bloodied sheets. Where'd they taken him?

"Dr. Johnson's in surgery with Zephyr," Anna said as she rushed toward us. Her eyes fell on Cassie, her eyes widening at her wounds. "Oh my Gods, let's get her in a bed."

"Something's wrong, Anna. She keeps clutching her chest," I said as Anna guided me to a clean bed. She pulled the curtains closed around us.

"Does she have a history of heart complications?" Anna asked as I lowered Cassie onto the bed.

"I... I don't know. She's never mentioned anything."

Anna leaned past the curtain, her words sharp and fast. "Mary! I need an EKG on bed three!"

"On it, Anna!" a female voice responded, her heavy footfalls echoing off the walls as she rushed down the hall.

"Cas, can you hear me?" Anna asked calmly, her voice kind and gentle despite the speed at which the words left her lips.

Everything was happening too fast, and yet... too slow at the same time. Cassie's lashes lifted, agony filling those hazel eyes I loved so much. Her lips parted as she panted, but no words came. She nodded, but then her eyes clamped shut as her face contorted again.

Had I missed something? I wracked my mind for any signs, any details I might have overlooked. I clenched my hands into fists at my side, resisting the urge to punch something as my skin crawled. I shouldn't have fucking left them. I should have stayed.

"Vincent, I'm going to need room," Anna said abruptly, her tone firm as she stepped around to a nearby monitor.

Vincent swallowed and nodded, stepping back through the curtain in a daze.

My heart twisted for him, for the hollow pain consuming him. His cousin was gone, Barrett was... "*Gods dammit.*"

"Cas, we're going to remove your armor, ok?" Cas didn't acknowledge her, and Anna lifted her eyes to me. "Damien, I need to open her armor. I can't check anything through this leather. Can you help me?" Anna reached for the buckles of her harnesses.

"Watch out," I said, brushing her hands aside as I pulled my dagger from its sheath and sliced through the harnesses. "Try to stay still, Cas."

"I'm sorry," she breathed, grimacing once more as tears dotted her eyes. Her voice was weak, barely above a whisper. "I'm so sorry..."

I'm so sorry.

My heart twisted, those very words I'd heard so long ago echoing in the recesses of my mind. Why was she apologizing? "Just relax for me."

Scissors wouldn't be able to cut through this leather, and I didn't want to cause her more pain by pulling it over her head. I carefully lifted the hem of her top, slipping my hand under it to protect her skin while I sliced the leather up the middle, the sting of the cut spreading across the top of my hand. Cassie tensed, her head falling back as a broken sound slipped from her lips.

"Sorry," I said as I finished cutting her out of her armor. I stopped breathing as my eyes drifted over her. Bruising painted the side of her rib cage, the skin already turning black and blue.

"You can leave her bra," Anna said as she pulled her stethoscope over her head, quickly fitting the earpieces as she pressed the end piece to Cassie's chest. She remained silent for a moment, a mask of concentration settling over her face.

"I think she's having a heart attack. Mary! Where's that EKG—"

My gaze snapped to her, the air halting in my lungs. "A heart attack?"

"I've got it right here," the other nurse said, nearly over top of me as Vincent lifted the curtain aside for her. He quickly averted his gaze at the sight of Cassie, exposed on the table.

A heart attack? Selene had warned us of the toll her magic would have on her body. Was this what she spoke of? Was this the beginning? Terror swept over me. I hadn't expected it to come so soon.

"I need to know her history. Is she on any medications? Anything you can get. I can't get into the human health systems to pull her files," Anna said as she prepped the machine.

I swallowed, my mind racing through everything. Medication? "She's not on any medication that I'm aware of. I think she's on birth control. I'll get James to see if he can pull her records," I said, stepping out of Anna's way as she got to work.

Anna immediately began giving Mary orders. "Mary, I need you to get her vitals. We need her on the cardiac monitor and—" Her voice blurred, the chaos erupting around me as my eyes fell on Cassie. Mary brushed past me to get to work.

Anna got back to work on the machine. "Kris!"

Another nurse echoed a response almost immediately. "Yes?"

Anna voice quickened. "I need you to see what we have in stock. Morphine—Lipitor—epinephrine—aspirin. Whatever we've got bring it, and we need to prep a cardiac cath—"

I pulled myself away, trying not to listen to the things Anna was preparing to do to Cassie. My hands shook as I grabbed my phone and quickly called James.

James' voice was groggy as he answered. "Hey, Dam—"

"I need you to pull up every medical file you can on Cassie. I don't care what you need to do."

His voice became clearer, concerned. "Is everythin' ok? Whit hap—"

"There's no time. I need that information, now. Where are you? I'm bringing you down to Johnson's office."

"Ah'm home," he groaned, and bedsheets rustled in the background. I hung up as I glanced to Vincent sitting in a chair just outside the curtains surrounding Cassie's bed. His head was tilted downward, his eyes staring at nothing.

"I'll be right back."

Vincent nodded in a daze, his gaze remaining fixed, and I slipped back through the shadows, emerging into James' living room.

"I'm here!" I called out. James rushed down the stairs, pulling his sweater over his head as he made it to the base of the stairs.

"Whit's goin' oon? Is everythin' ok?" he asked as he grabbed his coat and laptop case.

"Darklings attacked The Complex," I answered, turning back into the darkness swirling in the corner of his living room. He followed close behind, his laptop bag tucked under his arm. My feet were leaden, the drain of magic beginning to wear on me.

"*Christ*," James breathed as we emerged in Johnson's office, his eyes finding the numerous immortals taking shelter here. "Where's everyone? Ur they ok?"

I bit back the pain that rose at the question. "Anna thinks Cassie's having a heart attack. I think it's what Selene warned us about. I need everything on her medical history. How fast can you have that ready?"

James swallowed, finding a chair and table to set up his laptop. "Ah shuid be able tae get into eh EHR an' get ye somethin' quickly; mibbe ten minutes?"

"As quickly as you can," I pleaded, turning to head back toward Cassie's bed. James had plenty of experience hacking into medical systems and bypassing security for the occasional incidents where immortals had wound up unconscious and admitted into hospitals. We'd had to destroy medical records, security footage, and any other leads too many times. If anyone could get that information, it was him.

Anna's voice drifted from the curtain. "I'm calling a STEMI. We're going to need that cardiac cath. I want to get her moved into a room."

"How is she—" I froze at the sight of her as I drew back the curtain, unconscious, nodes stuck to various places on her chest as Anna worked.

"She's okay, Damien. The morphine knocked her out," Anna assured me, and I had to brace myself against the bed. Anna's eyes fell as she turned to look back at the machine.

The other nurse, Mary, was hard at work preparing IVs on the other side, and I'd come in just as she was sliding a second needle into a vein in the crook of Cassie's elbow.

"Is James getting that information?" Anna asked.

"He is. What did you find?" I asked.

She swallowed, Mary briefly meeting her gaze. "She *is* having a heart attack. We're giving her something to help, but..."

Her eyes dipped, unable to meet my gaze. "It's not good, Damien." She drew a deep breath. "I'm limited here. Heart issues aren't common in our race, and we don't have a heavy stock of the supplies we'd need to treat a human. We do keep a few things on hand for the humans who serve our kind, but we're limited."

"If I need to break into a hospital, I will. Just tell me what you nee—"

"This is the last of what we have, but I found some," a nurse, Kris, said as she emerged through the curtains, carrying an assortment of things.

Anna took the medications to look at them, rattling off how much to give.

"Ah hev it up, Anna," James called from the other side of the curtain.

Anna's head whipped to him, and she nodded to the two nurses to get to work. "Mary, remove the nodes and get her cleaned up. We need to start assessing her other wounds once she's fully stabilized. Kris, prep a room for her and let me know as soon as it's ready. We're going to have to do it without Dr. Johnson."

Mary and Kris glanced at each other grimly.

"Shouldn't we wait for him?" Mary asked.

I opened my mouth to speak, prepared to demand they do whatever they needed to ensure she lived, but Anna spoke first. "He's tied up in surgery. She might not make it that long," Anna responded, and the females nodded before getting to work.

She might not make it that long.

My eyes locked on Cassie, her face so peaceful despite the dirt and blood, her chest rising in a slow, steady rhythm. We needed more time. It couldn't end like this. I pulled myself from her, slipping past the curtain to find Anna already reading through her file. Anna's pale eyes flitted back and forth across the screen, her sepia skin paling, her inner brows curving upward.

"What is it?" I dared to ask, her sorrow filling the room, like freshly fallen rain. My heart dipped. "What did you find?"

"Damien, I—" She blinked, her own voice cutting off as she drew a sharp, uneven breath, trying to keep calm.

"What?" I asked.

378

"This... isn't her first heart attack."

All air left me. "What do you mean?"

"She... this isn't something new. She's been battling this for years," Anna said, her eyes falling back to the screen. "There are records in here going all the way back to nineteen ninety-three. She's been fighting this since she was a child."

The world shifted beneath my feet, and I had to grab hold of the table to keep myself upright. "What exactly has she been battling?"

"She has a rare form of cardiomyopathy. There's scar tissue buildup in her heart, inhibiting its ability to function. She—" Anna lifted her eyes to me. "She never told you anything about this?"

My eyes drifted to the curtain blocking my view from Cassie.

"No... she—" My eyes drifted back to the laptop sitting before Anna. "She never did."

Why had she hidden this from me?

"Can it be fixed?" I asked.

Her lips pressed into a thin line as she released a heavy sigh. "Looking at these files, it seems they've been trying to for years with no success. It would take me days to sort through just how many procedures she's been through already."

Her body will not be able to handle the powers at their peak. They will destroy her.

Selene's warning shot through me so painfully, I couldn't breathe. I was losing her.

"Damien," Anna started, and I shifted my gaze to her, her pale eyes dulled with sorrow. Gods, please don't say it. Don't tell me what I feared.

"She doesn't have much time left..."

379

CHAPTER 49

CASSIE

Something was beeping. God, it wouldn't shut up. I tried to open my eyes, tried to reach for what I thought must be an alarm to wake me up for... school? No. Training? I had training... or... No. What was I doing?

My body felt so heavy, leaden, and yet not, as if I were riding on waves. I couldn't move, couldn't lift my eyelids no matter how hard I tried. God, that damned beeping. Why wouldn't it stop? I swallowed, my mouth bone dry, throat even drier. I just wanted to sleep.

A throbbing pain rippled through my head, and the air was icy over my skin. Where were my blankets? Had I forgotten to set the heat? I managed enough strength to crack my eyes open, my lids heavy. I wanted nothing more than to close them again, allow myself to slip back into that deep sleep, but that damned beeping wouldn't stop. The room was a blur, and I frowned at the unfamiliar colors and objects.

Beep... Beep... Beep. I lifted my hand to try to reach for whatever the alarm was, tempted to throw it across the room, but something pulled at the crease in my elbow. I was attached to something. A sting crept in through the numbness, and I blinked, trying to focus enough to see what it was.

Something gripped my other hand, and I shifted my head to find someone sitting at my side, his head resting against the blankets next to me. Though I couldn't see quite clearly, I knew it was him, the scent of cedar and leather reaching me.

What was he doing? Why wasn't he in bed? I opened my mouth to try to speak, but the cold air hit my parched throat and I coughed. Sharp pain shot down my arm and back, and I grimaced, a groan ripping through my throat. Damien's head shot up, and then he was on his feet, looking over me.

"Easy; try not to move."

My brows furrowed as I looked up at him, dazed and confused.

"Are you in any pain? I can ask Anna to get you something."

"Anna?" I asked. I craved water so badly, and my eyes dragged from him, searching for where my nightstand should be, where I might have a glass of water. I was greeted with monitors. Why were there monitors in our room?

"Does anything hurt?" he asked again as I attempted to lift my hand to scratch my arm. It was suddenly so itchy. "Try not to move that arm. You dislocated your shoulder."

The room came into focus, and my gaze drifted over the bare white walls, the various monitors and IV drips on the other side of my bed.

"Where are we?" I groaned, my voice hoarse. God, did that horrible sound come from me?

"We're at Johnson's," Damien answered, lifting his hand to brush back my hair. Exhaustion painted his face, his eyes red and swollen. Why? Had he been crying?

I lifted my eyes to the TV mounted to the wall. The volume was muted, set to the news. Subtitles flew across the screen, my eyes unable to focus fast enough, and I couldn't make out what they were saying. It was an aerial view of the remnants of a big fire, nothing remaining. What had burned do—

Fly, spitfire.

The monitor started to beep faster, the room spinning as everything resurfaced.

"Cassie, you've got to slow your breathing. Look at me." Damien's voice was a rush, and his hands cupped my face, forcing my gaze to him. "Breathe, for me. You need to try to calm down."

My eyes flitted everywhere, panic creeping in. "Barrett. He—"

His jaw tensed, the inner corners of his dark brows curving up as he pressed his forehead to mine. His silence was deafening. I couldn't bear it; I wanted to hear him speak, hear him reassure me that he'd made it out.

"No. No. Please tell me you found him..." My voice quivered.

"He's gone, *mea luna*." His voice was heavy, as if it took everything in him to force the words past his lips.

It was a lie. He couldn't be. He was too stubborn for that, too hardheaded.

"He was bitten," I muttered, and Damien tensed.

Tears welled in my eyes, my chest so heavy, I thought it might cave in. "I couldn't..." My lips quivered, my throat burning as I fought the tears threatening to fall. "I couldn't do anything for him..." Realization shot across my thoughts, and my body went rigid. "Oh, God. What about Zephyr? Vincent? Are they ok?"

"They're both safe. Zephyr came out of surgery thirty minutes ago and is resting right now. He'll pull through."

"I want to see them," I said, pushing myself up. "Please, Damien. I need to see them."

"Anna said you can't stand. They had to run a catheter into your heart."

I froze. A catheter? To my heart? I lifted my eyes to him, and he met my gaze with sorrow-filled eyes. His throat bobbed.

"You..." His words fell short. "You had a heart attack, Cas."

I parted my lips, but I couldn't find the words. "Damien, I—"

"Damien? Cassie?" A voice shot out through the halls.

"Thalia, you can't come through here!"

"Damien!" she called out again, heavy footsteps echoing down the hall.

Icy dread and guilt swept over me.

Thalia appeared in the doorway, breathless, as if she ran the entire way here. Her silver eyes were wide, terrified, her cornsilk hair a windswept mess. She was pale, so pale, and her gaze found me. She rushed to my bedside, looking me over. "Thank the Gods you're okay, Cas."

Her hands were cold as they lifted to my face, and her smile wavered, as if she couldn't force it anymore as she looked at Damien. "Where is he?"

Damien swallowed, and his mouth opened to speak, but he fell short.

"Damien?" Her eyes flitted between us, and my heart squeezed. "I can't find Barrett. I heard Zephyr's in recovery, but..."

When neither of us could speak, she continued, the words spilling out. "When he didn't answer his phone, I checked his apartment to see if maybe he stopped there to change, but he wasn't home. I heard the sirens, but I didn't realize The Complex caught fire. I tried calling you all, but no one answered."

Tears welled in my eyes, my chest threatening to explode. "I'm so sorry, Thalia," I muttered, my voice breaking as my vision blurred.

She looked back at me as I reached for her, the denial in her expression breaking something inside me. "For what? He was just late for our date. It's okay."

"Thalia, I—"

"I don't feel good, Damien," she admitted, her breaths growing shallow as she swallowed, looking at him. Her hands quivered, her throat bobbing. She was so pale. "Something doesn't... feel right."

I cupped my hand over my mouth, trying to keep myself from breaking down.

"Where's my mate?" Thalia asked, her eyes glassy, tears welling.

Where's my mate? Where's my mate? That single sentence burned into me, carving itself so deep into my soul, I thought I might break. My eyes burned, my chest throbbing. What could I say? What could I do? He was gone because of me.... because he'd been protecting me.

It was my fault...

"Thalia," Damien said, turning to her. "I need you to sit down." She froze.

Damien's voice thickened. "When the darklings attacked The Complex, Vincent, Zephyr, Cas, and Barrett drew the darklings away so I could evacuate everyone. They came out of nowhere without warning."

My heart faltered as Barrett's face danced across my thoughts, the smile he'd worn to his last moment.

"He..." Damien's eyes fell downward, and Thalia stepped backward, her head slowly shaking in disbelief.

I wanted to hold her, to try to comfort her. "Thalia—"

"No..." Tears flooded her eyes.

"He ensured no darkling left that building," Damien said, withholding the information that he'd been bitten. Only him and I knew that. Knowing what I did about Micah, I knew it would've devastated her.

It should've been me. Barrett and Thalia deserved so much more. They'd finally found each other, were finding happiness.

"Thalia, I'm so sorry," Damien said.

"Please tell me you at least were able to recover him," Thalia said on uneven breaths.

Damien and I flinched at the request.

Her eyes flitted back and forth between us when we didn't answer. She cupped her hands over her mouth, her hands shaking. "No! If we don't have him, I can't lay him to rest. He'll never find peace!"

The sob tore through me, and I tried to push myself up, but my shoulder protested, pain shooting up my back and ribs. Tears welled in Damien's eyes. She turned, running out the door.

"Thalia!" Damien shouted, and he followed after her.

No! I groaned as I climbed out of bed, the monitors reacting, the beeps growing louder.

"Cassie!" Damien halted in the doorway, spinning back toward me as I stumbled.

I forced myself upright, gasping as pain shot across my upper back and over my shoulder. "Thalia, please!"

Damien's arms came around me. Supporting my weight, he tried to guide me back to the bed, but I refused, pushing toward the doorway. We reached it in time to see the black mist descend over Thalia, and a large gray wolf emerged from the darkness as she ran. Nurses and patients jumped out of her way, shouting in surprise.

Vincent stumbled into view as she shoved past him, turning into the hall where he'd come from. His eyes followed her, realization flashing across them before he met our gazes.

"Vincent, after her! She doesn't need to be alone!" Damien shouted, but he hadn't needed to. Vincent was already rushing after her.

My breaths came in short pants, and my legs couldn't hold my weight anymore. My knees gave out, and I winced at the pain in my ribs as Damien's arm supported me.

"I've got you, Cas."

"Cas! You can't be out of bed!" I jumped at the sound of Anna's voice as she found us in the doorway, coming from the hall opposite where Thalia had disappeared down. "What happened? I got an alert your monitors were going off. Was that Thalia I heard?"

Damien nodded, and Anna's lips pressed into a thin line.

"She knows," I muttered.

Anna drew a deep breath, and for a second, I saw the tears form before she shook her head and wiped them away, refocusing herself.

"I need you back in bed," Anna said to me, and I looked back down the hall. "We can't risk your insertion site reopening."

I tensed as Damien helped me turn back into the room, every part of my body protesting the movement. Anna and Damien got me back into bed, and I tried to focus on my breathing, tried to will my body to relax through the pain. I was so cold, the shivers washing over me.

Anna stood the IV stands back up and checked over the lines in the crook of my elbow. "I'm so sorry. I made such a mess of all this."

Anna offered a weak smile. "It's okay, hun. This isn't going to be easy for any of us. How is your shoulder feeling?"

"It hurts," I admitted, rubbing residual tears from my eyes.

"And your back?"

"What exactly did I injure? How bad is it?" I asked, and Anna glanced to Damien briefly.

"You dislocated your shoulder, and you have a few broken ribs on either side. Thankfully, you didn't puncture a lung, but you somehow managed to fracture both scapulae."

"Scapulae?" I echoed.

"Your shoulder blades," she confirmed.

"You had wings when you hit the fence," Damien said. "They were broken. The injuries you sustain when you're shifted affect your real body, so I'm assuming it had something to do with that."

I nodded, rubbing my arms together as the chills gripped me. Why was it so cold?

"I'll get her another blanket. The morphine's going to make her feel cold until it wears off." Anna glanced at Damien as she headed back out of the room.

"Thank you, Anna," I said as I melted into the pillow.

Damien didn't speak as he pulled up a seat beside me. I couldn't look at him as my mind wandered through every possibility. I had a heart attack. How was I still alive? Did they find out my history?

Did he know?

Anna returned quickly with a thick blanket. "Here you go, Cas." She tossed it over me, ensuring everything was covered. It was so warm that I moaned in response, my eyes slipping closed.

"Let me know if you need anything," she added.

The silence returned, and I almost wished she hadn't left.

"Would you like some water? I'm sure you're thirsty," Damien offered.

Thirsty was an understatement. "Water would be really nice."

He reached for the plastic cup, and it all felt too familiar, my mind flying to when Kat had been where I now lay.

This wasn't how I wanted this to happen...

He rose from his seat, his hand slipping behind my head to help me drink. The cool water hit my throat, hard and soothing at the same time. I coughed but lifted my hand when he started to pull away, desperate for more. I sank against his arm once I'd drank enough, unable to hold my own weight any longer.

Damien set the empty cup down on the rolling table before easing back down into his chair. God, I wanted to say something, wanted *him* to say something.

I opened my mouth to speak, to tell him what I'd been trying to for months, but he spoke first.

"Why didn't you tell me?"

CHAPTER 50

CASSIE

I'd thought about how this conversation could go countless times, had planned every possible response, every scenario, but the moment those words left his lips, every thought I had prepared vanished.

Guilt sank in.

"I..." I swallowed, something pressing into the back of my throat.

"Why couldn't you tell me about this?" he asked, his eyes burning into me, his pain, his hurt seeping into every part of my body. I tried to shut it down, tried to not pick up on his emotions, but they burned through every defense I could muster.

Words hung on my tongue, just out of reach as I tried to speak. "I... I wanted to."

"Then why didn't you, Cas?"

"I couldn't—"

"You couldn't?" he repeated, as if he couldn't understand what I meant.

"I wanted to, but..."

"But you *couldn't*," he reiterated, unable to look at me, and I flinched at the hurt in his voice. "Cas—"

"No one knows," I said before he could continue, and his eyes snapped back to me, the room falling quiet. He blinked, his lips parting but closing as he tried to process.

"Only my parents and Kat know. Or at least... they knew. I guess Kat's the only one who knows now. I'd kept it from her too, but I found out recently she knew all along."

His gaze slipped, whatever words he might have said halting on his tongue. The fact that he wasn't the only one who didn't know and the mention of my parents seemed to make him consider his words more carefully.

"I..." I tried to think of where to even begin. There was so much, too much. "I didn't mean to hide it from you. I never expected things to get this far, never imagined when we met that we'd become what we are. Things happened so fast, and I've tried to tell you so many times, but every time, something would come up."

He opened his mouth to respond but halted, realization dancing across his face. "You were trying to tell me before the darklings attacked..."

I nodded, fidgeting with the blanket.

"You should've told me earlier, Cas. If I'd known, I wouldn't have pushed your training so hard. I would have fought Selene on the urgency. I wouldn't have sent you out there on patrol if I'd—"

"That's exactly why I never told anyone; why I was afraid to tell you."

He drew back, frowning.

"I've lived my entire life dealing with doctors, nurses, and family members treating me like I'm fragile, breakable. I'm not glass, Damien. I don't have much time left, but I'll be damned if I live it sheltered. I've regretted every decision I've made in minding my parents' caution, letting them keep me home, keep me from school, from... everything."

He blinked, guilt flashing across his face, and he swallowed.

"When we met, you treated me like a normal person. You saw me, not my illness—you treated me the way I'd always wanted to be treated. Even though I was mortal and weaker than you, you didn't let it cloud your faith in me. You didn't try to protect me from everything, but instead encouraged me to become stronger. You encouraged me to push myself forward, to overcome my weaknesses and faults, to do things I'd never dreamed of doing. You showed me happiness and love."

"I was afraid that would change once you knew. When I began to regain my memories, I... All I could think about was the look on your face when you learned that we wouldn't get that time together, that you would lose me again." Tears welled in my eyes, my voice beginning to quiver. "I almost walked away so many times in the beginning. I nearly took you up on your offer to erase my memories, if only to spare you from what I knew was going to happen. No matter how many times I tried to reason with myself that it would be better if we went our separate ways, there was always something drawing me back, and now I know that it was my soul calling to yours. I've lived my entire life feeling incomplete, and I've never felt more whole than when I'm with you. I was afraid that would change."

He remained silent, eyes burning into the floor as he absorbed my words.

"I'm sorry I didn't tell you. I never meant for it to go on this long." He drew a deep breath, running his fingers through his hair, and my stomach dipped. What was he thinking? "I can't tell you how much it hurt to not tell you, to deal with it alone. You're the first person in my life I've actually *wanted* to tell."

His gaze lifted to me, his brows rising.

"I didn't want to feel alone anymore. I wanted... you to be there with me, to be at my side when I went to my checkup."

His eyes softened, and he took my hand in his. The tears overflowed then, that single touch breaking me down. His thumb brushed tender strokes along my skin, and I never wanted it to end, I wanted to always feel his touch on my skin, his presence at my side.

"It was the day we erased my parents' memory." His thumb froze. "I thought of you the entire time, of Vincent, Zephyr, Thalia... Barrett." My voice broke at his name. "I've lived more in these last four months than I have my entire life."

"Were you going to turn me down?" he asked, and my brows furrowed. "When I asked if you'd be bound to me."

"I wasn't, but... I needed you to kno—"

"It changes nothing."

My gaze shot to him, my chest swelling.

He spoke again, his words as sure as the earth beneath us, unyielding and unwavering. "No matter how little time we have left, I'd rather spend it together as a bonded pair, as one. Nothing would ever change that."

The tears spilled then, a sob breaking from my chest as I caved into him. His strong arm wrapped me in his warm embrace.

"I'm sorry you've dealt with this alone, that I couldn't help you carry that burden," he whispered into my ear.

"I'm so sorry I never told you. I'm so sorry."

"Would you have me as your bonded, Cassie Hites?"

I pulled away just enough to meet his gaze, the amber of his eyes bursting from the ashen gray. I laughed through the tears, butterflies fluttering in my chest at the sound of my full name on his lips.I pulled away just enough to meet his gaze, the amber of his eyes bursting from the ashen gray. I laughed through the tears, butterflies fluttering in my chest at the sound of my full name on his lips.

"Yes," I said, as he lifted his hand to brush away my tears.

"I want to hear you say it fully."

"I would love nothing more than to have you as my bonded, Damien Archonis."

"Hey, Cas."

I looked over my shoulder to see Zephyr's warm smile as Calista helped him through the entry into the living room.

"Zephyr!" I pushed myself up from the couch awkwardly with one hand, my other arm resting in a sling. Damien cursed as I winced.

"You can't just get up like that. Let me help you," he said, jumping to his feet.

"Sorry. I got ahead of myself," I said with a weak smile as Damien tried to help me without putting pressure on my ribs. He shook his head with a sigh, but smiled, helping me to my feet.

God, it was a relief to see his face. I hadn't been able to see Zephyr after his surgery, and I was discharged before him, so I'd been desperate for him to be released. He was kept for observation at

Johnson's clinic for thirty-six hours after his surgery, and I'd been on bedrest, unable to leave the house. Calista released Zephyr as I slipped from Damien's arm and Zephyr pulled me into a warm embrace.

I winced at the tenderness in my ribs, and Zephyr tensed. "Shit, sorry!"

"Don't be, it's okay," I said, holding onto him, not allowing him to step back as tears dotted my eyes. It was such a relief to see his face, to hear his voice. I pulled back to look at him. His tanned skin had paled a bit, but I knew after a few feedings the color would return quickly. "How're you feeling?"

"Sore, but I'll pull through," he assured me.

"Johnson managed to get all your guts back where they belong?" Damien joked.

"I don't know how he did it, but yeah," Zephyr said with a smile.

"Is 'at Zephyr ah hear?" Ethel called from the kitchen.

"Hey *Mitera*," Zephyr said as she appeared in the hallway. He released me before she gave him a monstrous hug. It was amazing how quickly immortals healed. To be on his feet so soon after the wound he'd suffered was incredible.

"Ah wis jus' makin' tea. Wuid ye lovelies care fer a cuppa?" she asked.

"Tea would be lovely, *Mitera*," Calista said, her smile lighting up her delicate silver eyes.

"Ah'll hev em ready in no time," Ethel said as she disappeared back into the kitchen.

Damien turned to me. "Back to the couch, now. You're supposed to be on bedrest, *mea luna*."

"Yes, m'lord," I teased, and Damien huffed a laugh.

"How's Anna holding up?" I asked as Damien helped me to the couch. "She worked so many hours that night. I know it can't be good for her and the baby." Air rushed from my lungs in a heavy sigh of relief as I eased onto the couch, but it was short-lived as my back met the cushion, my fractured shoulder blades still tender.

"She's home with Vincent now, resting," Zephyr said, settling onto the couch beside me.

"Johnson has her on a week's vacation," Calista added. "She resisted it of course, wanted to help anyway she could, but she gave in. There's only twelve more weeks until her due date. Our kind tend to go on bedrest at thirty weeks, as the toll grows heavier, and complications can arise."

I prayed she'd be okay. No, she *would* be okay. Medical procedures were better now, immortal deliveries more successful. It had been a huge topic at the meeting with The Council.

I wondered what sort of changes were coming after everything that happened. The Complex seemed to have been a central hub for the immortals, not just for The Order. It had been a place to live, a refuge, a command center, a medical facility... perfectly located too, in the middle of the city.

"She really took charge," Damien said, sliding me a glance. "I'm glad she was there."

That single look told me enough of why he was relieved she'd been there, and I was too. From what Damien told me, she'd taken no chances, and with Johnson stuck in surgery, she was likely the only reason I'd survived. She'd saved my life.

"Any news on Thalia?" Calista asked, and my stomach twisted.

Damien's eyes flitted to me, his shoulders sagging in defeat. "None. Vincent tried to follow her, but she lost him in the woods. We've been looking for any tracks she might've left behind, but the snow's making it nearly impossible. She could be anywhere by now."

I hated that she was alone, terrified of what she might do in her grief, and I feared for how she would hold up in the winter cold.

"I hope we find her soon."

CHAPTER 51

CASSIE

"Aleirene touen enlisno en solos."

Peace embrace his soul—that's what Damien had told me it meant. I dipped my head briefly as the warrior paid his respects, shrouded in black. Every immortal brought a single lit candle and laid them at the base of the intricately woven pile of wood surrounding the stone bed where Barrett's body would have been. On the stone bed lay bountiful arrangements of delicate flowers in place of his body.

I glanced over my shoulder and past the pyre to Moira's body resting beneath the moonlight from the crescent ceiling window. I knew the immortals believed in an afterlife, but I was still learning their customs and beliefs, so I didn't understand it fully. Thalia had been distraught when she'd learned we couldn't recover Barrett's body. There was no way we could've, not when the entire building, brick and all, had been reduced to ash.

"*Aleirene touen enlisno en solos.*" I slipped from my thoughts as another immortal approached, clutching a single candle in her hand. I recognized her as I lifted my gaze. She was the mother we'd encountered at The Complex, the one with an infant. She'd survived.

"My young and I are alive, thanks to Barrett. We will never forget his sacrifice."

"Thank you," I said, dipping my head as she gave a bow before continuing to the pyre. Countless candles sat around the base, casting a warm glow throughout Moira's Rest. Damien told me the flames were meant to offer a guiding light for his soul to find The River Styx. There seemed to be a bit of divide between the immortals on whether or not souls could be guided without the remains. Some believed their souls would wander with no rest, that they'd never reach the afterlife they called Elysium unless they were released from their body during the ceremonial burning, that ceremonial flame guiding their souls.

He'll never find peace!

Thalia's words tore through my mind, her fears etching their way into me. I couldn't let myself think that could be possible, not for Barrett.

A hollowness filled my chest as I stood at Damien's side, my eyes swollen and tired. I'd cried so much over the last few days, every tear exhausted at each step of planning this funeral.

Damien had offered to take care of everything, but I'd refused. I wanted to help in any way I could, yes, but the truth was that I needed to stay busy. I couldn't sit still, couldn't let the grief consume me. It would tear me down if I let it.

Damien comforted those who needed it as they offered their condolences, and countless faces I'd never seen passed in a blur. Little arms wrapped around my legs, catching me off guard, and my eyes fell to a little head of wavy black hair pulled back in two braids.

"Gentle, Aurelia. Lady Cas is still recovering," Lydia whispered as she approached.

My heart squeezed at the sight of the child, her hands quivering.

"It's okay, Lydia," I assured her, laying a hand against Aurelia's back, my chest swelling as she held me tightly. Lydia dropped her free hand to her side, her pale, reddened eyes falling to the tiny flame dancing on her candle. Aurelia lifted her head as I lowered myself to my knees before her. Her eyes were swollen and red, her cheeks stained with dried tears.

"*Aleir*..." She sniffled. "*Aleirene tou*..." She couldn't get it out, her voice breaking every time she tried to say the phrase. The fact that she knew it broke something inside me, and I knew it was likely from her own father passing last year.

I pulled her into my arms, tears welling in my eyes. She'd adored Barrett, and they'd grown close over the last few weeks. He'd always taken time to entertain her when she needed, play with her, teased her.

She cried into my shoulder, and I tensed as she squeezed her arms around my chest, my ribs protesting. Damien and Lydia seemed to notice immediately as they made a move to pull Aurelia back, but I shook my head.

"I miss him," she muttered, her voice shaken and hoarse. "I wish he didn't have to suffer like this."

"Me too, *Mikros*." My voice broke.

Lydia bowed her head to Damien and me, saying what Aurelia couldn't, the words of condolences Aurelia couldn't get past her lips, the words I'd heard too many times now.

"Come on, Aurelia. You want to place the candle?" Lydia offered, holding it out to her. Aurelia released me slowly as she turned back to her mother, wiping her tiny hands over her eyes. She nodded, and Lydia handed the candle to her.

"Careful now," Lydia whispered, and dipped her head to us once more before guiding Aurelia toward the pyre.

My eyes drifted across those in silent observance as I pushed myself to my feet, the movement taking every bit of my energy. There were so many immortals within these dark walls, so many who either knew Barrett or had been affected by him.

I caught sight of Semele consoling Eiko as she cried. I found Anna tucked tightly under Vincent's arm as they stared at the candles surrounding the pyre, her beautiful eyes swollen and red. At their side were Zephyr and Calista. The color had returned to Zephyr's tawny skin, and it was a relief to see him standing on his own again. Damien assured me he'd be fully healed and back to normal by the end of the week.

I continued searching for the one face I desperately wanted to see among the mourners, but she wasn't there.

No one had heard from or seen Thalia since she'd disappeared from Johnson's office six days ago. Her apartment had remained untouched in the days following her disappearance, and we all feared for her.

"Are you okay, *mea luna*?" Damien asked, and I blinked, realizing how tired I must have looked. "You can sit if you need."

"I'll be okay, *mea sol*. Thank you."

I was healing all right, had managed to come out of the sling supporting my dislocated shoulder the day before. My healing wasn't done, though. It would be six to eight weeks before my ribs and shoulder blades would fully heal and the bruising fade. The wounds weren't the only thing that lingered, either. An exhaustion had settled into my bones. The fact that I made it out of Johnson's clinic was nothing short of a miracle. I should, by all accounts be dead. Regardless, I knew the time I'd been originally allotted was far shorter now.

The room quieted, and I turned my eyes in time to find the goddess Selene emerging through the massive double doors. Her pale skin glowed against the black gossamer gown she wore, her silver hair hanging in loose waves. The immortals bowed lowly as she passed, her steps silent, her gown whispering along the black marble floor. Damien and I bowed our heads to her as she approached. She came to a stop beside us before the pyre, and everyone lifted their eyes.

"Revinia aleirene, mea belariôs. Leukós regis vôu solos etu Elysium."

I couldn't understand her words, but there was power in her voice, woven with a gentle calm, like a warm blanket. Her delicate hands rose from her sides, sweeping through the air in a wide arc across the mass of candles. The orange flames danced and shifted into a cool blue as all other candles lining the walls were extinguished.

She lifted her hands before her, and the flames of each candle rose, drifting to the stone bed surrounded by wood, the flames converging until they ignited into a pyre that sent blue embers climbing in the air.

Damien's arm came around me as my hand rose to my mouth, and I blinked back tears.

Words danced from Selene's lips, soft and delicate, like droplets of moonlight and stardust. *"Emei charisti etu Celestia."*

Damien's eyes lowered as he joined her, followed by a sea of voices echoing across the stone chamber. *"Ge dorai en nemos esti lampei."*

"Mea bellarios, mea asidia."

The words meant nothing to me, and yet... everything, and I could feel in my soul that I'd heard this hymn far too many times.

"Manýa èn nychtôs. Atresei ekein prin vôu. Vôu varyó èstin telôs."

All eyes locked on the flames; the immortals offered up their lament for Barrett's soul in song.

"Oreie etai skiasei ntropo. Afin leukô odigei vôu solos. Etu Elysium sei enlisnô."

My gaze shifted from the pyre to Selene as her hands continued their dance, the words continuing to pour from her lips as the hymn started anew.

I froze at the sight of the starlight tear rolling down her cheek.

CHAPTER 52

CASSIE

Lips brushed against my brow, and a soft whisper filtered into my ear in the darkness.

I love you, mea luna.

I opened my eyes, shivering under the covers. *"Mea sol?"*

He was gone, the room empty. What time was it? A piece of paper on my nightstand caught my attention. I grimaced as I pushed myself up, my shoulders and back stiff and protesting. Cold air nipped at my skin as the blankets fell, and I grabbed the note.

> *Need to take care of some work at The Outpost. Try to take it easy. I should be back this evening.*

I set the piece of paper back on my nightstand. I must have been too tired to wake up when he'd kissed me goodbye.

God, I was sore, the lingering stiffness of whiplash still clinging to my neck and back. I sat there a moment, exhausted and wanting to lie back down and go to sleep, but I couldn't. I needed to get up, needed to do more than just lay in bed all day. I looked at the clock; it was already past noon. I'd nearly slept the day away. I groaned as I forced myself to the edge of the bed. Maybe a hot shower would help ease the soreness in my body. I rose and headed for the bathroom.

The hot water rolled down my body, soothing, but not soothing enough. It wouldn't be. It had been a little over a week since everything happened, so it was no surprise I was still sore. Johnson told me to take it easy for the first five days, but to try to stay mobile after that, to get whatever exercise I could manage. Movement encouraged blood flow, and blood flow encouraged healing.

I turned the faucet, the hot water trickling to a stop. Cold air threatened to invade the warm space as the steam dispersed. A chill danced over my skin, and I stepped out, grabbing a towel to dry myself. I stopped before the vanity, my eyes drifting over my body in the mirror. Bruising painted my body; my left shoulder, along my ribs, my knees. It was beginning to fade, turning more yellow and less black and blue.

My gaze fell to the two bottles of medicine on the counter, no longer hidden from view. I drew a deep breath as I grabbed one. Did these even buy me time anymore? How much time did I have left? I twisted the cap and deposited a pill into my palm before grabbing the other and knocking them both back with a glass of water.

Fresh air would be good. I could go for a walk; I hadn't gone for a walk through the city in a while. Maybe I could stop by Kats, visit her for a bit. I moved to the closet, fishing through my clothes before finding a black sweater and pants. The pants weren't difficult to get on, but when I tried to put my sweater on...

"Shit." I couldn't lift my arm, the limb still weak from the dislocation. Damien had been helping me dress since I'd been released, and this was the first time I'd tried to do it myself. I drew a deep breath. I could figure this out. I used my good arm, slipping my hand downward into the sleeve, then pulled the sleeve up to my shoulder before pulling the sweater over my head. I barely managed to slide my good arm into the other sleeve unaided.

My shoulders sagged in relief, and triumph swelled in my chest that I'd managed it by myself. I eased down onto the bed, feeling a little winded after dressing. Exhaustion clung to me. I hadn't even started walking and I was already tired. I grabbed my phone, determined to get out of the house. I'd been cooped up here since we'd returned from Barrett's funeral a few days ago.

My fingers tapped away at the keyboard, texting Kat.

Hey love. I was going to go for a walk, you home?

I set my phone down beside me and pulled my thick socks on. My toes were freezing in the winter air permeating the space, despite the radiators. I couldn't seem to stay warm on my own. My phone vibrated, and I grabbed it.

I'm home studying. I could actually use a study partner. Anatomy and Physiology's kicking my ass.

I smiled, wondering how exactly I'd be able to help her, but it would be nice to see her face.

I'll head that way.

She responded quickly.

401

You don't want me to come pick you up?

I need the exercise. You study. I'll see you soon.

My phone pinged again.

Ok. See you soon! XO!

I drew a deep breath, building up the courage to leave the house. I looked out the window, the bare maple branches framing my view of the forest behind our house. It was warmer today, clear of snow for the first time in weeks, so it was a perfect day for a walk. I rose from the bed and headed for the door.

The kitchen was empty as I peered inside, so Ethel was gone for the day. How was she holding up? The house felt so empty, too quiet. This kitchen was always filled with life most mornings when the brothers would barge in and drive us nuts. Would we ever have breakfasts like that again? Would we still have shitty movie Sundays if Barrett wasn't there to choose the absolute worst movie he could find? Would it even be the same without him? I lingered in the doorway of the kitchen for a moment, sadness creeping back in, tears blurring my vision. My stomach growled, and I rubbed my eyes, drawing a deep breath. I needed to eat something.

I ruffled through the pantry, made some peanut butter toast, and headed for the door. A walk would be good for me. I needed a change in scenery. I stepped into my boots, tugging them on when they resisted. Thankfully, they still fit my swollen feet. I glanced down the empty hall, feeling unsettled at how lonely it felt to not have anyone to say goodbye to, then grabbed my keys before heading out the door.

Winter air kissed my cheeks as I pulled my coat on, starting with my weak left arm. I shoved my hands into my pockets, drawing a deep breath before heading down the steps of the front porch. The distant sounds of the city reached my ears as I made my way down the sidewalk, mortals going about their lives, unaware of everything happening in the darkness of night, unaware of what lurked in the not-so-distant future. Would this neighborhood be the same after the darklings attacked? My chest tightened as I thought of just how many people would get caught in the crossfire—how many would die? If only I'd been reborn as an immortal; I could've done more, could've made a difference.

I'd barely made it a few blocks when I had to stop and sit to catch my breath. I still had a couple blocks to the incline plane, and a couple miles beyond that before I made it to Kat's. Maybe this was a bad idea. I lifted my head, looking down the road to the incline plane, which would take me down the mountainside into the valley of the city.

"We can do this," I breathed as I hoisted myself up and started toward the overlook at the incline plane.

I realized I hadn't called Damien and pulled my phone from my pocket. It rang once before he answered.

"Hey, sleepyhead," he said, warm and sweet, and I smiled.

"Hey, *mea sol*. Sorry I didn't get to say goodbye when you left."

"You didn't wake when I kissed you goodbye, so I figured you were tired. I know the last week took a toll on you, so don't apologize. You needed the rest." He paused a moment. "Are you okay? You sound out of breath."

God, did I really sound that terrible?

"I went for a walk to get out of the house. I'm walking to Kat's," I said, coming to a stop at the incline plane's ticket window. The attendant greeted me with a warm smile, despite the cold.

"Shit, if I'd have known, I would've left the car for you to take. I can see if I can step away to come get you and take you there," he offered, concern in his voice.

"No, *mea sol*. Don't do that. Your work is too important." I paid the attendant, thanking her before heading onto the platform where the incline plane was already stationed. "Johnson told me to keep moving; it'll be good for me."

"If it gets to be too much and you need a lift, just call. I can send someone."

I smiled, coming to a stop at the railing of the lift as the attendant announced the gates were closing. My eyes drifted over the vast valley before me. "I'll be okay but thank you."

The wind snaked through my hair, and I shrugged my shoulders up to shield my neck from the icy claws raking along my skin. "How are things going at The Outpost?"

He cleared his throat on the other end. "It's going to be a rough transition. We're currently looking for a building to act as the new hub. The Outpost is too far out of town, and patrols have been a mess without The Complex." I could hear the stress in his voice. "Displaced immortals need a safe place to stay as well, but... they're afraid."

I didn't blame them for being afraid. The Complex was viewed as one of the safest places to stay—under the protection of The Order. We'd never expected the darklings to attack the building, and certainly not in such large numbers. A few darklings wouldn't have been an issue: the resident warriors would have made quick work of them. It had been a bold move for Melantha to make, but it had the effect she likely wanted.

The attack left The Order scattered, the immortals shaken.

"Have you had any luck?" I asked as the lift made its slow descent down the mountainside.

"We've found a few old apartment complexes, but they're going to need heavy renovations before we can put one to use." He sighed, and I wished I could be there with him, help him in some way. "I'm sorry I can't be with you today."

The incline plane came to a stop at the base of the mountainside, and I stepped off the lift as the gates opened. "It's okay. I can only imagine how much you have on your plate right now."

The muffled sound of someone talking came through on his end, and he acknowledged them briefly. "I have to go. James has something he needs to show me. I'll see you this evening."

"I can't wait," I said, a smile tugging at my lips.

"I love you, *mea luna*." The way he said it, his voice dripping with adoration and... something else, made my heart squeeze.

"I love you too, *mea sol*."

I slid the phone back into my pocket as I turned down the sidewalk, the sounds of the city filling my ears as I looked to the sky. It was nice today, the clearest it had been in weeks. A lone bird drifted high above, and the sight of it caused worry to resurface.

I prayed Thalia was okay, wherever she was.

The chilled air had permeated my coat and pants by the time I neared my old neighborhood, the cold seeping into my bones. My eyes drifted over the familiar sights: the sidewalks and back streets I'd walked my entire life, the old buildings me and the neighborhood kids got caught breaking in to play hide and seek. Dread crawled across my skin as I neared Matthew Street. The buildings next to The Complex were still standing, the church clock tower still there, visible high above the building blocking my view.

I'd yet to see the remains of The Complex, save what I barely remembered of the news footage. My stomach dipped, and my feet refusing to take another step.

There was truly nothing left but ashes; even the brick had burned to nothing. It had actually been good in the end that it had all burned. There was no evidence, nothing left to endanger our secret. The police had ruled it an arson and never figured out the building had been inhabited.

I pulled my eyes from the remains of what was, forcing my mind elsewhere. I'd passed Kat's road a few blocks back, with the intention of stopping in at the little corner store to get us some drinks and snacks. To everyone else, it was Ciscato's market, but to us, it was Al's. It was a place of memories; my parents took me there to buy penny candy and other treats as a child.

The bell over the door chimed as I approached, my eyes dragging along the sidewalk before me as I tucked my chin in, holding onto what little warmth remained in my jacket.

"Yins drive safe! I'll miss seein' you around here!" the shop owner's voice stretched from deep within the store as someone left.

"Thanks! We'll miss you too!"

I stiffened at the voice that echoed through every treasured memory I held onto, every memory that no longer existed outside of my own mind. I lifted my eyes to find myself standing before my parents, my father holding the door open for my mother.

"Watch your step, babe," Dad said.

"Thanks," she said, a warm smile lacing her voice.

I should move, should get out of sight, but I couldn't bring myself to take another step. My heart hammered as she lifted her gaze... the hazel eyes she'd given me found mine.

Air froze in my lungs, my knees threatening to come out from under me. *Shit.* What should I do? Would this mess up what I'd done to erase their memories? Would she not know who I was? Neither possibility felt better than the other.

"Oh, so sorry. Let me get out of your way," she said, hurrying out of the doorway and to the side as my father headed for the car.

My heart twisted, pain contorting my stomach, as if I'd been stabbed. She didn't know me. We were strangers. My eyes burned, and I blinked, trying to force my composure, trying to look as if I knew them as little as they now knew me.

"It's okay. Thank you." I averted my gaze, heading for the door.

"Wait."

I froze, my hand hovering over the handle, my pulse pounding in my ears as I turned to look back at her.

Her dirty blonde brows scrunched as she took in my face. "I'm sorry. Have we... have we met before?"

My throat tightened, and I forced a friendly smile, tilting my head. "I don't think so."

"Sorry, you... just look so familiar," she said, and I could almost see the gears turning in her mind. I needed to get away from her. I didn't know if it was possible for memories to resurface once they'd been erased.

"We've gotta get on the road, babe," my father called from the car.

She perked up, glancing back at him. "Coming!" She turned to me again. "Sorry, I didn't mean to sound weird. You have a good day."

"You too," I said, watching her turn and leave.

Something chipped away inside me as she climbed into the passenger side. They looked so happy, unweighted by struggles... By me. Their car pulled away, and I watched them disappear down the road.

It was better this way.

***

"Come in!"

I opened Kat's door, what little energy I'd had this morning sapped from me. Would I be any help to her in this state? Either way, I needed to talk to her. I still hadn't told her about my heart attack.

Her head popped out of the kitchen doorway, her coppery hair tied up in a loose bun. "Oooo! What did you bring me?"

I chuckled at her enthusiasm at the sight of the bag in my hand. I kicked my boots off, shrugging out of my jacket before heading down the hallway toward her. "I figured if I'm helping you study, I might as well bring snacks."

She wandered over, fern-green eyes glittering as she watched me unbag her favorite drink among the assortment of other snacks. The moment I pulled out the plastic case containing her favorite treat, she beamed.

"You got Gobs?" she nearly shrieked. "You know me too well!"

I snickered, watching as she grabbed a cake from the packaging.

"How are your parents settling into their new home? Did they find the arsonist?" she asked through a mouthful of the chocolate cake.

I swallowed, shoving down the agony those words brought to the surface. My mom not knowing who I was almost too much to bear.

"They're settling in well." The lie slid off my tongue all too easily. Had I become so well acquainted with lying now? God, my stomach twisted at the thought. It was only temporary. Cody would tell her everything, and I could finally be open with her about it all. "I haven't heard anything from the detectives, though. There was no evidence to point them in any direction, so they're probably going to close the case."

"I wonder if it's the same one who burned down that building on Short Street," she said as she took another bite.

I forced my face to remain unresponsive to the thought of the building I'd watched burn, the life that had been lost with it.

"What're you making?" I asked, noticing the stove was on and eager to change the subject.

"I didn't know you were gonna bring snacks, so I made us brownies! I need chocolate to fuel this brain."

I chuckled as I settled into the chair and rubbed my eyes. God, I was so tired.

"You okay?" she asked, copper brows scrunching.

I forced a smile. "Just tired."

"You look a bit pale," she said, taking the seat next to me. When she began to scrutinize me further, narrowing her eyes as she cocked her head. She knew something was up.

I sighed. "I... had another heart attack."

The color drained from her face, her lips parting, and the words poured from her mouth. "Oh my God. Are you okay? Are you *gonna* be okay? What're the doctors saying?"

"I—" I wanted to tell her yes, wanted to tell her I would be fine, but I couldn't. "I don't know."

She swallowed.

"I'm sorry. I didn't want to ruin the visit."

"You didn't," she assured me, and she drew a sharp breath. "Shit. Should you have walked all the way here? You should've let me pick you up!"

"I needed to get out and stretch my feet. Besides, I'm only a couple miles away. I've been in bed most of the week, and the exercise is good for me. I might have you drive me home though. I don't think I could make the trip back."

"Of course!"

"So, you needed help studying, right?"

She nodded, shoving the last bite into her mouth as she stood. "Come on, I've got my stuff in the living room."

My eyes fell on the flashcards scattered across the coffee table.

"I've got a big test tomorrow, so if you could just quiz me, that'd be great."

I settled into the couch and began gathering the flashcards. "Alright, let's get to work then."

We spent the next hour and a half going over muscles, the skeletal system, and the circulatory system. I peered at Kat from behind the stack of flashcards in my hand as she sat on the nearby loveseat. God, how could there be so many different names for different sections of one vein in your body? I didn't know how she absorbed all this. There was so much. This was the exact reason why I'd never gone into the medical field.

"Which group of muscles lift the leg at the hip?" I asked.

"Hip flexor?"

"Yep," I said, setting the flashcard face down in the stack. Before I could ask the next question, Kat spoke.

"Cody's been acting weird lately."

I frowned, lifting my eyes to her. "What do you mean?"

"I don't know. He's been like... secretive and nervous, but not in the cheating sort of way. I don't know how to explain it. I think he's going to propose or something,"

I bit my lip. Was he going to propose, or was he going to tell her he was immortal? Damien said he was going to reveal everything to her at some point. A combination of emotions bloomed in my chest, causing my heart to race: excitement, unease, fear. How would she react?

I shrugged. "I haven't talked to him in a while. He hasn't mentioned anything to me."

She chewed the inside of her lip, as if that statement disappointed her. "I was hoping he'd reach out to you to help him pick out a ring."

I blinked. "Wait, are you saying you'd say yes? You guys have only been together for like what, five months?"

"Honestly?" She went quiet for a moment, as if she couldn't believe she was admitting it. "I think I would. I don't know what it is, but it just feels... right. I never get tired of seeing his face, even when he's annoying me. I've never felt like this with any other guy I've dated. I'm just... drawn to him."

Her admission had me contemplating something: was the mating bond only limited to immortals? Could immortals find the other half of their soul in a mortal? It was heartbreaking to imagine, but the way she described it, it was very similar to what I felt for Damien. I couldn't talk to her about this stuff, though, which only frustrated me.

"You better call me the second he does." It was all I could think to say.

She tilted her head, as if pondering that notion. "Nah, I'll probably call Jessica and tell her first."

I threw my half-empty water bottle at her, and she snickered. "Shut up! You haven't talked to her since high school when she hit on your boyfriend."

She burst out laughing, throwing the bottle back at me. "Bitch, of course I'm gonna call you first!"

"Okay, no more distractions. You have a big test tomorrow." I grabbed the stack of flashcards I'd set aside and read off the next question.

I hoped Cody told her, and I prayed she took the news well, that she'd accept him. There was so much I wanted to talk to her about, wanted to show her. I wouldn't have to erase her memories. I could keep her in my life. I just hoped he'd do it sooner rather than later.

Before I ran out of time.

CHAPTER 53

DAMIEN

I pulled my coat on as I stepped out of the main building of The Outpost and into the training yard. The echoes of warriors barking instructions and the grunts of sparring filled my ears. More initiates had joined The Order over the last few weeks, each house sending more with each day, and it was a relief to see everyone coming together to help. They were training harder than ever, picking up extra shifts. Even those who couldn't fight were offering up their services to help in any way they could. I was afraid the attack on The Complex would break their spirits, but it seemed to have lit a fire within them.

You're still driving them forward, Barrett.

It wasn't the same here without him. I'd never thought I'd miss his annoying taunts, and I'd give anything to hear him crack a joke at Cas and make her cheeks redden, to see him hop over the bar at Stokers and drive Semele and Eiko crazy mixing his own drinks. Melantha may have failed in breaking us, but she'd taken something, taken a part of us, and we'd never be the same.

"Ah'm gunna go check oot eh buildin' we discussed, see 'ow much work it'll take tae mek it secure," James said as he slid his laptop case over his shoulder.

I nodded. "Keep me updated. I'm going to head home, try to spend some time with Cas."

He halted at the mention of her. "'Ow's she doin'?"

Everyone knew she'd been seriously injured, but only our inner circle knew the full extent of what she'd suffered. "She's doing okay. Went for a walk to Kat's house to get some exercise and fresh air."

I sounded optimistic, but unease remained anchored in my gut. She'd been exhausted, her body using every bit of energy to heal itself. The exhaustion in her eyes, though… it was an exhaustion that went beyond her injuries. I feared her body was waning, that I was running out of time.

"Mibbe we'll all get together fer breakfast when she's feelin' up tae it. Ah'm sure she's no' happy aboot stayin' home," he said, patting my shoulder.

She hadn't been. She hated that she couldn't be here helping the recruits train or go on patrols anymore. Sasha, Liam, and Zach asked about her every day, eager for her to work with them again, always understanding of how long it would take for her to heal, excited to see her back when she fully recovered.

But I feared she might not be able to return to training even after her healing was done.

"Ah'll see ye later," James said, and I waved as he left.

I shoved my hands into my coat pocket as I headed for my car, the few warriors who took notice of me dipping their heads in a quick bow as I passed.

"Lord Damien!" Aurelia's tiny voice startled me, and I stopped, turning as she ran for me.

I smiled, kneeling to her level. "Helping your mom train today?"

She nodded, her round cheeks flushed with the cold. "I wanted to give you this."

I frowned as she placed a cord of brightly colored braided thread in my palm. "What's this for?"

"They have lots, but I thought they might like the colors," she said as her eyes danced over the colorful threads.

I opened my mouth to question her, but Lydia called from across the yard. "Aurelia! It's time to go!"

"I've gotta go. Tell Lucia I said hi!" Aurelia said and took off before I could stop her.

My eyes fell to the braid in my hand. Who had she spoken of, and why did she call Cassie Lucia? Maybe it was one of the games she always played. I slid the braid into my pocket and continued toward my car.

The sun was already sinking behind the mountains. Cas should be home by now, and I realized she hadn't called for a ride. Had she walked home? I pulled my phone from my pocket to find that she'd texted me at some point, but I hadn't heard the notification.

> Kat gave me a ride home. I hope things are going good at The Outpost. I love you, mea sol.

Guilt slammed into me at the thought that I'd left her hanging. Gods, she'd sent it over an hour ago. I would've been deep in conversation with the accountant and the agent discussing the new complex, going over the finances and what repairs were needed. I quickly texted her back before slipping my phone into my pocket and getting into the car.

> Sorry I missed your text. I love you too, mea luna. I'm heading home now.

Trees blurred by as I drove through the dense forest surrounding The Outpost. I couldn't help but linger on thoughts of Thalia at the sight of them. I remembered the guilt on Vincent's face when he'd returned without her. He'd been taking Barrett's loss hard. It was no surprise; Vincent and Barrett did nearly everything together, had been inseparable for as long as I could remember. Vincent had even tried sneaking into training from time to time during Barrett's recruitment when he was still too young, before his settling. The cousins always seemed to get into trouble together, always had each other's backs even when they got on each other's nerves. Vincent was lost without him, and if it weren't for Anna, I feared what he might've done in his grief.

There had been no word from the scouts I'd sent out this morning to search for Thalia, which meant there was still no sign of her. A team had gone out every day, but the valley was massive, the forests endless, and she could be anywhere. Despite the melted snow, they hadn't been able to pick up on any tracks, any scent, and her apartment still remained untouched. I feared the worst.

By the time I pulled into the driveway, the sun had set. I checked my phone as I stepped out of the car. Cassie hadn't responded, and it seemed Ethel had finished her work for the day, her car gone. Most of the lights were off, but I could see the warm glow of the living room fireplace through the bay window.

The house was quiet as I opened the door and stepped inside. Was she in her study drawing? Reading?

"Cas?" I called as I hung my coat on the rack.

There was no response. I rubbed my hands together, warming them up as I headed down the hall. My heart dipped at the silence that answered. Was she ok? I grew dizzy, my mouth going dry as my mind wandered to the worst possibilities. She'd been home alone. How long ago had Ethel left?

"Cas?" I repeated as I entered the doorway to the living room. I could just barely make out the chestnut hair peeking over the top of the cushion. I rounded the couch, and relief washed over me.

She was curled up in a blanket, her head tilted to the side against the back of the couch, resting on her fist. A book laid her lap, open to the page she'd been reading before she fell asleep.

Asleep when I left this morning, and asleep when I got home tonight. My heart ached that I hadn't gotten to look into those beautiful hazel eyes today, but I wouldn't wake her.

I caught sight of her bookmark resting on the cushion next to her, so I grabbed it and placed it in her book before setting it aside for her to find tomorrow. Her face was so peaceful, her blush lips parting ever so slightly. I wanted to see her smile, see the flash of those teeth when that infectious grin would spread across her face. I lifted a stray curl, just basking in the sight of her for a moment, my heart swelling.

More time. I needed more time. There had to be a way to save her. I didn't care what it took. I wouldn't lose her again. I shifted, gently easing my hands under her, lifting her into my arms. She didn't wake, but the sweet sound she made as she curled into me was enough to make me weak.

My weakness. My strength. *"Mea luna,"* I whispered against her hair before pressing a kiss to the top of her head. Her skin was cold, despite the fire and the blanket. I hated how cold she felt. A smile tugged at her lips as she curled against me, a groan of relief slipping from her throat as she soaked up my warmth.

I smiled, heading down the hall and up the stairs to tuck her into bed. The wood floors threatened to creak beneath my feet, so I took them slowly, trying to be as quiet as possible. The radiator was already working hard to warm our room as I nudged the door open.

I eased her onto the bed and pulled the blankets over her. She melted into the pillow, shifting onto her side as she always did in her sleep. I wanted to climb into bed beside her, pull her against me, breathe in her scent. There was no time, though. There was something I needed to do.

"I'll be back," I whispered as I laid one final kiss to her forehead before turning to leave. I stole one final glance at her sweet face before I flipped the light switch and slipped through the door, heading back downstairs.

There had to be a way to save her, a way to heal her. Selene may not be able to do it, but surely someone else could. Darkness greeted me as I descended the stairs to the basement. As I reached the base of the stairs, I willed the candles to light in the Propylaea, the blue flames came to life around the altar.

Selene would give me answers, or I'd find someone who could.

I lowered to my knees before the altar, closing my eyes. The stone alter rippled with power as I stretched out my senses, energy cut across the veil, forming the gateway, and I reached out to it. Darkness descended around me, swallowing me whole until I was no longer part of the Mortalrealm.

Cold marble welcomed my knees as I settled onto the floor of Selene's chambers. It was oddly quiet, and when my eyes opened, the room felt almost darker than normal. My gaze swept over the dimós trees lining the chambers. Perhaps I was just imagining it, but they seemed... dull, not as bright. I shook my head.

I've got more important things to worry about.

I found Selene curled up on her altar, her silken white hair draped over her body, spilling over the edges and pooling on the floor of the dais. She was speaking to the stone horse at her side.

"I'm sorry I can't let you out to run, Arion..." Her hand halted against the stone warhorse and her voice faded as she noticed my presence, and she turned those opalescent eyes to me.

"What is the nature of your visit, warrior?" she asked, her melodic voice dancing across the stone chambers. "I was not expecting you."

"Tell me how to save Cassie," I demanded as I rose to my feet and approached her.

She stiffened at my words. "I've already told you; I cannot help Moi—"

"Then tell me who can," I insisted, and she cocked her head, blinking at me. I knew it was rare for someone to cut her off, if ever. I no longer cared, though, irritation pushing away any sense of self preservation. I didn't want to resort to it. It would be my final option, but if there was no other means of saving her... I'd choose her life over mine.

"I will pretend I did not hear you give me an order," she said, straightening as her opalescent eyes narrowed on me. Those same eyes that were once bright and kind flashed across my mind, and I hated that she'd become so cold.

"Pretend all you like. I'm done watching you act like her life doesn't matter," I said through gritted teeth. The blue flames dancing in the sconces flickered, and the starlit sky trapped in the ceiling dimmed to near darkness.

Her jaw clenched, eyes sharpening. "Watch your tongue, warrior."

"Or you'll do what? Kill me?" I challenged, stopping at the foot of the dais. "Do it, Selene! Kill me! If that's the only way to save her then do it! I'll die so she can live!"

She hesitated, conflict flitting across her face. "I would prefer not to do that, Damien."

"She's dying, Selene!" I yelled, and I nearly faltered at what I'd said. My voice broke as I spoke again, the air painful in my lungs. "She's... she's dying."

That single admission broke something in me. She was dying, and there was no option I could find to save her without ripping her heart out, without sentencing her to the endless suffering I'd been subjected to for centuries.

Selene's eyes fell from me, and my irritation smoldered in my veins, my teeth grinding against one another. "Will you just sit back and watch her die *again*? Does she mean nothing to you?"

"I cannot interfere," she muttered, her eyes still downcast.

"She's your daughter!"

She stiffened, the harshness marring her delicate face faltering for a moment. "I told you, Damien..."

She pushed herself down from the altar, and my thoughts halted. She'd always glided down from the dais. When she lifted her eyes to me, exhaustion clouded her eyes, and her skin didn't glow as brightly.

The inner corners of her white brows curved upward as she stopped at the top stair. "My hands are tied, Damien. I cannot help her. If I change her, and the twelve sentence me to oblivion..."

"So your life is more important than hers?" She flinched at my words and my brows furrowed. "I guess the only value she holds to you is how effective she is at destroying the darklings. Is that it?" Her lips parted, but she remained silent. "Are you just waiting for her to reincarnate into a form more suitable for you?"

She didn't respond, eyes flickering from me.

"Did the twelve promise to release you from your imprisonment on the far moon if you put an end to the darklings' chaos? Is that what all this is? Is that all we're good for?"

She didn't answer still, and my chest heaved, irritation turning into fury. "Well, maybe she's not important to you, Selene, but she's everything to me! You may not be willing to, but if it meant dying for her, I'd do it, and I will."

Pain flashed across her face. "It's not what you think, Dami—"

"Then send me to The Fates," I demanded, teeth bared. "Perhaps *they* will be of more use to me than you are."

CHAPTER 54

DAMIEN

Use this stone to call me when you're ready to return.

Selene's voice rippled through my mind as I took one final look at the far moon where I'd just been moments before at her temple. It was one of two massive moons that lit up the night sky—two moons for two moon goddesses. I'd been told stories as a child that there was a third moon, for a third goddess, Hecate—a dark moon, one you couldn't see. Whether it actually existed or not, I didn't know.

The stone was cold in my hand as I gripped it, the icy surface unaffected by my warmth. I couldn't lose this; I didn't have the ability to pass the stretch of distance between Elythia and Selene's moon through the shadows—I'd be stranded. I pushed the stone into my coat pocket and lowered my gaze from the night sky.

Rolling hills stretched out for miles around me, no sign of any cities nearby. I wondered if Zeus had noticed my presence. Would he come for me? The Fates resided in his domain, but they didn't answer to him. They answered to no one, so maybe he wouldn't interfere with my visit. There was no time to waste, regardless. I couldn't risk the delay. Time was running out.

I turned my gaze to the massive building before me. It wasn't a complex structure of towers and great halls like many of the other castles I'd visited in the Godsrealm, but the carvings in the stone were the most intricate I'd ever seen. I'd never visited the Fates, had never seen the stunning stained-glass windows framed out in carved stone pillars glowing in the darkness of night. The arched windows stretched up hundreds of feet, and I wondered just how big it was inside.

With each stone step, unease sank further and further into the pit of my stomach. Would the Fates be willing to help me, or would they turn me away? How difficult would it be to find them? Or would they find me first? Would they already know I'd come long before I decided to? I didn't have time to dwell on the possibilities. Either they'd give me answers to save Cassie's life or they'd end me for barging in uninvited.

Either way, she would live.

I steeled my nerves, stepping toward the massive glass doors. Before I could touch them, they opened, groaning as if they hadn't been opened in years. I halted, looking for any sign of guards or beasts, but nothing appeared, the only scent the nearby rolling meadows.

A whisper brushed against the back of my neck, too quiet for me to understand, but it pushed me forward. I gave in, stepping through the door.

Elythian magic was nothing short of amazing, the very walls seemed to be alive. Massive stained-glass windows stood before me, but they weren't like those of the Mortalrealm. No, the scenes before me breathed with life, each window depicting events across the history of Elythia, our continent within the Godsrealm, as if it were happening before my eyes. The inside of the Fates' castle was a spiral of staircases, crossing and intersecting, ascending all the way to the ceiling and descending far below the surface. I peered over the railing. It seemed to tunnel downward forever.

Gods, how the hell would I find them in all this?

That whisper brushed over my shoulder, winding down my arm until it tugged at my hand.

Down.

My stomach dipped, old magic leaving goosebumps on my flesh. Was this the Fates guiding me to them? Or trickery? I hesitated a moment, unsure if I should follow, but I had no other choice. I didn't know where they could possibly be, so I followed that soft whisper of power.

The stairs spiraled downward, on and on. I passed a scene of a black castle on a mountainside surrounded by death, life sprouting as gardens breaking from the ground overtook the dark castle, casting a domain that appeared once lifeless in an endless sea of blossoms and greenery.

I passed another glass scene. The image captured the motion of countless warriors charging for one another, Gods clashing in the skies above, a few falling to the earth below, never to get back up again. I frowned, looking to the one God falling from the sky, his form standing out from the rest. He was powerful, his battled scarred skin the color of a crimson sunset, as if war was woven into his very being. Ares?

My eyes continued over the scene, finding countless fae, immortals, and beasts, forever etched in glass moments from destroying each other. Was this the Godswar? My parents had fought in that war. I'd had nightmares of it as a child from the stories alone.

There were other moments in history, ones I didn't recognize, unsure of when they'd occurred, such as one depicting a male and a siren reaching out to each other, the male cloaked in black garbs that nearly resembled the armor we immortals used to wear.

Another scene held my attention for a time. It was a female, an elf from the looks of the delicate points of her long ears. Her silken silver hair glowed against her black cloak, a pair of massive moons hanging high in the night sky behind her. The glass captured her mid-leap as she descended on a person below, their back turned to her, her dagger lifted and prepared to strike. I frowned. There was something different about this pair of moons. One was damaged, another embedded into it as if they'd collided, the mist of moon debris lingering around the point of impact.

The whisper of power urged me on, and I gave in.

I continued down the seemingly endless spiral of stairs. The stairway split into three paths, and I hesitated. I let slip an irritated sigh. Gods, I didn't have time to navigate a maze. This was why I hated visiting this realm; everything seemed to be a game to the Elythians, something to entertain them in their boredom.

My eyes drifted to the left, and something drew my attention in the distance, a singular stained-glass depiction. It was darker than the rest, as if the glow didn't light this window as it did the others. I wandered toward it, and that whisper returned, beckoning me away from the dimmed glass. Did it not want me to see it?

The closer I grew, the more that whisper beckoned me away. I pushed past it, and something icy crawled over my skin with each step, as if my body understood what the glass before me revealed.

Horror was woven into the very glass itself—true horror and dread. Cascading down the center of the image was what appeared to be a glittering wall. The wall seemed alive with magic, thriving where it was still intact, but it was shattering into pieces, darkness descending where it fell. On either side of the crumbling wall, the earth was ripping apart, castles and structures crumbling, the inhabitants screaming as they ran for safety where none was to be had. Gods, what was I looking at?

This way...

That whisper returned, more powerful, and I turned, expecting to find someone, but I was alone. I glanced back at the scene, to the horror-filled faces of the humans, fae, and other creatures on either side of the wall. Every instinct came to life, telling me to get away, the terror trapped in time seeping into my bones.

Come...

I listened, letting it guide me back toward the staircase. I couldn't dwell on... whatever the hell it was I'd seen. Cassie didn't have much time, and I needed answers.

The stairway stretched on endlessly, and I grew tired of the countless steps, the windows growing dimmer and dimmer, until I reached a point where the glass seemed void of any scenes. That whisper tugged at my arm again, and I turned from the empty glass. I assumed they were moments in time that had yet to be determined. I halted as a pair of doors appeared before me. My eyes darted around; there had been stairs spiraling farther down just moments ago. Gods-damned Elythians and their magic; had they sent me on a wild goose chase? Had they been delaying me?

This way...

I drew a deep breath, staunching the irritation growing in me. I had no interest in these games, but I knew I'd get nowhere if I didn't play nice. The doors parted, and I stepped through, wondering just what awaited me.

420

The room looked nothing like the rest of the building. There was no glass, no color. The stone was carved just as intricately, the pillars and walls stretching up to the dome high above. It wasn't the lack of glass or the stone that left me speechless—it was the towering nearly fossilized dead trees growing into the walls, stretching hundreds of feet to the dome above. Countless threads were woven in a web across the massive chamber, crossing and overlapping in every direction, some intertwined in the branches of the trees.

The threads of fate.

"He comes, sisters," a soft, melodic voice echoed before me, near dripping with excitement. I turned my gaze to the center of the room where every thread intersected like a web, to find three females.

"Approach, Lord of Shadows," one of them said from where she sat on a golden framed chaise, the voice just as soft and melodic, but far calmer than the first, proper and refined.

I hesitated, wary. Were these the Fates? I'd been told horror stories as a child of three crones, misshapen and deformed, ancient beings who would string up and eat unwelcome trespassers. These were no old crones, creatures so deformed and decrepit that they could scarcely be considered Elythians. Before me were three beautiful females, identical in every way. Their hair fell in ashen blonde waves down their backs, complex braids woven through their loose curls. Bangs dusted large eyes that were almost the same color as their hair, their skin a grayish tone.

One stood at a small table, giggling as she poured something into a goblet. "I think he is unsure of us, sisters."

"We are not the creatures of your nursemaid's tales, Lord of Shadows." This voice was different. While the other two were a strange opposition of cheery and childish, proper and level, this one was... somber, sad even. She lifted her sorrowful eyes to me from behind the proper one, whose hair she was braiding. A glint caught my eyes, and I noticed a pair of golden scissors tucked into her braids. "We will not eat you."

It felt like an invasion, her words reigniting those very tales my nursemaid *had* told me as a child.

"You're too cute to eat." The cheerful one giggled once more, taking a sip of the goblet before setting it down. "No, I could think of far more entertaining things to do with you."

I ignored the comment as her eyes roamed over me.

The cheerful one stiffened at the table as her gaze snapped to me, eyes lighting with something I couldn't place. "You have a gift for us."

I blinked. "What?"

"A gift," the somber one said, her sad eyes roaming down my body. "In your pocket."

What were they talking about? I reached into my coat and froze. *They have lots, but I thought they might like the colors.*

Aurelia's words danced across my thoughts as I pulled the braid she'd given me just hours before from my pocket. My gaze fell to the cord resting in my palm, and I looked up to the countless threads intertwining above us. Any words I might have said halted on my tongue as my mind spiraled. How could Aurelia have known I'd come here tonight? I hadn't even known myself until I'd spoken with Selene.

"Oh, it's so colorful," the cheerful one said, and I jerked back as she appeared before me, eyes locked on the colorful braid. She took it from my hand, reappearing next to the chaise, whispering to her sisters. "It is her, sisters."

"You know Aurelia?" I asked. Gods, I was such an idiot. Of course they knew her.

"The fallen star made flesh again," the refined one said as she took the cord, inspecting the threads. "A child just as unnatural as Moira."

Unnatural? I stepped forward, opening my mouth to question further.

"You're late," the refined one said, ending the conversation that had barely begun as she set the braided cord in her lap. She leveled her gaze on me, as if I'd disappointed her.

I wanted to ask more, wanted to know what they knew about Aurelia, but time was limited. The cheerful one's eyes glittered as if hoping I'd ask a question.

"I didn't know I had an appointment," I said flatly.

"Oh, we've waited for you for centuries," the cheerful one said, glancing to her sisters. Their demeanors seemed to be the only way I would be able to tell these three apart.

"Then you know what I've come for."

"Of course—wait." The cheerful one glanced at her sisters again. "Is this the timeline where he asks for help with saving Moira, or the timeline where he seeks to aid the assassin—"

"You speak too openly, Clotho," the refined one said, lifting her chin as the one at her back continued to braid her hair. "He knows nothing, and it must remain that way. We cannot intercede."

Assassin? I tried not to linger on her words, but what did they mean by timelines? Did they not know what date it was?

423

"You're no fun, Lachesis." The cheerful one, Clotho, pouted, crossing her arms.

"And you're too cheerful, Clotho," the somber one said, her tone level and somber.

"Well, life is too short to be so down, Atropos," Clotho sneered, but it was more of a tease than actual anger. Their antics were dizzying, bickering like children, and wasting my time. These three were what determined our fates? Gods, no wonder the realms were in chaos.

"I've come to ask for help in finding a way to save Cassie," I said, interrupting their conversation, trying not to think too deeply into their nonsense.

The three fates turned their gazes on me, and the threads above us seemed to hum with power. I stared back, refusing to back down.

"The fated child..." Lachesis, the proper one, who seemed to be the most level-headed one here said. She stared down her nose at me from her chaise. Atropos, the somber one, let the last braid slip from her hand before pushing herself up.

I frowned. Fated child? What the hell was she talking about?

"It is best she die," Atropos said, a deep sadness lacing her voice, as if she was mourning the thought.

My heart lurched. "Why? She's done nothin—"

"Wrong?" Clotho finished all too cheerfully. "Moira's reincarnation will bring about the death of millions of innocents."

I froze. "Cassie would never—"

"And yet she will," Lachesis stated. "The balance has been disturbed thanks to Selene's intervention in Moira's death. Her existence is unnatural."

"So, you will let her die..." I scoffed, looking between the three. "Because of something you *think* will happen."

Clotho looked at me. "It will happen. The foundation has been laid; it *will* happen if she lives."

"One life against millions, Lord of Shadows. Would you condemn so many for the life of your mate?" Lachesis inquired. The way she said it sounded almost like a test.

"There are many things I would not hesitate to do for my mate." I said through gritted teeth. "Regardless, I would not condemn her for something that hasn't happened, for something that hasn't even been set in motion yet."

"The wheels are already turning, shadows creeping in the background, chaos churning," Atropos said, her voice flat, her attention suddenly fixated on a thread. She lifted her hand to the golden scissors in her hair.

"You're going to cut a mortal thread while we have a guest?" Clotho asked Atropos, as if it were a rude gesture.

"It is her time," Atropos said absentmindedly, reaching for the thread.

I stiffened, and my heart stuttered. A mortal's thread? Gods, please no. "Wai—"

"Do not fear, Lord of Shadows. It is not hers," Clotho said, passing a smile in my direction. The threads hummed again, a low rumble settling into the concrete beneath my feet, and I stumbled back, eyes falling downward.

"Her power is waning," Lachesis said to Clotho, her voice echoing off the stone walls and trees, gray eyes near glowing.

"It weakens with each reincarnation," Clotho continued, her eyes doing the same as Lachesis.

"If she dies, the chain will be broken," Atropos finished, glowing eyes fixated on the thread just out of her grasp as she inched closer to it.

My eyes flitted between them, my world threatening to cave in on itself. What were they saying? Would Cassie not return if I couldn't save her? Time had stretched longer than it should've before she'd reawakened after Lucia. Was that the reason? Was the chain of reincarnation failing?

"If she dies, she won't be reincarnated?" I asked, taking a step toward them.

"She wouldn't be able to tell you," Lachesis said, turning her near glowing gaze to me, her gray skin glittering. "Bound to secrecy."

"Silence was her cost," Atropos continued, as if they were one mind. She slid the thread between the outstretched blades of her golden scissors. "For the sin she committed."

"Whose cost? How can I stop it? Please tell me," I begged, looking between them.

Clotho settled into the chaise, lowering her head to rest on Lachesis' lap, her ashen blonde hair spilling out over the edge. "We cannot interfere."

"We can only watch," Lachesis continued.

"The cataclysm will come if Moira lives," Atropos said solemnly, and the snip of her scissors echoed throughout the chamber as she cut.

425

CHAPTER 55

CASSIE

It had been nearly two weeks since Thalia disappeared, and we still hadn't found her. God, I missed her, missed talking to her, hearing her jokes, I missed... watching her and Barrett tease each other. Damien hadn't verbalized it, but I knew he feared whether she was still alive as much as I did.

I almost ended it many times.

Damien's words rippled through my mind. He'd told me how badly it affected their kind when their true soul mate passed, that his own grief from my loss had pushed him to an end he could never attain due to Selene's curse. I'd been dead, so he'd been stuck in life. I couldn't let myself think it, couldn't bear to imagine the possibility that he could have...

Damien's hand brushed against mine, jolting me back to reality, and I realized I'd begun to drift off at the dining table. I lifted my eyes to him, finding the weak smile he offered, but I couldn't miss the concern in his eyes. I was worrying him again. I returned his smile, gently squeezing his hand.

"I'm okay. Just a little tired," I whispered, answering the question in his eyes.

"Ye shuid come see eh new complex, Cas." James said between bites of his eggs and bacon. "It's massive. Renovations ur startin' next week so it's a bit o' a mess right noo, but its gonnae look amazin' once its finished."

"Donnae talk wit yer mouth full, James," Ethel chastised, and I giggled.

"I'd love to see it," I said.

I noticed Zephyr's gaze flicker to my untouched plate. His lips parted, but he didn't speak. I should eat something, but I was so tired, my stomach not latching onto the aroma of the food before me. I swallowed, my stomach flipping at the thought of taking a bite, but I grabbed my fork and speared a bit of scrambled egg before lifting it to my mouth.

"How's Anna doing?" I asked, lifting my eyes to Vincent across the table. It was so nice to see his face. It was the first time in over a week I'd had the energy to see them all.

"She's on bedrest. We're down to the last several weeks," he said, and the light shining in his eyes was like a breath of fresh air. I'd been so worried about him.

"She's already tired of sitting still," Vincent said with a chuckle. "I keep catching her sneaking out of bed."

"Have you decided on a name?" I asked.

"We haven't settled on one yet."

I felt like I'd missed out on so much in the last two weeks. Damien kept me updated on things at The Outpost, told me when my recruits asked about me. I missed Sasha, Liam, and Zach, missed their antics and troublemaking. I wondered how their training was going. Was Aurelia still going to training with Lydia? I missed her sweet face, her voice. Maybe I could go to The Outpost with Damien soon, even if only to visit.

"How is planning for the binding ceremony going?" I asked Zephyr.

427

He seemed caught off guard by the question, and the guilt that danced across his face confused me. "We're thinking of postponing it."

My heart dipped. "Why?"

"Calista and I were afraid that, with… everything that's happened, it just isn't a good time," Zephyr explained.

I opened my mouth to speak, but hesitated. Damien looked at Zephyr. "You shouldn't."

Zephyr's eyes jumped to Damien, and I was glad to see I wasn't the only one thinking it.

"If anything, we need positivity right now, Zephyr," I admitted.

His pale green eyes drifted over me, and it seemed as if he almost didn't believe me.

"I agree with Cas and Damien," Vincent added, and my heart squeezed. While I knew his hands had been full and his mind occupied with thoughts of Anna and their young, the wounds he held were still far too fresh.

"Barrett…" It hurt to say his name, but I continued. "Barrett would have wanted you guys to be bound as soon as you could. He'd want you to be happy."

Zephyr's eyes wavered, his fork lingering in his hand. "I'll talk to Calista about it. We were originally going to hold it in two weeks, I just…"

I reached out to take his hand, and his eyes rose to mine.

It hurt to admit it, but it was something I knew all too well by now. "Don't hesitate, Zephyr. You guys deserve to be happy. Don't live to regret it."

"Are you sure you'll be good here, *mea luna*?" Damien asked as we stepped through the entrance to the Archivallia. The little librarians immediately took notice of me, their starlight eyes gleaming as they greeted me.

"I'll be okay, *mea sol*."

I'd gotten a bit more energy after breakfast and I was excited to really explore the Archivallia. Damien hated leaving me alone at the house while he oversaw the countless responsibilities that had piled up in recent weeks, and I'd hated being cooped up. This seemed like a good way to alleviate some of that.

"I'll be gone a few hours at least, probably more. James and I are meeting with the subcontractors at the new complex, and then I have to meet with Xander to go over paperwork on new recruits. Salwa is here somewhere, so if you need to go early, just ask her. She can bring you home anytime."

I smiled. "You're doting again."

A warm smile tugged at his lips; a genuine one, not one of concern or worry. "I love doting on you."

I giggled, the sight of his smile warming my heart, and I pushed myself up on my toes to press my lips to his. His arms swept around me, pulling me against him as he deepened the kiss, his scent fanning out over my skin. I'd never tire of it.

"I love you," he whispered, leaning his head against mine as he held me.

"I love you too, *mea sol*. Now go, you'll be late."

He reluctantly released me and pressed another kiss to my knuckles before heading back through the archway.

A tiny hand tugged at my loose joggers, and I looked down to find one of the astral sprites beckoning for my attention. I crouched down to its level.

"Hello to you, too," I said warmly.

It pointed off down the aisle between the towering bookshelves, and a whisper brushed against my thoughts. I frowned, blinking down at the creature.

You used to communicate with them somehow.

Damien had told me that, but how? The creature lifted its eyes to me, and I held out my hand. Its tiny claws settled onto my fingertips, and that whisper danced through my mind again, like a feather drifting on the breeze. I reached out, tethering my thoughts to it.

The creature spoke to me, but it was soft, like a mouse. It was strange how they communicated. Their speech didn't fully sound like actual words, more like intentions, their wishes and wills. Yet I somehow understood them now, or I guess... again.

"I wanted to read, but nothing's in my language. Is there a way you can help me read Elythian?" I asked.

Another sprite tugged at my shirt from the other side, and I held out my hand, its response resounding and bright. How exactly did their magic work? The feelings flowing through my skin where the sprites touched me were so warm, so positive in their response to help me read a language I knew nothing about.

Where did I even begin? There were countless books within these chambers, the shelves reaching high to the ceiling where stars sparkled amidst the pitch night sky. I noticed the lanterns were resting on the shelves, on the floors around them. They'd been floating the last time I'd come here... hadn't they?

I hoisted myself to my feet, groaning at the energy it took. God, I hated this.

A glint of gold caught my attention, and my eyes drifted over the illuminated glass case I'd seen my first time here. The three books lay within it, old and worn, and I wondered what they contained.

The sprites skittered alongside me as I drifted toward the case. The three books varied in color, the leather-bound covers dulled with age. Just how old were these books? I lifted the lid and dipped my hand inside, running my fingers over the text imprinted in the worn leather.

The Book of Lucia.

My hand recoiled as the words cascaded across my thoughts. I looked down to the sprite at my side, its tiny claws still holding onto my hand. I looked back to the books, reaching out to touch the next one.

The Book of Elena.

These books were about my past lives, but how did I know that? The sprites chittered at my side, starlight twinkling in the shadows of their bodies.

I reached out, running my finger over the engraved text on the third book, an imprint of what looked like a moth embossed in the leather. It almost resembled a lunar moth from the mortal realm, but... different.

"The Book of Moira," I whispered, the thoughts spilling from my lips as they echoed across my mind.

I wanted to read Moira's book, wanted to connect with those lost memories, but I needed to see if there were any hints of what Lucia had done to destroy Melantha. The sprites watched me with glittering, curious eyes as I pulled Lucia's book from the case. I turned, but halted, my eyes locked back on Moira's book. There might be time for me to skim through both. I caved, grabbing that one as well.

"Is there a comfortable place to sit and read?" I asked, the sprites gathering around me. A few of them tugged at my pants, urging me to follow. I giggled as they chittered and pointed with sparkling energy. "Okay, okay, lead the way."

I loved these sprites. They were so special, and I wondered just how they came to be here. How long had they resided in Selene's temple? Did they age? Would they exist as long as this ancient library would?

Their tiny feet patted along the floor as they led me down the aisle of shelves to a lone bench, others bringing pillows and piling them up. Had they communicated with each other that they were bringing me to this bench?

"Thank you so much. It looks super comfortable," I said, setting Moira's book down on the table. I settled into the cushions, pulling my feet up to tuck them under my legs as I laid the book out on my lap.

One of the sprites climbed onto the seat next to me, placing its tiny claws against my arm as it gazed down at the book.

"Are you going to help me?"

The creature nodded eagerly, and the others gathered at my feet, some standing, some sitting. Their excitement was infectious, but I didn't know what they were waiting for.

I drew a deep breath, turning the cover over to open the book, the pages worn and stained with age. As my eyes fell on the intricate inscriptions, the text took form in my mind. My jaw dropped as I read the text that had once made no sense.

"Lucia Archonis. Queen of the Immortals. 1435-1889." Wow. I'd lived over three hundred years. I lingered on that thought, on how amazing it would have been to be at Damien's side so long.

My vision rippled, and I blinked back tears, my chest growing heavy as I struggled to pull myself back. We wouldn't get that time now, but I'd return—

And we'd get that time together in the next life.

CHAPTER 56

DAMIEN

"Does she always look as tired as she did this morning?"

Zephyr's question caught me off guard as we stepped out of the building we'd been looking over. It was to become the new complex, seven stories of everything we'd need. It was run down, and it would take a lot of work to repair and update, but I knew once it was finished, it would be perfect.

"Yeah," I said, hating the admission. "She's been sleeping a lot more lately, nodding off when I'm not looking. She pretends she's not, that she's awake but..."

I knew the truth she was trying to hide, the truth I feared. Her body was shutting down, struggling to maintain itself. She'd tried to keep the brunt of what she was dealing with from me just this morning.

Cassie groaned as she pushed herself up from the bed. I stiffened at the sound; it wasn't a sleeping groan, like the sweet ones she made when she stretched. This groan was discomfort, pain. I stepped out of the closet, heading toward her side of the bed as she pulled her feet to the edge, lowering them to the floor.

Her feet were swollen, the tendons and veins, normally visible, were hidden beneath inflamed tissue and fluid.

"I'll be fine, mea sol. It's not that bad," she said with a forced smile. Gods, she was a terrible liar. She tried to push herself up, but the moment she put weight on her swollen feet she winced.

I lifted my hands, stopping her from pushing herself farther. "Let me help, mea luna. Tell me what you need."

Her eyes lifted to me, and for a moment I thought she might deny the help, but she caved. A somber smile tugged at her lips. "I need to take my morning meds. Can you get them off the bathroom vanity for me?"

I nodded, heading for the bathroom to get her medicine.

"A glass of water too, please," she called from the room. I grabbed the bottles and poured a glass of water.

"Here you go," I said as I returned to her, setting them on her nightstand.

"Thank you," she breathed, reaching for the bottles. She dropped a mix of tablets in her hand and tossed them back before downing them with the water.

"The others won't be here for another thirty minutes. I can call them. We can do breakfast another day if it's too much—"

"No, it's okay. I just... I just need to work out the stiffness," she grimaced, pushing herself up. I took hold of her hand, my other on her lower back as I helped her stabilize on her tender feet. "I miss them. I want to see them."

I swallowed, wishing I could take her discomfort away.

"I'm sorry you have to see me like this, mea sol."

It hurt to hear her say those words. "There's nothing to apologize for. I will be here at your side, healthy or ill. There's nowhere else I'd rather be."

"She barely touched her food," Zephyr said, pulling me from my thoughts of Cassie.

"She's been struggling with her appetite lately. Sometimes she's nauseous, sometimes she just isn't hungry. The medication's messing with her." I lifted my gaze to Zephyr, and I saw it there in his eyes, that same flicker of fear I held. I looked away, the sight too much to bear.

"Vincent said you visited the Fates."

"And they were no fucking help," I said, irritation building in my chest at the thought of the three females who spoke of life like it was nothing more than threads laid out before them. I should've known they'd be of no use. "I don't know what else to do."

I couldn't bring myself to mention the nonsense the Fates had spoken amongst themselves, and they'd refused to speak more on Aurelia. I didn't want to freak Lydia out, so I'd kept that information to myself these past few weeks.

My thoughts lingered on the vague riddles they'd spoken. They couldn't have meant Cassie. I refused to give into the thought that if I lost her...

She'd be gone for good.

"She's...." Zephyr started, but he couldn't seem to finish the sentence. "There's really no way to save her, is there?"

"Unless we can curry favor with a god." A sigh slipped through my lips as I prepared to admit defeat. "No."

Zephyr's sorrow filled my lungs, like the scent of freshly fallen rain. His eyes fell to the pavement as we approached the cars. "We've only just found her..."

It was a painful truth to swallow. I'd hoped that, despite her mortal form, we'd at least get to experience some time together. Gods dammit, this wasn't fair. Had we not sacrificed enough?

"Do you think Selene would give her a warrior's send off? Allow her a place in Moira's Rest even though she's mortal?"

I stopped breathing as the words left Zephyr's lips, and I turned to look at him. "I can't just... give up—"

"I don't want to either, Damien, but..."

He was right. I didn't want to admit it, but he was. I shouldn't waste what precious time I had left with her searching. I needed to be at her side.

"I'm passing responsibilities to James."

Zephyr frowned.

"I'm taking some time off, spend as much of it with her as possible before..." I couldn't finish the sentence, the pain seeping deep into me at the thought of losing her again.

Zephyr nodded. "Calista and I were talking about moving the binding ceremony up. I want her to be there if she has the energy."

"I don't think she'd miss it, even if she didn't," I said with a smile. "She'd fight all odds to make sure she was there to see it. I'll get a wheelchair for her if I have to."

Zephyr smiled, chuckling lightly, but it faded.

"At the end of the week I'll be caught up enough to pass the few remaining projects to you and James, if you're okay with that."

Zephyr nodded. "I'll see that everything's taken care of. If there's any way I can help beyond that, let me know."

"I will."

There was nothing more he could do, nothing any of them could do. I'd spend whatever time she had left at her side, soak up her light, etch every detail of her into my mind—

And end myself before her heart gave out.

CHAPTER 57

CASSIE

Damien stood before me, his eyes nearly glowing as rays of moonlight glinted down on us. He smiled warmly at me, his hands holding mine tightly as we stood on the dais surrounded by our friends, our family.

Anticipation built within me as Damien's lips parted to say the words I wanted so desperately to hear.

"I vow to protect you. My goddess. My queen. My mate," he said, and my heart fluttered, his thumb brushing over mine as he continued. "Until the end of everything. Until the sun burns up and the moon crumbles to dust. I will always love you. I will always be at your side. I will always be yours."

Something fell over me, embracing me in a way that it cut through my vision, and I awoke with a start. My eyes were leaden as I opened them, and I realized I'd fallen asleep reading Lucia's book. I groaned as I pushed myself up from the pillows the astral sprites had laid out for me on the bench.

It was a dream... No. It was a memory. My heart fluttered in my chest as Damien's words rippled through my mind.

Until the end of everything.

He'd said those words to me before, but I'd never known they were his vows. A smile spread across my face, and I wanted so badly to hold him, to kiss him, but he hadn't yet arrived to pick me up.

How long had I been asleep?

I turned, realizing a blanket had been draped over me. Had the sprites done it? A heavy yawn escaped me, and I stretched. I froze as I caught sight of a white glow disappearing around a corner at the far end of the bookshelf.

I looked down at Lucia's book, which lay open beside me. I'd found nothing, and I'd nearly gotten halfway through before I nodded off. I pushed the blanket off as I closed the book and set it on the table. What had I seen? What was here with me?

Goddamn feet. I winced as I lowered my feet onto the marble floor. They were already swollen again. I hated to make him worry more, but I needed to ask Damien to get me some compression socks. Damien had asked me to share the burden with him, and while I hated that he had to see me like this…

I needed him at my side through these final days.

My body protested as I pushed myself up from the bench. I was curious of what I'd seen disappear from my view. Every step was misery as I reached the end of the stretch of bookshelves to find—

I froze in place at the sight of Selene, her body reflecting a glow as pale and soft as the moon itself as she stepped through the entrance of the Archivallia. A pair of astral sprites skittered at her sides, holding her hands as they walked together, and I caught a glimpse of her face as she glanced down to one of them. She was… smiling, and it was so profoundly beautiful and sweet, it caused my heart to dance. I looked back, eyes finding the blanket that had been laid over me. Surely, she hadn't been the one to put it there. I assumed it was the sprites.

My feet moved on their own as I followed her. I'd only seen her a handful of times since meeting Damien, and not once had I ever held any sort of conversation with the goddess. She'd been so intimidating the first time we met, and I'd honestly been a little afraid of her, but

437

something seemed to be changing. I still had the letter she'd sent with Damien when she gifted me the silver gown, and I'd never spoken of it to him, but when Eris attacked me, what had pulled me back from that darkness... It had been a warm, guiding light that had reached out to me, a hand wrapped in kindness and love. Had that been her?

I leaned my head out the doorway of the Archivallia, searching for where she'd disappeared to.

"You're in pain."

I nearly leapt out of my skin at the sound of her voice, at the sight of those opalescent eyes meeting mine.

"Geez, you scared me!" I stiffened. "I mean, sorry. I—" Shit. Do I bow? What do I even say? Then, her words processed in my mind, and my gaze snapped back to her.

"Yes... I know." Her words were soft, and I couldn't read just what emotion her tone held, if any at all.

My lips parted, but once again, I was speechless. What exactly did she know, and how much? She'd known from the moment we first met about my heart condition, so I assumed she knew more than I'd have liked.

"I'm sorry…"

I blinked. "For what?"

"That I cannot stop this."

I frowned. That wasn't news. I'd known from our first meeting she wouldn't interfere.

"Damien is upset with me," she said, easing down onto the stone bench resting under the pale glow of the dimós tree beside us.

"Why?" I asked.

Her eyes lingered on the marble floor. "He blames me for it all."

I couldn't believe she was talking so openly with me. It was then that I noticed an exhaustion similar to my own reflected in those opalescent eyes.

"Are you okay?" I asked, easing down to sit next to her.

Her white brows lifted, as if it were strange that I'd even asked, and her shoulders sagged a little. "I'm just a little tired."

"I guess even gods and goddesses get tired from time to time," I said with a light chuckle, masking my disbelief with humor. I lifted my gaze to the pale glowing branches stretching out overhead, their light dim and yet still the most beautiful thing I'd ever seen. "I can only imagine how much magic it takes to maintain this place."

I glanced at her from the corner of my eye, realizing she was watching me, and my skin tingled. I couldn't believe I was sitting here

438

with Selene, talking casually. It felt strange, and yet not. I wondered if she once held casual conversations like this with Moira. Did we have a good relationship once? Her gaze lingered on me, and I tried to act like I didn't feel it.

"The astral sprites have been so welcoming. Have they always been here?"

"I created them shortly after my banishment."

My brows rose. "Banishment?"

"Damien didn't tell you?" She blinked, and her eyes drifted forward again. "I would have thought he'd tell you."

"I know he's been hesitant to overwhelm me, and it's been a lot to take in in the last few months." I hesitated but asked, "What happened?"

"It's complicated, but I violated the laws of The Twelve, so I was banished to the far moon."

I balked. "The far moon?"

"My temple resides on one of the three moons of Elythia."

I'd always thought she was just in the Godsrealm, but the moon? "I'll have to process that later," I admitted, letting slip a nervous laugh, trying not to cave under the thought that I'd been walking on a moon.

She giggled softly, the sound so melodic, I couldn't breathe as it danced through the halls. What few astral sprites resided in the hall, tending to the trees and cleaning, halted their tasks, glowing eyes locking on us.

"Sorry. It's been a while since I've spoken with someone like this, let alone a mortal," she said. "It is only ever business when I speak with Damien and the other Kyrios."

Her eyes fell to the astral sprite who'd wandered over, its tiny claws reaching up to touch her hand. "The astral sprites are the only true companions I have, but as you've figured out, they don't communicate as you and I do."

"They were helping me read earlier. I'm still not entirely sure how exactly," I said, smiling at the sprite as its round face turned to me, starlight glittering across its misty black body.

Her smile faded, and I was almost sad to see that flicker of her true self slip behind a mask of indifference. "Feel free to enjoy their company as much as you like."

She rose, and for a moment, she glanced back at me as if she wanted to say more. Instead, she turned to leave.

"Wait," I said without thinking.

She halted, curiosity lighting her eyes as she glanced back. "Yes?"

"Would… I don't know how it all works, but Damien asked if we could be bound."

She pondered the request, turning until she faced me once more, her delicate hands folding neatly in front of her.

"I—what I mean to ask is…" God, I didn't even know what exactly to ask. "You know how little time I have left. I know you oversaw the ceremonies for Barrett's funeral. Do you…"

"I perform the binding rituals, yes."

"Is that something we could do?"

She seemed surprised by the request. "If that is what you wish. It will take some planning; you'll have to select attendants, and guest—"

"I don't want anything big. Just… us."

The inner corners of her pale brows curved upward, then settled, as if she understood. "If that is your wish, come to me when you're ready."

A sense of relief washed over me. "Thank you."

The mask faded again, a flicker of her true self piercing through, allowing a glimpse of near adoration, a soft smile tugging at her lips. Her hand lifted toward me, and I stiffened as she halted just before her hand cupped my cheek. It was only a second, but it felt like minutes as we both stood frozen.

She blinked, her hand falling before our skin touched, and the hint of emotion that flickered in her eyes vanished as she dipped her head. "I hope you can forgive me one day."

Before I could say anything, she turned and left me alone in the hall, the tiny sprite waving to me as it skittered after her. My shoulders sagged. I didn't hold it against her for not helping. I wished she could, wished she could somehow heal me or change me, but I could never ask her to risk herself for my sake. I could only hope the chain of reincarnation would return to normal when I passed, that I would return as an immortal, as I was meant to be—

And Damien and I would have the time we deserved.

I sighed and rose from the bench, wincing with each tender step as I returned to the Archivallia. I wasn't sure what time it was, or how much longer I had until Damien would return for me. I wondered where Salwa was. This chamber was so massive, she could be anywhere, but I didn't want to disturb her work.

My chest swelled as I thought about the news I'd be able to share with Damien.

We would be bound to each other. We would be one. I didn't want to wait, didn't want to risk us not having enough time. I looked down at myself as I neared the bench. Joggers and a loose T-shirt. This was definitely not what I wanted to wear, so it wouldn't happen when he came to pick me up.

I couldn't deny it; I felt a little guilty about only wanting it to be us, but everyone had their own things to deal with. Vincent needed to focus on Anna and their baby. Zephyr and Calista were busy planning their own binding ceremony. I didn't want to take anything from them.

This was for us, and for no one else.

I reached down to grab Lucia's book, which was resting where I'd left it. I'd skimmed to The Fall of Kingdoms, but there'd been nothing in it on how she'd defeated Melantha—no details, just that she'd done it. It was frustrating.

My eyes drifted to Moira's book on the small table next to the bench. I wanted to know more of her, if only to feel a little more connected. The leather was cold against my hand as I grabbed it and set Lucia's book in its place. An astral sprite caught sight of me and approached, its head tilting as I settled onto the bench, turning the cover over to the first page.

"Mind helping me?"

The creature climbed onto the bench beside me, the act more like a toddler than a magical librarian, and I giggled. It scooted beside me and lifted its tiny clawed hand to my arm as I held the book. My eyes fell to the text before me, the words flowing into my mind once again. "Your magic is amazing."

The tiny sprite chittered, the cheerful pleasure it felt from the compliment seeping into my skin.

Moira Archonis. I smiled at the sound of Damien's last name in my mind. We'd been bound even then. Cassie Archonis. My smile grew wider, and I had to shake my head to focus on what I was reading.

Moira Archonis. 1025-1221. I hadn't lived as long as Lucia, just under two hundred years.

Parentage. Maternal: Selene, Goddess of the Moon. Paternal…

I frowned. There was no father listed. Why? I knew Moira's father had been an immortal, but who? I chewed the inside of my lip as I flipped through the pages, wishing I'd kept a diary of sorts, something to help me visit memories now lost to me. There were many major events listed, far more than in Lucia's book. I'd been more warrior than a princess, and the details of the first thirty to forty years seemed vague. Over the next hundred years, there were notations of many accomplishments, battles, and victories. It wasn't until 1082 that Damien and I had been bound to one another. What was the ceremony like?

What little I'd seen of Lunoscia castle had been glorious. I could only imagine how beautiful it would have been to hold a binding ceremony within its walls. I wished I could've experienced ceremony like that, the gowns, the music, the dancing. Hollow numbness spread through my chest, and I blinked back the burning in my eyes to refocus on the text before me.

Page after page, I read, battle after battle, victory after victory. God, Damien and I had fought so many battles, so many monsters. A name popped up from time to time, snagging my attention, almost always linked to a battle. Lupa. I wondered who it was. It almost sounded like the name of the shadow wolves Damien summoned, the Lupai. Another warrior, maybe?

The pages grew fewer and fewer until I reached the text describing The Darklings' Descent. A chill as icy as the winter wind crawled over my skin as I began to read. It had happened so fast, a dark power sweeping in with little warning. Immortals fell left and right to the warriors who'd turned, their minds seemingly twisted by Matthias' dark influence. My heart ached when I read the next line.

The darkness was far too strong, corrupting and unleashing the horror lingering at the core of House Skiá, turning immortals into darklings, friend into foe.

I halted at the end of that line, my stomach dipping. Damien had told me House Skiá fell when the darklings first appeared, but I'd assumed they'd been killed. They hadn't, though. They'd been changed—tethered to Matthias' will and the darkness he commanded.

My imagination ran wild, images of immortals falling one by one as the darklings descended on our kingdom. The immortal, Lee, flashed across my mind, the dark veins spreading across her skin. Had it been as gruesome a sight as that? I could only imagine how terrifying it must have been.

I continued reading.

The kingdom of Lunoscia was unprepared, the attack devastating. Thousands were killed or converted before Matthias was destroyed.

I turned the page, but it was blank.

Wait, what happened?

I flipped back, wondering if I'd missed a page, but there was nothing. It just... ended. What happened to Moira after The Darklings' Descent? I set the book aside and grabbed Lucia's book to flip through until I found the end, then scrolled over the last page with text.

Lucia Archonis passed in childbirth. She was survived by mate Damien Archonis and daughter Emilia Archonis.

The words hurt to read, but I pushed past the pain sinking into my chest at the sight of her name. I closed the book and grabbed Moira's. The astral sprite watched me with confused eyes as I pushed myself up from the bench, regretting that I hadn't propped my feet up as the throbbing pain seared through them. The sprite jumped down from the bench, tiny, clawed hands shooting up into the air frantically at me.

"I'm okay, just sore," I assured the creature, forcing a weak smile. We headed toward the front of the Archivallia where the glass case resided. I wanted to look at Elena's book, see what it said at the end. Did it have my cause of death listed there? I set Moira's and Lucia's books back in their places, then grabbed Elena's book and flipped through to the end.

Elena Archonis fell in battle during the darkling invasion of Moonhaven, survived by mate Damien Archonis and brother Zephyr Laskaris.

Why was there no record of Moira's death?

"Cas?"

"Jesus!" I gasped, nearly dropping Elena's book as Salwa's voice reached my ears.

"Oh gods, I'm so sorry. I didn't mean to scare you."

I giggled, my hand hovering over my fluttering heart. "It's okay. I was just a little focused."

Her eyes fell on Elena's book in my hand. "Ah, you're reading about your past lives."

"Yeah, I've been trying to remember anything I can. Some memories of Elena and Lucia have resurfaced, but I can't seem to regain any memories of Moira."

I turned back to the case, settling Elena's book back in. I lifted my hand to close the lid, but I stopped. Salwa was the Tabularius. She might know why information regarding Moira's death was missing.

"Hey…" Salwa perked, tilting her head to me. "I couldn't help but notice there's no information on Moira's death. It just leaves off at Matthias being destroyed."

Salwa's eyes flickered, and she drew a deep breath. "We don't know exactly what happened to Moira."

My brows furrowed. "No one knows?"

"There's only one person who knows what happened, and I've never been able to get him to tell me."

Something stirred within me, my heart dipping as something icy crawled over my skin, settling into the pit of my stomach. "Who knew?"

Salwa lifted her pale eyes to me, dulled with sorrow. "Damien."

CHAPTER 58

CASSIE

I lay curled up against Damien the following morning, the sun barely peaking over the ridge of the distant mountains, his warmth surrounding me. I couldn't believe I was awake; I hadn't been able to wake up this early for the last couple weeks, sleep holding me in its clutches until late morning or early afternoon most days.

Salwa's words lingered in my thoughts. What had happened to Moira when Matthias attacked? What did Damien know? The way the text described it, it was as if Moira had just... vanished.

I'd wanted to ask him, but if he hadn't even opened up to Salwa, their race's historian, it must've been terrible. When he'd arrived to pick me up from Selene's temple the night before, I couldn't bring myself to ask him. I'd wanted to tell him about my conversation with Selene, about how the astral sprites helped me read the books, but I'd been so tired. I didn't have the energy, and he'd had to carry me home—didn't even remember making it to bed.

His chest rose and fell in a fluid motion as he slept, the soft pump of his heart a steady beat threatening to lull me back to sleep. There was so much I wanted to do, so much I wanted to see, so much I wanted to tell him. I wanted to experience everything with him, wanted to hear him say those vows he'd said when were bound before, the words he'd shared with me just a few months ago.

Then it hit me, realization sinking like gravel into the pit of my stomach, and my excitement drained from every inch of my body. Time was running out, and we were no closer to knowing how to destroy Melantha. I knew I wouldn't be able to help them fight the darklings or defend the city. Would they be able to defeat Melantha without me? We'd barely destroyed her before when I was an immortal demigoddess. Would they fail? Would she annihilate them?

God, I wanted so badly to enjoy what little time we had left, but would the price of that bit of time be the lives of thousands? Millions?

Would the price be Damien's life?

The thought of Damien falling to the darklings terrified me. Vincent, Anna, Zephyr, Calista, everyone. If we didn't destroy Melantha, if I couldn't help them, the immortals might fall. If there were no immortals to keep the threat of the darklings at bay, would they spread across the state? The country? God, their numbers grew so quickly, that they could rise up and destroy... everything.

Melantha wanted to convert me into a darkling to serve her. If I went in search of her, would she find me? How would I destroy her before she could turn me? I hadn't been able to use my magic since the attack on The Complex; the only ability that didn't seem to take a toll on me was my Nous ability, as it didn't use nearly as much magic. Damien feared it still affected me, so I'd used it sparingly.

How could I defeat Melantha if I couldn't use my magic without putting too much strain on my heart?

I couldn't.

A sigh slipped from my lungs, my body sagging in defeat. I wouldn't walk away from it—I couldn't afford to walk away, couldn't allow her to turn me into a darkling. My eyes drifted back to Damien, his face peaceful as he slept. I didn't have much time left, but I could buy them more.

If I had to, I'd bring Melantha down with me to ensure he lived on until I could find him again.

Telos Pyrai... Flame's end.

I could use it like Barrett did, concentrate the destructive power of the flame Stoicheion, use it to wipe Melantha from existence. Surely, it would work. He'd destroyed countless darklings in a matter of minutes.

Looking up at Damien my heart twisted at the I thought of leaving him, of choosing to destroy Melantha instead of being at his side.

We'll get that time, in the next life.

My eyes burned.

I didn't want to wait. I wanted that time now.

Something built in the back of my throat, and I swallowed at the thought of him waking to find me gone. I wouldn't leave him to suffer the memory of it. I could make this easier for him, erase everything, as if none of this had ever happened.

It hurt to think about, hurt to imagine him not knowing me, but it would be worth it, if only to know he wouldn't suffer my loss again.

When I returned, Melantha would be gone—we could just be together. We could live the life we should've gotten to experience. No darklings, no war.

Just... us.

We could start a family, live a simple life.

My body fought against me as I pushed myself up, taking in the details of his face, the thick dark brows, the stubble growing in along his jaw from when he'd shaved just a few days prior, the shadows of his tattoo winding and twisting down his arm.

I could erase every trace of myself from him. Selene could take care of the others. I wondered if she would if I asked it of her. She couldn't do anything to me as a mortal, but surely she could remove any memories of me from everyone else's minds. That left Kat, Cody, and Ethel.

It would seem as if I'd never existed.

Tears dotted my eyes as I continued to watch him sleep. My mind wandered, imagining him waking without me, not thinking anything of it, not knowing that I'd been there when he'd fallen asleep.

More time. If only we had more time. I swallowed, lifting my hand. This was for the best; he wouldn't suffer this way. Melantha would be destroyed, and I'd return to him again.

I prayed I could do it.

My hand halted before I could touch his skin, my body, my soul, protesting with every fiber. Tears rolled down my cheeks as I struggled to breathe, droplets falling onto the bed.

Just do it. It's for the best…

I inhaled a shaky breath, my hands trembling as they hovered near his temples.

I couldn't do it. God, I couldn't go through with it. I'd lost my parents—I might still lose Kat. I needed him at my side.

He groaned softly, and I stiffened.

His lashes lifted, revealing those stunning amber and ashen eyes I loved so much, and the sight of them broke me as I imagined those eyes looking at me, not knowing who I was—the way my mother had looked at me. He blinked, dark brows scrunching as he realized I was awake. *"Mea luna?* Is everything okay?"

I rubbed my eyes and tried to compose myself, and his eyes flashed. "What's wrong? Did something happen? Was it another dream?"

"No, I just—" His question broke what little control I had, and the tears continued. I couldn't stop them, and the frustration only made the tears come harder, my breath catching in my throat as I sobbed. "I'm scared."

He pushed himself up and wrapped his strong arms around me as he pulled me into a tight embrace. I couldn't hold it back any longer—I broke down.

"I'm stepping away from work in a week."

My breath sucked in through my teeth, and my gaze snapped to him.

"I… I want to be at your side every moment I can. I just have to finish some things that can't be done without me, and then I'm coming home to stay."

He would be here, at my side. We would be together until my final moments, to make every second count.

His hand lifted to my face, and his thumb brushed along my jaw. It reminded me of our first kiss—the night he'd come to my house, when I'd been covered in charcoal. My heart swelled as I gazed into those beautiful eyes. There was no way I could've ever gone through with erasing myself from his memories. I hated myself for it, but I'd sacrificed so much, had bowed to everyone else's wishes, wants, and needs.

This was one sacrifice I couldn't make.

"I spoke with Selene last night," I said, eager to share the news that I hadn't been able to the night before.

His tanned skin paled. "What happened? Did she do anything to you? Why didn't you tell me?"

"Oh, God, no! It's okay! Everything's okay," I clarified, and I realized how that might've worried him. "It was actually a good conversation."

He eyed me warily, and I sighed at the speculation in his eyes. I nudged him back down onto the bed. "I'm not just saying that, so don't worry, *mea sol*. It was honestly a good conversation."

"What did you talk about?" he asked as I climbed over him to lay my head against his chest. His arms came around me again, careful of my still-tender, healing injuries, and I curled into his warmth.

I didn't want to linger on sad things; I wanted to share only good with him now. "I asked her about performing a binding ceremony for us."

He stilled, and I almost wondered if I shouldn't have been the one to ask. "Is it bad I asked?"

"No!" he said. "It isn't. I just... I didn't expect you to ask her." A smile crept across his face. "I was going to ask her when I saw her the other night."

I frowned, lifting my head to gaze up at him. "The other night?"

"I... don't want to talk about it. The conversation didn't go well with her, and I... I didn't want to talk to her after that," he explained, as his fingers traced idle strokes along my arms.

Damien is upset with me. Selene's words rippled through my mind. I hadn't understood what she meant at the time. Had they gotten into a fight?

"This is perfect, though. We'll have to start planni—"

"I..." His brows rose when I interrupted him. "I asked her if it could just be us."

Guilt immediately set in. I hadn't stopped to consider if he'd want others there, if he'd want to plan it out.

"Okay," he said simply, his eyes nearly glowing with adoration, a crooked smile curving the corners of his lips. "If that's what you want."

"I'm so sorry. I didn't think. It just sort of happened, and I want to have the full experience, but..." I was so tired. I didn't have the energy to plan out something big. It had taken so much out of me to help him plan Barrett's funeral, and I didn't want to waste any time.

"No apologies," he said. "We could be mated alone in the shadow steppes with not a soul for miles, and I'd be happy just to be joined with you."

My chest swelled. "Selene said for us to come to her when we're ready, that she'd be happy to perform the um... mating ritual."

"How's tonight sound?" he suggested, his crooked smile widening into a grin.

I giggled as he pulled me up to nuzzle his face against mine, the stubble on his jaw tickling. "It's a date."

CHAPTER 59

CASSIE

The house was quiet, save for the giggles that burst from my lips as Damien brushed kisses over the back of my shoulder.

"I'll never finish getting ready if you keep distracting me," I said, nudging him back. He released me so I could head into the closet to step into my gown.

He'd given Ethel the night off. No one would know we'd done this. It would just be us and Selene, and that was okay. This was for us, so we were united in every way we could be before the end. I slid the sleeve up my arm, the delicate chiffon glittering with my movements. I wondered what it would be like. Zephyr had told me how the binding ceremony was more than just an exchanging of rings like mortal marriages. It was a melding of souls.

"Can you help me with the back?" I asked as I stepped out of the closet, holding my gown in place. It was the same one I'd worn to the meeting with The Council. I loved this gown with starlight woven into pale gray gossamer fabric that hugged my body until it cascaded down from my hips into sweeping skirts.

Damien smiled, stepping over to help lace up the back as I pulled my hair over my shoulder. He wore an outfit similar to what he'd worn when I'd first met Selene. His chest was bare, a robe of delicate black fabric hanging from his shoulders, and he wore black pants.

My fingers passed over the glittering gemstones stitched into the bodice, depicting delicate vines of jasmine climbing across my chest, the fabric thinning just above my breasts and between them. I'd once felt too exposed in this gown, but now, I felt truly beautiful, and the way Damien's eyes roamed over me left my heart dancing.

Damien had helped me with my hair over the last half hour. I'd left the natural waves loose, and he'd braided sections of it, the braids crossing and overlapping across the back of my head. The act nearly made me cry, and my cheeks hurt from how wide I'd smiled watching him concentrate on my hair in the mirror.

"There, how does that feel?" he asked, finishing the ties in the back of my gown and stepping back.

"Perfect," I said, looking over myself in the mirror, at the intricate braids he'd so carefully woven into my hair. "How did you get so good at this?"

He smiled, and it was so warm, his eyes lowering as he touched the braids. "My mother taught me when I was little. She hoped that one day I could braid my future mate's hair. They're important to our culture, representing unity and strength," he paused a moment, and a wave of emotions surged across my skin—happiness, adoration, pride… sorrow. "I wish she could have seen us bound to one another…"

My chest swelled in both happiness that he had that piece of her, that in some way she was still with him, and sorrow for the pain her felt knowing he'd lost her so long ago. God, I wish I could have met her, or at least… remembered any times I might've shared with her as Moira. I couldn't help but let my mind wander, imagining a young Damien braiding his mother's hair.

"You ready?" he asked.

I drew a deep breath, my heart fluttered at the question, and the nerves I'd felt all evening resurfaced. "Yes… more than ready."

He took my hand, his fingers lacing with mine as he lifted my hand to brush a kiss against my knuckles. "You look stunning, *mea luna*."

My cheeks warmed, and my eyes burned. His smile softened, and his other hand lifted to brush the tears from my eyes.

"I love you," he breathed, his voice like a calm before the storm, unwavering and powerful.

My lips quivered, and I wrapped my arms around him, trying not to cry and ruin the makeup I'd worked so hard on.

"I love you too, *mea sol*."

Blue light fell from the sconces mounted high on the pillars, mixing with the pale glow of the dimós trees, the light cool yet warm at the same time. Stars glittered in the night sky, trapped within the ceiling of Selene's chambers above us, the delicate scent of night blooming jasmine filling my lungs with each breath.

I stood at the foot of the dais, nerves dancing through my fingertips as my eyes locked with Selene standing before us. She was radiant, her silver hair cascading around her in waves until it pooled at her feet, her silken white gown barely brushing the floor. Damien gave my hand a reassuring squeeze, and I drew a deep breath, steeling my nerves.

We were really doing this.

The marble was cold against my bare feet, which was oddly soothing. I'd been surprised when Damien had told me to leave my shoes off, explaining it was part of the binding ritual, something about an uninterrupted connection with the magic of the land. It was a relief, honestly, as my feet had been so swollen that only my boots fit me, and I didn't think black boots would go with the silver gown I wore.

We came to a stop at the top of the dais, my heart thundering in my ears as we stood before Selene, her head held high, opalescent eyes drifting over me before turning to Damien.

"You stand before me this day to exchange vows, to bind yourselves to one another."

"We do," we said in unison, and I'd barely managed to get the words out. Damien smiled to the side at me, and it was infectious enough to help ease my racing heart, my lips reflecting the smile he shared with me.

"Lift your hands," she said, and Damien did as she asked, our fingers still interlaced, my hand atop his.

452

Her delicate hand lifted to meet ours, and a thread of pure starlight stretched out from her fingertips, climbing around our joined hands like a ribbon. The magic tingled against my skin as it slid up our arms, and then I stiffened as it sank into our skin, the starlight fading, but the magic humming just beneath the surface.

"Damien Archonis, son of Darius Archonis and Cora Archonis, I bind you to Moira, from this day until her last day," Selene said, her words reaching to every corner of the chamber.

The magic in her voice glided over my skin, echoed in my ears, as if her words shifted the very fabric of reality. Her pale eyes nearly glowed as she turned her gaze to me, the sparkling constellation freckles dancing over her face.

"Moira, daughter of mine, I bind you to Damien, from this day, until his last day."

Damien turned to me, and I followed his lead, my mind failing to remember the steps Damien had tried to teach me in the short amount of time we had to prepare.

"I will remove your coat, warrior," Selene said, and my gaze snapped back to her. He hadn't mentioned anything like this.

Damien allowed Selene the room to remove the black robe he wore, revealing the rest of his tattoo—the crescent moon on his right pectoral, the runes and shadows stretching out until they spiraled and twisted down his arm.

Damien took my hand and lifted it to the crescent moon inked into his chest, pressing my palm to his skin.

"What are yo—"

He pressed his finger to his lips, that crooked smile I loved so much tugging at the corners.

"From this day, until my last, I vow to remain at your side." My heart fluttered as his intense gaze pierced through me, his hand bracing mine to his chest. "To help carry your burdens and soothe your sorrows." I drew a sharp breath as the skin beneath my palm grew warm, and my eyes fell to his chest.

"I vow to be your strength when you are at your weakest." The shadows inked into his skin shifted and moved, something fading into view in the gaps of his tattoo. "And your confidence when you feel doubt."

"I vow to protect you. My goddess... My queen... My mate," he said, and new runes formed amidst the others. "Until the end of everything. Until the sun burns up and the moon crumbles to dust. I

will always love you. I will always be at your side. I will always be yours."

Tears dotted my eyes as I lifted them to him, and he released my hand to reveal the newly inked skin, the imprint of his vows to me, his mate.

"Repeat after me, Moira," Selene said softly.

I blinked, my mind going blank. What was next? Was I supposed to recite those same vows?

"From this day, until my last," Selene started.

"Can I form a mark like he did?" I asked, and Selene's eyes widened slightly.

Damien hesitated. "It utilizes the user's magic. I don't want to risk—"

"Please," I breathed.

His face softened, and for a moment I thought I saw a soft smile form on Selene's lips.

"Damien, place your hand," Selene said.

He smiled, lifting his hand to place it against my chest, his palm settling between my breasts.

"From this day, until my last," Selene started again.

His eyes glistened as he watched me, and I drew a deep breath as I tried to find my voice. "From this day... until my last."

"I vow to remain at your side," Selene continued.

My skin warmed under his palm, my magic rising to meet his. "I vow to remain at your side."

"To help carry your burdens, and soothe your sorrows," Selene said, the blue flames flickering as the magic wound around us.

"To help—" My voice broke, my vision blurring as tears welled, and Damien offered me a smile, his other hand rising to brush the tears away. "To help carry your burdens... and soothe your sorrows."

"I vow to be your strength when you are at your weakest."

I drew a shaky breath, trying to calm my racing heart as the magic rippled around us, warmth spreading through my chest. "I vow to be your strength when you are at your weakest."

"And your confidence when you feel doubt."

"And—"I swallowed, and my smile widened. "Your confidence when you feel doubt."

"I vow to protect you," Selene continued. "Until my final breath, I am yours."

"I vow..." His words echoed across my mind, and I smiled when I realized he'd changed the vows. They weren't part of the ritual. They were his own.

"I vow to protect you. My king." His smile wavered, his eyes lighting up with awe as I continued. "My mate."

His smile returned, widening, and his amber and ashen eyes turned glassy as I continued, my own tears rolling down my cheeks.

"Until my final breath... I am yours."

He drew an uneven breath, and his hand slid from me. My eyes fell to see the newly inked skin—

Where a crescent moon, amidst shadow and runes now shown.

The blue flames came to life as we emerged from the shadows into the Propylaea, the silence of our home filling my ears. Damien lingered at my side, his hand in mine, and for a moment we just stood there. I couldn't form words, couldn't think straight as I tried to process what just happened, that we were...

My gaze lifted to Damien, his eyes glowing in the candlelight, and he spoke, his voice full of emotion and warmth. "Welcome home, Cassie Archonis."

The tears threatened to return, and Damien pulled me into his arms, his lips crashing against mine as he held me. I could feel him, all that he was, and not just the touch of his skin, the feel of his lips claiming mine. No, his magic *intertwined* with mine, his presence like an air of warmth and resounding completion. My heart soared, my blood sang, and my body came to life.

I was his, and he was mine, and the very air hummed with the magic of our bond, the connection between our souls woven into the fabric of everything we were.

His hands drifted down to my lower back, pulling me tighter against him as his tongue slid against the seam of my lips. I parted for him, welcoming him, wanting him. His touch was electric against my skin, the feeling dulled where our clothes divided us. My hands glided up his chest, his heart racing under my touch. I pushed his coat back off his shoulders, and he shrugged it the rest of the way, one arm at a time, so he never released me, letting the coat fall to the floor as he started working on the back of my gown.

I gasped when my ass met the stone altar behind us, and Damien let out a throaty laugh against my lips as he pulled the ribbon free from my dress, the back of my gown falling open. I'd nearly gotten all the buttons undone on his shirt when his hands took mine. He pulled the remaining free, shrugging it off and tossing it aside. I broke the kiss for a moment, my fingers tracing over the new runes inked into his smooth skin.

His eyes dipped to where my fingers glided along his skin. "I missed seeing these markings," he breathed.

My eyes lifted to him, my heart fluttering. "You…"

"They're my vow to my goddess. To my mate."

His eyes fell to my own markings, the skin between my breasts still tingling with the vow I'd made. He lifted his hand to brush his finger against the skin, and my breath hitched. "You honor me."

He grabbed hold of my hips and lifted me onto the altar. His hands disappeared under the skirts of my gown, my chest heaving as the electric current washed over my skin, my magic responding to his. I couldn't quite find words for how it felt, but each brush of our skin was different now, as if each touch was an echo of power, of perfection…

Of completion.

"Isn't this some sort of temple?" I asked, glancing down at the altar he'd placed me on.

"It is," he breathed against my lips, his fingers tracing along my thigh, back and forth in torturously slow strokes.

My breath hitched in my throat, my skin burning where he touched. "Isn't it a bit… I don't know sacrilegious to be doing this here?"

The corner of his lips kicked up into a wicked grin. "I *am* worshipping a goddess, am I not?"

Air flooded my lungs as his finger dragged up my center, and he groaned his pleasure at the feel of the liquid heat already pooling between my thighs. "And it seems the worship is being well received."

"You're terribl—" I moaned as his finger pushed past my underwear, plunging into me, his eyes burning as my head fell back.

"I'm *right*," he corrected, and his hand glided up my back until he took hold of the back of my neck, pulling me to him. "I promised you I'd enjoy making you call out my title in our bed once."

Tension coiled between my thighs, my body throbbing with each word that slipped through those wicked lips.

"But I'm pretty damned tempted to make you call it out on this altar," his eyes turned predatory, and the blue flame candles around us flickered, his magic rumbling through the room, the shadows in the corners shuddering in response.

My chest heaved as he withdrew his finger, all too slowly, the fire within me writhing and coiling, begging to be unleashed. "You are a wicked man, Damien Archonis."

"And you like it, Cassie Archonis."

A hum of laughter slipped from my throat as I bit my lip, eyes watching him. "Mmmm… *I do.*"

His hands pushed my gown up around my hips, and I shivered as he lifted it up and over my head, dropping it in a heap on the floor. His eyes drifted over me, over the delicate lace I wore. My cheeks warmed as my eyes flitted from his.

"I see you went exploring in the closet," Damien said, his hips coming to rest against the stone altar between my legs.

"It's a special occasion. Thought I'd surprise you with a treat," I said with a grin. I'd never gotten the courage, nor had the time, to try on the lingerie he'd gotten for me.

His finger dragged down my sternum, over the ink marking our vows, and further down along the delicate lace that plunged to my navel. Ripples of electric ecstasy danced across my skin in the wake of his touch. I shivered as he gripped my hip firmly. His lashes lowered as he took me in, every detail.

"Quite the treat, indeed."

He pulled me harder against him, his eyes lifting back to me. A rush of heat surged through me at the feel of his hot length pressed against me through his pants. He captured my lips with his own, his hands snaking around me to undo my teddy. God, he tasted divine, his tongue dancing with mine in a wild frenzy, as if we couldn't get enough of each other.

We couldn't.

The clasp came loose, and he pulled it down, before dipping down to take my nipple into his mouth. My back bowed, a moan slipping from my lips as he teased the sensitive flesh. I shivered as he worked his tongue against me, pulling it between his teeth, while his hands worked to slip the rest of the lace off, only breaking away to tug it off my feet.

He returned to me, his fingers gliding down my stomach until he found the agonizing heat between my thighs. My back arched as he brushed against me, just enough to leave me dying for more, and I moaned his name.

"That's not the name I want to hear, *mea luna*," he groaned, his hot breath spilling out over my breast.

He dipped two fingers inside me, and I gasped. His other hand captured the back of my neck, dragging my gaze back to his as he pumped his fingers into me. I parted my lips, but when his thumb brushed over that sensitive bundle of nerves, I moaned. *"Mea sol."*

"Closer," he said through gritted teeth, and he sank his fingers deeper, curling his fingertips, and my body bucked.

I reached for the buttons of his pants, wanting to feel him, to touch him. His hand grabbed mine, stopping me.

"What are yo—" He silenced me with his lips and lowered me down onto the altar.

"I'm worshipping my goddess," he growled against my lips, trailing kisses down my jaw, down my throat. His fingers worked in and out of me, his thumb sliding back and forth against that bundle of nerves until my body was a lit flame, my hips surging on their own to meet his deep strokes.

"I want to hear you say it."

I gasped as he nipped at my hip, his fang grazing my skin.

I bit my lip, a wry laugh slipping from my throat as I dipped my head back and taunted him further. "My... mate?"

A low growl rumbled from him, the vibrations dancing across my skin in a way that caused my heart to flutter. He withdrew his fingers from me, and the sight of him drawing those fingertips between his lips to taste me nearly made me come undone. "Such a tease."

God, did I *love* teasing him.

"You like it when I—" He dipped down, his tongue dragging up my center, and I gasped, my head falling back.

"What was that?" he whispered against my throbbing flesh.

I bit my lip, fighting the smile on my face. "You like it when I tease"—I gasped again as his tongue flicked against that sensitive bundle of nerves—"*you.*"

I tilted my head, finding his eyes already watching me as I shivered and shook on the stone altar. His hand slid up my stomach until he reached my breast, massaging the sensitive peak as he worked his tongue between my thighs.

"God…" I moaned.

"Still not what I'm looking for," he said against my heated flesh, and I cried out, back arching off the stone as he plunged two fingers deep into me with the next flick of his tongue.

The tension built higher, my body winding tighter and tighter with each thrust of his fingers, each stroke of his tongue, each word he whispered.

My breath came in heated pants, my chest heaving. "Damien, I—"

He lifted himself from between my thighs, his fingers still pumping into me as his other hand snaked around the back of my neck and pulled me up to his face. He didn't kiss me, though, his face inches from mine as his eyes devoured me.

"You what?" he breathed. "Say it."

"*Fuck,*" I moaned, my head falling back against his hand as my hips surged against him, meeting him with each thrust of his fingers.

"Such dirty words from such a pretty mouth," he crooned, that sinful grin curving the corners of his lips.

I met his gaze, the urge to tease him once more rising. "I'm sorry, my—"

He pumped harder, and I moaned as I drew closer to that edge.

"My what?" he ground out, his thrusts growing desperate, as if he needed my release as much as I did.

"I'm sorry, my—" He bit down on my throat, his fangs sinking in as he plunged his fingers into me, and I cried out the word originally meant to be a tease. "*King.*"

That wicked grin curved his lips as he watched me writhe against him. "That's my girl."

He'd already undone the buttons of his pants by the time I'd regained my senses. He pulled me to the edge, my skin dipping under the firm grasp of his fingertips, and he sank himself deep inside me, our magic erupting at the joining of our souls, the bond exploding between us.

"*Fuck,*" he moaned as every inch of him filled me. "You were fucking made for me."

I grabbed onto him as he drove himself into me, harder and harder, the wave I'd already been riding shattering around me. His name left my lips on a breathy moan, and the flames around us doused, plunging us into darkness as he joined me with his own groan of pleasure. He slammed into me again and again, his muscles cording and winding tight under my fingers as I grasped onto him. My thoughts scattered as he pulled my hips up to meet his deep thrusts, and my back bowed, chest pressing against his, my toes curling.

He came, his head falling against my shoulder as his body spasmed and tightened.

I held him against me, felt his chest heave, his heart pound, sweat rolling down his skin. He lifted his head to rest his forehead to mine, those beautiful eyes locking with mine. I smiled, air flooding and escaping my lungs in short bursts as I tried to regain control, muscles shivering as the orgasm echoed through every inch of my body.

"I am yours, *mea luna*," he panted, pure adoration gleaming in his eyes.

My chest swelled, my soul humming in response to his words.

"And I am yours, *mea sol*."

CHAPTER 60

CASSIE

There was a knock at the front door, and Damien and I perked up at the dining table where we were finishing breakfast.

"Is that Kat?" Damien asked as I pushed myself up from my chair.

"Yeah," I said, wincing as my swollen feet protested the movement.

"I'll get it, *mea luna*. You relax," Damien offered.

I smiled but lifted my hand. "I'm all right, *mea sol*. I feel good today. Besides, we're going for a walk. I need to get the blood flowing."

He'd gotten me some compression socks the day before, and they were helping tremendously, the swelling not as severe as it had been.

Kat wrapped her arms around me as I let her inside, and I winced at the tenderness in my back, my shoulder blades still healing.

"Cody's gonna join us for the walk, if that's okay with you," she said. "The park website said there's been a lot of wolf activity lately, something about a pack moving across from a nearby reserve. I wanted to make sure we had someone to trip so you and I could get away."

I chuckled as Cody stepped through the door, giving her a sideways glance. "I'm here and ready to be sacrificed."

It felt strange to see Cody. The last time I'd seen him, I thought he was human. To know now that he was half immortal just felt odd. I wondered if I'd get a chance to talk to him alone, get to know him, without the guise of mortality.

"Are you ready to go?" Kat asked, a wide grin forming on her face.

"Yeah."

Damien appeared at my back, wrapping his arms around me and pulling me against him. I giggled as he nuzzled against my cheek. Kat smiled warmly at me, and I briefly met her gaze.

"You guys have fun. Call me if you need anything," he said, his warmth enveloping me.

"We'll be in the car," Kat said as her and Cody headed outside.

"You're going to be working with James today, right?" I asked, turning in his arms so I could press against his chest.

"Yeah, I'll have my phone on me, though, so if you need me at all just call," he said as he pressed a kiss to my forehead. "Promise me you'll take it slow today."

He released me so I could slide my boots on. "I will. We're going to the Ghost Town Trail. I haven't been there in a while, but I'm excited to get out and see the forest again."

"Are you bringing your sketchbook?" he asked as I grabbed my bag from the table near the stairway.

I smiled, patting the bag as I pulled it over my shoulder, sketchbook and graphite already stowed away inside. "You know it."

He tugged my hand to pull me back toward him, his hand pressing against the inked skin between my breasts, the mark tingling in response. His lips brushed against mine. "I love you, *mate*."

My cheeks warmed, my chest swelling at the words, at the truth only we knew.

"I love you, too, *mate*."

The air was crisp against my skin, but it was warmer today than it had been in nearly a month. We hadn't had any snow recently, and the clouds had cleared to allow the sun to warm the ground. I couldn't believe spring was only a few weeks away.

Kat and Cody chatted away on either side of me as we walked. We'd come a long way in the last hour, despite my need to stop for periodic breaks. I missed this, missed seeing the sights, missed exercising.

"We should go camping when it gets warmer," Kat said. "Cody's got some great scary stories."

"As long as we roast marshmallows, I'll be there," I said, looping my arm with hers.

"God, roasted marshmallows and chocolate sound so good right now," Kat groaned, tilting her head back, her coppery braid swaying at her back.

"Anything with chocolate sounds good to you," Cody teased, and I chuckled in response.

The trees grew thicker around us, dead twigs and leaves crunching under our feet as we walked along the base of the mountain. A strange sensation crawled across my skin, and I shivered, rubbing my arms together.

"You okay, Cas?" Kat asked.

"I'm okay, just a chill," I said as we came to a stop. A cave came into view, carved out in the mountainside along the trail.

The hairs on the back of my neck stood on end, and something stirred in my chest.

"Creepy, isn't it?" Kat asked, startling me.

"Yeah," I answered warily, rubbing away the chills pebbling my skin.

"It's supposedly haunted," Cody said eerily, passing us to continue down the trail.

My gaze remained fixated on the dark void before me, every instinct coming to life, screaming to stay away.

"Legends say, anyone who enters never comes out," Kat whispered in my ear, putting on her creepiest voice as she loomed against my shoulder.

I pushed her back, giggling, and she laced her fingers with mine before we continued down the trail. "I don't know how you guys do those scary stories and horror movies. I had nightmares for weeks after that one ghost ship movie we watched."

I'd never been able to stand watching scary movies, my imagination far too wild for my own good, and it was enough these days to know monsters *did* exist.

"I love them," Kat said.

My eyes drifted to Cody, who'd gained some ground and was several steps ahead of us.

"Can you slow down, Cody? Us short girls can't keep up with your freakishly long legs!" Kat shouted, her voice bouncing off the mountainside and echoing through the forest. I snickered as he looked over his shoulder at us. It was a relief for her to speak up, because I couldn't match his pace, and I was already inching toward needing another break.

Cody huffed a laugh, slowing down to allow us to catch up. My gaze drifted to him as he settled into a slower pace at Kat's side, leaning in to brush a kiss to her cheek. Her responding giggle made me smile, her happiness a rush of warmth. It warmed my heart to hear her laughter, to see her so happy. Cody would take care of her. He'd be there to pick up the pieces. I just wished he would tell her soon so I could talk to her.

My eyes drifted upward across the bare branches of the trees, the sun warming my skin as I drew a deep breath of crisp mountain air. I couldn't seem to get enough, though, and I glanced at Kat to whisper. "I'm so sorry, Kat. I think I need another break."

The inner corners of her coppery brows curved upward. "That's okay, love. There's a place up ahead we can rest."

I nodded, and she helped support me, her arm looping with mine. We followed the curve of the mountainside, the trees parting to reveal a small clearing, and I lifted my eyes from the ground as Kat and Cody came to a stop. I frowned, no sign of any places to sit like Kat had said.

My heart stopped, my breath catching in my lungs.

Cold, black eyes leveled on me from across the small clearing, just twenty feet ahead of us as he emerged from behind a tree.

My knees weakened. "Cole?"

Cody slid in front of us, arms shooting out defensively.

"What a lovely surprise this is," Cole said flatly, tilting his head as he eyed me. I took a step back, terror surging through me. Kat stood at my side, her brows furrowing as she peered at Cole from around Cody.

"Cas, you and Kat get out of here," Cody said, his eyes fixed on Cole.

"What are *you* gonna do?" Cole taunted, taking a step closer, sizing Cody up. "You're no warrior. Besides, where will she go? How far could she get? Can you even run anymore, Cas?"

Oh God, how had he found us? Did he know about what happened to me? How? My hand dropped to my hip on instinct, and I cursed, realizing I'd left my daggers at home. Shit. Shit. Shit. I'd fallen out of the habit of carrying them with me. I hadn't left the house for weeks, so they'd sat untouched on my dresser.

"Kat, we need to get out of here, no—"

Kat released my arm and brushed past Cody, and my heart lurched as I reached for her, coming up short as she spoke, her voice calm and relaxed.

"You're late, Cole."

CHAPTER 61

CASSIE

The earth shifted beneath me, the forest spinning and silencing as the words left her lips, each crunch of the leaves under her feet echoing in dizzying clarity. Cody and I stood frozen as she walked toward Cole.

You're late, Cole.

My feet wouldn't move, couldn't move as I watched her approach him, my heart leaping into my throat. "Kat! Cole's not who you think he is!"

"Oh, I know exactly who he is," she crooned, each step threatening to stop my heart.

I swallowed, my throat so dry I nearly choked. "This isn't time for jokes, Kat. What're you talking about?"

Kat stopped at Cole's side, turning to face us as she propped an elbow on his shoulder. Cole didn't react, his eyes not meeting hers.

"Your time's almost up, so I had no choice but to push the plan into motion."

I couldn't breathe, couldn't see straight as the world spun. Cody didn't move, his eyes fixated on Kat and Cole.

"But you… you couldn't possibly—" Cody stammered, the color draining from his face.

Kat's eyes shifted to him, and I almost didn't recognize the look in her fern-green eyes. It wasn't my best friend standing before me; it was as if she were someone else entirely.

"I guess I can let you in on my little secret," she said, lifting her chin as she pushed away from Cole. As if she'd had a layer of magic over her, the shell of her appearance crumbled away like dust. Her coppery hair faded to black waves, her rosy cheeks turning pale and gray, blush lips tinting black. Her clothes broke down as well, revealing a slender body clothed in slivers of shadow that barely covered her. Long black claws replaced her manicured fingertips, sharp enough to skewer a man. Her lashes lifted, revealing bottomless black eyes, darkness swirling to every corner as she turned her gaze on me.

My heart stuttered. I'd never forgotten those eyes. The images I'd seen from Cole's memories flashed before me, and my own memories of the strange darkling I'd encountered in the alley jolted through me, a rush of panic taking root.

"Melantha," I muttered, and Cody stiffened at my side.

Her smile widened, lips parting. I stepped back at the sight of the serrated teeth they'd hidden.

Cody shook his head, disbelief painting his tongue as he spoke. "You were attacked by darklings…"

"It was too easy to fool you all into thinking I was the victim. I will admit, even my darklings got a bit too excited when I appeared before them in mortal skin," she said, Cole remaining still at her side, like an obedient lapdog.

Her eyes shifted back to me, her words full of pity as she spoke. "If you hadn't arrived in time to rescue me, they might've actually torn me apart. To think, you could have been rid of me all together, but you just had to save your best friend."

Cody's breaths grew uneven, his eyes flickering as if he were searching for any signs he missed. "This isn't possible. I… we—"

"Kept an eye on me?" Kat—no. *Melantha* finished, her black eyes flashing as she laughed.

I wanted to cry, scream, lash out. A maelstrom of emotions churned so violently within me I thought I might burst. My eyes burned as my mind began to put all the pieces together, and I ground out, "Did you turn the real Kat?"

"Oh, Cassie," she said, pity lighting those abysmal eyes.

My hands shook, anger and hurt flaring, my skin growing hotter. I didn't know which would be worse: if I'd lost my friend, or if she'd never been my friend to begin with.

"When you and your parents moved to town, I felt it immediately. I quickly sought you out to convert you, but you were so young, and you had no memories or use of your magic. So, I waited."

That last sentence nearly broke me.

My best friend… she'd never truly been that. She'd found me simply to use me.

"Why didn't you just convert me when you found me in that alley?" I bit out, tears threatening to fall. I wouldn't do it, wouldn't give her the satisfaction but, God; I couldn't bear this, couldn't bear the thought of Kat—

She'd never been real.

Melantha's eyes narrowed. "That was the original plan. I hoped encountering my darklings might somehow trigger your memories, that your powers might resurface."

I ground my teeth together, my hands clenching into fists at my sides as a coy grin formed on her lips. I couldn't stomach the sight of it. It was *her* smile, that smart smile she'd always made when she was eager to cause trouble or tease me. It was tarnished now, a smile that was once part of so many fond memories, was now a smile that would haunt me.

"Sadly, there was no magic, not even a hint. So, I encouraged you to join your long-lost mate. Surely, your other half would be enough to bring forth those memories and the powers lying dormant. To my disappointment, nothing happened, and when I had Marcus try again, nothing changed." She shifted her weight, and the darkness swirled in her eyes. "There was no point in converting you without your magic. You would've just become another darkling." Her annoyance painted her tongue as she said, "a weaker one at that." She let out a breath. "So, I had Marcus take you, rough you up a bit, put you in danger."

I winced as the mention of it brought forth memories; the blinding pain I'd felt as he'd forced his way into my mind, the markings he'd carved into my body, the scars he'd left. She'd done this, orchestrated it all, and then looked me in the eye when I'd returned to my parents' house as if none of it was her doing. I thought I might be sick. She'd hugged me that night, shared how relieved she was that I was alive, had made me tea. My skin crawled as horror surged within me. She'd been with my parents alone.

She huffed a laugh, my skin crawling at the sound of it. "And what do you know, it worked. Your memories began to resurface, the soul rising to defend its host, and your magic bloomed."

My eyes shifted to Cole, whose black eyes remained on me. He looked tired, his tawny skin pale and dull. He didn't speak, simply stood at Melantha's side, as if he were a willing soldier waiting for his orders. He looked nothing like the Cole I'd known.

"Is that really you standing there, Cole? Or is your mind corrupted?" I asked, and a cruel grin formed on Melantha's face. Cole didn't respond, didn't even react, and my stomach dipped.

"You like my handy work? He was the first. He didn't display the results I'd hoped, but that's okay. He was the beginning of my... experiments," she said as she pushed herself up to her toes to trace a claw along his jawline, her tongue passing over her serrated teeth. "It's taken time to perfect, but just wait until you see my newest projects. They're far closer to what I'd hoped he'd become, more than simple puppets."

Cole's eyes flickered for a moment before he returned to that stonelike glare. What did she mean by projects? Unease settled into the pit of my stomach as my gaze briefly switched to Cody. My heart twisted at the sight of him, at the utter heartbreak marring his face.

"Sadly, very few immortals we've taken have survived the trials," Melantha started, and my heart lurched.

"The innocent immortals *your* darklings kidnapped in the night? You're using them for some sick experimentation?" I asked, anger flaring. The poor immortal female who'd been bitten flashed across my mind, her agonizing pleas echoing across my thoughts.

"Those exact ones," she said, coy grin remaining on her face, her head tilting to rest against Cole's shoulder.

My chest heaved as I stared her down. I had to let go. I had to push past the building agony. This wasn't Kat. Kat never truly existed. The woman standing before me, whose black eyes lingered on Cole as if he were some prized piece of art, was a monster. She'd ruined everything, killed thousands. My mind spiraled, every memory of the cruelty Damien and I had faced at her hands resurfacing; the healers, countless immortals, and humans who'd been killed during the battle of

The Fall of Kingdoms… Marcus, who'd been corrupted and manipulated… Vivienne… Lydia and Aurelia, who'd had to lay their mate and father to rest…

Barrett…

"You're the reason for all our suffering," I said through gritted teeth, my blood boiling, my skin growing hot. "You took Barrett from us."

Her grin widened, her gaze heavy against my skin as she watched me from the corner of her eyes. "Yes, I did. It was supposed to be you, though."

It was like a punch to the gut.

It should've been me. It should've been me.

"We'd come for you that night, but no, someone had to go and be a hero," Melantha scoffed, as if Barrett's sacrifice were a mere annoyance. My skin turned molten, anger rising to the surface in the form of flames begging to be released. "You should have been mine the night Moonhaven fell."

I stiffened.

She inspected her black claws as she continued. "I wasn't yet strong enough to fully control them, and they were too driven by their hunger. They killed you before you could turn."

She'd been around when Moonhaven fell? I thought she'd first appeared before The Fall of Kingdoms. Did Damien know?

"I don't understand," Cody muttered, and my gaze snapped to him as he took a step forward. "We watched you. *I* watched you."

Her face turned to him, the smile fading. "You saw what I wanted you to see."

Cody halted. She pushed herself off Cole, taking short strides toward Cody, her movements graceful and predatory. Would she attack me if I reached for my phone? I didn't think I had the strength to reach Damien's thoughts, not from this distance.

Her head tilted to the side as she eyed Cody. "You know, I was quite surprised when I first met you, when I felt it."

Felt it? My brows furrowed.

"I am immortal too," she said. "So it's only natural that I should also have… another half."

Oh God. I turned my gaze to Cody, to the look of absolute horror and pain etched into his face.

She paused and pushed out her lower lip, pouting. "Oh, are you disappointed? That hurts, Cody." She gave a harsh laugh. "And to think,

I'd originally planned to make you my equal, to have a king of my own. It isn't fair she gets one and I don't," she added, glancing to me.

I stopped breathing. Cody was Melantha's... No, it couldn't be.

"No, when I found you talking with that fool of a red headed mortal who serves the Lord of Shadows"—Her expression soured, irritation lacing her voice—"I had to change plans, had to keep you around until I could take Moira's reincarnation. If I turned you it would raise too much suspicion."

She prowled toward him, and I stiffened, hating that I had no way to defend myself. This was bad. My eyes darted around. There was nowhere to run, nowhere to hide. Cole would catch me in a heartbeat, and Cody was too stunned to move an inch. I couldn't leave him behind.

"Do you know how much of a pain it's been to keep it all hidden, to keep up the façade? To pretend to be mortal..." Her black eyes trailed to me. "To pretend to be your friend..."

Those words sank into my heart like a dagger. Every happy memory we'd shared burned before me, every laugh, every tear, every joke. None of it was true, none of it had been real.

Everything had been a lie.

"But I don't have to anymore." She smiled, her chest expanding as she sighed. "Ugh, you don't know how good it feels to be able to just be *me*."

Dark tendrils shot out of her lower back, the darkness writhing and coiling together like tails. She locked that pitch gaze on Cody, and my heart lurched. This wasn't happening; this couldn't be happening.

I reached for him as the tendrils shot forward, the power so great, it surged across my skin. My scream pierced the sky as I cried out his name—

And her tendrils plunged through Cody's stomach.

CHAPTER 62

CASSIE

Melantha's manic laughter flooded the clearing, and Cody's gasps of pain filled my ears. She jerked him forward and away from my reach, suspending him above the ground as he grasped onto the darkness, struggling to pull away. The other coils writhing at her back stretched to the ground, lifting her up until her eyes were level with his.

Cody recoiled, fighting to get away as blood rolled down his leg, crimson droplets falling to the pool forming on the ground beneath him. My feet moved on their own as I lurched for them. I didn't know what I'd do. I didn't have any weapons, but I couldn't sit here and watch.

Melantha's darkness snaked up Cody's body, and his struggles weakened, his body giving up.

"Cody!" I yelled. The tendrils pulled his head to the side as she inched closer, cheeks splitting as her jaw widened, ready to strike. Oh God, she was going to convert him. "No!"

My hand shot out, fire burning beneath my skin, rising to the surface. If I could burn her, weaken her, we might stand a chance. I'd originally given up on the idea of using flames against Melantha, of using *Telos Pyrai*, flames end, to destroy her, but...

Damien's warm face flickered across my thoughts, his smile lighting his eyes as we exchanged our vows the night before.

I'm so sorry.

I didn't have any other choice. I had to get Cody away from her first, though; I wouldn't take him out with us. The heat built under my skin, and my hands extended out to Melantha as the flames sparked. Pain surged through me, my body recoiling as it pierced my chest, and the spark died out before it could come to life, the flame never surfacing. I fell to my knees, panting as the pain faded. *Shit.* I couldn't use my magic. My body couldn't sustain it anymore.

Horror settled in. I couldn't do anything. I was defenseless.

A pair of boots settled onto the ground before me, and I lifted my eyes to find Cole. His black eyes were hollow as he stared down at me, face void of emotion. He crouched, his hand shooting out to wrap around my throat. I fought against him as he rose, lifting me with him until my toes barely reached the ground.

"Cole—" I gasped for air as I grabbed at his hands, my feet kicking through the air. "Stop this!"

He didn't respond, those broken eyes staring through me.

"This isn't... you!" I barked out between gasps, my voice hoarse. "I know... you're being forced! Are you still in there?"

His eyes flickered for a moment but then narrowed as he bared his teeth, his fangs lengthening as his grip tightened around my windpipe. I gasped, but no air came, and panic set in. My heart pounded painfully as adrenaline surged through my body. There was no time, and only one option. I threw my hands out, one grasping his arm, my other slamming over his eyes as I dove into his thoughts.

Darkness welcomed me, the corruption oily in the air as I plunged into Cole's mind. There was no light here, no warmth, just an empty void of nothing. How deeply had it rooted into his mind? I had to destroy it, had to free him somehow.

I focused on the darkness, on the corruption writhing around me. God, how much had he suffered? He must still be in here, the true Cole, the Cole I knew. I'd burn this darkness out, purge it from his mind until none remained. He would be free.

White hot pain lanced my skin as claws sank into my legs, as if the darkness realized my presence, my intrusion. I bit back the scream threatening to spill from my lips.

Blinding light flooded me, the corruption pushing against me as I let it erupt, let it flow to every inch of my body before I unleashed it. The darkness rang out, its claws raking down my legs as it tried to pull me down into its depths. My heart dipped as the ground beneath my feet shifted and changed until it was an oily pit, and I began to sink.

Shit. Shit!

My feet dipped into the darkness beneath me, and my lungs squeezed as my body continued to suffocate on the outside. I couldn't let it suck me in, couldn't give in. I fought against it, the icy agony searing, and I cried out as I pushed it back. I would burn it all away, every trace. I let go, unleashing everything I had on the darkness surrounding me, and my heart stuttered—the warning of my limit resounding and clear. The darkness recoiled, ghastly shrieks piercing my ears until I thought my eardrums might burst as the flame surged through it, I would ensure nothing remained.

I slammed back into my body, pain sparking across every inch of me as I tried to breathe. Cole's grip on my neck loosened, and when I opened my eyes, I found him, those onyx eyes wide in horror.

"Cole?" I panted as I struggled to keep myself upright, my knees threatening to buckle under me. "Is it... really you?"

His wide eyes roamed over me, and his hand released my throat, arms recoiling. My knees gave out, but he caught me.

"Gods, Cas. I'm so sorry!" The words spilled from his lips in a flurry, horror painting his tongue. "I couldn't... I didn't have any control. I'm so sorry!"

Tears welled in my eyes at the sight of him, the real him, and I'd never been happier to see something real, something true. It had never been him who'd done those things. He was no longer shackled to Melantha's will, no longer suffering the horrors she'd laced through his mind.

"It's okay... You're free." I said through panted breaths, my chest heaving, heart hammering, and the world began to spin. "I know you... wouldn't have... done those things..."

"Can you ever forgive me?" he asked, tears flooding his eyes.

"It wasn't yo—" My body lurched forward, the wind slamming out of my lungs. Cole froze, the color draining from his face, and I tried to speak, tried to think. I gasped, air painful to inhale. Coppery liquid flooded my mouth, and panic shot through me as I tried to breathe, tried to calm myself. Cole's eyes widened as they fell downward, and my gaze followed his.

To the tendril of darkness protruding from my stomach.

I was ripped from Cole's grasp, and I cried out, but no sound came as I was thrown to the ground. Agony lanced across my back, across my still healing shoulder blades and ribs, and the wound in my gut. Cole ran for me, but Melantha ripped the tendril from my stomach and blocked his path, the dark power whipping through the air and slamming into him. He flew back, crashing into a nearby tree before crumpling to the ground.

"Cole!" I cried out, but my voice barely breached my lips. I couldn't move, my body twitching and jerking as I clutched my stomach, warm liquid coating my hand, seeping into my shirt. I tried to breathe, tried to calm myself as tears rolled down my cheeks, but I couldn't. Air came in too short pants, not enough to fill my lungs, not enough to get oxygen.

Melantha's dark gaze shot to me, the tendrils dancing through the air at her back. Where was Cody? My eyes darted around, searching. He lay nearby, unmoving, head turned from me.

The sobs built in my throat. "God, no."

"You just *had* to do that," Melantha hissed as she stalked toward me.

My feet slipped against the dirt as I tried to scoot away from her. The movement only caused more blood to gush from my wound, and I cried out, my head falling back into the dirt.

"Cole handled the conversion before. I'll just do to him what I did to the others," she said, and my heart stuttered as she lunged for me, grabbing hold of my arms. I fought against her, but my body was failing me, strength fading.

I kicked, but it did nothing as she pulled me close, her jaws parting. She bit down onto my shoulder, white-hot pain shooting up my neck, down my arm. I screamed, the sound guttural and hoarse as it echoed off the mountainside.

She pulled back, licking her lips as she dropped me onto the ground. A broken sob ripped from my throat.

"Now for the final step... Let's see if you can survive, this."

My eyes widened as she bit into her wrist, tearing the flesh, and black blood oozed, dripping down her arm. Her other hand shot out, grabbing hold of my face.

No! No, no, no, no!

A grin spread across her face as she lifted my head, thumb and index finger pressing into the sides of my cheeks until she forced my lips to part, lifting her bleeding wrist over me.

"*Drink*," she insisted, the oily liquid dripping down onto my lips. The substance was sickeningly sweet and acidic, causing my stomach to churn. No! I couldn't let myself drink it, couldn't let her do whatever she intended to. Her grip on my cheeks eased as the liquid flooded my mouth.

I spit it out, the inky liquid dotting her face. She ground her serrated teeth, forcing my lips open as she poured her blood into my mouth again, and she released my cheeks to clamp her hand over my mouth, forcing it closed as her other hand rose to pinch my nose closed.

"*Drink!*"

My chest heaved as my lungs tried to draw in air, my body bucking. I couldn't open my mouth to spit it out, couldn't breathe, couldn't—

I gagged, liquid slipping down my throat, and she released me, shoving my head back into the ground. The liquid burned its way down my throat as I gasped, coughing. God, what had she done to me? Her weight vanished as Cole dragged her back by her foot, throwing her to the side. She crashed into the ground, and he stood between us.

He glanced over his shoulder at me and caught sight of the wound in my stomach, of the blood seeping into my sweater and pooling on the ground. I clutched my stomach but failed to apply enough pressure to do any good, the pain too much to bear. His eyes found the wound on my shoulder.

He paled. "*Gods, no.*"

"I'm..." I winced, unable to breathe fully, every breath painful. The cough that forced its way out of my throat was ten times worse. "I'm okay."

Melantha pushed herself up, a growl ripping from her throat as she lunged for Cole. He braced himself, fully prepared to do anything to defend me. No! She was too powerful, and he was unarmed.

A loud snarl shot out from the woods as Melantha reached for Cole, and a massive gray wolf crashed into her. Melantha's shriek rang out through the trees as its jaws crunched down onto her arm.

My heart soared at the sight of her. "Thalia..."

They plowed into the ground, and Melantha cried out as Thalia tore her arm in half. Melantha pushed her up, baring her fangs as the tendrils at her back shot forward.

I tried to push myself up, desperate to see her. Cole's hands reached out, though, halting me. "Stay still, Cas."

A cold chill swept over me, icy needles scattering across the surface of my skin, sharp and painful. My eyes fluttered, exhaustion fighting to sink its claws into me, to drag me under. I tried to focus on him, his image splitting into two, then three. God, I was going to be sick. What had she done to me? Darklings didn't trade blood with their victims. They just bit them.

"Cas, keep your eyes open. Stay with me," Cole pleaded.

No, I couldn't be bitten. I couldn't change. What would happen if I was converted? I gasped, crying out as Cole applied pressure to my wound, trying to staunch the bleeding.

"Damie—" My breaths came in shorter and shorter pants, my heart slamming against my rib cage.

Thalia crashed into the ground beside us, and I looked in time to see Melantha rise from the dirt, her left forearm missing, black blood pouring from the wound and onto the forest floor. Thalia pushed herself to her feet, and when her eyes found Cole, she hunched low, a growl ripping from her barred teeth.

"Don't—" I gasped, and Thalia stilled, pale eyes falling to me. "He was—" I winced, a sob breaking free from my throat as the pain surged again. "Corrupted."

Thalia whimpered as her eyes roamed over me, lowering her muzzle to brush her tongue against my face.

"I'll be..." My eyes fluttered. "I'll be..."

Cole leaned over me. "Cas! Eyes on me!"

I couldn't, his face splitting and blurring as my eyes failed to focus. I shivered, my lips numbing, an icy chill crawling over my skin.

Damien.

I didn't know if I had the strength to reach him. I might not even have been able to reach Cole's mind.

Damien!

A whimper tore from Thalia, and Cole cried out as darkness erupted and he was torn from me, the tendrils whipping through the air in a frenzy. I couldn't see them, couldn't lift my head to search for them, the only thing visible the blur of the sky through the slumbering trees above.

"You filthy mutt. How dare you put your mouth on me!" Melantha growled, the leaves crunching under her feet as she approached me. She came into view above me, her form blurring as I fought to keep my eyes open.

No! I couldn't let it happen. I had to fight it, had to...

Melantha lowered herself to my side, her grin widening as she gazed down at me. My strength failed, my eyes falling closed as darkness swept over me, and I plummeted into the abyss.

"We'll bring the immortals and their goddess down together... Sister."

CHAPTER 63

DAMIEN

The crinkle of paper reached my ears over the distant pounding of hammers as James laid out the blueprints detailing the modifications the subcontractors proposed. We'd gone through every floor, discussing the rooms, their potential uses, ways we could improve on what we'd already had at the old complex. This building would have everything we could ever need.

Zephyr's weight pressed into my shoulder as he leaned in, eyes drifting over the large sheets of paper. James started marking out the adjustments we wanted with a pen; placement of lights, cabinets, anything of note we'd found on our walkthrough. They'd already begun demolition, the racket ringing through the building. It would be a few months before it was finished, but the transformation would be nothing short of amazing. This building had sat abandoned for years, and I was happy we could breathe new life into it.

"Thir'll be twice as many guest rooms, an' each will hev its own kitchenette," James explained.

"Is that a gym?" Vincent asked, peering between us to the plans.

James nodded. "Aye, thir'll be a workoot room fer evry'wan tae use, eh medical bay will take up eh entire underground level, an' it'll be stocked wi' all eh medical equipment Johnson cuid eva' need."

"This looks great, James," I said, patting his shoulder as I stepped back, eyes scanning the expanse of the room. One day, this would be a common room, where the residents, warriors, and recruits could gather. There'd be a fireplace, games, things for entertainment, and Cassie had even suggested a small library. I prayed she'd hold out long enough to see it all come to fruition.

"'appy I can lighten eh load," James said. He'd really come through on overseeing what he could when I was busy with other matters.

There'd been a lot going on in the background over the last few weeks. Calista had been hard at work on the new laws being put in place to protect females of the aristocracy, and I'd been at her side, helping her navigate it all. The female had her hands full with the responsibilities being Kyrios came with, but she'd taken to the challenge with a level of grace and diligence I never thought I'd see. She'd truly come out of her shell, and I knew Vivienne would have been proud of her niece.

Vincent had stepped up to take Barrett's position. He'd been hesitant, and I'd hated to ask it of him, but I needed my chain of command to be whole again. It wouldn't ever be the same, but I couldn't imagine anyone who'd do a better job.

My hand drifted to the corner of my chest, where the new ink of my vows was still fresh, the warm tingle of it settling in. Even if I knew they'd disappear again soon, to be able to feel them again, to feel the presence of our vows once more on my skin, in my soul, was enough. I glanced down at my hand, the hand that had held hers as Selene wove the ribbons of power around us the night before, magic humming beneath the surface.

"Where's Cas today?" Zephyr asked, and I turned to him, wondering if I'd made it obvious that I was thinking of her. Zephyr had always been too perceptive for his own good, so I wouldn't be surprised if he'd picked up on something.

"Her and Kat went for a hike. She wanted some exercise and fresh air."

Zephyr's brows furrowed. "Is she gonna be okay doing that? What if it's too much?"

I smiled somberly. I'd had the same reservations when she'd made the plans. "She needed it. She's been cooped up so much lately, hardly leaving the house. I don't want her to feel caged."

He spoke again, but his words became jumbled as a wave of nausea rolled over me. The room tilted and shifted, and I stumbled into the wall, my hand shooting out to brace myself.

"*Fuck*," I breathed, swallowing back the bile rising in my throat.

Zephyr grabbed hold of my arm. "Woah, Damien."

Vincent and James halted their conversation, their attention snapping to us.

I blinked, the air flooded my lungs in a deep breath. *Shit*. Why did I suddenly feel like I'd drank entirely way too much ambrosia liquor, as if I might hurl my guts up?

"What's going on?" Vincent asked as he approached, and his skin paled as he got a good look at my face. "Shit, Damien. What's wrong?"

"I... I don't know, I just feel..." Gods, I felt like shit. Immortals didn't get the flu, but I'd experienced this twice in my life, and neither of those instances were possible. "I don't feel good."

"Easy, man. You're whiter than a sheet," Zephyr said as he helped stabilize me.

I leaned against the wall as the room settled, but the nausea persisted. What the hell was going on? Why did I feel like this? Something rippled at the far end of the bond, as if I were being tugged, and my heart stuttered. Was something wrong with Cassie? Was she okay?

My eyes met Zephyr's as my mind flew to the worst possibilities, and realization flashed across his eyes.

"Damien?" he started, as if dreading the words I might say.

She was with Cody and Kat, but I hadn't gotten a call from Cody. He would've called me the moment something happened.

Damien!

I jerked at the sound of Cassie's voice shooting across my mind, but it was quiet, despite it sounding like a cry for help—distant, muffled, and almost too low for me to understand.

Cas?

"What happened?" Zephyr asked suddenly, his face grave.

I blinked, trying to calm myself, calling out to her again, but there was no answer. "I don't know. I just heard Cassie call out to me, but..."

Cassie!

My brothers stilled around me, and I looked at James. "James, track Cassie's phone. See if you can pick up a signal."

James' brows rose. "Oh—aye. Give me a sec." He grabbed his laptop and got to work quickly as he typed. Seconds felt like hours as he searched.

"Is she not responding?" Zephyr asked, his tawny skin paling.

I couldn't bring myself to answer him, terror creeping into me. Gods, she couldn't have... No, I couldn't let myself think that. She had to be ok. Her time couldn't have run out already. I'd feel it, feel the agonizing snap as the bond broke. She was alive. She had to be—

But something was very wrong.

"Here," James said, turning his laptop to show us her location. She was deep in the forest, and I could see the trail they'd taken, their tracks marked out on the program. I pulled my phone from my pocket, dialing her number.

"Come on, come on," I muttered under my breath, pacing as I held the phone to my ear.

It rang on and on until her voicemail picked up, her voice bright in my ear. "It's Cas! Leave a message at the tone!"

I cursed, clicking the screen before shoving my phone into my pocket. The park wasn't nearby, and it would be quite a jump, but I needed to get to her, make sure she was okay.

"Vincent, Zephyr." I said, glancing around to ensure none of the workers could see us. The coast was clear, the subcontractors all hard at work elsewhere. I drew a deep breath, focusing on that place. I'd not made a jump to a place I'd never been or couldn't physically see in a long time, but there was no time to make the drive. If I could just get us close enough, Zephyr could pick up their trail.

Vincent and Zephyr nodded, ready at my side as I tapped into the dark void, focusing on the map James had shown me. We just needed to get as close as possible. Ice skittered over my skin, a cold sweat breaking out as the nausea twisted my gut, but I pushed past it. I couldn't let my focus slip and risk sending us to Gods know where.

The shadows rippled and danced, stretching out until they joined together to form the doorway before us. I stepped through, Zephyr and Vincent close behind me.

Please be okay.

The forest was deathly quiet when we emerged from the darkness, void of any signs it had ever been inhabited by any creatures, as if they had all fled. I didn't know where exactly we were, whether we were close. Zephyr was already shifting, black fur coming into view through the black mist as it fell from his massive panther form. He dipped his head low, inhaling deeply for any scent.

A distant bark and growl shot through the forest and we stilled.

"Was that..." Vincent started, and it was clear I wasn't the only one who thought the sound familiar. I couldn't feel relief, though. The nausea had only intensified, and I blinked as the trees threatened to spin.

Zephyr took off ahead of us, leaves flying beneath his heavy black paws. Vincent and I followed, our feet barely touching the ground. She had to be okay, she had to.

Fates, don't take her from me.

The snarls and barks grew louder, and the darkness at my core rippled, disturbed and excited all at once. I swallowed, dread sinking deep into my gut. Were there darklings here? It was still daylight.

"You feel that too?" Vincent asked, pulling his trench knives from beneath his coat and sliding the weapons over his knuckles as he gripped the palms of the knives.

I couldn't acknowledge it. It couldn't be possible, but I couldn't deny the familiar feeling, the presence. There was no mistaking it. I descended into the dark void, calling forth my dagger until the weight fell into my hand.

"*Holy Gods,*" Vincent said under his breath as my worst fears came into view through the trees.

"Melantha," I growled, and my pace quickened at the sight of the creature, at the snake-like tendrils of darkness stretching out from her lower back, swaying like cobras poised to strike.

Vincent's eyes widened. "Thalia!"

It was such a relief to see her, her wolf form standing before Melantha. Anger flared at the sight of Cole kneeling behind her, but where was—

My heart stopped.

Cassie lay on the ground before Cole, her head tilted away from me, and the scent of blood reached my nose. That sickness I'd felt crawled over my skin, an icy sweat breaking out across my brow, and I burst from the tree line, eyes locked on Cole.

Every image of what Cassie had shared with me resurfaced, every moment he'd put his hands on her, every time he'd aided in Marcus' torture.

I couldn't look at Melantha, fury burning in my blood as I launched for Cole hovering over her. Cole's head jerked to me as I slammed into him, pinning him to the ground. His hands flew up, his eyes wide.

"Damie—" I slammed my hand over his mouth, raising my dagger to slam it into his chest.

"For what you fucking did to her," I ground out, flipping the dagger, prepared to end him. His eyes flashed, and he tried to speak against my palm, but I gripped tighter.

Thalia appeared at my side, her jaw clamping down on my arm before I could strike, and I froze as I looked at her. She didn't speak, her pale moon-lit eyes staring up at me as she held me back. Gods, the sight of her tore something apart in me, the utter look of brokenness and exhaustion in her eyes.

I looked back at Cole, his onyx eyes filled with terror, and my grip on his face relaxed.

He gasped, chest heaving under me as he panted. "Cas, she— she freed me."

Gods. It had been true. I jerked my gaze to Melantha, the monster watching us with an amusement that made my skin crawl. He'd been corrupted, just as Marcus had, as Cassie had nearly been. I turned to look back at Cassie, sprawled out on the ground. Time stopped at the sight of the blood that soaked through her sweater, seeping into the dirt and leaves beneath her. She was so pale, black veins crawling beneath her skin.

"*No.*"

I pushed off Cole and rushed to Cassie's side just as Zephyr crouched beside her. He whimpered, nuzzling against her cheek, but she didn't respond, didn't stir. My eyes roamed over her as Cole hurried to my side, his hand quickly pressing on the wound in her stomach. She'd been stabbed.

"You're too late, Lord of Shadows," Melantha crooned.

Thalia growled low, teeth bared as Zephyr joined her and Vincent to guard our backs.

Melantha looked over our group before she glanced back to… My heart lurched. Cody lay on the ground nearby.

The dark tendrils at Melantha's back stretched out and slipped under Cody's body to lift him. She looked back to us, those hollow black eyes locking on me and I barred my teeth, my fangs unsheathing, dagger drawn and ready.

"Enjoy her while you can," she mused, turning from us. Cody's body sagged as she lifted him, his limbs limp. "She'll come for me when she awakens."

Darkness flickered at her feet, writhing, coiling up and around her until she and Cody vanished. I looked around. What the hell had happened? Where was Kat?

"I'm so sorry," Cole muttered, holding onto Cassie's wound, his hands and clothes coated in her blood.

I hurried to Cassie's other side. "You couldn't help it."

"It was Kat."

I halted, air rushing from my lungs. "What?"

"Kat was Melantha," Cole clarified, and Zephyr and Vincent both whipped around to us.

"Son of a bitch!" I shoved down the rage as the nausea tore through me again, and I checked over Cassie for any other wounds. I halted when I found the shredded, bloodied fabric at her shoulder.

Gods, no.

I reached out, my hand shaking as I pulled back the ripped fabric of her sweater, exposing the torn flesh, the black veins already creeping out beneath her skin. She'd been bitten. Zephyr and Thalia stopped at Cassie's feet, rubbing their heads against one another. Their whimpers tore at me.

"She did something to her," Cole said, his dark skin pale and shallow.

"What do you mean?" I asked, pulling my coat off to make a pillow under her head.

"She didn't just bite her; she forced her to drink her blood."

Vincent tensed. "The fuck?"

Air rushed from my lungs. I couldn't lose her, couldn't let her turn. She'd be lost to me forever. I didn't hesitate, leaning forward to press my lips to the bite wound. I'd draw out the venom, the darkness.

"Damien!" Zephyr yelled, his hand plastering to my shoulder as he shifted.

I jerked from his grip. "I have to stop this!"

"You'll get infected too!"

I turned on him. "If I do, end me. I'll die, and she'll live. If she turns, we'll lose her forever!"

He tensed, his skin blanching, and his lips parted, but he didn't speak. I knew what he failed to say, what he couldn't bring himself to say.

"Don't ask me to kill her, Zephyr. Don't fucking ask that of me!"

I'd rather die with her than see her turned or end her life. I hesitated at her neck, my eyes trailing down to the wound in her stomach. She'd lost so much blood. She couldn't afford to lose anymore. I looked to Cole, to the terror etched in his face as he pressed the wound on her stomach.

"Cole," I started, his eyes flashed to me. "I need you to listen to me carefully."

He nodded. I'd never seen him so shaken, his eyes flickering to Cassie momentarily before I grabbed his arm, forcing his gaze back to me.

"You have to use your ability on her. Can you search out the darkness in her blood?"

His eyes fell to her. "I... I think so."

"Cole, I need you to be sure of what you're doing. If I draw out too much blood, we'll lose her. I just need to draw out the darkness. Can you isolate it for me? Push it back to her shoulder wound?"

Cole's chest heaved, but he nodded. "I... yeah, maybe?"

"No maybes, Cole. You can do this. Focus," I said, lowering my face to her neck.

Cole's eyes closed, his power rippling across her body, and he winced, gasping as he encountered something. "Gods, it's... so cold."

I pressed my mouth over the wound, her skin ice against mine. Gods, she *was* cold, her skin already turning gray, the black veins branching out beneath her shallow skin.

Just hold on, Cas.

CHAPTER 64

CASSIE

It was so cold, my bones clattering in the chill that consumed me as I plunged further and further into its depths.

"Don't do this, please!"

I couldn't see anything, darkness winding around me, enveloping me. My eyes darted around, looking for the voice echoing through the nothingness. Who'd spoken? The voice sounded so familiar…

Like home.

The darkness shifted and spun around me like a dust storm, and I turned, trying to see something. A sliver of pale light broke through, and I flinched away from it. A blurred image formed on the other side as my eyes adjusted to the brightness. His dark hair hung in loose waves around his face, his hands clutching his chest as he curled forward on his knees. He lifted his face to me, our gazes meeting.

It was Damien, and my heart lurched at the sight of the dark veins stretching and creeping out under his skin, shadows writhing and coiling on the ground beneath him, the tiny tendrils of dark magic climbing over him, as if welcoming him. Those pale amber and ashen eyes had turned pitch black, darkness trying to take root in the whites, wide with terror. He tried to stand, tried to get to me, but it was as if he were tethered in place, his body giving out.

"*Please*!" he begged, reaching out for me.

I don't know why, but I drew back from his reach, my heart twisting as I fought the urge to go to him, to hold him. "*I'm so sorry…*"

Something pulled me back, darkness crashing over the vision, and I cried out for him. No! What was wrong with him? What was happening? I reached out, fighting whatever it was. I needed to get to him, to pull him out before he slipped under.

Come back to me, Cassie. Please!

His voice flitted across my mind. I couldn't see him for the nothingness surrounding me, but I knew that voice, the voice I wanted so badly to hear every waking moment of my life.

Open your eyes for me.

I resurfaced and God, I was so tired, my body so heavy, but I forced my eyes to open, the light bright and blinding. My shoulder burned, the pain too intense, but there was no strength left for me to try to move. Where was I?

"She's awake!" someone said. Cole?

My eyes fluttered, and I nearly slipped back under before he lifted his head from my neck, absolute terror marring that beautiful face I loved so much. My eyes slid shut as I began to drift, exhaustion calling me back beneath the depths like a siren.

He spit something onto the ground before speaking, his words a rush of panic. "No, stay with me, Cas! Keep your eyes open for me!" he pleaded, and I was so relieved to be welcomed by those beautiful eyes, the amber glittering amidst the ashen gray. They'd been black, so black, and his skin had been so pale.

A weak smile tugged at my lips. I never thought I'd get to see him again.

490

"You came..." My voice was hoarse, and the air poured down my throat like a bag of needles, nearly causing me to cough.

"I promised I'd always find you, *mea luna*," he said, his bloodied hand lifting to cup my cheek. *Oh God*, he was covered in blood—his shirt, his hands, his lips. What happened?

My eyes widened at the sight of it, and I drew a deep breath. I regretted it instantly, pain lancing through my stomach and up my side. I gasped a cry, my face contorting as my body tensed.

"Easy, Cas. You'll reopen your wound." The voice was wrapped in a warm summer breeze, and a hand touched my arm, reassuring and calming.

"Did we get all of it? Is there anymore?" Damien asked, his words almost too fast for me to register. The forest spun above us, nausea leaving my breath uneven as my mouth watered.

"I don't feel anything in her blood. I think you got the venom out."

Oh God, Melantha had tried to turn me. How was I still—

My stomach churned, something rising in my throat, and I twisted, my body lurching as I heaved. It didn't help, the pain growing so unbearable that I cried out as I vomited onto the ground. Something black and oily spilled out of my mouth, and the taste left me heaving to get more out. Damien tried to support me, tried to aid any way he could, and when my strength gave out and I collapsed, he caught me before I could fall into it. I couldn't so much as lift my head as he turned me over, and I fell back, my eyes threatening to close again. It was cold, so cold.

"She's lost too much blood, Damien." This voice was marred with fear and concern.

"No, no, no, no, no. Don't you close your eyes on me, Cas." Damien's hand cupped my cheek, his forehead pressing against mine. They were speaking so fast, too fast, and I couldn't keep up with them, couldn't keep up with who spoke. I cried out as an arm slid under me, and Damien's face turned elsewhere as he spoke, his voice blurring. "We need to get her to Johnson's."

"We'll make the trek back. You focus on her," another voice said, the same voice I'd heard before, laced with warmth and kindness. I tried to lift my head to see them, to see who was with us, but no matter how much I tried, my body didn't heed my commands. Was it Zephyr? Was he here?

491

Damien nodded to whoever had spoken, his eyes falling back to me. Sharp burning pain shot across my shoulder and stomach as he lifted me into his arms.

"It hurts."

"I know, *mea luna*. I'm so sorry. I'm going to make it better. I'm going to fix it. Just bear with me, please," he said, voice full of pain as he turned, and something wet fell onto my face.

I clenched my eyes shut, air flooding my lungs in painful pants with every movement. Darkness swept over me again, the voices and movements blurring, the pain dulling, numbing.

Icy air crawled over my skin, and then the air was hot. His scent disappeared, the scent of cedarwood and leather fading into something sterile, something… bitter.

"Get her on a bed!"

"Damien?" I groaned as my back met something soft. Where was he? Movement ripped a pained cry from me.

"Stay with me. Please," his voice urged from the haze, but he wasn't near me anymore. I couldn't feel him. I was pulled under once more, something dragging me beneath the surface until I couldn't breathe, and I pushed back up, gasping for air.

"Her wound reopened!"

"Applying pressure!"

I cried out as the pain intensified, ripping through me from my lower back to my stomach, something pushing my body onto its side as they pressed onto me.

"I need that rapid infuser!"

Words flew through the air, overlapping and melding until I couldn't understand anything they were saying. Where had Damien gone? I wanted to feel him with me, wanted to feel his touch as the darkness crept in again, the agony too much to bear with each movement. Arms stabilized me as white-hot, searing pain shot across my stomach, and I cried out.

Damien!

CHAPTER 65

DAMIEN

The monitor's beep echoed through the doorway. The annoying, level sound was the only thing tethering me to this place, the only thing giving me hope. Zephyr and Vincent sat on the bench outside Cassie's room, quietly talking as they sipped their black coffee.

Thalia lay on the floor at the foot of Cassie's bed, still in her wolf form. She hadn't spoken a word or shifted since we'd found them in the woods. She slept, but the moment someone set foot in the room she would stir, her teeth baring as she gave a low warning growl until she knew the person didn't mean Cassie any harm.

Cassie's chest rose and fell in a rhythm that was far too slow, her heart beating just as slowly. She was hooked up to so many monitors, so many machines. They'd given her blood transfusions and worked over the last few hours to stabilize her, to treat her wounds. Her cries still echoed in my mind, my throat tightening as I remembered the look of agony on her face as the nurses held her still while Johnson worked.

That beautiful face that had been marred with so much pain just a few hours earlier was now nearly lifeless. I couldn't take the sight of it, couldn't bear how pale she was. She'd lost so much blood… too much.

I approached the doorway, and, as I expected, Thalia tensed at my approach. A low growl rippled from her throat before she lifted her head to see it was me. She settled, exhausted pale eyes fluttering as she lowered her head back down over her crossed paws. Gods, what had she gone through these last few weeks? What had she endured, alone?

I knelt at her side, running my hand through the gray fur on her head, grateful that she'd been there, that she'd defended Cassie. "Thank you."

Her back lifted under my hand, and she let out a heavy sigh, a whimper so faint I almost didn't hear it. She felt what we all did—the fear that Cassie might not make it, and the pain of watching her in agony.

She would, though. I didn't care what it took. I didn't want to leave them, didn't want to make her suffer, but I couldn't bear to lose her again, couldn't go on without her. For centuries I'd been cursed to live on in the wake of her death. I would use that very curse to ensure she survived.

A soft groan pulled my attention to Cassie. I shot to my feet and hurried to her bedside, heart leaping into my throat. Her face twisted, chestnut brows furrowing as she stirred.

"Try not to move," I whispered, and her lashes lifted, barely revealing those beautiful hazel eyes. I lifted my hand to brush a finger down her cheek, her skin cold under my touch. Gods, she was too cold.

"I'm going to get you more blankets," I said.

"No… please," she muttered, her hand shaking as she struggled to lift it.

I halted. "You're cold, *mea luna*."

"Please…" she said, her voice barely breeching her lips, laced with so much pain that I wondered if the morphine wasn't working.

"Let me call Zephyr, then." Her shoulders eased, her eyes lowering to the door before her bed. Her lashes fluttered as she tried to stay awake.

"Call me for what?" Zephyr asked, peering through the doorway. He stiffened when he caught sight of her, awake and somewhat aware. "Does she need something? You okay, Cas?"

495

"Can you get another blanket and call a nurse? I think she's in pain," I said, and Zephyr nodded, dipping back out the doorway.

I settled into the chair at her side, taking her hand in mine. "I'm here, *mea luna*."

She seemed to ease at that, her head settling back into the pillow, her hand going slack in mine. My eyes and ears narrowed in on the steady beep… beep… beep of the monitor, on the proof she was still here, still alive.

I ran my fingers through her hair as her eyes roamed over me. They fluttered again, the exhaustion heavy in them.

"It's ok. Rest. I'm not going anywhere."

She tried to smile, her lip twitching, but she gave up, her eyes slipping closed once more. The sight of it was enough to break me. Gods, I couldn't believe Kat was Melantha. How had we been so blind? How had she avoided detection for so long? I could only imagine how deeply it must have hurt Cassie—what she might be feeling now.

Cole appeared in the doorway, hesitant, and Thalia growled a warning, her eyes locked on him as if she was still weary.

"It's okay, Thalia," I said, and she gave a light huff as she lowered her head back onto her paws.

"She still hasn't shifted," Cole said.

I shook my head, my gaze drifting to her once more. "She hasn't spoken to any of us."

Cole lingered, his hesitation clear. I didn't know how to talk to him, my mind a mass of confliction. I was happy he was here, that he was safe, that it had never been him who'd done all those things, but that happiness was clouded with the images of his involvement with the torture Marcus had subjected Cassie to, of the families who'd been murdered or taken from their homes. I struggled to look at him, the sight of his face tainted.

"Here you go, Damien," Zephyr said as he entered the room with a few folded blankets in his arms. I rose, taking one from him, and we laid it out over her. I lifted her arms and lowered them back onto the new layers of blankets, careful not to disturb the IVs in the crooks of both arms and the monitor clamped to her fingertip. She didn't stir despite the movement, and I was both relieved and fearful of how deeply she slumbered.

Zephyr paused, his gaze latching onto her. "A nurse will be here shortly to check on her."

"Thanks, Zephyr," I said, and Zephyr glanced to Cole.

496

"I'll leave you to it. I'm gonna check in with Calista, update her on everything. Call me if you need anything," Zephyr's eyes flickered to Cassie. "Let me know if she wakes up."

I nodded, and Zephyr saw himself out, leaving Cole, Thalia, and me in an awkward silence.

"I want you to tell me everything that happened in those woods, Cole." My eyes drifted back to Cassie, to her chest rising and falling too faintly.

Cole drew a deep breath and began. He told me everything, every detail, from the moment she'd pulled him from the depths. Gods, she'd used her magic, even though she knew the cost. She'd saved him, and I couldn't decide whether I was proud of her for her sacrifice to save him or upset with her.

"Cody was Melantha's mate," I echoed as Cole finished.

Cole nodded.

"Is that why she took him?"

Cole shrugged. "I'm assuming that's the case. Melantha did the same thing to him that she did to Cassie. She bit him and then gave him her blood."

He'd tried to tell me more, but he struggled with the memories leading up to Cassie entering his mind, his vision mottled and blurred, only bits and pieces leaking through.

I pondered, rubbing my hand along my jaw. "I wonder if what she did has anything to do with these projects and experiments she mentioned, if she's doing that to other immortals."

"I'm sorry I can't offer any more insight. The last several months have been a... blur. I remember meeting Cas, and there were times when I'd seen glimpses—" He swallowed, his eyes falling, as if he were reliving whatever horrors had slipped through the haze. "I saw glimpses of her in Marcus' compound. Gods, I'm so sor—"

"Don't." My blood boiled at the thought, and I feared if he continued stirring that memory, I might slip over the edge into that conflicting feeling that made me want to slit his throat, regardless of whether he had a choice or not. I drew a deep breath. He'd been innocent this entire time. I could see it in his eyes. It was truly him looking back at me now.

"The next few months are going to be rough, if you live long enough. I just want you to be prepared," I warned, and Cole's tawny skin paled.

My eyes drifted back to Cassie, who'd slipped into a deep sleep now, her body so still that the monitor's beep was the only reason I

497

didn't check to make sure she was still breathing. "There are a lot of immortals who want your head."

"I understand, and I don't blame them," Cole muttered, his onyx eyes lifting to me.

Vincent peered into the room. "How's she doing?"

"Resting," I answered, settling back into the seat.

"I just got a call. The Council wants Cole brought in," Vincent said, his silver eyes slipping to him.

Shit, word had traveled fast. I met Cole's gaze, fearing how this would go for him.

"The more you cooperate, the better chance we have of convincing them of what truly transpired," I said, and Cole drew a deep breath.

"Vincent," I started, and his brows rose. "Let me know of any developments. It's going to be difficult to prove his innocence."

Vincent nodded, and my eyes drifted back to Cassie as I slumped into my chair. Fates be kind to him. The Council would likely tear him apart, and sadly, the only one who could prove his innocence... might not walk out of this hospital.

Tender hands combed through my hair, the touch warm, leaving rippling waves of ecstasy rippling across my skin. I groaned, my body moving on its own to get closer. Wait... I jolted awake, my eyes jerking upward. Cassie was conscious, a weak smile on her face as she watched me, but her hand halted the moment I woke.

"Sorry, I didn't mean..." She drew a deep breath, as if it took too much oxygen to speak. "I didn't mean... to wake you."

"It's okay, *mea luna*." I pushed myself up to press a kiss to her forehead. "Don't push yourself if it's too difficult to talk."

She inhaled again, her chest rising, and she winced briefly before settling back into her pillow. My chest tightened, the sight of her pain too much. I wished I could take every ounce of what she was feeling away.

"I hate these monitors," she admitted, eyes shifting to the ones sitting on the other side of her bed. How many times had she been hooked up to them in her life?

"How're you feeling? Are you in pain?" I asked, checking that the blankets were covering her.

She shook her head, and a reassuring smile tugged at the corners of her lips. "I'm okay, *mea sol.*"

I settled back into the chair, taking her hand in mine. A slight tremor rattled her fingers, and my mind raced through the possible causes. She hadn't eaten anything since we'd brought her in the day before. Could her blood sugar be low? Was it anxiety? Was she lying about the pain?

"Do you think you can stomach some food?" I asked.

Her brows scrunched together, her face souring as if the thought of food was foul. Gods, it had been nearly twenty-four hours since I'd seen her eat anything. Did remnants of Melantha's blood remain in her stomach? Had she not gotten it all out?

"You need to try to get something down soon, *mea luna.*"

She didn't respond and her eyes drifted, as if she were slipping back into that abyss that had claimed her the last several hours. I ran my thumb along her hand, if only to pull her back to me, to offer her some reassurance, some comfort. She smiled, and it was like warm rays of summer against my skin.

"Where's everyone?" she asked, looking to the open door, the hallway quiet in the evening hours.

"Zephyr went home to check on Calista and update her, and Vincent…" She didn't know about Cole and about the Council. Her hazel eyes lifted to me, flickering with exhaustion. "Vincent took Cole. The Council called for him to be brought in."

Her eyes widened slightly, and her head lifted. "What are they going to do to him?"

"They're going to try him for the crimes he committed."

"But he didn't—" She winced as her voice heightened, her body tensing, and I jumped to my feet.

"Easy." Gods, even a little too much excitement was too much.

"He didn't do those things!" she said, the panic creeping into her weak voice.

"I know, *mea luna.* I believe you." I let out a heavy sigh. "But there is no way to prove it. You're the only one who can bear witness to what was done to him."

"Then take me to them." She grimaced, pushing herself up, but I urged her back down.

"You can't leave this bed. I love Cole, and what happened to him is shit, but I won't risk losing you." I swallowed, wishing I could give her some hope. "It will be some time before the trial. We have time. You focus on recovering."

Her eyes met mine but then fell, the weight of something troubling that beautiful mind. I lifted my hand to cup her cheek, guiding her gaze back to me. I needed to see those sweet hazel eyes, take in every fleck of green and brown decorating her irises.

"I'll do everything I can for him. I promise."

She forced a smile that didn't reach her eyes, and it twisted something in my chest. We lingered in silence for a while, and I soaked up her presence, content to simply sit at her side.

She drew an uneven breath, and her lips parted. "There's…"

My brows rose, and I tilted my head, resting it on my fist as my gaze drifted across her face.

"There's a bank account I haven't touched… There's a paper with all the information in the drawer of my nightstand for you to access it. I've already added you as an authorized user. There's also a list of things…"

My blood turned icy.

"I don't have many things, but…" She'd made a will. There was a will in her nightstand drawer at home. I couldn't bear the thought, couldn't bear to think of another life after her.

"I haven't touched the account since I moved in with you, but I was on disability, and the money has been collecting in the account over the last six months. I want it to go to Aurelia."

I couldn't find words to say. How long had she been working on a will? Was this something she'd started recently? Had she started it before we'd even met?

"I hate to ask," she said. "But, if possible, could you find someone to help set it up so it can be managed for her until she's old enough? Maybe for college, or a house, anything. And my art supplies… I don't know if she likes to draw, but if she's interested, I'd like her to have it all."

I should say something, but I just sat there, lips parted, words lingering on my tongue but refusing to form. Her eyes warmed as she smiled at me despite the sadness lingering there. I couldn't stand the sight of it, my chest threatening to cave in as I tried to hold her warm gaze. How could she be so strong? How could she sit here before me and talk about these things, ready to face death?

I was frozen, unable to so much as speak as her words played on repeat in my mind.

"I tried to avoid you when we first met. I didn't want you to go through this."

My hand tightened on hers. "Don't talk like that."

She winced again, and I tensed, releasing her hand to stand. "I'm going to get the nurse. They're taking too long."

"No—" She grabbed my hand, her grip shaking, and I froze. Her eyes met mine, and though she tried to maintain a mask of calm, there was fear within those hazel eyes.

It broke me.

"Please, just…" Her eyes searched, as if the words lying just out of her reach were a tangible object she could find. "I want you here. I don't want to be alone."

"I'm not going anywhere, *mea luna*. I'm here with you." It pained me to say those words… because I wouldn't be. I had yet to find a way to save her, and with all other options exhausted—

I would have to leave her.

"Can you…" She drew a deep breath, exhaustion coating each inhale. "Can you lie with me?"

I hesitated, looking over the tubes, the IVs in the crooks of her elbows. I didn't want to risk damaging them. Carefully, I pushed myself up and moved things around so I wouldn't disturb them. I shirked my coat off and hung it on the back of the chair before carefully climbing into bed beside her.

The mattress groaned as I turned onto my side, the bed nowhere near large enough to hold the two of us, but I held myself on the edge, offering her any comfort and warmth I could. She tried to turn to me, but I stopped her.

"I don't want to risk messing with your IVs," I said, and she sighed, nuzzling her face into the crook of my shoulder instead. I stretched an arm across her, holding her against me as I rested my chin on her head.

I don't know how long we laid there like that. Time could've stopped; I wished it would have. If only we could slip from this world, slip from time and just be, just us.

Her breathing grew uneven, shaky, her chest heaving in a way that felt like she was trying to hide it, and a salty scent filled my nose. I pressed a kiss to her forehead.

"I'm so sorry," she said into my shoulder, her voice low.

"No apologies," I whispered. "Don't hold it back. Don't hide it. Let me share the burden. Let me be here with you."

"I didn't want this for you," she said, and it was enough to make me crumble, to leave me broken.

I didn't want this for *her*. Hadn't we sacrificed enough? Hadn't we lost enough? I would burn the Fates' temple to the ground for this, for their willingness to let her die over a bullshit prophecy that may or may not come true. Fuck their prophecies. She'd never do what they said, would never have a hand in the deaths of millions—

And even if she did...

"I wish I could've seen it all with you... the Godsrealm, the end of the war." Her voice broke as the sobs took over, and I held her, her head pressing under my chin.

I couldn't find the words, and it irritated me to no end that the only thing I could do for her was to hold her and allow her the time to cry. "Me too, *mea luna*. Me too."

She might see it, but it wouldn't be with me.

502

CHAPTER 66

CASSIE

"Guid mornin' deary," Ethel greeted as she entered my room. Her curly silver hair was tied back in a low ponytail, and she carried two bags with her. I didn't know what it was about her. This woman was magical, her very presence like sunshine and warm spring air lighting up the room whenever she entered.

"I've missed you so much, *Mitera*," I said, pushing myself up to sit.

Damien was on his feet, his arm coming to my back to help me sit up, and I smiled in thanks. My arms shook under my weight. I stifled the urge to grimace at the dull pain in my stomach, but I finally managed to balance upright.

She leaned over me, wrapping her arm around my neck and laying a kiss to my forehead. She tensed at the contact of our skin and reached down to rub my hands. "Oh child, yer so cold. Ah brought blanket from tae hoose fer ye. Ah also grabbed som' fuzzeh socks." She released me and reached into the bag strung over her shoulder to pull my favorite blanket free. I ran my hands over the soft fuzz as she laid it over my lap, and I pulled it up against my chest, pressing my nose into it to inhale the scent of our home. Damien's scent lingered on it, and it was the most comforting thing she could've brought.

"Ah figured ye cuid use a book tae keep ye entertained," she said with a wink as she reached into the bag again and slipped a couple of books from my library into my lap.

"Thank you so much, *Mitera*. This is perfect," I said.

She waved her hand as if it were nothing. "Hev ye bin able tae get anythin' down today?"

I gave a guilty smile, and Damien answered. "She ate a bit of applesauce earlier."

"Soonds tae meh like Johnson needs tae get a betteh cook in their kitchen. Ah brought ye a little somethin' Ah always mek James when he's sick," she said, pulling out a little Tupperware with some sort of soup. God, this woman was Mary Poppins the way she could pull all these things out of a bag. "Guid fer weak stomachs."

I swallowed, eyeing the Tupperware warily as she set it on the rolling table.

"I willny be insulted if ye donnae eat it, but try fer me," she said.

"I promise to try it, *Mitera*."

She smiled down at me, her eyes full of warmth as they roamed over me, and her shoulders sagged a little, as if the cheeriness was fading. She blinked, as if realizing it herself. She quickly headed for the nearby couch where a blanket lay strewn across the cushion in a messy heap. Damien had slept there the last few nights, and I could only imagine how uncomfortable it must be.

"Ah brought ye a couple changes of clothes, Lord Damien, as well as a few other things ye might need," she said, setting the bag down on the couch. "If ye need more, joos give meh a call an' Ah'll bring sum down an' grab yer dirty clothes tae wash." She paused momentarily at the couch before turning back to us. "Surely ye willny need too many changes of clothes. It'll be nice tae have ye both home again. Ah'll make yer favorite food fer yer first night home."

My eyes burned. I wanted so badly to go home, to just be there for whatever time I had left, but... Damien squeezed my hand and he

504

offered Ethel a smile. "I'm sure by then, Cas' appetite will have returned. I know these meds make her nauseous."

Ethel beamed before looking around briefly, as if to make sure she'd done all she'd intended. "Ah willny keep ye two. I kno' yer tired, deary. Ye rest up, and Ah'll stop back by tomorrow."

"Thank you, *Mitera*."

As soon as she dipped out the door, my shoulders sagged, and I nearly fell back on the pillow, the exhaustion too much to fight any longer. Damien's hand was already at my back, catching me to ease me back into the pillow.

"You didn't have to push yourself," Damien said with a forced smirk.

"She came all this way. I didn't want her to..." My eyes fell from him. I didn't want her to see just how bad I was, how weak I was.

He remained silent, his eyes trailing over my face.

"How's Anna doing? Any news on the baby?" I asked, eager to distract myself from the thoughts that lingered and the guilt at giving Ethel false hope.

Damien forced a smile, easing back into his seat. "Getting closer to her due date. She officially went on leave yesterday, so she's home. Vincent's been trying to juggle his new position while tending to her, but I told him not to worry too much. Zephyr and I are here to help carry the load until after she delivers, so he can be at her side whenever he's needed."

Images of Vincent and Anna together wandered through my thoughts, Vincent holding a beautiful little boy or girl in his arms. God, he'd be such a good dad, and Anna, she'd be the most loving mother. I could see Vincent playing in the snow with the child, making snowmen, Anna bringing out hot cocoa and chastising Vincent for not putting more clothes on the child.

"I wish I could've met their baby." I stiffened the moment the words left my lips, and I glanced at Damien, fearful he'd heard them. He had, pain clearly etched into the lines of his face as he watched me. The words had slipped out before I'd realized. I hadn't meant to say them. "I'm sorry, I didn't mean—"

"You will, Cas. I haven't given up on finding a way to save you." He drew a deep breath. "There must be a way, and I won't rest until I find it. As soon as Johnson gets you stable enough, we'll get you settled back in at home, and I'll continue looking."

I smiled at him, reaching up to cup his face. It warmed my heart that he refused to give up on me, and yet it shattered it. He leaned into my hand, his own rising to hold it to him, the subtle hum of magic dancing beneath his skin in response to my touch. It was still taking a lot to adjust to the mating bond between us. He turned his face to press a kiss into my palm.

"It's okay," I whispered, my eyes burning, and the sorrow crept in. There wasn't enough time, nowhere near enough.

"This is enough," I lied, and I tugged on him, trying to blink away tears threatening to fall. He lowered himself down to me, his forehead resting against mine, and I breathed in his scent, the aroma of cedarwood and leather so calming that it eased the growing fear. "It's enough that I got to spend this time with you. I wish we had more time, wish we had all the time in the world, but..." My eyes fell from his, to the place where our fingers were intertwined. "My life was never meant to last, and that I was able to meet you, if only for this brief time..." I lifted my eyes back to his, my lips quivering as I spoke. "It's more than I could've ever asked for."

His eyes flitted between mine, grief flickering across them, and his hand lifted to cup my cheek. There was a low hum where our skin touched, as if my very being sang out to his. It made me wish I could trap us in this moment, that I could just linger here with him forever, frozen in time. I drew a deep breath, the expansion too painful, and I winced as my heart fluttered unevenly. It was happening more often, the pain in my chest radiating more powerfully each day despite the medications. He lifted his head enough to settle back into his chair, his thumb passing in gentle strokes along my skin.

"I almost ended my own life..." His face remained neutral as he listened intently to every word. I knew he'd seen the thin scars on my wrists, but whether he'd put all the pieces together, he didn't let it show. "I'd struggled for so long, wondering why I kept holding on, why I kept going. I now know it was because of you, because part of me knew you were out there somewhere, looking for me, and you found me. You showed me what I've been missing out on, how wonderful life can be."

Tears welled in my eyes, the pain building in my chest until I almost couldn't stand it. "If I could do it all again, but the cost to not have suffered this condition meant I'd never have met you, I wouldn't change a thing."

He drew a deep breath, the pain in his eyes too much to bear.

"I just..." The pressure built in the back of my throat, the tears blurring my vision. "I hate that you have to suffer, that my happiness is costing you so much."

506

"Your happiness is not a cost, *mea luna*," he said. "It's my reward, and there is nothing I wouldn't do to see that beautiful smile light up your face."

Damien's lips parted again, but a soft knock on the door made him pause, and we turned our gazes to find a pair of nurses in the doorway. They'd been the ones tending to me since I'd awoken. I remembered them from the last time I'd been here after The Complex had been attacked.

"Hey, Mary. Hey Kris," I said, quickly wiping the tears away.

Kris smiled as she approached, her black braided hair slipping over her shoulder as she dipped her head in acknowledgement of Thalia. Thalia rose, and her tail wagged in response. "Hey, Cas. We're here to check over things. Just routine stuff."

Routine stuff.

I nodded.

"Lord Damien, Thalia, can you give us some room?" Mary asked, pulling her stethoscope from around her shoulders.

Damien nodded, glancing at Thalia whose ears perked at the sound of her name. He pressed a kiss to my forehead. "I'll be back as soon as they're done, *mea luna*. I'll be right in the hall if you need me."

I smiled. "Okay, *mea sol*."

Damien rose from his chair and headed for the door, followed closely by Thalia, who stopped right outside and turned around to sit where she could watch me, her tail swaying side to side. I smiled at her, glad she was here, alive. Mary and Kris headed for me, and I swallowed, drawing an uneven breath.

"You cut you hair," I said, noting how short Mary's mahogany waves were. It had been down to her back when I'd seen her yesterday.

She smiled sheepishly. "Yesterday after my shift. How does it look?"

"I love it," I said as Mary placed the stethoscope buds in her ears and leaned in to listen to my heart.

Kris headed for the other side. "How're you feeling today?"

I hesitated, but answered truthfully. "It's not been a good day. The pain's getting worse."

Kris paused at the bags, her smile faltering briefly but returning almost immediately. "Well, we'll see if we can get you something more for the pain. Your stitches are still healing, and it'll be a couple weeks before the wounds have sealed up, so some pain is to be exp—"

"It's not the stitches." Mary and Kris' eyes darted to each other before falling back to me. "The pain's getting worse here." I raised my hand to my chest, and as if on cue, my heart took an uneven beat, the chambers expanding and contracting irregularly. I flinched as the pain shot through my chest.

"It's getting worse."

CHAPTER 67

DAMIEN

    I eased down onto the bench just outside her room, resting my elbows on my knees as I settled my chin against my laced fingers. I probably should've grabbed the fresh clothes Ethel had brought me, used the brief time I couldn't be at Cassie's side to change, maybe grab a quick shower. Thalia's gray tail swished along the floor as she sat outside the doorway in quiet observation as the nurses spoke with Cassie. There was something about the way she watched Cassie now, like a guardian, and I knew she'd die before she let anyone harm Cassie again.

    My gaze settled back on the tile floor. I didn't know what I was going to do. Selene wouldn't help, The Fates were useless. I could try to petition Erebus, though I dreaded being in his presence and the thought of setting foot in his kingdom was enough to leave me in a cold sweat. Even if I did, what could I offer him that would be enticing enough to violate the laws of The Twelve?

The nurses spoke with Cassie in the nearby room, their words soft and kind. I knew how weary Cassie was of hospitals, and I hoped the familiarity of their presence might help make this easier for her. I'd requested them when they admitted her since Cassie remembered them from her last time here. They'd taken great care in her treatment, had brought her back to me.

I just needed a bit more time.

The fluorescent lights on the ceiling flickered, and I lifted my gaze to them, brows furrowing. I shook my head, reaching to fish my phone out of my pocket to check in with James when the temperature in the hallway dropped. A shiver ran through me and I stiffened as my eyes darted around. I jumped to my feet as the walls began to melt around me, the voices of the nurses growing slower, rippling and distant, until they halted entirely. I turned, stepping back from the bench as it melted into shadow, the lights above me flickering until they doused entirely. What the hell was happening?

"Thalia?" I called, but there was no response, no sound.

Shadow slithered up my chest, a hiss slipping through the darkness. Her cold presence was just as it had been in Selene's temple.

"It's a shame she suffers this way, Damien." Eris' body came into view as she pressed herself up to whisper, venom coating every word, her tongue like a snake as her voice slid into my ear in a hiss.

I jerked back from her touch. Black hair danced in near-weightless waves around her body, her eyes just as black as they settled on me. She tilted her head, popping a manicured hand on her hip.

"What do you want, Eris?" I said through gritted teeth as I glanced over my shoulder. I could no longer see Cassie's room, couldn't hear her voice. Had Eris taken me somewhere? Had she removed me from the Mortalrealm?

Eris wrapped an arm around her waist, propping her other elbow on it to inspect her long, sharp, black nails. "A little birdy told me you were searching for a means to save your precious mate."

Who could've told her that? The Fates? Selene? Had she been watching me? Her onyx eyes shifted to me when I didn't respond, narrowing.

"I'd think you'd be dropping at my feet, begging me to save her," she crooned with a grin that made my skin crawl.

510

I turned from her, ready to use whatever magic it took to leave this realm, to return to Cassie's side.

"I could do it, you know." I halted in my tracks, unable to take another step as she continued. "I could save her."

My feet remained in place, my mind roaring. I'd been searching for a god or goddess willing to go against the laws of The Twelve. Eris had violated the laws numerous times. If anyone would be willing to do it, it would be her. I turned, looking back to her over my shoulder, and the triumph in her eyes boiled my blood. My jaw clenched as I held back the urge to curse her. "You can't be trusted. I know what you did to Marcus, the corruption."

"Marcus." She pressed a tip of her finger to her lips as she thought. "What year would that have been? I've played with so many minds, I'm not sure who you speak of."

"Don't fucking play with me, Eris. I know you did it. You tried to do it to Cassie."

"I tried to help her. Do you know how many heart attacks she would have suffered had I not been there?"

I scoffed. "I won't risk your deception."

"Oh? What other options do you have?" she asked, the form before me melting into shadows. She reappeared within inches of me, her hand lifting to rest against my chest. The touch was enough to make the hairs on the back of my neck stand. "To end your own life?"

I didn't move, forcing my face to remain unreadable as I held her gaze.

"I know of your plan, Lord of Shadows. To end your own life, to trip the reincarnation cycle and its curse to force her to live." She lingered a moment, her onyx eyes falling to my chest where her cold hand rested. "It won't work, though."

"And how would you know?"

"Oh, I know things, Lord of Shadows. Many things. She would live, yes, but she would never recover."

I stopped breathing. "What do you mean?"

"Did you not consider the fact, she's human? Preventing her from dying won't fix the damage already done. She can't heal like the immortals. You would leave her trapped in the state she's in now."

My heart stuttered, my knees weakening under my weight. "No..."

"Yes." She lifted those depthless eyes to me. "Would you suffer her a lifetime of agony, Lord of Shadows?"

Dread spread through my chest. My eyes fell from hers as the thought of Cassie, trapped in this state, suffering this pain tore through me. Eris remained silent, allowing me time to think.

"How would it benefit you, though? What do you want in exchange?" I knew how this worked. You didn't bargain with gods and goddesses without paying a price. It was dangerous, reckless, even more so than bargaining with the fae. I'd exhausted all other possibilities, though, and Cassie was almost out of time.

Her form melted away into shadow again, and I braced myself, eyes searching the darkness for her. Her voice echoed through the nothingness around me. "I will claim something of yours at a time of my choosing."

"What is it you want, exactly?" I asked, taking a step back, trying to feel out where she might be.

"I haven't yet decided," she said from the shadows.

"Then the answer's no," I said through gritted teeth, irritated by these games.

Her cold presence appeared at my back, her arms lowering over my shoulders as she leaned in to whisper. *"I'm not the one who is running out of time."*

Before I could pull from her, she melted away, the shadows slipping downward as the walls returned into view. The fluorescent lights on the ceiling flickered back on, and slowly but surely the ambient sounds of Johnson's medical office filled my ears once more. My gaze jerked to the door, the sound of the conversations in Cassie's room returning, Thalia still wagging her tail as she watched. Had time stopped? Slowed?

Air rushed from me as I slumped onto the bench, a cold sweat breaking out over my skin as I panted. Gods... Eris had been willing to help Cassie, and I'd fucking turned her down. The chance had been right there, right in my grasp. What was I fucking thinking?

No, it was better this way. There was no telling what she had hidden up her sleeve, what sort of twisted games she might be trying to play. I had to find another way, there had to be one. Her warning left gravelly unease in the pit of my stomach.

You would leave her trapped in the state she is in now.

Was what she said true? If she'd been telling the truth, Cassie would never heal, might suffer the pain she was enduring until I returned, and the moment I resurrected... her heart would likely give out. Gods, I couldn't do that to her, *wouldn't* do that to her.

Something brushed against the walls of my mind, soft and tender, and it was enough to ground me, to tether me back to this realm. I smiled softly to myself as I reached out to meet that caress.

You shouldn't waste your strength using your abilities, mea luna.

Her warmth filled my senses, the feeling washing over every inch of me through our connection, and it was enough to ease the tension that had built in my shoulders.

I let out a sigh, resting back against the wall as my eyes lifted to the ceiling.

I wish I could take you home. I wish I could take you away from all this.

Her voice echoed through my thoughts again, defeat clear with each word.

I know, mea sol.

The pain in her voice was too much to bear.

I love you, mea luna.

I love you too.

I swallowed, my toe tapping on the floor, eager to be back at her side. I spoke through the connection again.

You really should take it easy. Try not to use your magic if you can help it.

I just want to be close to you while I can —

Her voice cut off abruptly, her presence ripping from my mind, and I flinched as she clung to me, as she fought against what pulled her from my thoughts. The connection snapped, as if my thoughts had been torn in two, and I lurched, the pain leaving me breathless.

"Cas?" The nurse's voice reached my ears from the room. "Cassie, can you hear me? What's going on?"

I leapt to my feet and dashed for the doorway as Thalia did the same. I halted in the threshold as my eyes found her. Her hazel eyes were wide, mouth agape. Her hand clutched her chest as she tried but failed to breathe.

"Cassie?" I rushed for her, and her hand reached for me. Her nails dug into my skin as she grabbed hold of me, as if she might be falling from a cliff. "I'm here. Speak to me."

Mary rushed out the room, calling out something down the hall, but the words were inaudible over the roar in my mind, over Cassie's short gasps.

"What's going on?" I shouted to the nurse on the other side of the bed.

Cassie's eyes rolled back in her head as she fell back. I caught her, my heart lurching as her body began convulsing. My thoughts scattered, and terror sank into me. *Gods, no.*

"She's going into cardiac arrest!" Kris yelled as she rushed to gather supplies and equipment.

The beeps I'd clung to since I'd arrived rang out in a long ringing sound as Cassie's body went still, her head falling to the side, and the world stopped.

"Cassie!"

CHAPTER 68

DAMIEN

"Lord Damien, I need you to step out," a nurse repeated, her voice muffled, as if my ears had stopped working. She tugged at my arm as I stood there, unable to think straight, unable to move as people poured into the room. My body wouldn't respond, legs wouldn't move, eyes wouldn't leave her.

The room spun as I stumbled back, allowing whoever it was gripping my arm to guide me out. She left me in the hallway just outside the door, watching as my entire world fell apart, as everything around me crumbled.

Voices blurred as Johnson rushed past me, barking orders to a nurse who was already working on chest compressions. Thalia's whimpers and yips tore through the muddy sounds as she paced at my feet.

This couldn't be happening.

Johnson shouted something as he readied the paddles in his hands, and the nurses lifted their hands from Cassie's body as he pressed them to her chest. Her body surged, chest jolting off the bed and then everyone remained frozen, looking to the flat green line on the monitor. The empty, blaring ring persisted.

This wasn't happening....

I'm so sorry...

Moira's voice drifted through my mind. The nurses rushed around in blurred motions, voices flooding the room as a nurse began forcing air into her lungs.

No...

Please be careful...

Elena's voice flitted through my mind as the nurses shouted murky words at each other, Cassie unmoving on the bed as Johnson prepared to try again.

I love you... mea sol.

Cassie's body jolted again as Lucia's voice shot across my mind. Her body fell limp again, the blaring ring shooting out across the room so piercing it was the only thing I heard, the only thing my mind would latch onto.

She was...

I just want to be close to you while I can.

The world shuddered, the earth beneath my feet threatening to break open and plunge me into the abyss. Time slowed as Johnson placed the paddles to her chest.

Again.

Again.

Again.

Darkness threatened to descend on me, my skin growing cold, and a voice slithered into my ear. "All you have to do is say yes..." Eris whispered, the air at my back icy.

Say yes...

All thoughts eddied out of my mind, all rationale leaving me. Those beautiful eyes remained closed, and I couldn't take the thought of them never opening again, the thought of never seeing her smile again, never hearing her laugh.

"Time's running out," Eris whispered, and my heart stuttered.

I will claim something of yours at a later time.

The only thing I couldn't bear to lose was Cassie. There was nothing I possessed that held the same weight as she did. The bond grew taut, winding and winding, nearly ready to snap, my chest growing so tight, I might crumple to my knees. I couldn't lose her, couldn't lay her to rest again. I wouldn't. I didn't care what it cost, didn't care who suffered.

I would burn the world to ashes and dust if it meant she lived.

The words flew from my lips. "Swear to me you won't hurt Cassie, that you won't lay a finger on her."

Eris remained silent for a moment, seeming almost irritated by that stipulation. Time slipped by at a snail's crawl as Cassie settled into the bed.

"Fine," she hissed in my ear, and she took my hand as she appeared before me, a wry grin tugging on her black lips. "It's a deal."

The fluorescents flickered as time resumed, the world shuddering, and Johnson and the nurses halted, their eyes darting around as their machinery malfunctioned, screens blipping. The ringing persisted, the green line flat across the monitor as I stood there.

She didn't move, didn't stir, and Johnson's head dipped in defeat.

"No... Wait..." I breathed. It couldn't be. Eris was supposed to...

"Time... 5:23pm..." Johnson breathed, eyes on his wristwatch. The nurses stood frozen in place, their eyes sorrowful as they looked over Cassie's unmoving body on the bed.

Thalia's whimpers and painful yips faded, the room growing silent despite their mouths moving.

I just want to be close to you while I can.

The nurses began the slow work of removing the ports from Cassie's arms.

Icy air swept across the room, and the equipment screens flickered again, the fluorescent lights flickered. The nurses and Johnson froze, their eyes drifting around them.

Darkness erupted, and the nurses screamed as black mist surrounded Cassie's bed. Johnson and the staff fell back from it, their shrieks echoing off the walls.

Eris' voice hissed in my ear once more, poisonous and triumphant. "I hope you're ready, Lord of Shadows."

Shadows consumed me, swallowing me until there was nothing. The floor disappeared from beneath me, and I slammed into stone. I grimaced, my bones rattling. The shadows receded. Stone walls surrounded me in a near perfect circle, a stone bed before me, and my heart lurched as I found Cassie lying on it.

"Cassie?"

I rushed to her side, her skin pale, her face peaceful, as if she were only sleeping. She didn't move, her hospital gown replaced with white silk. My arms jerked up, invisible bindings lifting them, and I was torn from her.

Eris melted into view from the shadows on the other side of the stone bed. Her black gown billowed around her as she glided toward us, her onyx eyes wholly locked on Cassie.

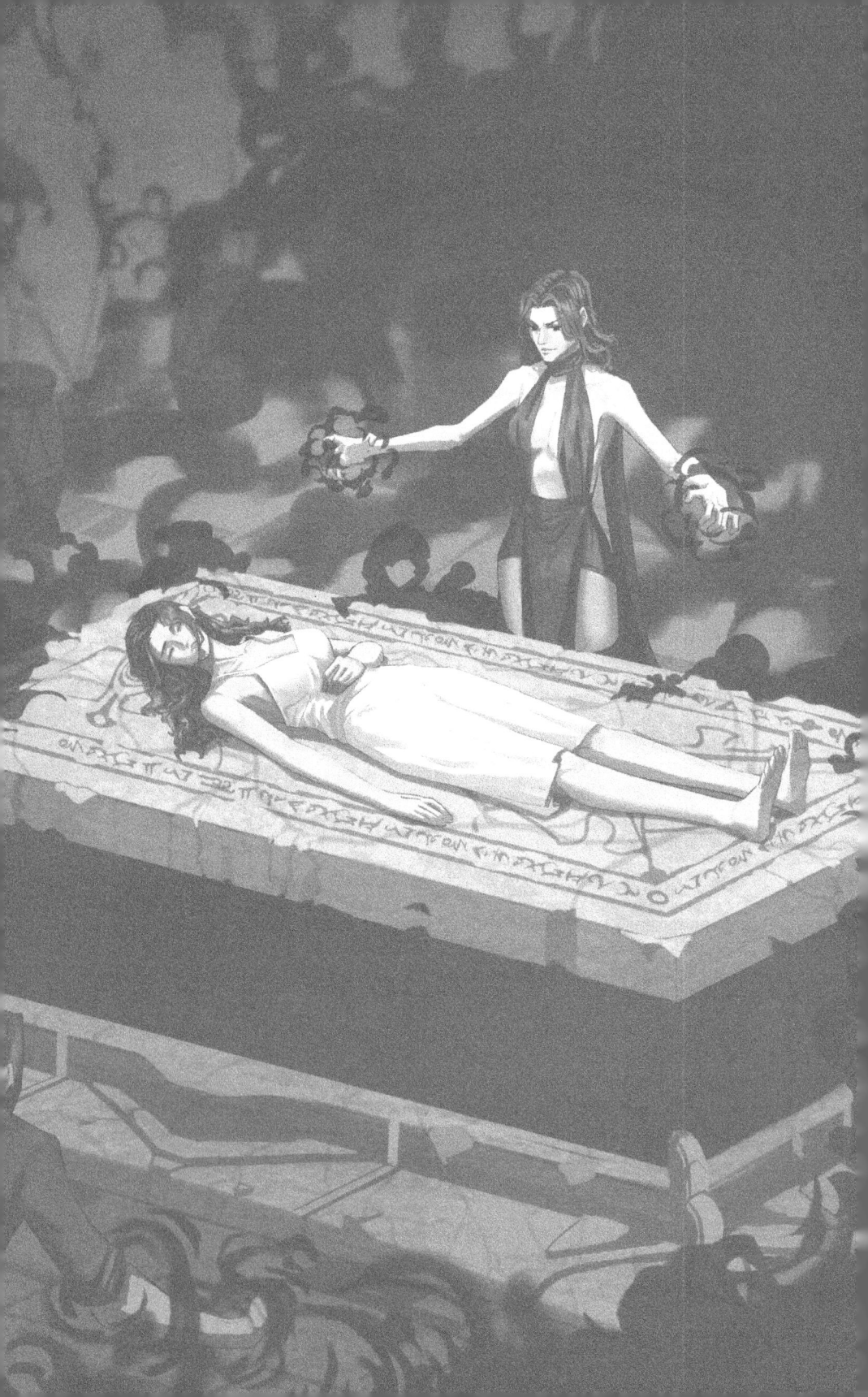

"What are you doing?" I demanded, fighting against the bindings.

"What you asked," she said, eyes remaining on Cassie. Eris lifted her grayish hands out before her, palms downward, and darkness poured out of them.

My chest heaved as it drifted down over her body. Eris lifted her onyx eyes to me, and she lifted her chin. Pain lanced across my wrist, and the air hissed through my teeth as I flinched. I jerked my gaze to my arm, to the wrist that now oozed blood.

Eris chanted something, words I didn't recognize as the darkness pouring from her hands spilled out over the stone bed where Cassie's body lay, the darkness climbing up my legs until it reached my wrist, and I gasped as it tore into the wound.

White hot pain shot down my arm. "What is this?"

"This is old magic. Dark magic long forgotten," Eris whispered, her eyes falling back on Cassie. Words continued to flow from Eris' lips, her voice echoing off the walls. Distant voices whispered from the shadows around us, speaking in ancient dead languages I couldn't understand, their words and voices melding and mixing as they echoed what she spoke.

Eris' hands lowered toward Cassie, and I instinctively tugged on the invisible bindings to get to her, to protect her from the unknown. The coiling shadows latched onto me tighter, and I felt the draw. The room spun as darkness pulled blood from my wound. It released me then, slithering back down my body and toward its mistress. Eris' hand came to rest on Cassie's forehead, her other hand laying on her unmoving chest.

Eris continued the chant, the whispers growing louder, the very air humming with icy power, the shadowy mist retreating from every corner as it converged above Cassie's body. The shadows swept in, black mist slipping into Cassie's parted lips and nose, as if she were inhaling it.

My heart lurched. What had I done? Why had I trusted Eris? What was she doing to her?

Eris' smile turned wicked, onyx eyes lighting with something as she recited the words. The darkness disappeared into Cassie and her body lurched, muscles spasming before she went limp on the table.

Cassie's chest expanded, a deep gasp drawing in a gulp of breath before she settled. Her chest rose and fell again, the color returning to her skin almost immediately. Relief washed over me, but the smile hadn't faded from Eris' face, and unease settled in my gut.

"What did you do to her?" I asked, my chest heaving as I pulled against the invisible bindings, desperate to get to Cassie, to feel her, to hold her.

"She is now as she was meant to be," Eris said, rising to her full height, the shadows disappearing. She lifted her onyx eyes to me, that wicked smile tugging at the corners of her lips as she lifted her hand. "Be careful. She may be a bit... bitey."

She snapped her fingers, and I plummeted through the stone, darkness swallowing me whole once more.

I slammed into wood floors, the shadows slithering back into the far corners of the room, our room. I jumped to my feet, eyes searching. Where had she gone?

The softest breath caught my attention, and I spun to our bed to find Cassie resting on the blankets, still clothed in white silk. Her chest rose and fell in a fluid motion, and I rushed to her bedside. I reached out reluctantly, afraid that this might be a dream or a trick. Had Eris truly saved her? Had she done something to her?

She is now as she was meant to be.

What did she mean by that? Had she healed her? Had she...

Oh Gods, had she changed her? I leaned over her, my eyes falling to her slightly parted lips. I couldn't tell if she had fangs.

"Cas?" I whispered, reaching out to run a hand against her cheek. It was warm, and the bond danced between us, the tingle rippling across my hand where our skin met, and I could've wept for how wonderful it was to feel it, to feel her.

"Cas?"

She didn't stir.

A loud bang shook through the house as the front door slammed open downstairs.

"Damien?" It was Vincent whose voice rang out across the house, his words laced with panic. "Are you here?"

I hesitated, but left Cassie and headed for the door, dipping my head into the hall to call to him. "I'm up here!"

His feet thundered against the wood steps as he rushed upstairs, and I returned to Cassie's bedside.

"What the hell happened? Anna got a call from Johnson about darkness exploding in Cassie's room, and..." His words trailed off as he entered the room, his eyes landing on Cassie. His chest heaved, as if he'd run the whole way here. "Is she?"

I nodded my head. "She's alive."

"But... but how? Johnson said she... she flatlined." Vincent's voice broke, and when I got a good look at him I realized how red his eyes were. He'd known she'd died.

I opened my mouth to answer, but considered my words. "I found a way."

"You mean—" he gaped, his eyes snapping to her again. "Is she... How?"

I couldn't tell him about Eris, couldn't risk the consequences if the knowledge got out, if The Twelve might come after us. "An old spell... Forgotten magic."

He eyed me but approached the bed. "Johnson's office is freaking out. They thought you lost it when they couldn't revive her. You weren't answering your phone. No one knew where you'd gone."

"Sorry, it's..." I drew a deep breath, the nerves still leaving my body shaken. "It's complicated, but she's alive."

My eyes drifted back to her, taking in every detail of her beautiful face.

"She's still with us."

CHAPTER 69

CASSIE

I was hollow... I was empty... I was void... I was...
What was I?
Something delicious filled my senses, my lungs, and... Oh gods, I was starving, as if I'd never tasted food, never drank water. My bones ached as if every inch of my body had been broken down, as if it were mending itself back together piece by piece. My mouth watered, my lips parting as I inhaled that delicious fragrance. I wanted it.
Someone was speaking, but their voice.... It was as if water divided us, as if I were sitting beneath the surface, listening. I couldn't understand anything they said, their words, their voice so muffled I couldn't even discern who it was. I didn't care, though. The pain in my

stomach and my mouth was too much to bear. An intense throbbing echoed to my core, my teeth hurting so badly. Why did it hurt? Why—

A pounding flooded my ears, a rhythmic beat so melodic, so beautiful, that my mind, my thoughts narrowed in on it. It was all I heard, all I cared about.

My eyes were leaden, but I opened them, the dim light burning, and I groaned. Something touched my arm, but I couldn't see straight, couldn't think straight as the person spoke, their voice murky and rippling like a pond surface disturbed by a stray stone. The sweet scent filled my lungs as I breathed, and the pounding picked up, a steady, exciting thump... thump... thump. The throbbing in my teeth became too much to bear, my stomach so hollowed I thought I might die... I *would* die.

My body hummed, my bones singing, and... Gods, my throat. It burned so badly, so dry, I thought it might be on fire. I panted as I pushed myself up, the fibers of the blankets like sandpaper against my skin.

The person spoke again, but I didn't care to try to discern what they were saying as they pressed against my skin. My ears narrowed in on the pounding that nearly drowned out their muffled words, the sound growing louder and louder until nothing else occupied my mind.

My gaze latched onto the person leaning over me, their features blurred and melted, dark and covered in red shadows. Everything was red, energy rippling off every object around me like steam, but their body... Gods, their body was white hot, pumping with veins of liquid life. My mouth watered as my vision latched onto the pulsing, as if I could see the flow of what my body wanted, the liquid concentrating in one place. I inhaled the scent so delicious that I couldn't want anything more. I needed it.

I pushed myself up, my body taking over, and I couldn't get to them fast enough, couldn't latch onto whatever it was I saw, the scent too much to resist. I slammed into them, my breath coming in shallow gasps as my body protested every movement. The air was icy against my skin, the scratch of the fabric clothing my body far too irritating. I wanted to rip it off, but I needed what they had, needed it above all else. My lips parted as I inhaled the scent beneath the surface, that source I so desperately needed to taste.

Someone grabbed hold of my arms from behind, pulling me away. I pulled against their hold, desperate to taste that power, that life, my stomach howling, throat burning. They persisted, struggling to drag me away, and I jerked my gaze over my shoulder. How dare they put their hands on me, come between me and what was mine? White hot anger flared within me as I bared my teeth at them. The hands released me with a shout, and I dropped down, thrusting my foot out to swipe their legs out from under them. Their body hit the floor with a thud, and I leapt, pinning them to the floor beneath me. They didn't smell nearly as nice, but Gods, I didn't care. I was so desperate, so thirsty.

The pounding grew louder and louder, the glowing red energy pulsing so brightly that I couldn't pull myself away from it, from the luscious scent lingering just beneath the surface. I lowered myself, and the pain grew more unbearable the closer I got to tasting it. My lips parted, the throbbing concentrating into two points.

A voice from behind me shouted, but I didn't care, couldn't stop myself as I—

I froze as a stronger, richer scent flooded my senses from behind me, decadent and everything I could have ever wanted. I lifted my head, turning my gaze to the figure standing behind me, the source of life, the power, the rich red liquid dripping from the person's wrist as they held it out to me.

The body beneath me remained frozen, and I pushed myself up from them, my gaze locked on the liquid dripping to the floor, the bright light of power fading to darkness as it hit the wood. My body quaked, hollow stomach howling as I watched it fall.

I needed it, more than anything.

CHAPTER 70

DAMIEN

I stood frozen, the dagger gripped in my hand, blood oozing from my wrist as I held it out to her. Vincent lay frozen on the floor beneath her, his burned hands held out in surrender, wide eyes locked with mine as his chest heaved.

"That's right. Come to me," I said. "I have what you need."

Her blush lips parted, her tongue sweeping across the small fangs peeking into view, but it wasn't the fangs my gaze latched onto. Pale orbs stared back at me, the only remnants of those hazel eyes now a sliver in the silver of her right iris, a fragment of what she once was. She'd been changed. She *was* immortal, and she was dangerous.

I could tell by the way her glazed eyes locked onto the blood dripping from my wrist, crystalline veins lighting her silver iris', pupils expanding and contracting at the subtlest movement, and how the pain and hunger had etched into her beautiful face, that she wasn't herself, wasn't in her right mind. She didn't even seem to recognize me or Vincent. I'd seen very few immortals get this bad in my lifetime, had experienced it myself once. It wasn't a place our kind dared to risk falling into.

Bloodlust.

Be careful, she may be a bit... bitey.

Fucking Eris. She knew this was going to happen, must be sitting in her castle in the Godsrealm laughing to herself. Cassie didn't deserve this kind of suffering.

She grimaced briefly, before her eyes locked back on my wrist.

"It's okay, *mea luna*. I know it hurts," I breathed. "I can fix it."

She climbed off Vincent, pale eyes flickering as she pushed herself to her feet. I prayed Ethel didn't show up, that no one else did.

"You okay, Vincent? Don't speak, just nod."

Vincent nodded hesitantly. I knew it wouldn't take him long to heal, but Gods, she'd burned him, his skin red and peeling in places already, the scent of burned flesh lingering in the air. It was dangerous enough that Vincent was here. I didn't care if she hurt me, but Anna needed Vincent. I couldn't let Cassie hurt him more than she already had.

Vincent lifted himself up, but I gave a short harsh shake of my head, praying he saw and remained still. We couldn't risk drawing her attention from me again. We might not be so lucky a second time. He froze, heeding my warning, his eyes flickering to Cassie as she tilted her head.

I braced myself as she lurched forward, crossing the few feet between us. My ass slammed into the dresser as she crashed into me, her lips finding their mark.

Vincent shot to his feet, ready to intervene. I threw my other hand up. "No!"

He halted, eyes wide as Cassie bit into my already sliced wrist, and I ground my teeth together at the searing pain. "But she—"

"I'm okay. Get out of here, now."

I bit down against the pain as she drew on my wrist, and he hesitated.

"What if she takes too much, Damien?"

"I'll be okay, I promise. Make sure no one else enters the house until I give the all clear."

Vincent's eyes flitted to Cassie once more before cursing under his breath and slipping out the door quietly. Cassie's body tensed as the door clicked shut, her lips threatening to release me. Shit. I couldn't let her stop. She needed the blood. I didn't know exactly what Eris' magic had done to her, what her body had undergone during the change. I flexed my hand, causing the blood to flow faster, and she immediately lost all sense of anything as the blood flooded her mouth, and latched onto my wrist again.

There was nothing gentle about her feeding, and I braced myself against the nightstand as she drew deeply at my wrist. She wasn't getting enough, and her pulls grew more desperate. I needed to get her to my throat where she could get more blood. She broke the contact before I could do anything, hot panted breaths spilling out over the wound on my wrist. Blood dripped down her lips, droplets staining the white silk of her gown, and... Gods, if the sight of those blood tipped fangs didn't stir something in me.

My body tightened, and I tried to ignore it, tried to ignore every instinct roaring to life as she fed from me.

Her eyes wandered, as if she were realizing her surroundings, and for a moment I caught a glimpse of her beneath the surface of the predator that had taken over. I slid my hand down her back, and she stiffened, her gaze jerking to me, pupils expanding as our gazes locked. She resurfaced again at the sight of me, if only for a moment, her brows scrunching as she blinked.

"Here," I coaxed, pulling my hair from the side of my neck, and her eyes dropped to my throat, to the vein thrumming with what she wanted.

"I don't..." Her voice was pained, and she withdrew as if fighting with herself, with the instinct to feed. Gods, I could only imagine how confused she must have been.

I stopped her, pulling her back against me. "Don't fight it, *mea luna*. It's going to be okay. I'm going to make it better."

Her gaze flickered between my eyes and my throat, and her scent flooded the room. Gods, I wanted to feel those fangs sink into me, feel her take from my throat. My skin tightened at the mere thought of it, at the thought of all the things I wanted to do to her while she took from my vein.

"Take from me. *Use me*," I said, trying to hold myself back as my cock pressed against the fly of my jeans, begging to be touched by those

527

delicate hands, those soft lips. I ground my teeth together, my own fangs lengthening at the sight of her flushed cheeks, of the blood painting her lips.

Fucking hell. I forced myself to let her take lead, resisting the urge to pull her to me, hike up that blood-stained gown she wore and bury myself inside her—feel that slick heat consume me.

She panted, and thank the gods, stopped resisting my hold, stopped fighting as her gaze latched wholly on my throat. Her hands glided up my chest, each inch torturous, each second leading my mind into a spiral of all the ways I wanted those hands to touch me. I tilted my head to the side, my hand sweeping down her back in encouraging strokes. Her heated breath spilled out against my skin, and I inhaled sharply. She tensed before she could bite down, her hands twitching as they gripped my shirt tightly.

"Don't hesitate," I breathed into her hair, lifting my hand to the back of her head.

She bit down, those glorious little fangs piercing into my throat, and my body bucked, the sharp pain immediately melting into something sinful.

"*Fuck.*"

A moan slipped from her lips as she drank down the first gulp, and I nearly came right there. I calmed the roaring in my blood, the need threatening to ignite me. I wanted to feel her around me, feel her ride my cock as she fed from my vein, let her taste every bit of the pleasure she sent coursing through my body. Our bond roared to life in electric waves.

She drew another deep pull before her knees buckled. I wrapped my arms around her waist, pulling her against me so she could continue. She moaned against my skin as I slid my knee between her thighs, allowing her to settle against me. I cursed at the molten heat at her core, and I realized she was bare beneath her gown.

Her scent heightened, the scent of jasmine and citrus strong, mixed with the sweet scent of her arousal. I wanted to taste her, to throw her up on the dresser and drop to my knees before her. My hands drifted down her back, over her hips where the gown bunched as she straddled my thigh. I gripped her hips, pulling them forward against my knee, and she broke from my neck to gasp a moan.

"*Sorry,*" I breathed, but she latched back on. Her hips rocked forward against my thigh again, and the moan that slipped from her throat broke my focus, broke my control. My hands slid around to grab her ass, and I pulled her firmly against me as she rocked against my leg and...

"Fucking hell, Cas," I breathed into her ear. "Gods, I want to feel you on me."

The scent of her arousal told me she wanted it just as badly, and I'd let her use me however she needed—my vein, my lips, my leg, my cock. She could have it all.

Her hand fell to the front of my pants, making quick work of the button and zipper. Was she aware yet? Or was this the effects of the feeding, of the bloodlust? I couldn't see her eyes, and I didn't want to risk pulling her away, didn't want to stop her before she'd gotten what she needed.

Her hand slid into my jeans, the tips of her fingers brushing against—

"*Gods*," I groaned, my head falling back.

She moaned as the taste of my pleasure slid down her throat, as it echoed to every inch of her body, just as it did for me when I drank down every ounce of her ecstasy as she cried out my name. I could lose myself in that taste, in the sensation, in her.

Her hand wrapped around my cock. She stroked me from base to tip and back down again, and I dropped my head against her shoulder, sweat breaking out across my skin as I held myself back. I wanted to take her, to lift her up and feel that wet heat envelop me as I plunged myself into her so deeply she screamed my name.

She paused her strokes as she broke the connection with my throat to catch a breath, and I grabbed hold of her hand before she could pull free of my jeans. I pressed a kiss to her shoulder, gripping her hand around my cock, unable to hold myself back anymore, needing to feel her in some way. A moan slipped from my lips as she continued to glide her hand over me, and my hips pumped against her, meeting each stroke.

My fangs lengthened, throbbing, desperate to taste her as she tasted me, but not yet. That would come later when she was fully recovered and strong enough. My pants sagged down on my hips, and I held her hand to me, my fingers wrapping on hers as she pumped me until I thought I might shatter.

I ran my tongue up her neck, and the moan that tore from her throat nearly caused me to slip and bite down. Her chest heaved against mine as she gasped for air, her back bowing as she caved into me.

She didn't return to my neck, her head dipping forward to rest against my shoulder. Had she taken enough? Had she returned to me? I pulled back just enough to see her face, my hand rising to tilt her chin up to see those dazzling eyes meet mine. She blinked, as if her vision was focusing, and her hand halted its strokes.

Her lips parted as her eyes drifted over my face. That hunger lingered in her eyes, though, that little fleck of hazel gleaming amidst the silver glow.

"Damien, I... I don't—"

I kissed her, the sound of her voice the most beautiful music I'd ever heard. I'd nearly lost her, possibly for good, but she was here, alive.

Her hand slipped free of my pants and reached up to ensnare her fingers in my hair. She pulled me closer, her lips crashing into my own, and I groaned. I felt her hunger with each stroke of her lips, each brush of her tongue against mine. She broke the kiss, eyes falling back to my throat, the hunger lingering.

"If you need more, it's okay," I breathed, cupping her face, eager for her to take me again. Immeasurable pride swelled within me that I could give her what her body needed, that I could give her strength.

Her fingers dug into my arm, and I groaned at the feel of her skin against mine. Her hands dropped to the hem of my shirt, and she lifted it up and over my head before she passed her tongue against the puncture wounds on my neck. Waves of ecstasy rippled out to every inch of my body. I wanted her, couldn't wait another moment to feel her fangs sink into me as my cock plunged into her.

I grabbed hold of her hips and pulled her against me as I dropped my head to press kisses against her shoulder, up her neck. I stepped back to the bed, kicking off my jeans and boxers before I eased down to sit before her. She didn't hesitate, climbing up until she straddled me, my cock free and pressed up against her slick heat. The feel of it was almost too much, but I held back, resisted the urge to let myself go.

Her lips crashed against mine for one, much too short, heated kiss before she pushed me back onto the bed. Her glossy eyes roamed my chest, her tongue passing over her bloodied lips as those fangs caught the dim light of the lamps. My cock twitched at the sight of them.

"Tell me what you want, *mea luna*."

Her chest heaved, her nipples pebbling against the thin silk of her gown. I wanted to taste them, wanted to nip and lick them until she was writhing.

"You," she breathed.

"Take me," I dared her. "I'm yours."

Her eyes fell to my throat once more, blushed lips parting, and she crawled up my chest, each brush of her silken gown, of her skin, leaving rippling need in its wake. She tilted her head as she lowered her face to the crook of my neck. I tilted my head back as she bit down, the rush of pleasure surging through me, my cock twitching against her damp heat, desperate to slide inside.

"Lift your hips for me," I groaned into her ear as I grabbed hold of her hips. This would be my invitation; she could stay right where she was, drink from me and rest if she wanted, but gods, I wanted her, wanted to feel her.

She lifted herself just enough, and I guided myself to her entrance before pulling her down onto me. We both cried out in unison, our moans flooding the room as we met each other in one, deep thrust. She took me, every fucking inch. I lifted my hips to meet her as I dragged her forward and back until she found that balance, that rhythm between pulls at my throat and roll of her hips as she rode my cock.

Gods, she was so wet, so slick and warm, and she moaned as I thrust into her with each rock of her hips. I wasn't going to last much longer, my skin too sensitive, the feeding sending me over the edge. She tightened around me, her lips breaking contact with my throat to moan my name and—

"*Fuck*," I groaned, my body coiled, release rolling through me as her silken heat gripped my cock. I grasped her hips, pulling her against me as her own orgasm exploded. I deepened the thrusts, the friction, driving myself deeper as I came, and we moaned together as we shattered, breaking into millions of glorious pieces.

She collapsed against me, our breaths mingling, our bodies drenched in sweat, every brush of skin electric. Her forehead pressed to mine as our gazes locked, and I could cry at the sight of her staring back at me. I lifted my hand to cup her cheek, taking in every detail of her face, every detail of the new eyes staring into mine.

"How is this possible?" she asked, her eyes shifting back and forth between mine.

"I found a way. I promised you I would."

"But… how?"

I hesitated. I couldn't bring myself to tell her about Eris, didn't want the weight of what that cost might one day bear down on her shoulders. "Old magic, and it worked."

Her lips curved into a smile, tears welling in her eyes. "I'm truly immortal?"

"You are, *mea luna*." I pressed a kiss to her soft lips and smiled up at her. "And nothing will separate us again."

CHAPTER 71

CASSIE

My eyes burned as I awoke, the sun's rays leaking through the curtains, much too bright. It was just barely a stream of light, but even the tiniest bit seemed to be nearly unbearable. I groaned, turning over under the comforter and the feel of the fibers against my skin was almost too much. Every sensation was heightened, every touch, every sound amplified so much that I wished I could shut it out.

A throbbing pain had taken root in my head—thoughts, images, and memories surging in a whirlwind. There was so much, as if many of the memories of my past lives that had been just out of reach all resurfaced. Everything fit somehow, as if they were simply distant memories I'd forgotten. Despite the pieces falling into place, I felt like myself, and yet... not.

Was I still... me?

My eyes drifted to the picture frame of my parents sitting on my nightstand. They were still my parents, but... they weren't my first. I had another mother and father... the ones I shared with Zephyr. Adrian and Thea. Thea was my mother, but not Zephyr's. His mother had passed before I was born. My brows narrowed. Maya was her name. I could remember the small painting of her that had adorned the mantle of the fireplace in our home. Zephyr looked so much like her, while I'd resembled our father more, inheriting his blond hair.

The memories around my parents as Lucia were... not pleasant. I shied away from them, of the horror I'd experienced at their hands. The only other parent I should know better was Selene, and every time her name crossed my mind, I felt nothing but cold resentment. She'd been cold to me, and I could never understand why. It irritated me to no end that, despite my memories from my lives as Elena and Lucia, Moira's memories still remained just out of my reach.

There was so much, so many lives, so many memories, wonderful memories and terrible ones. How did it all fit into one mind?

A soft, sleepy groan slipped from Damien's throat as he shifted against me. His scent chased all thoughts from my mind, and my mouth watered, teeth throbbing at the brush of his skin, body heating until I thought I might catch fire.

Pressure built in the top of my mouth, a weight settling into place on my upper teeth, and my eyes latched onto his throat as he pulled me closer to him. His heart thrummed in my ear, though I wasn't pressed against his chest. I shouldn't be able to hear it, and yet I did, and it sent my own heart into a frenzy. I couldn't resist the urge to reach out, to run my finger over the thrumming vein I could somehow sense beneath his skin.

"Go ahead, *mea luna*."

I jumped at the sound of Damien's voice. I had become so entranced, I hadn't even realized he awoke. Gods, I wanted it so badly. "But..."

"It's okay. Our blood replenishes quickly. Take what you need," he said, his arm sliding around my lower back to pull me closer.

My cheeks heated, thinking of all the ways I'd *taken* what I needed the night before. I couldn't understand how I could need more already. "I kept you up almost all night. You must be exhausted."

He pulled me tightly against him, his body bare against my own, his voice husky as he spoke. "I'm *blissfully* exhausted, happy for every second you've taken from me, and I can't tell you how eager I am to satisfy your hunger again and again, with my blood, my cock, whatever you need. I'm yours."

I smiled and pressed a kiss to his lips, his skin so warm and soft, the salt of his sweat mingling with the rich scent of cedarwood and leather. We were a mess, hadn't showered since I'd awoken in our bed the night before, but I'd been so lost, balancing precariously on the edge of hunger, exhaustion, and pure need. I'd lost count of how many times I'd fed, how many times we'd made love to each other, how few hours of sleep we'd managed in between.

"Will I be like this forever?" I asked, almost fearful of what I'd become. Damien had told me a human had never been turned into an immortal, that there were no records of anything like this happening.

"You shouldn't. You just underwent a massive change. Your body's been completely remade, healed. It takes a lot to repair the damage your mortal body harbored. I'm sure you'll feel normal again soon. There's a period similar to this for our kind we call the settling, when we reach our prime, stop aging, and come into our magic. It's then that we develop the need to feed. It's just as intense. I've helped you through your settling once before."

I blinked, scanning through the countless memories screaming to be seen. He had... had helped me as Lucia through my settling. It was hazy, but I vaguely remember bits and pieces.

He tilted his head, and my eyes fell to the skin of his throat, the vein pulsing just beneath the surface, the skin black and blue from all the times I'd fed. My breath caught in my throat as his hand trailed over my hip, the hum of my magic rising to the surface to meet his, the bond so strong, I couldn't imagine never having felt it to begin with. The pull had been there before when I was human, and it had strengthened when we'd done the binding ceremony, but this...

This was more than I could've ever imagined.

His emotions surged—happiness, pride, love, adoration, need, hunger. It was overwhelming, almost too much to register all at once, and my own emotions rose to meet his, crashing into each other like a tidal wave. I lifted my eyes to his once more, smiling as I cupped his cheek.

"*Mine.*"

His amber and ashen eyes brightened, lighting with such profound adoration, I could have cried. "*Yours.*"

I kissed him, and he rolled over, pulling me until I straddled him. His hard length pressed against me, the movement enough to tear a gasp from me as he brushed against that sensitive bundle of nerves between my thighs. My body shuddered against him.

"*Gods,*" I breathed, grabbing onto his shoulders as he sat up. His hands slid down my waist to my hips, his eyes burning as he gazed into mine. I lowered myself to his throat, my fangs throbbing with the promise of the sweet, luscious taste of his blood, of the power within it. I bit down, the rich dark liquid spilling onto my tongue like dark chocolate, and Damien's moan mirrored my own.

Within seconds, he gripped my hips and lifted me just enough to plunge himself into me, my body absorbing every glorious inch of him, and I cried out as we burned together.

We'd spent the entire morning tangled up in each other, and I'd finally started to adjust to the light leaking through the curtain, to the feel of the fabric, the very air against my skin. It was all so strange to adjust to the sounds, the smells, everything.

If it were possible to melt, I would have been a puddle of useless limbs—my body nearly one with the blankets as I lay beneath Damien, his body twitching against mine as I shuddered through the remnants of my orgasm. His skin was slick with sweat. His dark hair hung in damp waves around his face as he gazed down at me, and I lifted my hand to tuck a stray curl behind his ear. A crooked grin formed on his face.

"I don't know which I like more: the sounds you make, or the way you taste on my tongue," he said as he leaned down to brush his lips against mine.

I giggled and shivered at the feel of the stubble along his jaw tickling my skin. "You keep talking like that, and I may just enjoy making *you* call out *my* title in bed."

One of his dark brows cocked up. "I'm awfully tempted to keep you here just to see what you'd do to make that happen."

I pushed at his chest, giggling as he rolled off me.

"In all honesty, while I'd love to hog you all to myself, I'm sure the others are desperate to see you," he said, shifting to the edge of the bed.

"Before that..." I grunted as I pushed myself up, my body protesting the movements. "I need a shower."

"A shower would definitely be nice," Damien agreed with a chuckle. He pressed a kiss to my forehead before pushing himself off the bed.

"I'm going to need a minute," I said, my body still shivering as my orgasm faded.

"I'll go get the shower started," he said, and headed for the bathroom. I turned over onto my side, tilting my head to enjoy the view of his ass.

I couldn't resist; and I blew out a whistle, to which he smirked over his shoulder at me. "Don't tempt me."

I giggled and rolled over onto my stomach, drawing a deep breath as I tried to find control of my body. My gaze fell to the white gown I'd worn the night before, now discarded on the floor. I couldn't remember much of what happened before I'd come to in Damien's arms, his wrist bleeding, my body wracked with so much pain and hunger, I could barely think straight. The pain was gone now—my ribs no longer broken, my shoulder blades healed as well, and the hunger I'd felt last night, while not quite gone, was much more tolerable.

My heart? It didn't hurt anymore, didn't beat the same way—pumping in three powerful beats instead of two...

It was amazing, all the things I could hear now—the wind whistling through the magnolia branches beyond the window, the hum of the radiators throughout the house, the faint, distant sound of cars driving in the city. The shower came to life in the bathroom, the scent of the minerals in the water drifting on the air through the open doorway mixed with Damien's scent of cedarwood and leather, mixed with... my cheeks heated at the sweet and salty scent of what we'd been busy doing for the last several hours.

The sheets rustled as I pushed myself up to sit. Damien returned from the bathroom and his pace quickened when he caught sight of me pushing off the bed. "You okay to stand?"

I nodded, tentatively reaching out to his extended hand, bracing myself as I lowered my feet to the floor. The wood was icy against my skin, but I pushed through it, rising. Gods, I was unsteady, as if I had new legs, which I guess I sort of did in a strange way. My eyes fell to my wrists, and I stiffened. I pulled my hand from Damien's grasp, staring down at the new skin of my arms. The scars left from Marcus' torture were gone—the thin lines on my wrists I had left years ago... gone.

Damien's eyes fell to my unmarred skin, and I wasn't sure if I felt happiness or sadness that every mark, every reminder, had vanished—as if it had never happened. I was new, remade. It was as if I had a chance at a fresh start, unburdened by what had been done to me. I wasn't sure how to feel about it. I should be happy, but...

"Are you okay, *mea luna*?" Damien asked, his hand reaching for my elbow.

"I will be. It's just... a lot to process," I admitted. I wouldn't hide anything from him, no more secrets. He was here at my side, and I his, and we would no longer face the darkness alone.

I drew a deep breath and lifted my eyes to him, a smile tugging at my lips. "About that shower."

He met my smile with his own. "I'll follow your lead. Take your time."

My chest swelled, and my eyes fell to the icy wood floors beneath my feet, every bit of wood grain crystal clear. Damien offered his hand once more, and I took it, leaning into him as I took each step. It wasn't that I felt weak, but more like if I took too big a step, I might lurch forward, or if my steps were too heavy, I might crash through the floor.

"You mentioned before that immortals go through a settling when they come of age." I tried to remember, but the memory was hazy, as if too much time had passed, or it was still settling into place among the countless memories of two lives.

Damien nodded. "They do."

"Is it like this for them?" I asked, lifting my gaze to him then quickly dropping it back to the floor, as I had lost track of where my feet were meant to go.

"Almost. It's very similar. It can be painful for some, and it takes them a while afterward to recover and feel normal in their own skin again," he explained.

We gradually made it to the bathroom, steam licking my skin in heated waves, and I shivered at the all too sensitive feel of it. I halted as we passed the vanity, at the sight of silver eyes staring back at me. My breath caught in my throat, and I pulled from Damien's hold. I braced myself against the vanity as I stared at my reflection. My mother's eyes... one of the few pieces of her I had left—

I leaned forward, my gaze latching onto my right eye, to the small sliver of hazel that still remained, blending into the silver like a brushstroke of paint.

"She's still here," I muttered without meaning to as my hand lifted to my face, my finger brushing my cheek just beneath the silver and hazel. Everything else looked almost the same; my body hadn't seemed to change much, just... healed. New. Damien's arms came around me, and his lips brushed my temple as I relaxed into him.

"Am I still... me, Damien?" I asked, my gaze faltering from my face, from the stranger's eyes staring back at me.

"It's a lot to take in, I know, but you're still you. You're still Cassie, regardless of what form you take," he said against my cheek, his head leaning forward to settle against my own. "You are you, and no one else."

CHAPTER 72

CASSIE

"Easy, now, one step at a time," Damien said as he stood on the stair below me, his hand bracing mine as I took the next step down. His eyes flitted between my face and my feet with each step, ready to catch me if I fell. "Don't rush."

I started to grumble, but my center of gravity shifted the slightest bit, threatening to send me tumbling down the stairs, and I grabbed onto Damien's hand tighter. "Gods, I hope this doesn't last long."

Damien's eyes flickered to me a moment before he chuckled. "You'll get used to it soon enough. Parts of you are likely still settling. Give it time. You should be back to normal in a few days. You'll probably be able to walk on your own in a few hours. It'll come. Just be patient, *mea luna*."

I sighed. I didn't want to be patient. I wanted to get out of this house, wanted to go see everything, hear everything. I wanted to try using my powers again. With the memories came a sense of how to use them, albeit a little hazy. I was excited to try them out, to train again.

A number of scents and smells flooded my senses as we neared the bottom of the steps, and quiet mutterings reached my ears. Damien had notified everyone to come over in the later afternoon, allowing me enough time to shower and dress. The showering part had taken a while, the water like needles on my skin at first.

Zephyr and the others were already downstairs. I could only imagine what the last twenty-four hours had been like for them. I'd died, or I thought I had, it was all a blur.

The thunder of paws echoed down the hall, and Thalia appeared at the foot of the stairs. Her tired, pale eyes found mine, the sliver of her scar pronounced against her dappled gray fur. She whined and yipped as she hovered at the base of the steps, watching us descend. Her scent filled my lungs, woodsy and fresh like black spruce and wintergreen.

"She's unsteady but she's okay, Thalia; just getting used to her new legs," Damien assured her. She stepped back as I lowered myself from the final step onto flat ground. I'd never been happier to be at the base of the stairs, and I didn't know if I'd be able to make it back up them.

Thalia's head slid under my free hand as she pressed into me, her fur soft enough that I wanted to bury myself in it. I smiled, running my fingers over her head. I wondered when she might shift back, when I'd get to see her face again, hear her voice.

"The moment she heard you were here, she was on the front porch with Vincent, standing guard," Damien said.

I wondered what she might be thinking, whether she thought at all or had fled into the bare instincts guiding her to escape the feelings that had plagued her. I lowered to my knees and wrapped my arms around her. She was so warm, and her scent was so calming.

"I won't invade your thoughts, but I'm here if you want to talk," I whispered into her ear. Her ears twitched and perked, and she leaned her head into me, whining softly.

"Cas?" a hesitant voice reached my ears from down the hall—a voice wrapped in a warm summer breeze, one I'd known for centuries.

I lifted my head to gaze upon Zephyr, his face stark, pale green eyes wide as he took me in.

"Gods, it's really true," he breathed, heading for me.

I grunted, pushing myself to my feet, and Damien reached out to help me.

Zephyr's massive arms wrapped around me; his scent so strong. I didn't know how I'd never noticed it before, comforting and warm, like sage and pine. He held me for the longest time, and I leaned into him. Tears welled in my eyes as memories that flooded my mind within the last twelve hours resurfaced—of times when he'd first taught me to shift as a freshly settled teenager, times when he'd taken me out into the woods to hunt for dinner. We'd been so close. He was the best big brother I could've ever asked for.

I breathed, my chest contracting as I tried to hold back the emotions. "There's so much I want to talk to you about, so much I want to know."

Zephyr's body tensed and he pulled back just enough to gaze down at me. His eyes widened, tears dotting his lashes, and he glanced at Damien, who nodded. He wrapped his arms around me once more, his adoration filling my lungs like wildflowers and sweet tobacco. "I thought we'd lost you."

"I thought so too," I admitted. Those final moments were hazy. The last thing I remembered was the terror that flooded me and the words I'd shared with Damien. Gods, I was so glad they weren't my last, that we would be able to have that time I'd wanted.

"Everyone's in the living room," Zephyr said, releasing me, and Thalia nudged my leg toward the hallway. Damien and Zephyr both took my hands, helping me that way.

The crackle of the fire in the fireplace reached my ears before we entered the living room, but the moment I turned into the doorway, all sounds of the house quieted—the crackling of the fire, the hum of the radiators, everything.

They were all here—Vincent, Anna, Calista, James, Ethel, Salwa, Eiko, Semele; they all stood before me, eyes wide with shock and joy. I pulled from Damien and Zephyr, stumbling forward before Calista caught me, and I wrapped my arms around her, letting the tears fall as I held onto her. Warmth enveloped me as the others slowly surrounded me, their arms wrapping me in a tight hug.

"Thank the Fates," Vincent breathed before releasing me, the sight of his grin and tear-filled eyes only causing my own to fall harder.

I turned to find Anna smiling warmly at me. Gods, it felt like ages since I'd seen her last, since I'd felt the kick of the sweet babe growing in her womb. Realization and profound joy surged through me as my eyes met Anna's.

I wouldn't have to miss out on anything.

Laughter echoed throughout the house, and it was more than I could ever want, more than I could ever ask for. Semele had broken out a few bottles of ambrosia liquor, and we'd spent the last few hours celebrating. Damien, Zephyr, and Vincent knocked back a shot before staring each other down, waiting to see who caved first. Vincent wavered and threw his hand up, bowing out, and the laughter returned, Anna running her fingers through Vincent's dirty blond curls as he leaned back against the couch in drunken defeat. I snickered before light caught my eye. The sun was setting outside, the blanket of night working to cover the city.

I glanced once more to Damien as he turned on Zephyr, ready to take him out next. I took a tentative step back and slipped out of the room, holding onto the blanket Damien had given me when I'd become chilled. I headed for the back door. Cheering and hollering echoed throughout the house, and I wondered if either of the two had caved. Just as I reached for the doorknob, I felt the brush of fur against my hip, and I glanced down to see Thalia at my side. She nudged her nose against my elbow, and I smiled.

"Join me for some fresh air?" I asked, and Thalia's silver eyes fell to the doorway in silent confirmation.

I turned the doorknob and pushed the door open, the cold crisp evening air skating over my skin. I pulled my blanket tighter around me as I stepped out. The woodsy and earthy scents of the forest behind the house flooded my lungs, and it was the most wonderful thing to breathe in. The door eased closed behind me, and I took it one step at a time as Thalia leapt down the stairs into the grass before turning back to me.

"I'm coming, I'm coming," I said, reaching out for the railing and taking each step carefully, the wood creaking and groaning beneath my feet. I delighted in the feel of it against my skin, every groove, every imperfection, but it was nothing compared to the soft feel of the grass as I stepped down into it.

My chest expanded with a deep breath, inhaling the scents around me as I walked farther from the back porch and closer to the forest. I lowered to my knees, Thalia standing nearby as she watched, and the Dendron magic within me called out to the grass, to the trees, to the plants surrounding us. It was peaceful, and yet... not. The sounds were louder with my heightened senses—mixing and mingling with the animals skittering around in the forest, the distant sound of cars driving in the city.

I could lose myself in the hum of the magic, though, like music singing in my very veins. It didn't last, and the magic faltered beneath the weight of everything else, of every memory dancing through my mind, of all that had happened...

Of Kat.

Thalia settled into the grass, stretching her legs out to lay down at my back. I settled against her. We laid there for a long while, and I tried to focus on the sun setting over the ridge, the purples and blues of the sky as the moon rose at the far end of the valley. I drew a deep breath and turned onto my side, burrowing into the warmth of her fur, trying to focus on the steady rhythm of her heart, of her breath. It wasn't enough, though, for in the quiet calm, everything surfaced. How did I find normalcy in it all, in the countless lives trying to fit into one mind, one body?

Kat.

I didn't want to believe it, didn't want to think about everything she'd revealed, everything she'd done, that it was because of her we'd lost Barrett. Something stirred deep inside my chest, something I hadn't felt before: a void, as if at the very core of my being, there was a central mass of... nothing. It rippled, as if stirred by the bitter anger and hurt swelling in my chest at the thought of her and everything she'd done.

None of it had ever been real.

"Cas?"

I jerked and looked over my shoulder. "Hey."

"Is everything ok?" Damien asked as he settled into the grass beside me. Thalia didn't budge, and I couldn't tell if she was awake or if she'd drifted into a nap.

"I just needed some fresh air," I said, my gaze lifting to the moon now hanging just above the ridge, a few stars just becoming visible as the light faded. "Who won? You or Zephyr?"

"Are you kidding?" he said with a smug grin. "I could drink those guys under the table."

I snickered, but the thoughts returned, and I pressed my lips together as the question lingered on my tongue. "Any news on Cole?" I asked, glancing back at him.

He let out a sigh, his shoulders sagging. "They're holding him until they can pass judgement. It'll probably be a couple of months before they hold his trial."

"Any news of Ka—" I drew a deep breath, wishing I could purge that name from my mind. "Of Melantha? Of Cody?"

His amber and ashen eyes lingered on me, as if watching for any hint of the pain that had worked its way into me. "None."

I slumped against Thalia, my eyes falling on the dark forest before us.

"I'm sorry about everything with Kat," he said, and I hated the sound of her name on his lips.

"Don't be... It was never real for her, so why should it be for me?" I wished I could believe those words, wished I could will the pain in my chest to vanish.

"It's okay to feel hurt by her betrayal, Cas."

I swallowed, hating that I *did* feel the hurt.

"I do... And I hate it. I'm so hurt... and sad... and angry." I turned my gaze to him, something sparking within me, something else stirring in that abysmal void at my core.

"And I will destroy her for everything she's done."

545

EPILOGUE

Melantha's shriek rang out through the cavern, followed closely by a loud crack as the tendrils of dark magic launched a stray boulder to the far stone wall. Darklings scattered out of the way as best they could, but a few lay broken and shattered on the ground, black blood oozing into a pool beneath a pile of mangled limbs.

I... *We* remained where we stood, silent, listening… waiting.

That was all we could do. Wait. Wait for a command, an attack, an itch we couldn't scratch. Our chest twisted, the unending nausea and hunger clawing in our gut, our fangs throbbing.

I needed to get back to—

We don't need anything but to serve. We are a tool.

What... did I need to get back to? What had I been fighting for? What had I been protecting?

Melantha's chest heaved, her hollow black eyes wild and furious. "She was mine!"

Another boulder flew through the cavern as she shrieked again, and the darklings' clicks were drowned out by the thunderous sound of

LUNA LAURIER

crushing stone. More black blood, more shrieks. "That filthy mutt! How did she find us?"

A darkling crawled past me, baring its sharp teeth, and my fingers twitched as I fought for control of my limbs to strike—

They are us. We are them.

We... are them.

We rolled our neck, easing the building tension, and turned our gaze back to our injured queen. She examined her arm, half of it had been torn from her body by the immortal shifter. The flesh was sealed, her body already working to grow back the missing limb. "I finally had her!"

Our skin bristled at the mention of her, and something icy sliced deep at the memory. She is our enemy. *They* are our enemy. They are to be destroyed. And we will do it all for the glory of our queen. We will destroy all who stand in her path.

No…

Yes…

I didn't want—

We *want this.* **We** *want to be used.* **We** *are hers.*

We... are hers...

We lifted our eyes as our queen turned to us, her chest heaving. Her tendrils of darkness staked into the ground, lifting her up, carrying her closer. The sea of darklings parted as they crawled and slinked out of her way without need of command, her will their own. They shifted and moved, each step building dread and awe in our very core.

She lowered before me, her eyes level with mine. "You."

Me.

Us.

"I may have use for you after all."

My teeth ground, biting back the words clawing up my throat. "Use us," we said, every word a poison coating my—our tongue.

"We are yours."

547

Thank you so much for taking a chance on the shadow and moonlight series. I cannot wait for you to read what comes next.

I would love for you to join my reader group on discord so we can all chat about your thoughts and feelings on the Shadow and Moonlight Series. This group is the first to find out about cover reveals, books news, new releases, sneak peeks, ARC opportunities, and a way to meet other like-minded readers.

Once again, thank you so much for taking the time to read my book.

XOXO,
Luna Laurier
www.lunalaurier.com

If you enjoyed the book, please consider leaving an honest review on Goodreads & Amazon

https://www.goodreads.com/book/show/
60626092-of-shadow-and-moonlight

CONTINUED IN BOOK 2.5
OF THE SHADOW AND
MOONLIGHT SERIES

SHE WHO BITES THE FLAME

COMING
SPRING 2024

ADD ON GOODREADS

Luna laurier's Taste of Darkness

Can't get enough of the Shadow and Moonlight Universe and it's characters? Join the Patreon to gain access to bonus scenes and content not in the books, bonus spicy scenes between characters (both canon and non-canon *eyes the spicy scene between Cassie, Damien, and Marcus*), NSFW artwork, ARC Team access, discounts on merch and signed books, and more!

www.patreon.com/lunalaurier

SHOP THE OFFICIAL MERCH STORE

LUNALAURIER.COM

GLOSSARY

Aleirene touen/tauen enlisnó en solos - A phrase spoken to honor the fallen meaning "peace embrace his/her soul".

Ambrosia Liquor - A potent drink that is distilled and bottled in the Godsrealm. Due to the high metabolism of immortals and other beings of the Godsrealm, alcohols of the mortalrealm have little to no effect. Humans should never drink as a single sip could cause sever alcohol poisoning and possibly even death.

Archivallia (ark-i-vall-E-uh) - The massive library housing every record of the immortal race.

Aristocracy - A group of pure-blooded immortals.

Astral Sprites (Librarians) - Sprites created by Selene to tend to the Archivallia and the rest of the temple. They are small standing about two feet tall, their bodies are made up of night sky and starlight and have little tails. Majority of them reside in the Archivallia, assisting Salwa and caring for the books. They do not speak, but they do chitter to each other, communication with feelings and intentions rather than words.

Brierleaf (br-eye-er-leaf) - a potent herb that when smoked can give psychoactive affects similar to that of marijuana.

Celestia - The single deity worshipped by the Elythians and many of the residents of the Godsrealm.

Coronis (cor-O-nis) - A swarm of crow-like birds summoned by House Skiá from the Godsrealm. In the Godsrealm their forms are more like large crows, but when summoned by House Skiá, they take on a form of black mist and shadow and are often used to swarm enemies. They were turned against the immortals by Melantha during The Fall of Kingdoms. Anyone who falls prey to them suffer a slow and agonizing death.

Dimós trees (deem-yOs) - A tree of the Godsrealm, with velvety smooth bark that is pale and glows. These trees have no leaves and are ageless, living for millennia. They are believed to have sprouted from the tears of

Celestia, the one deity the Elythian's worship, when she cast her mate from the heavens.

Elythia (el-i-thia) - One of 26 countries in the Godsrealm. It is divided into 12 kingdoms/domains which are governed by 12 Elythian's. There are many races that inhabit Elythia: elythians, elves, fae, wyverns, and many other creatures of myth and legend.

Elythians - A race of ancient beings who were worshipped in Ancient Greece when they wandered across the veil and met humans. They among one of the most ancient races, descendants of the first created by Celestia. Elythian's inhabit the continent of Elythia within the Godsrealm.

Godsrealm - A realm, parallel to the Mortalrealm, where magic exists, everything creature of myth and legends resides within this realm. The myths and legends within the Mortalrealm are formed when creatures of the Godsrealm wander through "ripples" in the veil that separates the Godsrealm from the Mortalrealm. The greek gods exist within the realm which are an ancient race known as Elythians. There are many continents housing many other ancient races much like the Elythians, which have each had their own impact on certain places in the Mortalrealm.

The Twelve - A group of Elythians that govern the continent of Elythia.

Houses of Power - A number of guilds within the immortal race where immortals are sorted or aligned based on which magical affinity they have.

House of Skiá́ (skee-uh) - Users skilled in shadowmancy

House of Nous (noos) - Users skilled in mindbending

House of Stoicheion (st-eye-chyon) - Users skilled in element magic

House of Thiríon (ther-E-on) – Users skilled in beast shifting

House of Psukhé́ (tsu-kay) – Users skilled in telekinesis

House of Dendron – Users skilled in plant magic

House of Leukos (loo-k-O-s) - Users skilled in lightmancy

House of Aíma (eye-ma) – Users skilled in blood manipulation

House of Latros (lat-r-O-s) – Users skilled in healing magic

Kyrios (ker-E-O-s) - Leaders of the Houses of Power.

Lunassia Flower - A pale flower from the Godsrealm that only blooms on the Astral Mountains once a year during the lunar solstice.

Lupai (loo-p-eye) - Wolves summoned by House Skiá from the Godsrealm, in the Godsrealm their forms are more like large wolves, but when summoned by House Skiá, they take on a form of black mist and shadow.

Mikros (mee-kr-O-s) - A term of endearment referring to children meaning "little one", or from parent to offspring.

Moonhaven - A village built by the immortals to be a new home after they moved to the Mortalrealm to hunt the darklings.

Oneiroi (O-near-ee) - A nous user with unique amplified abilities that only a rare few are born with. The few immortals with this ability were trained during the Godswar as spies and assassins, infiltrating enemy domains to "tether" themselves to their target and use their unique dreamwalking ability to gain information or assassinate their target.

Pantheon - Refers to the individual groups those who descended from the origin race within the Godsrealm. The Elythians are one of the groups. Different pantheons rule over their own continents and domains.

Tabularius - The historian of the immortal race. The title is only given to one immortal, only passed on from teacher to student when the title's holder dies.

Telos Pyrai (teh-l-O-s-pear-eye) - An ability used by the flame Stoicheion that builds up the flame magic and unleashes it all at one like a bomb. It is not often that the user survives the use of this ability and it is often used as a last resort. If the user survives they are left vulnerable and depleted.

The Order - A group of warriors serving under Selene that are tasked with fighting the darklings.

ELYTHIAN TRANSLATIONS

adôs *(odd-Os)* - brother

afin *(ah-fin)* - let, allow

Aleirene *(al-ir-ee-n)* - Peace, peaceful

asidia *(ah-s-id-ya)* - shield

atresei *(at-res-eye)* - As, like

belariôs *(bel-ar-ee-Os)* - Warrior

charisti *(cah-ree-stee)* - to give thanks

dorai *(door-eye)* - gift, to gift

Dýnamis - strength

ekein *(eh-keen)* - those

emei *(em-ee)* - We, us, our

emôs *(em-yo-s)* - Mine

èn *(connective word)* - in, on, of

enlisnô *(en-lis-nO)* - Embrace, to hold

esti *(es-tee)* - so

èstin *(es-tin)* - is, has

etai *(e-t-eye)* - from

etu *(e-too)* - to

ge *(zsh-ay)* - for

gravôsia *(gra-v-O-shia)* - to carry, pregnant

hallôs *(hal-Os)* - Heart, love

kalôsa *(k-al-O-sa)* - welcome

kelisa *(k-el-ee-sa)* - Most beautiful

lamprei *(lamp-r-eye)* - bright, shining

leukôs / leukô *(l-ewk-Os)* - Light

llispsais *(ill-ip-s-eye)* - missed you, miss you

luna *(l-oo-na)* - Moon

manya *(m-ah-n-ya)* - cloak, cloaked, to cloak

Mávrôsia *(mav-ro-shya)* - black, blackened

mea *(may)* - My, my own

Metai *(met-eye)* - Mother

miño *(m-een-yo)* - no

mouèn *(m-O-en)* - I, me

nalas *(n-o-las)* - will

nemos *(n-Ay-m-O-s)* - life

nôlôs *(no-l-O-s)* - will not

ntrosi *(tro-see)* - disgrace, shame

nychtôs *(n-ee-k-tos)* - night

odigei *(O-d-ee-g-eye)* - lead, guide, take

Oneiroi *(O-near-ee)* - dream walker

paiôs *(pie-Os)* - Child

Pètai *(pet-eye)* - Father

prin - before

règis *(re-zsh-ee)* - Guide, guiding

Retala - Rite, rite of passage, ceremony

rńvinia *(re-v-een-ya)* - Rest

saliestas *(sal-yes-tas)* - Hello, greetings

sei *(say)* - Shows ownership

solos *(s-O-l-Os)* - soul, spirit

stellarôs *(stel-ar-Os)* - Star

styllaris *(stil-ar-is)* - Afterlife

ELYTHIAN TRANSLATIONS

tauńn (t-ow-en) - she, her
telôs (tel-O-s) - end, completion
Telôs pyrai (Tel-O-s Peer-eye) - flames end
tenes (ten-es) - to hold, hold
tôuèn (toe-en) - he, him, his
vai (v-eye) - yes
varyó (var-yO) - Hunter, to hunt
vôu (voe) - you, your

WARRIOR'S LAMENT

Emei charisti etu Celestia, Ge dorai en nemos esti lampei, Mea bellarios, mea asidia.
We offer thanks to Celestia, For gifts of a life so bright, My warrior, my shield.

Manýa èn nychtôs, Atresei ekein prin vôu, Vôu varyó èstin telôs.
Cloaked in night, As those before you, Your hunt has ended.

Oreie etai skiasei ntropo, Afin leukô odigei vôu solos, Etu Elysium sei enlisnô.
Risen from shadow's disgrace, Let light guide your soul, to Elysium's embrace.

ACKNOWLEDGEMENT

I never thought I would ever have published a book, and to be here in this moment releasing my second book, there are no amount of words I could form to express my thanks to everyone who had a hand in the this journey.

To my husband, my love, you continue to push and support me when I need it most. You don't know how much influence you have had on this series and the shaping of the characters and their relationships and love you've inspired.

To my son who never lets me talk down about myself and my writing when the imposter syndrome gets to be too much. You will always be my biggest little hype man.

To Ocean, though you are no longer with us, your Shitty Movie Sunday tradition will forever live on in our lives and the lives of these characters. We miss you dearly.

To Rachel Parker, thank you for letting me talk your ears off about potential plot and twists and lore and helping me develop and design the most amazing tattoos and things for the series!

To Fey, my most amazing alpha reader, thank you for letting my rip your heart out first!

To my amazing developmental editor, Natalie Cammaratta. You have helped me become so much stronger as a writer since my journey began with book 1. Thank you so much for everything you have done for this series. We are now even for you taking away all my comfort ellipses and em dashes after chapter 47. I can't wait to rip your heart out again.

To my amazing copy editor/proofreader, Alexa with The Fiction Fix. Thank you for finding all my bad grammar and typos! You've helped me so much in my overall grammar and vocabulary, and I cannot wait to work with you again!

To my amazing artist, Huangja. You never cease to amaze me with your talent. You have a gift, and I am honored to be able to work with you and see you bring every scene and character to life.

To my fellow authors: Kristen M. Long, K.A. Lee, Amber Nicole, Kalista Neith, Nicole Kimmons, and Jordan A. Day, thank you for pushing me forward and being such an encouraging presence every step of the way! I love our writing sprint marathons we host live, and I know I wouldn't have gotten so far in writing without you all!!!

To my amazing ARC Team, you have done more for this series that no amount of thanks would ever be enough. You helped this this series up on its feet and you are the reason we are where we are today!

To my amazing friends, followers, and supporters on TikTok, Instagram, and Facebook. You're kind words, your encouragement, your excitement push me forward, and it has been a light in my life when I was ready to give up.

And lastly, to my readers. Thank you for taking a chance on me. I could not have done this without you. Thank you for all your support. I am forever grateful.

Milton Keynes UK
Ingram Content Group UK Ltd.
UKHW041844291223
435208UK00014B/267/J

9 798985 972375